The Works
of
Nathaniel
Hawthorne

One Volume Edition

BLACK'S READERS SERVICE COMPANY

NEW YORK, N. Y.

Contents

THE SCARLET LETTER

CHAPTER I

THE PRISON-DOOR

A THRONG of bearded men, in sad-colored garments, and gray, steeple-crowned hats, intermixed with women, some wearing hoods, and others bare-headed, was assembled in front of a wooden edifice, the door of which was heavily timbered with oak, and studded with iron spikes.

The founders of a new colony, whatever Utopia of human virtue and happiness they might originally project, have invariably recognized it among their earliest practical necessities to allot a portion of the virgin soil as a cemetery, and another portion as the site of a prison. In accordance with this rule, it may safely be assumed that the forefathers of Boston had built the first prison-house somewhere in the vicinity of Cornhill, almost as seasonably as they marked out the first burial-ground, on Isaac Johnson's lot, and round about his grave, which subsequently became the nucleus of all the congregated sepulchres in the old church-yard of King's Chapel. Certain it is, that, some fifteen or twenty years after the settlement of the town, the wooden jail was already marked with weather-stains and other indications of age, which gave a yet darker aspect to its beetle-browed and gloomy front. The rust on the ponderous iron-work of its oaken door looked more antique than anything else in the New World. Like all that pertains to crime, it seemed never to have known a youthful era. Before this ugly edifice, and between it and the wheel-track of the street, was a grass-plot, much overgrown with burdock, pig-weed, apple-peru, and such unsightly vegetation, which evidently found something congenial in the soil that had so early borne the black flower of civilized society, a prison. But, on one side of the portal, and rooted almost at the threshold, was a wild rose-bush, covered, in this month of June, with its delicate gems, which might be imagined to offer their fragrance and fragile beauty to the prisoner as he went in, and to the condemned criminal as he came forth to his doom, in token that the deep heart of Nature could pity and be kind to him.

This rose-bush, by a strange chance, has been kept alive in history; but whether it had merely survived out of the stern old wilderness, so long after the fall of the gigantic pines and oaks that originally overshadowed it,—or whether, as there is fair authority for believing, it had sprung up under the footsteps of the sainted Ann Hutchinson, as she entered the prison-door,—we shall not take upon us to determine. Finding it so directly on the threshold of our narrative, which is now about to issue from that inauspicious portal, we could hardly do otherwise than pluck one of its flowers, and present it to the reader. It may serve, let us hope, to symbolize some sweet moral blossom, that may be found along the track, or relieve the darkening close of a tale of human frailty and sorrow.

CHAPTER II

THE MARKET-PLACE

THE grass-plot before the jail, in Prison-lane, on a certain summer morning, not less than two centuries ago, was occupied by a pretty large number of the inhabitants of Boston; all with their eyes intently fastened on the iron-clamped oaken door. Amongst any other population, or at a later period in the history of New England, the grim rigidity that petrified the bearded physiognomies of these good people would have augured some awful business in hand. It could have betokened nothing short of the anticipated execution of some noted culprit, on whom the sentence of a legal tribunal had but confirmed the verdict of public sentiment. But, in that early severity of the Puritan character, an inference of this kind could not so indubitably be drawn. It might be that a sluggish bond-servant, or an undutiful child, whom his parents had given over to the civil authority, was to be corrected at the whipping-post. It might be, that an Antinomian, a Quaker, or other heterodox religionist, was to be scourged out of the town, or an idle and vagrant Indian, whom the white man's fire-water had made riotous about the streets, was to be driven with stripes into the shadow of the forest. It might be, too, that a witch, like old Mistress Hibbins, the bitter-tempered widow of the magistrate, was to die upon the gallows. In either case, there was very much the same solemnity of demeanor on the part of the spectators; as befitted a people amongst whom religion and law were almost identical, and in whose character both were so thoroughly interfused, that the mildest and the severest acts of public discipline were alike made venerable and awful. Meagre, indeed, and cold, was the sympathy that a transgressor might look for, from such bystanders, at the scaffold. On the other hand, a penalty which, in our days, would infer a degree of mocking infamy and ridicule, might then be invested with almost as stern a dignity as the punishment of death itself.

It was a circumstance to be noted, on the summer morning when our story begins its course, that the women, of whom there were several in the crowd, appeared to take a peculiar interest in whatever penal infliction might be expected to ensue. The age had not so much refinement, that any sense of impropriety restrained the wearers of petticoat and farthingale from stepping forth into the public ways, and wedging their not unsubstantial persons, if occasion were, into the throng nearest to the scaffold at an execution. Morally, as well as materially, there was a coarser fibre in those wives and maidens of old English birth and breeding, than in their fair descendants, separated from them by a series of six or seven generations; for, throughout that chain of ancestry, every successive mother has transmitted to her child a fainter bloom, a more delicate and briefer beauty, and a slighter physical frame, if not a character of less force and solidity, than her own. The women who were now standing about the prison-door stood within less than half a century of the period when the man-like Elizabeth had been the not altogether unsuitable representative of the sex. They were her countrywomen; and the beef and ale of their native land, with a moral diet not a whit more refined, entered largely into their composition. The bright morning sun, therefore, shone on broad shoulders and well-developed busts, and on round and ruddy cheeks, that had ripened in the far-off island, and had hardly yet grown paler or thinner in the atmosphere of New England. There was, moreover, a boldness and rotundity of speech among these matrons, as most of them seemed to be, that would startle us at the present day, whether in respect to its purport or its volume of tone.

"Goodwives," said a hard-featured dame of fifty, "I'll tell ye a piece of my mind. It would be greatly for the public behoof, if we women, being of mature age and church-members in good repute, should have the handling of such malefactresses as this Hester Prynne. What think ye, gossips? If the hussy stood up for judgment be-

fore us five, that are now here in a knot together, would she come off with such a sentence as the worshipful magistrates have awarded? Marry, I trow not!"

"People say," said another, "that the Reverend Master Dimmesdale, her godly pastor, takes it very grievously to heart that such a scandal should have come upon his congregation."

"The magistrates are God-fearing gentlemen, but merciful overmuch,—that is a truth," added a third autumnal matron. "At the very least, they should have put the brand of a hot iron on Hester Prynne's forehead. Madam Hester would have winced at that, I warrant me. But she, the naughty baggage,—little will she care what they put upon the bodice of her gown! Why, look you, she may cover it with a brooch, or such like heathenish adornment, and so walk the streets as brave as ever!"

"Ah, but," interposed, more softly, a young wife, holding a child by the hand, "let her cover the mark as she will, the pang of it will be always in her heart."

"What do we talk of marks and brands, whether on the bodice of her gown, or the flesh of her forehead?" cried another female, the ugliest as well as the most pitiless of these self-constituted judges. "This woman has brought shame upon us all, and ought to die. Is there not law for it? Truly there is, both in the Scripture and the statute-book. Then let the magistrates, who have made it of no effect, thank themselves if their own wives and daughters go astray!"

"Mercy on us, goodwife," exclaimed a man in the crowd, "is there no virtue in woman, save what springs from a wholesome fear of the gallows? That is the hardest word yet! Hush, now, gossips! for the lock is turning in the prison door, and here comes Mistress Prynne herself."

The door of the jail being flung open from within, there appeared, in the first place, like a black shadow emerging into sunshine, the grim and grisly presence of the town-beadle, with a sword by his side, and his staff of office in his hand. This personage prefigured and represented in his aspect the whole dismal severity of the Puritanic code of law, which it was his business to administer in its final and closest application to the offender. Stretching forth the official staff in his left hand, he laid his right upon the shoulder of a young woman, whom he thus drew forward; until, on the threshold of the prison-door, she repelled him, by an action marked with natural dignity and force of character, and stepped into the open air, as if by her own free will. She bore in her arms a child, a baby of some three months old, who winked and turned aside its little face from the too vivid light of day; because its existence, heretofore, had brought it acquainted only with the gray twilight of a dungeon, or other darksome apartment of the prison.

When the young woman—the mother of this child—stood fully revealed before the crowd, it seemed to be her first impulse to clasp the infant closely to her bosom; not so much by an impulse of motherly affection, as that she might thereby conceal a certain token, which was wrought or fastened into her dress. In a moment, however, wisely judging that one token of her shame would but poorly serve to hide another, she took the baby on her arm, and, with a burning blush, and yet a haughty smile, and a glance that would not be abashed, looked around at her townspeople and neighbors. On the breast of her gown, in fine red cloth, surrounded with an elaborate embroidery and fantastic flourishes of gold thread, appeared the letter A. It was so artistically done, and with so much fertility and gorgeous luxuriance of fancy, that it had all the effect of a last and fitting decoration to the apparel which she wore; and which was of a splendor in accordance with the taste of the age, but greatly beyond what was allowed by the sumptuary regulations of the colony.

The young woman was tall, with a figure of perfect elegance on a large scale. She had dark and abundant hair, so glossy that it threw off the sunshine with a gleam, and a face which, besides being beautiful from regularity of feature and richness of complexion, had the impressiveness belonging to a marked brow and deep black eyes. She was lady-like, too, after the manner of the feminine gentility of those days; characterized by a certain state and dignity, rather than by the delicate, evanescent, and indescribable grace, which is now recognized as its indication. And never had Hester Prynne appeared more lady-like, in the antique interpretation of the term, than as she issued from the prison. Those who had before known her, and had expected to behold her dimmed and obscured by a disastrous cloud, were astonished, and even startled, to perceive how her beauty shone out, and made a halo of the misfortune and ignominy in which she was enveloped. It may be true, that, to a sensitive observer, there was something exquisitely painful in it. Her attire, which, indeed, she had wrought for the occasion, in prison, and had modelled much after her own fancy, seemed to express the attitude of her spirit, the desperate recklessness of her mood, by its wild and picturesque peculiarity. But the point which drew all eyes, and, as it were, transfigured the wearer,—so that both men and women, who had been familiarly acquainted with Hester Prynne, were now impressed as if they beheld her for the first time,—was that SCARLET LETTER, so fantastically embroidered and illuminated upon her bosom. It had the effect of a spell, taking her out of the ordinary relations with humanity, and enclosing her in a sphere by herself.

"She hath good skill at her needle, that's certain," remarked one of her female spectators; "but did ever a woman, before this brazen hussy, contrive such a way of showing it! Why, gossips, what is it but to laugh in the faces of our godly magistrates, and make a pride out of what they, worthy gentlemen, meant for a punishment?"

"It were well," muttered the most iron-visaged of the old dames, "if we stripped Madam Hester's rich gown off her dainty shoulders; and as for the red letter, which she hath stitched so curiously, I'll bestow a rag of mine own rheumatic flannel, to make a fitter one!"

"O, peace, neighbors, peace!" whispered their youngest companion; "do not let her hear you! Not a stitch in that embroidered letter, but she has felt it in her heart."

The grim beadle now made a gesture with his staff.

"Make way, good people, make way, in the King's name!" cried he. "Open a passage; and, I promise ye, Mistress Prynne shall be set where man, woman and child, may have a fair sight of her brave apparel, from this time till an hour past meridian. A blessing on the righteous Colony of the Massachusetts, where iniquity is dragged out into the sunshine! Come along, Madam Hester, and show your scarlet letter in the market-place!"

A lane was forthwith opened through the crowd of spectators. Preceded by the beadle, and attended by an irregular procession of stern-browed men and unkindly visaged women, Hester Prynne set forth towards the place appointed for her punishment. A crowd of eager and curious school-boys, understanding little of the matter in hand, except that it gave them a half-holiday, ran before her progress, turning their heads continually to stare into her face, and at the winking baby in her arms, and at the ignominious letter on her breast. It was no great distance, in those days, from the prison-door to the market-place. Measured by the prisoner's experience, however, it might be reckoned a journey of some length; for, haughty as her demeanor was, she perchance underwent an agony from every footstep of those that thronged to see her, as if her heart had been flung into the street for them all to spurn and trample upon. In our nature, however, there is a provision, alike marvellous and merciful, that the sufferer should never know the intensity of what he endures by its present torture, but chiefly by the pang that rankles after it. With almost a serene deportment, therefore, Hester Prynne passed through this portion of her ordeal, and came to a sort of scaffold, at the western extremity of the market-place. It stood nearly beneath the eaves of Boston's earliest church, and appeared to be a fixture there.

In fact, this scaffold constituted a portion of a penal machine, which now, for two or three generations past, has been merely historical and traditionary among us, but was held, in the old time, to be as effectual an agent, in the promotion of good citizenship, as ever was the guillotine among the terrorists of France. It was, in short, the platform of the pillory; and above it rose the framework of that instrument of discipline, so fashioned as to confine the human head in its tight grasp, and thus hold it up to the public gaze. The very ideal of ignominy was embodied and made manifest in this contrivance of wood and iron. There can be no outrage, methinks, against our common nature,—whatever be the delinquencies of the individual,—no outrage more flagrant than to forbid the culprit to hide his face for shame; as it was the essence of this punishment to do. In Hester Prynne's instance, however, as not unfrequently in other cases, her sentence bore, that she should stand a certain time upon the platform, but without undergoing that gripe about the neck and confinement of the head, the proneness to which was the most devilish characteristic of this ugly engine. Knowing well her part, she ascended a flight of wooden steps, and was thus displayed to the surrounding multitude, at about the height of a man's shoulders above the street.

Had there been a Papist among the crowd of Puritans, he might have seen in this beautiful woman, so picturesque in her attire and mien, and with the infant at her bosom, an object to remind him of the image of Divine Maternity, which so many illustrious painters have vied with one another to represent; something which should remind him, indeed, but only by contrast, of that sacred image of sinless motherhood, whose infant was to redeem the world. Here, there was the taint of deepest sin in the most sacred quality of human life, working such effect, that the world was only the darker for this woman's beauty, and the more lost for the infant that she had borne.

The scene was not without a mixture of awe, such as must always invest the spectacle of guilt and shame in a fellow-creature, before society shall have grown corrupt enough to smile, instead of shuddering, at it. The witnesses of Hester Prynne's disgrace had not yet passed beyond their simplicity. They were stern enough to look upon her death, had that been the sentence, without a murmur at its severity, but had none of the heartlessness of another social state, which would find only a theme for jest in an exhibition like the present. Even had there been a disposition to turn the matter into ridicule, it must have been repressed and overpowered by the solemn presence of men no less dignified than the Governor, and several of his counsellors, a judge, a general, and the ministers of the town; all of whom sat or stood in a balcony of the meeting-house, looking down upon the platform. When such personages could constitute a part of the spectacle, without risking the majesty or reverence of rank and office, it was safely to be inferred that the infliction of a legal sentence would have an earnest and effectual meaning. Accordingly, the crowd was sombre and grave. The unhappy culprit sustained herself as best a woman might, under the heavy weight of a thousand unrelenting eyes, all fastened upon her, and concentrated at her bosom. It was almost intolerable to be borne. Of an impulsive and passionate nature, she had fortified herself to encounter the stings and venomous stabs of public contumely, wreaking itself in every variety of insult; but there was a quality so much more terrible in the solemn mood of the popular mind, that she longed rather to behold all those rigid countenances contorted with scornful merriment, and herself the object. Had a roar of laughter burst from the multitude,—each man, each woman, each little shrill-voiced child, contributing their individual parts,—Hester Prynne might have repaid them all with a bitter and disdainful smile. But, under the leaden infliction which it was her doom to endure, she felt, at moments, as if she must needs shriek out with the full power of her lungs, and cast herself from the scaffold down upon the ground, or else go mad at once.

Yet there were intervals when the whole scene, in which she was the most conspicuous object, seemed to vanish from her eyes, or, at least, glimmered indistinctly before them, like a mass of imperfectly shaped and spectral images. Her mind, and especially her memory, was preternaturally active, and kept bringing up other scenes than this roughly hewn street of a little town, on the edge of the Western wilderness; other faces than were lowering upon her from beneath the brims of those steeple-crowned hats. Reminiscences, the most trifling and immaterial, passages of infancy and school-days, sports, childish quarrels, and the little domestic traits of her maiden years, came swarming back upon her, intermingled with recollections of whatever was gravest in her subsequent life; one picture precisely as vivid as another; as if all were of similar importance, or all alike a play. Possibly, it was an instinctive device of her spirit, to relieve itself, by the exhibition of these phantasmagoric forms, from the cruel weight and hardness of the reality.

Be that as it might, the scaffold of the pillory was a point of view that revealed to Hester Prynne the entire track along which she had been treading, since her happy infancy. Standing on that miserable eminence, she saw again her native village, in Old England, and her paternal home; a decayed house of gray stone, with a poverty-stricken aspect, but retaining a half-obliterated shield of arms over the portal, in token of antique gentility. She saw her father's face, with its bald brow, and reverend white beard, that flowed over the old-fashioned Elizabethan ruff; her mother's, too, with the look of heedful and anxious love which it always wore in her remembrance, and which, even since her death, had so often laid the impediment of a gentle remonstrance in her daughter's pathway. She saw her own face, glowing with girlish beauty, and illuminating all the interior of the dusky mirror in which she had been wont to gaze at it. There she beheld another countenance, of a man well stricken in years, a pale, thin, scholar-like visage, with eyes dim and bleared by the lamp-light that had served them to pore over many ponderous books. Yet those same bleared optics had a strange, penetrating power, when it was their owner's purpose to read the human soul. This figure of the study and the cloister, as Hester Prynne's womanly fancy failed not to recall, was slightly deformed, with the left shoulder a trifle higher than the right. Next rose before her, in memory's picture-gallery, the intricate and narrow thoroughfares, the tall, gray houses, the huge cathedrals, and the public edifices, ancient in date and quaint in architecture, of a Continental city; where a new life had awaited her, still in connection with the misshapen scholar; a new life, but feeding itself on time-worn materials, like a tuft of green moss on a crumbling wall. Lastly, in lieu of these shifting scenes, came back the rude market-place of the Puritan settlement, with all the townspeople assembled and levelling their stern regards at Hester Prynne,—yes, at herself,—who stood on the scaffold of the pillory, an infant on her arm, and the letter A, in scarlet, fantastically embroidered with gold thread, upon her bosom!

Could it be true? She clutched the child so fiercely to her breast, that it sent forth a cry; she turned her eyes downward at the scarlet letter, and even touched it with her finger, to assure herself that the infant and the shame were real. Yes!—these were her realities,—all else had vanished!

CHAPTER III

THE RECOGNITION

FROM this intense consciousness of being the object of severe and universal observation, the wearer of the scarlet letter was at length relieved, by discerning, on the outskirts of the crowd, a figure which irresistibly took possession of her thoughts. An Indian, in his native garb, was standing there; but the red men were not so infrequent visitors of the English settlements, that one of them would have attracted any notice from Hester Prynne, at such a time; much less would he have excluded all other objects and ideas from her mind. By the Indian's side, and evidently sustaining a companionship with him, stood a white man, clad in a strange disarray of civilized and savage costume.

He was small in stature, with a furrowed visage, which, as yet, could hardly be termed aged. There was a remarkable intelligence in his features, as of a person who had so cultivated his mental part that it could not fail to mould the physical to itself, and become manifest by unmistakable tokens. Although, by a seemingly careless arrangement of his heterogeneous garb, he had endeavored to conceal or abate the peculiarity, it was sufficiently evident to Hester Prynne, that one of this man's shoulders rose higher than the other. Again, at the first instant of perceiving that thin visage, and the slight deformity of the figure, she pressed her infant to her bosom, with so convulsive a force that the poor babe uttered another cry of pain. But the mother did not seem to hear it.

At his arrival in the market-place, and some time before she saw him, the stranger had bent his eyes on Hester Prynne. It was carelessly, at first, like a man chiefly accustomed to look inward, and to whom external matters are of little value and import, unless they bear relation to something within his mind. Very soon, however, his look became keen and penetrative. A writhing horror twisted itself across his features, like a snake gliding swiftly over them, and making one little pause, with all its wreathed intervolutions in open sight. His face darkened with some powerful emotion, which, nevertheless, he so instantaneously controlled by an effort of his will, that, save at a single moment, its expression might have passed for calmness. After a brief space, the convulsion grew almost imperceptible, and finally subsided into the depths of his nature. When he found the eyes of Hester Prynne fastened on his own, and saw that she appeared to recognize him, he slowly and calmly raised his finger, made a gesture with it in the air, and laid it on his lips.

Then, touching the shoulder of a townsman who stood next to him, he addressed him, in a formal and courteous manner.

"I pray you, good Sir," said he, "who is this woman?—and wherefore is she here set up to public shame?"

"You must needs be a stranger in this region, friend," answered the townsman, looking curiously at the questioner and his savage companion, "else you would surely have heard of Mistress Hester Prynne, and her evil doings. She hath raised a great scandal, I promise you, in godly Master Dimmesdale's church."

"You say truly," replied the other. "I am a stranger, and have been a wanderer, sorely against my will. I have met with grievous mishaps by sea and land, and have been long held in bonds among the heathen-folk, to the southward; and am now brought hither by this Indian, to be redeemed out of my captivity. Will it please you, therefore, to tell me of Hester Prynne's,—have I her name rightly?—of this woman's offences, and what has brought her to yonder scaffold?"

"Truly, friend; and methinks it must gladden your heart, after your troubles and sojourn in the wilderness," said the townsman, "to find yourself, at length, in a land where iniquity is searched out, and punished in the sight of rulers and people; as here in our godly New England. Yonder woman, Sir, you must know, was the wife of a certain learned man, English by birth, but who had long dwelt in Amsterdam, whence, some good time agone, he was minded to cross over and cast in his lot with us of the Massachusetts. To this purpose, he sent his wife before him, remaining himself to look after some necessary affairs. Marry, good Sir, in some two years, or less, that the woman has been a dweller here in Boston, no tidings have come of this learned gentleman, Master Prynne; and his young wife, look you, being left to her own misguidance—"

"Ah!—aha!—I conceive you," said the stranger, with a bitter smile. "So learned a man as you speak of should have learned this too in his books. And who, by your favor, Sir, may be the father of yonder babe—it is some three or four months old, I should judge—which Mistress Prynne is holding in her arms?"

"Of a truth, friend, that matter remaineth a riddle; and the Daniel who shall expound it is yet a-wanting," answered the townsman. "Madam Hester absolutely refuseth to speak, and the magistrates have laid their heads together in vain. Peradventure the guilty one stands looking on at this sad spectacle, unknown of man, and forgetting that God sees him."

"The learned man," observed the stranger, with another smile, "should come himself, to look into the mystery."

"It behooves him well, if he be still in life," responded the townsman. "Now, good Sir, our Massachusetts magistracy, bethinking themselves that this woman is youthful and fair, and doubtless was strongly tempted to her fall;—and that, moreover, as is most likely, her husband may be at the bottom of the sea;—they have not been bold to put in force the extremity of our righteous law against her. The penalty thereof is death. But in their great mercy and tenderness of heart, they have doomed Mistress Prynne to stand only a space of three hours on the platform of the pillory, and then and thereafter, for the remainder of her natural life, to wear a mark of shame upon her bosom."

"A wise sentence!" remarked the stranger, gravely bowing his head. "Thus she will be a living sermon against sin, until the ignominious letter be engraved upon her tomb-stone. It irks me, nevertheless, that the partner of her iniquity should not, at least,

stand on the scaffold by her side. But he will be known!—he will be known! —he will be known!"

He bowed courteously to the communicative townsman, and, whispering a few words to his Indian attendant, they both made their way through the crowd.

While this passed, Hester Prynne had been standing on her pedestal, still with a fixed gaze towards the stranger; so fixed a gaze, that, at moments of intense absorption, all other objects in the visible world seemed to vanish, leaving only him and her. Such an interview, perhaps, would have been more terrible than even to meet him as she now did, with the hot, midday sun burning down upon her face, and lighting up its shame; with the scarlet token of infamy on her breast; with the sinborn infant in her arms; with a whole people, drawn forth as to a festival, staring at the features that should have been seen only in the quiet gleam of the fireside, in the happy shadow of a home, or beneath a matronly veil, at church. Dreadful as it was, she was conscious of a shelter in the presence of these thousand witnesses. It was better to stand thus, with so many betwixt him and her, than to greet him, face to face, they two alone. She fled for refuge, as it were, to the public exposure, and dreaded the moment when its protection should be withdrawn from her. Involved in these thoughts, she scarcely heard a voice behind her, until it had repeated her name more than once, in a loud and solemn tone, audible to the whole multitude.

"Hearken unto me, Hester Prynne!" said the voice.

It has already been noticed, that directly over the platform on which Hester Prynne stood was a kind of balcony, or open gallery, appended to the meeting-house. It was the place whence proclamations were wont to be made, amidst an assemblage of the magistracy, with all the ceremonial that attended such public observances in those days. Here, to witness the scene which we are describing, sat Governor Bellingham himself, with four sergeants about his chair, bearing halberds, as a guard of honor. He wore a dark feather in his hat, a border of embroidery on his cloak, and a black velvet tunic beneath; a gentleman advanced in years, with a hard experience written in his wrinkles. He was not ill fitted to be the head and representative of a community, which owed its origin and progress, and its present state of development, not to the impulses of youth, but to the stern and tempered energies of manhood, and the sombre sagacity of age; accomplishing so much, precisely because it imagined and hoped so little. The other eminent characters, by whom the chief ruler was surrounded, were distinguished by a dignity of mien, belonging to a period when the forms of authority were felt to possess the sacredness of Divine institutions. They were, doubtless, good men, just, and sage. But, out of the whole human family, it would not have been easy to select the same number of wise and virtuous persons, who should be less capable of sitting in judgment on an erring woman's heart, and disentangling its mesh of good and evil, than the sages of rigid aspect towards whom Hester Prynne now turned her face. She seemed conscious, indeed, that whatever sympathy she might expect

lay in the larger and warmer heart of the multitude; for, as she lifted her eyes towards the balcony, the unhappy woman grew pale and trembled.

The voice which had called her attention was that of the reverend and famous John Wilson, the eldest clergyman of Boston, a great scholar, like most of his contemporaries in the profession, and withal a man of kind and genial spirit. This last attribute, however, had been less carefully developed than his intellectual gifts, and was, in truth, rather a matter of shame than self-congratulation with him. There he stood, with a border of grizzled locks beneath his skull-cap; while his gray eyes, accustomed to the shaded light of his study, were winking, like those of Hester's infant, in the unadulterated sunshine. He looked like the darkly engraved portraits which we see prefixed to old volumes of sermons; and had no more right than one of those portraits would have, to step forth, as he now did, and meddle with a question of human guilt, passion and anguish.

"Hester Prynne," said the clergyman, "I have striven with my young brother here, under whose preaching of the word you have been privileged to sit," —here Mr. Wilson laid his hand on the shoulder of a pale young man beside him,—"I have sought, I say, to persuade this godly youth, that he should deal with you, here in the face of Heaven, and before these wise and upright rulers, and in hearing of all the people, as touching the vileness and blackness of your sin. Knowing your natural temper better than I, he could the better judge what arguments to use, whether of tenderness or terror, such as might prevail over your hardness and obstinacy; insomuch that you should no longer hide the name of him who tempted you to this grievous fall. But he opposes to me, (with a young man's over-softness, albeit wise beyond his years,) that it were wronging the very nature of woman to force her to lay open her heart's secrets in such broad daylight, and in presence of so great a multitude. Truly, as I sought to convince him, the shame lay in the commission of the sin, and not in the showing of it forth. What say you to it, once again, brother Dimmesdale? Must it be thou, or I, that shall deal with this poor sinner's soul?"

There was a murmur among the dignified and reverend occupants of the balcony; and Governor Bellingham gave expression to its purport, speaking in an authoritative voice, although tempered with respect towards the youthful clergyman whom he addressed.

"Good Master Dimmesdale," said he, "the responsibility of this woman's soul lies greatly with you. It behooves you, therefore, to exhort her to repentance, and to confession, as a proof and consequence thereof."

The directness of this appeal drew the eyes of the whole crowd upon the Reverend Mr. Dimmesdale; a young clergyman, who had come from one of the great English universities, bringing all the learning of the age into our wild forest-land. His eloquence and religious fervor had already given the earnest of high eminence in his profession. He was a person of very striking aspect, with a white, lofty, and impending brow, large, brown, melancholy eyes, and a mouth which, unless when he forcibly compressed it, was apt to be tremulous, expressing both nervous sensibility and a vast power of self-restraint. Notwithstanding his high native gifts and scholar-like attainments, there was an air about this young minister,—an apprehensive, a startled, a half-frightened look,—as of a being who felt himself quite astray and at a loss in the pathway of human existence, and could only be at ease in some seclusion of his own. Therefore, so far as his duties would permit, he trod in the shadowy by-paths, and thus kept himself simple and child-like; coming forth, when occasion was with a freshness, and fragrance, and dewy purity of thought, which, as many people said, affected them like the speech of an angel.

Such was the young man whom the Reverend Mr. Wilson and the Governor had introduced so openly to the public notice, bidding him speak, in the hearing of all men, to that mystery of a woman's soul, so sacred even in its pollution. The trying nature of his position drove the blood from his cheek, and made his lips tremulous.

"Speak to the woman, my brother," said Mr. Wilson. "It is of moment to her soul, and therefore, as the worshipful Governor says, momentous to thine own, in whose charge hers is. Exhort her to confess the truth!"

The Reverend Mr. Dimmesdale bent his head, in silent prayer, as it seemed, and then came forward.

"Hester Prynne," said he, leaning over the balcony, and looking down steadfastly into her eyes, "thou hearest what this good man says, and seest the accountability under which I labor. If thou feelest it to be for thy soul's peace, and that thy earthly punishment will thereby be made more effectual to salvation, I charge thee to speak out the name of thy fellow-sinner and fellow-sufferer! Be not silent from any mistaken pity and tenderness for him; for, believe me, Hester, though he were to step down from a high place, and stand there beside thee, on thy pedestal of shame, yet better were it so, than to hide a guilty heart through life. What can thy silence do for him, except it tempt him—yea, compel him, as it were —to add hypocrisy to sin? Heaven hath granted thee an open ignominy, that thereby thou mayest work out an open triumph over the evil within thee, and the sorrow without. Take heed how thou deniest to him—who, perchance, hath not the courage to grasp it for himself —the bitter, but wholesome, cup that is now presented to thy lips!"

The young pastor's voice was tremulously sweet, rich, deep, and broken. The feeling that it so evidently manifested, rather than the direct purport of the words, caused it to vibrate within all hearts, and brought the listeners into one accord of sympathy. Even the poor baby, at Hester's bosom, was affected by the same influence; for it directed its hitherto vacant gaze towards Mr. Dimmesdale, and held up its little arms, with a half pleased, half plaintive murmur. So powerful seemed the minister's appeal, that the people could not believe but that Hester Prynne would speak out the guilty name; or else that the guilty one himself, in whatever high or lowly place he stood, would be drawn forth by an inward and inevitable necessity, and compelled to ascend the scaffold.

Hester shook her head.

"Woman, transgress not beyond the limits of Heaven's mercy!" cried the Reverend Mr. Wilson, more harshly than before. "That little babe hath been gifted with a voice, to second and confirm the counsel which thou hast heard. Speak out the name! That, and thy repentance, may avail to take the scarlet letter off thy breast."

"Never!" replied Hester Prynne, looking, not at Mr. Wilson, but into the deep and troubled eyes of the younger clergyman. "It is too deeply branded. Ye cannot take it off. And would that I might endure his agony, as well as mine!"

"Speak, woman!" said another voice, coldly and sternly, proceeding from the crowd about the scaffold. "Speak; and give your child a father!"

"I will not speak!" answered Hester, turning pale as death, but responding to this voice, which she too surely recognized. "And my child must seek a heavenly Father; she shall never know an earthly one!"

"She will not speak!" murmured Mr. Dimmesdale, who, leaning over the balcony, with his hand upon his heart, had awaited the result of his appeal. He now drew back, with a long respiration. "Wondrous strength and generosity of a woman's heart! She will not speak!"

Discerning the impracticable state of the poor culprit's mind, the elder clergyman, who had carefully prepared himself for the occasion, addressed to the multitude a discourse on sin, in all its branches, but with continual reference to the ignominious letter. So forcibly did he dwell upon this symbol, for the hour or more during which his periods were rolling over the people's heads, that it assumed new terrors in their imagination, and seemed to derive its scarlet hue from the flames of the infernal pit. Hester Prynne, meanwhile, kept her place upon the pedestal of shame, with glazed eyes, and an air of weary indifference. She had borne, that morning, all that nature could endure; and as her temperament was not of the order that escapes from too intense suffering by a swoon, her spirit could only shelter itself beneath a stony crust of insensibility, while the faculties of animal life remained entire. In this state, the voice of the preacher thundered remorselessly, but unavailingly, upon her ears. The infant, during the latter portion of her ordeal, pierced the air with its wailings and screams; she strove to hush it, mechanically, but seemed scarcely to sympathize with its trouble. With the same hard demeanor, she was led back to prison, and vanished from the public gaze within its iron-clamped portal. It was whispered, by those who peered after her, that the scarlet letter threw a lurid gleam along the dark passage-way of the interior.

CHAPTER IV

THE INTERVIEW

AFTER her return to the prison, Hester Prynne was found to be in a state of nervous excitement that demanded constant watchfulness, lest she should perpetrate violence on herself, or do some half-frenzied mischief to the poor babe. As night approached, it proving impossible to quell her insubordination by rebuke or threats of punishment, Master Brackett, the jailer, thought fit to introduce a physician. He described him as a man of skill in all Christian modes of physical science, and likewise familiar with whatever the savage people could teach, in respect to medicinal herbs and roots that grew in the forest. To say the truth, there was much need of professional assistance, not merely for Hester herself, but still more urgently for the child; who, drawing its sustenance from the maternal bosom, seemed to have drank in with it all the turmoil, the anguish and despair, which pervaded the mother's system. It now writhed in convulsions of pain, and was a forcible type, in its little frame, of the moral agony which Hester Prynne had borne throughout the day.

Closely following the jailer into the dismal apartment, appeared that individual, of singular aspect, whose presence in the crowd had been of such deep interest to the wearer of the scarlet letter. He was lodged in the prison, not as suspected of any offence, but as the most convenient and suitable mode of disposing of him, until the magistrates should have conferred with the Indian sagamores respecting his ransom. His name was announced as Roger Chillingworth. The jailer, after ushering him into the room, remained a moment, marvelling at the comparative quiet that followed his entrance; for Hester Prynne had immediately become as still as death, although the child continued to moan.

"Prithee, friend, leave me alone with

my patient," said the practitioner. "Trust me, good jailer, you shall briefly have peace in your house; and, I promise you, Mistress Prynne shall hereafter be more amenable to just authority than you may have found her heretofore."

"Nay, if your worship can accomplish that," answered Master Brackett, "I shall own you for a man of skill indeed! Verily, the woman hath been like a possessed one; and there lacks little, that I should take in hand to drive Satan out of her with stripes."

The stranger had entered the room with the characteristic quietude of the profession to which he announced himself as belonging. Nor did his demeanor change, when the withdrawal of the prison-keeper left him face to face with the woman, whose absorbed notice of him, in the crowd, had intimated so close a relation between himself and her. His first care was given to the child; whose cries, indeed, as she lay writhing on the trundle-bed, made it of peremptory necessity to postpone all other business to the task of soothing her. He examined the infant carefully, and then proceeded to unclasp a leathern case, which he took from beneath his dress. It appeared to contain medical preparations, one of which he mingled with a cup of water.

"My old studies in alchemy," observed he, "and my sojourn, for above a year past, among a people well versed in the kindly properties of simples, have made a better physician of me than many that claim the medical degree. Here, woman! The child is yours,— she is none of mine,—neither will she recognize my voice or aspect as a father's. Administer this draught, therefore, with thine own hand."

Hester repelled the offered medicine, at the same time gazing with strongly marked apprehension into his face.

"Wouldst thou avenge thyself on the innocent babe?" whispered she.

"Foolish woman!" responded the physician, half coldly, half soothingly. "What should ail me, to harm this misbegotten and miserable babe? The medicine is potent for good; and were it my child,—yea, mine own, as well as thine!—I could do no better for it."

As she still hesitated, being, in fact, in no reasonable state of mind, he took the infant in his arms, and himself administered the draught. It soon proved its efficacy, and redeemed the leech's pledge. The moans of the little patient subsided; its convulsive tossings gradually ceased; and, in a few moments, as is the custom of young children after relief from pain, it sank into a profound and dewy slumber. The physician, as he had a fair right to be termed, next bestowed his attention on the mother. With calm and intent scrutiny, he felt her pulse, looked into her eyes, —a gaze that made her heart shrink and shudder, because so familiar, and yet so strange and cold, and, finally, satisfied with his investigation, proceeded to mingle another draught.

"I know not Lethe nor Nepenthe," remarked he; "but I have learned many new secrets in the wilderness, and here is one of them,—a recipe that an Indian taught me, in requital of some lessons of my own, that were as old as Paracelsus. Drink it! It may be less soothing than a sinless conscience. That I cannot give thee. But it will calm the swell and heaving of thy passion, like oil thrown on the waves of a tempestuous sea."

He presented the cup to Hester, who

received it with a slow, earnest look into his face; not precisely a look of fear, yet full of doubt and questioning, as to what his purposes might be. She looked also at her slumbering child.

"I have thought of death," said she, —"have wished for it,—would even have prayed for it, were it fit that such as I should pray for anything. Yet, if death be in this cup, I bid thee think again, ere thou beholdest me quaff it. See! It is even now at my lips."

"Drink, then," replied he, still with the same cold composure. "Dost thou know me so little, Hester Prynne? Are my purposes wont to be so shallow? Even if I imagine a scheme of vengeance, what could I do better for my object than to let thee live,—than to give thee medicines against all harm and peril of life,—so that this burning shame may still blaze upon thy bosom?" As he spoke, he laid his long forefinger on the scarlet letter, which forthwith seemed to scorch into Hester's breast, as if it had been red-hot. He noticed her involuntary gesture, and smiled. "Live, therefore, and bear about thy doom with thee, in the eyes of men and women,—in the eyes of him whom thou didst call thy husband,—in the eyes of yonder child! And, that thou mayest live, take off this draught."

Without further expostulation or delay, Hester Prynne drained the cup, and, at the motion of the man of skill, seated herself on the bed where the child was sleeping; while he drew the only chair which the room afforded, and took his own seat beside her. She could not but tremble at these preparations; for she felt that—having now done all that humanity, or principle, or, if so it were. a refined cruelty, impelled him

to do, for the relief of physical suffering—he was next to treat with her as the man whom she had most deeply and irreparably injured.

"Hester," said he, "I ask not wherefore, nor how, thou hast fallen into the pit, or say, rather, thou hast ascended to the pedestal of infamy, on which I found thee. The reason is not far to seek. It was my folly, and thy weakness. I,—a man of thought,—the bookworm of great libraries,—a man already in decay, having given my best years to feed the hungry dream of knowledge, —what had I to do with youth and beauty like thine own! Misshapen from my birth-hour, how could I delude myself with the idea that intellectual gifts might veil physical deformity in a young girl's fantasy! Men call me wise. If sages were ever wise in their own behoof, I might have foreseen all this. I might have known that, as I came out of the vast and dismal forest, and entered this settlement of Christian men, the very first object to meet my eyes would be thyself, Hester Prynne, standing up, a statue of ignominy, before the people. Nay, from the moment when we came down the old church-steps together, a married pair, I might have beheld the bale-fire of that scarlet letter blazing at the end of our path!"

"Thou knowest," said Hester,—for depressed as she was, she could not endure this last quiet stab at the token of her shame,—"thou knowest that I was frank with thee. I felt no love, nor feigned any."

"True," replied he. "It was my folly! I have said it. But, up to that epoch of my life, I had lived in vain. The world had been so cheerless! My heart was a habitation large enough for many guests, but lonely and chill, and without a household fire. I longed to kindle one! It seemed not so wild a dream,—old as I was, and sombre as I was, and mis-shapen as I was,—that the simple bliss, which is scattered far and wide, for all mankind to gather up, might yet be mine. And so, Hester, I drew thee into my heart, into its innermost chamber, and sought to warm thee by the warmth which thy presence made there!"

"I have greatly wronged thee," mur-mured Hester.

"We have wronged each other," an-swered he. "Mine was the first wrong, when I betrayed thy budding youth into a false and unnatural relation with my decay. Therefore, as a man who has not thought and philosophized in vain, I seek no vengeance, plot no evil against thee. Between thee and me, the scale hangs fairly balanced. But, Hester, the man lives who has wronged us both! Who is he?"

"Ask me not!" replied Hester Prynne, looking firmly into his face. "That thou shalt never know!"

"Never, sayest thou?" rejoined he, with a smile of dark and self-relying intelligence. "Never know him! Be-lieve me, Hester, there are few things, —whether in the outward world, or, to a certain depth, in the invisible sphere of thought,—few things hidden from the man who devotes himself earnestly and unreservedly to the solution of a mystery. Thou mayest cover up thy secret from the prying multitude. Thou mayest conceal it, too, from the minis-ters and magistrates, even as thou didst this day, when they sought to wrench the name out of thy heart, and give thee a partner on thy pedestal. But, as for me, I come to the inquest with other senses than they possess. I shall seek this man, as I have sought truth in books; as I have sought gold in al-chemy. There is a sympathy that will make me conscious of him. I shall see him tremble. I shall feel myself shud-der, suddenly and unawares. Sooner or later, he must needs be mine!"

The eyes of the wrinkled scholar glowed so intensely upon her, that Hes-ter Prynne clasped her hands over her heart, dreading lest he should read the secret there at once.

"Thou wilt not reveal his name? Not the less he is mine," resumed he, with a look of confidence, as if destiny were at one with him. "He bears no letter of infamy wrought into his garment, as thou dost; but I shall read it on his heart. Yet fear not for him! Think not that I shall interfere with Heaven's own method of retribution, or, to my own loss, betray him to the gripe of human law. Neither do thou imagine that I shall contrive aught against his life; no, nor against his fame, if, as I judge, he be a man of fair repute. Let him live! Let him hide himself in out-ward honor, if he may! Not the less he shall be mine!"

"Thy acts are like mercy," said Hes-ter, bewildered and appalled. "But thy words interpret thee as a terror!"

"One thing, thou that wast my wife, I would enjoin upon thee," continued the scholar. "Thou hast kept the secret of thy paramour. Keep, likewise, mine! There are none in this land that know me. Breathe not, to any human soul, that thou didst ever call me husband! Here, on this wild outskirt of the earth, I shall pitch my tent; for, elsewhere a wanderer, and isolated from human in-terests. I find here a woman, a man, a child, amongst whom and myself there exist the closest ligaments. No matter whether of love or hate; no matter whether of right or wrong! Thou and thine, Hester Prynne, belong to me. My home is where thou art, and where he is. But betray me not!"

"Wherefore dost thou desire it?" inquired Hester, shrinking, she hardly knew why, from this secret bond. "Why not announce thyself openly, and cast me off at once?"

"It may be," he replied, "because I will not encounter the dishonor that besmirches the husband of a faithless woman. It may be for other reasons. Enough, it is my purpose to live and die unknown. Let, therefore, thy husband be to the world as one already dead, and of whom no tidings shall ever come. Recognize me not, by word, by sign, by look! Breathe not the secret, above all, to the man thou wottest of. Shouldst thou fail me in this, beware!

His fame, his position, his life, will be in my hands. Beware!"

"I will keep thy secret, as I have his," said Hester.

"Swear it!" rejoined he.

And she took the oath.

"And now, Mistress Prynne," said old Roger Chillingworth, as he was hereafter to be named, "I leave thee alone; alone with thy infant, and the scarlet letter! How is it, Hester? Doth thy sentence bind thee to wear the token in thy sleep? Art thou not afraid of nightmares and hideous dreams?"

"Why dost thou smile so at me?" inquired Hester, troubled at the expression of his eyes. "Art thou like the Black Man that haunts the forest round about us? Hast thou enticed me into a bond that will prove the ruin of my soul?"

"Not thy soul," he answered, with another smile. "No, not thine!"

CHAPTER V

HESTER AT HER NEEDLE

HESTER PRYNNE'S term of confinement was now at an end. Her prison-door was thrown open, and she came forth into the sunshine, which, falling on all alike, seemed, to her sick and morbid heart, as if meant for no other purpose than to reveal the scarlet letter on her breast. Perhaps there was a more real torture in her first unattended footsteps from the threshold of the prison, than even in the procession and spectacle that have been described,

where she was made the common infamy, at which all mankind was summoned to point its finger. Then, she was supported by an unnatural tension of the nerves, and by all the combative energy of her character, which enabled her to convert the scene into a kind of lurid triumph. It was, moreover, a separate and insulated event, to occur but once in her lifetime, and to meet which, therefore, reckless of economy, she might call up the vital strength that would have sufficed for many quiet years. The very law that condemned her —a giant of stern features, but with vigor to support, as well as to annihilate, in his iron arm—had held her up, through the terrible ordeal of her ignominy. But now, with this unattended walk from her prison-door, began the daily custom; and she must either sustain and carry it forward by the ordinary resources of her nature, or sink beneath it. She could no longer borrow from the future to help her through the present grief. To-morrow would bring its own trial with it; so would the next day, and so would the next; each its own trial, and yet the very same that was now so unutterably grievous to be borne. The days of the far-off future would toil onward, still with the same burden for her to take up, and bear along with her, but never to fling down; for the accumulating days, and added years, would pile up their misery upon the heap of shame. Throughout them all, giving up her individuality, she would become the general symbol at which the preacher and moralist might point, and in which they might vivify and embody their images of woman's frailty and sinful passion. Thus the young and pure would be taught to look at her, with the scarlet letter flaming on her breast,—at her, the child of honorable parents,—at her, the mother of a babe, that would hereafter be a woman,—at her, who had once been innocent,—as the figure, the body, the reality of sin. And over her grave, the infamy that she must carry thither would be her only monument.

It may seem marvellous, that, with the world before her,—kept by no restrictive clause of her condemnation within the limits of the Puritan settlement, so remote and so obscure,—free to return to her birth-place, or to any other European land, and there hide her character and identity under a new exterior, as completely as if emerging into another state of being,—and having also the passes of the dark, inscrutable forest open to her, where the wildness of her nature might assimilate itself with a people whose customs and life were alien from the law that had condemned her,—it may seem marvellous, that this woman should still call that place her home, where, and where only, she must needs be the type of shame. But there is a fatality, a feeling so irresistible and inevitable that it has the force of doom, which almost invariably compels human beings to linger around and haunt, ghost-like, the spot where some great and marked event has given the color to their lifetime; and still the more irresistibly, the darker the tinge that saddens it. Her sin, her ignominy, were the roots which she had struck into the soil. It was as if a new birth, with stronger assimilations than the first, had converted the forest-land, still so uncongenial to every other pilgrim and wanderer, into Hester Prynne's wild and dreary, but life-long home. All other scenes of earth—even that village of rural England, where happy infancy and stainless maidenhood seemed yet to be in her mother's keeping, like garments put off long ago —were foreign to her, in comparison. The chain that bound her here was of iron links, and galling to her inmost soul, but could never be broken.

It might be, too,—doubtless it was so, although she hid the secret from herself, and grew pale whenever it struggled out of her heart, like a serpent from its hole,—it might be that another feeling kept her within the scene and pathway that had been so fatal. There dwelt, there trode the feet of one with whom she deemed herself connected in a union, that, unrecognized on earth, would bring them together before the bar of final judgment, and make that their marriage-altar, for a joint futurity of endless retribution. Over and over again, the tempter of souls had thrust this idea upon Hester's contemplation, and laughed at the passionate and desperate joy with which she seized, and then strove to cast it from her. She barely looked the idea in the face, and hastened to bar it in its dungeon. What she compelled herself to believe,—what, finally, she reasoned upon, as her motive for continuing a resident of New England,—was half a truth, and half a self-delusion. Here, she said to herself, had been the scene of her guilt, and here should be the scene of her earthly punishment; and so, perchance, the torture of her daily shame would at length purge her soul, and work out another purity than that which she had lost; more saint-like, because the result of martyrdom.

Hester Prynne, therefore, did not flee. On the outskirts of the town, within the verge of the peninsula, but not in close vicinity to any other habitation, there was a small thatched cottage. It had been built by an earlier settler, and abandoned, because the soil about it was too sterile for cultivation, while its comparative remoteness put it out of the sphere of that social activity which already marked the habits of the emigrants. It stood on the shore, looking across a basin of the sea at the forest-covered hills, towards the west. A clump of scrubby trees, such as alone grew on the peninsula, did not so much conceal the cottage from view, as seem to denote that here was some object which would fain have been, or at least ought to be, concealed. In this little, lonesome dwelling, with some slender means that she possessed, and by the license of the magistrates, who still kept an inquisitorial watch over her, Hester established herself, with her infant child. A mystic shadow of suspicion immediately attached itself to the spot. Children, too young to comprehend wherefore this woman should be shut out from the sphere of human charities, would creep nigh enough to behold her plying her needle at the cottage-window, or standing in the doorway, or laboring in her little garden, or coming forth along the pathway that led townward; and, discerning the scarlet letter on her breast, would scamper off with a strange, contagious fear.

Lonely as was Hester's situation, and without a friend on earth who dared to show himself, she, however, incurred no risk of want. She possessed an art that sufficed, even in a land that afforded comparatively little scope for its exercise, to supply food for her thriving infant and herself. It was the art—then, as now, almost the only one within a woman's grasp—of needle-work. She bore on her breast, in the curiously embroidered letter, a specimen of her delicate and imaginative skill, of which the dames of a court might gladly have availed themselves, to add the richer and more spiritual adornment of human ingenuity to their fabrics of silk and gold. Here, indeed, in the sable simplicity that generally characterized the

Puritanic modes of dress, there might be an infrequent call for the finer productions of her handiwork. Yet the taste of the age, demanding whatever was elaborate in compositions of this kind, did not fail to extend its influence over our stern progenitors, who had cast behind them so many fashions which it might seem harder to dispense with. Public ceremonies, such as ordinations, the installation of magistrates, and all that could give majesty to the forms in which a new government manifested itself to the people, were, as a matter of policy, marked by a stately and well-conducted ceremonial, and a sombre, but yet a studied magnificence. Deep ruffs, painfully wrought bands, and gorgeously embroidered gloves, were all deemed necessary to the official state of men assuming the reins of power; and were readily allowed to individuals dignified by rank or wealth, even while sumptuary laws forbade these and similar extravagances to the plebeian order. In the array of funerals, too,—whether for the apparel of the dead body, or to typify, by manifold emblematic devices of sable cloth and snowy lawn, the sorrow of the survivors,—there was a frequent and characteristic demand for such labor as Hester Prynne could supply. Baby-linen—for babies then wore robes of state—afforded still another possibility of toil and emolument.

By degrees, nor very slowly, her handiwork became what would now be termed the fashion. Whether from commiseration for a woman of so miserable a destiny; or from the morbid curiosity that gives a fictitious value even to common or worthless things; or by whatever other intangible circumstance was then, as now, sufficient to bestow, on some persons, what others might seek in vain; or because Hester really filled a gap which must otherwise have remained vacant; it is certain that she had ready and fairly requited employment for as many hours as she saw fit to occupy with her needle. Vanity, it may be, chose to mortify itself, by putting on, for ceremonials of pomp and state, the garments that had been wrought by her sinful hands. Her needle-work was seen on the ruff of the Governor; military men wore it on their scarfs, and the minister on his band; it decked the baby's little cap; it was shut up, to be mildewed and moulder away, in the coffins of the dead. But it is not recorded that, in a single instance, her skill was called in aid to embroider the white veil which was to cover the pure blushes of a bride. The exception indicated the ever relentless vigor with which society frowned upon her sin.

Hester sought not to acquire anything beyond a subsistence, of the plainest and most ascetic description, for herself, and a simple abundance for her child. Her own dress was of the coarsest materials and the most sombre hue: with only that one ornament,—the scarlet letter,—which it was her doom to wear. The child's attire, on the other hand, was distinguished by a fanciful, or, we might rather say, a fantastic ingenuity, which served, indeed, to heighten the airy charm that early began to develop itself in the little girl, but which appeared to have also a deeper meaning. We may speak further of it hereafter. Except for that small expenditure in the decoration of her infant, Hester bestowed all her superfluous means in charity, on wretches less miserable than herself, and who not unfrequently insulted the hand that fed them. Much of the time, which she might readily have applied to the better efforts of her art, she employed in making coarse garments for the poor. It is probable that there was an idea of penance in this mode of occupation, and that she offered up a real sacrifice of enjoyment, in devoting so many hours to such rude handiwork. She had in her nature a rich, voluptuous, Oriental characteristic,—a taste for the gorgeously beautiful, which, save in the exquisite productions of her needle, found nothing else, in all the possibilities of her life, to exercise itself upon. Women derive a pleasure, incomprehensible to the other sex, from the delicate toil of the needle. To Hester Prynne it might have been a mode of expressing, and therefore soothing, the passion of her life. Like all other joys, she rejected it as sin. This morbid meddling of conscience with an immaterial matter betokened, it is to be feared, no genuine and steadfast penitence, but something doubtful, something that might be deeply wrong, beneath.

In this manner, Hester Prynne came to have a part to perform in the world. With her native energy of character, and rare capacity, it could not entirely cast her off, although it had set a mark upon her, more intolerable to a woman's heart than that which branded the brow of Cain. In all her intercourse with society, however, there was nothing that made her feel as if she belonged to it. Every gesture, every word, and even the silence of those with whom she came in contact, implied, and often expressed, that she was banished. and as much alone as if she inhabited another sphere, or communicated with the common nature by other organs and senses than the rest of human kind. She stood apart from moral interests, yet close beside them, like a ghost that revisits the familiar fireside, and can no longer make itself seen or felt; no more smile with the household joy, nor mourn with the kindred sorrow; or, should it succeed in manifesting its forbidden sympathy, awakening only terror and horrible repugnance. These emotions, in fact, and its bitterest scorn besides, seemed to be the sole portion that she retained in the universal heart. It was not an age of delicacy; and her position, although she understood it well, and was in little danger of forgetting it, was often brought before her vivid self-perception, like a new anguish, by the rudest touch upon the tenderest spot. The poor, as we have already said, whom she sought out to be the objects of her bounty, often reviled the hand that was stretched forth to succor them. Dames of elevated rank, likewise, whose doors she entered in the way of her occupation, were accustomed to distil drops of bitterness into her heart; sometimes through that alchemy of quiet malice, by which women can concoct a subtile poison from ordinary trifles; and sometimes, also, by a coarser expression, that fell upon the sufferer's defenceless breast like a rough blow upon an ulcerated wound. Hester had schooled herself long and well; she never responded to these attacks, save by a flush of crimson that rose irrepressibly over her pale cheek, and again subsided into the depths of her bosom. She was patient,—a martyr, indeed,—but she forebore to pray for her enemies; lest, in spite of her forgiving aspirations, the words of the blessing should stubbornly twist themselves into a curse.

Continually, and in a thousand other ways, did she feel the innumerable throbs of anguish that had been so cunningly contrived for her by the undying, the ever-active sentence of the Puritan tribunal. Clergymen paused in the street to address words of exhortation, that brought a crowd, with its mingled grin and frown, around the poor, sinful woman. If she entered a church, trusting to share the Sabbath smile of the Universal Father, it was often her mishap to find herself the text of the discourse. She grew to have a dread of children; for they had imbibed from their parents a vague idea of something horrible in this dreary woman, gliding silently through the town, with never any companion but one only child. Therefore, first allowing her to pass, they pursued her at a distance with shrill cries, and the utterance of a word that had no distinct purport to their own minds, but was none the less terrible to her, as proceeding from lips that babbled it unconsciously. It seemed to argue so wide a diffusion of her shame, that all nature knew of it; it could have caused her no deeper pang, had the leaves of the trees whispered the dark story among themselves, —had the summer breeze murmured about it—had the wintry blast shrieked it aloud! Another peculiar torture was felt in the gaze of a new eye. When strangers looked curiously at the scarlet letter,—and none ever failed to do so,—they branded it afresh into Hester's soul; so that, oftentimes, she could scarcely refrain, yet always did refrain,

from covering the symbol with her hand. But then, again, an accustomed eye had likewise its own anguish to inflict. Its cool stare of familiarity was intolerable. From first to last, in short, Hester Prynne had always this dreadful agony in feeling a human eye upon the token; the spot never grew callous; it seemed, on the contrary, to grow more sensitive with daily torture.

But sometimes, once in many days, or perchance in many months, she felt an eye—a human eye—upon the ignominious brand, that seemed to give a momentary relief, as if half of her agony were shared. The next instant, back it all rushed again, with still a deeper throb of pain; for, in that brief interval, she had sinned anew. Had Hester sinned alone?

Her imagination was somewhat affected, and, had she been of a softer moral and intellectual fibre, would have been still more so, by the strange and solitary anguish of her life. Walking to and fro, with those lonely footsteps, in the little world with which she was outwardly connected, it now and then appeared to Hester,—if altogether fancy, it was nevertheless too potent to be resisted,—she felt or fancied, then, that the scarlet letter had endowed her with a new sense. She shuddered to believe, yet could not help believing, that it gave her a sympathetic knowledge of the hidden sin in other hearts. She was terror-stricken by the revelations that were thus made. What were they? Could they be other than the insidious whispers of the bad angel, who would fain have persuaded the struggling woman, as yet only half his victim, that the outward guise of purity was but a lie, and that, if truth were everywhere to be shown, a scarlet letter would blaze forth on many a bosom besides Hester Prynne's? Or, must she receive those intimations—so obscure, yet so distinct—as truth? In all her miserable experience, there was nothing else so awful and so loathsome as this sense. It perplexed, as well as shocked her, by the irreverent inopportuneness of the occasions that brought it into vivid action. Sometimes the red infamy upon her breast would give a sympathetic throb, as she passed near a venerable minister or magistrate, the model of piety and justice, to whom that age of antique reverence looked up, as to a mortal man in fellowship with angels. "What evil thing is at hand?" would Hester say to herself. Lifting her reluctant eyes, there would be nothing human within the scope of view, save the form of this earthly saint! Again, a mystic sisterhood would contumaciously assert itself, as she met the sanctified frown of some matron, who, according to the rumor of all tongues, had kept cold snow within her bosom throughout life. That unsunned snow in the matron's bosom, and the burning shame on Hester Prynne's, what had the two in common? Or, once more, the electric thrill would give her warning,—"Behold, Hester, here is a companion!"—and, looking up, she would detect the eyes of a young maiden glancing at the scarlet letter, shyly and aside, and quickly averted, with a faint, chill crimson in her cheeks; as if her purity were somewhat sullied by that momentary glance. O Fiend, whose talisman was that fatal symbol, wouldst thou leave nothing, whether in youth or age, for this poor sinner to revere? —such loss of faith is ever one of the saddest results of sin. Be it accepted as a proof that all was not corrupt in this poor victim of her own frailty, and man's hard law, that Hester Prynne yet struggled to believe that no fellow-mortal was guilty like herself.

The vulgar, who, in those dreary old times, were always contributing a grotesque horror to what interested their imaginations, had a story about the scarlet letter which we might readily work up into a terrific legend. They averred, that the symbol was not mere scarlet cloth, tinged in an earthly dye-pot, but was red-hot with infernal fire, and could be seen glowing all alight, whenever Hester Prynne walked abroad in the night-time. And we must needs say, it seared Hester's bosom so deeply, that perhaps there was more truth in the rumor than our modern incredulity may be inclined to admit.

CHAPTER VI

PEARL

WE have as yet hardly spoken of the infant; that little creature, whose innocent life had sprung, by the inscrutable decree of Providence, a lovely and immortal flower, out of the rank luxuriance of a guilty passion. How strange it seemed to the sad woman, as she watched the growth, and the beauty that became every day more brilliant, and the intelligence that threw its quivering sunshine over the tiny features of this child! Her Pearl!—For so had Hester called her; not as a name expressive of her aspect, which had nothing of the calm, white, unimpassioned lustre that would be indicated by the comparison. But she named the infant "Pearl," as being of great price,—purchased with all she had,—her mother's only treasure! How strange, indeed! Man had marked this woman's sin by a scarlet letter, which had such potent and disastrous efficacy that no human sympathy could reach her, save it were sinful like herself. God, as a direct consequence of the sin which man thus punished, had given her a lovely child, whose place was on that same dishonored bosom, to connect her parent forever with the race and descent of mortals, and to be finally a blessed soul in heaven! Yet these thoughts affected Hester Prynne less with hope than apprehension. She knew that her deed had been evil; she could have no faith, therefore, that its result would be good. Day after day, she looked fearfully into the child's expanding nature; ever dreading to detect some dark and wild peculiarity, that should correspond with the guiltiness to which she owed her being.

Certainly, there was no physical defect. By its perfect shape, its vigor, and its natural dexterity in the use of all its untried limbs, the infant was worthy to have been brought forth in Eden; worthy to have been left there, to be the plaything of the angels, after the world's first parents were driven out. The child had a native grace which does not invariably coëxist with faultless beauty; its attire, however simple, always impressed the beholder as if it were the very garb that precisely became it best. But little Pearl was not clad in rustic weeds. Her mother, with a morbid purpose that may be better understood hereafter, had bought the richest tissues that could be procured, and allowed her imaginative faculty its full play in the arrangement and decoration of the dresses which the child wore, before the public eye. So magnificent was the small figure, when thus arrayed, and such was the splendor of Pearl's own proper beauty, shining through the gorgeous robes which might have extinguished a paler loveliness, that there was an absolute circle of radiance around her, on the darksome cottage floor. And yet a russet gown, torn and soiled with the child's rude play, made a picture of her just as perfect. Pearl's aspect was imbued with a spell of infinite variety; in this one child there were many children, comprehending the full scope between the wild-flower prettiness of a peasant-baby, and the pomp, in little, of an infant princess. Throughout all, however, there was a trait of passion, a certain depth of hue, which she never lost; and if, in any of her changes, she had grown fainter or paler, she would have ceased to be herself;—it would have been no longer Pearl!

This outward mutability indicated, and did not more than fairly express, the various properties of her inner life. Her nature appeared to possess depth, too, as well as variety; but—or else Hester's fears deceived her—it lacked reference and adaptation to the world into which she was born. The child could not be made amenable to rules. In giving her existence, a great law had been broken; and the result was a being whose elements were perhaps beautiful and brilliant, but all in disorder; or with an order peculiar to themselves, amidst which the point of variety and arrangement was difficult or impossible to be discovered. Hester could only account for the child's character—and even then most vaguely and imperfectly—by recalling what she herself had been, during that momentous period while Pearl was imbibing her soul from the spiritual world, and her bodily frame from its material of earth. The mother's impassioned state had been the medium through which were transmitted to the unborn infant the rays of its moral life; and, however white and clear originally, they had taken the deep stains of crimson and gold, the fiery lustre, the black shadow, and the untempered light, of the intervening substance. Above all, the warfare of Hester's spirit, at that epoch, was perpetuated in Pearl. She could recognize her wild, desperate, defiant mood, the flightiness of her temper, and even some of the very cloud-shapes of gloom and despondency that had brooded in her heart. They were now illuminated by the morning radiance of a young child's disposition, but, later in the day of earthly existence, might be prolific of the storm and whirlwind.

The discipline of the family, in those days, was of a far more rigid kind than now. The frown, the harsh rebuke, the frequent application of the rod, enjoined by Scriptural authority, were used, not merely in the way of punishment for actual offences, but as a wholesome regimen for the growth and promotion of all childish virtues. Hester Prynne, nevertheless, the lonely mother of this one child, ran little risk of erring on the side of undue severity. Mindful, however, of her own errors and misfortunes, she early sought to impose a tender, but strict control over the infant immortality that was committed to her charge. But the task was beyond her skill. After testing both smiles and frowns, and proving that neither mode of treatment possessed any calculable influence, Hester was ultimately compelled to stand aside, and permit the child to be swayed by her own impulses. Physical compulsion or restraint was effectual, of course, while it lasted. As to any other kind of discipline, whether addressed to her mind or heart, little Pearl might or might not be within its reach, in accordance with the caprice that ruled the moment. Her mother, while Pearl was yet an infant, grew acquainted with a certain peculiar look, that warned her when it would be labor thrown away to insist, persuade, or plead. It was a look so intelligent, yet inexplicable, so perverse, sometimes so malicious, but generally accompanied by a wild flow of spirits, that Hester could not help questioning, at such moments, whether Pearl was a human child. She seemed rather an airy sprite, which, after playing its fantastic sports for a little while upon the cottage-floor, would flit away with a mocking smile. Whenever that look appeared in her wild, bright, deeply black eyes, it invested her with a strange remoteness and intangibility; it was as if she were hovering in the air and might vanish, like a glimmering light, that comes we know not whence, and goes we know not whither. Beholding it, Hester was constrained to rush towards the child, —to pursue the little elf in the flight which she invariably began,—to snatch her to her bosom, with a close pressure and earnest kisses,—not so much from overflowing love, as to assure herself that Pearl was flesh and blood, and not utterly delusive. But Pearl's laugh, when she was caught, though full of merriment and music, made her mother more doubtful than before.

Heart-smitten at this bewildering and baffling spell, that so often came between herself and her sole treasure, whom she had bought so dear, and who was all her world, Hester sometimes burst into passionate tears. Then, perhaps,—for there was no foreseeing how it might affect her,—Pearl would frown, and clench her little fist, and harden her small features into a stern, unsympathizing look of discontent. Not seldom, she would laugh anew, and louder than before, like a thing incapable and unintelligent of human sorrow. Or—but this more rarely happened—she would be convulsed with a rage of grief, and sob out her love for her mother, in broken words, and seem intent on proving that she had a heart, by breaking it. Yet Hester was hardly safe in confiding herself to that gusty tenderness; it passed, as suddenly as it came. Brooding over all these matters, the mother felt like one who has evoked a spirit, but, by some irregularity in the process of conjuration, has failed to win the master-word that should control this new and incomprehensible intelligence. Her only real comfort was when the child lay in the placidity of sleep. Then she was sure of her, and tasted hours of quiet, sad, delicious happiness; until

—perhaps with that perverse expression glimmering from beneath her opening lids—little Pearl awoke!

How soon—with what strange rapidity, indeed!—did Pearl arrive at an age that was capable of social intercourse, beyond the mother's ever-ready smile and nonsense-words! And then what a happiness would it have been, could Hester Prynne have heard her clear, bird-like voice mingling with the uproar of other childish voices, and have distinguished and unravelled her own darling's tones, amid all the entangled outcry of a group of sportive children! But this could never be. Pearl was a born outcast of the infantile world. An imp of evil, emblem and product of sin, she had no right among christened infants. Nothing was more remarkable than the instinct, as it seemed, with which the child comprehended her loneliness; the destiny that had drawn an inviolable circle round about her; the whole peculiarity, in short, of her position in respect to other children. Never, since her release from prison, had Hester met the public gaze without her. In all her walks about the town, Pearl, too, was there; first as the babe in arms, and afterwards as the little girl, small companion of her mother, holding a forefinger with her whole grasp, and tripping along at the rate of three or four footsteps to one of Hester's. She saw the children of the settlement, on the grassy margin of the street, or at the domestic thresholds, disporting themselves in such grim fashion as the Puritanic nurture would permit; playing at going to church, perchance; or at scourging Quakers; or taking scalps in a sham-fight with the Indians; or scaring one another with freaks of imitative witchcraft. Pearl saw, and gazed intently, but never sought to make acquaintance. If spoken to, she would not speak again. If the children gathered about her, as they sometimes did, Pearl would grow positively terrible in her puny wrath, snatching up stones to fling at them, with shrill, incoherent exclamations, that made her mother tremble, because they had so much the sound of a witch's anathemas in some unknown tongue.

The truth was, that the little Puritans, being of the most intolerant brood that ever lived, had got a vague idea of something outlandish, unearthly, or at variance with ordinary fashions, in the mother and child; and therefore scorned them in their hearts, and not unfrequently reviled them with their tongues. Pearl felt the sentiment, and requited it with the bitterest hatred that can be supposed to rankle in a childish bosom. These outbreaks of a fierce temper had a kind of value, and even comfort, for her mother; because there was at least an intelligible earnestness in the mood, instead of the fitful caprice that so often thwarted her in the child's manifestations. It appalled her, nevertheless, to discern here, again, a shadowy reflection of the evil that had existed in herself. All this enmity and passion had Pearl inherited, by inalienable right, out of Hester's heart. Mother and daughter stood together in the same circle of seclusion from human society; and in the nature of the child seemed to be perpetuated those unquiet elements that had distracted Hester Prynne before Pearl's birth, but had since begun to be soothed away by the softening influences of maternity.

At home, within and around her mother's cottage, Pearl wanted not a wide and various circle of acquaintance. The spell of life went forth from her ever creative spirit, and communicated itself to a thousand objects, as a torch kindles a flame wherever it may be applied. The unlikeliest materials,—a stick, a bunch of rags, a flower,—were the puppets of Pearl's witchcraft, and without undergoing any outward change became spiritually adapted to whatever drama occupied the stage of her inner world. Her one baby-voice served a multitude of imaginary personages, old and young, to talk withal. The pine-trees, aged, black and solemn, and flinging groans and other melancholy utterances on the breeze, needed little transformation to figure as Puritan elders; the ugliest weeds of the garden were their children, whom Pearl smote down and uprooted, most unmercifully. It was wonderful, the vast variety of forms into which she threw her intellect, with no continuity, indeed, but darting up and dancing, always in a state of preternatural activity,—soon sinking down as if exhausted by so rapid and feverish a tide of life,—and succeeded by other shapes of a similar wild energy. It was like nothing so much as the phantasmagoric play of the northern lights. In the mere exercise of the fancy, however, and the sportiveness of a growing mind, there might be little more than was observable in other children of bright faculties; except as Pearl, in the dearth of human playmates, was thrown more upon the visionary throng which she created. The singularity lay in the hostile feelings with which the child regarded all these offspring of her own heart and mind. She never created a friend, but seemed always to be sowing broadcast the dragon's teeth, whence sprung a harvest of armed enemies, against whom she rushed to battle. It was inexpressibly sad—then what depth of sorrow to a mother, who felt in her own heart the cause!—to observe, in one so young, this constant recognition of an adverse world, and so fierce a training of the energies that were to make good her cause, in the contest that must ensue.

Gazing at Pearl, Hester Prynne often dropped her work upon her knees, and cried out with an agony which she would fain have hidden, but which made utterance for itself, betwixt speech and a groan,—"O Father in Heaven,—if Thou art still my Father,—what is this being which I have brought into the world!" And Pearl, overhearing the ejaculation, or aware through some more subtile channel, of those throbs of anguish, would turn her vivid and beautiful little face upon her mother, smile with sprite-like intelligence, and resume her play.

One peculiarity of the child's deportment remains yet to be told. The very first thing which she had noticed, in her life, was—what?—not the mother's smile, responding to it, as other babies do, by that faint, embryo smile of the little mouth, remembered so doubtfully afterwards, and with such fond discussion whether it were indeed a smile. By no means! But the first object of which Pearl seemed to become aware was—shall we say it?—the scarlet letter on Hester's bosom! One day, as her mother stooped over the cradle, the infant's eyes had been caught by the glimmering of the gold embroidery about the letter; and, putting up her little hand, she grasped at it, smiling, not doubtfully,

but with a decided gleam, that gave her face the look of a much older child. Then, gasping for breath, did Hester Prynne clutch the fatal token, instinctively endeavoring to tear it away; so infinite was the torture inflicted by the intelligent touch of Pearl's baby-hand. Again, as if her mother's agonized gesture were meant only to make sport for her, did little Pearl look into her eyes, and smile! From that epoch, except when the child was asleep, Hester had never felt a moment's safety; not a moment's calm enjoyment of her. Weeks, it is true, would sometimes elapse, during which Pearl's gaze might never once be fixed upon the scarlet letter; but then, again, it would come at unawares, like the stroke of sudden death, and always with that peculiar smile, and odd expression of the eyes.

Once, this freakish, elvish cast came into the child's eyes, while Hester was looking at her own image in them, as mothers are fond of doing; and, suddenly,—for women in solitude, and with troubled hearts, are pestered with unaccountable delusions,—she fancied that she beheld, not her own miniature portrait, but another face, in the small black mirror of Pearl's eye. It was a face, fiend-like, full of smiling malice, yet bearing the semblance of features that she had known full well, though seldom with a smile, and never with malice in them. It was as if an evil spirit possessed the child, and had just then peeped forth in mockery. Many a time afterwards had Hester been tortured, though less vividly, by the same illusion.

In the afternoon of a certain summer's day, after Pearl grew big enough to run about, she amused herself with gathering handfuls of wild-flowers, and flinging them, one by one, at her mother's bosom; dancing up and down, like a little elf, whenever she hit the scarlet letter. Hester's first motion had been to cover her bosom with her clasped hands. But, whether from pride or resignation, or a feeling that her penance might best be wrought out by this unutterable pain, she resisted the impulse, and sat erect, pale as death, looking sadly into little Pearl's wild eyes. Still came the battery of flowers, almost invariably hitting the mark, and covering the mother's breast with hurts for which she could find no balm in this world, nor knew how to seek it in another. At last, her shot being all expended, the child stood still and gazed at Hester, with that little, laughing image of a fiend peeping out—or, whether it peeped or no, her mother so imagined it—from the unsearchable abyss of her black eyes.

"Child, what art thou?" cried the mother.

"O, I am your little Pearl!" answered the child.

But, while she said it, Pearl laughed, and began to dance up and down, with the humorsome gesticulation of a little imp, whose next freak might be to fly up the chimney.

"Art thou my child, in very truth?" asked Hester.

Nor did she put the question altogether idly, but, for the moment, with a portion of genuine earnestness; for, such was Pearl's wonderful intelligence, that her mother half doubted whether she were not acquainted with the secret spell of her existence, and might not now reveal herself.

"Yes; I am little Pearl!" repeated the child, continuing her antics.

"Thou are not my child! Thou art no Pearl of mine!" said the mother, half playfully; for it was often the case that a sportive impulse came over her, in the midst of her deepest suffering. "Tell me, then, what thou art, and who sent thee hither?"

"Tell me, mother!" said the child, seriously, coming up to Hester, and pressing herself close to her knees. "Do thou tell me!"

"Thy Heavenly Father sent thee!" answered Hester Prynne.

But she said it with a hesitation that did not escape the acuteness of the child. Whether moved only by her ordinary freakishness, or because an evil spirit prompted her, she put up her small forefinger, and touched the scarlet letter.

"He did not send me!" cried she, positively. "I have no Heavenly Father!"

"Hush, Pearl, hush! Thou must not talk so!" answered the mother, suppressing a groan. "He sent us all into this world. He sent even me, thy mother. Then, much more, thee! Or, if not, thou strange and elfish child, whence didst thou come?"

"Tell me! Tell me!" repeated Pearl, no longer seriously, but laughing, and capering about the floor. "It is thou that must tell me!"

But Hester could not resolve the query, being herself in a dismal labyrinth of doubt. She remembered—betwixt a smile and a shudder—the talk of the neighboring townspeople; who, seeking vainly elsewhere for the child's paternity, and observing some of her odd attributes, had given out that poor little Pearl was a demon offspring; such as, ever since old Catholic times, had occasionally been seen on earth, through the agency of their mother's sin, and to promote some foul and wicked purpose Luther, according to the scandal of his monkish enemies, was a brat of that hellish breed; nor was Pearl the only child to whom this inauspicious origin was assigned, among the New England Puritans.

CHAPTER VII

THE GOVERNOR'S HALL

HESTER PRYNNE went, one day, to the mansion of Governor Bellingham, with a pair of gloves, which she had fringed and embroidered to his order, and which were to be worn on some great occasion of state; for, though the chances of a popular election had caused this former ruler to descend a step or two from the highest rank, he still held an honorable and influential place among the colonial magistracy.

Another and far more important reason than the delivery of a pair of embroidered gloves impelled Hester, at his time, to seek an interview with a personage of so much power and activity in the affairs of the settlement. It had reached her ears, that there was a design on the part of some of the leading inhabitants, cherishing the more rigid order of principles in religion and government, to deprive her of her child. On the supposition that Pearl, as already hinted, was of demon origin, these good people not unreasonably argued that a Christian interest in the mother's soul required them to remove such a stumbling-block from her path. If the child, on the other hand, were really capable of moral and religious growth, and possessed the elements of ultimate salvation, then, surely, it would enjoy all the fairer prospect of these advantages, by being transferred to wiser and better guardianship than Hester Prynne's. Among those who promoted the design, Governor Bellingham was said to be one of the most busy. It may appear singular, and, indeed, not a little ludicrous, that an affair of this kind, which, in later days, would have been referred to no higher jurisdiction than that of the selectmen of the town, should then have been a question publicly discussed, and on which statesmen of eminence took sides. At that epoch of pristine simplicity, however, matters of even slighter public interest, and of far less intrinsic weight, than the welfare of Hester and her child, were strangely mixed up with the deliberations of legislators and acts of state. The period was hardly, if at all, earlier than that of our story, when a dispute concerning the right of property in a pig, not only caused a fierce and bitter contest in the legislative body of the colony, but resulted in an important modification of the framework itself of the legislature.

Full of concern, therefore,—but so conscious of her own right that it seemed scarcely an unequal match between the public, on the one side, and a lonely woman, backed by the sympathies of nature, on the other,—Hester Prynne set forth from her solitary cottage. Little Pearl, of course, was her companion. She was now of an age to run lightly along by her mother's side, and, constantly in motion, from morn till sunset, could have accomplished a much longer journey than that before her. Often, nevertheless, more from caprice than necessity, she demanded to be taken up in arms; but was soon as imperious to be set down again, and frisked onward before Hester on the grassy pathway, with many a harmless trip and tumble. We have spoken of Pearl's rich and luxuriant beauty; a beauty that shone with deep and vivid tints; a bright complexion, eyes possessing intensity both of depth and glow, and hair already of a deep, glossy brown, and which, in after years, would be nearly akin to black. There was fire in her and throughout her; she seemed the unpremeditated offshoot of a passionate moment. Her mother, in contriving the child's garb, had allowed the gorgeous tendencies of her imagination their full play; arraying her in a crimson velvet tunic, of peculiar cut, abundantly embroidered with fantasies and flourishes of gold thread. So much strength of coloring, which must have given a wan and pallid aspect to cheeks of a fainter bloom, was admirably adapted to Pearl's beauty, and made her the very brightest little jet of flame that ever danced upon the earth.

But it was a remarkable attribute of this garb, and, indeed, of the child's whole appearance, that it irresistibly and inevitably reminded the beholder of the token which Hester Prynne was doomed to wear upon her bosom. It was the scarlet letter in another form; the scarlet letter endowed with life! The mother herself—as if the red ignominy were so deeply scorched into her brain that all her conceptions assumed its form—had carefully wrought out the similitude; lavishing many hours of morbid ingenuity, to create an analogy between the object of her affection and the emblem of her guilt and torture. But, in truth, Pearl was the one, as well as the other; and only in consequence of that identity had Hester contrived so perfectly to represent the scarlet letter in her appearance.

As the two wayfarers came within the precincts of the town, the children of the Puritans looked up from their play,—or what passed for play with those sombre little urchins,—and spake gravely one to another:—

"Behold, verily, there is the woman of the scarlet letter; and, of a truth, moreover, there is the likeness of the scarlet letter running along by her side! Come, therefore, and let us fling mud at them!"

But Pearl, who was a dauntless child, after frowning, stamping her foot, and shaking her little hand with a variety of threatening gestures, suddenly made a rush at the knot of her enemies, and put them all to flight. She resembled, in her fierce pursuit of them, an infant pestilence,—the scarlet fever, or some such half-fledged angel of judgment,—whose mission was to punish the sins of the rising generation. She screamed and shouted, too, with a terrific volume of sound, which, doubtless, caused the hearts of the fugitives to quake within them. The victory accomplished,

Pearl returned quietly to her mother, and looked up, smiling, into her face.

Without further adventure, they reached the dwelling of Governor Bellingham. This was a large wooden house, built in a fashion of which there are specimens still extant in the streets of our elder towns; now moss-grown, crumbling to decay, and melancholy at heart with the many sorrowful or joyful occurrences, remembered or forgotten, that have happened, and passed away, within their dusky chambers. Then, however, there was the freshness of the passing year on its exterior, and the cheerfulness, gleaming forth from the sunny windows, of a human habitation, into which death had never entered. It had, indeed, a very cheery aspect; the walls being overspread with a kind of stucco, in which fragments of broken glass were plentifully intermixed; so that, when the sunshine fell aslant-wise over the front of the edifice, it glittered and sparkled as if diamonds had been flung against it by the double handful. The brilliancy might have befitted Aladdin's palace, rather than the mansion of a grave old Puritan ruler. It was further decorated with strange and seemingly cabalistic figures and diagrams, suitable to the quaint taste of the age, which had been drawn in the stucco when newly laid on, and had now grown hard and durable, for the admiration of after times.

Pearl, looking at this bright wonder of a house, began to caper and dance, and imperatively required that the whole breadth of sunshine should be stripped off its front, and given her to play with.

"No, my little Pearl!" said her mother. "Thou must gather thine own sunshine. I have none to give thee!"

They approached the door; which was of an arched form, and flanked on each side by a narrow tower or projection of the edifice, in both of which were lattice-windows, with wooden shutters to close over them at need. Lifting the iron hammer that hung at the portal, Hester Prynne gave a summons, which was answered by one of the Governor's bond-servants; a free-born Englishman, but now a seven years' slave. During that term he was to be the property of his master, and as much a commodity of bargain and sale as an ox, or ? joint-stool. The serf wore the blue coat, which was the customary garb of serving-men at that period, and long before, in the old hereditary halls of England.

"Is the worshipful Governor Bellingham within?" inquired Hester.

"Yea, forsooth," replied the bond-servant, staring with wide-open eyes at the scarlet letter, which, being a newcomer in the country, he had never before seen. "Yea, his honorable worship is within. But he hath a godly minister or two with him, and likewise a leech. Ye may not see his worship now."

"Nevertheless, I will enter," answered Hester Prynne; and the bondservant, perhaps judging from the decision of her air, and the glittering symbol in her bosom, that she was a great lady in the land, offered no opposition.

So the mother and little Pearl were admitted into the hall of entrance. With many variations, suggested by the nature of his building-materials, diversity of climate, and a different mode of social life, Governor Bellingham had planned his new habitation after the residences of gentlemen of fair estate in his native land. Here, then, was a wide and reasonably lofty hall, extending through the whole depth of the house, and forming a medium of general communication, more or less directly, with all the other apartments. At one extremity, this spacious room was lighted by the windows of the two towers, which formed a small recess on either side of the portal. At the other end, though partly muffled by a curtain, it was more powerfully illuminated by one of those embowed hall-windows which we read of in old books, and which was provided with a deep and cushioned seat. Here, on the cushion, lay a folio tome, probably of the Chronicles of England, or other such substantial literature; even as, in our own days, we scatter gilded volumes on the centre-table, to be turned over by the casual guest. The furniture of the hall consisted of some ponderous chairs, the backs of which were elaborately carved with wreaths of oaken flowers; and likewise a table in the same taste; the whole being of the Elizabethan age, or perhaps earlier, and heirlooms, transferred hither from the Governor's paternal home. On the table —in token that the sentiment of old English hospitality had not been left behind—stood a large pewter tankard, at the bottom of which, had Hester or Pearl peeped into it, they might have seen the frothy remnant of a recent draught of ale.

On the wall hung a row of portraits, representing the forefathers of the Bellingham lineage, some with armor on their breasts, and others with stately ruffs and robes of peace. All were characterized by the sternness and severity which old portraits so invariably put on; as if they were the ghosts, rather than the pictures, of departed worthies, and were gazing with harsh and intolerant criticism at the pursuits and enjoyments of living men.

At about the centre of the oaken panels, that lined the hall, was suspended a suit of mail, not, like the pictures, an ancestral relic, but of the most modern date; for it had been manufactured by a skilful armorer in London, the same year in which Governor Bellingham came over to New England. There was a steel headpiece, a cuirass, a gorget, and greaves, with a pair of gauntlets and a sword hanging beneath; all, and especially the helmet and breastplate, so highly burnished as to glow with white radiance, and scatter an illumination everywhere about upon the floor. This bright panoply was not meant for mere idle show, but had been worn by the Governor on many a solemn muster and training field, and had glittered, moreover, at the head of a regiment in the Pequod war. For, though bred a lawyer, and accustomed to speak of Bacon, Coke, Noye, and Finch, as his professional associates, the exigences of this new country had transformed Governor Bellingham into a soldier, as well as a statesman and ruler.

Little Pearl—who was as greatly pleased with the gleaming armor as she had been with the glittering frontispiece of the house—spent some time looking into the polished mirror of the breastplate.

"Mother," cried she, "I see you here. Look! Look!"

Hester looked, by way of humoring the child; and she saw that, owing to the peculiar effect of this convex mirror, the scarlet letter was represented in exaggerated and gigantic proportions, so as to be greatly the most prominent feature of her appearance. In truth, she seemed absolutely hidden behind it. Pearl pointed upward, also, at a similar picture in the headpiece; smiling at her mother, with the elfish intelligence that was so familiar an expression on her small physiognomy. That look of naughty merriment was likewise reflected in the mirror, with so much breadth and intensity of effect, that it made Hester Prynne feel as if it could not be the image of her own child, but of an imp who was seeking to mould itself into Pearl's shape.

"Come along, Pearl," said she, drawing her away. "Come and look into this fair garden. It may be, we shall see flowers there; more beautiful ones than we find in the woods."

Pearl, accordingly, ran to the bow-window, at the further end of the hall, and looked along the vista of a garden-walk, carpeted with closely shaven grass, and bordered with some rude and immature attempt at shrubbery. But the proprietor appeared already to have relinquished, as hopeless, the effort to perpetuate on this side of the Atlantic, in a hard soil and amid the close struggle for subsistence, the native English taste for ornamental gardening. Cabbages

grew in plain sight; and a pumpkin-vine, rooted at some distance, had run across the intervening space, and deposited one of its gigantic products directly beneath the hall-window; as if to warn the Governor that this great lump of vegetable gold was as rich an ornament as New England earth would offer him. There were a few rose-bushes, however, and a number of apple-trees, probably the descendants of those planted by the Reverend Mr. Blackstone, the first settler of the peninsula; that half mythological personage, who rides through our early annals, seated on the back of a bull.

Pearl, seeing the rose-bushes, began to cry for a red rose, and would not be pacified.

"Hush, child, hush!" said her mother, earnestly. "Do not cry, dear little Pearl! I hear voices in the garden. The Governor is coming, and gentlemen along with him!"

In fact, adown the vista of the garden avenue, a number of persons were seen approaching towards the house. Pearl, in utter scorn of her mother's attempt to quiet her, gave an eldritch scream, and then became silent; not from any notion of obedience, but because the quick and mobile curiosity of her disposition was excited by the appearance of these new personages.

CHAPTER VIII

THE ELF-CHILD AND THE MINISTER

GOVERNOR BELLINGHAM, in a loose gown and easy cap,—such as elderly gentlemen loved to endue themselves with, in their domestic privacy,—walked foremost, and appeared to be showing off his estate, and expatiating on his projected improvements. The wide circumference of an elaborate ruff, beneath his gray beard, in the antiquated fashion of King James' reign, caused his head to look not a little like that of John the Baptist in a charger. The impression made by his aspect, so rigid and severe, and frost-bitten with more than autumnal age, was hardly in keeping with the appliances of worldly enjoyment wherewith he had evidently done his utmost to surround himself. But it is an error to suppose that our grave forefathers—though accustomed to speak and think of human existence as a state merely of trial and warfare, and though unfeignedly prepared to sacrifice goods and life at the behest of duty—made it a matter of conscience to reject such means of comfort, or even luxury, as lay fairly within their grasp. This creed was never taught, for instance, by the venerable pastor, John Wilson, whose beard, white as a snowdrift, was seen over Governor Bellingham's shoulder; while its wearer suggested that pears and peaches might yet be naturalized in the New England climate, and that purple grapes might possibly be compelled to flourish, against the sunny garden-wall. The old clergyman, nurtured at the rich bosom of the English Church, had a long-established and legitimate taste for all good and comfortable things; and however stern he might show himself in the pulpit, or in his public reproof of such transgressions as that of Hester Prynne, still, the genial benevolence of his private life had won him warmer affection than was accorded to any of his professional contemporaries.

Behind the Governor and Mr. Wilson came two other guests; one, the Reverend Arthur Dimmesdale, whom the reader may remember, as having taken a brief and reluctant part in the scene of Hester Prynne's disgrace; and, in close companionship with him, old Roger Chillingworth, a person of great skill in physic, who, for two or three years past, had been settled in the town. It was understood that this learned man was the physician as well as friend of the young minister, whose health had severely suffered, of late, by his too unreserved self-sacrifice to the labors and duties of the pastoral relation.

The Governor, in advance of his visitors, ascended one or two steps, and, throwing open the leaves of the great hall window, found himself close to little Pearl. The shadow of the curtain fell on Hester Prynne, and partially concealed her.

"What have we here?" said Governor Bellingham, looking with surprise at the scarlet little figure before him. "I profess, I have never seen the like, since my days of vanity, in old King James' time, when I was wont to esteem it a high favor to be admitted to a court mask! There used to be a swarm of these small apparitions, in holiday time; and we called them children of the Lord of Misrule. But how gat such a guest into my hall?"

"Ay, indeed!" cried good old Mr. Wilson. "What little bird of scarlet plumage may this be? Methinks I have seen just such figures, when the sun has been shining through a richly painted window, and tracing out the golden and crimson images across the floor. But that was in the old land. Prithee, young one, who art thou, and what has ailed thy mother to bedizen thee in this strange fashion? Art thou a Christian child,—ha? Dost know thy catechism? Or art thou one of those naughty elfs or fairies, whom we thought to have left behind us, with other relics of Papistry, in merry old England?"

"I am mother's child," answered the scarlet vision, "and my name is Pearl!"

"Pearl?—Ruby, rather!—or Coral!—or Red Rose, at the very least, judging from thy hue!" responded the old minister, putting forth his hand in a vain attempt to pat little Pearl on the cheek. "But where is this mother of thine? Ah! I see," he added; and, turning to Governor Bellingham, whispered, "This is the selfsame child of whom we have held speech together; and behold here the unhappy woman, Hester Prynne, her mother!"

"Sayest thou so?" cried the Governor. "Nay, we might have judged that such a child's mother must needs be a scarlet woman, and a worthy type of her of Babylon! But she comes at a good time; and we will look into this matter forthwith."

Governor Bellingham stepped through the window into the hall, followed by his three guests.

"Hester Prynne," said he, fixing his naturally stern regard on the wearer of the scarlet letter, "there has been much question concerning thee, of late. The point hath been weightily discussed, whether we, that are of authority and influence, do well discharge our consciences by trusting an immortal soul, such as there is in yonder child, to the guidance of one who hath stumbled and fallen, amid the pitfalls of this world. Speak thou, the child's own mother! Were it not, thinkest thou, for thy little one's temporal and eternal welfare, that she be taken out of thy charge, and clad soberly, and disciplined strictly, and instructed in the truths of heaven and earth? What canst thou do for the child, in this kind?"

"I can teach my little Pearl what I have learned from this!" answered Hester Prynne, laying her finger on the red token.

"Woman, it is thy badge of shame!" replied the stern magistrate. "It is because of the stain which that letter indicates, that we would transfer thy child to other hands."

"Nevertheless," said the mother, calmly, though growing more pale, "this badge hath taught me,—it daily teaches me,—it is teaching me at this moment, —lessons whereof my child may be the wiser and better, albeit they can profit nothing to myself."

"We will judge warily," said Bellingham, "and look well what we are about to do. Good Master Wilson, I pray you, examine this Pearl,—since that is her name,—and see whether she hath had such Christian nurture as befits a child of her age."

The old minister seated himself in an

arm-chair, and made an effort to draw Pearl betwixt his knees. But the child, unaccustomed to the touch of familiarity of any but her mother, escaped through the open window, and stood on the upper step, looking like a wild tropical bird, of rich plumage, ready to take flight into the upper air. Mr. Wilson, not a little astonished at this outbreak,—for he was a grandfatherly sort of personage, and usually a vast favorite with children,—essayed, however, to proceed with the examination.

"Pearl," said he, with great solemnity, "thou must take heed to instruction, that so, in due season, thou mayest wear in thy bosom the pearl of great price. Canst thou tell me, my child, who made thee?"

Now Pearl knew well enough who made her; for Hester Prynne, the daughter of a pious home, very soon after her talk with the child about her Heavenly Father, had begun to inform her of those truths which the human spirit, at whatever stage of immaturity, imbibes with such eager interest. Pearl, therefore, so large were the attainments of her three years' lifetime, could have borne a fair examination in the New England Primer, or the first column of the Westminster Catechisms, although unacquainted with the outward form of either of those celebrated works. But that perversity, which all children have more or less of, and of which little Pearl had a ten-fold portion, now, at the most inopportune moment, took thorough possession of her, and closed her lips, or impelled her to speak words amiss. After putting her finger in her mouth, with many ungracious refusals to answer good Mr. Wilson's question, the child finally announced that she

had not been made at all, but had been plucked by her mother off the bush of wild roses that grew by the prison-door.

This fantasy was probably suggested by the near proximity of the Governor's red roses, as Pearl stood outside of the window; together with her recollection of the prison rose-bush, which she had passed in coming hither.

Old Roger Chillingworth, with a smile on his face, whispered something in the young clergyman's ear. Hester Prynne looked at the man of skill, and even then, with her fate hanging in the balance, was startled to perceive what a change had come over his features,— how much uglier they were,—how his dark complexion seemed to have grown duskier, and his figure more misshapen, —since the days when she had familiarly known him. She met his eyes for an instant, but was immediately constrained to give all her attention to the scene now going forward.

"This is awful!" cried the Governor, slowly recovering from the astonishment into which Pearl's response had thrown him. "Here is a child of three years old, and she cannot tell who made her! Without question, she is equally in the dark as to her soul, its present depravity, and future destiny! Methinks, gentlemen, we need inquire no further."

Hester caught hold of Pearl, and drew her forcibly into her arms, confronting the old Puritan magistrate with almost a fierce expression. Alone in the world, cast off by it, and with this sole treasure to keep her heart alive, she felt that she possessed indefeasible rights against the world, and was ready to defend them to the death.

"God gave me the child!" cried she.

"He gave her in requital of all things else, which ye had taken from me. She is my happiness!—she is my torture, none the less! Pearl keeps me here in life! Pearl punishes me too! See ye not, she is the scarlet letter, only capable of being loved, and so endowed with a million-fold the power of retribution for my sin? Ye shall not take her! I will die first!"

"My poor woman," said the not unkind old minister, "the child shall be well cared for!—far better than thou canst do it."

"God gave her into my keeping," repeated Hester Prynne, raising her voice almost to a shriek. "I will not give her up!"—And here, by a sudden impulse, she turned to the young clergyman, Mr. Dimmesdale, at whom, up to this moment, she had seemed hardly so much as once to direct her eyes.—"Speak thou for me!" cried she. "Thou wast my pastor, and hadst charge of my soul, and knowest me better than these men can. I will not lose the child! Speak for me! Thou knowest,—for thou hast sympathies which these men lack!—thou knowest what is in my heart, and what are a mother's rights, and how much the stronger they are, when that mother has but her child and the scarlet letter! Look thou to it! I will not lose the child! Look to it!"

At this wild and singular appeal, which indicated that Hester Prynne's situation had provoked her to little less than madness, the young minister at once came forward, pale, and holding his hand over his heart, as was his custom whenever his peculiarly nervous temperament was thrown into agitation. He looked now more careworn and ema-ciated than as we described him at the scene of Hester's public ignomy; and whether it were his failing health, or whatever the cause might be, his large dark eyes had a world of pain in their troubled and melancholy depth.

"There is truth in what she says," began the minister, with a voice sweet, tremulous, but powerful, insomuch that the hall reëchoed, and the hollow armor rang with it,—"truth in what Hester says, and in the feeling which inspires her! God gave her the child, and gave her, too, an instinctive knowledge of its nature and requirements,—both seemingly so peculiar,—which no other mortal being can possess. And, more-over, is there not a quality of awful sacredness in the relation between this mother and this child?"

"Ay!—how is that, good Master Dimmesdale?" interrupted the Governor. "Make that plain, I pray you."

"It must be even so," resumed the minister. "For, if we deem it other-wise, do we not thereby say that the Heavenly Father, the Creator of all flesh, hath lightly recognized a deed of sin, and made of no account the distinction between unhallowed lust and holy love? This child of its father's guilt and its mother's shame hath come from the hand of God, to work in many ways upon her heart, who pleads so earnestly, and with such bitterness of spirit, the right to keep her. It was meant for a blessing; for the one bless-ing of her life! It was meant, doubt-less, as the mother herself hath told us, for a retribution too; a torture to be felt at many an unthought-of mo-ment; a pang, a sting, an ever-recurring agony, in the midst of a troubled joy! Hath she not expressed this thought in the garb of the poor child, so forcibly reminding us of that red symbol which sears her bosom?"

"Well said, again!" cried good Mr. Wilson. "I feared the woman had no better thought than to make a mountebank of her child!"

"O, not so!—not so!" continued Mr. Dimmesdale. "She recognizes, believe me, the solemn miracle which God hath wrought, in the existence of that child. And may she feel, too,—what, methinks, is the very truth,—that this boon was meant, above all things else, to keep the mother's soul alive, and to preserve her from blacker depths of sin into which Satan might else have sought to plunge her! Therefore it is good for this poor, sinful woman that she hath an infant immortality, a being capable of eternal joy or sorrow, confided to her care,—to be trained up by her to righteousness,—to remind her, at every moment, of her fall,—but yet to teach her, as it were by the Creator's sacred pledge, that, if she bring the child to heaven, the child also will bring its parent thither! Herein is the sinful mother happier than the sinful father. For Hester Prynne's sake, then, and no less for the poor child's sake, let us leave them as Providence hath seen fit to place them!"

"You speak, my friend, with a strange earnestness," said old Roger Chillingworth, smiling at him.

"And there is a weighty import in what my young brother hath spoken," added the Reverend Mr. Wilson. "What say you, worshipful Master Bellingham? Hath he not pleaded well for the poor woman?"

"Indeed hath he," answered the magistrate, "and hath adduced such arguments, that we will even leave the matter as it now stands; so long, at least, as there shall be no further scandal in the woman. Care must be had, nevertheless, to put the child to due and stated examination in the catechism, at thy hands or Master Dimmesdale's. Moreover, at a proper season, the tithing-men must take heed that she go both to school and to meeting."

The young minister, on ceasing to speak, had withdrawn a few steps from the group, and stood with his face partially concealed in the heavy folds of the window-curtain; while the shadow of his figure, which the sunlight cast upon the floor, was tremulous with the vehemence of his appeal. Pearl, that wild and flighty little elf, stole softly towards him, and taking his hand in the grasp of both her own, laid her cheek against it; a caress so tender, and withal so unobtrusive, that her mother, who was looking on, asked herself,—"Is that my Pearl?" Yet she knew that there was love in the child's heart, although it mostly revealed itself in passion, and hardly twice in her lifetime had been softened by such gentleness as now. The minister,—for, save the long-sought regards of woman, nothing is sweeter than these marks of childish preference, accorded spontaneously by a spiritual instinct, and therefore seeming to imply in us something truly worthy to be loved,—the minister looked round, laid his hand on the child's head, hesitated an instant, and then kissed her brow. Little Pearl's unwonted mood of sentiment lasted no longer; she laughed and went capering down the hall, so airily, that old Mr. Wilson raised a question whether even her tiptoes touched the floor.

"The little baggage hath witchcraft in her, I profess," said he to Mr. Dimmesdale. "She needs no old woman's broomstick to fly withal!"

"A strange child!" remarked old Roger Chillingworth. "It is easy to see the mother's part in her. Would it be beyond a philosopher's research, think ye, gentlemen, to analyze that child's nature, and, from its make and mould, to give a shrewd guess at the father?"

"Nay; it would be sinful, in such a question, to follow the clew of profane philosophy," said Mr. Wilson. "Better to fast and pray upon it; and still better, it may be, to leave the mystery as we find it, unless Providence reveal it of its own accord. Thereby, every good Christian man hath a title to show a father's kindness towards the poor, deserted babe."

The affair being so satisfactorily concluded, Hester Prynne, with Pearl, departed from the house. As they descended the steps, it is averred that the lattice of a chamber-window was thrown open, and forth into the sunny day was thrust the face of Mistress Hibbins, Governor Bellingham's bitter-tempered sister, and the same who, a few years later, was executed as a witch.

"Hist, hist!" said she, while her ill omened physiognomy seemed to cast a shadow over the cheerful newness of the house. "Wilt thou go with us tonight? There will be a merry company in the forest; and I well-nigh promised the Black Man that comely Hester Prynne should make one."

"Make my excuse to him, so please you!" answered Hester, with a triumphant smile. "I must tarry at home, and keep watch over my little Pearl. Had they taken her from me, I would willingly have gone with thee into the forest, and signed my name in the Black Man's book too, and that with mine own blood!"

"We shall have thee there anon!" said the witch-lady, frowning as she drew back her head.

But here—if we suppose this interview betwixt Mistress Hibbins and Hester Prynne to be authentic, and not a parable—was already an illustration of the young minister's argument against sundering the relation of a fallen mother to the offspring of her frailty. Even thus early had the child saved her from Satan's snare.

CHAPTER IX

THE LEECH

UNDER the appellation of Roger Chillingworth, the reader will remember, was hidden another name, which its former wearer had resolved should never more be spoken. It has been related, how, in the crowd that witnessed Hester Prynne's ignominious exposure, stood a man, elderly, travel-worn, who, just emerging from the perilous wilderness, beheld the woman, in whom he hoped to find embodied the warmth and cheerfulness of home, set up as a type of sin before the people. Her matronly frame was trodden under all men's feet. Infamy was babbling around her in the public market-place. For her kindred, should the tidings ever reach them, and for the companions of her unspotted life, there remained nothing but the contagion of her dishonor; which would not fail to be distributed in strict accordance and proportion with the intimacy and sacredness of their previous relationship. Then why—since the choice was with himself—should the individual, whose connection with the fallen woman had been the most intimate and sacred of them all, come forward to vindicate his claim to an inheritance so little desirable? He resolved not to be pilloried beside her on her pedestal of shame. Unknown to all but Hester Prynne, and possessing the lock and key of her silence, he chose to withdraw his name from the roll of mankind, and, as regarded his former ties and interest, to vanish out of life as completely as if he indeed lay at the bottom of the ocean, whither rumor had long ago consigned him. This purpose once effected, new interests would immediately spring up, and likewise a new purpose; dark, it is true, if not guilty, but of force enough to engage the full strength of his faculties.

In pursuance of this resolve, he took up his residence in the Puritan town, as Roger Chillingworth, without other introduction than the learning and intelligence of which he possessed more than a common measure. As his studies, at a previous period of his life, had made him extensively acquainted with the medical science of the day, it was as a physician that he presented himself, and as such was cordially received.

Skillful men, of the medical and chirurgical profession, were of rare occurrence in the colony. They seldom, it would appear, partook of the religious zeal that brought other emigrants across the Atlantic. In their researches into the human frame, it may be that the higher and more subtile faculties of such men were materialized, and that they lost the spiritual view of existence amid the intricacies of that wondrous mechanism, which seemed to involve art enough to comprise all of life within itself. At all events, the health of the good town of Boston, so far as medicine had aught to do with it, had hitherto lain in the guardianship of an aged deacon and apothecary, whose piety and godly deportment were stronger testimonials in his favor than any that he could have produced in the shape of a diploma. The only surgeon was one who combined the occasional exercise of that noble art with the daily and habitual flourish of a razor. To such a professional body Roger Chillingworth was a brilliant acquisition. He soon manifested his familiarity with the ponderous and imposing machinery of antique physic; in which every remedy contained a multitude of far-fetched and heterogeneous ingredients, as elaborately compounded as if the proposed result had been the Elixir of Life. In his Indian captivity, moreover, he had gained much knowledge of the properties of native herbs and roots; nor did he conceal from his patients, that these simple medicines, Nature's boon to the untutored savage, had quite as large a share of his own confidence as the European pharmacopœia, which so many learned doctors had spent centuries in elaborating.

This learned stranger was exemplary, as regarded, at least, the outward forms of a religious life, and, early after his arrival, had chosen for his spiritual guide the Reverend Mr. Dimmesdale. The young divine, whose scholar-like renown still lived in Oxford, was considered by his more fervent admirers as little less than a heavenly-ordained apostle, destined, should he live and labor for the ordinary term of life, to do as great deeds for the now feeble New England Church, as the early Fathers had achieved for the infancy of the Christian faith. About this period, however, the health of Mr. Dimmesdale had evidently begun to fail. By those best acquainted with his habits, the paleness of the young minister's cheek was accounted for by his too earnest devotion to study, his scrupulous fulfilment of parochial duty, and, more than all, by the fasts and vigils of which he made a frequent practice, in order to keep the grossness of this earthly state from clogging and obscuring his spiritual lamp. Some declared, that, if Mr. Dimmesdale were really going to die, it was cause enough, that the world was not worthy to be any longer trodden by his feet. He himself, on the other hand, with characteristic humility, avowed his belief, that, if Providence should see fit to remove him, it would be because of his own unworthiness to perform its humblest mission here on earth. With all this difference of opinion as to the cause of his decline, there could be no question of the fact. His form grew emaciated; his voice, though still rich and sweet, had a certain melancholy prophecy of decay in it; he was often observed, on any slight alarm or other sudden accident, to put his hand over his heart, with first a flush and then a paleness, indicative of pain.

Such was the young clergyman's condition, and so imminent the prospect that his dawning light would be extinguished, all untimely, when Roger Chillingworth made his advent to the town. His first entry on the scene, few people could tell whence, dropping down, as it were, out of the sky, or starting from the nether earth, had an aspect of mystery, which was easily heightened to the miraculous. He was now known to be a man of skill; it was observed that he gathered herbs, and the blossoms of wild-flowers, and dug up roots, and plucked off twigs from the forest-trees, like one acquainted with hidden virtues in what was valueless to common eyes. He was heard to speak of Sir Kenelm Digby, and other famous men,—whose scientific attainments were esteemed hardly less than supernatural, —as having been his correspondents or associates. Why, with such rank in the learned world, had he come hither? What could he, whose sphere was in great cities, be seeking in the wilderness? In answer to this query a rumor gained ground,—and, however absurd, was entertained by some very sensible people,—that Heaven had wrought an absolute miracle, by transporting an eminent Doctor of Physic, from a German university, bodily through the air, and setting him down at the door of Mr. Dimmesdale's study! Individuals of wiser faith, indeed, who knew that Heaven promotes its purposes without aiming at the stage-effect of what is called miraculous interposition, were inclined to see a providential hand in Roger Chillingworth's so opportune arrival.

This idea was countenanced by the strong interest which the physician ever manifested in the young clergyman; he attached himself to him as a parishioner, and sought to win a friendly regard and confidence from his naturally reserved sensibility. He expressed great alarm at his pastor's state of health, but was anxious to attempt the cure, and, if early undertaken, seemed not despondent of a favorable result. The elders, the deacons, the motherly dames, and the young and fair maidens, of Mr. Dimmesdale's flock, were alike importunate that he should make trial of the physician's frankly offered skill. Mr. Dimmesdale gently repelled their entreaties.

"I need no medicine," said he.

But how could the young minister say so, when, with every successive Sabbath, his cheek was paler and thinner, and his voice more tremulous than before,—when it had now become a constant habit, rather than a casual gesture, to press his hand over his heart? Was he weary of his labors? Did he wish to die? These questions were solemnly propounded to Mr. Dimmesdale by the elder ministers of Boston and the deacons of his church, who, to use their own phrase, "dealt with him" on the sin of rejecting the aid which Providence so manifestly held out. He listened in silence, and finally promised to confer with the physician.

"Were it God's will," said the Reverend Mr. Dimmesdale, when, in fulfilment of this pledge, he requested old Roger Chillingworth's professional advice, "I could be well content, that my labors, and my sorrows, and my sins, and my pains, should shortly end with

me, and what is earthly of them be buried in my grave, and the spiritual go with me to my eternal state, rather than that you should put your skill to the proof in my behalf."

"Ah," replied Roger Chillingworth, with that quietness which, whether imposed or natural, marked all his deportment, "it is thus that a young clergyman is apt to speak. Youthful men, not having taken a deep root, give up their hold of life so easily! And saintly men, who walk with God on earth, would fain be away, to walk with Him on the golden pavements of the New Jerusalem."

"Nay," rejoined the young minister, putting his hand to his heart, with a flush of pain flitting over his brow, "were I worthier to walk there, I could be better content to toil here."

"Good men ever interpret themselves too meanly," said the physician.

In this manner, the mysterious old Roger Chillingworth became the medical adviser of the Reverend Mr. Dimmesdale. As not only the disease interested the physician, but he was strongly moved to look into the character and qualities of the patient, these two men, so different in age, came gradually to spend much time together. For the sake of the minister's health, and to enable the leech to gather plants with healing balm in them, they took long walks on the sea-shore, or in the forest; mingling various talk with the plash and murmur of the waves, and the solemn wind-anthem among the tree-tops. Often, likewise, one was the guest of the other, in his place of study and retirement. There was a fascination for the minister in the company of the man of science, in whom he recognized an intellectual cultivation of no moderate depth or scope; together with a range and freedom of ideas, that he would have vainly looked for among the members of his own profession. In truth, he was startled, if not shocked, to find this attribute in the physician. Mr. Dimmesdale was a true priest, a true religionist, with the reverential sentiment largely developed, and an order of mind that impelled itself powerfully along the track of a creed, and wore its passage continually deeper with the lapse of time. In no state of society would he have been what is called a man of liberal views; it would always be essential to his peace to feel the pressure of a faith about his, supporting, while it confined him within its iron framework. Not the less, however, though with a tremulous enjoyment, did he feel the occasional relief of looking at the universe through the medium of another kind of intellect than those with which he habitually held converse. It was as if a window were thrown open, admitting a freer atmosphere into the close and stifled study, where his life was wasting itself away, amid lamplight, or obstructed day-beams, and the musty fragrance, be it sensual or moral, that exhales from books. But the air was too fresh and chill to be long breathed with comfort. So the minister, and the physician with him, withdrew again within the limits of what their church defined as orthodox.

Thus Roger Chillingworth scrutinized his patient carefully, both as he saw him in his ordinary life, keeping an accustomed pathway in the range of thoughts familiar to him, and as he appeared when thrown amidst other moral scenery, the novelty of which might call out something new to the surface of his character. He deemed it essential, it would seem, to know the man, before attempting to do him good. Wherever there is a heart and an intellect, the diseases of the physical frame are tinged with the peculiarities of these. In Arthur Dimmesdale, thought and imagination were so active, and sensibility so intense, that the bodily infirmity would be likely to have its groundwork there. So Roger Chillingworth—the man of skill, the kind and friendly physician—strove to go deep into his patient's bosom, delving among his principles, prying into his recollections, and probing everything with a cautious touch, like a treasure-seeker in a dark cavern. Few secrets can escape an investigator, who has opportunity and license to undertake such a quest, and skill to follow it up. A man burdened with a secret should especially avoid the intimacy of his physician. If the latter possess native sagacity, and a nameless something more,— let us call it intuition; if he show no intrusive egotism, nor disagreeably prominent characteristics of his own; if he have the power, which must be born with him, to bring his mind into such affinity with his patient's, that this last shall unawares have spoken what he imagines himself only to have thought; if such revelations be received without tumult, and acknowledged not so often by an uttered sympathy as by silence, an inarticulate breath, and here and there a word, to indicate that all is understood; if to these qualifications of a confidant be joined the advantages afforded by his recognized character as a physician;—then, at some inevitable moment, will the soul of the sufferer be dissolved, and flow forth in a dark, but transparent stream, bringing all its mysteries into the daylight.

Roger Chillingworth possessed all, or most, of the attributes above enumerated. Nevertheless, time went on; a kind of intimacy, as we have said, grew up between these two cultivated minds, which had as wide a field as the whole sphere of human thought and study, to meet upon; they discussed every topic of ethics and religion, of public affairs, and private character; they talked much, on both sides, of matters that seemed personal to themselves; and yet no secret, such as the physician fancied must exist there, ever stole out of the minister's consciousness into his companion's ear. The latter had his suspicions, indeed, that even the nature of Mr. Dimmesdale's bodily disease had never fairly been revealed to him. It was a strange reserve! After a time, at a hint from Roger Chillingworth, the friends of Mr. Dimmesdale effected an arrangement by which the two were lodged in the same house; so that every ebb and flow of the minister's life-tide might pass under the eye of his anxious and attached physician. There was much joy throughout the town when this greatly desirable object was attained. It was held to be the best possible measure for the young clergyman's welfare; unless, indeed, as often urged by such as felt authorized to do so, he had selected some one of the many blooming damsels, spiritually devoted to him, to become his devoted wife. This latter step, however, there was no present prospect that Arthur Dimmesdale would be prevailed upon to take; he rejected all suggestions of the kind, as if priestly celibacy were one of his articles of church-discipline. Doomed by nis own choice, therefore, as Mr. Dimmesdale so evidently was, to eat his unsavory morsel always at another's board, and endure the life-long chill which must be his lot who seeks to warm himself only at another's fireside, it truly seemed that his sagacious, experienced, benevolent old physician, with his concord of paternal and reverential love for the young pastor, was the very man, of all mankind, to be constantly within reach of his voice.

The new abode of the two friends was with a pious widow, of good social rank, who dwelt in a house covering pretty nearly the site on which the venerable structure of King's Chapel has since been built. It had the grave-yard, originally Isaac Johnson's homefield, on one side, and so was well adapted to call up serious reflections, suited to their respective employments, in both minister and man of physic. The motherly care of the good widow assigned to Mr. Dimmesdale a front apartment, with a sunny exposure, and heavy window-curtains, to create a noontide shadow, when desirable. The walls were hung round with tapestry, said to be from the Gobelin looms, and, at all events, representing the Scriptural story of David and Bathsheba, and Nathan the Prophet, in colors still unfaded, but which made the fair woman of the scene almost as grimly picturesque as the woe-denouncing seer. Here, the pale clergyman piled up his library, rich with parchment-bound folios of the Fathers, and the lore of Rabbis, and monkish erudition, of which the Protestant divines, even while they vilified and decried that class of writers, were yet constrained often to avail themselves. On the other side of the house, old Roger Chillingworth arranged his study and laboratory; not such as a modern man of science would reckon even tolerably complete, but provided with a distilling apparatus, and the means of compounding drugs and chemicals, which the practised alchemist knew well how to turn to purpose. With such commodiousness of situation, these two learned persons sat themselves down, each in his own domain, yet familiarly passing from one apartment to the other, and bestowing a mutual and not incurious inspection into one another's business.

And the Reverend Arthur Dimmesdale's best discerning friends, as we have intimated, very reasonably imagined that the hand of Providence had done all this, for the purpose—besought in so many public, and domestic, and secret prayers—of restoring the young minister to health. But—it must now be said—another portion of the community had latterly begun to take its own view of the relation betwixt Mr. Dimmesdale and the mysterious old physician. When an uninstructed multitude attempts to see with its eyes, it is exceedingly apt to be deceived. When, however, it forms its judgment, as it usually does, on the intuitions of its great and warm heart, the conclusions thus attained are often so profound and so unerring, as to possess the character of truths supernaturally revealed. The people, in the case of which we speak, could justify its prejudice against Roger Chillingworth by no fact or argument worthy of serious refutation. There was an aged handicraftsman, it is true, who had been a citizen of London at the period of Sir Thomas Overbury's murder, now some thirty years agone; he testified to having seen the physician, under some other name, which the narrator of the story had now forgotten, in company with Doctor Forman, the famous old conjurer, who was implicated in the affair of Overbury. Two or three individuals hinted, that the man of skill, during his Indian captivity, had enlarged his medical attainments by joining in the incantations of the savage priests; who were universally acknowledged to be powerful enchanters, often performing seemingly miraculous cures by their skill in the black art. A large number—and many of these were persons of such sober sense and practical observation that their opinions would have been valuable, in other matters—affirmed that Roger Chillingworth's aspect had undergone a remarkable change while he had dwelt in town, and especially since his abode with Mr. Dimmesdale. At first, his expression had been calm, meditative, scholar-like. Now, there was something ugly and evil in his face, which they had not previously noticed, and which grew still the more obvious to sight, the oftener they looked upon him. According to the vulgar idea, the fire in his laboratory had been brought from the lower regions, and was fed with infernal fuel; and so, as might be expected, his visage was getting sooty with the smoke.

To sum up the matter, it grew to be a widely diffused opinion, that the Reverend Arthur Dimmesdale, like many other personages of especial sanctity, in all ages of the Christian world, was haunted either by Satan himself, or Satan's emissary, in the guise of old Roger Chillingworth. This diabolical agent had the Divine permission, for a season, to burrow into the clergyman's intimacy, and plot against his soul. No sensible man, it was confessed, could doubt on which side the victory would turn. The people looked, with an unshaken hope, to see the minister come forth out of the conflict, transfigured with the glory which he would unquestionably win. Meanwhile, nevertheless, it was sad to think of the perchance mortal agony through which he must struggle towards his triumph.

Alas! to judge from the gloom and terror in the depths of the poor minister's eyes, the battle was a sore one, and the victory anything but secure.

CHAPTER X

THE LEECH AND HIS PATIENT

OLD Roger Chillingworth, throughout life, had been calm in temperament, kindly, though not of warm affections, but ever, and in all his relations with the world, a pure and upright man. He had begun an investigation, as he imagined, with the severe and equal integrity of a judge, desirous only of truth, even as if the question involved no more than the air-drawn lines and figures of a geometrical problem, instead of human passions, and wrongs inflicted on himself. But, as he proceeded, a terrible fascination, a kind of fierce, though still calm, necessity seized the old man within its gripe, and never set him free again, until he had done all its bidding. He now dug into the poor clergyman's heart, like a miner searching for gold; or, rather, like a sexton delving into a grave, possibly in quest of a jewel that had been buried on the dead man's bosom, but likely to find nothing save mortality and corruption. Alas for his own soul, if these were what he sought!

Sometimes, a light glimmered out of the physician's eyes, burning blue and ominous, like the reflection of a furnace, or, let us say, like one of those gleams of ghastly fire that darted from Bunyan's awful doorway in the hill-side, and quivered on the pilgrim's face. The soil where this dark miner was working had perchance shown indications that encouraged him.

"This man," said he, at one such moment, to himself, "pure as they deem him,—all spiritual as he seems,—hath inherited a strong animal nature from his father or his mother. Let us dig a little further in the direction of this vein!"

Then, after long search into the minister's dim interior, and turning over many precious materials, in the shape of high aspirations for the welfare of his race, warm love of souls, pure sentiments, natural piety, strengthened by thought and study, and illuminated by revelation,—all of which invaluable gold was perhaps no better than rubbish to the seeker,—he would turn back, discouraged, and begin his quest towards another point. He groped along as stealthily, with as cautious a tread, and as wary an outlook, as a thief entering a chamber where a man lies only half asleep,—or, it may be, broad awake,—with the purpose to steal the very treasure which this man guards as the apple of his eye. In spite of his premeditated carefulness, the floor would now and then creak; his garments would rustle; the shadow of his presence, in a forbidden proximity, would be thrown across his victim. In other words, Mr. Dimmesdale, whose sensibility of nerve often produced the effect of spiritual intuition, would become vaguely aware that something inimical to his peace had thrust itself into relation with him. But old Roger Chillingworth, too, had perceptions that were almost intuitive; and when the minister threw his startled eyes towards him, there the physician sat; his kind, watchful, sympathizing, but never intrusive friend.

Yet Mr. Dimmesdale would perhaps have seen this individual's character more perfectly, if a certain morbidness, to which sick hearts are liable, had not rendered him suspicious of all mankind. Trusting no man as his friend, he could not recognize his enemy when the latter actually appeared. He therefore still kept up a familiar intercourse with him, daily receiving the old physician in his study; or visiting the laboratory, and, for recreation's sake, watching the processes by which weeds were converted into drugs of potency.

One day, leaning his forehead on his hand, and his elbow on the sill of the open window, that looked towards the grave-yard, he talked with Roger Chillingworth, while the old man was examining a bundle of unsightly plants.

"Where," asked he, with a look askance at them,—for it was the clergyman's peculiarity that he seldom, nowadays, looked straightforth at any object, whether human or inanimate—"where, my kind doctor, did you gather those herbs, with such a dark, flabby leaf?"

"Even in the grave-yard here at hand," answered the physician, continuing his employment. "They are new to me. I found them growing on a grave, which bore no tomb-stone, nor other memorial of the dead man, save these ugly weeds, that have taken upon themselves to keep him in remembrance. They grew out of his heart, and typify, it may be, some hideous secret that was buried with him, and which he had done better to confess during his lifetime."

"Perchance," said Mr. Dimmesdale, "he earnestly desired it, but could not."

"And wherefore?" rejoined the physician. "Wherefore not; since all the powers of nature call so earnestly for the confession of sin, that these black weeds have sprung up out of a buried heart, to make manifest an unspoken crime?"

"That, good Sir, is but a fantasy of yours," replied the minister. "There can be, if I forebode aright, no power, short of the Divine mercy, to disclose, whether by uttered words or by type or emblem, the secrets that may be buried with a human heart. The heart, making itself guilty of such secrets, must perforce hold them, until the day when all hidden things shall be revealed. Nor have I so read or interpreted Holy Writ, as to understand that the disclosure of human thoughts and deeds, then to be made, is intended as a part of the retribution. That, surely, were a shallow view of it. No; these revelations, unless I greatly err, are meant merely to promote the intellectual satisfaction of all intelligent beings, who will stand waiting, on that day, to see the dark problem of this life made plain. A knowledge of men's hearts will be needful to the completest solution of that problem. And I conceive, moreover, that the hearts holding such miserable secrets as you speak of will yield them up, at that last day, not with reluctance, but with a joy unutterable."

"Then why not reveal them here?" asked Roger Chillingworth, glancing quietly aside at the minister. "Why should not the guilty ones sooner avail themselves of this unutterable solace?"

"They mostly do," said the clergyman, griping hard at his breast, as if afflicted with an importunate throb of pain. "Many, many a poor soul hath given its confidence to me, not only on the death-bed, but while strong in life, and fair in reputation. And ever, after such an outpouring, O, what a relief have I witnessed in those sinful brethren! even as in one who at last draws free air, after long stifling with his own polluted breath. How can it be otherwise? Why should a wretched man, guilty, we will say, of murder, prefer to keep the dead corpse buried in his own heart, rather than fling it forth at once, and let the universe take care of it!"

"Yet some men bury their secrets thus," observed the calm physician.

"True; there are such men," answered Mr. Dimmesdale. "But, not to suggest more obvious reasons, it may be that they are kept silent by the very constitution of their nature. Or,—can we not suppose it?—guilty as they may be, retaining, nevertheless, a zeal for God's glory and man's welfare, they shrink from displaying themselves black and filthy in the view of men; because, thenceforward, no good can be achieved by them; no evil of the past be redeemed by better service. So, to their own unutterable torment, they go about among their fellow-creatures, looking pure as new-fallen snow; while their hearts are all speckled and spotted with iniquity of which they cannot rid themselves."

"These men deceive themselves," said Roger Chillingworth, with somewhat more emphasis than usual, and making a slight gesture with his forefinger. "They fear to take up the shame that rightfully belongs to them. Their love for man, their zeal for God's service,—these holy impulses may or may not coëxist in their hearts with the evil inmates to which their guilt has unbarred the door, and which must needs propagate a hellish breed within them. But, if they seek to glorify God, let them not lift heavenward their unclean hands! If they would serve their fellow-men, let them do it by making manifest the power and reality of conscience, in constraining them to penitential self-abasement! Wouldst thou have me to believe, O wise and pious friend, that a false show can be better —can be more for God's glory, or man's welfare—than God's own truth? Trust me, such men deceive themselves!"

"It may be so," said the young clergyman, indifferently, as waiving a discussion that he considered irrelevant or unseasonable. He had a ready faculty, indeed, of escaping from any topic that agitated his too sensitive and nervous temperament.—"But, now, I would ask of my well-skilled physician, whether, in good soothe, he deems me to have profited by his kindly care of this weak frame of mine?"

Before Roger Chillingworth could answer, they heard the clear, wild laughter of a young child's voice, proceeding from the adjacent burial-ground. Looking instinctively from the open window,—for it was summer-time, —the minister beheld Hester Prynne and little Pearl passing along the footpath that traversed the enclosure. Pearl looked as beautiful as the day, but was in one of those moods of perverse merriment which, whenever they occurred, seemed to remove her entirely out of the sphere of sympathy or human contact. She now skipped irreverently from one grave to another; until, coming to the broad, flat, armorial tombstone of a departed worthy,—perhaps of Isaac Johnson himself,—she began to dance upon it. In reply to her mother's command and entreaty that she would behave more decorously, little Pearl paused to gather the prickly burrs from a tall burdock which grew beside the tomb. Taking a handful of these, she arranged them along the lines of the scarlet letter that decorated the maternal bosom, to which the burrs, as their nature was, tenaciously adhered. Hester did not pluck them off.

Roger Chillingworth had by this time approached the window, and smiled grimly down.

"There is no law, nor reverence for authority, no regard for human ordinances or opinions, right or wrong, mixed up with that child's composition," remarked he, as much to himself as to his companion. "I saw her, the other day, bespatter the Governor himself with water, at the cattle-trough in Spring-lane. What, in Heaven's name, is she? Is the imp altogether evil? Hath she affections? Hath she any discoverable principle of being?"

"None,—save the freedom of a broken law," answered Mr. Dimmesdale, in a quiet way, as if he had been discussing the point within himself. "Whether capable of good, I know not."

The child probably overheard their voices; for, looking up to the window, with a bright, but naughty smile of mirth and intelligence, she threw one of the prickly burrs at the Reverend Mr. Dimmesdale. The sensitive clergyman shrank, with nervous dread, from the light missile. Detecting his emotion, Pearl clapped her little hands, in the most extravagant ecstasy. Hester Prynne, likewise, had involuntarily looked up; and all these four persons, old and young, regarded one another in silence, till the child laughed aloud, and shouted,—"Come away, mother! Come away, or yonder old Black Man will catch you! He hath got hold of the minister already. Come away, mother, or he will catch you! But he cannot catch little Pearl!"

So she drew her mother away, skipping, dancing, and frisking fantastically, among the hillocks of the dead people, like a creature that had nothing in common with a bygone and buried generation, nor owned herself akin to it. It was as if she had been made afresh, out of new elements, and must perforce be permitted to live her own life, and be a law unto herself, without her eccentricities being reckoned to her for a crime.

"There goes a woman," resumed Roger Chillingworth, after a pause, "who, be her demerits what they may, hath none of that mystery of hidden sinfulness which you deem so grievous to be borne. Is Hester Prynne the less miserable, think you, for that scarlet letter on her breast?"

"I do verily believe it," answered the clergyman. "Nevertheless, I cannot answer for her. There was a look of pain in her face, which I would gladly have been spared the sight of. But still, methinks, it must needs be better for the sufferer to be free to show his pain, as this poor woman Hester is, than to cover it all up in his heart."

There was another pause; and the physician began anew to examine and arrange the plants which he had gathered.

"You inquired of me, a little time agone," said he, at length, "my judgment as touching your health."

"I did," answered the clergyman, "and would gladly learn it. Speak frankly, I pray you, be it for life or death."

"Freely, then, and plainly," said the physician, still busy with his plants, but keeping a wary eye on Mr. Dimmesdale, "the disorder is a strange one; not so much in itself, nor as outwardly manifested,—in so far, at least, as the symptoms have been laid open to my observation. Looking daily at you, my good Sir, and watching the tokens of your aspect, now for months gone by, I should deem you a man sore sick, it may be, yet not so sick but that an instructed and watchful physician might well hope to cure you. But—I know not what to say—the disease is what I seem to know, yet know it not."

"You speak in riddles, learned Sir," said the pale minister, glancing aside out of the window.

"Then, to speak more plainly," continued the physician, "and I crave pardon, Sir,—should it seem to require pardon,—for this needful plainness of my speech. Let me ask,—as your friend, —as one having charge, under Providence, of your life and physical wellbeing,—hath all the operation of this disorder been fairly laid open and recounted to me?"

"How can you question it?" asked the minister. "Surely, it were child's play, to call in a physician, and then hide the sore!"

"You would tell me, then, that I know all?" said Roger Chillingworth, deliberately, and fixing an eye, bright with intense and concentrated intelligence, on the minister's face. "Be it so! But, again! He to whom only the outward and physical evil is laid open, knoweth, oftentimes, but half the evil which he is called upon to cure. A bodily disease, which we look upon as whole and entire within itself, may, after all, be but a symptom of some ailment in the spiritual part. Your pardon, once again, good Sir, if my speech give the shadow of offence. You, Sir, of all men whom I have known, are he whose body is the closest conjoined, and imbued, and identified, so to speak, with the spirit whereof it is the instrument."

"Then I need ask no further," said the clergyman, somewhat hastily rising from his chair. "You deal not, I take it, in medicine for the soul!"

"Thus, a sickness," continued Roger Chillingworth, going on, in an unaltered tone, without heeding the interruption, —but standing up, and confronting the emaciated and white-cheeked minister, with his low, dark and misshapen fig-are,—"a sickness, a sore place, if we may so call it, in your spirit hath immediately its appropriate manifestation in your bodily frame. Would you, therefore, that your physician heal the bodily evil? How may this be, unless you first lay open to him the wound or trouble in your soul?"

"No!—not to thee!—not to an earthly physician!" cried Mr. Dimmesdale, passionately, and turning his eyes, full and bright, with a kind of fierceness, on old Roger Chillingworth. "Not to thee! But if it be the soul's disease, then do I commit myself to the one Physician of the soul! He, if it stand with his good pleasure, can cure; or he can kill! Let him do with me as, in his justice and wisdom, he shall see good. But who art thou, that meddlest in this matter?—that dares thrust himself between the sufferer and his God?"

With a frantic gesture, he rushed out of the room.

"It is as well to have made this step," said Roger Chillingworth to himself, looking after the minister, with a grave smile. "There is nothing lost. We shall be friends again anon. But see, now, how passion takes hold upon this man, and hurrieth him out of himself! As with one passion, so with another! He hath done a wild thing ere now, this pious Master Dimmesdale, in the hot passion of his heart!"

It proved not difficult to reëstablish the intimacy of the two companions, on the same footing and in the same degree as heretofore. The young clergyman, after a few hours of privacy, was sensible that the disorder of his nerves had hurried him into an unseemly outbreak of temper, which there had been nothing in the physician's words to excuse or palliate. He marvelled, indeed, at the violence with which he had thrust back the kind old man when merely proffering the advice which it was his duty to bestow, and which the minister himself had expressly sought. With these remorseful feelings, he lost no time in making the amplest apologies, and besought his friend still to continue the care, which, if not successful in restoring him to health, had, in all probability, been the means of prolonging his feeble existence to that hour. Roger Chillingworth readily assented, and went on with his medical supervision of the minister; doing his best for him, in all good faith, but always quitting the patient's apartment, at the close of a professional interview, with a mysterious and puzzled smile upon his lips. This expression was invisible in Mr. Dimmesdale's presence, but grew strongly evident as the physician crossed the threshold.

"A rare case!" he muttered. "I must needs look deeper into it. A strange sympathy betwixt soul and body! Were it only for the art's sake, I must search this matter to the bottom!"

It came to pass, not long after the scene above recorded, that the Reverend Mr. Dimmesdale, at noon-day, and entirely unawares, fell into a deep, deep slumber, sitting in his chair, with a large black-letter volume open before him on the table. It must have been a work of vast ability in the somniferous school of literature. The profound depth of the minister's repose was the more remarkable, inasmuch as he was one of those persons whose sleep, ordinarily, is as light, as fitful, and as easily scared away, as a small bird hopping on a twig. To such an unwonted remoteness, however, had his spirit now withdrawn into itself, that he stirred not in his chair, when old Roger Chillingworth, without any extraordinary precaution, came into the room. The physician advanced directly in front of his patient, laid his hand upon his bosom, and thrust aside the vestment, that, hitherto, had always covered it even from the professional eye.

Then, indeed, Mr. Dimmesdale shuddered, and slightly stirred.

After a brief pause, the physician turned away.

But, with what a wild look of wonder, joy, and horror! With what a ghastly rapture, as it were, too mighty to be expressed only by the eye and features, and, therefore bursting forth through the whole ugliness of his figure, and making itself even riotously manifest by the extravagant gestures with which he threw up his arms towards the ceiling, and stamped his foot upon the floor! Had a man seen old Roger Chillingworth, at that moment of his ecstasy, he would have had no need to ask how Satan comports himself, when a precious human soul is lost to heaven, and won into his kingdom.

But what distinguished the physician's ecstasy from Satan's was the trait of wonder in it!

CHAPTER XI

THE INTERIOR OF A HEART

AFTER the incident last described, the intercourse between the clergyman and the physician, though externally the same, was really of another character than it had previously been. The intellect of Roger Chillingworth had now a sufficiently plain path before it. It was not, indeed, precisely that which he had laid out for himself to tread. Calm, gentle, passionless, as he appeared, there was yet, we fear, a quiet depth of malice, hitherto latent, but active now, in this unfortunate old man, which led him to imagine a more intimate revenge than any mortal had ever wreaked upon an enemy. To make himself the one trusted friend, to whom should be confided all the fear, the remorse, the agony, the ineffectual repentance, the backward rush of sinful thoughts, expelled in vain! All that guilty sorrow, hidden from the world, whose great heart would have pitied and forgiven, to be revealed to him, the Pitiless, to him, the Unforgiving! All that dark treasure to be lavished on the very man, to whom nothing else could so adequately pay the debt of vengeance!

The clergyman's shy and sensitive reserve had balked this scheme. Roger Chillingworth, however, was inclined to be hardly, if at all, less satisfied with the aspect of affairs, which Providence —using the avenger and his victim for its own purposes, and, perchance, pardoning, where it seemed most to punish —had substituted for his black devices. A revelation, he could almost say, had been granted to him. It mattered little, for his object, whether celestial, or from what other region. By its aid, in all the subsequent relations betwixt him and Mr. Dimmesdale, not merely the external presence, but the very inmost soul, of the latter, seemed to be brought out before his eyes, so that he could see and comprehend its every movement. He became, thenceforth, not a spectator only, but a chief actor, in the poor minister's interior world. He could play upon him as he chose. Would he arouse him with a throb of agony? The victim was forever on the rack; it needed only to know the spring that controlled the engine;—and the physician knew it well! Would he startle him with sudden fear? As at the waving of a magician's wand, uprose a grisly phantom,—uprose a thousand phantoms,—in many shapes, of death, or more awful shame, all flocking round about the clergyman, and pointing with their fingers at his breast!

All this was accomplished with a subtlety so perfect, that the minister, though he had constantly a dim perception of some evil influence watching over him, could never gain a knowledge of its actual nature. True, he looked doubtfully, fearfully,—even, at times, with horror and the bitterness of hatred, —at the deformed figure of the old physician. His gestures, his gait, his grizzled beard, his slightest and most indifferent acts, the very fashion of his garments, were odious in the clergyman's sight; a token implicitly to be relied on, of a deeper antipathy in the breast of the latter than he was willing to acknowledge to himself. For, as it was impossible to assign a reason for such distrust and abhorrence, so Mr. Dimmesdale, conscious that the poison

of one morbid spot was infecting his heart's entire substance, attributed all his presentiments to no other cause. He took himself to task for his bad sympathies in reference to Roger Chillingworth, disregarded the lesson that he should have drawn from them, and did his best to root them out. Unable to accomplish this, he nevertheless, as a matter of principle, continued his habits of social familiarity with the old man, and thus gave him constant opportunities for perfecting the purpose to which—poor, forlorn creature that he was, and more wretched than his victim—the avenger had devoted himself.

While thus suffering under bodily disease, and gnawed and tortured by some black trouble of the soul, and given over to the machinations of his deadliest enemy, the Reverend Mr. Dimmesdale had achieved a brilliant popularity in his sacred office. He won it, indeed, in great part, by his sorrows. His intellectual gifts, his moral perceptions, his power of experiencing and communicating emotion, were kept in a state of preternatural activity by the prick and anguish of his daily life. His fame, though still on its upward slope, already overshadowed the soberer reputations of his fellow-clergymen, eminent as several of them were. There were scholars among them, who had spent more years in acquiring abstruse lore, connected with the divine profession, than Mr. Dimmesdale had lived; and who might well, therefore, be more profoundly versed in such solid and valuable attainments than their youthful brother. There were men, too, of a sturdier texture of mind than his, and endowed with a far greater share of shrewd, hard, iron, or granite understanding; which, duly mingled with a fair proportion of doctrinal ingredient, constitutes a highly respectable, efficacious, and unamiable variety of the clerical species. There were others, again, true saintly fathers, whose faculties had been elaborated by weary toil among their books, and by patient thought, and etherealized, moreover, by spiritual communications with the better world, into which their purity of life had almost introduced these holy personages, with their garments of mortality still clinging to them. All that they lacked was the gift that descended upon the chosen disciples at Pentecost, in tongues of flame; symbolizing, it would seem. not the power of speech in foreign and unknown languages, but that of addressing the whole human brotherhood in the heart's native language. These fathers, otherwise so apostolic, lacked Heaven's last and rarest attestation of their office, the Tongue of Flame. They would have vainly sought —had they ever dreamed of seeking— to express the highest truths through the humblest medium of familiar words and images. Their voices came down, afar and indistinctly, from the upper heights where they habitually dwelt.

Not improbably, it was to this latter class of men that Mr. Dimmesdale, by many of his traits of character, naturally belonged. To the high mountain-peaks of faith and sanctity he would have climbed, had not the tendency been thwarted by the burden, whatever it might be, of crime or anguish, beneath which it was his doom to totter. It kept him down, on a level with the lowest; him, the man of ethereal attributes, whose voice the angels might else have listened to and answered! But this very burden it was, that gave him sympathies so intimate with the sinful brotherhood of mankind; so that his heart vibrated in unison with theirs, and received their pain into itself, and sent its own throb of pain through a thousand other hearts, in gushes of sad, persuasive eloquence. Oftenest persuasive, but sometimes terrible! The people knew not the power that moved them thus. They deemed the young clergyman a miracle of holiness. They fancied him the mouthpiece of Heaven's messages of wisdom, and rebuke, and love. In their eyes, the very ground on which he trod was sanctified. The virgins of his church grew pale around him, victims of a passion so imbued with religious sentiment that they imagined it to be all religion, and brought it openly, in their white bosoms, as their most acceptable sacrifice before the altar. The aged members of his flock, beholding Mr. Dimmesdale's frame so feeble, while they were themselves so rugged in their infirmity, believed that he would go heavenward before them, and enjoined it upon their children, that their old bones should be buried close to their young pastor's holy grave. And, all this time, perchance, when poor Mr. Dimmesdale was thinking of his grave, he questioned with himself whether the grass would ever grow on it, because an accursed thing must there be buried!

It is inconceivable, the agony with which this public veneration tortured him! It was his genuine impulse to adore the truth, and to reckon all things shadow-like, and utterly devoid of weight or value, that had not its divine essence as the life within their life. Then. what was he?—a substance?—or the dimmest of all shadows? He longed to speak out, from his own pulpit, at the full height of his voice, and tell the people what he was. "I, whom you behold in these black garments of the priesthood,—I, who ascend the sacred desk, and turn my pale face heavenward, taking upon myself to hold communion, in your behalf, with the Most High Omniscience,—I, in whose daily life you discern the sanctity of Enoch, —I, whose footsteps, as you suppose, leave a gleam along my earthly track, whereby the pilgrims that shall come after me may be guided to the regions of the blest,—I, who have laid the hand of baptism upon your children,—I, who have breathed the parting prayer on your dying friends, to whom the Amen sounded faintly from a world which they had quitted,—I, your pastor, whom you so reverence and trust, am utterly a pollution and a lie!"

More than once, Mr. Dimmesdale had gone into the pulpit, with a purpose never to come down its steps, until he should have spoken words like the above. More than once, he had cleared his throat, and drawn in the long, deep, and tremulous breath, which, when sent forth again, would come burdened with the black secret of his soul. More than once—nay, more than a hundred times—he had actually spoken! Spoken! But how? He had told his hearers that he was altogether vile, a viler companion of the vilest, the worst of sinners, an abomination, a thing of unimaginable iniquity; and that the only wonder was, that they did not see his wretched body shrivelled up before their eyes, by the burning wrath of the Almighty! Could there be plainer speech than this? Would not the peo-

ple start up in their seats, by a simultaneous impulse, and tear him down out of the pulpit which he defiled? Not so, indeed! They heard it all, and did but reverence him the more. They little guessed what deadly purport lurked in those self-condemning words. "The godly youth!" said they among themselves. "The saint on earth! Alas, if he discern such sinfulness in his own white soul, what horrid spectacle would he behold in thine or mine!" The minister well knew—subtle, but remorseful hypocrite that he was!—the light in which his vague confession would be viewed. He had striven to put a cheat upon himself by making the avowal of a guilty conscience, but had gained only one other sin, and a self-acknowledged shame, without the momentary relief of being self-deceived. He had spoken the very truth, and transformed it into the veriest falsehood. And yet, by the constitution of his nature, he loved the truth, and loathed the lie, as few men ever did. Therefore, above all things else, he loathed his miserable self!

His inward trouble drove him to practices more in accordance with the old, corrupted faith of Rome, than with the better light of the church in which he had been born and bred. In Mr. Dimmesdale's secret closet, under lock and key, there was a bloody scourge. Oftentimes, this Protestant and Puritan divine had plied it on his own shoulders; laughing bitterly at himself the while, and smiting so much the more pitilessly because of that bitter laugh. It was his custom, too, as it has been that of many other pious Puritans, to fast,—not, however, like them, in order to purify the body and render it the fitter medium of celestial illumination but rigorously, and until his knees trembled beneath him, as an act of penance. He kept vigils, likewise, night after night, sometimes in utter darkness; sometimes with a glimmering lamp; and sometimes viewing his own face in a looking-glass, by the most powerful light which he could throw upon it. He thus typified the constant introspection wherewith he tortured, but could not purify, himself. In these lengthened vigils, his brain often reeled, and visions seemed to flit before him; perhaps seen doubtfully, and by a faint light of their own, in the remote dimness of the chamber, or more vividly, and close beside him, within the looking-glass. Now it was a herd of diabolic shapes, that grinned and mocked at the pale minister, and beckoned him away with them; now a group of shining angels, who flew upward heavily, as sorrow-laden, but grew more ethereal as they rose. Now came the dead friends of his youth, and his white-bearded father, with a saint-like frown, and his mother, turning her face away as she passed by. Ghost of a mother,—thinnest fantasy of a mother,—methinks she might yet have thrown a pitying glance towards her son! And now, through the chamber which these spectral thoughts had made so ghastly, glided Hester Prynne, leading along little Pearl, in her scarlet garb, and pointing her forefinger, first at the scarlet letter on her bosom, and then at the clergyman's own breast.

None of these visions ever quite deluded him. At any moment, by an effort of his will, he could discern substances through their misty lack of substance, and convince himself that they were not solid in their nature, like yonder table of carved oak, or that big, square, leathern-bound and brazen-clasped volume of divinity. But, for all that, they were, in one sense, the truest and most substantial things which the poor minister now dealt with. It is the unspeakable misery of a life so false as his, that it steals the pith and substance out of whatever realities there are around us, and which were meant by Heaven to be the spirit's joy and nutriment. To the untrue man, the whole universe is false,—it is impalpable,—it shrinks to nothing with his grasp. And he himself, in so far as he shows himself in a false light, becomes a shadow, or, indeed, ceases to exist. The only truth that continued to give Mr. Dimmesdale a real existence on this earth, was the anguish in his inmost soul, and the undissembled expression of it in his aspect. Had he once found power to smile, and wear a face of gayety, there would have been no such man!

On one of those ugly nights, which we have faintly hinted at, but forborne to picture forth, the minister started from his chair. A new thought had struck him. There might be a moment's peace in it. Attiring himself with as much care as if it had been for public worship, and precisely in the same manner, he stole softly down the staircase, undid the door, and issued forth.

CHAPTER XII

THE MINISTER'S VIGIL

WALKING in the shadow of a dream, as it were, and perhaps actually under the influence of a species of somnambulism, Mr. Dimmesdale reached the spot, where, now so long since, Hester Prynne had lived through her first hours of public ignominy. The same platform or scaffold, black and weather-stained with the storm or sunshine of seven long years, and foot-worn, too, with the tread of many culprits who had since ascended it, remained standing beneath the balcony of the meeting-house. The minister went up the steps.

It was an obscure night of early May. An unvaried pall of cloud muffled the whole expanse of sky from zenith to horizon. If the same multitude which had stood as eye-witnesses while Hester Prynne sustained her punishment could now have been summoned forth, they would have discerned no face above the platform, nor hardly the outline of a human shape, in the dark gray of the midnight. But the town was all asleep. There was no peril of discovery. The minister might stand there, if it so pleased him, until morning should redden in the east, without other risk than that the dank and chill night-air would creep into his frame, and stiffen his joints with rheumatism, and clog his throat with catarrh and cough; thereby defrauding the expectant audience of to-morrow's prayer and sermon. No eye could see him, save that ever-wakeful one which had seen him in his closet, wielding the bloody scourge. Why, then, had he come hither? Was

it but the mockery of penitence? A mockery, indeed, but in which his soul trifled with itself! A mockery at which angels blushed and wept, while fiends rejoiced, with jeering laughter! He had been driven hither by the impulse of that Remorse which dogged him everywhere, and whose own sister and closely linked companion was that Cowardice which invariably drew him back, with her tremulous gripe, just when the other impulse had hurried him to the verge of a disclosure. Poor, miserable man! what right had infirmity like his to burden itself with crime? Crime is for the iron-nerved, who have their choice either to endure it, or, if it press too hard, to exert their fierce and savage strength for a good purpose, and fling it off at once! This feeble and most sensitive of spirits could do neither, yet continually did one thing or another, which intertwined, in the same inextricable knot, the agony of heaven-defying guilt and vain repentance.

And thus, while standing on the scaffold, in this vain show of expiation, Mr. Dimmesdale was overcome with a great horror of mind, as if the universe were gazing at a scarlet token on his naked breast, right over his heart. On that spot, in very truth, there was, and there had long been, the gnawing and poisonous tooth of bodily pain. Without any effort of his will, or power to restrain himself, he shrieked aloud; an outcry that went pealing through the night, and was beaten back from one house to another, and reverberated from the hills in the background; as if a company of devils, detecting so much misery and terror in it, had made a plaything of the sound, and were bandying it to and fro.

"It is done!" muttered the minister, covering his face with his hands. "The whole town will awake, and hurry forth, and find me here!"

But it was not so. The shriek had perhaps sounded with a far greater power, to his own startled ears, than it actually possessed. The town did not awake, or, if it did, the drowsy slumberers mistook the cry either for something frightful in a dream, or for the noise of witches; whose voices, at that period, were often heard to pass over the settlements or lonely cottages, as they rode with Satan through the air. The clergyman, therefore, hearing no symptoms of disturbance, uncovered his eyes and looked about him. At one of the chamber-windows of Governor Bellingham's mansion, which stood at some distance, on the line of another street, he beheld the appearance of the old magistrate himself, with a lamp in his hand, a white night-cap on his head, and a long white gown enveloping his figure. He looked like a ghost, evoked unseasonably from the grave. The cry had evidently startled him. At another window of the same house, moreover, appeared old Mistress Hibbins, the Governor's sister, also with a lamp, which, even thus far off, revealed the expression of her sour and discontented face. She thrust forth her head from the lattice, and looked anxiously upward. Beyond the shadow of a doubt, this venerable witch-lady had heard Mr. Dimmesdale's outcry, and interpreted it, with its multitudinous echoes and reverberations, as the clamor of the fiends and night-hags, with whom she was well known to make excursions into the forest.

Detecting the gleam of Governor Bellingham's lamp the old lady quickly extinguished her own, and vanished. Possibly, she went up among the clouds. The minister saw nothing further of her motions. The magistrate, after a wary observation of the darkness—into which, nevertheless, he could see but little further than he might into a millstone—retired from the window.

The minister grew comparatively calm. His eyes, however, were soon greeted by a little, glimmering light, which, at first a long way off, was approaching up the street. It threw a gleam of recognition on here a post, and there a garden-fence, and here a latticed window-pane, and there a pump, with its full trough of water, and here, again, an arched door of oak, with an iron knocker, and a rough log for the door-step. The Reverend Mr. Dimmesdale noted all these minute particulars, even while firmly convinced that the doom of his existence was stealing onward, in the footsteps which he now heard; and that the gleam of the lantern would fall upon him, in a few moments more, and reveal his long-hidden secret. As the light grew nearer, he beheld, within its illuminated circle, his brother clergyman,—or, to speak more accurately, his professional father, as well as highly valued friend,—the Reverend Mr. Wilson; who, as Mr. Dimmesdale now conjectured, had been praying at the bedside of some dying man. And so he had. The good old minister came freshly from the death-chamber of Governor Winthrop, who had passed from earth to heaven within that very hour. And now, surrounded, like the saint-like personages of olden times, with a radiant halo, that glorified him amid this gloomy night of sin,— as if the departed Governor had left him an inheritance of his glory, or as if he had caught upon himself the distant shine of the celestial city, while looking thither-ward to see the triumphant pilgrim pass within its gates,— now, in short, good Father Wilson was moving homeward, aiding his footsteps with a lighted lantern! The glimmer of this luminary suggested the above conceits to Mr. Dimmesdale, who smiled,—nay, almost laughed at them, —and then wondered if he were going mad.

As the Reverend Mr. Wilson passed beside the scaffold, closely muffling his Geneva cloak about him with one arm, and holding the lantern before his breast with the other, the minister could hardly restrain himself from speaking.

"A good evening to you, venerable Father Wilson! Come up hither, I pray you, and pass a pleasant hour with me!"

Good heavens! Had Mr. Dimmesdale actually spoken? For one instant, he believed that these words had passed his lips. But they were uttered only within his imagination. The venerable Father Wilson continued to step slowly onward, looking carefully at the muddy pathway before his feet, and never once turning his head towards the guilty platform. When the light of the glimmering lantern had faded quite away, the minister discovered, by the faintness which came over him, that the last few moments had been a crisis of terrible anxiety; although his mind had made an involuntary effort to relieve it-

self by a kind of lurid playfulness.

Shortly afterwards, the like grisly sense of the humorous again stole in among the solemn phantoms of his thought. He felt his limbs growing stiff with the unaccustomed chilliness of the night, and doubted whether he should be able to descend the steps of the scaffold. Morning would break, and find him there. The neighborhood would begin to rouse itself. The earliest riser, coming forth in the dim twilight, would perceive a vaguely defined figure aloft on the place of shame; and, half crazed betwixt alarm and curiosity, would go, knocking from door to door, summoning all the people to behold the ghost— as he needs must think it—of some defunct transgressor. A dusky tumult would flap its wings from one house to another. Then—the morning light still waxing stronger—old patriarchs would rise up in great haste, each in his flannel gown, and matronly dames, without pausing to put off their night-gear. The whole tribe of decorous personages, who had never heretofore been seen with a single hair of their heads awry would start into public view, with the disorder of a nightmare in their aspects. Old Governor Bellingham would come grimly forth, with his King James' ruff fastened askew; and Mistress Hibbins, with some twigs of the forest clinging to her skirts, and looking sourer than ever, as having hardly got a wink of sleep after her night ride; and good Father Wilson, too, after spending half the night at a death-bed, and liking ill to be disturbed, thus early, out of his dreams about the glorified saints. Hither, likewise, would come the elders and deacons of Mr. Dimmesdale's church, and the young virgins who so idolized their minister, and had made a shrine for him in their white bosoms; which now, by the by, in their hurry and confusion, they would scantly have given themselves time to cover with their kerchiefs. All people, in a word, would come stumbling over their thresholds, and turning up their amazed and horror-stricken visages around the scaffold. Whom would they discern there, with the red eastern light upon his brow? Whom, but the Reverend Arthur Dimmesdale, half frozen to death, overwhelmed with shame, and standing where Hester Prynne had stood!

Carried away by the grotesque horror of this picture, the minister, unawares, and to his own infinite alarm, burst into a great peal of laughter. It was immediately responded to by a light, airy, childish laugh, in which a thrill of the heart,—but he knew not whether of exquisite pain, or pleasure as acute, —he recognized the tones of little Pearl.

"Pearl! Little Pearl!" cried he, after a moment's pause; then, suppressing his voice,—"Hester! Hester Prynne! Are you there?"

"Yes; it is Hester Prynne!" she replied, in a tone of surprise; and the minister heard her footsteps approaching from the sidewalk, along which she had been passing. "It is I, and my little Pearl."

"Whence come you, Hester?" asked the minister. "What sent you hither?"

"I have been watching at a death-bed," answered Hester Prynne;—"at Governor Winthrop's death-bed, and have taken his measure for a robe, and am now going homeward to my dwelling."

"Come up hither, Hester, thou and little Pearl," said the Reverend Mr.

Dimmesdale. "Ye have both been here before, but I was not with you. Come up hither once again, and we will stand all three together!"

She silently ascended the steps, and stood on the platform, holding little Pearl by the hand. The minister felt for the child's other hand, and took it. The moment that he did so, there came what seemed a tumultuous rush of new life, other life than his own, pouring like a torrent into his heart, and hurrying through all his veins, as if the mother and the child were communicating their vital warmth to his half-torpid system. The three formed an electric chain.

"Minister!" whispered little Pearl.

"What wouldst thou say, child?" asked Mr. Dimmesdale.

"Wilt thou stand here with mother and me, to-morrow noon-tide?" inquired Pearl.

"Nay; not so, my little Pearl," answered the minister; for, with the new energy of the moment, all the dread of public exposure, that had so long been the anguish of his life, had returned upon him; and he was already trembling at the conjunction in which—with a strange joy, nevertheless—he now found himself. "Not so, my child. I shall, indeed, stand with thy mother and thee one other day, but not to-morrow."

Pearl laughed, and attempted to pull away her hand. But the minister held it fast.

"A moment longer, my child!" said he.

"But wilt thou promise," asked Pearl, "to take my hand, and mother's hand, to-morrow noontide?"

"Not then, Pearl," said the minister, "but another time."

"And what other time?" persisted the child.

"At the great judgment day," whispered the minister,—and, strangely enough, the sense that he was a professional teacher of the truth impelled him to answer the child so. "Then, and there, before the judgment-seat, thy mother, and thou, and I, must stand together. But the daylight of this world shall not see our meeting!"

Pearl laughed again.

But before Mr. Dimmesdale had done speaking, a light gleamed far and wide over all the muffled sky. It was doubtless caused by one of those meteors, which the night-watcher may so often observe burning out to waste, in the vacant regions of the atmosphere. So powerful was its radiance, that it thoroughly illuminated the dense medium of cloud betwixt the sky and earth. The great vault brightened, like the dome of an immense lamp. It showed the familiar scene of the street, with the distinctness of mid-day, but also with the awfulness that is always imparted to familiar objects by an unaccustomed light. The wooden houses, with their jutting stories and quaint gable-peaks; the doorsteps and thresholds, with the early grass springing up about them; the garden-plots, black with freshly turned earth; the wheel-track, little worn, and, even in the market-place, margined with green on either side;—all were visible, but with a singularity of aspect that seemed to give another moral interpretation to the things of this world than they had ever borne before. And there stood the minister, with his hand over his heart; and Hester Prynne, with the embroidered letter glimmering on her bosom; and little Pearl, herself a symbol, and the connecting link between those two. They stood in the noon of that strange and solemn splendor, as if it were the light that is to reveal all secrets, and the daybreak that shall unite all who belong to one another.

There was witchcraft in little Pearl's eyes; and her face, as she glanced upward at the minister, wore that naughty smile which made its expression frequently so elvish. She withdrew her hand from Mr. Dimmesdale's, and pointed across the street. But he clasped both his hands over his breast, and cast his eyes towards the zenith.

Nothing was more common, in those days, than to interpret all meteoric appearances, and other natural phenomena, that occurred with less regularity than the rise and set of sun and moon, as so many revelations from a supernatural source. Thus, a blazing spear, a sword of flame, a bow, or a sheaf of arrows, seen in the midnight sky, prefigured Indian warfare. Pestilence was known to have been foreboded by a shower of crimson light. We doubt whether any marked event, for good or evil, ever befell New England, from its settlement down to Revolutionary times, of which the inhabitants had not been previously warned by some spectacle of this nature. Not seldom, it had been seen by multitudes. Oftener, however, its credibility rested on the faith of some lonely eye-witness, who beheld the wonder through the colored, magnifying, and distorting medium of his imagination, and shaped it more distinctly in his after-thought. It was, indeed, a majestic idea, that the destiny of nations should be revealed, in these awful hieroglyphics, on the cope of heaven. A scroll so wide might not be deemed too expansive for Providence to write a people's doom upon. The belief was a favorite one with our forefathers, as betokening that their infant commonwealth was under a celestial guardianship of peculiar intimacy and strictness. But what shall we say, when an individual discovers a revelation, addressed to himself alone, on the same vast sheet of record! In such a case, it could only be the symptom of a highly disordered mental state, when a man, rendered morbidly self-contemplative by long, intense, and secret pain, had extended his egotism over the whole expanse of nature, until the firmament itself should appear no more than a fitting page for his soul's history and fate!

We impute it, therefore, solely to the disease in his own eye and heart, that the minister, looking upward to the zenith, beheld there the appearance of an immense letter,—the letter A,—marked out in lines of dull red light. Not but the meteor may have shown itself at that point, burning duskily through a veil of cloud; but with no such shape as his guilty imagination gave it; or, at least, with so little definiteness, that another's guilt might have seen another symbol in it.

There was a singular circumstance that characterized Mr. Dimmesdale's psychological state, at this moment. All the time that he gazed upward to the zenith, he was, nevertheless, perfectly aware that little Pearl was pointing her finger towards old Roger Chillingworth, who stood at no great distance from the scaffold. The minister appeared to see him, with the same glance that discerned the miraculous letter. To his features, as to all other objects, the mete-

oric light imparted a new expression; or it might well be that the physician was not careful then, as at all other times, to hide the malevolence with which he looked upon his victim. Certainly, if the meteor kindled up the sky, and disclosed the earth, with an awfulness that admonished Hester Prynne and the clergyman of the day of judgment, then might Roger Chillingworth have passed with them for the arch-fiend, standing there with a smile and scowl, to claim his own. So vivid was the expression, or so intense the minister's perception of it, that it seemed still to remain painted on the darkness, after the meteor had vanished, with an effect as if the street and all things else were at once annihilated.

"Who is that man, Hester?" gasped Mr. Dimmesdale, overcome with terror. "I shiver at him! Dost thou know the man? I hate him, Hester!"

She remembered her oath, and was silent.

"I tell thee, my soul shivers at him!" muttered the minister again. "Who is he? Who is he? Canst thou do nothing for me? I have a nameless horror of the man!"

"Minister," said little Pearl, "I can tell thee who he is!"

"Quickly, then, child!" said the minister, bending his ear close to her lips. "Quickly!—and as low as thou canst whisper."

Pearl mumbled something into his ear, that sounded, indeed, like human language, but was only such gibberish as children may be heard amusing themselves with, by the hour together. At all events, if it involved any secret information in regard to old Roger Chillingworth, it was in a tongue unknown to the erudite clergyman, and did but increase the bewilderment of his mind. The elvish child then laughed aloud.

"Dost thou mock me now?" said the minister.

"Thou wast not bold!—thou wast not true!"—answered the child. "Thou wouldst not promise to take my hand, and mother's hand, to-morrow noontide!"

"Worthy Sir," answered the physician, who had now advanced to the foot of the platform. "Pious Master Dimmesdale! can this be you? Well, well, indeed! We men of study, whose heads are in our books, have need to be straitly looked after! We dream in our waking moments, and walk in our sleep. Come, good Sir, and my dear friend, I pray you, let me lead you home!"

"How knewest thou that I was here?" asked the minister, fearfully.

"Verily, and in good faith," answered Roger Chillingworth, "I knew nothing of the matter. I had spent the better part of the night at the bedside of the worshipful Governor Winthrop, doing what my poor skill might to give him ease. He going home to a better world, I, likewise, was on my way homeward, when this strange light shone out. Come with me, I beseech you, Reverend Sir; else you will be poorly able to do Sabbath duty to-morrow. Aha! see now, how they trouble the brain,—these books!—these books! You should study less, good Sir, and take a little pastime; or these night-whimsies will grow upon you."

"I will go home with you," said Mr. Dimmesdale.

With a chill despondency, like one awaking, all nerveless, from an ugly dream, he yielded himself to the physician, and was led away.

The next day, however, being the Sabbath, he preached a discourse which was held to be the richest and most powerful, and the most replete with heavenly influences, that had ever proceeded from his lips. Souls, it is said, more souls than one, were brought to the truth by the efficacy of that sermon, and vowed within themselves to cherish a holy gratitude towards Mr. Dimmesdale throughout the long hereafter. But, as he came down the pulpit steps, the gray-bearded sexton met him, holding up a black glove, which the minister recognized as his own.

"It was found," said the sexton, "this morning, on the scaffold where evil-doers are set up to public shame. Satan dropped it there, I take it, intending a scurrilous jest against your reverence. But, indeed, he was blind and foolish, as he ever and always is. A pure hand needs no glove to cover it!"

"Thank you, my good friend," said the minister, gravely, but startled at heart; for, so confused was his remembrance, that he had almost brought himself to look at the events of the past night as visionary. "Yes, it seems to be my glove, indeed!"

"And, since Satan saw fit to steal it, your reverence must needs handle him without gloves, henceforward," remarked the old sexton, grimly smiling. "But did your reverence hear of the portent that was seen last night?—a great red letter in the sky,—the letter A, which we interpret to stand for Angel. For, as our good Governor Winthrop was made an angel this past night, it was doubtless held fit that there should be some notice thereof!"

"No," answered the minister, "I have not heard of it."

CHAPTER XIII

ANOTHER VIEW OF HESTER

In her late singular interview with Mr. Dimmesdale, Hester Prynne was shocked at the condition to which she found the clergyman reduced. His nerve seemed absolutely destroyed. His moral force was abased into more than childish weakness. It grovelled helpless on the ground, even while his intellectual faculties retained their pristine strength, or had perhaps acquired a morbid energy, which disease only could have given them. With her knowledge of a train of circumstances hidden from all others, she could readily infer that, besides that legitimate action of his own conscience, a terrible machinery had been brought to bear, and was still operating, on Mr. Dimmesdale's well-being and repose. Knowing what this poor, fallen man had once been, her whole soul was moved by the shuddering terror with which he had appealed to her, —the outcast woman,—for support against his instinctively discovered enemy. She decided, moreover, that he had a right to her utmost aid. Little accustomed, in her long seclusion from society, to measure her ideas of right and wrong by any standard external to herself, Hester saw—or seemed to see—that there lay a responsibility upon her, in reference to the clergyman, which she owed to no other, nor to the whole world besides. The links that

united her to the rest of human kind —links of flowers, or silk, or gold, or whatever the material—had all been broken. Here was the iron link of mutual crime, which neither he nor she could break. Like all other ties, it brought along with it its obligations.

Hester Prynne did not now occupy precisely the same position in which we beheld her during the earlier periods of her ignominy. Years had come and gone. Pearl was now seven years old. Her mother, with the scarlet letter on her breast, glittering in its fantastic embroidery, had long been a familiar object to the townspeople. As is apt to be the case when a person stands out in any prominence before the community, and, at the same time, interferes neither with public nor individual interests and convenience, a species of general regard had ultimately grown up in reference to Hester Prynne. It is to the credit of human nature, that, except where its selfishness is brought into play, it loves more readily than it hates. Hatred, by a gradual and quiet process, will even be transformed to love, unless the change be impeded by a continually new irritation of the original feeling of hostility. In this matter of Hester Prynne, there was neither irritation nor irksomeness. She never battled with the public, but submitted, uncomplainingly, to its worst usage; she made no claim upon it, in requital for what she suffered; she did not weigh upon its sympathies. Then, also, the blameless purity of her life during all these years in which she had been set apart to infamy, was reckoned largely in her favor. With nothing now to lose, in the sight of mankind, and with no hope, and seemingly no wish, of gaining anything, it could only be a genuine regard for virtue that had brought back the poor wanderer to its path.

It was perceived, too, that while Hester never put forward even the humblest title to share in the world's privileges,—further than to breathe the common air, and earn daily bread for little Pearl and herself by the faithful labor of her hands,—she was quick to acknowledge her sisterhood with the race of man, whenever benefits were to be conferred. None so ready as she to give of her little substance to every demand of poverty; even though the bitter-hearted pauper threw back a gibe in requital of the food brought regularly to his door, or the garments wrought for him by the fingers that could have embroidered a monarch's robe. None so self-devoted as Hester, when pestilence stalked through the town. In all seasons of calamity, indeed, whether general or of individuals, the outcast of society at once found her place. She came, not as a guest, but as a rightful inmate, into the household that was darkened by trouble; as if its gloomy twilight were a medium in which she was entitled to hold intercourse with her fellow-creatures. There glimmered the embroidered letter, with comfort in its unearthly ray. Elsewhere the token of sin, it was the taper of the sick-chamber. It had even thrown its gleam, in the sufferer's hard extremity, across the verge of time. It had shown him where to set his foot, while the light of earth was fast becoming dim, and ere the light of futurity could reach him In such emergencies, Hester's nature showed itself warm and rich; a well-spring of human tenderness, unfailing to every real demand and inexhaustible by the largest. Her breast, with its badge of shame, was but the softer pillow for the head that needed one. She was self-ordained a Sister of Mercy; or, we may rather say, the world's heavy hand had so ordained her, when neither the world nor she looked forward to this result. The letter was the symbol of her calling. Such helpfulness was found in her,—so much power to do, and power to sympathize,—that many people refused to interpret the scarlet A by its original signification. They said that it meant Able; so strong was Hester Prynne, with a woman's strength.

It was only the darkened house that could contain her. When sunshine came again, she was not there. Her shadow had faded across the threshold. The helpful inmate had departed, without one backward glance to gather up the meed of gratitude, if any were in the hearts of those whom she had served so zealously. Meeting them in the street, she never raised her head to receive their greeting. If they were resolute to accost her, she laid her finger on the scarlet letter, and passed on. This might be pride, but was so like humility, that it produced all the softening influence of the latter quality on the public mind The public is despotic in its temper; it is capable of denying common justice, when too strenuously demanded as a right; but quite as frequently it awards more than justice, when the appeal is made, as despots love to have it made, entirely to its generosity. Interpreting Hester Prynne's deportment as an appeal of this nature, society was inclined to show its former victim a more benign countenance than she cared to be favored with, or, perchance, than she deserved.

The rulers, and the wise and learned men of the community, were longer in acknowledging the influence of Hester's good qualities than the people. The prejudices which they shared in common with the latter were fortified in themselves by an iron framework of reasoning, that made it a far tougher labor to expel them. Day by day, nevertheless, their sour and rigid wrinkles were relaxing into something which, in the due course of years, might grow to be an expression of almost benevolence. Thus it was with the men of rank, on whom their eminent position imposed the guardianship of the public morals. Individuals in private life, meanwhile, had quite forgiven Hester Prynne for her frailty; nay, more, they had begun to look upon the scarlet letter as the token, not of that one sin, for which she had borne so long and dreary a penance, but of her many good deeds since. "Do you see that woman with the embroidered badge?" they would say to strangers. "It is our Hester,—the town's own Hester,—who is so kind to the poor, so helpful to the sick, so comfortable to the afflicted!" Then, it is true, the propensity of human nature to tell the very worst of itself, when embodied in the person of another, would constrain them to whisper the black scandal of bygone years.

It was none the less a fact, however, that, in the eyes of the very men who spoke thus, the scarlet letter had the effect of the cross on a nun's bosom. It imparted to the wearer a kind of sacredness, which enabled her to walk securely amid all peril. Had she fallen among thieves, it would have kept her safe. It was reported, and believed by many, that an Indian had drawn his arrow against the badge, and that the missile struck, but fell harmless to the ground.

The effect of the symbol—or, rather, of the position in respect to society that was indicated by it—on the mind of Hester Prynne herself, was powerful and peculiar. All the light and graceful foliage of her character had been withered up by this red-hot brand, and had long ago fallen away, leaving a bare and harsh outline, which might have been repulsive, had she possessed friends or companions to be repelled by it. Even the attractiveness of her person had undergone a similar change. It might be partly owing to the studied austerity of her dress, and partly to the lack of demonstration in her manners. It was a sad transformation, too, that her rich and luxuriant hair had either been cut off, or was so completely hidden by a cap, that not a shining lock of it ever once gushed into the sunshine. It was due in part to all these causes, but still more to something else, that there seemed to be no longer anything in Hester's face for Love to dwell upon; nothing in Hester's form, though majestic and statue-like, that Passion would ever dream of clasping in its embrace; nothing in Hester's bosom, to make it ever again the pillow of Affection. Some attribute had departed from her, the permanence of which had been essential to keep her a woman. Such is frequently the fate, and such the stern development, of the feminine character and person, when the woman has encountered, and lived through, an experience of peculiar severity. If she be all tenderness, she will die. If she survive, the tenderness will either be crushed out of her, or—and the outward semblance is the same—crushed so deeply into her heart that it can never show itself more. The latter is perhaps the truest theory. She who has once been woman, and ceased to be so, might at any moment become a woman again, if there were only the magic touch to effect the transfiguration. We shall see whether Hester Prynne were ever afterwards so touched, and so transfigured.

Much of the marble coldness of Hester's impression was to be attributed to the circumstance, that her life had turned, in a great measure, from passion and feeling, to thought. Standing alone in the world,—alone, as to any dependence on society, and with little Pearl to be guided and protected,—alone, and hopeless of retrieving her position, even had she not scorned to consider it desirable,—she cast away the fragments of a broken chain. The world's law was no law for her mind. It was an age in which the human intellect, newly emancipated, had taken a more active and a wider range than for many centuries before. Men of the sword had overthrown nobles and kings. Men bolder than these had overthrown and rearranged—not actually, but within the sphere of theory, which was their most real abode—the whole system of ancient prejudice, wherewith was linked much of ancient principle. Hester Prynne imbibed this spirit. She assumed a freedom of speculation, then common enough on the other side of the Atlantic, but which our forefathers, had they known it, would have held to be a deadlier crime than that stigmatized by the scarlet letter. In her lonesome cottage, by the seashore, thoughts visited her, such as dared to enter no other dwelling in New England; shadowy guests, that would have been as perilous as demons to their entertainer, could they have been seen so much as knocking at her door.

It is remarkable, that persons who speculate the most boldly often conform with the most perfect quietude to the external regulations of society. The thought suffices them, without investing itself in the flesh and blood of action. So it seemed to be with Hester. Yet, had little Pearl never come to her from the spiritual world, it might have been far otherwise. Then, she might have come down to us in history, hand in hand with Ann Hutchinson, as the foundress of a religious sect. She might, in one of her phases, have been a prophetess. She might, and not improbably would, have suffered death from the stern tribunals of the period, for attempting to undermine the foundations of the Puritan establishment. But, in the education of her child, the mother's enthusiasm of thought had something to wreak itself upon. Providence, in the person of this little girl, had assigned to Hester's charge the germ and blossom of womanhood, to be cherished and developed amid a host of difficulties. Everything was against her. The world was hostile. The child's own nature had something wrong in it, which continually betokened that she had been born amiss,—the effluence of her mother's lawless passion,—and often impelled Hester to ask, in bitterness of heart, whether it were for ill or good that the poor little creature had been born at all.

Indeed, the same dark question often rose into her mind, with reference to the whole race of womanhood. Was existence worth accepting, even to the happiest among them? As concerned her own individual existence, she had long ago decided in the negative, and dismissed the point as settled. A tendency to speculation, though it may keep woman quiet, as it does man, yet makes her sad. She discerns, it may be, such a hopeless task before her. As a first step, the whole system of society is to be torn down, and built up anew. Then, the very nature of the opposite sex, or its long hereditary habit, which has become like nature, is to be essentially modified, before woman can be allowed to assume what seems a fair and suitable position. Finally, all other difficulties being obviated, woman cannot take advantage of these preliminary reforms, until she herself shall have undergone a still mightier change; in which, perhaps, the ethereal essence, wherein she has her truest life, will be found to have evaporated. A woman never overcomes these problems by any exercise of thought. They are not to be solved, or only in one way. If her heart chance to come uppermost, they vanish. Thus, Hester Prynne, whose heart had lost its regular and healthy throb, wandered without a clew in the dark labyrinth of mind; now turned aside by an insurmountable precipice; now starting back from a deep chasm. There was wild and ghastly scenery all around her, and a home and comfort nowhere. At times, a fearful doubt strove to possess her soul, whether it were not better to send Pearl at once to heaven, and go herself to such futurity as Eternal Justice should provide.

The scarlet letter had not done its office.

Now, however, her interview with the Reverend Mr. Dimmesdale, on the night of his vigil, had given her a new theme of reflection, and held up to her an object that appeared worthy of any exertion and sacrifice for its attainment. She had witnessed the intense misery beneath which the minister struggled, or, to speak more accurately, had ceased to struggle. She saw that he stood on the verge of lunacy, if he had not already stepped across it. It was impossible to doubt, that, whatever painful efficacy there might be in the secret sting of remorse, a deadlier venom had been infused into it by the hand that proffered relief. A secret enemy had been continually by his side, under the semblance of a friend and helper, and had availed himself of the opportunities thus afforded for tampering with the delicate springs of Mr. Dimmesdale's nature. Hester could not but ask herself, whether there had not originally been a defect of truth, courage and loyalty, on her own part, in allowing the minister to be thrown into a position where so much evil was to be foreboded, and nothing auspicious to be hoped. Her only justification lay in the fact, that she had been able to discern no method of rescuing him from a blacker ruin than had overwhelmed herself, except by acquiescing in Roger Chillingworth's scheme of disguise. Under that impulse, she had made her choice, and had chosen, as it now appeared, the more wretched alternative of the two. She determined to redeem her error, so far as it might yet be possible. Strengthened by years of hard and solemn trial, she felt herself no longer so inadequate to cope with Roger Chillingworth as on that night, abased by sin, and half maddened by the ignominy that was still new, when they had talked together in the prison-chamber. She had climbed her way, since then, to a higher point. The old man, on the other hand, had brought himself nearer to her level, or perhaps below it, by the revenge which he had stooped for.

In fine, Hester Prynne resolved to meet her former husband, and do what might be in her power for the rescue of the victim on whom he had so evidently set his gripe. The occasion was not long to seek. One afternoon, walking with Pearl in a retired part of the peninsula, she beheld the old physician, with a basket on one arm, and a staff in the other hand, stooping along the ground, in quest of roots and herbs to concoct his medicines withal.

CHAPTER XIV

HESTER AND THE PHYSICIAN

HESTER bade little Pearl run down to the margin of the water, and play with the shells and tangled seaweed, until she should have talked awhile with yonder gatherer of herbs. So the child flew away like a bird, and, making bare her small white feet, went pattering along the moist margin of the sea. Here and there she came to a full stop, and peeped curiously into a pool, left by the retiring tide as a mirror for Pearl to see her face in. Forth peeped at her, out of the pool, with dark, glistening curls around her head, and an elf-smile in her eyes, the image of a little maid, whom Pearl, having no other playmate, invited to take her hand, and run a race with her. But the visionary little maid, on her part, beckoned likewise, as if to say,—"This is a better place! Come thou into the pool!" And Pearl, stepping in, mid-leg deep, beheld her own white feet at the bottom; while, out of a still lower depth, came the gleam of a kind of fragmentary smile, floating to and fro in the agitated water.

Meanwhile, her mother had accosted the physician.

"I would speak a word with you," said she,—"a word that concerns us much."

"Aha! and is it Mistress Hester that has a word for old Roger Chillingworth?" answered he, raising himself from his stooping posture. "With all my heart! Why, Mistress, I hear good tidings of you, on all hands! No longer ago than yester-eve, a magistrate, a wise and godly man, was discoursing of your affairs, Mistress Hester, and whispered me that there had been question concerning you in the council. It was debated whether or no, with safety to the common weal, yonder scarlet letter might be taken off your bosom. On my life, Hester, I made my entreaty to the worshipful magistrate that it might be done forthwith!"

"It lies not in the pleasure of the magistrates to take off this badge," calmly replied Hester. "Were I worthy to be quit of it, it would fall away of its own nature, or be transformed into something that should speak a different purport."

"Nay, then, wear it, if it suit you better," rejoined he. "A woman must needs follow her own fancy, touching the adornment of her person. The letter is gayly embroidered, and shows right bravely on your bosom!"

All this while, Hester had been looking steadily at the old man, and was shocked, as well as wonder-smitten, to discern what a change had been wrought upon him within the past seven years. It was not so much that he had grown older; for though the traces of advancing life were visible, he bore his age well, and seemed to retain a wiry vigor and alertness. But the former aspect of an intellectual and studious man, calm and quiet, which was what she best remembered in him, had altogether vanished, and been succeeded by an eager, searching, almost fierce, yet carefully guarded look. It seemed to be his wish and purpose to mask this expression with a smile; but the latter played him false, and flickered over his visage so derisively, that the spectator could see his blackness all the better for it. Ever and anon, too, there came a glare of red light out of his eyes; as if the old man's soul were on fire, and kept on smouldering duskily within

his breast, until, by some casual puff of passion, it was blown into a momentary flame. This he repressed, as speedily as possible, and strove to look as if nothing of the kind had happened.

In a word, old Roger Chillingworth was a striking evidence of a man's faculty of transforming himself into a devil, if he will only, for a reasonable space of time, undertake a devil's office. This unhappy person had effected such a transformation, by devoting himself, for seven years, to the constant analysis of a heart full of torture, and deriving his enjoyment thence, and adding fuel to those fiery tortures which he analyzed and gloated over.

The scarlet letter burned on Hester Prynne's bosom. Here was another ruin, the responsibility of which came partly home to her.

"What see you in my face," asked the physician, "that you look at it so earnestly?"

"Something that would make me weep, if there were any tears bitter enough for it," answered she. "But let it pass! It is of yonder miserable man that I would speak."

"And what of him?" cried Roger Chillingworth, eagerly, as if he loved the topic, and were glad of an opportunity to discuss it with the only person of whom he could make a confidant. "Not to hide the truth, Mistress Hester, my thoughts happen just now to be busy with the gentleman. So speak freely; and I will make answer."

"When we last spake together," said Hester, "now seven years ago, it was your pleasure to extort a promise of secrecy, as touching the former relation betwixt yourself and me. As the life and good fame of yonder man were in your hands, there seemed no choice to me, save to be silent, in accordance with your behest. Yet it was not without heavy misgivings that I thus bound myself; for, having cast off all duty towards other human beings, there remained a duty towards him; and something whispered me that I was betraying it, in pledging myself to keep your counsel. Since that day, no man is so near to him as you. You tread behind his every footstep. You are beside him, sleeping and waking. You search his thoughts. You burrow and rankle in his heart! Your clutch is on his life, and you cause him to die daily a living death; and still he knows you not. In permitting this, I have surely acted a false part by the only man to whom the power was left me to be true!"

"What choice had you?" asked Roger Chillingworth. "My finger, pointed at this man, would have hurled him from his pulpit into a dungeon,—thence, peradventure, to the gallows!"

"It had been better so!" said Hester Prynne.

"What evil have I done the man?" asked Roger Chillingworth again. "I tell thee, Hester Prynne, the richest fee that ever physician earned from monarch could not have bought such care as I have wasted on this miserable priest! But for my aid, his life would have burned away in torments, within the first two years, after the perpetration of his crime and thine. For, Hester, his spirit lacked the strength that could have borne up, as thine has, beneath a burden like thy scarlet letter. O, I could reveal a goodly secret! But enough! What art can do, I have exhausted on him. That he now breathes, and creeps about on earth, is owing

all to me!"

"Better he had died at once!" said Hester Prynne.

"Yea, woman, thou sayest truly!" cried old Roger Chillingworth, letting the lurid fire of his heart blaze out before her eyes. "Better had he died at once! Never did mortal suffer what this man has suffered. And all, all, in the sight of his worst enemy! He has been conscious of me. He has felt an influence dwelling always upon him like a curse. He knew, by some spiritual sense,—for the Creator never made another being so sensitive as this,—he knew that no friendly hand was pulling at his heart-strings, and that an eye was looking curiously into him, which sought only evil, and found it. But he knew not that the eye and hand were mine! With the superstition common to his brotherhood, he fancied himself given over to a fiend, to be tortured with frightful dreams, and desperate thoughts, the sting of remorse, and despair of pardon; as a foretaste of what awaits him beyond the grave. But it was the constant shadow of my presence!—the closest propinquity of the man whom he had most vilely wronged!—and who had grown to exist only by this perpetual poison of the direst revenge! Yea, indeed!—he did not err!—there was a fiend at his elbow! A mortal man, with once a human heart, has become a fiend for his especial torment!"

The unfortunate physician, while uttering these words, lifted his hands with a look of horror, as if he had beheld some frightful shape, which he could not recognize, usurping the place of his own image in a glass. It was one of those moments—which sometimes occur only at the interval of years—when a man's moral aspect is faithfully revealed to his mind's eye. Not improbably, he had never before viewed himself as he did now.

"Hast thou not tortured him enough?" said Hester, noticing the old man's look. "Has he not paid thee all?"

"No!—no!—He has but increased the debt!" answered the physician; and as he proceeded, his manner lost its fiercer characteristics, and subsided into gloom. "Dost thou remember me, Hester, as I was nine years agone? Even then, I was in the autumn of my days, nor was it the early autumn. But all my life had been made up of earnest, studious, thoughtful, quiet years, bestowed faithfully for the increase of mine own knowledge, and faithfully, too, though this latter object was but casual to the other,—faithfully for the advancement of human welfare. No life had been more peaceful and innocent than mine; few lives so rich with benefits conferred. Dost thou remember me? Was I not, though you might deem me cold, nevertheless a man thoughtful for others, craving little for himself,—kind, true, just, and of constant, if not warm affections? Was I not all this?"

"All this, and more," said Hester.

"And what am I now?" demanded he, looking into her face, and permitting the whole evil within him to be written on his features. "I have already told thee what I am! A fiend! Who made me so?"

"It was myself!" cried Hester, shuddering. "It was I, not less than he. Why hast thou not avenged thyself on me?"

"I have left thee to the scarlet letter," replied Roger Chillingworth. "If that have not avenged me, I can do no more!"

He laid his finger on it, with a smile.

"It has avenged thee!" answered Hester Prynne.

"I judged no less," said the physician. "And now, what wouldst thou with me touching this man?"

"I must reveal the secret," answered Hester, firmly. "He must discern thee in thy true character. What may be the result, I know not. But this long debt of confidence, due from me to him, whose bane and ruin I have been, shall at length be paid. So far as concerns the overthrow or preservation of his fair fame and his earthly state, and perchance his life, he is in thy hands. Nor do I,—whom the scarlet letter has disciplined to truth, though it be the truth of red-hot iron, entering into the living soul,—nor do I perceive such advantage in his living any longer a life of ghastly emptiness, that I shall stoop to implore thy mercy. Do with him as thou wilt! There is no good for him,—no good for me,—no good for thee! There is no good for little Pearl! There is no path to guide us out of this dismal maze!"

"Woman, I could well-nigh pity thee!" said Roger Chillingworth, unable to restrain a thrill of admiration too; for there was a quality almost majestic in the despair which she expressed. "Thou hadst great elements. Peradventure, hadst thou met earlier with a better love than mine, this evil had not been. I pity thee, for the good that has been wasted in thy nature!"

"And I thee," answered Hester Prynne, "for the hatred that has transformed a wise and just man to a fiend! Wilt thou yet purge it out of thee, and be once more human? If not for his sake, then doubly for thine own! Forgive, and leave his further retribution to the Power that claims it! I said, but now, that there could be no good event for him, or thee, or me, who are here wandering together in this gloomy maze of evil, and stumbling, at every step, over the guilt wherewith we have strewn our path. It is not so! There might be good for thee, and thee alone, since thou hast been deeply wronged, and hast it at thy will to pardon. Wilt thou give up that only privilege? Wilt thou reject that priceless benefit?"

"Peace, Hester, Peace!" replied the old man, with gloomy sternness. "It is not granted me to pardon. I have no such power as thou tellest me of. My old faith, long forgotten, comes back to me, and explains all that we do, and all we suffer. By thy first step awry, thou didst plant the germ of evil; but since that moment, it has all been a dark necessity. Ye that have wronged me are not sinful, save in a kind of typical illusion; neither am I fiend-like, who have snatched a fiend's office from his hands. It is our fate. Let the black flower blossom as it may! Now go thy ways, and deal as thou wilt with yonder man."

He waved his hand, and betook himself again to his employment of gathering herbs.

CHAPTER XV

HESTER AND PEARL

So Roger Chillingworth—a deformed old figure, with a face that haunted men's memories longer than they liked —took leave of Hester Prynne, and went stooping away along the earth. He gathered here and there an herb, or grubbed up a root, and put it into the basket on his arm. His gray beard almost touched the ground, as he crept onward. Hester gazed after him a little while, looking with a half fantastic curiosity to see whether the tender grass of early spring would not be blighted beneath him, and show the wavering track of his footsteps, sere and brown, across its cheerful verdure. She wondered what sort of herbs they were, which the old man was so sedulous to gather. Would not the earth, quickened to an evil purpose by the sympathy of his eye, greet him with poisonous shrubs, of species hitherto unknown, that would start up under his fingers? Or might it suffice him, that every wholesome growth should be converted into something deleterious and malignant at his touch? Did the sun, which shone so brightly everywhere else, really fall upon him? Or was there, as it rather seemed, a circle of ominous shadow moving along with his deformity, whichever way he turned himself? And whither was he now going? Would he not suddenly sink into the earth, leaving a barren and blasted spot, where, in due course of time, would be seen deadly nightshade, dogwood, henbane, and whatever else of vegetable wickedness the climate could produce, all flourishing with hideous luxuriance? Or would he spread bat's wings and flee away, looking so much the uglier, the higher he rose towards heaven?

"Be it sin or no," said Hester Prynne, bitterly, as she still gazed after him, "I hate the man!"

She upbraided herself for the sentiment, but could not overcome or lessen it. Attempting to do so, she thought of those long-past days, in a distant land, when he used to emerge at eventide from the seclusion of his study, and sit down in the fire-light of their home, and in the light of her nuptial smile. He needed to bask himself in that smile, he said, in order that the chill of so many lonely hours among his books might be taken off the scholar's heart. Such scenes had once appeared not otherwise than happy, but now, as viewed through the dismal medium of her subsequent life, they classed themselves among her ugliest remembrances. She marvelled how such scenes could have been! She marvelled how she could ever have been wrought upon to marry him! She deemed it a crime most to be repented of, that she had ever endured, and reciprocated, the lukewarm grasp of his hand, and had suffered the smile of her lips and eyes to mingle and melt into his own. And it seemed a fouler offence committed by Roger Chillingworth, than any which had since been done him, that, in the time when her heart knew no better, he had persuaded her to fancy herself happy by his side.

"Yes, I hate him!" repeated Hester, more bitterly than before. "He betrayed me! He has done me worse wrong than I did him!"

Let men tremble to win the hand of woman, unless they win along with it the utmost passion of her heart! Else it may be their miserable fortune, as it was Roger Chillingworth's, when some mightier touch than their own may have awakened all her sensibilities, to be reproached even for the calm content, the marble image of happiness, which they will have imposed upon her as the warm reality. But Hester ought long ago to have done with this injustice. What did it betoken? Had seven long years, under the torture of the scarlet letter, inflicted so much of misery, and wrought out no repentance?

The emotions of that brief space, while she stood gazing after the crooked figure of old Roger Chillingworth, threw a dark light on Hester's state of mind, revealing much that she might not otherwise have acknowledged to herself.

He being gone, she summoned back her child.

"Pearl! Little Pearl! Where are you?"

Pearl, whose activity of spirit never flagged, had been at no loss for amusement while her mother talked with the old gatherer of herbs. At first, as already told, she had flirted fancifully with her own image in a pool of water, beckoning the phantom forth, and—as it declined to venture—seeking a passage for herself into its sphere of impalpable earth and unattainable sky. Soon finding, however, that either she or the image was unreal, she turned elsewhere for better pastime. She made little boats out of birch-bark, and freighted them with snail-shells, and sent out more ventures on the mighty deep than any merchant in New England; but the larger part of them foundered near the shore. She seized a live horse-shoe by the tail, and made prize of several five-fingers, and laid out a jelly-fish to melt in the warm sun. Then she took up the white foam, that streaked the line of the advancing tide, and threw it upon the breeze, scampering after it, with winged footsteps, to catch the great snow-flakes ere they fell. Perceiving a flock of beach-birds, that fed and fluttered along the shore, the naughty child picked up her apron full of pebbles, and, creeping from rock to rock after these small sea-fowl, displayed remarkable dexterity in pelting them. One little gray bird, with a white breast, Pearl was almost sure, had been hit by a pebble, and fluttered away with a broken wing. But then the elf-child sighed, and gave up her sport; because it grieved her to have done harm to a little being that was as wild as the sea-breeze, or as wild as Pearl herself.

Her final employment was to gather sea-weed, of various kinds, and make herself a scarf, or mantle, and a head-dress, and thus assume the aspect of a little mermaid. She inherited her mother's gift for devising drapery and costume. As the last touch to her mermaid's garb, Pearl took some eel-grass, and imitated, as best she could, on her own bosom, the decoration with which she was so familiar on her mother's. A letter,—the letter A,—but freshly green, instead of scarlet! The child bent her chin upon her breast, and contemplated this device with strange interest; even as if the one only thing for which she had been sent into the world was to make out its hidden import.

"I wonder if mother will ask me what it means?" thought Pearl.

Just then, she heard her mother's voice, and flitting along as lightly as one of the little sea-birds, appeared before Hester Prynne, dancing, laughing, and pointing her finger to the ornament upon her bosom.

"My little Pearl," said Hester, after a moment's silence, "the green letter, and on thy childish bosom, has no purport. But dost thou know, my child, what this letter means which thy mother is doomed to wear?"

"Yes, mother," said the child. "It is the great letter A. Thou hast taught me in the horn-book."

Hester looked steadily into her little face; but, though there was that singular expression which she had so often remarked in her black eyes, she could not satisfy herself whether Pearl really attached any meaning to the symbol. She felt a morbid desire to ascertain the point.

"Dost thou know, child, wherefore thy mother wears this letter?"

"Truly do I!" answered Pearl, looking brightly into her mother's face. "It is for the same reason that the minister keeps his hand over his heart!"

"And what reason is that?" asked Hester, half smiling at the absurd incongruity of the child's observation; but, on second thoughts, turning pale. "What has the letter to do with any heart, save mine?"

"Nay, mother, I have told all I know," said Pearl, more seriously than she was wont to speak. "Ask yonder old man whom thou hast been talking with! It may be he can tell. But in good earnest now, mother dear, what does this scarlet letter mean?—and why dost thou wear it on thy bosom?—and why does the minister keep his hand over his heart?"

She took her mother's hand in both her own, and gazed into her eyes with an earnestness that was seldom seen in her wild and capricious character. The thought occurred to Hester, that the child might really be seeking to approach her with child-like confidence, and doing what she could, and as intelligently as she knew how, to establish a meeting-point of sympathy. It showed Pearl in an unwonted aspect. Heretofore, the mother, while loving her child with the intensity of a sole affection, had schooled herself to hope for little other return than the waywardness of an April breeze; which spends its time in airy sport, and has its gusts of inexplicable passion, and is petulant in its best of moods, and chills oftener than caresses you, when you take it to your bosom; in requital of which misdemeanors, it will sometimes, of its own vague purpose, kiss your cheek with a kind of doubtful tenderness, and play gently with your hair, and then begone about its other idle business, leaving a dreamy pleasure at your heart. And this, moreover, was a mother's estimate of the child's disposition. Any other observer might have seen few but unamiable traits, and have given them a far darker coloring. But now the idea came strongly into Hester's mind, that Pearl, with her remarkable precocity and acuteness, might already have approached the age when she could be made a friend, and intrusted with as much of her mother's sorrows as could be imparted, without irreverence either to the parent or the child. In the little chaos of Pearl's character, there might be seen emerging—and could have been,

from the very first—the steadfast principles of an unflinching courage,—an uncontrollable will,—a sturdy pride, which might be disciplined into self-respect,—and a bitter scorn of many things, which, when examined, might be found to have the taint of falsehood in them. She possessed affections, too, though hitherto acrid and disagreeable, as are the richest flavors of unripe fruit. With all these sterling attributes, thought Hester, the evil which she inherited from her mother must be great indeed, if a noble woman do not grow out of this elfish child.

Pearl's inevitable tendency to hover about the enigma of the scarlet letter seemed an innate quality of her being. From the earliest epoch of her conscious life, she had entered upon this as her appointed mission. Hester had often fancied that Providence had a design of justice and retribution, in endowing the child with this marked propensity; but never, until now, had she bethought herself to ask, whether, linked with that design, there might not likewise be a purpose of mercy and beneficence. If little Pearl were entertained with faith and trust, as a spirit messenger no less than an earthly child, might it not be her errand to soothe away the sorrow that lay cold in her mother's heart, and converted it into a tomb—and to help her to overcome the passion, once so wild, and even yet neither dead nor asleep, but only imprisoned within the same tomb-like heart?

Such were some of the thoughts that now stirred in Hester's mind, with as much vivacity of impression as if they had actually been whispered into her ear. And there was little Pearl, all this while, holding her mother's hand in both her own, and turning her face upward, while she put these searching questions once, and again, and still a third time.

"What does the letter mean, mother? —and why dost thou wear it?—and why does the minister keep his hand over his heart?"

"What shall I say?" thought Hester to herself. "No! If this be the price of the child's sympathy, I cannot pay it."

Then she spoke aloud.

"Silly Pearl," said she, "what questions are these? There are many things in this world that a child must not ask about. What know I of the minister's heart? And as for the scarlet letter, I wear it for the sake of its gold thread."

In all the seven bygone years, Hester Prynne had never before been false to the symbol on her bosom. It may be that it was the talisman of a stern and severe, but yet a guardian spirit, who now forsook her; as recognizing that, in spite of his strict watch over her heart, some new evil had crept into

it, or some old one had never been expelled. As for little Pearl, the earnestness soon passed out of her face.

But the child did not see fit to let the matter drop. Two or three times, as her mother and she went homeward, and as often at supper-time, and while Hester was putting her to bed, and once after she seemed to be fairly asleep, Pearl looked up, with mischief gleaming in her black eyes.

"Mother," said she, "what does the scarlet letter mean?"

And the next morning, the first indication the child gave of being awake was by propping up her head from the pillow, and making that other inquiry, which she had so unaccountably connected with her investigations about the scarlet letter:—

"Mother!—Mother!—Why does the minister keep his hand over his heart?"

"Hold thy tongue, naughty child!" answered her mother, with an asperity that she had never permitted to herself before. "Do not tease me; else I shall shut thee into the dark closet!"

CHAPTER XVI

A FOREST WALK

HESTER PRYNNE remained constant in her resolve to make known to Mr. Dimmesdale, at whatever risk of present pain or ulterior consequences, the true character of the man who had crept into his intimacy. For several days, however, she vainly sought an opportunity of addressing him in some of the meditative walks which she knew him to be

in the habit of taking, along the shores of the peninsula, or on the wooded hills of the neighboring country. There would have been no scandal, indeed, nor peril to the holy whiteness of the clergyman's good fame, had she visited him in his own study; where many a penitent, ere now, had confessed sins of perhaps as deep a dye as the one betokened by the scarlet letter. But, partly that she dreaded the secret or undisguised interference of old Roger Chillingworth, and partly that her conscious heart imputed suspicion where none could have been felt, and partly that both the minister and she would need the whole wide world to breathe in, while they talked together,—for all these reasons, Hester never thought of meeting him in any narrower privacy than beneath the open sky.

At last, while attending in a sick-chamber, whither the Reverend Mr. Dimmesdale had been summoned to make a prayer, she learnt that he had gone, the day before, to visit the Apostle Eliot, among his Indian converts. He would probably return, by a certain hour, in the afternoon of the morrow. Betimes, therefore, the next day, Hester took little Pearl,—who was necessarily the companion of all her mother's expeditions, however inconvenient her presence,—and set forth.

The road, after the two wayfarers had crossed from the peninsula to the mainland, was no other than a footpath. It straggled onward into the mystery of the primeval forest. This hemmed it in so narrowly, and stood so black and dense on either side, and disclosed such imperfect glimpses of the sky above, that, to Hester's mind, it imaged not amiss the moral wilderness in which she had so long been wandering. The day was chill and sombre. Overhead was a gay expanse of cloud, slightly stirred, however, by a breeze; so that a gleam of flickering sunshine might now and then be seen at its solitary play along the path. This flitting cheerfulness was always at the further extremity of some long vista

through the forest. The sportive sunlight—feebly sportive, at best, in the predominant pensiveness of the day and scene—withdrew itself as they came nigh, and left the spots where it had danced the drearier, because they had hoped to find them bright.

"Mother," said little Pearl, "the sunshine does not love you. It runs away and hides itself, because it is afraid of something on your bosom. Now, see! There it is, playing, a good way off. Stand you here, and let me run and catch it. I am but a child. It will not flee from me; for I wear nothing on my bosom yet!"

"Nor ever will, my child, I hope," said Hester.

"And why not, mother?" asked Pearl, stopping short, just at the beginning of her race. "Will not it come of its own accord, when I am a woman grown?"

"Run away, child," answered her mother, "and catch the sunshine! It will soon be gone."

Pearl set forth, at a great pace, and, as Hester smiled to perceive, did actually catch the sunshine, and stood laughing in the midst of it, all brightened by its splendor, and scintillating with the vivacity excited by rapid motion. The light lingered about the lonely child, as if glad of such a playmate, until her mother had drawn almost nigh enough to step into the magic circle too.

"It will go now," said Pearl, shaking her head.

"See!" answered Hester, smiling. "Now I can stretch out my hand, and grasp some of it."

As she attempted to do so, the sunshine vanished; or, to judge from the bright expression that was dancing on Pearl's features, her mother could have fancied that the child had absorbed it into herself, and would give it forth again, with a gleam about her path, as they should plunge into some gloomier shade. There was no other attribute that so much impressed her with a sense of new and untransmitted vigor in Pearl's nature, as this never-failing vivacity of spirits; she had not the disease of sadness, which almost all children, in these latter days, inherit, with the scrofula, from the troubles of their ancestors. Perhaps this too was a disease, and but the reflex of the wild energy with which Hester had fought against her sorrows, before Pearl's birth. It was certainly a doubtful charm, imparting a hard, metallic lustre to the child's character. She wanted—what some people want throughout life—a grief that should deeply touch her, and thus humanize and make her capable of sympathy. But there was time enough yet for little Pearl.

"Come, my child!" said Hester, looking about her from the spot where Pearl had stood still in the sunshine. "We will sit down a little way within the wood, and rest ourselves."

"I am not aweary, mother," replied the little girl. "But you may sit down, if you will tell me a story meanwhile."

"A story, child!" said Hester. "And about what?"

"O, a story about the Black Man," answered Pearl, taking hold of her mother's gown, and looking up half earnestly, half mischievously, into her face. "How he haunts this forest, and carries a book with him,—a big, heavy book, with iron clasps; and how this ugly Black Man offers his book and

an iron pen to everybody that meets him here among the trees; and they are to write their names with their own blood. And then he sets his mark on their bosoms! Didst thou ever meet the Black Man, mother?"

"And who told you this story, Pearl?" asked her mother, recognizing a common superstition of the period.

"It was the old dame in the chimney-corner, at the house where you watched last night," said the child. "But she fancied me asleep while she was talking of it. She said that a thousand and a thousand people had met him here, and had written in his book, and have his mark on them. And that ugly-tempered lady, old Mistress Hibbins, was one. And, mother, the old dame said that this scarlet letter was the Black Man's mark on thee, and that it glows like a red flame when thou meetest him at midnight, here in the dark wood. Is it true, mother? And dost thou go to meet him in the night-time?"

"Didst thou ever awake, and find thy mother gone?" asked Hester.

"Not that I remember," said the child. "If thou fearest to leave me in our cottage, thou mightest take me along with thee. I would very gladly go! But, mother, tell me now! Is there such a Black Man? And didst thou ever meet him? And is this his mark?"

"Wilt thou let me be at peace, if I once tell thee?" asked her mother.

"Yes, if thou tellest me all," answered Pearl.

"Once in my life I met the Black Man!" said her mother. "This scarlet letter is his mark!"

Thus conversing, they entered sufficiently deep into the wood to secure themselves from the observation of any casual passenger along the forest track. Here they sat down on a luxuriant heap of moss; which, at some epoch of the preceding century, had been a gigantic pine, with its roots and trunk in the darksome shade, and its head aloft in the upper atmosphere. It was a little dell where they had seated themselves, with a leaf-strewn bank rising gently on either side, and a brook flowing through the midst, over a bed of fallen and drowned leaves. The trees impending over it had flung down great branches, from time to time, which choked up the current, and compelled it to form eddies and black depths at some points; while, in its swifter and livelier passages, there appeared a channel-way of pebbles, and brown, sparkling sand. Letting the eyes follow along the course of the stream, they could catch the reflected light from its water, at some short distance within the forest, but soon lost all traces of it amid the bewilderment of tree-trunks and underbrush, and here and there a huge rock covered over with gray lichens. All these giant trees and boulders of granite seemed intent on making a mystery of the course of this small brook; fearing, perhaps, that, with its never-ceasing loquacity, it should whisper tales out of the heart of the old forest whence it flowed, or mirror its revelations on the smooth surface of a pool. Continually, indeed, as it stole onward, the streamlet kept up a babble, kind, quiet, soothing, but melancholy, like the voice of a young child that was spending its infancy without playfulness, and knew not how to be merry among sad acquaintance and events of sombre hue.

"O brook! O foolish and tiresome little brook!" cried Pearl, after listening awhile to its talk. "Why art thou so sad? Pluck up a spirit, and do not be all the time sighing and murmuring!"

But the brook, in the course of its little lifetime among the forest-trees, had gone through so solemn an experience that it could not help talking about it, and seemed to have nothing else to say. Pearl resembled the brook, inasmuch as the current of her life gushed from a well-spring as mysterious, and had flowed through scenes shadowed as heavily with gloom. But, unlike the little stream, she danced and sparkled, and prattled airily along her course.

"What does this sad little brook say, mother?" inquired she.

"If thou hadst a sorrow of thine own, the brook might tell thee of it," answered her mother, "even as it is telling me of mine! But now, Pearl, I hear a foot-step along the path, and the noise of one putting aside the branches. I would have thee betake thyself to play, and leave me to speak with him that comes yonder."

"Is it the Black Man?" asked Pearl.

"Wilt thou go and play, child?" repeated her mother. "But do not stray far into the wood. And take heed that thou come at my first call."

"Yes, mother," answered Pearl. "But if it be the Black Man, wilt thou not let me stay a moment, and look at him, with his big book under his arm?"

"Go, silly child!" said her mother, impatiently. "It is no Black Man! Thou canst see him now, through the trees. It is the minister!"

"And so it is!" said the child. "And, mother, he has his hand over his heart! Is it because, when the minister wrote his name in the book, the Black Man set his mark in that place? But why does he not wear it outside his bosom, as thou dost, mother?"

"Go now, child, and thou shalt tease me as thou wilt another time," cried Hester Prynne. "But do not stray far. Keep where thou canst hear the babble of the brook."

The child went singing away, following up the current of the brook, and striving to mingle a more lightsome cadence with its melancholy voice. But the little stream would not be comforted, and still kept telling its unintelligible secret of some very mournful mystery that had happened—or making a prophetic lamentation about something that was yet to happen—within the verge of the dismal forest. So Pearl, who had enough of shadow in her own little life, chose to break off all acquaintance with this repining brook. She set herself, therefore, to gathering violets and wood-anemones, and some scarlet columbines that she found growing in the crevices of a high rock.

When her elf-child had departed, Hester Prynne made a step or two towards the track that led through the forest, but still remained under the deep shadow of the trees. She beheld the minister advancing along the path, entirely alone, and leaning on a staff which he had cut by the way-side. He looked haggard and feeble, and betrayed a nerveless despondency in his air, which had never so remarkably characterized him in his walks about the settlement, nor in any other situation where he deemed himself liable to notice. Here it was wofully visible, in this intense seclusion of the forest, which of itself would have been a heavy trial to the spirits. There was a listlessness in his gait; as if he saw no reason for taking one step further, nor felt any desire to do so, but would have been glad, could he be glad of anything, to fling himself down at the root of the nearest tree, and lie there passive, forevermore. The leaves might bestrew him, and the soil gradually accumulate and form a little hillock over his frame, no matter whether there were life in it or no. Death was too definite an object to be wished for, or avoided.

To Hester's eye, the Reverend Mr. Dimmesdale exhibited no symptom of positive and vivacious suffering, except that, as little Pearl had remarked, he kept his hand over his heart.

CHAPTER XVII

THE PASTOR AND HIS PARISHIONER

SLOWLY as the minister walked, he had almost gone by, before Hester Prynne could gather voice enough to attract his observation. At length, she succeeded.

"Arthur Dimmesdale!" she said, faintly at first; then louder, but hoarsely. "Arthur Dimmesdale!"

"Who speaks?" answered the minister.

Gathering himself quickly up, he stood more erect, like a man taken by surprise in a mood to which he was reluctant to have witnesses. Throwing his eyes anxiously in the direction of the voice, he indistinctly beheld a form under the trees, clad in garments so sombre, and so little relieved from the gray twilight into which the clouded sky and the heavy foliage had darkened the noontide, that he knew not whether it were a woman or a shadow. It may be, that his pathway through life was haunted thus, by a spectre that had stolen out from among his thoughts.

He made a step nigher, and discovered the scarlet letter.

"Hester! Hester Prynne!" said he. "Is it thou? Art thou in life?"

"Even so!" she answered. "In such life as has been mine these seven years past! And thou, Arthur Dimmesdale, dost thou yet live?"

It was no wonder that they thus questioned one another's actual and bodily existence, and even doubted of their own. So strangely did they meet, in the dim wood, that it was like the first encounter, in the world beyond the grave, of two spirits who had been intimately connected in their former life, but now stood coldly shuddering, in mutual dread; as not yet familiar with their state, nor wonted to the companionship of disembodied beings. Each a ghost, and awe-stricken at the other ghost! They were awe-stricken likewise at themselves; because the crisis flung back to them their consciousness, and revealed to each heart its history and experience, as life never does, except at such breathless epochs. The soul beheld its features in the mirror of the passing moment. It was

with fear, and tremulously, and, as it were, by a slow, reluctant necessity, that Arthur Dimmesdale put forth his hand, chill as death, and touched the chill hand of Hester Prynne. The grasp, cold as it was, took away what was dreariest in the interview. They now felt themselves, at least, inhabitants of the same sphere.

Without a word more spoken,—neither he nor she assuming the guidance, but with an unexpressed consent, —they glided back into the shadow of the woods, whence Hester had emerged, and sat down on the heap of moss where she and Pearl had before been sitting. When they found voice to speak, it was, at first, only to utter remarks and inquiries such as any two acquaintances might have made, about the gloomy sky, the threatening storm, and, next, the health of each. Thus they went onward, not boldly, but step by step, into the themes that were brooding deepest in their hearts. So long estranged by fate and circumstances, they needed something slight and casual to run before, and throw open the doors of intercourse, so that their real thoughts might be led across the threshold.

After a while, the minister fixed his eyes on Hester Prynne's.

"Hester," said he, "hast thou found peace?"

She smiled drearily, looking down upon her bosom.

"Hast thou?" she asked.

"None!—nothing but despair!" he answered. "What else could I look for, being what I am, and leading such a life as mine? Were I an atheist,—a man devoid of conscience,—a wretch with coarse and brutal instincts,—I might have found peace, long ere now.

Nay, I never should have lost it! But, as matters stand with my soul, whatever of good capacity there originally was in me, all of God's gifts that were the choicest have become the ministers of spiritual torment. Hester, I am most miserable!"

"The people reverence thee," said Hester. "And surely thou workest good among them! Dost this bring thee no comfort?"

"More misery, Hester!—only the more misery!" answered the clergyman, with a bitter smile. "As concerns the good which I may appear to do, I have no faith in it. It must needs be a delusion. What can a ruined soul, like mine, effect towards the redemption of other souls?—or a polluted soul, towards their purification? And as for the people's reverence, would that it were turned to scorn and hatred! Canst thou deem it, Hester, a consolation, that I must stand up in my pulpit, and meet so many eyes turned upward to my face, as if the light of heaven were beaming from it!—must see my flock hungry for the truth, and listening to my words as if a tongue of Pentecost were speaking!—and then look inward, and discern the black reality of what they idolize? I have laughed, in bitterness and agony of heart, at the contrast between what I seem and what I am! And Satan laughs at it!"

"You wrong yourself in this," said Hester, gently. "You have deeply and sorely repented. Your sin is left behind you, in the days long past. Your present life is not less holy, in very truth, than it seems in people's eyes. Is there no reality in the penitence thus sealed and witnessed by good works? And wherefore should it not

bring you peace?"

"No, Hester, no!" replied the clergyman. "There is no substance in it! It is cold and dead, and can do nothing for me! Of penance, I have had enough! Of penitence, there has been none! Else, I should long ago have thrown off these garments of mock holiness, and have shown myself to mankind as they will see me at the judgment-seat. Happy are you, Hester, that wear the scarlet letter openly upon your bosom! Mine burns in secret! Thou little knowest what a relief it is, after the torment of a seven years' cheat, to look into an eye that recognizes me for what I am! Had I one friend,—or were it my worst enemy!—to whom, when sickened with the praises of all other men, I could daily betake myself, and be known as the vilest of all sinners, methinks my soul might keep itself alive thereby. Even thus much of truth would save me! But now, it is all falsehood!—all emptiness!—all death!"

Hester Prynne looked into his face, but hesitated to speak. Yet, uttering his long-restrained emotions so vehemently as he did, his words here offered her the very point of circumstances in which to interpose what she came to say. She conquered her fears, and spoke.

"Such a friend as thou hast even now wished for," said she, "with whom to weep over thy sin, thou hast in me, the partner of it!"—Again she hesitated, but brought out the words with an effort.—"Thou hast long had such an enemy, and dwellest with him, under the same roof."

The minister started to his feet, gasping for breath, and clutching at his heart, as if he would have torn it out of his bosom.

"Ha! What sayest thou!" cried he. "An enemy! And under mine own roof! What mean you?"

Hester Prynne was now fully sensible of the deep injury for which she was responsible to this unhappy man, in permitting him to lie for so many years, or, indeed, for a single moment, at the mercy of one whose purposes could not be other than malevolent. The very contiguity of his enemy, beneath whatever mask the latter might conceal himself- was enough to disturb the magnetic sphere of a being so sensitive as Arthur Dimmesdale. There had been a period when Hester was less alive to this consideration; or, perhaps, in the misanthropy of her own trouble, she left the minister to bear what she might picture to herself as a more tolerable doom. But of late, since the night of his vigil, all her sympathies towards him had been both softened and invigorated. She now read his heart more accurately. She doubted not, that the continual presence of Roger Chillingworth,—the secret poison of his malignity, infecting all the air about him,— and his authorized interference, as a physician, with the minister's physical and spiritual infirmities,—that these bad opportunities had been turned to a cruel purpose. By means of them, the sufferer's conscience had been kept in an irritated state, the tendency of which was, not to cure by wholesome pain, but to disorganize and corrupt his spiritual being. Its result, on earth, could hardly fail to be insanity, and hereafter, that eternal alienation from the Good and True, of which madness is perhaps the earthly type.

Such was the ruin to which she had brought the man, once,—nay, why

should we not speak it?—still so passionately loved! Hester felt that the sacrifice of the clergyman's good name, and death itself, as she had already told Roger Chillingworth, would have been infinitely preferable to the alternative which she had taken upon herself to choose. And now, rather than have had this grievous wrong to confess, she would gladly have lain down on the forest-leaves, and died there, at Arthur Dimmesdale's feet.

"O Arthur," cried she, "forgive me! In all things else, I have striven to be true! Truth was the one virtue which I might have held fast, and did hold fast, through all extremity; save when thy good,—thy life,—thy fame,—were put in question! Then I consented to a deception. But a lie is never good, even though death threaten on the other side! Dost thou not see what I would say? That old man!—the physician!—he whom they call Roger Chillingworth!— he was my husband!"

The minister looked at her, for an instant, with all that violence of passion, which—intermixed, in more shapes than one, with his higher, purer, softer qualities,—was, in fact, the portion of him which the Devil claimed, and through which he sought to win the rest. Never was there a blacker or a fiercer frown than Hester now encountered. For the brief space that it lasted, it was a dark transfiguration. But his character had been so much enfeebled by suffering, that even its lower energies were incapable of more than a temporary struggle. He sank down on the ground, and buried his face in his hands.

"I might have known it," murmured he. "I did know it! Was not the secret told me, in the natural recoil of my heart, at the first sight of him, and as often as I have seen him since? Why did I not understand? O Hester Prynne, thou little, little knowest all the horror of this thing! And the shame!—the indelicacy!—the horrible ugliness of this exposure of a sick and guilty heart to the very eye that would gloat over it! Woman, woman, thou art accountable for this! I cannot forgive thee!"

"Thou shalt forgive me!" cried Hester, flinging herself on the fallen leaves beside him. "Let God punish! Thou shalt forgive!"

With sudden and desperate tenderness, she threw her arms around him, and pressed his head against her bosom; little caring though his cheek rested on the scarlet letter. He would have released himself, but strove in vain to do so. Hester would not set him free, lest he should look her sternly in the face. All the world had frowned on her,—for seven long years had it frowned upon this lonely woman,—and still she bore it all, nor ever once turned away her firm, sad eyes. Heaven, likewise, had frowned upon her, and she had not died. But the frown of this pale, weak, sinful, and sorrow-stricken man was what Hester could not bear, and live!

"Wilt thou yet forgive me?" she repeated, over and over again. "Wilt thou not frown? Wilt thou forgive?"

"I do forgive you, Hester," replied the minister, at length, with a deep utterance, out of an abyss of sadness, but no anger. "I freely forgive you now. May God forgive us both! We are not, Hester, the worst sinners in the world. There is one worse than even the polluted priest! That old man's

revenge has been blacker than my sin. He has violated, in cold blood, the sanctity of a human heart. Thou and I, Hester, never did so!"

"Never, never!" whispered she. "What we did had a consecration of its own. We felt it so! We said so to each other! Hast thou forgotten it?"

"Hush, Hester!" said Arthur Dimmesdale, rising from the ground. "No; I have not forgotten!"

They sat down again, side by side, and hand clasped in hand, on the mossy trunk of the fallen tree. Life had never brought them a gloomier hour; it was the point whither their pathway had so long been tending, and darkening ever, as it stole along;—and yet it enclosed a charm that made them linger upon it, and claim another, and another, and, after all, another moment. The forest was obscure around them, and creaked with a blast that was passing through it. The boughs were tossing heavily above their heads; while one solemn old tree groaned dolefully to another, as if telling the sad story of the pair that sat beneath, or constrained to forebode evil to come.

And yet they lingered. How dreary looked the forest-track that led backward to the settlement, where Hester Prynne must take up again the burden of her ignominy, and the minister the hollow mockery of his good name! So they lingered an instant longer. No golden light had ever been so precious as the gloom of this dark forest. Here, seen only by his eyes, the scarlet letter need not burn into the bosom of the fallen woman! Here, seen only by her eyes, Arthur Dimmesdale, false to God and man, might be, for one moment, true!

He started at a thought that suddenly occurred to him.

"Hester," cried he, "here is a new horror! Roger Chillingworth knows your purpose to reveal his true character. Will he continue, then, to keep our secret? What will now be the course of his revenge?"

"There is a strange secrecy in his nature," replied Hester, thoughtfully; "and it has grown upon him by the hidden practices of his revenge. I deem it not likely that he will betray the secret. He will doubtless seek other means of satiating his dark passion."

"And I!—how am I to live longer, breathing the same air with this deadly enemy?" exclaimed Arthur Dimmesdale, shrinking within himself, and pressing his hand nervously against his heart, —a gesture that had grown involuntary with him. "Think for me, Hester! Thou art strong. Resolve for me!"

"Thou must dwell no longer with this man," said Hester, slowly and firmly. "Thy heart must be no longer under his evil eye!"

"It were far worse than death!" replied the minister. "But how to avoid it? What choice remains to me? Shall I lie down again on these withered leaves, where I cast myself when thou didst tell me what he was? Must I sink down there, and die at once?"

"Alas, what a ruin has befallen thee!" said Hester, with the tears gushing into her eyes. "Wilt thou die for very weakness? There is no other cause!"

"The judgment of God is on me," answered the conscience-stricken priest. "It is too mighty for me to struggle with!"

"Heaven would show mercy," rejoined Hester, "hadst thou but the strength to take advantage of it."

"Be thou strong for me!" answered he. "Advise me what to do."

"Is the world, then, so narrow?" exclaimed Hester Prynne, fixing her deep eyes on the minister's, and instinctively exercising a magnetic power over a spirit so shattered and subdued that it could hardly hold itself erect. "Doth the universe lie within the compass of yonder town, which only a little time ago was but a leaf-strewn desert, as lonely as this around us? Whither leads yonder forest track? Backward to the settlement, thou sayest! Yes; but onward, too! Deeper it goes, and deeper, into the wilderness, less plainly to be seen at every step; until, some few miles hence, the yellow leaves will show no vestige of the white man's tread. There thou art free! So brief a journey would bring thee from a world where thou hast been most wretched, to one where thou mayest still be happy! Is there not shade enough in all this boundless forest to hide thy heart from the gaze of Roger Chillingworth?"

"Yes, Hester; but only under the fallen leaves!" replied the minister, with a sad smile.

"Then there is the broad pathway of the sea!" continued Hester. "It brought thee hither. If thou so choose, it will bear thee back again. In our native land, whether in some remote rural village or in vast London,—or, surely, in Germany, in France, in pleasant Italy,—thou wouldst be beyond his power and knowledge! And what hast thou to do with all these iron men, and their opinions? They have kept thy better part in bondage too long already!"

"It cannot be!" answered the minister, listening as if he were called upon to realize a dream. "I am powerless to go! Wretched and sinful as I am, I have had no other thought than to drag on my earthly existence in the sphere where Providence hath placed me. Lost as my own soul is, I would still do what I may for other human souls! I dare not quit my post, though an unfaithful sentinel, whose sure reward is death and dishonor, when his dreary watch shall come to an end!"

"Thou art crushed under this seven years' weight of misery," replied Hester, fervently resolved to buoy him up with her own energy. "But thou shalt leave it all behind thee! It shall not cumber thy steps, as thou treadest along the forest-path; neither shalt thou freight the ship with it, if thou prefer to cross the sea. Leave this wreck and ruin here where it hath happened. Meddle no more with it! Begin all new! Hast thou exhausted possibility in the failure of this one trial? Not so! The future is yet full of trial and success. There is happiness to be enjoyed! There is good to be done! Exchange this false life of thine for a true one. Be, if thy spirit summon thee to such a mission, the teacher and apostle of the red men. Or,—as is more

thy nature,—be a scholar and a sage among the wisest and the most renowned of the cultivated world. Preach! Write! Act! Do anything, save to lie down and die! Give up this name of Arthur Dimmesdale, and make thyself another, and a high one, such as thou canst wear without fear or shame. Why shouldst thou tarry so much as one other day in the torments that have so gnawed into thy life!—that have made thee feeble to will and to do!—that will leave thee powerless even to repent! Up, and away!"

"O Hester!" cried Arthur Dimmesdale, in whose eyes a fitful light, kindled by her enthusiasm, flashed up and died away, "thou tellest of running a race to a man whose knees are tottering beneath him! I must die here! There is not the strength or courage left me to venture into the wide, strange, difficult world, alone!"

It was the last expression of the despondency of a broken spirit. He lacked energy to grasp the better fortune that seemed within his reach.

He repeated the word.

"Alone, Hester!"

"Thou shalt not go alone!" answered she, in a deep whisper.

Then, all was spoken!

CHAPTER XVIII

A FLOOD OF SUNSHINE

ARTHUR DIMMESDALE gazed into Hester's face with a look in which hope and joy shone out, indeed, but with fear betwixt them. and a kind of hor-

ror at her boldness, who had spoken what he vaguely hinted at, but dared not speak.

But Hester Prynne, with a mind of

native courage and activity, and for so long a period not merely estranged, but outlawed, from society, had habituated herself to such latitude of speculation as was altogether foreign to the clergyman. She had wandered, without rule or guidance, in a moral wilderness; as vast, as intricate and shadowy, as the untamed forest, amid the gloom of which they were now holding a colloquy that was to decide their fate. Her intellect and heart had their home, as it were, in desert places, where she roamed as freely as the wild Indian in his woods. For years past she had looked from this estranged point of view at human institutions, and whatever priests or legislators had established; criticising all with hardly more reverence than the Indian would feel for the clerical band, the judicial robe, the pillory, the gallows, the fireside, or the church. The tendency of her fate and fortunes had been to set her free. The scarlet letter was her passport into regions where other women dared not tread. Shame, Despair, Solitude! These had been her teachers,— stern and wild ones,—and they had made her strong, but taught her much amiss.

The minister, on the other hand, had never gone through an experience calculated to lead him beyond the scope of generally received laws; although, in a single instance, he had so fearfully transgressed one of the most sacred of them. But this had been a sin of passion, not of principle, nor even purpose. Since that wretched epoch, he had watched, with morbid zeal and minuteness, not his acts,—for those it was easy to arrange,—but each breath of emotion, and his every thought. At the

head of the social system, as the clergymen of that day stood, he was only the more trammelled by its regulations, its principles, and even its prejudices. As a priest, the framework of his order inevitably hemmed him in. As a man who had once sinned, but who kept his conscience all alive and painfully sensitive by the fretting of an unhealed wound, he might have been supposed safer within the line of virtue than if he had never sinned at all.

Thus, we seem to see that, as regarded Hester Prynne, the whole seven years of outlaw and ignominy had been little other than a preparation for this very hour. But Arthur Dimmesdale! Were such a man once more to fall, what plea could be urged in extenuation of his crime? None; unless it avail him somewhat, that he was broken down by long and exquisite suffering; that his mind was darkened and confused by the very remorse which harrowed it; that, between fleeing as an avowed criminal, and remaining as a hypocrite, conscience might find it hard to strike the balance; that it was human to avoid the peril of death and infamy, and the inscrutable machinations of an enemy; that, finally, to this poor pilgrim, on his dreary and desert path, faint, sick, miserable, there appeared a glimpse of human affection and sympathy, a new life, and a true one, in exchange for the heavy doom which he was now expiating. And be the stern and sad truth spoken, that the breach which guilt has once made into the human soul is never, in this mortal state, repaired. It may be watched and guarded; so that the enemy shall not force his way again into the citadel, and might even, in his subsequent assaults, select some other avenue, in preference to that where he had formerly succeeded. But there is still the ruined wall, and, near it, the stealthy tread of the foe that would win over again his unforgotten triumph.

The struggle, if there were one, need not be described. Let it suffice, that the clergyman resolved to flee, and not alone.

"If, in all these past seven years," thought he, "I could recall one instant of peace or hope, I would yet endure, for the sake of that earnest of Heaven's mercy. But now,—since I am irrevocably doomed,—wherefore should I not snatch the solace allowed to the condemned culprit before his execution? Or, if this be the path to a better life, as Hester would persuade me, I surely give up no fairer prospect by pursuing it! Neither can I any longer live without her companionship; so powerful is she to sustain,—so tender to soothe! O Thou to whom I dare not lift mine eyes, wilt Thou yet pardon me!"

"Thou wilt go!" said Hester, calmly, as he met her glance.

The decision once made, a glow of strange enjoyment threw its flickering brightness over the trouble of his breast. It was the exhilarating effect—upon a prisoner just escaped from the dungeon of his own heart—of breathing the wild, free atmosphere of an unredeemed, unchristianized, lawless region. His spirit rose, as it were, with a bound, and attained a nearer prospect of the sky, than throughout all the misery which had kept him grovelling on the earth. Of a deeply religious temperament, there was inevitably a tinge of the devotional in his mood.

"Do I feel joy again?" cried he,

wondering at himself. "Methought the germ of it was dead in me! O Hester, thou art my better angel! I seem to have flung myself—sick, sin-stained, and sorrow-blackened—down upon these forest-leaves, and to have risen up all made anew, and with new powers to glorify Him that hath been merciful! This is already the better life! Why did we not find it sooner?"

"Let us not look back," answered Hester Prynne. "The past is gone! Wherefore should we linger upon it now? See! With this symbol, I undo it all, and make it as it had never been!"

So speaking, she undid the clasp that fastened the scarlet letter, and, taking it from her bosom, threw it to a distance among the withered leaves. The mystic token alighted on the hither verge of the stream. With a hand's breadth further flight it would have fallen into the water, and have given the little brook another woe to carry onward, besides the unintelligible tale which it still kept murmuring about. But there lay the embroidered letter, glittering like a lost jewel, which some ill-fated wanderer might pick up, and thenceforth be haunted by strange phantoms of guilt, sinkings of the heart, and unaccountable misfortune.

The stigma gone, Hester heaved a long, deep sigh, in which the burden of shame and anguish departed from her spirit. O exquisite relief! She had not known the weight, until she felt the freedom! By another impulse, she took off the formal cap that confined her hair; and down it fell upon her shoulders, dark and rich, with at once a shadow and a light in its abundance, and imparting the charm of softness to her features. There played around her mouth, and beamed out of her eyes, a radiant and tender smile, that seemed gushing from the very heart of womanhood. A crimson flush was glowing on her cheek, that had been long so pale. Her sex, her youth, and the whole richness of her beauty, came back from what men call the irrevocable past, and clustered themselves, with her maiden hope, and a happiness before unknown, within the magic circle of this hour. And, as if the gloom of the earth and sky had been but the effluence of these two mortal hearts, it vanished with their sorrow. All at once, as with a sudden smile of heaven, forth burst the sunshine, pouring a very flood into the obscure forest, gladdening each green leaf, transmuting the yellow fallen ones to gold, and gleaming adown the gray trunks of the solemn trees. The objects that had made a shadow hitherto, embodied the brightness now. The course of the little brook might be traced by its merry gleam afar into the wood's heart of mystery, which had become a mystery of joy.

Such was the sympathy of Nature —that wild, heathen Nature of the forest, never subjugated by human law, nor illumined by higher truth—with the bliss of these two spirits! Love, whether newly born, or aroused from a death-like slumber, must always create a sunshine, filling the heart so full of radiance, that it overflows upon the outward world. Had the forest still kept its gloom, it would have been bright in Hester's eyes, and bright in Arthur Dimmesdale's.

Hester looked at him with the thrill of another joy.

"Thou must know Pearl!" said she.

"Our little Pearl! Thou hast seen her —yes, I know it!—but thou wilt see her now with other eyes. She is a strange child! I hardly comprehend her. But thou wilt love her dearly, as I do, and wilt advise me how to deal with her."

"Dost thou think the child will be glad to know me?" asked the minister somewhat uneasily. "I have long shrunk from children, because they often show a distrust,—a backwardness to be familiar with me. I have even been afraid of little Pearl!"

"Ah, that was sad!" answered the mother. "But she will love thee dearly, and thou her. She is not far off. I will call her! Pearl! Pearl!"

"I see the child," observed the minister. "Yonder she is, standing in a streak of sunshine, a good way off, on the other side of the brook. So thou thinkest the child will love me?"

Hester smiled, and again called to Pearl, who was visible, at some distance, as the minister had described her, like a bright-apparelled vision, in a sunbeam, which fell down upon her through an arch of boughs. The ray quivered to and fro, making her figure dim or distinct,—now like a real child, now like a child's spirit,—as the splendor went and came again. She heard her mother's voice, and approached slowly through the forest.

Pearl had not found the hour pass wearisomely, while her mother sat talking with the clergyman. The great black forest—stern as it showed itself to those who brought the guilt and troubles of the world into its bosom—became the playmate of the lonely infant, as well as it knew how. Sombre as it was, it put on the kindest of its mood

welcome her. It offered her the par-
idge-berries, the growth of the preced-
g autumn but ripening only in the
pring, and now red as drops of blood
pon the withered leaves. These Pearl
athered, and was pleased with their
ild flavor. The small denizens of the
ilderness hardly took pains to move
ut of her path. A partridge, indeed,
ith a brood of ten behind her, ran
rward threateningly, but soon repented
f her fierceness, and clucked to her
oung ones not to be afraid. A pigeon,
one on a low branch, allowed Pearl
o come beneath, and uttered a sound
s much of greeting as alarm. A squir-
el, from the lofty depths of his domes-
c tree, chattered either in anger or
erriment,—for a squirrel is such a
holeric and humorous little personage,
hat it is hard to distinguish between
is moods,—so he chattered at the child,
nd flung down a nut upon her head.
t was a last year's nut, and already
nawed by his sharp tooth. A fox,
artled from his sleep by her light
ootstep on the leaves, looked inquisi-
ively at Pearl, as doubting whether it
vere better to steal off, or renew his

nap on the same spot. A wolf, it is
said,—but here the tale has surely
lapsed into the improbable,—came up,
and smelt of Pearl's robe, and offered
his savage head to be patted by her
hand. The truth seems to be, however,
that the mother-forest, and these wild
things which it nourished, all recognized a kindred wildness in the human
child.

And she was gentler here than in
the grassy-margined streets of the settlement, or in her mother's cottage. The
flowers appeared to know it; and one
and another whispered as she passed,
"Adorn thyself with me, thou beautiful
child, adorn thyself with me!"—and,
to please them, Pearl gathered the violets, and anemones, and columbines, and
some twigs of the freshest green, which
the old trees held down before her eyes.
With these she decorated her hair, and
her young waist, and became a nymph-
child, or an infant dryad, or whatever
else was in closest sympathy with the
antique wood. In such guise had Pearl
adorned herself, when she heard her
mother's voice, and came slowly back.

Slowly; for she saw the clergyman!

CHAPTER XIX

THE CHILD AT THE BROOK-SIDE

"THOU wilt love her dearly," repeated
Hester Prynne, as she and the minister
sat watching little Pearl. "Dost thou not
think her beautiful? And see with what
natural skill she has made those simple
flowers adorn her! Had she gathered
pearls, and diamonds, and rubies, in

the wood, they could not have become
her better. She is a splendid child! But
I know whose brow she has!"

"Dost thou know, Hester," said
Arthur Dimmesdale, with an unquiet
smile, "that this dear child, tripping
about always at thy side, hath caused

me many an alarm? Methought—O
Hester, what a thought is that, and how
terrible to dread it!—that my own features were partly repeated in her face,
and so strikingly that the world might
see them! But she is mostly thine!"

"No, no! Not mostly!" answered the
mother, with a tender smile. "A little
longer, and thou needest not to be
afraid to trace whose child she is. But
how strangely beautiful she looks, with
those wild flowers in her hair! It is as
if one of the fairies, whom we left in
our dear old England, had decked her
out to meet us."

It was with a feeling which neither
of them had ever before experienced,
that they sat and watched Pearl's slow
advance. In her was visible the tie that
united them. She had been offered to
the world, these seven years past, as
the living hieroglyphic, in which was
revealed the secret they so darkly sought
to hide,—all written in this symbol,—
all plainly manifest,—had there been
a prophet or magician skilled to read
the character of flame! And Pearl was
the oneness of their being. Be the
foregone evil what it might, how could
they doubt that their earthly lives and
future destinies were conjoined, when
they beheld at once the material union,
and the spiritual idea, in whom they
met, and were to dwell immortally together? Thoughts like these—and perhaps other thoughts, which they did
not acknowledge or define—threw an
awe about the child, as she came onward.

"Let her see nothing strange—no passion nor eagerness—in thy way of ac-
costing her," whispered Hester. "Our
Pearl is a fitful and fantastic little elf,
sometimes. Especially, she is seldom tol-

erant of emotion, when she does n
fully comprehend the why and wher
fore. But the child hath strong affe
tions! She loves me, and will lo
thee!"

"Thou canst not think," said the mi
ister, glancing aside at Hester Prynn
"how my heart dreads this intervie
and yearns for it! But, in truth, as
already told thee, children are not rea
ily won to be familiar with me. The
will not climb my knee, nor prattle
my ear, nor answer to my smile; b
stand apart, and eye me strangely. Eve
little babes, when I take them in m
arms, weep bitterly. Yet Pearl, twice
her little lifetime, hath been kind
me! The first time,—thou knowest
well! The last was when thou led
her with thee to the house of yond
stern old Governor."

"And thou didst plead so bravely
her behalf and mine!" answered th
mother. "I remember it; and so sha
little Pearl. Fear nothing! She may
strange and shy at first, but will soo
learn to love thee!"

By this time Pearl had reached th
margin of the brook, and stood on th
further side, gazing silently at Hest
and the clergyman, who still sat t
gether on the mossy tree-trunk, waitir
to receive her. Just where she h
paused, the brook chanced to form
pool, so smooth and quiet that it r
flected a perfect image of her litt
figure with all the brilliant picturesqu
ness of her beauty, in its adornment
flowers and wreathed foliage, but mo
refined and spiritualized than the realit
This image, so nearly identical wi
the living Pearl, seemed to communica
somewhat of its own shadowy and i
tangible quality to the child herself.

s strange, the way in which Pearl
ood, looking so steadfastly at them
rough the dim medium of the forest-
oom; herself, meanwhile, all glorified
ith a ray of sunshine, that was at-
acted thitherward as by a certain sym-
thy. In the brook beneath stood an-
her child,—another and the same,—
ith likewise its ray of golden light.
ester felt herself, in some indistinct
d tantalizing manner, estranged from
earl; as if the child, in her lonely
mble through the forest, had strayed
t of the sphere in which she and her
other dwelt together, and was now
ainly seeking to return to it.

There was both truth and error in
ie impression; the child and mother
ere estranged, but through Hester's
ult, not Pearl's. Since the latter
mbled from her side, another inmate
id been admitted within the circle of
ie mother's feelings, and so modified
ie aspect of them all, that Pearl, the
eturning wanderer, could not find her
onted place, and hardly knew where
ie was.

"I have a strange fancy," observed
ie sensitive minister, "that this brook
the boundary between two worlds,
id that thou canst never meet thy
earl again. Or is she an elfish spirit,
ho, as the legends of our childhood
aught us, is forbidden to cross a run-
ing stream? Pray hasten her; for this
elay has already imparted a tremor
> my nerves."

"Come, dearest child!" said Hester,
ncouragingly, and stretching out both
er arms. "How slow thou art! When
ast thou been so sluggish before now?
Here is a friend of mine, who must
e thy friend also. Thou wilt have twice
s much love, henceforward, as thy

mother alone could give thee! Leap
across the brook, and come to us. Thou
canst leap like a young deer!"

Pearl, without responding in any manner to these honey-sweet expressions,
remained on the other side of the brook.
Now she fixed her bright, wild eyes
on her mother, now on the minister,
and now included them both in the same
glance; as if to detect and explain to
herself the relation which they bore to
one another. For some unaccountable
reason, as Arthur Dimmesdale felt the
child's eyes upon himself, his hand—
with that gesture so habitual as to have
become involuntary—stole over his
heart. At length, assuming a singular air
of authority, Pearl stretched out her
hand, with the small forefinger extended
and pointing evidently towards her
mother's breast. And beneath, in the
mirror of the brook, there was the
flower-girdled and sunny image of little
Pearl, pointing her small forefinger too.

"Thou strange child, why dost thou
not come to me?" exclaimed Hester.

Pearl still pointed with her forefinger;
and a frown gathered on her brow; the
more impressive from the childish, the
almost baby-like aspect of the features
that conveyed it. As her mother still
kept beckoning to her, and arraying her
face in a holiday suit of unaccustomed
smiles, the child stamped her foot with
a yet more imperious look and gesture.
In the brook, again, was the fantastic
beauty of the image, with its reflected
frown, its pointed finger, and imperious
gesture, giving emphasis to the aspect
of little Pearl.

"Hasten, Pearl; or I shall be angry
with thee!" cried Hester Prynne, who,
however inured to such behavior on the
elf-child's part at other seasons, was

naturally anxious for a more seemly deportment now. "Leap across the brook, naughty child, and run hither! Else I must come to thee!"

But Pearl, not a whit startled at her mother's threats, any more than mollified by her entreaties, now suddenly burst into a fit of passion, gesticulating violently, and throwing her small figure into the most extravagant contortions. She accompanied this wild outbreak with piercing shrieks, which the woods reverberated on all sides; so that, alone as she was in her childish and unreasonable wrath, it seemed as if a hidden multitude were lending her their sympathy and encouragement. Seen in the brook, once more, was the shadowy wrath of Pearl's image, crowned and girdled with flowers, but stamping its foot, wildly gesticulating, and, in the midst of all, still pointing its small forefinger at Hester's bosom!

"I see what ails the child," whispered Hester to the clergyman, and turning pale in spite of a strong effort to conceal her trouble and annoyance. "Children will not abide any, the slightest, change in the accustomed aspect of things that are daily before their eyes. Pearl misses something which she has always seen me wear!"

"I pray you," answered the minister, "if thou hast any means of pacifying the child, do it forthwith! Save it were the cankered wrath of an old witch, like Mistress Hibbins," added he, attempting to smile, "I know nothing that I would not sooner encounter than this passion in a child. In Pearl's young beauty, as in the wrinkled witch, it has a preternatural effect. Pacify her, if thou lovest me!"

Hester turned again towards Pearl,

with a crimson blush upon her chee a conscious glance aside at the clerg man, and then a heavy sigh; whi even before she had time to speak, th blush yielded to a deadly pallor.

"Pearl," said she, sadly, "look dow at thy feet! There!—before thee!—c the hither side of the brook!"

The child turned her eyes to the poi indicated; and there lay the scarlet le ter, so close upon the margin of th stream, that the gold embroidery w reflected in it.

"Bring it hither," said Hester.

"Come thou and take it up!" a swered Pearl.

"Was ever such a child!" observe Hester, aside to the minister. "O, I hav much to tell thee about her! But, i very truth, she is right as regards th hateful token. I must bear its tortu yet a little longer,—only a few da longer,—until we shall have left th region, and look back hither as to land which we have dreamed of. Th forest cannot hide it! The mid-ocea shall take it from my hand, and swallo it up forever!"

With these words, she advanced t the margin of the brook, took up th scarlet letter, and fastened it agai into her bosom. Hopefully, but a mo ment ago, as Hester had spoken drowning it in the deep sea, there wa a sense of inevitable doom upon he as she thus received back this dead symbol from the hand of fate. She ha flung it into infinite space!—she ha drawn an hour's free breath!—and her again was the scarlet misery, glitterin on the old spot! So it ever is, whethe thus typified or no, that an evil dee invests itself with the character doom. Hester next gathered up th

avy tresses of her hair, and confined
em beneath her cap. As if there were
withering spell in the sad letter, her
auty, the warmth and richness of her
omanhood, departed, like fading sun-
ine; and a gray shadow seemed to
ll across her.

When the dreary change was wrought,
e extended her hand to Pearl.

"Dost thou know thy mother now,
ild?" asked she, reproachfully, but
th a subdued tone. "Wilt thou come
ross the brook, and own thy mother,
w that she has her shame upon her,
now that she is sad?"

"Yes; now I will!" answered the
ild, bounding across the brook, and
asping Hester in her arms. "Now thou
t my mother indeed! And I am thy
tle Pearl!"

In a mood of tenderness that was not
ual with her, she drew down her moth-
's head, and kissed her brow and
th her cheeks. But then—by a kind of
cessity that always impelled this child
 alloy whatever comfort she might
ance to give with a throb of anguish
Pearl put up her mouth, and kissed
e scarlet letter too!

"That was not kind!" said Hester.
Vhen thou hast shown me a little
ve, thou mockest me!"

"Why doth the minister sit yonder?"
ked Pearl.

"He waits to welcome thee," replied
r mother. "Come thou, and entreat
s blessing! He loves thee, my little
arl, and loves thy mother too. Wilt
ou not love him? Come! he longs to
eet thee!"

"Doth he love us?" said Pearl, look-
g up, with acute intelligence, into her
other's face. "Will he go back with

us, hand in hand, we three together,
into the town?"

"Not now, dear child," answered
Hester. "But in days to come he will
walk hand in hand with us. We will
have a home and fireside of our own;
and thou shalt sit upon his knee; and
he will teach thee many things, and
love thee dearly. Thou wilt love him;
wilt thou not?"

"And will he always keep his hand
over his heart?" inquired Pearl.

"Foolish child, what a question is
that!" exclaimed her mother. "Come
and ask his blessing!"

But, whether influenced by the jealousy that seems instinctive with every
petted child towards a dangerous rival,
or from whatever caprice of her freakish nature, Pearl would show no favor
to the clergyman. It was only by an
exertion of force that her mother
brought her up to him, hanging back,
and manifesting her reluctance by odd
grimaces; of which, ever since her babyhood, she had possessed a singular variety, and could transform her mobile
physiognomy into a series of different
aspects, with a new mischief in them,
each and all. The minister—painfully
embarrassed, but hoping that a kiss
might prove a talisman to admit him
into the child's kindlier regards—bent
forward, and impressed one on her brow.
Hereupon, Pearl broke away from her
mother, and, running to the brook,
stooped over it, and bathed her forehead, until the unwelcome kiss was
quite washed off, and diffused through
a long lapse of the gliding water. She
then remained apart, silently watching
Hester and the clergyman; while they
talked together, and made such arrange-

ments as were suggested by their new position, and the purposes soon to be filled.

And now this fateful interview had come to a close. The dell was to be left a solitude among its dark, old trees, which, with their multitudinous tongues, would whisper long of what had passed there, and no mortal be t wiser. And the melancholy brook wou add this other tale to the mystery wi which its little heart was already ove burdened, and whereof it still kept a murmuring babble, with not a wh more cheerfulness of tone than for ag heretofore.

CHAPTER XX

THE MINISTER IN A MAZE

As the minister departed, in advance of Hester Prynne and little Pearl, he threw a backward glance; half expecting that he should discover only some faintly traced features or outline of the mother and the child, slowly fading into the twilight of the woods. So great a vicissitude in his life could not at once be received as real. But there was Hester, clad in her gray robe, still standing beside the tree-trunk, which some blast had overthrown a long antiquity ago, and which time had ever since been covering with moss, so that these two fated ones, with earth's heaviest burden on them, might there sit down together, and find a single hour's rest and solace. And there was Pearl, too, lightly dancing from the margin of the brook,—now that the intrusive third person was gone,—and taking her old place by her mother's side. So the minister had not fallen asleep, and dreamed!

In order to free his mind from this indistinctness and duplicity of impression, which vexed it with a strange disquietude, he recalled and more thoroughly defined the plans which Hester and himself had sketched for their d parture. It had been determined betwe them, that the Old World, with i crowds and cities, offered them a mo eligible shelter and concealment tha the wilds of New England, or all Ame ica, with its alternatives of an Indi. wigwam, or the few settlements of Eur peans, scattered thinly along the se board. Not to speak of the clergymar health, so inadequate to sustain the har ships of a forest life, his native gif his culture, and his entire developmer would secure him a home only in t midst of civilization and refinement; t higher the state, the more delicate adapted to it the man. In furtheran of this choice, it so happened that ship lay in the harbor; one of tho questionable cruisers, frequent at th day, which, without being absolute outlaws of the deep, yet roamed ov its surface with a remarkable irrespo sibility of character. This vessel had r cently arrived from the Spanish Mai and, within three days' time, would s for Bristol. Hester Prynne—whose v cation, as a self-enlisted Sister of Cha

y, had brought her acquainted with
e captain and crew—could take upon
rself to secure the passage of two in-
viduals and a child, with all the se-
ecy which circumstances rendered
ore than desirable.

The minister had inquired of Hester,
ith no little interest, the precise time
which the vessel might be expected
depart. It would probably be on the
urth day from the present. "That is
ost fortunate!" he had then said to
mself. Now, why the Reverend Mr.
immesdale considered it so very for-
nate, we hesitate to reveal. Neverthe-
ss,—to hold nothing back from the
ader,—it was because, on the third
y from the present, he was to preach
e Election Sermon; and, as such an
casion formed an honorable epoch
the life of a New England clergy-
an, he could not have chanced upon
more suitable mode and time of ter-
inating his professional career. "At
ast, they shall say of me," thought
is exemplary man, "that I leave no
blic duty unperformed, nor ill per-
rmed!" Sad, indeed, that an intro-
ection so profound and acute as this
oor minister's should be so miserably
ceived! We have had, and may still
ve, worse things to tell of him; but
ne, we apprehend, so pitiably weak;
evidence, at once so slight and ir-
fragable, of a subtle disease, that had
ng since begun to eat into the real
bstance of his character. No man,
r any considerable period, can wear
e face to himself, and another to the
ultitude, without finally getting be-
ildered as to which may be the true.
The excitement of Mr. Dimmesdale's
elings, as he returned from his inter-
ew with Hester, lent him unaccus-

tomed physical energy, and hurried him
townward at a rapid pace. The pathway among the woods seemed wilder,
more uncouth with its rude natural ob-
stacles, and less trodden by the foot
of man, than he remembered it on his
outward journey. But he leaped across
the plashy places, thrust himself through
the clinging underbrush, climbed the
ascent, plunged into the hollow, and
overcame, in short, all the difficulties
of the track, with an unweariable activity that astonished him. He could not
but recall how feebly, and with what
frequent pauses for breath, he had
toiled over the same ground, only two
days before. As he drew near the town,
he took an impression of change from
the series of familiar objects that presented themselves. It seemed not yesterday, not one, nor two, but many
days, or even years ago, since he had
quitted them. There, indeed, was each
former trace of the street, as he remembered it, and all the peculiarities
of the houses, with the due multitude
of gable-peaks, and a weather-cock at
every point where his memory suggested one. Not the less, however, came
this importunately obtrusive sense of
change. The same was true as regarded
the acquaintances whom he met, and
all the well-known shapes of human life,
about the little town. They looked
neither older nor younger now; the
beards of the aged were no whiter, nor
could the creeping babe of yesterday
walk on his feet to-day; it was impossible to describe in what respect they
differed from the individuals on whom
he had so recently bestowed a parting
glance; and yet the minister's deepest
sense seemed to inform him of their
mutability. A similar impression struck

him most remarkably, as he passed under the walls of his own church. The edifice had so very strange, and yet so familiar, an aspect, that Mr. Dimmesdale's mind vibrated between two ideas; either that he had seen it only in a dream hitherto, or that he was merely dreaming about it now.

This phenomenon, in the various shapes which it assumed, indicated no external change, but so sudden and important a change in the spectator of the familiar scene, that the intervening space of a single day had operated on his consciousness like the lapse of years. The minister's own will, and Hester's will, and the fate that grew between them, had wrought this transformation. It was the same town as heretofore; but the same minister returned not from the forest. He might have said to the friends who greeted him,—"I am not the man for whom you take me! I left him yonder in the forest, withdrawn into a secret dell, by a mossy tree-trunk, and near a melancholy brook! Go, seek your minister, and see if his emaciated figure, his thin cheek, his white, heavy, pain-wrinkled brow, be not flung down there, like a cast-off garment!" His friends, no doubt, would still have insisted with him,—"Thou art thyself the man!"—but the error would have been their own, not his.

Before Mr. Dimmesdale reached home, his inner man gave him other evidences of a revolution in the sphere of thought and feeling. In truth, nothing short of a total change of dynasty and moral code, in that interior kingdom, was adequate to account for the impulses now communicated to the unfortunate and startled minister. At every step he was incited to do some strange, wild, wicked thing or other, with a sense that it would be at once involuntary and intentional; in spite of himself, yet growing out of a profounder self than that which opposed the impulse. For instance, he met one of his own deacons. The good old man addressed him with the paternal affection and patriarchal privilege, which his venerable age, his upright and holy character, and his station in the Church, entitled him to use; and, conjoined with this, the deep, almost worshipping respect, which the minister's profession and private claims alike demanded. Never was there a more beautiful example of how the majesty of age and wisdom may comport with the obeisance and respect enjoined upon it, as from a lower social rank, and inferior order of endowment, towards a higher. Now, during a conversation of some two or three moments between the Reverend Mr. Dimmesdale and this excellent and hoary-bearded deacon, it was only by the most careful self-control that the former could refrain from uttering certain blasphemous suggestions that rose into his mind, respecting the communion-supper. He absolutely trembled and turned pale as ashes, lest his tongue should wag itself, in utterance of these horrible matters, and plead his own consent for so doing, without his having fairly given it. And, even with this terror in his heart, he could hardly avoid laughing, to imagine how the sanctified old patriarchal deacon would have been petrified by his minister's impiety!

Again, another incident of the same nature. Hurrying along the street, the Reverend Mr. Dimmesdale encountered the eldest female member of his church, a most pious and exemplary old dame, poor, widowed, lonely, and with a heart as full of reminiscences about her dead husband and children, and her dead friends of long ago, as a burial-ground is full of storied gravestones. Yet all this, which would else have been such heavy sorrow, was made almost a solemn joy to her devout old soul, by religious consolations and the truths of Scripture, wherewith she had fed herself continually for more than thirty years. And, since Mr. Dimmesdale had taken her in charge, the good grandam's chief earthly comfort—which, unless it had been likewise a heavenly comfort, could have been none at all —was to meet her pastor, whether casually, or of set purpose, and be refreshed with a word of warm, fragrant, heaven-breathing Gospel truth, from his beloved lips, into her dulled, but rapturously attentive ear. But, on this occasion, up to the moment of putting his lips to the old woman's ear, Mr. Dimmesdale, as the great enemy of souls would have it, could recall no text of Scripture, nor aught else, except a brief, pithy, and, as it then appeared to him, unanswerable argument against the immortality of the human soul. The instilment thereof into her mind would probably have caused this aged sister to drop down dead, at once, as by the effect of an intensely poisonous infusion. What he really did whisper, the minister could never afterwards recollect. There was, perhaps, a fortunate disorder in his utterance, which failed to impart any distinct idea to the good widow's comprehension, or which Providence interpreted after a method of its own. Assuredly, as the minister looked back, he beheld an expression of divine gratitude and ecstasy that seemed like the shine of the celestial city on her face, so wrinkled and ashy pale.

Again, a third instance. After parting from the old church-member, he met the youngest sister of them all. It was a maiden newly won—and won by the Reverend Mr. Dimmesdale's own sermon, on the Sabbath after his vigil —to barter the transitory pleasures of the world for the heavenly hope, that was to assume brighter substance as life grew dark around her, and which would gild the utter gloom with final glory. She was fair and pure as a lily that had bloomed in Paradise. The minister knew well that he was himself enshrined within the stainless sanctity of her heart, which hung its snowy curtains about his image, imparting to religion the warmth of love, and to love a religious purity. Satan, that afternoon, had surely led the poor young girl away from her mother's side, and thrown her into the pathway of this sorely tempted, or—shall we not rather say? —this lost and desperate man. As she drew nigh, the arch-fiend whispered him to condense into small compass and drop into her tender bosom a germ of evil that would be sure to blossom darkly soon, and bear black fruit betimes. Such was his sense of power over this virgin soul, trusting him as she did, that the minister felt potent to blight all the field of innocence with but one wicked look, and develop all its opposite with but a word. So—with a mightier struggle than he had yet sustained—he held his Geneva cloak before his face, and hurried onward, making no sign of recognition, and leaving the young sister to digest his rudeness as she might. She ransacked her conscience,—which was full of harmless little matters, like her pocket or her work-bag,—and took herself to task, poor thing! for a thousand imaginary faults; and went about her household duties with swollen eyelids the next morning.

Before the minister had time to celebrate his victory over this last temptation, he was conscious of another impulse, more ludicrous, and almost as horrible. It was,—we blush to tell it,—it was to stop short in the road, and teach some very wicked words to a knot of little Puritan children who were playing there, and had but just begun to talk. Denying himself this freak, as unworthy of his cloth, he met a drunken seaman, one of the ship's crew from the Spanish Main. And, here, since he had so valiantly forborne all other wickedness, poor Mr. Dimmesdale longed, at least, to shake hands with the tarry blackguard, and recreate himself with a few improper jests, such as dissolute sailors so abound with, and a volley of good, round, solid, satisfactory, and heaven-defying oaths! It was not so much a better principle, as partly his natural good taste, and still more his buckramed habit of clerical decorum, that carried him safely through the latter crisis.

"What is it that haunts and tempts me thus?" cried the minister to himself, at length, pausing in the street, and striking his hand against his forehead. "Am I mad? or am I given over utterly to the fiend? Did I make a contract with him in the forest, and sign it with my blood? And does he now summon me to its fulfilment, by suggesting the performance of every wickedness which his most foul imagination can conceive?"

At the moment when the Reverend Mr. Dimmesdale thus communed with himself, and struck his forehead with his hand, old Mistress Hibbins, the reputed witch-lady, is said to have been passing by. She made a very grand appearance; having on a high head-dress, a rich gown of velvet, and a ruff done up with the famous yellow starch of which Ann Turner, her especial friend, had taught her the secret, before this last good lady had been hanged for Sir Thomas Overbury's murder. Whether the witch had read the minister's thoughts, or no, she came to a full stop, looked shrewdly into his face, smiled craftily, and—though little given to converse with clergymen—began a conversation.

"So, reverend Sir, you have made a visit into the forest," observed the witch-lady, nodding her high head-dress at him. "The next time, I pray you to allow me only a fair warning, and I shall be proud to bear you company. Without taking overmuch upon myself, my good word will go far towards gaining any strange gentleman a fair reception from yonder potentate you wot of!"

"I profess, madam," answered the clergyman, with a grave obeisance, such as the lady's rank demanded, and his own good-breeding made imperative,—"I profess, on my conscience and character, that I am utterly bewildered as touching the purport of your words! I went not into the forest to seek a potentate; neither do I, at any future time, design a visit thither, with a view to gaining the favor of such personage. My one sufficient object was to greet that pious friend of mine, the Apostle Eliot, and rejoice with him over the many precious souls he hath won from heathendom!"

"Ha, ha, ha!" cackled the old witch-lady, still nodding her high head-dress at the minister. "Well, well, we must needs talk thus in the daytime! You carry it off like an old hand! But at midnight, and in the forest, we shall have other talk together!"

She passed on with her aged stateliness, but often turning back her head and smiling at him, like one willing to recognize a secret intimacy of connection.

"Have I then sold myself," thought the minister, "to the fiend whom, if men say true, this yellow-starched and velveted old hag has chosen for her prince and master!"

The wretched minister! He had made a bargain very like it! Tempted by a dream of happiness, he had yielded himself, with deliberate choice, as he had never done before, to what he knew was deadly sin. And the infectious poison of that sin had been thus rapidly diffused throughout his moral system. It had stupefied all blessed impulses, and awakened into vivid life the whole brotherhood of bad ones. Scorn, bitterness, unprovoked malignity, gratuitous desire of ill, ridicule of whatever was good and holy, all awoke, to tempt, even while they frightened him. And his encounter with old Mistress Hibbins, if it were a real incident, did but show his sympathy and fellowship with wicked mortals, and the world of perverted spirits.

He had, by this time, reached his dwelling, on the edge of the burial-ground, and, hastening up the stairs, took refuge in his study. The minister was glad to have reached this shelter, without first betraying himself to the world

by any of those strange and wicked eccentricities to which he had been continually impelled while passing through the streets. He entered the accustomed room, and looked around him on its books, its windows, its fireplace, and the tapestried comfort of the walls, with the same perception of strangeness that had haunted him throughout his walk from the forest-dell into the town, and thitherward. Here he had studied and written; here, gone through fast and vigil, and come forth half alive; here, striven to pray; here, borne a hundred thousand agonies! There was the Bible, in its rich old Hebrew, with Moses and the Prophets speaking to him, and God's voice through all! There, on the table, with the inky pen beside it, was an unfinished sermon, with a sentence broken in the midst, where his thoughts had ceased to gush out upon the page, two days before. He knew that it was himself, the thin and white-cheeked minister, who had done and suffered these things, and written thus far into the Election Sermon! But he seemed to stand apart, and eye this former self with scornful, pitying, but half-envious curiosity. That self was gone. Another man had returned out of the forest; a wiser one; with a knowledge of hidden mysteries which the simplicity of the former never could have reached. A bitter kind of knowledge that!

While occupied with these reflections, a knock came at the door of the study, and the minister said, "Come in!"—not wholly devoid of an idea that he might behold an evil spirit. And so he did! It was old Roger Chillingworth that entered. The minister stood, white and speechless, with one hand on the Hebrew Scriptures, and the other spread upon his breast.

"Welcome home, reverend Sir," said the physician. "And how found you that godly man, the Apostle Eliot? But methinks, dear Sir, you look pale; as if the travel through the wilderness had been too sore for you. Will not my aid be requisite to put you in heart and strength to preach your Election Sermon?"

"Nay, I think not so," rejoined the Reverend Mr. Dimmesdale. "My journey, and the sight of the holy Apostle yonder, and the free air which I have breathed, have done me good, after so long confinement in my study. I think to need no more of your drugs, my kind physician, good though they be, and administered by a friendly hand."

All this time, Roger Chillingworth was looking at the minister with the grave and intent regard of a physician towards his patient. But, in spite of his outward show, the latter was almost convinced of the old man's knowledge, or, at least, his confident suspicion, with respect to his own interview with Hester Prynne. The physician knew then, that, in the minister's regard, he was no longer a trusted friend, but his bitterest enemy. So much being known, it would appear natural that a part of it should be expressed. It is singular, however, how long a time often passes before words embody things; and with what security two persons, who choose to avoid a certain subject, may approach its very verge, and retire without disturbing it. Thus, the minister felt no apprehension that Roger Chillingworth would touch, in express words, upon the real position which they sustained towards one another. Yet did the physi-

cian, in his dark way, creep frightfully near the secret.

"Were it not better," said he, "that you use my poor skill to-night? Verily, dear Sir, we must take pains to make you strong and vigorous for this occasion of the Election discourse. The people look for great things from you; apprehending that another year may come about, and find their pastor gone."

"Yea, to another world," replied the minister, with pious resignation. "Heaven grant it be a better one; for, in good sooth, I hardly think to tarry with my flock through the flitting seasons of another year! But, touching your medicine, kind Sir, in my present frame of body, I need it not."

"I joy to hear it," answered the physician. "It may be that my remedies, so long administered in vain, begin now to take due effect. Happy man were I, and well deserving of New England's gratitude, could I achieve this cure!"

"I thank you from my heart, most watchful friend," said the Reverend Mr. Dimmesdale, with a solemn smile. "I thank you, and can but requite your good deeds with my prayers."

"A good man's prayers are golden recompense!" rejoined old Roger Chillingworth, as he took his leave. "Yea, they are the current gold coin of the New Jerusalem, with the King's own mint-mark on them!"

Left alone, the minister summoned a servant of the house, and requested food, which, being set before him, he ate with ravenous appetite. Then, flinging the already written pages of the Election Sermon into the fire, he forthwith began another, which he wrote with such an impulsive flow of thought and emotion, that he fancied himself inspired; and only wondered that Heaven should see fit to transmit the grand and solemn music of its oracles through so foul an organ-pipe as he. However, leaving that mystery to solve itself, or go unsolved forever, he drove his task onward, with earnest haste and ecstasy. Thus the night fled away. as if it were a winged steed, and he careering on it; morning came, and peeped, blushing, through the curtains; and at last sunrise threw a golden beam into the study, and laid it right across the minister's bedazzled eyes. There he was, with the pen still between his fingers, and a vast, immeasurable tract of written space behind him!

CHAPTER XXI

THE NEW ENGLAND HOLIDAY

BETIMES in the morning of the day on which the new Governor was to receive his office at the hands of the people, Hester Prynne and little Pearl came into the market-place. It was already thronged with the craftsmen and other plebeian inhabitants of the town, in considerable numbers; among whom, likewise, were many rough figures, whose attire of deer-skins marked them as belonging to some of the forest settlements, which surrounded the little metropolis of the colony.

On this public holiday, as on all other occasions, for seven years past, Hester was clad in a garment of coarse gray cloth. Not more by its hue than by some indescribable peculiarity in its fashion, it had the effect of making her fade personally out of sight and outline; while, again, the scarlet letter brought her back from this twilight indistinctness, and revealed her under the moral aspect of its own illumination. Her face, so long familiar to the townspeople, showed the marble quietude which they were accustomed to behold there. It was like a mask; or, rather, like the frozen calmness of a dead woman's features; owing this dreary resemblance to the fact that Hester was actually dead, in respect to any claim of sympathy, and had departed out of the world with which she still seemed to mingle.

It might be, on this one day, that there was an expression unseen before, nor, indeed, vivid enough to be detected now; unless some preternaturally gifted observer should have first read the heart, and have afterwards sought a corresponding development in the countenance and mien. Such a spiritual seer might have conceived, that, after sustaining the gaze of the multitude through seven miserable years as a necessity, a penance, and something which it was a stern religion to endure, she now, for one last time more, encountered it freely and voluntarily, in order to convert what had so long been agony into a kind of triumph. "Look your last on the scarlet letter and its wearer!"—the people's victim and life-long bond-slave, as they fancied her, might say to them. "Yet a little while, and she will be beyond your reach! A few hours longer, and the deep, mysterious ocean will quench and hide forever the symbol which ye have caused to burn upon her bosom!" Nor were it an inconsistency too improbable to be assigned to human nature, should we suppose a feeling of regret in Hester's mind, at the moment when she was about to win her freedom from the pain which had been thus deeply incorporated with her being. Might there not be an irresistible desire to quaff a lost, long, breathless draught of the cup of wormwood and aloes, with which nearly all her years of womanhood had been perpetually flavored? The wine of life, henceforth to be presented to her lips, must be indeed rich, delicious, and exhilarating, in its chased and golden beaker; or else leave an inevitable and weary languor, after the lees of bitterness wherewith she had been drugged, as with a cordial of intensest potency.

Pearl was decked out with airy gayety. It would have been impossible to guess that this bright and sunny apparition owed its existence to the shape of gloomy gray; or that a fancy, at once so gorgeous and so delicate as must have been requisite to contrive the child's apparel, was the same that had achieved a task perhaps more difficult, in imparting so distinct a peculiarity to Hester's simple robe. The dress, so proper was it to little Pearl, seemed an effluence, or inevitable development and outward manifestation of her character, no more to be separated from her than the many hued brilliancy from a butterfly's wing, or the painted glory from the leaf of a bright flower. As with these, so with the child; her garb was all of one idea with her nature. On this eventful day, moreover, there was a certain singular inquietude and excitement in her mood, resembling nothing so much as the shimmer of a diamond, that sparkles and flashes with the varied throbbings of the breast on which it is displayed. Children have always a sympathy in the agitations of those connected with them; always, especially, a sense of any trouble or impending revolution, of whatever kind, in domestic circumstances; and therefore Pearl, who was the gem on her mother's unquiet bosom, betrayed, by the very dance of her spirits, the emotions which none could detect in the marble passiveness of Hester's brow.

This effervescence made her flit with a bird-like movement, rather than walk by her mother's side. She broke continually into shouts of a wild, inarticulate, and sometimes piercing music. When they reached the market-place, she became still more restless, on perceiving the stir and bustle that enlivened the spot; for it was usually more like the broad and lonesome green before a village meeting-house, than the centre of a town's business.

"Why, what is this, mother?" cried she. "Wherefore have all the people left their work to-day? Is it a playday for the whole world? See, there is the blacksmith! He has washed his sooty face, and put on his Sabbath-day clothes, and looks as if he would gladly be merry, if any kind body would only teach him how! And there is Master Brackett, the old jailer, nodding and smiling at me. Why does he do so, mother?"

"He remembers thee a little babe,

ay child," answered Hester.

"He should not nod and smile at me, or all that,—the black, grim, ugly-eyed old man!" said Pearl. "He may nod at thee, if he will; for thou art clad in gray, and wearest the scarlet letter. But see, mother, how many faces of strange people, and Indians among them, and sailors! What have they all come to do, here in the market-place?"

"They wait to see the procession pass," said Hester. "For the Governor and the magistrates are to go by, and the ministers, and all the great people and good people, with the music and the soldiers marching before them."

"And will the minister be there?" asked Pearl. "And will he hold out both his hands to me, as when thou ledst me to him from the brook-side?"

"He will be there, child," answered her mother. "But he will not greet thee to-day; nor must thou greet him."

"What a strange, sad man is he!" said the child, as if speaking partly to herself. "In the dark night-time he calls us to him, and holds thy hand and mine, as when we stood with him on the scaffold yonder! And in the deep forest, where only the old trees can hear, and the strip of sky see it, he talks with thee, sitting on a heap of moss! And he kisses my forehead, too, so that the little brook would hardly wash it off! But here, in the sunny day, and among all the people, he knows us not; nor must we know him! A strange, sad man is he, with his hand always over his heart!"

"Be quiet, Pearl! Thou understandest not these things," said her mother. "Think not now of the minister, but look about thee, and see how cheery is everybody's face to-day. The chil-dren have come from their schools, and the grown people from their workshops, and their fields, on purpose to be happy. For, to-day, a new man is beginning to rule over them; and so—as has been the custom of mankind ever since a nation was first gathered—they make merry and rejoice; as if a good and golden year were at length to pass over the poor old world!"

It was as Hester said, in regard to the unwonted jollity that brightened the faces of the people. Into this festal season of the year—as it already was, and continued to be during the greater part of two centuries—the Puritans compressed whatever mirth and public joy they deemed allowable to human infirmity; thereby so far dispelling the customary cloud, that, for the space of a single holiday, they appeared scarcely more grave than most other communities at a period of general affliction.

But we perhaps exaggerate the gray or sable tinge, which undoubtedly characterized the mood and manners of the age. The persons now in the market-place of Boston had not been born to an inheritance of Puritanic gloom. They were native Englishmen, whose fathers had lived in the sunny richness of the Elizabethan epoch; a time when the life of England, viewed as one great mass, would appear to have been as stately, magnificent, and joyous, as the world has ever witnessed. Had they followed their hereditary taste, the New England settlers would have illustrated all events of public importance by bonfires, banquets, pageantries, and processions. Nor would it have been impracticable, in the observance of majestic ceremonies, to combine mirthful recreation with solemnity, and give, as it were, a grotesque and brilliant embroidery to the great robe of state, which a nation, at such festivals, puts on. There was some shadow of an attempt of this kind in the mode of celebrating the day on which the political year of the colony commenced. The dim reflection of a remembered splendor, a colorless and manifold diluted repetition of what they had beheld in proud old London, —we will not say at a royal coronation, but at a Lord Mayor's show,—might be traced in the customs which our forefathers instituted, with reference to the annual installation of magistrates. The fathers and founders of the commonwealth—the statesman, the priest, and the soldier—deemed it a duty then to assume the outward state and majesty, which, in accordance with antique style, was looked upon as the proper garb of public or social eminence. All came forth, to move in procession before the people's eye, and thus impart a needed dignity to the simple framework of a government so newly constructed.

Then, too, the people were countenanced, if not encouraged, in relaxing the severe and close application to their various modes of rugged industry, which, at all other times, seemed of the same piece and material with their religion. Here, it is true, were none of the appliances which popular merriment would so readily have found in the England of Elizabeth's time, or that of James;—no rude shows of a theatrical kind; no minstrel, with his harp and legendary ballad, nor gleeman, with an ape dancing to his music; no juggler, with his tricks of mimic witchcraft; no Merry Andrew, to stir up the multitude with jests, perhaps hundreds of

years old, but still effective, by their appeals to the very broadest sources of mirthful sympathy. All such professors of the several branches of jocularity would have been sternly repressed, not only by the rigid discipline of law, but by the general sentiment which gives law its vitality. Not the less, however, the great, honest face of the people smiled, grimly, perhaps, but widely too. Nor were sports wanting, such as the colonists had witnessed, and shared in, long ago, at the country fairs and on the village-greens of England; and which it was thought well to keep alive on this new soil, for the sake of the courage and manliness that were essential in them. Wrestling-matches, in the different fashions of Cornwall and Devonshire, were seen here and there about the market-place: in one corner, there was a friendly bout at quarterstaff; and—what attracted most interest of all—on the platform of the pillory, already so noted in our pages, two masters of defence were commencing an exhibition with the buckler and broadsword. But, much to the disappointment of the crowd, this latter business was broken off by the interposition of the town beadle, who had no idea of permitting the majesty of the law to be violated by such an abuse of one of its consecrated places.

It may not be too much to affirm, on the whole, (the people being then in the first stages of joyless deportment, and the offspring of sires who had known how to be merry, in their day,) that they would compare favorably, in point of holiday keeping, with their descendants, even at so long an interval as ourselves. Their immediate posterity, the generation next to the early emigrants, wore the blackest shade of Puritanism, and so darkened the national visage with it, that all the subsequent years have not sufficed to clear it up. We have yet to learn again the forgotten art of gayety.

The picture of human life in the market-place, though its general tint was the sad gray, brown, or black of the English emigrants, was yet enlivened by some diversity of hue. A party of Indians—in their savage finery of curiously embroidered deer-skin robes; wampum-belts, red and yellow ochre, and feathers, and armed with the bow and arrow and stone-headed spear—stood apart, with countenances of inflexible gravity, beyond what even the Puritan aspect could attain. Nor, wild as were these painted barbarians, were they the wildest feature of the scene. This distinction could more justly be claimed by some mariners,—a part of the crew of the vessel from the Spanish Main,—who had come ashore to see the humors of Election Day. They were rough-looking desperadoes, with sun-blackened faces, and an immensity of beard; their wide, short trousers were confined about the waist by belts, often clasped with a rough plate of gold, and sustaining always a long knife, and, in some instances, a sword. From beneath their broad-brimmed hats of palm-leaf, gleamed eyes which, even in good nature and merriment, had a kind of animal ferocity. They transgressed, without fear or scruple, the rules of behavior that were binding on all others; smoking tobacco under the beadle's very nose, although each whiff would have cost a townsman a shilling; and quaffing, at their pleasure, draughts of wine or aqua-vitæ from pocket-flasks, which

they freely tendered to the gaping crowd around them. It remarkably characterized the incomplete morality of the age, rigid as we call it, that a license was allowed the seafaring class, not merely for their freaks on shore, but for far more desperate deeds on their proper element. The sailor of that day would go near to be arraigned as a pirate in our own. There could be little doubt, for instance, that this very ship's crew, though no unfavorable specimens of the nautical brotherhood, had been guilty, as we should phrase it, of depredations on the Spanish commerce, such as would have perilled all their necks in a modern court of justice.

But the sea, in those old times, heaved, swelled and foamed very much at its own will, or subject only to the tempestuous wind, with hardly any attempts at regulation by human law. The buccaneer on the wave might relinquish his calling, and become at once, if he chose, a man of probity and piety on land; nor, even in the full career of his reckless life, was he regarded as a personage with whom it was disreputable to traffic, or casually associate. Thus, the Puritan elders, in their black cloaks, starched bands, and steeple-crowned hats, smiled not unbenignantly at the clamor and rude deportment of these jolly seafaring men; and it excited neither surprise nor animadversion, when so reputable a citizen as old Roger Chillingworth, the physician, was seen to enter the market-place, in close and familiar talk with the commander of the questionable vessel.

The latter was by far the most showy and gallant figure, so far as apparel went, anywhere to be seen among the multitude. He wore a profusion of ribbons on his garment, and gold lace on his hat, which was also encircled by a gold chain, and surmounted with a feather. There was a sword at his side, and a sword-cut on his forehead, which, by the arrangement of his hair, he seemed anxious rather to display than hide. A landsman could hardly have worn this garb and shown this face, and worn and shown them both with such a galliard air, without undergoing stern question before a magistrate, and probably incurring fine or imprisonment, or perhaps an exhibition in the stocks. As regarded the shipmaster, however, all was looked upon as pertaining to the character, as to a fish his glistening scales.

After parting from the physician, the commander of the Bristol ship strolled idly through the market-place; until, happening to approach the spot where Hester Prynne was standing, he appeared to recognize, and did not hesitate to address her. As was usually the case wherever Hester stood, a small vacant area—a sort of magic circle—had formed itself about her, into which, though the people were elbowing one another at a little distance, none ventured, or felt disposed to intrude. It was a forcible type of the moral solitude in which the scarlet letter enveloped its fated wearer; partly by her own reserve, and partly by the instinctive, though no longer so unkindly, withdrawal of her fellow-creatures. Now, if never before, it answered a good purpose, by enabling Hester and the seaman to speak together without risk of being overheard; and so changed was Hester Prynne's repute before the public, that the matron in town most eminent for rigid morality could not have held such intercourse with less result of scandal than herself.

"So, mistress," said the mariner, "I must bid the steward make ready one more berth than you bargained for! No fear of scurvy or ship-fever, this voyage! What with the ship's surgeon and this other doctor, our only danger will be from drug or pill; more by token, as there is a lot of apothecary's stuff aboard, which I traded for with a Spanish vessel."

"What mean you?" inquired Hester, startled more than she permitted to appear. "Have you another passenger?"

"Why, know you not," cried the shipmaster, "that this physician here—Chillingworth, he calls himself—is minded to try my cabin-fare with you? Ay, ay, you must have known it; for he tells me he is of your party, and a close friend to the gentleman you spoke of, —he that is in peril from these sour old Puritan rulers!"

"They know each other well, indeed," replied Hester, with a mien of calmness, though in the utmost consternation. "They have dwelt together."

Nothing further passed between the mariner and Hester Prynne. But, at that instant, she beheld old Roger Chillingworth himself, standing in the remotest corner of the market-place, and smiling on her; a smile which—across the wide and bustling square, and through all the talk and laughter, and various thoughts, moods, and interests of the crowd,—conveyed secret and fearful meaning.

CHAPTER XXII

THE PROCESSION

BEFORE Hester Prynne could call together her thoughts, and consider what was practicable to be done in this new and startling aspect of affairs, the sound of military music was heard approaching along a contiguous street. It denoted the advance of the procession of magistrates and citizens, on its way towards the meeting-house; where, in compliance with a custom thus early established, and ever since observed, the Reverend Mr. Dimmesdale was to deliver an Election Sermon.

Soon the head of the procession showed itself, with a slow and stately march, turning a corner, and making its way across the market-place. First came the music. It comprised a variety of instruments, perhaps imperfectly adapted to one another, and played with no great skill; but yet attaining the great object for which the harmony of drum and clarion addresses itself to the multitude,—that of imparting a higher and more heroic air to the scene of life that passes before the eye. Little Pearl at first clapped her hands, but then lost, for an instant, the restless agitation that had kept her in a continual effervescence throughout the morning; she gazed silently, and seemed to be borne upward, like a floating sea-bird, on the long heaves and swells of sound. But she was brought back to her former mood by the shimmer of the sunshine on the weapons and bright armor of the military company, which followed after the music, and formed the honorary escort of the procession.

This body of soldiery—which still sustains a corporate existence, and marches down from past ages with an ancient and honorable fame—was composed of no mercenary materials. Its ranks were filled with gentlemen, who felt the stirrings of martial impulse, and sought to establish a kind of College of Arms, where, as in an association of Knights Templars, they might learn the science, and, so far as peaceful exercise would teach them, the practices of war. The high estimation then placed upon the military character might be seen in the lofty port of each individual member of the company. Some of them, indeed, by their services in the Low Countries and on other fields of European warfare, had fairly won their title to assume the name and pomp of soldiership. The entire array, moreover, clad in burnished steel, and with plumage nodding over their bright morions, had a brilliancy of effect which no modern display can aspire to equal.

And yet the men of civil eminence, who came immediately behind the military escort, were better worth a thoughtful observer's eye. Even in outward demeanor, they showed a stamp of majesty that made the warrior's haughty stride look vulgar, if not absurd. It was an age when what we call talent had far less consideration than now, but the massive materials which produce stability and dignity of character a great deal more. The people possessed, by hereditary right, the quality of reverence; which, in their descendants, if it survive at all, exists in smaller proportion, and with a vastly diminished force, in the selection and estimate of public men. The change may be for good or ill, and is partly, perhaps, for both. In that old day, the English settler on these rude shores—having left king, nobles, and all degrees of awful rank behind, while still the faculty and necessity of reverence were strong in him—bestowed it on the white hair and venerable brow of age; on long-tried integrity; on solid wisdom and sad-colored experience; on endowments of that grave and weighty order which gives the idea of permanence, and comes under the general definition of respectability. These primitive statesmen, therefore,—Bradstreet, Endicott, Dudley, Bellingham, and their compeers,—who were elevated to power by the early choice of the people, seem to have been not often brilliant, but distinguished by a ponderous sobriety, rather than activity of intellect. They had fortitude and self-reliance, and, in time of difficulty or peril, stood up for the welfare of the state like a line of cliffs against a tempestuous tide. The traits of character here indicated were well represented in the square cast of countenance and large physical development of the new colonial magistrates. So far as a demeanor of natural authority was concerned, the mother country need not have been ashamed to see these foremost men of an actual democracy adopted into the House of Peers, or made the Privy Council of the sovereign.

Next in order to the magistrates came the young and eminently distinguished divine, from whose lips the religious discourse of the anniversary was expected.

His was the profession, at that era, in which intellectual ability displayed itself far more than in political life; for —leaving a higher motive out of the question—it offered inducements powerful enough, in the almost worshipping respect of the community, to win the most aspiring ambition into its service. Even political power—as in the case of Increase Mather—was within the grasp of a successful priest.

It was the observation of those who beheld him now, that never, since Mr. Dimmesdale first set his foot on the New England shore, had he exhibited such energy as was seen in the gait and air with which he kept his pace in the procession. There was no feebleness of step, as at other times; his frame was not bent; nor did his hand rest ominously upon his heart. Yet, if the clergyman were rightly viewed, his strength seemed not of the body. It might be spiritual, and imparted to him by angelic ministrations. It might be the exhilaration of that potent cordial, which is distilled only in the furnace-glow of earnest and long-continued thought. Or, perchance, his sensitive temperament was invigorated by the loud and piercing music, that swelled heavenward, and uplifted him on its ascending wave. Nevertheless, so abstracted was his look, it might be questioned whether Mr. Dimmesdale even heard the music. There was his body, moving onward, and with an unaccustomed force. But where was his mind? Far and deep in its own region, busying itself, with preternatural activity, to marshal a procession of stately thoughts that were soon to issue thence; and so he saw nothing, heard nothing, knew nothing, of what was around him; but the spiritual element took up the feeble frame, and carried it along, unconscious of the burden, and converting it to spirit like itself. Men of uncommon intellect, who have grown morbid, possess this occasional power of mighty effort, into which they throw the life of many days, and then are lifeless for as many more.

Hester Prynne, gazing steadfastly at the clergyman, felt a dreary influence come over her, but wherefore or whence she knew not; unless that he seemed so remote from her own sphere, and utterly beyond her reach. One glance of recognition, she had imagined, must needs pass between them. She thought of the dim forest, with its little dell of solitude, and love, and anguish, and the mossy tree-trunk, where, sitting hand in hand, they had mingled their sad and passionate talk with the melancholy murmur of the brook. How deeply had they known each other then! And was this the man? She hardly knew him now! He, moving proudly past, enveloped, as it were, in the rich music, with the procession of majestic and venerable fathers; he, so unattainable in his worldly position, and still more so in that far vista of his unsympathizing thoughts, through which she now beheld him! Her spirit sank with the idea that all must have been a delusion, and that, vividly as she had dreamed it, there could be no real bond betwixt the clergyman and herself. And thus much of woman was there in Hester, that she could scarcely forgive him, —least of all now, when the heavy footstep of their approaching Fate might be heard, nearer, nearer, nearer!—for being able so completely to withdraw himself from their mutual world: while

she groped darkly, and stretched forth her cold hands, and found him not.

Pearl either saw and responded to her mother's feelings, or herself felt the remoteness and intangibility that had fallen around the minister. While the procession passed, the child was uneasy, fluttering up and down, like a bird on the point of taking flight. When the whole had gone by, she looked up into Hester's face.

"Mother," said she, "was that the same minister that kissed me by the brook?"

"Hold thy peace, dear little Pearl!" whispered her mother. "We must not always talk in the market-place of what happens to us in the forest."

"I could not be sure that it was he, so strange he looked," continued the child. "Else I would have run to him, and bid him kiss me now, before all the people; even as he did yonder among the dark old trees. What would the minister have said, mother? Would he have clapped his hand over his heart, and scowled on me, and bid me begone?"

"What should he say, Pearl," answered Hester, "save that it was no time to kiss, and that kisses are not to be given in the market-place? Well for thee, foolish child, that thou didst not speak to him!"

Another shade of the same sentiment in reference to Mr. Dimmesdale, was expressed by a person whose eccentricities—or insanity, as we should term it —led her to do what few of the townspeople would have ventured on; to begin a conversation with the wearer of the scarlet letter, in public. It was Mistress Hibbins, who, arrayed in great magnificence, with a triple ruff, a broidered stomacher, a gown of rich velvet, and a gold-headed cane, had come forth to see the procession. As this ancient lady had the renown (which subsequently cost her no less a price than her life) of being a principal actor in all the works of necromancy that were continually going forward, the crowd gave way before her, and seemed to fear the touch of her garment, as if it carried the plague among its gorgeous folds. Seen in conjunction with Hester Prynne,—kindly as so many now felt towards the latter,—the dread inspired by Mistress Hibbins was doubled, and caused a general movement from that part of the market-place in which the two women stood.

"Now, what mortal imagination could conceive it!" whispered the old lady, confidentially, to Hester. "Yonder divine man! That saint on earth, as the people uphold him to be, and as—I must needs say—he really looks! Who, now, that saw him pass in the procession, would think how little while it is since he went forth out of his study,—chewing a Hebrew text of Scripture in his mouth, I warrant,—to take an airing in the forest! Aha! we know what that means, Hester Prynne! But, truly, forsooth, I find it hard to believe him the same man. Many a church-member saw I, walking behind the music, that has danced in the same measure with me, when Somebody was fiddler, and, it might be, an Indian powwow or a Lapland wizard changing hands with us! That is but a trifle, when a woman knows the world. But this minister! Couldst thou surely tell, Hester, whether he was the same man that encountered thee on the forest-path?"

"Madam, I know not of what you speak," answered Hester Prynne, feeling Mistress Hibbins to be of infirm mind; yet strangely startled and awe-stricken by the confidence with which she affirmed a personal connection between so many persons (herself among them) and the Evil One. "It is not for me to talk lightly of a learned and pious minister of the Word, like the Reverend Mr. Dimmesdale!"

"Fie, woman, fie!" cried the old lady, shaking her finger at Hester. "Dost thou think I have been to the forest so many times, and have yet no skill to judge who else has been there? Yea; though no leaf of the wild garlands, which they wore while they danced, be left in their hair! I know thee, Hester; for I behold the token. We may all see it in the sunshine; and it glows like a red flame in the dark. Thou wearest it openly; so there need be no question about that. But this minister! Let me tell thee, in thine ear! When the Black Man sees one of his own servants, signed and sealed, so shy of owning to the bond as is the Reverend Mr. Dimmesdale, he hath a way of ordering matters so that the mark shall be disclosed in open daylight to the eyes of all the world! What is it that the minister seeks to hide, with his hand always over his heart? Ha, Hester Prynne!"

"What is it, good Mistress Hibbins?" eagerly asked little Pearl. "Hast thou seen it?"

"No matter, darling!" responded Mistress Hibbins, making Pearl a profound reverence. "Thou thyself wilt see it, one time or another. They say, child, thou art of the lineage of the Prince of the Air! Wilt thou ride with me, some fine night, to see thy father?

Then thou shalt know wherefore the minister keeps his hand over his heart!"

Laughing so shrilling that all the market-place could hear her, the weird old gentlewoman took her departure.

By this time the preliminary prayer had been offered in the meeting-house, and the accents of the Reverend Mr. Dimmesdale were heard commencing his discourse. An irresistible feeling kept Hester near the spot. As the sacred edifice was too much thronged to admit another auditor, she took up her position close beside the scaffold of the pillory. It was in sufficient proximity to bring the whole sermon to her ears, in the shape of an indistinct, but varied, murmur and flow of the minister's very peculiar voice.

This vocal organ was in itself a rich endowment; insomuch that a listener, comprehending nothing of the language in which the preacher spoke, might still have been swayed to and fro by the mere tone and cadence. Like all other music, it breathed passion and pathos, and emotions high or tender, in a tongue native to the human heart, wherever educated. Muffled as the sound was by its passage through the church-walls, Hester Prynne listened with such intentness, and sympathized so intimately, that the sermon had throughout a meaning for her, entirely apart from its indistinguishable words. These, perhaps, if more distinctly heard, might have been only a grosser medium, and have clogged the spiritual sense. Now she caught the low undertone, as of the wind sinking down to repose itself; then ascended with it, as it rose through progressive gradations of sweetness and power, until its volume seemed to envelop her with an atmosphere of awe and solemn grandeur. And yet, majestic as the voice sometimes became, there was forever in it an essential character of plaintiveness. A loud or low expression of anguish,—the whisper, or the shriek, as it might be conceived, of suffering humanity, that touched a sensibility in every bosom! At times this deep strain of pathos was all that could be heard, and scarcely heard, sighing amid a desolate silence. But even when the minister's voice grew high and commanding,—when it gushed irrepressibly upward,—when it assumed its utmost breadth and power, so overfilling the church as to burst its way through the solid walls, and diffuse itself in the open air,—still, if the auditor listened intently, and for the purpose, he could detect the same cry of pain. What was it? The complaint of a human heart, sorrow-laden, perchance guilty, telling its secret, whether of guilt or sorrow, to the great heart of mankind; beseeching its sympathy or forgiveness, —at every moment,—in each accent,— and never in vain! It was this profound and continual undertone that gave the clergyman his most appropriate power.

During all this time, Hester stood, statue-like, at the foot of the scaffold. If the minister's voice had not kept her there, there would nevertheless have been an inevitable magnetism in that spot, whence she dated the first hour of her life of ignominy. There was a sense within her,—too ill-defined to be made a thought, but weighing heavily on her mind,—that her whole orb of life, both before and after, was connected with this spot, as with the one point that gave it unity.

Little Pearl, meanwhile, had quitted her mother's side, and was playing at her own will about the market-place. She made the sombre crowd cheerful by her erratic and glistening ray; even as a bird of bright plumage illuminates a whole tree of dusky foliage, by darting to and fro, half seen and half concealed amid the twilight of the clustering leaves. She had an undulating, but, oftentimes, a sharp and irregular movement. It indicated the restless vivacity of her spirit, which to-day was doubly indefatigable in its tiptoe dance, because it was played upon and vibrated with her mother's disquietude. Whenever Pearl saw anything to excite her ever active and wandering curiosity, she flew thitherward, and, as we might say, seized upon that man or thing as her own property, so far as she desired it; but without yielding the minutest degree of control over her motions in requital. The Puritans looked on, and, if they smiled, were none the less inclined to pronounce the child a demon offspring, from the indescribable charm of beauty and eccentricity that shone through her little figure, and sparkled with its activity. She ran and looked the wild Indian in the face; and he grew conscious of a nature wilder than his own. Thence, with native audacity, but still with a reserve as characteristic, she flew into the midst of a group of mariners, the swarthy-cheeked wild men of the ocean, as the Indians were of the land; and they gazed wonderingly and admiringly at Pearl, as if a flake of the sea-foam had taken the shape of a little maid, and were gifted with a soul of the sea-fire, that flashes beneath the prow in the night-time.

One of these seafaring men—the shipmaster, indeed, who had spoken to Hester Prynne—was so smitten with Pearl's aspect, that he attempted to lay hands upon her, with purpose to snatch a kiss. Finding it as impossible to touch her as to catch a humming-bird in the air, he took from his hat the gold chain that was twisted about it, and threw it to the child. Pearl immediately twined it around her neck and waist, with such happy skill, that, once seen there, it became a part of her, and it was difficult to imagine her without it.

"Thy mother is yonder woman with the scarlet letter," said the seaman. "Wilt thou carry her a message from me?"

"If the message pleases me, I will," answered Pearl.

"Then tell her," rejoined he, "that I spake again with the black-a-visaged, hump-shouldered old doctor, and he engages to bring his friend, the gentleman she wots of, aboard with him. So let thy mother take no thought, save for herself and thee. Wilt thou tell her this, thou witch-baby?"

"Mistress Hibbins says my father is the Prince of the Air!" cried Pearl, with a naughty smile. "If thou callest me that ill name, I shall tell him of thee; and he will chase thy ship with a tempest!"

Pursuing a zigzag course across the market-place, the child returned to her mother, and communicated what the mariner had said. Hester's strong, calm, steadfastly enduring spirit almost sank, at last, on beholding this dark and grim countenance of an inevitable doom, which—at the moment when a passage seemed to open for the minister and herself out of their labyrinth of misery —showed itself, with an unrelenting smile, right in the midst of their path. With her mind harassed by the terrible perplexity in which the shipmaster's intelligence involved her, she was also subjected to another trial. There were many people present, from the country round about, who had often heard of the scarlet letter, and to whom it had been made terrific by a hundred false or exaggerated rumors, but who had never beheld it with their own bodily eyes. These, after exhausting other modes of amusement, now thronged about Hester Prynne with rude and boorish intrusiveness. Unscrupulous as it was, however, it could not bring them nearer than a circuit of several yards. At that distance they accordingly stood, fixed there by the centrifugal force of the repugnance which the mystic symbol inspired. The whole gang of sailors, likewise, observing the press of spectators, and learning the purport of the scarlet letter, came and thrust their sunburnt and desperado-looking faces into the ring. Even the Indians were affected by a sort of cold shadow of the white man's curiosity, and, gliding through the crowd, fastened their snake-like black eyes on Hester's bosom; conceiving, perhaps, that the wearer of this brilliantly embroidered badge must needs be a personage of high dignity among her people. Lastly the inhabitants of the town (their own interest in this worn-out subject languidly reviving itself by sympathy with what they saw others feel) lounged idly to the same quarter, and tormented Hester Prynne, perhaps more than all the rest, with their cool, well-acquainted gaze at her familiar shame. Hester saw and recognized the self-same faces of that group of matrons, who had awaited her forthcoming from the prison-door, seven years ago; all save one, the youngest and only compassionate among them, whose burial-robe she had since made. At the final hour, when she was so soon to fling aside the burning letter, it had strangely become the centre of more remark and excitement, and was thus made to sear her breast more painfully, than at any time since the first day she put it on.

While Hester stood in that magic circle of ignominy, where the cunning cruelty of her sentence seemed to have fixed her forever, the admirable preacher was looking down from the sacred pulpit upon an audience, whose very inmost spirits had yielded to his control. The sainted minister in the church! The woman of the scarlet letter in the market-place! What imagination would have been irreverent enough to surmise that the same scorching stigma was on them both!

CHAPTER XXIII

THE REVELATION OF THE SCARLET LETTER

THE eloquent voice, on which the souls of the listening audience had been borne aloft as on the swelling waves of the sea, at length came to a pause. There was a momentary silence, profound as what should follow the utterance of oracles. Then ensued a murmur and half-hushed tumult; as if the auditors, released from the high spell that had transported them into the region of another's mind, were returning into themselves, with all their awe and wonder still heavy on them. In a moment more, the crowd began to gush forth from the doors of the church. Now that there was an end, they needed other breath, more fit to support the gross and earthly life into which they relapsed, than that atmosphere which the preacher had converted into words of flame, and had burdened with the rich fragrance of his thought.

In the open air their rapture broke into speech. The street and the marketplace absolutely babbled, from side to side, with applause of the minister. His hearers could not rest until they had told one another of what each knew better than he could tell or hear. According to their united testimony, never had man spoken in so wise, so high, and so holy a spirit, as he that spake this day; nor had inspiration ever breathed through mortal lips more evidently than it did through his. Its influence could be seen, as it were, descending upon him, and possessing him, and continually lifting him out of the written discourse that lay before him, and filling him with ideas that must have been as marvellous to himself as to his audience. His subject, it appeared, had been the relation between the Deity and the communities of mankind, with a special reference to the New England which they were here planting in the wilderness. And, as he drew towards the close, a spirit as of prophecy had come upon him, constraining him to its purpose as mightily as the old prophets of Israel were constrained; only with this difference, that, whereas the Jewish seers had denounced judgments and ruin on their country, it was his mission to foretell a high and glorious destiny for the newly gathered people of the Lord. But, throughout it all, and through the whole discourse, there had been a certain deep, sad undertone of pathos, which could not be interpreted otherwise than as the natural regret of one soon to pass away. Yes; their minister whom they so loved—and who so loved them all, that he could not depart heavenward without a sigh—had the foreboding of untimely death upon him, and would soon leave them in their tears! This idea of his transitory stay on earth gave the last emphasis to the effect which the preacher had produced; it was as if an angel, in his passage to the skies, had shaken his bright wings over the people for an instant,—at once a shadow and a splendor,—and had shed down a shower of golden truths upon them.

Thus, there had come to the Reverend Mr. Dimmesdale—as to most men, in their various spheres, though seldom recognized until they see it far behind them—an epoch of life more brilliant and full of triumph than any previous one. or than any which could hereafter be. He stood, at this moment, on the very proudest eminence of superiority, to which the gifts of intellect, rich lore, prevailing eloquence, and a reputation of whitest sanctity, could exalt a clergyman in New England's earliest days, when the professional character was of itself a lofty pedestal. Such was the position which the minister occupied, as he bowed his head forward on the cushions of the pulpit, at the close of his

Election Sermon. Meanwhile Hester Prynne was standing beside the scaffold of the pillory, with the scarlet letter still burning on her breast!

Now was heard again the clangor of the music, and the measured tramp of the military escort, issuing from the church-door. The procession was to be marshalled thence to the town-hall, where a solemn banquet would complete the ceremonies of the day.

Once more, therefore, the train of venerable and majestic fathers was seen moving through a broad pathway of the people, who drew back reverently, on either side, as the Governor and magistrates, the old and wise men, the holy ministers, and all that were eminent and renowned, advanced into the midst of them. When they were fairly in the market-place, their presence was greeted by a shout. This—though doubtless it might acquire additional force and volume from the childlike loyalty which the age awarded to its rulers— was felt to be an irrepressible outburst of enthusiasm kindled in the auditors by that high strain of eloquence which was yet reverberating in their ears. Each felt the impulse in himself, and, in the same breath, caught it from his neighbor. Within the church, it had hardly been kept down; beneath the sky, it pealed upward to the zenith. There were human beings enough, and enough of highly wrought and symphonious feeling, to produce that more impressive sound than the organ tones of the blast, or the thunder, or the roar of the sea; even that mighty swell of many voices, blended into one great voice by the universal impulse which makes likewise one vast heart out of the many. Never, from the soil of New England, had gone up such a shout! Never, on New England soil, had stood the man so honored by his mortal brethren as the preacher!

How fared it with him then? Were there not the brilliant particles of a halo in the air about his head? So etherealized by spirit as he was, and so apotheosized by worshipping admirers, did his footsteps, in the procession, really tread upon the dust of earth?

As the ranks of military men and civil fathers moved onward, all eyes were turned towards the point where the minister was seen to approach among them. The shout died into a murmur, as one portion of the crowd after another obtained a glimpse of him. How feeble and pale he looked, amid all his triumph! The energy—or say, rather, the inspiration which had held him up, until he should have delivered the sacred message that brought its own strength along with it from heaven— was withdrawn, now that it had so faithfully performed its office. The glow, which they had just before beheld burning on his cheek, was extinguished, like a flame that sinks down hopelessly among the late-decaying embers. It seemed hardly the face of a man alive, with such a deathlike hue; it was hardly a man with life in him, that tottered on his path so nervelessly, yet tottered, and did not fall!

One of his clerical brethren,—it was the venerable John Wilson,—observing the state in which Mr. Dimmesdale was left by the retiring wave of intellect and sensibility, stepped forward hastily to offer his support. The minister tremulously, but decidedly, repelled the old man's arm. He still walked onward, if that movement could be so described, which rather resembled the wavering effort of an infant, with its mother's arms in view, outstretched to tempt him forward. And now, almost imperceptible as were the latter steps of his progress, he had come opposite the well-remembered and weather-darkened scaffold, where, long since, with all that dreary lapse of time between, Hester Prynne had encountered the world's ignominious stare. There stood Hester, holding little Pearl by the hand! And there was the scarlet letter on her breast! The minister here made a pause; although the music still played the stately and rejoicing march to which the procession moved. It summoned him onward,—onward to the festival!—but here he made a pause.

Bellingham, for the last few moments, had kept an anxious eye upon him. He now left his own place in the procession, and advanced to give assistance; judging, from Mr. Dimmesdale's aspect, that he must otherwise inevitably fall. But there was something in the latter's expression that warned back the magistrate, although a man not readily obeying the vague intimations that pass from one spirit to another. The crowd, meanwhile, looked on with awe and wonder. This earthly faintness was, in their view, only another phase of the minister's celestial strength; nor would it have seemed a miracle too high to be wrought for one so holy, had he ascended before their eyes, waxing dimmer and brighter, and fading at last into the light of heaven!

He turned towards the scaffold, and stretched forth his arms.

"Hester," said he, "come hither! Come, my little Pearl!"

It was a ghastly look with which he regarded them; but there was something at once tender and strangely triumphant in it. The child, with the bird-like motion which was one of her characteristics, flew to him, and clasped her arms about his knees. Hester Prynne—slowly, as if impelled by inevitable fate, and against her strongest will—likewise drew near, but paused before she reached him. At this instant, old Roger Chillingworth thrust himself through the crowd,—or, perhaps, so dark, disturbed and evil, was his look, he rose up out of some nether region,—to snatch back his victim from what he sought to do! Be that as it might, the old man rushed forward, and caught the minister by the arm.

"Madman, hold! what is your purpose?" whispered he. "Wave back that woman! Cast off this child! All shall be well! Do not blacken your fame, and perish in dishonor! I can yet save you! Would you bring infamy on your sacred profession?"

"Ha, tempter! Methinks thou art too late!" answered the minister, encountering his eye, fearfully, but firmly. "Thy power is not what it was! With God's help, I shall escape thee now!"

He again extended his hand to the woman of the scarlet letter.

"Hester Prynne," cried he, with a piercing earnestness, "in the name of Him, so terrible and so merciful, who gives me grace, at this last moment, to do what—for my own heavy sin and miserable agony—I withheld myself from doing seven years ago, come hither now, and twine thy strength about me! Thy strength, Hester; but let it be guided by the will which God hath granted me! This wretched and wronged old man is opposing it with all his might!—with all his own might, and he fiend's! Come, Hester, come! Support me up yonder scaffold!"

The crowd was in a tumult. The men of rank and dignity, who stood more immediately around the clergyman, were so taken by surprise, and so perplexed as to the purport of what they saw, —unable to receive the explanation which most readily presented itself, or to imagine any other,—that they remained silent and inactive spectators of the judgment which Providence seemed about to work. They beheld the minister, leaning on Hester's shoulder, and supported by her arm around him, approach the scaffold, and ascend its steps; while still the little hand of the sin-born child was clasped in his. Old Roger Chillingworth followed, as one intimately connected with the drama of guilt and sorrow in which they had all been actors, and well entitled, therefore, to be present, at its closing scene.

"Hadst thou sought the whole earth over," said he, looking darkly at the clergyman, "there was no one place so secret,—no high place nor lowly place, where thou couldst have escaped me,—save on this very scaffold!"

"Thanks be to Him who hath led me hither!" answered the minister.

Yet he trembled, and turned to Hester with an expression of doubt and anxiety in his eyes, not the less evidently betrayed, that there was a feeble smile upon his lips.

"Is not this better," murmured he, "than what we dreamed of in the forest?"

"I know not! I know not!" she hurriedly replied. "Better? Yea; so we may both die, and little Pearl die with us!"

"For thee and Pearl, be it as God shall order," said the minister; "and God is merciful! Let me now do the will which he hath made plain before my sight. For, Hester, I am a dying man. So let me make haste to take my shame upon me!"

Partly supported by Hester Prynne, and holding one hand of little Pearl's, the Reverend Mr. Dimmesdale turned to the dignified and venerable rulers; to the holy ministers, who were his brethren; to the people, whose great heart was thoroughly appalled, yet overflowing with tearful sympathy, as knowing that some deep life-matter—which, if full of sin, was full of anguish and repentance likewise—was now to be laid open to them. The sun, but little past its meridian, shone down upon the clergyman, and gave a distinctness to his figure, as he stood out from all the earth, to put in his plea of guilty at the bar of Eternal Justice!

"People of New England!" cried he, with a voice that rose over them, high, solemn, and majestic,—yet had always a tremor through it, and sometimes a shriek, struggling up out of a fathomless depth of remorse and woe,—"ye, that have loved me!—ye, that have deemed me holy!—behold me here, the one sinner of the world! At last!—at last!—I stand upon the spot where seven years since, I should have stood; here, with this woman, whose arm, more than the little strength wherewith I have crept hitherward, sustains me, at this dreadful moment, from grovelling down upon my face! Lo, the scarlet letter which Hester wears! Ye have all shuddered at it! Wherever her walk hath been,—wherever, so miserably burdened, she may have hoped to find repose,— it hath cast a lurid gleam of awe and horrible repugnance round about her.

But there stood one in the midst of you, at whose brand of sin and infamy ye have not shuddered!"

It seemed, at this point, as if the minister must leave the remainder of his secret undisclosed. But he fought back the bodily weakness,—and, still more, the faintness of heart,—that was striving for the mastery with him. He threw off all resistance, and stepped passionately forward a pace before the woman and the child.

"It was on him!" he continued, with a kind of fierceness; so determined was he to speak out the whole. "God's eye beheld it! The angels were forever pointing at it! The Devil knew it well, and fretted it continually with the touch of his burning finger! But he hid it cunningly from men, and walked among you with the mien of a spirit, mournful, because so pure in a sinful world! —and sad, because he missed his heavenly kindred! Now, at the death-hour, he stands up before you! He bids you look again at Hester's scarlet letter! He tells you, that, with all its mysterious horror, it is but the shadow of what he bears on his own breast, and that even this, his own red stigma, is no more than the type of what has seared his inmost heart! Stand any here that question God's judgment on a sinner? Behold! Behold a dreadful witness of it!"

With a convulsive motion, he tore away the ministerial band from before his breast. It was revealed! But it were irreverent to describe that revelation. For an instant, the gaze of the horror-stricken multitude was concentred on the ghastly miracle; while the minister stood, with a flush of triumph in his face, as one who, in the crisis of acutest pain, had won a victory. Then, down he

sank upon the scaffold! Hester partly raised him, and supported his head against her bosom. Old Roger Chillingworth knelt down beside him, with a blank, dull countenance, out of which the life seemed to have departed.

"Thou hast escaped me!" he repeated more than once. "Thou hast escaped me!"

"May God forgive thee!" said the minister. "Thou, too, hast deeply sinned!"

He withdrew his dying eyes from the old man, and fixed them on the woman and the child.

"My little Pearl," said he, feebly,— and there was a sweet and gentle smile over his face, as of a spirit sinking into deep repose; nay, now that the burden was removed, it seemed almost as if he would be sportive with the child,—"dear little Pearl, wilt thou kiss me now? Thou wouldst not, yonder, in the forest! But now thou wilt?"

Pearl kissed his lips. A spell was broken. The great scene of grief, in which the wild infant bore a part, had developed all her sympathies; and as her tears fell upon her father's cheek, they were the pledge that she would grow up amid human joy and sorrow, nor forever do battle with the world, but be a woman in it. Towards her mother, too, Pearl's errand as a messenger of anguish was all fulfilled.

"Hester," said the clergyman, "farewell!"

"Shall we not meet again?" whispered she, bending her face down close to his. "Shall we not spend our immortal life together? Surely, surely, we have ransomed one another, with all this woe! Thou lookest far into eternity, with those bright dying eyes! Then tell me what thou seest?"

"Hush, Hester, hush!" said he, with tremulous solemnity. "The law we broke!—the sin here so awfully revealed!—let these alone be in thy thoughts! I fear! I fear! It may be, that, when we forgot our God,—when we violated our reverence each for the other's soul,—it was thenceforth vain to hope that we could meet hereafter, in an everlasting and pure reunion. God knows; and he is merciful! He hath proved his mercy, most of all, in my afflictions. By giving me this burning torture to bear upon my breast! By sending yonder dark and terrible old man, to keep the torture always at red-heat! By bringing me hither, to die this death of triumphant ignominy before the people! Had either of these agonies been wanting, I had been lost forever! Praised be his name! His will be done! Farewell!"

That final word came forth with the minister's expiring breath. The multitude, silent till then, broke out in a strange, deep voice of awe and wonder, which could not as yet find utterance, save in this murmur that rolled so heavily after the departed spirit.

CHAPTER XXIV

CONCLUSION

AFTER many days, when time sufficed for the people to arrange their thoughts in reference to the foregoing scene, there was more than one account of what had been witnessed on the scaffold.

Most of the spectators testified to having seen, on the breast of the unhappy minister, a SCARLET LETTER—the very semblance of that worn by Hester Prynne—imprinted in the flesh. As regarded its origin, there were various explanations, all of which must necessarily have been conjectural. Some affirmed that the Reverend Mr. Dimmesdale, on the very day when Hester Prynne first wore her ignominious badge, had begun a course of penance, —which he afterwards, in so many futile methods, followed out,—by inflicting a hideous torture on himself. Others contended that the stigma had not been produced until a long time subsequent, when old Roger Chillingworth, being a potent necromancer, had caused it to appear, through the agency of magic and poisonous drugs. Others, again,—and those best able to appreciate the minister's peculiar sensibility, and the wonderful operation of his spirit upon the body,—whispered their belief, that the awful symbol was the effect of the ever active tooth of remorse, gnawing from the inmost heart outwardly, and at last manifesting Heaven's dreadful judgment by the visible presence of the letter. The reader may choose among these theories. We have thrown all the light we could acquire upon the portent, and would gladly, now that it has done its office, erase its deep print out of our own brain; where long meditation has fixed it in very undesirable distinctness.

It is singular, nevertheless, that certain persons, who were spectators of the whole scene, and professed never once to have removed their eyes from the Reverend Mr. Dimmesdale, denied that there was any mark whatever on his breast, more than on a new-born infant's. Neither, by their report, had his dying words acknowledged, nor even remotely implied, any, the slightest connection, on his part, with the guilt for which Hester Prynne had so long worn the scarlet letter. According to these highly respectable witnesses, the minister, conscious that he was dying,—conscious, also, that the reverence of the multitude placed him already among saints and angels,—had desired, by yielding up his breath in the arms of that fallen woman, to express to the world how utterly nugatory is the choicest of man's own righteousness. After exhausting life in his efforts for mankind's spiritual good, he had made the manner of his death a parable, in order to impress on his admirers the mighty and mournful lesson, that, in the view of Infinite Purity, we are sinners all alike. It was to teach them, that the holiest among us has but attained so far above his fellows as to discern more clearly the Mercy which looks down, and repudiate more utterly the phantom of human merit, which would look aspiringly upward. Without disputing a truth so momentous, we must be allowed to consider this version of Mr. Dimmesdale's story as only an instance of that stubborn fidelity with which a man's friends—and especially a clergyman's —will sometimes uphold his character, when proofs, clear as the mid-day sunshine on the scarlet letter, establish him

a false and sin-stained creature of the dust.

The authority which we have chiefly followed,—a manuscript of old date, drawn up from the verbal testimony of individuals, some of whom had known Hester Prynne, while others had heard the tale from contemporary witnesses,—fully confirms the view taken in the foregoing pages. Among many morals which press upon us from the poor minister's miserable experience, we put only this into a sentence:—"Be true! Be true! Be true! Show freely to the world, if not your worst, yet some trait whereby the worst may be inferred!"

Nothing was more remarkable than the change which took place, almost immediately after Mr. Dimmesdale's death, in the appearance and demeanor of the old man known as Roger Chillingworth. All his strength and energy —all his vital and intellectual force— seemed at once to desert him; insomuch that he positively withered up, shrivelled away, and almost vanished from mortal sight, like an uprooted weed that lies wilting in the sun. This unhappy man had made the very principle of his life to consist in the pursuit and systematic exercise of revenge; and when, by its completest triumph and consummation, that evil principle was left with no further material to support it, when, in short, there was no more Devil's work on earth for him to do, it only remained for the unhumanized mortal to betake himself whither his Master would find him tasks enough, and pay him his wages duly. But, to all these shadowy beings, so long our near acquaintances,—as well Roger Chillingworth as his companions,—we would fain be merciful. It is a curious subject of observation and inquiry, whether hatred and love be not the same thing at bottom. Each, in its utmost development, supposes a high degree of intimacy and heart-knowledge; each renders one individual dependent for the food of his affections and spiritual life upon another; each leaves the passionate lover, or the no less passionate hater, forlorn and desolate by the withdrawal of his subject. Philosophically considered, therefore, the two passions seem essentially the same, except that one happens to be seen in a celestial radiance, and the other in a dusky and lurid glow. In the spiritual world, the old physician and the minister—mutual victims as they have been—may, unawares, have found their earthly stock of hatred and antipathy transmuted into golden love.

Leaving this discussion apart, we have a matter of business to communicate to the reader. At old Roger Chillingworth's decease, (which took place within the year,) and by his last will and testament, of which Governor Bellingham and the Reverend Mr. Wilson were executors, he bequeathed a very considerable amount of property, both here and in England, to little Pearl, the daughter of Hester Prynne.

So Pearl—the elf-child,—the demon offspring, as some people, up to that epoch, persisted in considering her,—became the richest heiress of her day, in the New World. Not improbably, this circumstance wrought a very material change in the public estimation; and, had the mother and child remained here, little Pearl, at a marriageable period of life, might have mingled her wild blood with the lineage of the devoutest Puritan among them all. But, in no long time after the physician's death, the wearer of the scarlet letter disappeared, and Pearl along with her. For many years, though a vague report would now and then find its way across the sea,—like a shapeless piece of driftwood tost ashore, with the initials of a name upon it,—yet no tidings of them unquestionably authentic were received. The story of the scarlet letter grew into a legend. Its spell, however, was still potent, and kept the scaffold awful where the poor minister had died, and likewise the cottage by the sea-shore, where Hester Prynne had dwelt. Near this latter spot, one afternoon, some children were at play, when they beheld a tall woman, in a gray robe, approach the cottage-door. In all those years it had never once been opened; but either she unlocked it, or the decaying wood and iron yielded to her hand, or she glided shadowlike through these impediments,—and, at all events, went in.

On the threshold she paused,—turned partly round,—for, perchance, the idea of entering all alone, and all so changed, the home of so intense a former life, was more dreary and desolate than even she could bear. But her hesitation was only for an instant, though long enough to display a scarlet letter on her breast.

And Hester Prynne had returned, and taken up her long-forsaken shame! But where was little Pearl? If still alive, she must now have been in the flush and bloom of early womanhood. None knew—nor ever learned, with the fulness of perfect certainty—whether the elf-child had gone thus untimely to a maiden grave; or whether her wild, rich nature had been softened and subdued, and made capable of a woman's gentle happiness. But, through the remainder of Hester's life, there were indications that the recluse of the scarlet letter was the object of love and interest with some inhabitant of another land. Letters came, with armorial seals upon them, though of bearings unknown to English heraldry. In the cottage there were articles of comfort and luxury, such as Hester never cared to use, but which only wealth could have purchased, and affection have imagined for her. There were trifles, too, little ornaments, beautiful tokens of a continual remembrance, that must have been wrought by delicate fingers, at the impulse of a fond heart. And, once, Hester was seen embroidering a baby garment, with such a lavish richness of golden fancy as would have raised a public tumult, had any infant, thus apparelled, been shown to our sober-hued community.

In fine, the gossips of that day believed,—and Mr. Surveyor Pue, who made investigations a century later, believed,—and one of his recent successors in office, moreover, faithfully believes,—that Pearl was not only alive, but married, and happy, and mindful of her mother; and that she would most joyfully have entertained that sad and lonely mother at her fireside.

But there was a more real life for Hester Prynne, here, in New England, than in that unknown region where Pearl had found a home. Here had been her sin; here, her sorrow; and here was yet to be her penitence. She had returned, therefore, and resumed,—of her own free will, for not the sternest magistrate of that iron period would have imposed it,—resumed the symbol of which we have related so dark a tale. Never afterwards did it quit her

bosom. But, in the lapse of the toilsome, thoughtful, and self-devoted years that made up Hester's life, the scarlet letter ceased to be a stigma which attracted the world's scorn and bitterness, and became a type of something to be sorrowed over, and looked upon with awe, yet with reverence too. And, as Hester Prynne had no selfish ends, nor lived in any measure for her own profit and enjoyment, people brought all their sorrows and perplexities, and besought her counsel, as one who had herself gone through a mighty trouble. Women, more especially,—in the continually recurring trials of wounded, wasted, wronged, misplaced, or erring and sinful passion,—or with the dreary burden of a heart unyielded, because unvalued and unsought,—came to Hester's cottage, demanding why they were so wretched, and what the remedy! Hester comforted and counselled them, as best she might. She assured them, too, of her firm belief that, at some brighter period, when the world should have grown ripe for it in Heaven's own time, a new truth would be revealed, in order to establish the whole relation between man and woman on a surer ground of mutual happiness. Earlier in life, Hester had vainly imagined that she herself might be the destined prophetess, but had long since recognized the impossibility that any mission of divine and mysterious truth should be confided to a woman stained with sin, bowed down with shame, or even burdened with a lifelong sorrow. The angel and apostle of the coming revelation must be a woman indeed, but lofty, pure, and beautiful and wise, moreover, not through dusky grief, but the ethereal medium of joy and showing how sacred love shoul make us happy, by the truest test of a life successful to such an end!

So said Hester Prynne, and glanced her sad eyes downward at the scarlet letter. And, after many, many years, a new grave was delved, near an old and sunken one, in that burial-ground beside which King's Chapel has since been built. It was near that old and sunken grave, yet with a space between, as if the dust of the two sleepers had no right to mingle. Yet one tombstone served for both. All around, there were monuments carved with armorial bearings; and on this simple slab of slate —as the curious investigator may still discern, and perplex himself with the purport—there appeared the semblance of an engraved escutcheon. It bore a device, a herald's wording of which might serve for a motto and brief description of our now concluded legend; so sombre is it, and relieved only by one ever-glowing point of light gloomier than the shadow:—

"ON A FIELD, SABLE, THE LETTER A, GULES."

TWICE-TOLD TALES

———

THE GRAY CHAMPION

THERE was once a time when New England groaned under the actual pressure of heavier wrongs than those threatened ones which brought on the Revolution. James II., the bigoted successor of Charles the Voluptuous, had annulled the charters of all the colonies, and sent a harsh and unprincipled soldier to take away our liberties and endanger our religion. The Administration of Sir Edmund Andros lacked scarcely a single characteristic of tyranny: a Governor and Council, holding office from the King, and wholly independent of the country; laws made and taxes levied without concurrence of the people, immediate or by their representatives; the rights of private citizens violated, and the titles of all landed property declared void; the voice of complaint stifled by restrictions on the press; and, finally, disaffection overawed by the first band of mercenary troops that ever marched on our free soil. For two years our ancestors were kept in sullen submission, by that filial love which had invariably secured their allegiance to the mother country, whether its head chanced to be a Parliament, Protector, or Popish Monarch. Till these evil times, however, such allegiance had been merely nominal, and the colonists had ruled themselves, enjoying far more freedom than is even yet the privilege of the native subjects of Great Britain.

At length a rumor reached our shores that the Prince of Orange had ventured on an enterprise, the success of which would be the triumph of civil and religious rights and the salvation of New England. It was but a doubtful whisper; it might be false, or the attempt might fail; and, in either case, the man that stirred against King James would lose his head. Still the intelligence produced a marked effect. The people smiled mysteriously in the streets, and threw bold glances at their oppressors; while, far and wide, there was a subdued and silent agitation, as if the slightest signal would rouse the whole land from its sluggish despondency. Aware of their danger, the rulers resolved to avert it by an imposing display of strength, and perhaps to confirm their despotism by yet harsher measures. One afternoon in April, 1689, Sir Edmund Andros and his favorite councillors, being warm with wine, assembled the redcoats of the Governor's Guard, and made their appearance in the streets of Boston. The sun was near setting when the march commenced.

The roll of the drum, at that unquiet crisis, seemed to go through the streets, less as the martial music of the soldiers, than as a muster call to the inhabitants themselves. A multitude, by various avenues, assembled in King Street, which was destined to be the scene, nearly a century afterwards, of another encounter between the troops of Britain, and a people struggling against her tyranny. Though more than sixty years had elapsed, since the Pilgrims came, this crowd of their descendants still showed the strong and sombre features of their character, perhaps more strikingly in such a stern emergency than on happier occasions. There were the sober garb, the general severity of mien, the gloomy but undismayed expression, the scriptural forms of speech, and the confidence in Heaven's blessing on a righteous cause, which would have marked a band of the original Puritans, when threatened by some peril of the wilderness. Indeed, it was not yet time for the old spirit to be extinct; since there were men in the street, that day, who had worshipped there beneath the trees, before a house was reared to the God for whom they had become exiles. Old soldiers of the Parliament were here, too, smiling grimly at the thought, that their aged arms might strike another blow against the house of Stuart. Here, also, were the veterans of King Philip's war, who had burned villages and slaughtered young and old, with pious fierceness, while the godly souls throughout the land were helping them with prayer. Several ministers were scattered among the crowd which, unlike all other mobs, regarded them with such reverence, as if there were sanctity in their very garments. These holy men exerted their influence to quiet the people, but not to disperse them. Meantime, the purpose of the Governor, in disturbing the peace of the town, at a period when the slightest commotion might throw the country into a ferment, was almost the universal subject of inquiry, and variously explained.

"Satan will strike his master-stroke presently," cried some, "because he knoweth that his time is short. All our godly pastors are to be dragged to prison! We shall see them at a Smithfield fire in King Street!"

Hereupon the people of each parish gathered closer round their minister, who looked calmly upwards and assumed a more apostolic dignity, as well befitted a candidate for the highest honor of his profession, the crown of martyrdom. It was actually fancied, at that period, that New England might have a John Rogers of her own, to take the place of that worthy in the Primer.

"The Pope of Rome has given orders for a new St. Batholomew!" cried others. "We are to be massacred, man and male child!"

Neither was this rumor wholly discredited, although the wiser class believed the Governor's object somewhat less atrocious. His predecessor under the old charter, Bradstreet, a venerable companion of the first settlers, was known to be in town. There were grounds for conjecturing, that Sir Edmund Andros intended, at once, to strike terror, by a parade of military force, and to confound the opposite faction, by possessing himself of their chief.

"Stand firm for the old charter Governor!" shouted the crowd, seizing upon the idea. "The good old Governor Bradstreet!"

While this cry was at the loudest, the people were surprised by the well-known figure of Governor Bradstreet himself, a patriarch of nearly ninety, who appeared on the elevated steps of a door and, with characteristic mildness, besought them to submit to the constituted authorities.

"My children," concluded this venerable person, "do nothing rashly. Cry not aloud, but pray for the welfare of New England, and expect patiently what the Lord will do in this matter!"

The event was soon to be decided. All this time, the roll of the drum had been approaching through Cornhill, louder and deeper, till with reverberations from house to house, and the regular tramp of martial footsteps, it burst into the street. A double rank of soldiers made their appearance, occupying the whole breadth of the passage, with shouldered matchlocks, and matches burning, so as to present a row of fires in the dusk. Their steady march was like the progress of a machine, that would roll irresistibly over everything in its way. Next, moving slowly, with a confused clatter of hoofs on the pavement, rode a party of mounted gentlemen, the central figure being Sir Edmund Andros, elderly, but erect and soldier-like. Those around him were his favorite councillors, and the bitterest foes of New England. At his right hand rode Edward Randolph, our arch-enemy, that "blasted wretch," as Cotton Mather calls him, who achieved the downfall of our ancient government, and was followed with a sensible curse, through life and to his grave. On the other side was Bullivant, scattering jests and mockery as he rode along. Dudley came behind, with a down-cast look, dreading, as well he might, to meet the indignant gaze of the people, who beheld him, their only countryman by birth, among the oppressors of his native land. The captain of a frigate in the harbor, and two or three civil officers under the Crown, were also there. But the figure which most attracted the public eye, and stirred up the deepest feeling, was the Episcopal clergyman of King's Chapel, riding haughtily among the magistrates in his priestly vestments, the fitting representative of prelacy and persecution, the union of church and state, and all those abominations which had driven the Puritans to the wilderness. Another guard of soldiers, in double rank, brought up the rear.

The whole scene was a picture of the condition of New England, and its moral, the deformity of any government that does not grow out of the nature of things and the character of the people. On one side the religious multitude, with their sad visages and dark attire, and on the other, the group of despotic rulers, with the high churchman in the midst, and here and there a crucifix at their bosoms, all magnificently clad, flushed with wine, proud of unjust authority, and scoffing at the universal groan. And the mercenary soldiers, waiting but the word to deluge the street with blood, showed the only means by which obedience could be secured.

"O Lord of Hosts," cried a voice among the crowd, "provide a Champion for thy people!"

This ejaculation was loudly uttered, and served as a herald's cry, to introduce a remarkable personage. The crowd had rolled back, and were now huddled together nearly at the extremity of the street, while the soldiers had advanced no more than a third of its length. The intervening space was empty,—a paved solitude, between lofty edifices, which threw almost a twilight shadow over it. Suddenly, there was seen the figure of an ancient man, who seemed to have emerged from among the people, and was walking by himself along the centre of the street, to confront the armed band. He wore the old Puritan dress, a dark cloak and a steeple-crowned hat, in the fashion of at least fifty years before, with a heavy sword upon his thigh, but a staff in his hand to assist the tremulous gait of age.

When at some distance from the multitude, the old man turned slowly round, displaying a face of antique majesty, rendered doubly venerable by the hoary beard that descended on his breast. He made a gesture at once of encouragement and warning, then turned again, and resumed his way.

"Who is this gray patriarch?" asked the young men of their sires.

"Who is this venerable brother?" asked the old men among themselves.

But none could make reply. The fathers of the people, those of fourscore years and upwards, were disturbed, deeming it strange that they should forget one of such evident authority, whom they must have known in their early days, the associate of Winthrop, and all the old councillors, giving laws, and making prayers, and leading them against the savage. The elderly men ought to have remembered him, too, with locks as gray in their youth, as their own were now. And the young! How could he have passed so utterly from their memories,—that hoary sire, the relic of long-departed times, whose awful benediction had surely been bestowed on their uncovered heads, in childhood?

"Whence did he come? What is his purpose? Who can this old man be?" whispered the wondering crowd.

Meanwhile, the venerable stranger, staff in hand, was pursuing his solitary walk along the centre of the street. As he drew near the advancing soldiers and as the roll of their drum came full upon his ear, the old man raised himself to a loftier mien, while the decrepitude of age seemed to fall from his shoulders, leaving him in gray but unbroken dignity. Now, he marched onward with a warrior's step, keeping time to the military music. Thus the aged form advanced on one side, and the whole parade of soldiers and magistrates on the other, till, when scarcely twenty yards remained between, the old man grasped his staff by the middle, and held it before him like a leader's truncheon.

"Stand!" cried he.

The eye, the face, and attitude of command; the solemn, yet warlike peal of that voice, fit either to rule a host in the battle-field or be raised to God in prayer, were irresistible. At the old man's word and outstretched arm, the roll of the drum was hushed at once and the advancing line stood still. A tremulous enthusiasm seized upon the multitude. That stately form, combining the leader and the saint, so gray so dimly seen, in such an ancient garb could only belong to some old champion of the righteous cause, whom the oppressor's drum had summoned from his grave. They raised a shout of awe and exaltation, and looked for the deliverance of New England.

The Governor, and the gentlemen of his party, perceiving themselves brought to an unexpected stand, rode hastily forward, as if they would have pressed their snorting and affrighted horses right against the hoary apparition. He, however, blenched not a step, but glancing his severe eye round the group, which half encompassed him, at last bent it sternly on Sir Edmund Andros. One would have thought that the dark old man was chief ruler there, and that the Governor and Council, with soldiers at their back, representing the whole power and authority of the Crown, had no alternative but obedience.

"What does this old fellow here?" cried Edward Randolph, fiercely. "On, Sir Edmund! Bid the soldiers forward, and give the dotard the same choice that you give all his countrymen,—to stand aside or be trampled on!"

"Nay, nay, let us show respect to the good grandsire," said Bullivant, laughing. "See you not, he is some old round-headed dignitary, who hath lain asleep these thirty years, and knows nothing of the change of times? Doubtless, he thinks to put us down with a proclamation in Old Noll's name!"

"Are you mad, old man?" demanded Sir Edmund Andros, in loud and harsh tones. "How dare you stay the march of King James's Governor?"

"I have stayed the march of a King himself, ere now," replied the gray figure, with stern composure. "I am here, Sir Governor, because the cry of an oppressed people hath disturbed me in my secret place; and beseeching this favor earnestly of the Lord, it was vouchsafed me to appear once again on earth, in the good old cause of his saints. And what speak ye of James? There is no longer a Popish tyrant on the throne of England, and by to-morrow noon, his name shall be a by-word in this very street, where ye would make it a word of terror. Back, thou that wast a Governor, back! With this night thy power is ended,—to-morrow.

the prison!—back, lest I foretell the scaffold!"

The people had been drawing nearer and nearer, and drinking in the words of their champion, who spoke in accents long disused, like one unaccustomed to converse, except with the dead of many years ago. But his voice stirred their souls. They confronted the soldiers, not wholly without arms, and ready to convert the very stones of the street into deadly weapons. Sir Edmund Andros looked at the old man; then he cast his hard and cruel eye over the multitude, and beheld them burning with that lurid wrath, so difficult to kindle or to quench; and again he fixed his gaze on the aged form, which stood obscurely in an open space, where neither friend nor foe had thrust himself. What were his thoughts, he uttered no word which might discover. But whether the oppressor were overawed by the Gray Champion's look, or perceived his peril in the threatening attitude of the people, it is certain that he gave back, and ordered his soldiers to commence a slow and guarded retreat. Before another sunset, the Governor, and all that rode so proudly with him, were prisoners, and long ere it was known that James had abdicated, King William was proclaimed throughout New England.

But where was the Gray Champion? Some reported that, when the troops had gone from King Street, and the people were thronging tumultuously in their rear, Bradstreet, the aged Governor, was seen to embrace a form more aged than his own. Others soberly affirmed, that while they marvelled at the venerable grandeur of his aspect, the old man had faded from their eyes, melting slowly into the hues of twilight, till, where he stood, there was an empty space. But all agreed that the hoary shape was gone. The men of that generation watched for his reappearance, in sunshine and in twilight, but never saw him more, nor knew when his funeral passed, nor where his gravestone was.

And who was the Gray Champion? Perhaps his name might be found in the records of that stern Court of Justice which passed a sentence, too mighty for the age, but glorious in all after times for its humbling lesson to the monarch and its high example to the subject. I have heard that, whenever the descendants of the Puritans are to show the spirit of their sires, the old man appears again. When eighty years had passed, he walked once more in King Street. Five years later, in the twilight of an April morning, he stood on the green, beside the meeting-house, at Lexington, where now the obelisk of granite, with a slab of slate inlaid, commemorates the first fallen of the Revolution. And when our fathers were toiling at the breastwork on Bunker's Hill, all through that night the old warrior walked his rounds. Long, long may it be, ere he comes again! His hour is one of darkness and adversity and peril. But should domestic tyranny oppress us, or the invader's step pollute our soil, still may the Gray Champion come; for he is the type of New England's hereditary spirit; and his shadowy march, on the eve of danger, must ever be the pledge that New England's sons will vindicate their ancestry.

SUNDAY AT HOME

EVERY Sabbath morning in the summer time, I thrust back the curtain to watch the sunrise stealing down a steeple, which stands opposite my chamber window. First, the weathercock begins to flash; then, a fainter lustre gives the spire an airy aspect; next it encroaches on the tower, and causes the index of the dial to glisten like gold, as it points to the gilded figure of the hour. Now, the loftiest window gleams, and now the lower. The carved framework of the portal is marked strongly out. At length the morning glory, in its descent from heaven, comes down the stone steps, one by one; and there stands the steeple, glowing with fresh radiance, while the shades of twilight still hide themselves among the nooks of the adjacent buildings. Methinks, though the same sun brightens it every fair morning, yet the steeple has a peculiar robe of brightness for the Sabbath.

By dwelling near a church, a person soon contracts an attachment for the edifice. We naturally personify it, and conceive its massy walls, and its dim emptiness, to be instinct with a calm and meditative and somewhat melancholy spirit. But the steeple stands foremost in our thoughts as well as locally. It impresses us as a giant, with a mind comprehensive and discriminating enough to care for the great and small concerns of all the town. Hourly, while it speaks a moral to the few that think, it reminds thousands of busy individuals of their separate and most secret affairs. It is the steeple, too, that flings abroad the hurried and irregular accents of general alarm; neither have gladness and festivity found a better utterance than by its tongue; and when the dead are slowly passing to their home, the steeple has a melancholy voice to bid them welcome. Yet, in spite of this connection with human interests, what a moral loneliness on week days broods round about its stately height! It has no kindred with the houses above which it towers; it looks down into the narrow thoroughfare, the lonelier, because the crowd are elbowing their passage at its base. A glance at the body of the church deepens this impression. Within, by the light of distant windows, amid refracted shadows, we discern the vacant pews and empty galleries, the silent organ, the voiceless pulpit, and the clock, which tells to solitude how time is passing. Time,—where man lives not,—what is it but eternity? And in the church, we might suppose, are garnered up, throughout the week, all thoughts and feelings that have reference to eternity, until the holy day comes round again to let them forth. Might not, then, its more appropriate site be in the outskirts of the town, with space for old trees to wave around it, and throw their solemn shadows over a quiet green? We will say more of this hereafter.

But on the Sabbath I watch the earliest sunshine, and fancy that a holier brightness marks the day when there shall be no buzz of voices on the exchange, nor traffic in the shops, nor crowd, nor business, anywhere but at church. Many have fancied so. For my own part, whether I see it scattered down among tangled woods, or beaming broad across the fields, or hemmed in between brick buildings, or tracing out the figure of the casement on my chamber floor, still I recognize the Sabbath sunshine. And ever let me recognize it! Some illusions, and this among them, are the shadows of great truths. Doubts may flit around me, or seem to close their evil wings, and settle down; but, so long as I imagine that the earth is hallowed and the light of heaven retains its sanctity on the Sabbath,—while that blessed sunshine lives within me,—never can my soul have lost the instinct of its faith. If it have gone astray, it will return again.

I love to spend such pleasant Sabbaths, from morning till night, behind the curtain of my open window. Are they spent amiss? Every spot, so near the church as to be visited by the circling shadow of the steeple, should be deemed consecrated ground, to-day. With stronger truth be it said, that a devout heart may consecrate a den of thieves, as an evil one may convert a temple to the same. My heart, perhaps, has not such holy, nor, I would fain trust, such impious potency. It must suffice, that, though my form be absent, my inner man goes constantly to church, while many, whose bodily presence fills the accustomed seats, have left their souls at home. But I am there, even before my friend, the sexton. At length, he comes,—a man of kindly, but sombre aspect, in dark gray clothes, and hair of the same mixture,—he comes and applies his key to the wide portal.

Now, my thoughts may go in among the dusty pews, or ascend the pulpit without sacrilege, but soon come forth again to enjoy the music of the bell. How glad, yet solemn too! All the steeples in town are talking together, aloft in the sunny air, and rejoicing among themselves, while their spires point heavenward. Meantime, here are the children assembling to the Sabbath school, which is kept somewhere within the church. Often, while looking at the arched portal I have been gladdened by the sight of a score of these little girls and boys, in pink, blue, yellow, and crimson frocks, bursting suddenly forth into the sunshine, like a swarm of gay butterflies that had been shut up in the solemn gloom. Or I might compare them to cherubs, haunting that holy place.

About a quarter of an hour before the second ringing of the bell, individuals of the congregation begin to appear. The earliest is invariably an old woman in black, whose bent frame and rounded shoulders are evidently laden with some heavy affliction, which she is eager to rest upon the altar. Would that the Sabbath came twice as often, for the sake of that sorrowful old soul! There is an elderly man, also, who arrives in good season, and leans against the corner of the tower, just within the line of its shadow, looking downward with a darksome brow. I sometimes fancy that the old woman is the happier of the two. After these, others drop in singly, and by twos and threes, either disappearing through the doorway, or taking their stand in its vicinity. At last, and always with an unexpected sensation, the bell turns in the steeple overhead, and throws out an irregular clangor, jarring the tower to its foundation. As if there were magic in the sound, the sidewalks of the street, both up and down along, are immediately thronged with two long lines of people, all converging hitherward, and streaming into the church. Perhaps the far-off roar of a coach draws nearer,—a deeper thunder by its contrast with the surrounding stillness,—until it sets down the wealthy worshippers at the portal, among their humblest brethren. Beyond that entrance, in theory at least, there are no distinctions of earthly rank; nor, indeed, by the goodly apparel which is flaunting in the sun, would there seem to be such, on the hither side. Those pretty girls! Why will they disturb my pious meditations! Of all days in the week, they should strive to look least fascinating on the Sabbath, instead of heightening their mortal loveliness, as if to rival the blessed angels, and keep our thoughts from heaven. Were I the minister himself, I must needs look. One girl is white muslin from the waist upwards, and black silk downwards to her slippers; a second, blushes from topknot to shoetie, one universal scarlet; another shines of a pervading yellow, as if she had made a garment of the sunshine. The greater part, however, have adopted a milder cheerfulness of hue. Their veils, especially when the wind raises them, give a lightness to the general effect, and make them appear like airy phantoms, as they flit up the steps, and vanish into the sombre doorway. Nearly all—though it is very strange that I should know it—wear white stockings, white as snow, and neat slippers, laced crosswise with black ribbon, pretty high above the ankles. A white stocking is infinitely more effective than a black one.

Here comes the clergyman, slow and solemn, in severe simplicity, needing no black-silk gown to denote his office. His aspect claims my reverence, but cannot win my love. Were I to picture Saint Peter, keeping fast the gate of Heaven, and frowning more stern than pitiful, on the wretched applicants, that face should be my study. By middle age, or sooner, the creed has generally wrought upon the heart, or been attempered by it. As the minister passes into the church, the bell holds its iron tongue, and all the low murmur of the congregation dies away. The gray sexton looks up and down the street, and then at my window curtain, where, through the small peephole, I half fancy that he has caught my eye. Now, every loiterer has gone in, and the street lies asleep in the quiet sun, while a feeling of loneliness comes over me, and brings also an uneasy sense of neglected privileges and duties. O, I ought to have gone to church! The bustle of the rising congregation reaches my ears. They are standing up to pray. Could I bring my heart into unison with those who are praying in yonder church, and lift it heavenward, with a fervor of supplication, but no distinct request, would not that be the safest kind of prayer? "Lord, look down upon me in mercy!" With that sentiment gushing from my soul, might I not leave all the rest to Him?

Hark! the hymn. This, at least, is a portion of the service which I can enjoy better than if I sat within the walls, where the full choir, and the massive melody of the organ would fall with a weight upon me. At this distance, it thrills through my frame, and plays upon my heart-strings, with a pleasure both of the sense and spirit. Heaven be praised, I know nothing of music, as a science; and the most elaborate harmonies, if they please me, please as simply as a nurse's lullaby. The strain has ceased, but prolongs itself in my mind, with fanciful echoes, till I start from my reverie, and find that the sermon has commenced. It is my misfortune seldom to fructify, in a regular way, by any but printed sermons. The first strong idea which the preacher utters gives birth to a train of thought, and leads me onward, step by step, quite out of hearing of the good man's voice, unless he be indeed a son of thunder. At my open window, catching now and then a sentence of the "parson's saw," I am as well situated as at the foot of the pulpit stairs. The broken and scattered fragments of this one discourse will be the texts of many sermons, preached by those colleague pastors,—colleagues, but often disputants,—my Mind and Heart. The former pretends to be a scholar, and perplexes me with doctrinal points; the latter takes me on the score of feeling; and both, like several other preachers, spend their strength to very little purpose. I, their sole auditor, cannot always understand them.

Suppose that a few hours have passed, and behold me still behind my curtain, just before the close of the afternoon service. The hour-hand on the dial has passed beyond four o'clock. The declining sun is hidden behind the steeple, and throws its shadow straight across the street, so that my chamber is darkened as with a cloud. Around the church door all is solitude, and an impenetrable obscurity beyond the threshold. A commotion is heard. The seats are slammed down, and the pew-doors thrown back, —a multitude of feet are trampling along the unseen aisles,—and the congregation burst suddenly through the portal. Foremost, scampers a rabble of boys, behind whom moves a dense and dark phalanx of grown men, and lastly, a crowd of females, with young children, and a few scattered husbands. This instantaneous outbreak of life into loneliness is one of the pleasantest scenes of the day. Some of the good people are rubbing their eyes, thereby intimating that they have been wrapped, as it were, in a sort of holy trance by the fervor of their devotion. There is a young man, a third-rate coxcomb, whose first care is always to flourish a white handkerchief, and brush the seat of a tight pair of black-silk pantaloons, which shine as if varnished. They must have been made of the stuff called "everlasting," or perhaps of the same piece as Christian's garments in the Pilgrim's Progress, for he put them on two summers ago, and has not yet worn the gloss off. I have taken a great liking to those black-silk pantaloons. But, now, with nods and greetings among friends, each matron takes her husband's arm, and paces gravely homeward, while the girls also flutter away, after arranging sunset walks with their favored bachelors. The Sabbath eve is the eve of love. At length, the whole congregation is dispersed. No; here, with faces as glossy as black satin, come two sable ladies and a sable gentleman, and close in their rear the minister, who softens his severe visage, and bestows a kind word on each. Poor souls! To them the most captivating picture of bliss in heaven is,—"There we shall be white!"

All is solitude again. But, hark!—a broken warbling of voices, and now, attuning its grandeur to their sweetness, a stately peal of the organ. Who are the choristers? Let me dream that the angels, who came down from Heaven, this blessed morn, to blend themselves with the worship of the truly good, are playing and singing their farewell to the earth. On the wings of that rich melody they were borne upward.

This, gentle reader, is merely a flight of poetry. A few of the singing men and singing women had lingered behind their fellows, and raised their voices fitfully, and blew a careless note upon the organ. Yet it lifted my soul higher than all their former strains. They are gone,—the sons and daughters of music,—and the gray sexton is just closing the portal. For six days more there will be no face of man in the pews and aisles and galleries, nor a voice in the pulpit, nor music in the choir. Was it worth while to rear this massive edifice to be a desert in the heart of the town, and populous only for a few hours of each seventh day? O, but the church is a symbol of religion. May its site, which was consecrated on the day when the first tree was felled, be kept holy forever, a spot of solitude and peace, amid the trouble and vanity of our week-day world! There is a moral, and a religion too, even in the silent walls. And may the steeple still point heavenward, and be decked with the hallowed sunshine of the Sabbath morn!

THE WEDDING KNELL

THERE is a certain church in the city of New York, which I have always regarded with peculiar interest, on account of a marriage there solemnized, under very singular circumstances, in my grandmother's girlhood. That venerable lady chanced to be a spectator of the scene, and ever after made it her favorite narrative. Whether the edifice now standing on the same site be the identical one to which she referred, I am not antiquarian enough to know; nor would it be worth while to correct myself, perhaps, of an agreeable error, by reading the date of its erection on the tablet over the door. It is a stately church, surrounded by an enclosure of the loveliest green, within which appear urns, pillars, obelisks, and other forms of monumental marble, the tributes of private affection, or more splendid memorials of historic dust. With such a place, though the tumult of the city rolls beneath its tower, one would be willing to connect some legendary interest.

The marriage might be considered as the result of an early engagement, though there had been two intermediate weddings on the lady's part, and forty years of celibacy on that of the gentleman. At sixty-five, Mr. Ellenwood was a shy, but not quite a secluded man; selfish, like all men who brood over their own hearts, yet manifesting, on rare occasions, a vein of generous sentiment; a scholar, throughout life, though always an indolent one, because his studies had no definite object, either of public advantage or personal ambition; a gentleman, high bred and fastidiously delicate, yet sometimes requiring a considerable relaxation, in his behalf, of the common rules of society. In truth, there were so many anomalies in his character, and though shrinking with diseased sensibility from public notice, it had been his fatality so often to become the topic of the day, by some wild eccentricity of conduct, that people searched his lineage for an hereditary taint of insanity. But there was no need of this. His caprices had their origin in a mind that lacked the support of an engrossing purpose, and in feelings that preyed upon themselves, for want of other food. If he were mad, it was the consequence, and not the cause, of an aimless and abortive life.

The widow was as complete a contrast to her third bridegroom, in everything but age, as can well be conceived. Compelled to relinquish her first engagement, she had been united to a man of twice her own years, to whom she became an exemplary wife, and by whose death she was left in possession of a splendid fortune. A Southern gentleman, considerably younger than herself, succeeded to her hand, and carried her to Charleston, where, after many uncomfortable years, she found herself again a widow. It would have been singular, if any uncommon delicacy of feeling had survived through such a life as Mrs. Dabney's; it could not but be crushed and killed by her early disappointment, the cold duty of her first marriage, the dislocation of the heart's principles consequent on a second union, and the unkindness of her Southern husband, which had inevitably driven her to connect the idea of his death with that of her comfort. To be brief, she was that wisest, but unloveliest variety of woman, a philosopher, bearing troubles of the heart with equanimity, dispensing with all that should have been her happiness, and making the best of what remained. Sage in most matters, the widow was perhaps the more amiable, for the one frailty that made her ridiculous. Being childless, she could not remain beautiful by proxy, in the person of a daughter; she therefore refused to grow old and ugly, on any consideration; she struggled with Time, and held fast her roses in spite of him, till the venerable thief appeared to have relinquished the spoil, as not worth the trouble of acquiring it.

The approaching marriage of this woman of the world with such an unworldly man as Mr. Ellenwood was announced soon after Mrs. Dabney's return to her native city. Superficial observers, and deeper ones, seemed to concur in supposing that the lady must have borne no inactive part in arranging the affair; there were considerations of expediency, which she would be far more likely to appreciate than Mr. Ellenwood; and there was just the specious phantom of sentiment and romance, in this late union of two early lovers, which sometimes makes a fool of a woman, who has lost her true feelings among the accidents of life. All the wonder was, how the gentleman, with his lack of worldly wisdom, and agonizing consciousness of ridicule, could have been induced to take a measure at once so prudent and so laughable. But while people talked, the wedding-day arrived. The ceremony was to be solemnized according to the Episcopalian forms,

and in open church, with a degree of publicity that attracted many spectators, who occupied the front seats of the galleries, and the pews near the altar and along the broad aisle. It had been arranged, or possibly it was the custom of the day, that the parties should proceed separately to church. By some accident, the bridegroom was a little less punctual than the widow and her bridal attendants; with whose arrival, after this tedious, but necessary preface, the action of our tale may be said to commence.

The clumsy wheels of several old-fashioned coaches were heard, and the gentlemen and ladies composing the bridal party came through the church door, with the sudden and gladsome effect of a burst of sunshine. The whole group, except the principal figure, was made up of youth and gayety. As they streamed up the broad aisle, while the pews and pillars seemed to brighten on either side, their steps were as buoyant as if they mistook the church for a ball-room, and were ready to dance hand in hand to the altar. So brilliant was the spectacle, that few took notice of a singular phenomenon that had marked its entrance. At the moment when the bride's foot touched the threshold, the bell swung heavily in the tower above her, and sent forth its deepest knell. The vibrations died away and returned, with prolonged solemnity, as she entered the body of the church.

"Good heavens! what an omen," whispered a young lady to her lover.

"On my honor," replied the gentleman, "I believe the bell has the good taste to toll of its own accord. What has she to do with weddings? If you, dearest Julia, were approaching the altar, the bell would ring out its merriest peal. It has only a funeral knell for her."

The bride, and most of her company, had been too much occupied with the bustle of entrance to hear the first boding stroke of the bell, or at least to reflect on the singularity of such a welcome to the altar. They therefore continued to advance with undiminished gayety. The gorgeous dresses of the time, the crimson velvet coats, the gold-laced hats, the hoop petticoats, the silk, satin, brocade, and embroidery, the buckles, canes, and swords, all displayed to the best advantage on persons suited to such finery, made the group appear more like a bright-colored picture than anything real. But by what perversity of taste had the artist represented his principal figure as so wrinkled and decayed, while yet he had decked her out in the brightest splendor of attire, as if the loveliest maiden had suddenly withered into age and become a moral to the beautiful around her! On they went, however, and had glittered along about a third of the aisle, when another stroke of the bell seemed to fill the church with a visible gloom, dimming and obscuring the bright pageant till it shone forth again as from a mist.

This time the party wavered, stopped, and huddled closer together, while a slight scream was heard from some of the ladies, and a confused whispering among the gentlemen. Thus tossing to and fro, they might have been fancifully compared to a splendid bunch of flowers suddenly shaken by a puff of wind, which threatened to scatter the leaves of an old, brown, withered rose, on the same stalk with two dewy buds; such being the emblem of the widow between

her fair young bridemaids. But her heroism was admirable. She had started with an irrepressible shudder, as if the stroke of the bell had fallen directly on her heart; then, recovering herself, while her attendants were yet in dismay, she took the lead, and paced calmly up the aisle. The bell continued to swing, strike, and vibrate with the same doleful regularity as when a corpse is on its way to the tomb.

"My young friends here have their nerves a little shaken," said the widow, with a smile, to the clergyman at the altar. "But so many weddings have been ushered in with the merriest peal of the bells, and yet turned out unhappily, that I shall hope for better fortune under such different auspices."

"Madam," answered the rector, in great perplexity, "this strange occurrence brings to my mind a marriage sermon of the famous Bishop Taylor, wherein he mingles so many thoughts of mortality and future woe, that, to speak somewhat after his own rich style, he seems to hang the bridal chamber in black, and cut the wedding garment out of a coffin pall. And it has been the custom of divers nations to infuse something of sadness into their marriage ceremonies; so to keep death in mind while contracting that engagement which is life's chiefest business. Thus we may draw a sad but profitable moral from this funeral knell."

But, though the clergyman might have given his moral even a keener point, he did not fail to despatch an attendant to inquire into the mystery, and stop those sounds so dismally appropriate to such a marriage. A brief space elapsed, during which the silence was broken only by whispers and a few suppressed titterings among the wedding party and the spectators, who, after the first shock, were disposed to draw an ill-natured merriment from the affair. The young have less charity for aged follies than the old for those of youth. The widow's glance was observed to wander for an instant towards a window of the church, as if searching for the time-worn marble that she had dedicated to her first husband; then her eyelids dropped over their faded orbs, and her thoughts were drawn irresistibly to another grave. Two buried men, with a voice at her ear, and a cry afar off, were calling her to lie down beside them. Perhaps, with momentary truth of feeling, she thought how much happier had been her fate if, after years of bliss, the bell were now tolling for her funeral, and she were followed to the grave by the old affection of her earliest lover, long her husband. But why had she returned to him, when their cold hearts shrank from each other's embrace?

Still the death bell tolled so mournfully that the sunshine seemed to fade in the air. A whisper, communicated from those who stood nearest the windows, now spread through the church; a hearse, with a train of several coaches, was creeping along the street, conveying some dead man to the churchyard, while the bride awaited a living one at the altar. Immediately after, the footsteps of the bridegroom and his friends were heard at the door. The widow looked down the aisle, and clinched the arm of one of her bridemaids in her bony hand with such unconscious violence that the fair girl trembled.

"You frighten me, my dear madam!" cried she. "For Heaven's sake, what is the matter?"

"Nothing, my dear, nothing," said the widow; then whispering close to her ear,—"There is a foolish fancy that I cannot get rid of. I am expecting my bridegroom to come into the church with my first two husbands for groomsmen!"

"Look, look!" screamed the bridesmaid. "What is here? The funeral!"

As she spoke, a dark procession paced into the church. First came an old man and woman, like chief mourners at a funeral, attired from head to foot in the deepest black, all but their pale features and hoary hair; he leaning on a staff, and supporting her decrepit form with his nerveless arm. Behind appeared another, and another pair, as aged, as black, and mournful as the first. As they drew near, the widow recognized in every face some trait of former friends, long forgotten, but now returning, as if from their old graves, to warn her to prepare a shroud; or, with purpose almost as unwelcome, to exhibit their wrinkles and infirmity, and claim her as their companion by the tokens of her own decay. Many a merry night had she danced with them, in youth. And now, in joyless age, she felt that some withered partner should request her hand, and all unite, in a dance of death, to the music of the funeral bell.

While these aged mourners were passing up the aisle, it was observed that, from pew to pew, the spectators shuddered with irrepressible awe, as some object, hitherto concealed by the intervening figures, came full in sight. Many turned away their faces; others kept a fixed and rigid stare; and a young girl giggled hysterically, and fainted with the laughter on her lips. When the spectral procession approached the altar, each couple separated, and slowly diverged, till in the centre appeared a form that had been worthily ushered in with all this gloomy pomp, the death knell, and the funeral. It was the bridegroom in his shroud!

No garb but that of the grave could have befitted such a deathlike aspect; the eyes, indeed, had the wild gleam of a sepulchral lamp; all else was fixed in the stern calmness which old men wear in the coffin. The corpse stood motionless, but addressed the widow in accents that seemed to melt into the clang of the bell, which fell heavily on the air while he spoke.

"Come, my bride!" said those pale lips, "the hearse is ready. The sexton stands waiting for us at the door of the tomb. Let us be married; and then to our coffins!"

How shall the widow's horror be represented? It gave her the ghastliness of a dead man's bride. Her youthful friends stood apart, shuddering at the mourners, the shrouded bridegroom, and herself; the whole scene expressed, by the strongest imagery, the vain struggle of the gilded vanities of this world, when opposed to age, infirmity, sorrow, and death. The awe-stricken silence was first broken by the clergyman.

"Mr. Ellenwood," said he soothingly, yet with somewhat of authority, "you are not well. Your mind has been agitated by the unusual circumstances in which you are placed. The ceremony must be deferred. As an old friend, let me entreat you to return home."

"Home! yes; but not without my bride," answered he, in the same hollow accents. "You deem this mockery; perhaps madness. Had I bedizened my aged and broken frame with scarlet and embroidery,—had I forced my withered lips to smile at my dead heart,—that might have been mockery, or madness. But now, let young and old declare, which of us has come hither without a wedding garment,—the bridegroom or the bride!"

He stepped forward at a ghostly pace, and stood beside the widow, contrasting the awful simplicity of his shroud with the glare and glitter in which she had arrayed herself for this unhappy scene. None that beheld them could deny the terrible strength of the moral which his disordered intellect had contrived to draw.

"Cruel! cruel!" groaned the heart-stricken bride.

"Cruel!" repeated he; then losing his death-like composure in a wild bitterness,—"Heaven judge, which of us has been cruel to the other! In youth, you deprived me of my happiness, my hopes, my aims; you took away all the substance of my life, and made it a dream, without reality enough even to grieve at,—with only a pervading gloom, through which I walked wearily and cared not whither. But after forty years, when I have built my tomb, and would not give up the thought of resting there, —no, not for such a life as we once pictured,—you call me to the altar. At your summons I am here. But other husbands have enjoyed your youth, your beauty, your warmth of heart, and all that could be termed your life. What is there for me but your decay and death? And therefore I have bidden these funeral friends, and bespoken the sexton's deepest knell, and am come, in my shroud, to wed you, as with a burial service, that we may join our hands at the door of the sepulchre, and enter it together."

It was not frenzy; it was not merely the drunkenness of strong emotion, in a heart unused to it, that now wrought upon the bride. The stern lesson of the day had done its work; her worldliness was gone. She seized the bridegroom's hand.

"Yes!" cried she. "Let us wed, even at the door of the sepulchre! My life is gone in vanity and emptiness. But at its close, there is one true feeling. It has made me what I was in youth; it makes me worthy of you. Time is no more for both of us. Let us wed for eternity!"

With a long and deep regard, the bridegroom looked into her eyes, while a tear was gathering in his own. How strange that gush of human feeling from the frozen bosom of a corpse! He wiped away the tear even with his shroud.

"Beloved of my youth," said he, "I have been wild. The despair of my whole lifetime had returned at once, and maddened me. Forgive; and be forgiven. Yes; it is evening with us now; and we have realized none of our morning dreams of happiness. But let us join our hands before the altar, as lovers, whom adverse circumstances have separated through life, yet who meet again as they are leaving it, and find their earthly affection changed into something holy as religion. And what is Time, to the married of Eternity?"

Amid the tears of many, and a swell of exalted sentiment, in those who felt aright, was solemnized the union of two immortal souls. The train of withered mourners, the hoary bridegroom in his shroud, the pale features of the aged bride, and the death bell tolling through the whole, till its deep voice overpowered the marriage words, all marked the funeral of earthly hopes. But as the ceremony proceeded, the organ, as if stirred by the sympathies of this impressive scene, poured forth an anthem, first mingling with the dismal knell, then rising to a loftier strain, till the soul looked down upon its woe. And when the awful rite was finished, and with cold hand in cold hand, the Married of Eternity withdrew, the organ's peal of solemn triumph drowned the Wedding Knell.

THE MINISTER'S BLACK VEIL

A PARABLE *

THE sexton stood in the porch of Milford meeting-house, pulling busily at the

* Another clergyman in New England, Mr. Joseph Moody, of York, Maine, who died about eighty years since, made himself remarkable by the same eccentricity that is here related of the Reverend Mr. Hooper. In his case, however, the symbol had a different import. In early life he had accidentally killed a beloved friend; and from that day till the hour of his own death he hid his face from men.

bell-rope. The old people of the village came stooping along the street. Children with bright faces tripped merrily beside their parents, or mimicked a graver gait, in the conscious dignity of their Sunday clothes. Spruce bachelors looked sidelong at the pretty maidens, and fancied that the Sabbath sunshine made them prettier than on week days. When the throng had mostly streamed into the porch, the sexton began to toll the bell, keeping his eye on the Reverend Mr. Hooper's door. The first glimpse of the clergyman's figure was the signal for the bell to cease its summons.

"But what has good Parson Hooper got upon his face?" cried the sexton in astonishment.

All within hearing immediately turned about, and beheld the semblance of Mr. Hooper, pacing slowly his meditative way towards the meeting-house. With one accord they started, expressing more wonder than if some strange minister were coming to dust the cushions of Mr. Hooper's pulpit.

"Are you sure it is our parson?" inquired Goodman Gray of the sexton.

"Of a certainty it is good Mr. Hooper," replied the sexton. "He was to have exchanged pulpits with Parson Shute, of Westbury; but Parson Shute sent to excuse himself yesterday, being to preach a funeral sermon."

The cause of so much amazement may appear sufficiently slight. Mr. Hooper, a gentlemanly person, of about thirty, though still a bachelor, was dressed with due clerical neatness, as if a careful wife had starched his band, and brushed the weekly dust from his Sunday's garb. There was but one thing remarkable in his appearance. Swathed about his forehead, and hanging down over his face so low as to be shaken by his breath, Mr. Hooper had on a black veil. On a nearer view, it seemed to consist of two folds of crape, which entirely concealed his features, except the mouth and chin, but probably did not intercept his sight, further than to give a darkened aspect to all living and inanimate things. With this gloomy shade

before him, good Mr. Hooper walked onward, at a slow and quiet pace, stooping somewhat, and looking on the ground, as is customary with abstracted men, yet nodding kindly to those of his parishioners who still waited on the meeting-house steps. But so wonderstruck were they, that his greeting hardly met with a return.

"I can't really feel as if good Mr. Hooper's face was behind that piece of crape," said the sexton.

"I don't like it," muttered an old woman, as she hobbled into the meeting-house. "He has changed himself into something awful, only by hiding his face."

"Our parson has gone mad!" cried Goodman Gray, following him across the threshold.

A rumor of some unaccountable phenomenon had preceded Mr. Hooper into the meeting-house, and set all the congregation astir. Few could refrain from twisting their heads towards the door; many stood upright, and turned directly about; while several little boys clambered upon the seats, and came down again with a terrible racket. There was a general bustle, a rustling of the women's gowns and shuffling of the men's feet, greatly at variance with that hushed repose which should attend the entrance of the minister. But Mr. Hooper appeared not to notice the perturbation of his people. He entered with an almost noiseless step, bent his head mildly to the pews on each side, and bowed as he passed his oldest parishioner, a white-haired great-grandsire, who occupied an arm-chair in the centre of the aisle. It was strange to observe how slowly this venerable man became conscious of something singular in the appearance of his pastor. He seemed not fully to partake of the prevailing wonder, till Mr. Hooper had ascended the stairs, and showed himself in the pulpit, face to face with his congregation, except for the black veil. That mysterious emblem was never once withdrawn. It shook with his measured breath as he gave out the psalm; it threw its obscurity between him and the holy page, as he read the Scriptures; and while he prayed, the veil lay heavily on his uplifted countenance. Did he seek to hide it from the dread Being whom he was addressing?

Such was the effect of this simple piece of crape, that more than one woman of delicate nerves was forced to leave the meeting-house. Yet perhaps the pale-faced congregation was almost as fearful a sight to the minister as his black veil to them.

Mr. Hooper had the reputation of a good preacher, but not an energetic one: he strove to win his people heavenward by mild, persuasive influences, rather than to drive them thither by the thunders of the Word. The sermon which he now delivered was marked by the same characteristics of style and manner as the general series of his pulpit oratory. But there was something, either in the sentiment of the discourse itself, or in the imagination of the auditors, which made it greatly the most powerful effort that they had ever heard from their pastor's lips. It was tinged rather more darkly than usual with the gentle gloom of Mr. Hooper's temperament. The subject had reference to secret sin, and those sad mysteries which we hide from our nearest and dearest, and would fain conceal from our own consciousness, even forgetting that the Omniscient can detect them. A subtle power was breathed into his words. Each member of the congregation, the most innocent girl, and the man of hardened breast, felt as if the preacher had crept upon them, behind his awful veil, and discovered their hoarded iniquity of deed or thought. Many spread their clasped hands on their bosoms. There was nothing terrible in what Mr. Hooper said; at least, no violence; and yet with every tremor of his melancholy voice the hearers quaked. An unsought pathos came hand in hand with awe. So sensible were the audience of some unwonted attribute in their minister, that they longed for a breath of wind to blow aside the veil, almost believing that a stranger's visage would be discovered, though the form, gesture, and voice were those of Mr. Hooper.

At the close of the services, the people hurried out with indecorous confusion, eager to communicate their pent-up amazement, and conscious of lighter spirits the moment they lost sight of the black veil. Some gathered in little circles, huddled closely together, with their mouths all whispering in the centre; some went homeward alone, wrapt in silent meditation; some talked loudly, and profaned the Sabbath day with ostentatious laughter. A few shook their sagacious heads, intimating that they could penetrate the mystery; while one or two affirmed that there was no mystery at all, but only that Mr. Hooper's eyes were so weakened by the midnight lamp as to require a shade. After a brief interval, forth came good Mr. Hooper also, in the rear of his flock. Turning his veiled face from one group to another, he paid due reverence to the hoary heads, saluted the middle aged with kind dignity, as their friend and spiritual guide, greeted the young with mingled authority and love, and laid his hands on the little children's heads to bless them. Such was always his custom on the Sabbath day. Strange and bewildered looks repaid him for his courtesy. None, as on former occasions, aspired to the honor of walking by their pastor's side. Old Squire Saunders, doubtless by an accidental lapse of memory, neglected to invite Mr. Hooper to his table, where the good clergyman had been wont to bless the food almost every Sunday since his settlement. He returned, therefore, to the parsonage, and, at the moment of closing the door, was observed to look back upon the people, all of whom had their eyes fixed upon the minister. A sad smile gleamed faintly from beneath the black veil, and flickered about his mouth, glimmering as he disappeared.

"How strange," said a lady, "that a simple black veil, such as any woman might wear on her bonnet, should become such a terrible thing on Mr. Hooper's face!"

"Something must surely be amiss with Mr. Hooper's intellects," observed her husband, the physician of the village. "But the strangest part of the affair is the effect of this vagary, even on a sober-minded man like myself. The black veil, though it covers only our pastor's face, throws its influence over his whole person, and makes him ghost-like from head to foot. Do you not feel it so?"

"Truly do I," replied the lady; "and I would not be alone with him for the world. I wonder he is not afraid to be alone with himself!"

"Men sometimes are so," said her husband.

The afternoon service was attended with similar circumstances. At its conclusion, the bell tolled for the funeral of a young lady. The relatives and friends were assembled in the house, and the more distant acquaintances stood about the door, speaking of the good qualities of the deceased, when their talk was interrupted by the appearance of Mr. Hooper, still covered with his black veil. It was now an appropriate emblem. The clergyman stepped into the room where the corpse was laid, and bent over the coffin, to take a last farewell of his deceased parishioner. As he stooped, the veil hung straight down from his forehead, so that, if her eyelids had not been closed forever, the dead maiden might have seen his face. Could Mr. Hooper be fearful of her glance, that he so hastily caught back the black veil? A person who watched the interview between the dead and living, scrupled not to affirm, that, at the instant when the clergyman's features were disclosed, the corpse had slightly shuddered, rustling the shroud and muslin cap, though the countenance retained the composure of death. A superstitious old woman was the only witness of this prodigy. From the coffin Mr. Hooper passed into the chamber of the mourners, and thence to the head of the staircase, to make the funeral prayer. It was a tender and heart-dissolving prayer, full of sorrow, yet so imbued with celestial hopes, that the music of a heavenly harp, swept by the fingers of the dead, seemed faintly to be heard among the saddest accents of the minister. The people trembled, though they but darkly understood him when he prayed that they, and himself, and all of mortal race, might be ready, as he trusted this young maiden had been, for the dreadful hour that should snatch the veil from their faces. The bearers went heavily forth, and the mourners followed, saddening all the street, with the dead before them, and Mr. Hooper in his black veil behind.

"Why do you look back?" said one in the procession to his partner.

"I had a fancy," replied she, "that the minister and the maiden's spirit were walking hand in hand."

"And so had I, at the same moment," said the other.

That night, the handsomest couple in Milford village were to be joined in wedlock. Though reckoned a melancholy man, Mr. Hooper had a placid cheerfulness for such occasions, which often excited a sympathetic smile, where livelier merriment would have been thrown away. There was no quality of his disposition which made him more beloved than this. The company at the wedding awaited his arrival with impatience, trusting that the strange awe which had gathered over him throughout the day would now be dispelled. But such was not the result. When Mr. Hooper came, the first thing that their eyes rested on was the same horrible black veil, which had added deeper gloom to the funeral, and could portend nothing but evil to the wedding. Such was its immediate effect on the guests, that a cloud seemed to have rolled duskily from beneath the black crape, and dimmed the light of the candles. The bridal pair stood up before the minister. But the bride's cold fingers quivered in the tremulous hand of the bridegroom, and her deathlike paleness caused a whisper, that the maiden who had been buried a few hours before was come from her grave to be married. If ever another wedding was so dismal, it was that famous one where they tolled the wedding knell. After performing the ceremony, Mr. Hooper raised a glass of wine to his lips, wishing happiness to the new-married couple, in a strain of mild pleasantry that ought to have brightened the features of the guests, like a cheerful gleam from the hearth. At that instant, catching a glimpse of his figure in the looking-glass, the black veil involved his own spirit in the horror with which it overwhelmed all others. His frame shuddered,—his lips grew white,—he spilt the untasted wine upon the carpet,—and rushed forth into the darkness. For the Earth, too, had on her Black Veil.

The next day, the whole village of Milford talked of little else than Parson Hooper's black veil. That, and the mystery concealed behind it, supplied a topic for discussion between acquaintances meeting in the street, and good women gossiping at their open windows. It was the first item of news that the tavern-keeper told to his guests. The children babbled of it on their way to school. One imitative little imp covered his face with an old black handkerchief, thereby so affrighting his playmates that the panic seized himself, and he wellnigh lost his wits by his own waggery.

It was remarkable that, of all the busybodies and impertinent people in the parish, not one ventured to put the plain question to Mr. Hooper, wherefore he did this thing. Hitherto, whenever there appeared the slightest call for such interference, he had never lacked advisers, nor shown himself averse to be guided by their judgment. If he erred at all, it was by so painful a degree of self-distrust, that even the mildest censure would lead him to consider an indifferent action as a crime. Yet, though so well acquainted with this amiable weakness, no individual among his parishioners chose to make the black veil a subject of friendly remonstrance. There was a feeling of dread, neither plainly confessed nor carefully concealed, which caused each to shift the responsibility upon another, till at length it was found expedient to send a deputation of the church, in order to deal with Mr. Hooper about the mystery, before it should grow into a scandal. Never did an embassy so ill discharge its duties. The minister received them with friendly courtesy, but became silent, after they were seated, leaving to his visitors the whole burden of introducing their important business. The topic, it might be supposed, was obvious enough. There was the black veil, swathed round Mr. Hooper's forehead, and concealing every feature above his placid mouth, on which, at times, they could perceive the glimmering of a melancholy smile. But that piece of crape, to their imagination, seemed to hang down before his heart, the symbol of a fearful secret between him and them. Were the veil but cast aside, they might speak freely of it, but not till then. Thus they sat a considerable time, speechless, confused, and shrinking uneasily from Mr. Hooper's eye, which they felt to be fixed upon them with an invisible glance. Finally, the deputies returned abashed to their constituents, pronouncing the matter too weighty to be handled, except by a council of the churches, if, indeed, it might not require a general synod.

But there was one person in the village, unappalled by the awe with which the black veil had impressed all beside herself. When the deputies returned without an explanation, or even venturing to demand one, she, with the calm energy of her character, determined to chase away the strange cloud that appeared to be settling round Mr. Hooper, every moment more darkly than before. As his plighted wife, it should be her privilege to know what the black veil concealed. At the minister's first visit, therefore, she entered upon the subject, with a direct simplicity, which made the task easier both for him and her. After he had seated himself, she fixed her eyes steadfastly upon the veil, but could discern nothing of the dreadful gloom that had so overawed the multitude: it was but a double fold of crape, hanging down from his forehead to his mouth, and slightly stirring with his breath.

"No," said she aloud, and smiling, "there is nothing terrible in this piece of crape, except that it hides a face which I am always glad to look upon. Come, good sir, let the sun shine from behind the cloud. First lay aside your black veil; then tell me why you put it on."

Mr. Hooper's smile glimmered faintly.

"There is an hour to come," said he, "when all of us shall cast aside our veils. Take it not amiss, beloved friend, if I wear this piece of crape till then."

"Your words are a mystery too," returned the young lady. "Take away the veil from them, at least."

"Elizabeth, I will," said he, "so far as my vow may suffer me. Know, then, this veil is a type and a symbol, and I am bound to wear it ever, both in light and darkness, in solitude and before the gaze of multitudes, and as with strangers, so with my familiar friends. No mortal eye will see it withdrawn. This dismal shade must separate me from the world: even you, Elizabeth, can never come behind it!"

"What grievous affliction hath befallen you," she earnestly inquired, "that you should thus darken your eyes forever?"

"If it be a sign of mourning," replied Mr. Hooper, "I, perhaps, like most other mortals, have sorrows dark enough to be typified by a black veil."

"But what if the world will not believe that it is the type of an innocent sorrow?" urged Elizabeth. "Beloved and respected as you are, there may be whispers, that you hide your face under the consciousness of secret sin. For the sake of your holy office, do away this scandal!"

The color rose into her cheeks as she intimated the nature of the rumors that were already abroad in the village. But Mr. Hooper's mildness did not forsake him. He even smiled again,—that same sad smile, which always appeared like a faint glimmering of light, proceeding from the obscurity beneath the veil.

"If I hide my face for sorrow, there is cause enough," he merely replied; "and if I cover it for secret sin, what mortal might not do the same?"

And with this gentle, but unconquerable obstinacy did he resist all her entreaties. At length Elizabeth sat silent. For a few moments she appeared lost in thought, considering, probably, what new methods might be tried, to withdraw her lover from so dark a fantasy, which, if it had no other meaning, was

perhaps a symptom of mental disease. Though of a firmer character than his own, the tears rolled down her cheeks. But, in an instant, as it were, a new feeling took the place of sorrow: her eyes were fixed insensibly on the black veil, when, like a sudden twilight in the air, its terrors fell around her. She arose, and stood trembling before him.

"And do you feel it then at last?" said he, mournfully.

She made no reply, but covered her eyes with her hand, and turned to leave the room. He rushed forward and caught her arm.

"Have patience with me, Elizabeth!" cried he, passionately. "Do not desert me, though this veil must be between us here on earth. Be mine, and hereafter there shall be no veil over my face, no darkness between our souls! It is but a mortal veil,—it is not for eternity! O, you know not how lonely I am, and how frightened, to be alone, behind my black veil! Do not leave me in this miserable obscurity forever!"

"Lift the veil but once, and look me in the face," said she.

"Never! It cannot be!" replied Mr. Hooper.

"Then, farewell!" said Elizabeth.

She withdrew her arm from his grasp, and slowly departed, pausing at the door, to give one long, shuddering gaze, that seemed almost to penetrate the mystery of the black veil. But, even amid his grief, Mr. Hooper smiled to think that only a material emblem had separated him from happiness, though the horrors which it shadowed forth must be drawn darkly between the fondest of lovers.

From that time no attempts were made to remove Mr. Hooper's black veil, or, by a direct appeal, to discover the secret which it was supposed to hide. By persons who claimed a superiority to popular prejudice, it was reckoned merely an eccentric whim, such as often mingles with the sober actions of men otherwise rational, and tinges them all with its own semblance of insanity. But with the multitude, good Mr. Hooper was irreparably a bugbear. He could not walk the street with any peace of mind, so conscious was he that the gentle and timid would turn aside to avoid him, and that others would make it a point of hardihood to throw themselves in his way. The impertinence of the latter class compelled him to give up his customary walk, at sunset, to the burial-ground; for when he leaned pensively over the gate, there would always be faces behind the gravestones, peeping at his black veil. A fable went the rounds, that the stare of the dead people drove him thence. It grieved him, to the very depth of his kind heart, to observe how the children fled from his approach, breaking up their merriest sports, while his melancholy figure was yet afar off. Their instinctive dread caused him to feel, more strongly than aught else, that a preternatural horror was interwoven with the threads of the black crape. In truth, his own antipathy to the veil was known to be so great, that he never willingly passed before a mirror, nor stooped to drink at a still fountain, lest, in its peaceful bosom, he should be affrighted by himself. This was what gave plausibility to the whispers, that Mr. Hooper's conscience tortured him for some great crime too horrible to be entirely concealed, or otherwise than so obscurely intimated. Thus, from beneath the black veil, there rolled a cloud into the sunshine, an ambiguity of sin or sorrow, which enveloped the poor minister, so that love or sympathy could never reach him. It was said, that ghost and fiend consorted with him there. With self-shudderings and outward terrors, he walked continually in its shadow, groping darkly within his own soul, or gazing through a medium that saddened the whole world. Even the lawless wind, it was believed, respected his dreadful secret, and never blew aside the veil. But still good Mr. Hooper sadly smiled at the pale visages of the worldly throng as he passed by.

Among all its bad influences, the black veil had the one desirable effect, of making its wearer a very efficient clergyman. By the aid of his mysterious emblem—for there was no other apparent cause—he became a man of awful power, over souls that were in agony for sin. His converts always regarded him with a dread peculiar to themselves, affirming, though but figuratively, that, before he brought them to celestial light, they had been with him behind the black veil. Its gloom, indeed, enabled him to sympathize with all dark affections. Dying sinners cried aloud for Mr. Hooper, and would not yield their breath till he appeared; though ever, as he stooped to whisper consolation, they shuddered at the veiled face so near their own. Such were the terrors of the black veil, even when Death had bared his visage! Strangers came long distances to attend service at his church, with the mere idle purpose of gazing at his figure, because it was forbidden them to behold his face. But many were made to quake ere they departed! Once, during Governor Belcher's administration, Mr. Hooper was appointed to preach the election sermon. Covered with his black veil, he stood before the chief magistrate, the council, and the representatives, and wrought so deep an impression, that the legislative measures of that year were characterized by all the gloom and piety of our earliest ancestral sway.

In this manner Mr. Hooper spent a long life, irreproachable in outward act, yet shrouded in dismal suspicions; kind and loving, though unloved, and dimly feared; a man apart from men, shunned in their health and joy, but ever summoned to their aid in mortal anguish. As years wore on, shedding their snows above his sable veil, he acquired a name throughout the New England churches, and they called him Father Hooper. Nearly all his parishioners, who were of mature age when he was settled, had been borne away by many a funeral: he had one congregation in the church, and a more crowded one in the churchyard; and having wrought so late into the evening, and done his work so well, it was now good Father Hooper's turn to rest.

Several persons were visible by the shaded candlelight in the death-chamber of the old clergyman. Natural connections he had none. But there was the decorously grave, though unmoved physician, seeking only to mitigate the last pangs of the patient whom he could not save. There were the deacons, and other eminently pious members of his church. There, also, was the Reverend Mr. Clark, of Westbury, a young and zealous divine, who had ridden in haste to pray by the bedside of the expiring minister. There was the nurse, no hired handmaiden of death, but one whose

calm affection had endured thus long in secrecy, in solitude, amid the chill of age, and would not perish, even at the dying hour. Who, but Elizabeth! And there lay the hoary head of good Father Hooper upon the death pillow, with the black veil still swathed about his brow, and reaching down over his face, so that each more difficult gasp of his faint breath caused it to stir. All through life that piece of crape had hung between him and the world: it had separated him from cheerful brotherhood and woman's love, and kept him in that saddest of all prisons, his own heart; and still it lay upon his face, as if to deepen the gloom of his darksome chamber, and shade him from the sunshine of eternity.

For some time previous, his mind had been confused, wavering doubtfully between the past and the present, and hovering forward, as it were, at intervals, into the indistinctness of the world to come. There had been feverish turns, which tossed him from side to side, and wore away what little strength he had. But in his most convulsive struggles, and in the wildest vagaries of his intellect, when no other thought retained its sober influence, he still showed an awful solicitude lest the black veil should slip aside. Even if his bewildered soul could have forgotten, there was a faithful woman at his pillow, who, with averted eyes, would have covered that aged face, which she had last beheld in the comeliness of manhood. At length the death-stricken old man lay quietly in the torpor of mental and bodily exhaustion, with an imperceptible pulse, and breath that grew fainter and fainter, except when a long, deep, and irregular inspiration

~eemed to prelude the flight of his spirit.

The minister of Westbury approached the bedside.

"Venerable Father Hooper," said he, "the moment of your release is at hand. Are you ready for the lifting of the veil, that shuts in time from eternity?"

Father Hooper at first replied merely by a feeble motion of his head; then, apprehensive, perhaps, that his meaning might be doubtful, he exerted himself to speak.

"Yea," said he, in faint accents, "my soul hath a patient weariness until that veil be lifted."

"And is it fitting," resumed the Reverend Mr. Clark, "that a man so given to prayer, of such a blameless example, holy in deed and thought, so far as mortal judgment may pronounce; is it fitting that a father in the Church should leave a shadow on his memory, that may seem to blacken a life so pure? I pray you, my venerable brother, let not this thing be! Suffer us to be gladdened by your triumphant aspect, as you go to your reward. Before the veil of eternity be lifted, let me cast aside this black veil from your face!"

And thus speaking, the Reverend Mr. Clark bent forward to reveal the mystery of so many years. But, exerting a sudden energy, that made all the beholders stand aghast, Father Hooper snatched both his hands from beneath the bedclothes, and pressed them strongly on the black veil, resolute to struggle, if the minister of Westbury would contend with a dying man.

"Never!" cried the veiled clergyman. "On earth, never!"

"Dark old man!" exclaimed the affrighted minister, "with what horrible crime upon your soul are you now passing to the judgment?"

Father Hooper's breath heaved; it rattled in his throat; but, with a mighty effort, grasping forward with his hands, he caught hold of life, and held it back till he should speak. He even raised himself in bed; and there he sat, shivering with the arms of death around him, while the black veil hung down, awful, at that last moment, in the gathered terrors of a lifetime. And yet the faint, sad smile, so often there, now seemed to glimmer from its obscurity, and linger on Father Hooper's lips.

"Why do you tremble at me alone?" cried he, turning his veiled face round the circle of pale spectators. "Tremble also at each other! Have men avoided me, and women shown no pity, and children screamed and fled, only for my black veil? What, but the mystery which it obscurely typifies, has made this piece of crape so awful? When the friend shows his inmost heart to his friend; the lover to his best beloved; when man does not vainly shrink from the eye of his Creator, loathsomely treasuring up the secret of his sin; then deem me a monster, for the symbol beneath which I have lived, and died! I look around me, and, lo! on every visage a Black Veil!"

While his auditors shrank from one another, in mutual affright, Father Hooper fell back upon his pillow, a veiled corpse, with a faint smile lingering on the lips. Still veiled, they laid him in his coffin, and a veiled corpse they bore him to the grave. The grass of many years has sprung up and withered on that grave, the burial stone is moss-grown, and good Mr. Hooper's face is dust; but awful is still the thought, that it mouldered beneath the Black Veil!

THE MAYPOLE OF MERRY MOUNT

There is an admirable foundation for a philosophic romance, in the curious history of the early settlement of Mount Wollaston, or Merry Mount. In the slight sketch here attempted, the facts, recorded on the grave pages of our New England annalists, have wrought themselves, almost spontaneously, into a sort of allegory. The masques, mummeries, and festive customs described in the text are in accordance with the manners of the age. Authority on these points may be found in Strutt's Book of English Sports and Pastimes.

BRIGHT were the days at Merry Mount, when the Maypole was the banner staff of that gay colony! They who reared it, should their banner be triumphant, were to pour sunshine over New England's rugged hills, and scatter flower-seeds throughout the soil. Jollity and gloom were contending for an empire. Midsummer eve had come, bringing deep verdure to the forest, and roses in her lap, of a more vivid hue than the tender buds of Spring. But May, or her mirthful spirit, dwelt all the year round at Merry Mount, sporting with the summer months, and revelling with Autumn, and basking in the glow of Winter's fireside. Through a world of toil and care she flitted with a dreamlike smile, and came hither to find a home among the lightsome hearts of Merry Mount.

Never had the Maypole been so gayly decked as at sunset on midsummer eve. This venerated emblem was a pine-tree, which had preserved the slender grace of youth, while it equalled the loftiest height of the old wood monarchs. From its top streamed a silken banner, colored like the rainbow. Down nearly to the ground the pole was dressed with birchen boughs, and others of the liveliest green, and some with silvery leaves, fastened by ribbons that fluttered in fantastic knots of twenty different colors, but no sad ones. Garden flowers, and blossoms of the wilderness, laughed gladly forth amid the verdure, so fresh and dewy, that they must have grown by magic on that happy pine-tree. Where this green and flowery splendor terminated, the shaft of the Maypole was stained with the seven brilliant hues of the banner at its top. On the lowest green bough hung an abundant wreath of roses, some that had been gathered in the sunniest spots of the forest, and others, of still richer blush, which the colonists had reared from English seed. O people of the Golden Age, the chief of your husbandry was to raise flowers!

But what was the wild throng that stood hand in hand about the Maypole? It could not be, that the fauns and nymphs, when driven from their classic groves and homes of ancient fable, had sought refuge, as all the persecuted did, in the fresh woods of the West. These were Gothic monsters, though perhaps of Grecian ancestry. On the shoulders of a comely youth uprose the head and branching antlers of a stag; a second, human in all other points, had the grim visage of a wolf; a third, still with the trunk and limbs of a mortal man, showed the beard and horns of a venerable he-goat. There was the likeness of a bear erect, brute in all but his hind legs, which were adorned with pink silk stockings. And here again, almost as wondrous, stood a real bear of the dark forest, lending each of his fore paws to the grasp of a human hand, and as ready for the dance as any in that circle. His inferior nature rose half way, to meet his companions as they stooped. Other faces wore the similitude of man or woman, but distorted or extravagant, with red noses pendulous before their mouths, which seemed of awful depth, and stretched from ear to ear in an eternal fit of laughter. Here might be seen the Salvage Man, well known in heraldry, hairy as a baboon, and girdled with green leaves. By his side, a nobler figure, but still a counterfeit, appeared an Indian hunter, with feathery crest and wampum belt. Many of this strange company wore foolscaps, and had little bells appended to their garments, tinkling with a silvery sound, responsive to the inaudible music of their gleesome spirits. Some youths and maidens were of soberer garb, yet well maintained their places in the irregular throng, by the expression of wild revelry upon their features. Such were the colonists of Merry Mount, as they stood in the broad smile of sunset, round their venerated Maypole.

Had a wanderer, bewildered in the melancholy forest, heard their mirth, and stolen a half-affrighted glance, he might have fancied them the crew of Comus, some already transformed to brutes, some midway between man and beast, and the others rioting in the flow of tipsy jollity that foreran the change. But a band of Puritans, who watched the scene, invisible themselves, compared the masks to those devils and ruined souls with whom their superstition peopled the black wilderness.

Within the ring of monsters appeared the two airiest forms that had ever trodden on any more solid footing than a purple and golden cloud. One was a youth in glistening apparel, with a scarf of the rainbow pattern crosswise on his breast. His right hand held a gilded staff, the ensign of high dignity among the revellers, and his left grasped the slender fingers of a fair maiden not less gayly decorated than himself. Bright roses glowed in contrast with the dark and glossy curls of each, and were scattered round their feet, or had sprung up spontaneously there. Behind this lightsome couple, so close to the Maypole that its boughs shaded his jovial face, stood the figure of an English priest, canonically dressed, yet decked with flowers, in heathen fashion, and wearing a chaplet of the native vine-leaves. By the riot of his rolling eye, and the pagan decorations of his holy garb, he seemed the wildest monster there, and the very Comus of the crew.

"Votaries of the Maypole," cried the flower-decked priest, "merrily, all day long, have the woods echoed to your mirth. But be this your merriest hour, my hearts! Lo, here stand the Lord and Lady of the May, whom I, a clerk of Oxford, and high-priest of Merry Mount, am presently to join in holy matrimony. Up with your nimble spirits, ye morris dancers, green men, and glee maidens, bears and wolves, and horned gentlemen! Come; a chorus now, rich with the old mirth of Merry England, and the wilder glee of this fresh forest; and then a dance, to show the youthful pair what life is made of, and how airily they should go through it! All ye that love the Maypole, lend your voices to the nuptial song of the Lord and Lady of the May!"

This wedlock was more serious than most affairs of Merry Mount, where jest and delusion, trick and fantasy, kept up a continual carnival. The Lord and Lady of the May, though their titles must be laid down at sunset, were really and truly to be partners for the dance of life, beginning the measure that same bright eve. The wreath of roses that hung from the lowest green bough of the Maypole had been twined for them, and would be thrown over both their heads, in symbol of their flowery union. When the priest had spoken, therefore, a riotous uproar burst from the rout of monstrous figures.

"Begin you the stave, reverend Sir," cried they all, "and never did the woods ring to such a merry peal as we of the Maypole shall send up!"

Immediately a prelude of pipe, cithern, and viol, touched with practised minstrelsy, began to play from a neighboring thicket in such a mirthful cadence that the boughs of the Maypole quivered to the sound. But the May Lord, he of the gilded staff, chancing to look into his Lady's eyes, was wonderstruck at the almost pensive glance that met his own.

"Edith, sweet Lady of the May," whispered he, reproachfully, "is yon wreath of roses a garland to hang above our graves, that you look so sad? O Edith, this is our golden time! Tarnish it not by any pensive shadow of the mind; for it may be that nothing of futurity will be brighter than the mere remembrance of what is now passing."

"That was the very thought that saddened me! How came it in your mind, too?" said Edith, in a still lower tone than he; for it was high treason to be sad at Merry Mount. "Therefore do I sigh amid this festive music. And besides, dear Edgar, I struggle as with a dream, and fancy that these shapes of our jovial friends are visionary, and their mirth unreal, and that we are no true Lord and Lady of the May. What is the mystery in my heart?"

Just then, as if a spell had loosened them, down came a little shower of withering rose-leaves from the Maypole. Alas for the young lovers! No sooner had their hearts glowed with real passion than they were sensible of something vague and unsubstantial in their former pleasures, and felt a dreary presentiment of inevitable change. From the moment that they truly loved, they had subjected themselves to earth's doom of care and sorrow and troubled joy, and had no more a home at Merry Mount. That was Edith's mystery. Now leave we the priest to marry them, and the maskers to sport round the Maypole, till the last sunbeam be withdrawn from its summit, and the shadows of the forest mingle gloomily in the dance. Meanwhile, we may discover who these gay people were.

Two hundred years ago, and more the Old World and its inhabitants became mutually weary of each other Men voyaged by thousands to the West; some to barter glass beads, and such like jewels for the furs of the Indian hunter; some to conquer virgin mpires; and one stern band to pray. But none of these motives had much weight with the colonists of Merry Mount. Their leaders were men who had sported so long with life that, when Thought and Wisdom came, even these unwelcome guests were led astray by the crowd of vanities which they should have put to flight. Erring Thought and perverted Wisdom were made to put on masks and play the fool. The men of whom we speak, after losing the heart's fresh gayety, imagined a wild philosophy of pleasure, and came hither to act out their latest day-dream. They gathered followers from all that giddy tribe, whose whole life is like the festal days of soberer men. In their train were minstrels, not unknown in London streets; wandering players, whose theatres had been the halls of noblemen; mummers, rope-dancers, and mountebanks, who would long be missed at wakes, church ales, and fairs; in a word, mirth-makers of every sort, such as abounded in that age, but now began to be discountenanced by the rapid growth of Puritanism. Light had their footsteps been on land, and as lightly they came across the sea. Many had been maddened by their previous troubles into a gay despair; others were as madly gay in the flush of youth, like the May Lord and his Lady; but whatever might be the quality of their mirth, old and young were gay at Merry Mount. The young deemed themselves happy. The elder spirits, if they knew that mirth was but the counterfeit of happiness, yet followed the false shadow wilfully, because at least her garments glittered brightest. Sworn triflers of a lifetime, they would not venture among the sober truths of life, not even to be truly blest.

All the hereditary pastimes of Old England were transplanted hither. The King of Christmas was duly crowned, and the Lord of Misrule bore potent sway. On the eve of Saint John they felled whole acres of the forest to make bonfires, and danced by the blaze all night, crowned with garlands, and throwing flowers into the flame. At harvest time, though their crop was of the smallest, they made an image with the sheaves of Indian corn, and wreathed it with autumnal garlands, and bore it home triumphantly. But what chiefly characterized the colonists of Merry Mount was their veneration for the Maypole. It has made their true history a poet's tale. Spring decked the hallowed emblem with young blossoms and fresh green boughs; Summer brought roses of the deepest blush, and the perfected foliage of the forest; Autumn enriched it with that red and yellow gorgeousness which converts each wildwood leaf into a painted flower; and Winter silvered it with sleet and hung it round with icicles till it flashed in the cold sunshine, itself a frozen sunbeam. Thus each alternate season did homage to the Maypole, and paid it a tribute of its own richest splendor. Its votaries danced round it, once, at least, in every month; sometimes they called it their religion, or their altar; but always it was the banner-staff of Merry Mount.

Unfortunately, there were men in the New World of a sterner faith than these Maypole worshippers. Not far from Merry Mount was a settlement of Puritans, most dismal wretches, who said their prayers before daylight, and then wrought in the forest or the cornfield till evening made it prayer time again. Their weapons were always at hand, to shoot down the straggling savage. When they met in conclave, it was never to keep up the old English mirth, but to hear sermons three hours long, or to proclaim bounties on the heads of wolves and the scalps of Indians. Their festivals were fast days, and their chief pastime the singing of psalms. Woe to the youth or maiden who did but dream of a dance! The selectman nodded to the constable; and there sat the light-heeled reprobate in the stocks; or if he danced, it was round the whipping-post, which might be termed the Puritan Maypole.

A party of these grim Puritans, toiling through the difficult woods, each with a horseload of iron armor to burden his footsteps, would sometimes draw near the sunny precincts of Merry Mount. There were the silken colonists, sporting round their Maypole; perhaps teaching a bear to dance, or striving to communicate their mirth to the grave Indian; or masquerading in the skins of deer and wolves, which they had hunted for that especial purpose. Often, the whole colony were playing at blindman's bluff, magistrates and all with their eyes bandaged, except a single scapegoat, whom the blinded sinners pursued by the tinkling of the bells at his garments. Once, it is said, they were seen following a flower-decked corpse, with merriment and festive music, to his grave. But did the dead man laugh? In their quietest times, they sang ballads and told tales, for the edification of their pious visitors; or perplexed them with juggling tricks; or grinned at them through horse-collars; and when sport itself grew wearisome, they made game of their own stupidity, and began a yawning match. At the very least of

these enormities, the men of iron shook their heads and frowned so darkly, that the revellers looked up, imagining that a momentary cloud had overcast the sunshine, which was to be perpetual there. On the other hand, the Puritans affirmed, that, when a psalm was pealing from their place of worship, the echo which the forest sent them back seemed often like the chorus of a jolly catch, closing with a roar of laughter. Who but the fiend, and his bond-slaves the crew of Merry Mount, had thus disturbed them? In due time, a feud arose, stern and bitter on one side, and as serious on the other as anything could be among such light spirits as had sworn allegiance to the Maypole. The future complexion of New England was involved in this important quarrel. Should the grizzly saints establish their jurisdiction over the gay sinners, then would their spirits darken all the clime, and make it a land of clouded visages, of hard toil, of sermon and psalm for ever. But should the banner staff of Merry Mount be fortunate, sunshine would break upon the hills, and flowers would beautify the forest, and late posterity do homage to the Maypole.

After these authentic passages from history, we return to the nuptials of the Lord and Lady of the May. Alas! we have delayed too long, and must darken our tale too suddenly. As we glance again at the Maypole, a solitary sunbeam is fading from the summit, and leaves only a faint, golden tinge, blended with the hues of the rainbow banner. Even that dim light is now withdrawn, relinquishing the whole domain of Merry Mount to the evening gloom, which had rushed so instantaneously from the black surrounding woods. But some of

ese black shadows have rushed forth
human shape.

Yes, with the setting sun, the last
ay of mirth had passed from Merry
Mount. The ring of gay maskers was
sordered and broken; the stag lowered
s antlers in dismay; the wolf grew
eaker than a lamb; the bells of the
orris dancers tinkled with tremulous
fright. The Puritans had played a
aracteristic part in the Maypole mum-
eries. Their darksome figures were
termixed with the wild shapes of their
es, and made the scene a picture of
e moment, when waking thoughts start
amid the scattered fantasies of a
ream. The leader of the hostile party
ood in the centre of the circle, while
e rout of monsters cowered around
m, like evil spirits in the presence of
dread magician. No fantastic foolery
uld look him in the face. So stern was
e energy of his aspect, that the whole
an, visage, frame, and soul, seemed
rought of iron, gifted with life and
ought, yet all of one substance with
is headpiece and breastplate. It was
e Puritan of Puritans; it was Endicott
mself!

"Stand off, priest of Baal!" said he,
ith a grim frown, and laying no rever-
nt hand upon the surplice. "I know
ee, Blackstone! * Thou art the man.
ho couldst not abide the rule even of
ine own corrupted church, and hast
ome hither to preach iniquity, and to
ive example of it in thy life. But now
all it be seen that the Lord hath sanc-
fied this wilderness for his peculiar
eople. Woe unto them that would de-

* Did Governor Endicott speak less posi-
vely, we should suspect a mistake here. The
ev. Mr. Blackstone, though an eccentric, is
ot known to have been an immoral man. We
ther doubt his identity with the priest of
erry Mount.

file it! And first for this flower-decked
abomination, the altar of thy worship!"

And with his keen sword, Endicott
assaulted the hallowed Maypole. Nor
long did it resist his arm. It groaned
with a dismal sound; it showered leaves
and rosebuds upon the remorseless enthusiast; and finally, with all its green
boughs, and ribbons, and flowers, symbolic of departed pleasures, down fell
the banner staff of Merry Mount. As it
sank, tradition says, the evening sky
grew darker, and the woods threw forth
a more sombre shadow.

"There," cried Endicott, looking triumphantly on his work, "there lies the
only Maypole in New England! The
thought is strong within me, that by its
fall is shadowed forth the fate of light
and idle mirthmakers, amongst us
and our posterity. Amen, saith John
Endicott."

"Amen!" echoed his followers.

But the votaries of the Maypole gave
one groan for their idol. At the sound,
the Puritan leader glanced at the crew
of Comus, each a figure of broad mirth,
yet, at this moment, strangely expressive of sorrow and dismay.

"Valiant captain," quoth Peter Palfrey, the Ancient of the band, "what
order shall be taken with the prisoners?"

"I thought not to repent me of cutting
down a Maypole," replied Endicott,
"yet now I could find in my heart to
plant it again, and give each of these
bestial pagans one other dance round
their idol. It would have served rarely
for a whipping-post!"

"But there are pine-trees enow," suggested the lieutenant.

"True, good Ancient," said the leader.
"Wherefore, bind the heathen crew, and
bestow on them a small matter of

stripes apiece, as earnest of our future justice. Set some of the rogues in the stocks to rest themselves, so soon as Providence shall bring us to one of our own well-ordered settlements, where such accommodations may be found. Further penalties, such as branding and cropping of ears, shall be thought of hereafter."

"How many stripes for the priest?" inquired Ancient Palfrey.

"None as yet," answered Endicott, bending his iron frown upon the culprit. "It must be for the Great and General Court to determine, whether stripes and long imprisonment, and other grievous penalty, may atone for his transgressions. Let him look to himself! For such as violate our civil order, it may be permitted us to show mercy. But woe to the wretch that troubleth our religion!"

"And this dancing bear," resumed the officer. "Must he share the stripes of his fellows?"

"Shoot him through the head!" said the energetic Puritan. "I suspect witchcraft in the beast."

"Here be a couple of shining ones," continued Peter Palfrey, pointing his weapon at the Lord and Lady of the May. "They seem to be of high station among these misdoers. Methinks their dignity will not be fitted with less than a double share of stripes."

Endicott rested on his sword, and closely surveyed the dress and aspect of the hapless pair. There they stood, pale, downcast, and apprehensive. Yet there was an air of mutual support, and of pure affection, seeking aid and giving it, that showed them to be man and wife, with the sanction of the priest upon their love. The youth, in the peril of the moment, had dropped his gilded

staff, and thrown his arm about the Lady of the May, who leaned against his breast, too lightly to burden him, but with weight enough to express that their destinies were linked together, for good or evil. They looked first at each other and then into the grim captain's face. There they stood, in the first hour of wedlock, while the idle pleasures, of which their companions were the emblems, had given place to the sternest care of life, personified by the dark Puritans. But never had their youthful beauty seemed so pure and high, as when its glow was chastened by adversity.

"Youth," said Endicott, "ye stand in an evil case, thou and thy maiden wife. Make ready presently; for I am minded that ye shall both have a token to remember your wedding-day!"

"Stern man," cried the May Lord, "how can I move thee? Were the means at hand, I would resist to the death. Being powerless, I entreat! Do with me as thou wilt, but let Edith go untouched!"

"Not so," replied the immitigable zealot. "We are not wont to show an idle courtesy to that sex, which requireth the stricter discipline. What sayest thou, maid? Shall thy silken bridegroom suffer thy share of the penalty besides his own?"

"Be it death," said Edith, "and lay it all on me!"

Truly, as Endicott had said, the poor lovers stood in a woful case. Their foes were triumphant, their friends captive and abased, their home desolate, the benighted wilderness around them, and a rigorous destiny, in the shape of the Puritan leader, their only guide. Yet the deepening twilight could not altogether conceal that the iron man was softened;

e smiled at the fair spectacle of early
ove; he almost sighed for the inevitable
light of early hopes.

"The troubles of life have come
astily on this young couple," observed
ndicott. "We will see how they com-
ort themselves under their present
rials, ere we burden them with greater.
f, among the spoil, there be any gar-
ents of a more decent fashion, let
em be put upon this May Lord and
is Lady, instead of their glistening
anities. Look to it, some of you."

"And shall not the youth's hair be
ut?" asked Peter Palfrey, looking with
bhorrence at the love-lock and long
lossy curls of the young man.

"Crop it forthwith, and that in the
ue pumpkin-shell fashion," answered
e captain. "Then bring them along
ith us, but more gently than their fel-
ws. There be qualities in the youth
hich may make him valiant to fight,
d sober to toil, and pious to pray;
d in the maiden, that may fit her to
ecome a mother in our Israel, bringing
up babes in better nurture than her own
hath been. Nor think ye, young ones,
that they are the happiest, even in our
lifetime of a moment, who misspend it
in dancing round a Maypole!"

And Endicott, the severest Puritan of
all who laid the rock foundation of New
England, lifted the wreath of roses from
the ruin of the Maypole, and threw it,
with his own gauntleted hand, over the
heads of the Lord and Lady of the May.
It was a deed of prophecy. As the moral
gloom of the world overpowers all systematic gayety, even so was their home
of wild mirth made desolate amid the
sad forest. They returned to it no more.
But as their flowering garland was
wreathed of the brightest roses that had
grown there, so in the tie that united
them were intertwined all the purest
and best of their early joys. They went
heavenward, supporting each other along
the difficult path which it was their lot
to tread, and never wasted one regretful
thought on the vanities of Merry
Mount.

THE GENTLE BOY

In the course of the year 1656, sev-
al of the people called Quakers, led, as
ey professed, by the inward movement
the spirit, made their appearance in
ew England. Their reputation, as
olders of mystic and pernicious prin-
ples, having spread before them, the
uritans early endeavored to banish, and
prevent the further intrusion of the
sing sect. But the measures by which
was intended to purge the land of
resy, though more than sufficiently
vigorous, were entirely unsuccessful.
The Quakers, esteeming persecution as
a divine call to the post of danger, laid
claim to a holy courage, unknown to the
Puritans themselves, who had shunned
the cross, by providing for the peaceable
exercise of their religion in a distant
wilderness. Though it was the singular
fact, that every nation of the earth rejected the wandering enthusiasts who
practised peace towards all men, the
place of greatest uneasiness and peril,

and therefore, in their eyes the most eligible, was the province of Massachusetts Bay.

The fines, imprisonments, and stripes, liberally distributed by our pious forefathers; the popular antipathy, so strong that it endured nearly a hundred years after actual persecution had ceased, were attractions as powerful for the Quakers, as peace, honor, and reward would have been for the worldly-minded. Every European vessel brought new cargoes of the sect, eager to testify against the oppression which they hoped to share; and, when shipmasters were restrained by heavy fines from affording them passage, they made long and circuitous journeys through the Indian country, and appeared in the province as if conveyed by a supernatural power. Their enthusiasm, heightened almost to madness by the treatment which they received, produced actions contrary to the rules of decency, as well as of rational religion, and presented a singular contrast to the calm and staid deportment of their sectarian successors of the present day. The command of the spirit, inaudible except to the soul, and not to be controverted on grounds of human wisdom, was made a plea for most indecorous exhibitions, which, abstractedly considered, well deserved the moderate chastisement of the rod. These extravagances, and the persecution which was at once their cause and consequence, continued to increase, till, in the year 1659, the government of Massachusetts Bay indulged two members of the Quaker sect with the crown of martyrdom.

An indelible stain of blood is upon the hands of all who consented to this act, but a large share of the awful responsibility must rest upon the perso, then at the head of the government. H was a man of narrow mind and im perfect education, and his uncompromis ing bigotry was made hot and mischie vous by violent and hasty passions; h exerted his influence indecorously an unjustifiably to compass the death o the enthusiasts; and his whole conduct in respect to them, was marked b brutal cruelty. The Quakers, whose re vengeful feelings were not less deep be cause they were inactive, remembere this man and his associates in afte times. The historian of the sect affirm that, by the wrath of Heaven, a bligh fall upon the land in the vicinity of th "bloody town" of Boston, so that n wheat would grow there; and he take his stand, as it were, among the grave of the ancient persecutors, and triumph antly recounts the judgments that over took them, in old age or at the partin hour. He tells us that they died sud denly, and violently, and in madness but nothing can exceed the bitte mockery with which he records th loathsome disease, and "death b rottenness," of the fierce and cru governor.

*   *   *   *   *

On the evening of the autumn da that had witnessed the martyrdom o two men of the Quaker persuasion, Puritan settler was returning from th metropolis to the neighboring countr town in which he resided. The air wa cool, the sky clear, and the lingerin twilight was made brighter by the ra of a young moon, which had now near reached the verge of the horizon. Th traveller, a man of middle age, wrappe in a gray frieze cloak, quickened h pace when he reached the outskirts c

he town, for a gloomy extent of nearly
our miles lay between him and his
ome. The low, straw-thatched houses
vere scattered at considerable intervals
long the road, and the country having
een settled but about thirty years, the
racts of original forest still bore no
mall proportion to the cultivated
round. The autumn wind wandered
mong the branches, whirling away the
aves from all except the pine trees,
nd moaning as if it lamented the deso-
ation of which it was the instrument.
he road had penetrated the mass of
oods that lay nearest to the town, and
as just emerging into an open space,
hen the traveller's ears were saluted
y a sound more mournful than even
hat of the wind. It was like the wailing
f some one in distress, and it seemed
o proceed from beneath a tall and lone-
y fir-tree, in the centre of a cleared, but
nenclosed and uncultivated field. The
uritan could not but remember that
his was the very spot, which had been
ade accursed a few hours before, by
he execution of the Quakers, whose
odies had been thrown together into
ne hasty grave, beneath the tree on
hich they suffered. He struggled, how-
ver, against the superstitious fears
hich belonged to the age, and com-
elled himself to pause and listen.

"The voice is most likely mortal, nor
ave I cause to tremble if it be other-
ise," thought he, straining his eyes
hrough the dim moonlight. "Methinks
: is like the wailing of a child; some
nfant, it may be, which has strayed
rom its mother, and chanced upon this
lace of death. For the ease of mine
wn conscience, I must search this mat-
er out."

He therefore left the path, and walked
somewhat fearfully across the field.
Though now so desolate, its soil was
pressed down and trampled by the thousand footsteps of those who had witnessed the spectacle of that day, all of
whom had now retired, leaving the
dead to their loneliness. The traveller
at length reached the fir-tree, which
from the middle upward was covered
with living branches, although a scaffold
had been erected beneath, and other
preparations made for the work of
death. Under this unhappy tree, which
in after times was believed to drop
poison with its dew, sat the one solitary
mourner for innocent blood. It was a
slender and light clad little boy, who
leaned his face upon a hillock of fresh-
turned and half-frozen earth, and wailed
bitterly, yet in a suppressed tone, as if
his grief might receive the punishment
of crime. The Puritan, whose approach
had been unperceived, laid his hand upon
the child's shoulder, and addressed him
compassionately.

"You have chosen a dreary lodging,
my poor boy, and no wonder that you
weep," said he. "But dry your eyes, and
tell me where your mother dwells. I
promise you if the journey be not too
far, I will leave you in her arms to-
night."

The boy had hushed his wailing at
once, and turned his face upward to the
stranger. It was a pale, bright-eyed
countenance, certainly not more than
six years old, but sorrow, fear, and want
had destroyed much of its infantile expression. The Puritan, seeing the boy's
frightened gaze, and feeling that he
trembled under his hand, endeavored to
reassure him.

"Nay, if I intended to do you harm,
little lad, the readiest way were to leave

you here. What! you do not fear to sit beneath the gallows on a new-made grave, and yet you tremble at a friend's touch. Take heart, child, and tell me what is your name, and where is your home?"

"Friend," replied the little boy, in a sweet, though faltering voice, "they call me Ilbrahim, and my home is here."

The pale, spiritual face, the eyes that seemed to mingle with the moonlight, the sweet, airy voice, and the outlandish name, almost made the Puritan believe that the boy was in truth a being which had sprung up out of the grave on which he sat. But perceiving that the apparition stood the test of a short mental prayer, and remembering that the arm which he had touched was life-like, he adopted a more rational supposition. "The poor child is stricken in his intellect," thought he, "but verily his words are fearful, in a place like this." He then spoke soothingly, intending to humor the boy's fantasy.

"Your home will scarce be comfortable, Ilbrahim, this cold autumn night, and I fear you are ill provided with food. I am hastening to a warm supper and bed, and if you will go with me, you shall share them!"

"I thank thee, friend, but though I be hungry, and shivering with cold, thou wilt not give me food nor lodging," replied the boy, in the quiet tone which despair had taught him, even so young. "My father was of the people whom all men hate. They have laid him under this heap of earth, and here is my home."

The Puritan, who had laid hold of little Ilbrahim's hand, relinquished it as if he were touching a loathsome reptile. But he possessed a compassionate heart, which not even religious prejudice

could harden into stone.

"God forbid that I should leave th child to perish, though he comes of t accursed sect," said he to himself. "I we not all spring from an evil root? A we not all in darkness till the lig doth shine upon us? He shall not peris neither in body, nor, if prayer and i struction may avail for him, in soul He then spoke aloud and kindly Ilbrahim, who had again hid his fa in the cold earth of the grave. "W every door in the land shut against yo my child, that you have wandered this unhallowed spot?"

"They drove me forth from the pris when they took my father thence," sa the boy, "and I stood afar off, watchir the crowd of people, and when the were gone I came hither, and found on this grave. I knew that my father w sleeping here, and I said, This shall b my home."

"No, child, no; not while I have roof over my head or a morsel to shar with you!" exclaimed the Puritan, whos sympathies were now fully excite "Rise up and come with me, and fea not any harm."

The boy wept afresh, and clung to th heap of earth, as if the cold heart be neath it were warmer to him than an in a living breast. The traveller, how ever, continued to entreat him tenderl and, seeming to acquire some degree c confidence, he at length arose. But hi slender limbs tottered with weaknes his little head grew dizzy, and he leane against the tree of death for support.

"My poor boy, are you so feeble? said the Puritan "When did you tast food last?"

"I ate of bread and water with m father in the prison," replied Ilbrahim "but they brought him none neither yesterday nor to-day, saying that he had eaten enough to bear him to his journey's end. Trouble not thyself for my hunger, kind friend, for I have lacked food many times ere now."

The traveller took the child in his arms and wrapped his cloak about him, while his heart stirred with shame and anger against the gratuitous cruelty of the instruments in this persecution. In the awakened warmth of his feelings he resolved that, at whatever risk, he would not forsake the poor little defenceless being whom Heaven had confided to his care. With this determination he left the accursed field and resumed the homeward path from which the wailing of the boy had called him. The light and motionless burden scarcely impeded his progress, and he soon beheld the fire rays from the windows of the cottage which he, a native of a distant clime, had built in the Western wilderness. It was surrounded by a considerable extent of cultivated ground, and the dwelling was situated in the nook of a wood-covered hill, whither it seemed to have crept for protection.

"Look up, child," said the Puritan to Ilbrahim, whose faint head had sunk upon his shoulder, "there is our home."

At the word "home" a thrill passed through the child's frame, but he continued silent. A few moments brought them to the cottage door, at which the owner knocked; for at that early period, when savages were wandering everywhere among the settlers, bolt and bar were indispensable to the security of the dwelling. The summons was answered by a bond-servant, a coarse-clad and dull-featured piece of humanity, who, after ascertaining that his master was

the applicant, undid the door, and held a flaring pine-knot torch to light him in. Farther back in the passage-way, the red blaze discovered a matronly woman, but no little crowd of children came bounding forth to greet their father's return. As the Puritan entered he thrust aside his cloak, and displayed Ilbrahim's face to the female.

"Dorothy, here is a little outcast whom Providence hath put into our hands," observed he. "Be kind to him, even as if he were of those dear ones who have departed from us."

"What pale and bright-eyed little boy is this, Tobias?" she inquired. "Is he one whom the wilderness folk have ravished from some Christian mother?"

"No, Dorothy, this poor child is no captive from the wilderness," he replied. "The heathen savage would have given him to eat of his scanty morsel, and to drink of his birchen cup; but Christian men, alas! had cast him out to die."

Then he told her how he had found him beneath the gallows, upon his father's grave; and how his heart had prompted him, like the speaking of an inward voice, to take the little outcast home, and be kind unto him. He acknowledged his resolution to feed and clothe him as if he were his own child, and to afford him the instruction which should counteract the pernicious errors hitherto instilled into his infant mind. Dorothy was gifted with even a quicker tenderness than her husband, and she approved of all his doings and intentions.

"Have you a mother, dear child?" she inquired.

The tears burst forth from his full heart as he attempted to reply; but Dorothy at length understood that he had a mother, who, like the rest of her sect, was a persecuted wanderer. She had been taken from the prison a short time before, carried into the uninhabited wilderness, and left to perish there by hunger or wild beasts. This was no uncommon method of disposing of the Quakers, and they were accustomed to boast that the inhabitants of the desert were more hospitable to them than civilized man.

"Fear not, little boy, you shall not need a mother, and a kind one," said Dorothy, when she had gathered this information. "Dry your tears, Ilbrahim, and be my child, as I will be your mother."

The good woman prepared the little bed from which her own children had successively been borne to another resting-place. Before Ilbrahim would consent to occupy it, he knelt down, and as Dorothy listened to his simple and affecting prayer, she marvelled how the parents that had taught it to him could have been judged worthy of death. When the boy had fallen asleep, she bent over his pale and spiritual countenance, pressed a kiss upon his white brow, drew the bed-clothes up about his neck, and went away with a pensive gladness in her heart.

Tobias Pearson was not among the earliest emigrants from the old country. He had remained in England during the first years of the civil war, in which he had borne some share as a cornet of dragoons, under Cromwell. But when the ambitious designs of his leader began to develop themselves, he quitted the army of the Parliament and sought a refuge from the strife, which was no longer holy, among the people of his persuasion in the colony of Massachu-

setts. A more worldly consideration had perhaps, an influence in drawing him thither; for New England offered advantages to men of unprosperous fortunes as well as to dissatisfied religionists, and Pearson had hitherto found it difficult to provide for a wife and increasing family. To this supposed impurity of motive, the more bigoted Puritans were inclined to impute the removal by death of all the children, for whose earthly good the father had been overthoughtful. They had left their native country blooming like roses, and like roses they had perished in a foreign soil. Those expounders of the ways of Providence, who had thus judged their brother, and attributed his domestic sorrows to his sin, were not more charitable when they saw him and Dorothy endeavoring to fill up the void in their hearts by the adoption of an infant of the accursed sect. Nor did they fail to communicate their disapprobation to Tobias; but the latter, in reply, merely pointed at the little, quiet, lovely boy, whose appearance and deportment were indeed as powerful arguments as could possibly have been adduced in his own favor. Even his beauty, however, and his winning manners, sometimes produced an effect ultimately unfavorable; for the bigots, when the outer surfaces of their iron hearts had been softened and again grew hard, affirmed that no merely natural cause could have so worked upon them.

Their antipathy to the poor infant was also increased by the ill success of divers theological discussions, in which it was attempted to convince him of the errors of his sect. Ilbrahim, it is true, was not a skilful controversialist; but the feeling of his religion was strong as instinct in him, and he could neither be enticed nor driven from the faith which his father had died for. The odium of this stubbornness was shared in a great measure by the child's protectors, insomuch that Tobias and Dorothy very shortly began to experience a most bitter species of persecution, in the cold regards of many a friend whom they had valued. The common people manifested their opinions more openly. Pearson was a man of some consideration, being a representative to the General Court, and an approved lieutenant in the trainbands, yet within a week after his adoption of Ilbrahim, he had been both hissed and hooted. Once, also, when walking through a solitary piece of woods, he heard a loud voice from some invisible speaker; and it cried, "What shall be done to the backslider? Lo! the scourge is knotted for him, even the whip of nine cords, and every cord three knots!" These insults irritated Pearson's temper for the moment; they entered also into his heart, and became imperceptible but powerful workers towards an end, which his most secret thought had not yet whispered.

*　　*　　*　　*　　*　　*

On the second Sabbath after Ilbrahim became a member of their family, Pearson and his wife deemed it proper that he should appear with them at public worship. They had anticipated some opposition to this measure from the boy, but he prepared himself in silence, and at the appointed hour was clad in the new mourning suit which Dorothy had wrought for him. As the parish was then, and during many subsequent years, unprovided with a bell, the signal for the commencement of religious exercises was the beat of a drum. At the first sound of that martial call to the place of holy and quiet thoughts, Tobias and Dorothy set forth, each holding a hand of little Ilbrahim, like two parents linked together by the infant of their love. On their path through the leafless woods, they were overtaken by many persons of their acquaintance, all of whom avoided them, and passed by on the other side; but a severer trial awaited their constancy when they had descended the hill, and drew near the pine-built and undecorated house of prayer. Around the door, from which the drummer still sent forth his thundering summons, was drawn up a formidable phalanx, including several of the oldest members of the congregation, many of the middle aged, and nearly all the younger males. Pearson found it difficult to sustain their united and disapproving gaze, but Dorothy, whose mind was differently circumstanced, merely drew the boy closer to her, and faltered not in her approach. As they entered the door, they overheard the muttered sentiments of the assemblage, and when the reviling voices of the little children smote Ilbrahim's ear, he wept.

The interior aspect of the meeting-house was rude. The low ceiling, the unplastered walls, the naked woodwork, and the undrapered pulpit, offered nothing to excite the devotion, which, without such external aids, often remains latent in the heart. The floor of the building was occupied by rows of long, cushionless benches, supplying the place of pews, and the broad aisle formed a sexual division, impassable except by children beneath a certain age.

Pearson and Dorothy separated at the door of the meeting-house, and Ilbrahim, being within the years of infancy was retained under the care of the latter. The wrinkled beldams involved themselves in their rusty cloaks as he passed by; even the mild-featured maidens seemed to dread contamination; and many a stern old man arose, and turned his repulsive and unheavenly countenance upon the gentle boy, as if the sanctuary were polluted by his presence. He was a sweet infant of the skies, that had strayed away from his home, and all the inhabitants of this miserable world closed up their impure hearts against him, drew back their earth-soiled garments from his touch, and said, "We are holier than thou."

Ilbrahim, seated by the side of his adopted mother, and retaining fast hold of her hand, assumed a grave and decorous demeanor, such as might befit a person of matured taste and understanding, who should find himself in a temple dedicated to some worship which he did not recognize, but felt himself bound to respect. The exercises had not yet commenced, however, when the boy's attention was arrested by an event, apparently of trifling interest. A woman, having her face muffled in a hood, and a cloak drawn completely about her form, advancing slowly up the broad aisle, and took a place upon the foremost bench. Ilbrahim's faint color varied, his nerves fluttered, he was unable to turn his eyes from the muffled female.

When the preliminary prayer and hymn were over, the minister arose, and having turned the hour-glass which stood by the great Bible, commenced his discourse. He was now well-stricken in years, a man of pale, thin countenance, and his gray hairs were closely covered by a black-velvet skullcap. In his younger days he had practically learned the meaning of persecution from Archbishop Laud, and he was not now disposed to forget the lesson against which he had murmured then. Introducing the often discussed subject of the Quakers, he gave a history of that sect, and a description of their tenets, in which error predominated, and prejudice distorted the aspect of what was true. He adverted to the recent measures in the province, and cautioned his hearers of weaker parts against calling in question the just severity, which God-fearing magistrates had at length been compelled to exercise. He spoke of the danger of pity, in some cases a commendable and Christian virtue, but inapplicable to this pernicious sect. He observed that such was their devilish obstinacy in error, that even the little children, the sucking babes, were hardened and desperate heretics. He affirmed that no man, without Heaven's especial warrant, should attempt their conversion, lest while he lent his hand to draw them from the slough, he should himself be precipitated into its lowest depths.

The sands of the second hour were principally in the lower half of the glass, when the sermon concluded. An approving murmur followed, and the clergyman, having given out a hymn, took his seat with much self-congratulation, and endeavored to read the effect of his eloquence in the visages of the people. But while voices from all parts of the house were tuning themselves to sing, a scene occurred, which, though not very unusual at that period in the province, happened to be without precedent in this parish.

The muffled female, who had hitherto

sat motionless in the front rank of the audience, now arose, and with slow, stately, and unwavering step, ascended the pulpit stairs. The quiverings of incipient harmony were hushed, and the divine sat in speechless and almost terrified astonishment, while she undid the door, and stood up in the sacred desk from which his maledictions had just been thundered. She then divested herself of the cloak and hood, and appeared in a most singular array. A shapeless robe of sackcloth was girded about her waist with a knotted cord; her raven hair fell down upon her shoulders, and its blackness was defiled by pale streaks of ashes, which she had strown upon her head. Her eyebrows, dark and strongly defined, added to the deathly whiteness of a countenance, which, emaciated with want, and wild with enthusiasm and strange sorrows, retained no trace of earlier beauty. This figure stood gazing earnestly on the audience, and there was no sound, nor any movement, except a faint shuddering which every man observed in his neighbor, but was scarcely conscious of in himself. At length, when her fit of inspiration came, she spoke, for the first few moments, in a low voice, and not invariably distinct utterance. Her discourse gave evidence of an imagination hopelessly entangled with her reason; it was a vague and incomprehensible rhapsody, which, however, seemed to spread its own atmosphere round the hearer's soul, and to move his feelings by some influence unconnected with the words. As she proceeded, beautiful but shadowy images would sometimes be seen, like bright things moving in a turbid river; or a strong and singularly-shaped idea leaped forth, and seized at once on the understanding or the heart. But the course of her unearthly eloquence soon led her to the persecutions of her sect, and from thence the step was short to her own peculiar sorrows. She was naturally a woman of mighty passions, and hatred and revenge now wrapped themselves in the garb of piety; the character of her speech was changed, her images became distinct though wild, and her denunciations had an almost hellish bitterness.

"The Governor and his mighty men," she said, "have gathered together, taking counsel among themselves and saying, 'What shall we do unto this people, —even unto the people that have come into this land to put our iniquity to the blush?' And lo! the Devil entereth into the council-chamber, like a lame man of low stature and gravely apparelled, with a dark and twisted countenance, and a bright, downcast eye. And he standeth up among the rulers; yea, he goeth to and fro, whispering to each; and every man lends his ear, for his word is 'slay, slay!' But I say unto ye, Woe to them that slay! Woe to them that shed the blood of saints! Woe to them that have slain the husband, and cast forth the child, the tender infant, to wander homeless and hungry and cold, till he die; and have saved the mother alive, in the cruelty of their tender mercies! Woe to them in their lifetime, cursed are they in the delight and pleasure of their hearts! Woe to them in their death hour, whether it come swiftly with blood and violence, or after long and lingering pain! Woe, in the dark house, in the rottenness of the grave, when the children's children shall revile the ashes of the fathers! Woe, woe, woe, at the judgment, when all the persecuted and all the slain in this bloody land, and the father, the mother, and the child, shall await them in a day that they cannot escape! Seed of the faith, seed of the faith, yet whose hearts are moving with a power that ye know not, arise, wash your hands of this innocent blood! Life your voices, chosen ones, cry aloud, and call down a woe and a judgment with me!"

Having thus given vent to the flood of malignity which she mistook for inspiration, the speaker was silent. Her voice was succeeded by the hysteric shrieks of several women, but the feelings of the audience generally had not been drawn onward in the current with her own. They remained stupefied, stranded as it were, in the midst of a torrent, which deafened them by its roaring, but might not move them by its violence. The clergyman, who could not hitherto have ejected the usurper of his pulpit otherwise than by bodily force, now addressed her in the tone of just indignation and legitimate authority.

"Get you down, woman, from the holy place which you profane," he said. "Is it to the Lord's house that you come to pour forth the foulness of your heart, and the inspiration of the Devil? Get you down, and remember that the sentence of death is on you; yea, and shall be executed, were it but for this day's work."

"I go, friend, I go, for the voice hath had its utterance," replied she, in a depressed and even mild tone. "I have done my mission unto thee and to thy people. Reward me with stripes, imprisonment, or death, as ye shall be permitted."

The weakness of exhausted passion caused her steps to totter as she descended the pulpit stairs. The people, in the mean while, were stirring to and fro on the floor of the house, whispering among themselves, and glancing towards the intruder. Many of them now recognized her as the woman who had assaulted the governor with frightful language, as he passed by the window of her prison; they knew, also, that she was adjudged to suffer death, and had been preserved only by an involuntary banishment into the wilderness. The new outrage, by which she had provoked her fate, seemed to render further lenity impossible; and a gentleman in military dress, with a stout man of inferior rank, drew towards the door of the meeting-house, and awaited her approach. Scarcely did her feet press the floor, however, when an unexpected scene occurred. In that moment of her peril, when every eye frowned with death, a little timid boy pressed forth, and threw his arms round his mother.

"I am here, mother, it is I, and I will go with thee to prison," he exclaimed.

She gazed at him with a doubtful and almost frightened expression, for she knew that the boy had been cast out to perish, and she had not hoped to see his face again. She feared, perhaps, that it was but one of the happy visions, with which her excited fancy had often deceived her, in the solitude of the desert, or in prison. But when she felt his hand warm within her own, and heard his little eloquence of childish love, she began to know that she was yet a mother.

"Blessed art thou, my son," she sobbed. "My heart was withered; yea, dead with thee and with thy father; and now it leaps as in the first moment when I pressed thee to my bosom."

She knelt down and embraced him again and again, while the joy that could find no words, expressed itself in broken accents, like the bubbles gushing up to vanish at the surface of a deep fountain. The sorrows of past years, and the darker peril that was nigh, cast not a shadow on the brightness of that fleeting moment. Soon, however, the spectators saw a change upon her face, as the consciousness of her sad estate returned, and grief supplied the fount of tears which joy had opened. By the words she uttered, it would seem that the indulgence of natural love had given her mind a momentary sense of its errors, and made her know how far she had strayed from duty, in following the dictates of a wild fanaticism.

"In a doleful hour art thou returned to me, poor boy," she said, "for thy mother's path has gone darkening onward, till now the end is death. Son, son, I have borne thee in my arms when my limbs were tottering, and I have fed thee with the food that I was fainting for; yet I have ill performed a mother's part by thee in life, and now I leave thee no inheritance but woe and shame. Thou wilt go seeking through the world, and find all hearts closed against thee, and their sweet affections turned to bitterness for my sake. My child, my child, how many a pang awaits thy gentle spirit, and I the cause of all!"

She hid her face on Ilbrahim's head, and her long, raven hair, discolored with the ashes of her mourning, fell down about him like a veil. A low and interrupted moan was the voice of her heart's anguish, and it did not fail to move the sympathies of many who mistook their involuntary virtue for a sin. Sobs were audible in the female section of the house, and every man who was a father drew his hand across his eyes. Tobias Pearson was agitated and uneasy, but a certain feeling like the consciousness of guilt oppressed him, so that he could not go forth and offer himself as the protector of the child. Dorothy, however, had watched her husband's eye. Her mind was free from the influence that had begun to work on his, and she drew near the Quaker woman, and addressed her in the hearing of all the congregation.

"Stranger, trust this boy to me, and I will be his mother," she said, taking Ilbrahim's hand. "Providence has signally marked out my husband to protect him, and he has fed at our table and lodged under our roof, now many days, till our hearts have grown very strongly unto him. Leave the tender child with us, and be at ease concerning his welfare."

The Quaker rose from the ground, but drew the boy closer to her, while she gazed earnestly in Dorothy's face. Her mild, but saddened features, and neat matronly attire, harmonized together, and were like a verse of fireside poetry. Her very aspect proved that she was blameless, so far as mortal could be so, in respect to God and man; while the enthusiast, in her robe of sackcloth and girdle of knotted cord, had as evidently violated the duties of the present life and the future, by fixing her attention wholly on the latter. The two females, as they held each a hand of Ilbrahim, formed a practical allegory; it was rational piety and unbridled fanaticism, contending for the empire of a young heart.

"Thou art not of our people," said the Quaker, mournfully.

"No, we are not of your people," replied Dorothy, with mildness, "but we are Christians, looking upward to the same Heaven with you. Doubt not that your boy shall meet you there, if there be a blessing on our tender and prayerful guidance of him. Thither, I trust, my own children have gone before me, for I also have been a mother. I am no longer so," she added, in a faltering tone, "and your son will have all my care."

"But will ye lead him in the path which his parents have trodden?" demanded the Quaker. "Can ye teach him the enlightened faith which his father has died for, and for which I, even I, am soon to become an unworthy martyr? The boy has been baptized in blood; will ye keep the mark fresh and ruddy upon his forehead?"

"I will not deceive you," answered Dorothy. "If your child become our child, we must breed him up in the instruction which Heaven has imparted to us; we must pray for him the prayers of our own faith; we must do towards him according to the dictates of our own consciences, and not of yours. Were we to act otherwise, we should abuse your trust, even in complying with your wishes."

The mother looked down upon her boy with a troubled countenance, and then turned her eyes upward to heaven. She seemed to pray internally, and the contention of her soul was evident.

"Friend," she said at length to Dorothy, "I doubt not that my son shall receive all earthly tenderness at thy hands. Nay, I will believe that even thy imperfect lights may guide him to a better world; for surely thou art on the path thither. But thou hast spoken of a husband. Doth he stand here among this multitude of people? Let him come forth, for I must know to whom I commit this most precious trust."

She turned her face upon the male auditors, and after a momentary delay, Tobias Pearson came forth from among them. The Quaker saw the dress which marked his military rank, and shook her head; but then she noted the hesitating air, the eyes that struggled with her own, and were vanquished; the color that went and came, and could find no resting-place. As she gazed an unmirthful smile spread over her features, like sunshine that grows melancholy in some desolate spot. Her lips moved inaudibly, but at length she spake.

"I hear it, I hear it. The voice speaketh within me and saith, 'Leave thy child, Catharine, for his place is here, and go hence, for I have other work for thee. Break the bonds of natural affection, martyr thy love, and know that in all these things eternal wisdom hath its ends.' I go, friends, I go. Take ye my boy, my precious jewel. I go hence, trusting that all shall be well, and that even for his infant hands there is a labor in the vineyard."

She knelt down and whispered to Ilbrahim, who at first struggled and clung to his mother, with sobs and tears, but remained passive when she had kissed his cheek and arisen from the ground. Having held her hands over his head in mental prayer, she was ready to depart.

"Farewell, friends in mine extremity," she said to Pearson and his wife; "the good deed ye have done me is a treasure laid up in Heaven, to be returned a thousand-fold hereafter. And farewell ye, mine enemies, to whom it is not permitted to harm so much as a hair of my head, nor to stay my footsteps even for a moment. The day is coming when ye shall call upon me to witness for ye to this one sin uncommitted, and I will rise up and answer."

She turned her steps towards the door, and the men, who had stationed themselves to guard it, withdrew, and suffered her to pass. A general sentiment of pity overcame the virulence of religious hatred. Sanctified by her love and her affliction, she went forth, and all the people gazed after her till she had journeyed up the hill, and was lost behind its brow. She went, the apostle of her own unquiet heart, to renew the wanderings of past years. For her voice had been already heard in many lands of Christendom; and she had pined in the cells of a Catholic Inquisition, before she felt the lash, and lay in the dungeons of the Puritans. Her mission had extended also to the followers of the Prophet, and from them she had received the courtesy and kindness which all the contending sects of our purer religion united to deny her. Her husband and herself had resided many months in Turkey, where even the Sultan's countenance was gracious to them; in that pagan land, too, was Ilbrahim's birthplace, and his Oriental name was a mark of gratitude for the good deeds of an unbeliever.

*   *   *   *   *   *

When Pearson and his wife had thus acquired all the rights over Ilbrahim that could be delegated, their affection for him became, like the memory of their native land, or their mild sorrow for the dead, a piece of the immovable furniture of their hearts. The boy, also, after a week or two of mental disquiet,

began to gratify his protectors by many inadvertent proofs that he considered them as parents, and their house as home. Before the winter snows were melted, the persecuted infant, the little wanderer from a remote and heathen country, seemed native in the New England cottage, and inseparable from the warmth and security of its hearth. Under the influence of kind treatment, and in the consciousness that he was loved, Ilbrahim's demeanor lost a premature manliness, which had resulted from his earlier situation; he became more childlike, and his natural character displayed itself with freedom. It was in many respects a beautiful one, yet the disordered imagination of both his father and mother had perhaps propagated a certain unhealthiness in the mind of the boy. In his general state, Ilbrahim would derive enjoyment from the most trifling events, and from every object about him; he seemed to discover rich treasures of happiness, by a faculty analogous to that of the witch hazel, which points to hidden gold where all is barren to the eye. His airy gayety, coming to him from a thousand sources, communicated itself to the family, and Ilbrahim was like a domesticated sunbeam, brightening moody countenances, and chasing away the gloom from the dark corners of the cottage.

On the other hand, as the susceptibility of pleasure is also that of pain, the exuberant cheerfulness of the boy's prevailing temper sometimes yielded to moments of deep depression. His sorrows could not always be followed up to their original source, but most frequently they appeared to flow, though Ilbrahim was young to be sad for such a cause, from wounded love. The flightiness of his mirth rendered him often guilty of offences against the decorum of a Puritan household, and on these occasions he did not invariably escape rebuke. But the slightest word of real bitterness, which he was infallible in distinguishing from pretended anger, seemed to sink into his heart and poison all his enjoyments, till he became sensible that he was entirely forgiven. Of the malice, which generally accompanies a superfluity of sensitiveness, Ilbrahim was altogether destitute; when trodden upon, he would not turn; when wounded, he could but die. His mind was wanting in the stamina for self-support; it was a plant that would twine beautifully round something stronger than itself, but if repulsed or torn away, it had no choice but to wither on the ground. Dorothy's acuteness taught her that severity would crush the spirit of the child, and she nurtured him with the gentle care of one who handles a butterfly. Her husband manifested an equal affection, although it grew daily less productive of familiar caresses.

The feelings of the neighboring people, in regard to the Quaker infant and his protectors, had not undergone a favorable change, in spite of the momentary triumph which the desolate mother had obtained over their sympathies. The scorn and bitterness of which he was the object, were very grievous to Ilbrahim, especially when any circumstance made him sensible that the children, his equals in age, partook of the enmity of their parents. His tender and social nature had already overflowed in attachments to everything about him, and still there was a residue of unappropriated love, which he yearned to bestow upon the little ones who were taught to hate him. As the warm days of spring came on, Ilbraham was accustomed to remain for hours, silent and inactive, within hearing of the children's voices at their play; yet, with his usual delicacy of feeling, he avoided their notice, and would flee and hide himself from the smallest individual among them. Chance, however, at length seemed to open a medium of communication between his heart and theirs; it was by means of a boy about two years older than Ilbrahim, who was injured by a fall from a tree in the vicinity of Pearson's habitation. As the sufferer's own home was at some distance, Dorothy willingly received him under her roof and became his tender and careful nurse.

Ilbrahim was the unconscious possessor of much skill in physiognomy, and it would have deterred him, in other circumstances, from attempting to make a friend of this boy. The countenance of the latter immediately impressed a beholder disagreeably, but it required some examination to discover that the cause was a very slight distortion of the mouth, and the irregular, broken line, and near approach of the eyebrows. Analogous, perhaps, to these trifling deformities, was an almost imperceptible twist of every joint, and the uneven prominence of the breast; forming a body, regular in its general outline, but faulty in almost all its details. The disposition of the boy was sullen and reserved, and the village schoolmaster stigmatized him as obtuse in intellect; although, at a later period of life, he evinced ambition and very peculiar talents. But whatever might be his personal or moral irregularities, Ilbrahim's heart seized upon, and clung to him, from the moment that he was brought wounded into the cottage; the child of persecution seemed to compare his own fate with that of the sufferer, and to feel that even different modes of misfortune had created a sort of relationship between them. Food, rest, and the fresh air, for which he languished, were neglected; he nestled continually by the bedside of the little stranger, and, with a fond jealousy, endeavored to be the medium of all the cares that were bestowed upon him. As the boy became convalescent, Ilbrahim contrived games suitable to his situation, or amused him by a faculty which he had perhaps breathed in with the air of his barbaric birthplace. It was that of reciting imaginary adventures, on the spur of the moment, and apparently in inexhaustible succession. His tales were of course monstrous, disjointed, and without aim; but they were curious on account of a vein of human tenderness, which ran through them all, and was like a sweet, familiar face, encountered in the midst of wild and unearthly scenery. The auditor paid much attention to these romances, and sometimes interrupted them by brief remarks upon the incidents, displaying shrewdness above his years, mingled with a moral obliquity which grated very harshly against Ilbrahim's instinctive rectitude. Nothing, however, could arrest the progress of the latter's affection, and there were many proofs that it met with a response from the dark and stubborn nature on which it was lavished. The boy's parents at length removed him, to complete his cure under their own roof.

Ilbrahim did not visit his new friend after his departure; but he made anxious and continual inquiries respecting him, and informed himself of the day when he was to reappear among his playmates. On a pleasant summer afternoon, the children of the neighborhood had assembled in the little forest-crowned amphitheatre behind the meeting-house, and the recovering invalid was there, leaning on a staff. The glee of a score of untainted bosoms was heard in light and airy voices, which danced among the trees like sunshine become audible; the grown men of this weary world, as they journeyed by the spot, marvelled why life, beginning in such brightness, should proceed in gloom; and their hearts, or their imaginations, answered them and said, that the bliss of childhood gushes from its innocence. But it happened that an unexpected addition was made to the heavenly little band. It was Ilbrahim, who came towards the children with a look of sweet confidence on his fair and spiritual face, as if, having manifested his love to one of them, he had no longer to fear a repulse from their society. A hush came over their mirth the moment they beheld him, and they stood whispering to each other while he drew nigh; but, all at once, the devil of their fathers entered into the unbreeched fanatics, and sending up a fierce, shrill cry, they rushed upon the poor Quaker child. In an instant, he was the centre of a brood of baby-fiends, who lifted sticks against him, pelted him with stones, and displayed an instinct of destruction far more loathsome than the bloodthirstiness of manhood.

The invalid, in the mean while, stood apart from the tumult, crying out with a loud voice, "Fear not, Ilbrahim, come hither and take my hand"; and his unhappy friend endeavored to obey him.

After watching the victim's struggling approach, with a calm smile and unabashed eye, the foul-hearted little villain lifted his staff, and struck Ibrahim on the mouth, so forcibly that the blood issued in a stream. The poor child's arms had been raised to guard his head from the storm of blows; but now he dropped them at once. His persecutors beat him down, trampled upon him, dragged him by his long, fair locks, and Ibrahim was on the point of becoming as veritable a martyr as ever entered bleeding into Heaven. The uproar, however, attracted the notice of a few neighbors, who put themselves to the trouble of rescuing the little heretic, and of conveying him to Pearson's door.

Ibrahim's bodily harm was severe, but long and careful nursing accomplished his recovery; the injury done to his sensitive spirit was more serious, though not so visible. Its signs were principally of a negative character, and to be discovered only by those who had previously known him. His gait was thenceforth slow, even, and unvaried by the sudden bursts of sprightlier motion, which had once corresponded to his overflowing gladness; his countenance was heavier, and its former play of expression, the dance of sunshine reflected from moving water, was destroyed by the cloud over his existence; his notice was attracted in a far less degree by passing events, and he appeared to find greater difficulty in comprehending what was new to him, than at a happier period. A stranger, founding his judgment upon these circumstances, would have said that the dulness of the child's intellect widely contradicted the promise of his features;

but the secret was in the direction of Ibrahim's thoughts, which were brooding within him when they should naturally have been wandering abroad. An attempt of Dorothy to revive his former sportiveness was the single occasion, on which his quiet demeanor yielded to a violent display of grief; he burst into passionate weeping, and ran and hid himself, for his heart had become so miserably sore, that even the hand of kindness tortured it like fire. Sometimes, at night, and probably in his dreams, he was heard to cry, "Mother! Mother!" as if her place, which a stranger had supplied while Ibrahim was happy, admitted of no substitute in his extreme affliction. Perhaps, among the many life-weary wretches then upon the earth, there was not one who combined innocence and misery like this poor, broken-hearted infant, so soon the victim of his own heavenly nature.

While this melancholy change had taken place in Ibrahim, one of an earlier origin and of different character, had come to its perfection in his adopted father. The incident with which this tale commences found Pearson in a state of religious dulness, yet mentally disquieted, and longing for a more fervid faith than he possessed. The first effect of his kindness to Ibrahim was to produce a softened feeling, and incipient love for the child's whole sect; but joined to this, and resulting perhaps from self-suspicion, was a proud and ostentatious contempt of their tenets and practical extravagances. In the course of much thought, however, for the subject struggled irresistibly into his mind, the foolishness of the doctrine began to be less evident, and the points which had particularly offended his reason assumed another aspect, or vanished entirely away. The work within him appeared to go on even while he slept, and that which had been a doubt, when he laid down to rest, would often hold the place of a truth, confirmed by some forgotten demonstration, when he recalled his thoughts in the morning. But while he was thus becoming assimilated to the enthusiasts, his contempt, in no wise decreasing towards them, grew very fierce against himself; he imagined, also, that every face of his acquaintance wore a sneer, and that every word addressed to him was a gibe. Such was his state of mind at the period of Ilbrahim's misfortune; and the emotions consequent upon that event completed the change, of which the child had been the original instrument.

In the mean time, neither the fierceness of the persecutors, nor the infatuation of their victims, had decreased. The dungeons were never empty; the streets of almost every village echoed daily with the lash; the life of a woman, whose mild and Christian spirit no cruelty could embitter, had been sacrificed; and more innocent blood was yet to pollute the hands that were so often raised in prayer. Early after the Restoration, the English Quakers represented to Charles II. that a "vein of blood was open in his dominions"; but though the displeasure of the voluptuous king was roused, his interference was not prompt. And now the tale must stride forward over many months, leaving Pearson to encounter ignominy and misfortune; his wife to a firm endurance of a thousand sorrows; poor Ilbrahim to pine and droop like a cankered rosebud; his mother to wander on a mistaken errand, neglectful of the

holiest trust which can be committed to a woman.

*   *   *   *   *   *

A winter evening, a night of storm, had darkened over Pearson's habitation, and there were no cheerful faces to drive the gloom from his broad hearth. The fire, it is true, sent forth a glowing heat and a ruddy light, and large logs, dripping with half-melted snow, lay ready to be cast upon the embers. But the apartment was saddened in its aspect by the absence of much of the homely wealth which had once adorned it; for the exaction of repeated fines, and his own neglect of temporal affairs, had greatly impoverished the owner. And with the furniture of peace, the implements of war had likewise disappeared; the sword was broken, the helm and cuirass were cast away forever; the soldier had done with battles, and might not lift so much as his naked hand to guard his head. But the Holy Book remained, and the table on which it rested was drawn before the fire, while two of the persecuted sect sought comfort from its pages.

He who listened, while the other read, was the master of the house, now emaciated in form, and altered as to the expression and healthiness of his countenance; for his mind had dwelt too long among visionary thoughts, and his body had been worn by imprisonment and stripes. The hale and weatherbeaten old man, who sat beside him, had sustained less injury from a far longer course of the same mode of life. In person he was tall and dignified, and, which alone would have made him hateful to the Puritans, his gray locks fell from beneath the broadbrimmed hat, and rested on his shoulders. As the old man read the sacred page, the snow drifted against the windows, or eddied in at the crevices of the door, while a blast kept laughing in the chimney, and the blaze leaped fiercely up to seek it. And sometimes, when the wind struck the hill at a certain angle, and swept down by the cottage across the wintry plain, its voice was the most doleful that can be conceived; it came as if the Past were speaking, as if the Dead had contributed each a whisper, as if the Desolation of Ages were breathed in that one lamenting sound.

The Quaker at length closed the book, retaining however his hand between the pages which he had been reading, while he looked steadfastly at Pearson. The attitude and features of the latter might have indicated the endurance of bodily pain; he leaned his forehead on his hands, his teeth were firmly closed, and his frame was tremulous at intervals with a nervous agitation.

"Friend Tobias," inquired the old man, compassionately, "hast thou found no comfort in these many blessed passages of Scripture?"

"Thy voice has fallen on my ear like a sound afar off and indistinct," replied Pearson, without lifting his eyes. "Yea, and when I have hearkened carefully, the words seemed cold and lifeless, and intended for another and a lesser grief than mine. Remove the book," he added, in a tone of sullen bitterness. "I have no part in its consolations, and they do but fret my sorrow the more."

"Nay, feeble brother, be not as one who hath never known the light," said the elder Quaker, earnestly, but with mildness. "Art thou he that wouldst

be content to give all, and endure all for conscience' sake; desiring even peculiar trials, that thy faith might be purified, and thy heart weaned from worldly desires? And wilt thou sink beneath an affliction which happens alike to them that have their portion here below, and to them that lay up treasure in heaven? Faint not, for thy burden is yet light."

"It is heavy! It is heavier than I can bear!" exclaimed Pearson, with the impatience of a variable spirit. "From my youth upward I have been a man marked out for wrath; and year by year, yea, day after day, I have endured sorrows, such as others know not in their lifetime. And now I speak not of the love that has been turned to hatred, the honor to ignominy, the ease and plentifulness of all things to danger, want, and nakedness. All this I could have borne, and counted myself blessed. But when my heart was desolate with many losses I fixed it upon the child of a stranger, and he became dearer to me than all my buried ones; and now he too must die as if my love were poison. Verily, I am an accursed man, and I will lay me down in the dust, and lift up my head no more."

"Thou sinnest, brother, but it is not for me to rebuke thee; for I also have had my hours of darkness, wherein I have murmured against the cross," said the old Quaker. He continued, perhaps in the hope of distracting his companion's thoughts from his own sorrows. "Even of late was the light obscured within me, when the men of blood had banished me on pain of death, and the constables led me onward from village to village, towards the wilderness. A strong and cruel hand was wielding the knotted cords; they sunk deep into the flesh, and thou mightst have tracked every reel and totter of my footsteps by the blood that followed. As we went on—"

"Have I not borne all this; and have I murmured?" interrupted Pearson, impatiently.

"Nay, friend, but hear me," continued the other. "As we journeyed on, night darkened on our path, so that no man could see the rage of the persecutors, or the constancy of my endurance, though Heaven forbid that I should glory therein. The lights began to glimmer in the cottage windows, and I could discern the inmates as they gathered in comfort and security, every man with his wife and children by their own evening hearth. At length we came to a tract of fertile land; in the dim light the forest was not visible around it; and behold! there was a straw-thatched dwelling, which bore the very aspect of my home, far over the wild ocean, far in our own England. Then came bitter thoughts upon me; yea, remembrances that were like death to my soul. The happiness of my early days was painted to me; the disquiet of my manhood, the altered faith of my declining years. I remembered how I had been moved to go forth a wanderer, when my daughter, the youngest, the dearest of my flock, lay on her dying bed, and—"

"Couldst thou obey the command at such a moment?" exclaimed Pearson, shuddering.

"Yea, yea," replied the old man, hurriedly. "I was kneeling by her bedside when the voice spoke loud within me; but immediately I rose, and took my staff, and gat me gone. O, that it were

permitted me to forget her woful look when I thus withdrew my arm, and left her journeying through the dark valley alone! for her soul was faint, and she had leaned upon my prayers. Now in that night of horror I was assailed by the thought that I had been an erring Christian, and a cruel parent; yea, even my daughter, with her pale, dying features, seemed to stand by me and whisper, 'Father, you are deceived; go home and shelter your gray head.' O Thou, to whom I have looked in my farthest wanderings," continued the Quaker, raising his agitated eyes to Heaven, "inflict not upon the bloodiest of our persecutors the unmitigated agony of my soul, when I believed that all I had done and suffered for Thee was at the instigation of a mocking fiend! But I yielded not; I knelt down and wrestled with the tempter, while the scourge bit more fiercely into the flesh. My prayer was heard, and I went on in peace and joy towards the wilderness."

The old man, though his fanaticism had generally all the calmness of reason, was deeply moved while reciting this tale; and his unwonted emotion seemed to rebuke and keep down that of his companion. They sat in silence, with their faces to the fire, imagining perhaps, in its red embers, new scenes of persecution yet to be encountered. The snow still drifted hard against the windows, and sometimes, as the blaze of the logs had gradually sunk, came down the spacious chimney and hissed upon the hearth. A cautious footstep might now and then be heard in a neighboring apartment, and the sound invariably drew the eyes of both Quakers to the door which led thither. When a fierce and riotous gust of wind had led his thoughts, by a natural association, to homeless travellers on such a night, Pearson resumed the conversation.

"I have wellnigh sunk under my own share of this trial," observed he, sighing heavily; "yet I would that it might be doubled to me, if so the child's mother could be spared. Her wounds have been deep and many, but this will be the sorest of all."

"Fear not for Catharine," replied the old Quaker; "for I know that valiant woman, and have seen how she can bear the cross. A mother's heart, indeed, is strong in her, and may seem to contend mightily with her faith; but soon she will stand up and give thanks that her son has been thus early an accepted sacrifice. The boy hath done his work, and she will feel that he is taken hence in kindness both to him and her. Blessed, blessed are they, that with so little suffering can enter into peace!"

The fitful rush of the wind was now disturbed by a portentous sound; it was a quick and heavy knocking at the outer door. Pearson's wan countenance grew paler, for many a visit of persecution had taught him what to dread; the old man, on the other hand, stood up erect, and his glance was firm as that of the tried soldier, who awaits his enemy.

"The men of blood have come to seek me," he observed, with calmness. "They have heard how I was moved to return from banishment; and now am I to be led to prison, and thence to death. It is an end I have long looked for. I will open unto them, lest they say, 'Lo, he feareth!'"

"Nay, I will present myself before them," said Pearson, with recovered fortitude. "It may be that they seek me alone, and know not that thou abidest with me."

"Let us go boldly, both one and the other," rejoined his companion. "It is not fitting that thou or I should shrink."

They therefore proceeded through the entry to the door, which they opened, bidding the applicant "Come in, in God's name!" A furious blast of wind drove the storm into their faces, and extinguished the lamp; they had barely time to discern a figure, so white from head to foot with the drifted snow, that it seemed like Winter's self, come in human shape to seek refuge from its own desolation.

"Enter, friend, and do thy errand, be it what it may," said Pearson. "It must needs be pressing, since thou comest on such a bitter night."

"Peace be with this household," said the stranger, when they stood on the floor of the inner apartment.

Pearson started, the elder Quaker stirred the slumbering embers of the fire, till they sent up a clear and lofty blaze; it was a female voice that had spoken; it was a female form that shone out, cold and wintry, in that comfortable light.

"Catharine, blessed woman," exclaimed the old man, "art thou come to this darkened land again? art thou come to bear a valiant testimony as in former years? The scourge hath not prevailed against thee, and from the dungeon hast thou come forth triumphant; but strengthen, strengthen now thy heart, Catharine, for Heaven will prove thee yet this once, ere thou go to thy reward."

"Rejoice, friends!" she replied. "Thou who hast long been of our people, and thou whom a little child hath led to us, rejoice! Lo! I come, the messenger of glad tidings, for the day of persecution is overpast. The heart of the king, even Charles, hath been moved in gentleness towards us, and he hath sent forth his letters to stay the hands of the men of blood. A ship's company of our friends hath arrived at yonder town, and I also sailed joyfully among them."

As Catharine spoke, her eyes were roaming about the room, in search of him for whose sake security was dear to her. Pearson made a silent appeal to the old man, nor did the latter shrink from the painful task assigned him.

"Sister," he began, in a softened yet perfectly calm tone, "thou tellest us of His love, manifested in temporal good; and now must we speak to thee of that selfsame love, displayed in chastenings. Hitherto, Catharine, thou hast been as one journeying in a darksome and difficult path, and leading an infant by the hand; fain wouldst thou have looked heavenward continually, but still the cares of that little child have drawn thine eyes and thy affections to the earth. Sister, go on rejoicing, for his tottering footsteps shall impede thine own no more."

But the unhappy mother was not thus to be consoled; she shook like a leaf, she turned white as the very snow that hung drifted into her hair. The firm old man extended his hand and held her up, keeping his eye upon hers, as if to repress any outbreak of passion.

"I am a woman, I am but a woman; will He try me above my strength?" said Catharine, very quickly, and almost in a whisper. "I have been wounded sore; I have suffered much; many things in the body, many in the mind; crucified in myself, and in them that were dearest to me. Surely," added she, with a long shudder, "He hath spared me in this one thing." She broke forth with sudden and irrepressible violence. "Tell me, man of cold heart, what has God done to me? Hath He cast me down, never to rise again? Hath He crushed my very heart in his hand? And thou, to whom I committed my child, how hast thou fulfilled thy trust? Give me back the boy, well, sound, alive, alive; or earth and heaven shall avenge me!"

The agonized shriek of Catharine was answered by the faint, the very faint voice of a child.

On this day it had become evident to Pearson, to his aged guest, and to Dorothy, that Ilbrahim's brief and troubled pilgrimage drew near its close. The two former would willingly have remained by him, to make use of the prayers and pious discourses which they deemed appropriate to the time, and which, if they be impotent as to the departing traveller's reception in the world whither it goes, may at least sustain him in bidding adieu to earth. But though Ilbrahim uttered no complaint, he was disturbed by the faces that looked upon him; so that Dorothy's entreaties, and their own conviction that the child's feet might tread Heaven's pavement and not soil it, had induced the two Quakers to remove. Ilbrahim then closed his eyes and grew calm, and, except for now and then a kind and low word to his nurse, might have been thought to slumber. As nightfall came on, however, and the storm began to rise, something seemed to trouble the repose of the boy's mind, and to render his sense of hearing active and acute. If a passing wind lingered to shake the casement, he strove to turn his head towards it; if the door jarred to and fro upon its hinges, he looked long and anxiously thitherward; if the heavy voice of the old man, as he read the Scriptures, rose but a little higher, the child almost held his dying breath to listen; if a snow-drift swept by the cottage, with a sound like the trailing of a garment, Ilbrahim seemed to watch that some visitant should enter.

But, after a little time, he relinquished whatever secret hope had agitated him, and, with one low, complaining whisper, turned his cheek upon the pillow. He then addressed Dorothy with his usual sweetness, and besought her to draw near him; she did so, and Ilbrahim took her hand in both of his, grasping it with a gentle pressure, as if to assure himself that he retained it. At intervals, and without disturbing the repose of his countenance, a very faint trembling passed over him from head to foot, as if a mild but somewhat cool wind had breathed upon him, and made him shiver. As the boy thus led her by the hand in his quiet progress over the borders of eternity, Dorothy almost imagined that she could discern the near, though dim delightfulness, of the home he was about to reach; she would not have enticed the little wanderer back, though she bemoaned herself that she must leave him and return. But just when Ilbrahim's feet were pressing on the soil of Paradise, he heard a voice behind him, and it recalled him a few, few paces of the weary path which he had travelled. As Dorothy looked upon his features, she perceived that their placid expression

was again disturbed; her own thoughts had been so wrapped in him, that all sounds of the storm, and of human speech, were lost to her; but when Catharine's shriek pierced through the room, the boy strove to raise himself.

"Friend, she is come! Open unto her!" cried he.

In a moment, his mother was kneeling by the bedside; she drew Ilbrahim to her bosom, and he nestled there, with no violence of joy, but contentedly as if he were hushing himself to sleep. He looked into her face, and reading its agony, said, with feeble earnestness, "Mourn not, dearest Mother. I am happy now." And with these words, the gentle boy was dead.

*   *   *   *   *   *

The king's mandate to stay the New England persecutors was effectual in preventing further martyrdoms; but the colonial authorities, trusting in the remoteness of their situation, and perhaps in the supposed instability of the royal government, shortly renewed their severities in all other respects. Catharine's fanaticism had become wilder by the sundering of all human ties; and wherever a scourge was lifted, there was she to receive the blow; and whenever a dungeon was unbarred, thither she came to cast herself upon the floor. But in process of time, a more Christian spirit,—a spirit of forbearance, though not of cordiality or approbation, began to pervade the land in regard to the persecuted sect. And then, when the rigid old Pilgrims eyed her rather in pity than in wrath; when the matrons fed her with the fragments of their children's food, and offered her a lodging on a hard and lowly bed; when no little crowd of school-boys left their sports to cast stones after the roving enthusiast; then did Catharine return to Pearson's dwelling, and made that her home.

As if Ilbrahim's sweetness yet lingered round his ashes; as if his gentle spirit came down from Heaven to teach his parent a true religion, her fierce and vindictive nature was softened by the same griefs which had once irritated it. When the course of years had made the features of the unobtrusive mourner familiar in the settlement, she became a subject of not deep, but general interest; a being on whom the otherwise superfluous sympathies of all might be bestowed. Every one spoke of her with that degree of pity which it is pleasant to experience; every one was ready to do her the little kindnesses, which are not costly, yet manifest good will; and when at last she died, a long train of her once bitter persecutors followed her, with decent sadness and tears that were not painful, to her place by Ilbrahim's green and sunken grave.

MR. HIGGINBOTHAM'S CATASTROPHE

A YOUNG fellow, a tobacco pedler by trade, was on his way from Morristown, where he had dealt largely with the Deacon of the Shaker settlement, to the village of Parker's Falls, on Salmon River. He had a neat little cart, painted green, with a box of cigars depicted on each side pannel, and an Indian chief, holding a pipe and a golden tobacco-stalk, on the rear. The pedler drove a smart little mare, and was a young man of excellent character, keen at a bargain, but none the worse liked by the Yankees; who, as I have heard them say, would rather be shaved with a sharp razor than a dull one. Especially was he beloved by the pretty girls along the Connecticut, whose favor he used to court by presents of the best smoking tobacco in his stock; knowing well that the country lasses of New England are generally great performers on pipes. Moreover, as will be seen in the course of my story, the pedler was inquisitive, and something of a tattler, always itching to hear the news, and anxious to tell it again.

After an early breakfast at Morristown, the tobacco pedler, whose name was Dominicus Pike, had travelled seven miles through a solitary piece of woods, without speaking a word to anybody but himself and his little gray mare. It being nearly seven o'clock, he was as eager to hold a morning gossip as a city shopkeeper to read the morning paper. An opportunity seemed at hand, when, after lighting a cigar with a sunglass, he looked up, and perceived a man coming over the brow of the hill, at the foot of which the pedler had stopped his green cart. Dominicus watched him as he descended, and noticed that he carried a bundle over his shoulder on the end of a stick, and travelled with a weary, yet determined pace. He did not look as if he had started in the freshness of the morning, but had footed it all night: and meant to do the same all day.

"Good morning, mister," said Dominicus, when within speaking distance. "You go a pretty good jog. What's the latest news at Parker's Falls?"

The man pulled the broad brim of a gray hat over his eyes, and answered, rather sullenly, that he did not come from Parker's Falls, which, as being the limit of his own day's journey, the pedler had naturally mentioned in his inquiry.

"Well, then," rejoined Dominicus Pike, "let's have the latest news where you did come from. I'm not particular about Parker's Falls. Any place will answer."

Being thus importuned, the traveller —who was as ill looking a fellow as one would desire to meet, in a solitary piece of woods—appeared to hesitate a little, as if he was either searching his memory for news, or weighing the expediency of telling it. At last mounting on the step of the cart, he whispered in the ear of Dominicus, though he might have shouted aloud, and no other mortal would have heard him.

"I do remember one little trifle of news," said he. "Old Mr. Higginbotham, of Kimballton, was murdered in his orchard, at eight o'clock last night, by an Irishman and a nigger. They strung him up to the branch of a St. Michael's pear-tree, where nobody would find him till the morning."

As soon as this horrible intelligence was communicated, the stranger betook himself to his journey again, with more speed than ever, not even turning his head when Dominicus invited him to smoke a Spanish cigar and relate all the particulars. The pedler whistled to his mare and went up the hill, pondering on the doleful fate of Mr. Higginbotham, whom he had known in the way of trade, having sold him many a bunch of long nines, and a great deal of pigtail, lady's twist, and fig tobacco. He was rather astonished at the rapidity with which the news had spread. Kimballton was nearly sixty miles distant in a straight line; the murder had been perpetrated only at eight o'clock the preceding night; yet Dominicus had heard of it at seven in the morning, when, in all probability, poor Mr. Higginbotham's own family had but just discovered his corpse, hanging on the St. Michael's pear-tree. The stranger on foot must have worn seven-league boots, to travel at such a rate.

"Ill news flies fast, they say," thought Dominicus Pike; "but this beats railroads. The fellow ought to be hired to go express with the President's Message."

The difficulty was solved, by supposing that the narrator had made a mistake of one day, in the date of the occurrence; so that our friend did not hesitate to introduce the story at every tavern and country store along the road, expending a whole bunch of Spanish wrappers among at least twenty horrified audiences. He found himself invariably the first bearer of the intelligence, and was so pestered with questions that he could not avoid filling up the outline, till it became quite a respectable narrative. He met with one piece of corroborative evidence. Mr. Higginbotham was a trader; and a former clerk of his, to whom Dominicus related the facts, testified that the old gentleman was accustomed to return home through the orchard, about nightfall, with the money and valuable papers of the store in his pocket. The clerk manifested but little grief at Mr. Higginbotham's catastrophe, hinting, what the pedler had discovered in his own dealings with him, that he was a crusty old fellow, as close as a vice. His property would descend to a pretty niece who was now keeping school in Kimballton.

What with telling the news for the public good, and driving bargains for his own, Dominicus was so much delayed on the road, that he chose to put up at a tavern, about five miles short of Parker's Falls. After supper, lighting one of his prime cigars, he seated himself in the bar-room, and went through the story of the murder, which had grown so fast that it took him half an hour to tell. There were as many as twenty people in the room, nineteen of whom received it all for gospel. But the twentieth was an elderly farmer, who had arrived on horseback a short time before, and was now seated in a corner, smoking his pipe. When the story was concluded, he rose up very deliberately, brought his chair right in front of Dominicus, and stared him full in the face, puffing out the vilest tobacco smoke the pedler had ever smelt.

"Will you make affidavit," demanded he, in the tone of a country justice taking an examination, "that old Squire Higginbotham of Kimballton was murdered in his orchard the night before last, and found hanging on his great pear-tree yesterday morning?"

"I tell the story as I heard it, mister," answered Dominicus, dropping his half-burnt cigar; "I don't say that I saw the thing done. So I can't take my oath that he was murdered exactly in that way."

"But I can take mine," said the farmer, "that if Squire Higginbotham was murdered night before last, I drank a glass of bitters with his ghost this morning. Being a neighbor of mine, he called me into his store, as I was riding by, and treated me, and then asked me to do a little business for him on the road. He didn't seem to know any more about his own murder than I did."

"Why, then, it can't be a fact!" exclaimed Dominicus Pike.

"I guess he'd have mentioned, if it was," said the old farmer; and he removed his chair back to the corner, leaving Dominicus quite down in the mouth.

Here was a sad resurrection of old Mr. Higginbotham! The pedler had no heart to mingle in the conversation any more, but comforted himself with a glass of gin and water, and went to bed, where, all night long, he dreamed of hanging on the St. Michael's pear-tree. To avoid the old farmer, (whom he so detested, that his suspicion would have pleased him better than Mr. Higginbotham's,) Dominicus rose in the gray of the morning, put the little mare into the green cart, and trotted swiftly away towards Parker's Falls. The fresh breeze, the dewy road, and the pleasant summer dawn revived his spirits, and might have encouraged him to repeat the old story, had there been anybody awake to hear it. But he met neither ox team, light wagon, chaise, horseman, nor foot traveller, till, just as he crossed Salmon River, a man came trudging down to the bridge with a bundle over his shoulder, on the end of a stick.

"Good morning, mister," said the pedler, reining in his mare. "If you come from Kimballton or that neighborhood, may be you can tell me the real fact about this affair of old Mr. Higginbotham. Was the old fellow actually murdered two or three nights ago, by an Irishman and a nigger?"

Dominicus had spoken in too great a hurry to observe, at first, that the stranger himself had a deep tinge of negro blood. On hearing this sudden question, the Ethiopian appeared to change his skin, its yellow hue becoming a ghastly white, while, shaking and stammering, he thus replied:—

"No! no! There was no colored man! It was an Irishman that hanged him last night, at eight o'clock. I came away at seven! His folks can't have looked for him in the orchard yet."

Scarcely had the yellow man spoken when he interrupted himself, and though he seemed weary enough before, continued his journey at a pace which would have kept the pedler's mare on a smart trot. Dominicus stared after him in great perplexity. If the murder had not been committed till Tuesday night, who was the prophet that had foretold it, in all its circumstances, on Tuesday morning? If Mr. Higginbotham's corpse were not yet discovered by his own family, how came the mulatto, at above thirty miles' distance, to know that he was hanging in the orchard, especially as he had left Kimballton before the unfortunate man was hanged at all? These ambiguous circumstances, with the stranger's surprise and terror, made Dominicus think of raising a hue and cry after him, as an accomplice in the murder; since a murder, it seemed, had really been perpetrated.

"But let the poor devil go," thought the pedler. "I don't want his black blood on my head; and hanging the nigger wouldn't unhang Mr. Higginbotham. Unhang the old gentleman! It's a sin, I know; but I should hate to have him come to life a second time, and give me the lie!"

With these meditations, Dominicus Pike drove into the street of Parker's Falls, which, as everybody knows, is as thriving a village as three cotton-factories and a slitting-mill can make it. The machinery was not in motion, and but a few of the shop-doors unbarred, when he alighted in the stable-yard of the tavern, and made it his first business to order the mare four quarts of oats. His second duty, of course, was to impart Mr. Higginbotham's catastrophe to the ostler. He deemed it advisable, however, not to be too positive as to the date of the direful fact, and also to be uncertain whether it were perpetrated by an Irishman and a mulatto, or by the son of Erin alone. Neither did he profess to relate it on his own authority, or that of any one person; but mentioned it as a report generally diffused.

The story ran through the town like fire among girdled trees, and became so much the universal talk, that nobody could tell whence it had originated. Mr. Higginbotham was as well known at Parker's Falls as any citizen of the place, being part owner of the slitting-mill, and a considerable stockholder in the cotton-factories. The inhabitants felt their own prosperity interested in his fate. Such was the excitement, that the Parker's Falls Gazette anticipated its regular day of publication, and came out with half a form of blank paper and a column of double pica emphasized with capitals, and headed HORRID MURDER OF MR. HIGGINBOTHAM!

Among other dreadful details, the printed account described the mark of the cord round the dead man's neck, and stated the number of thousand dollars of which he had been robbed; there was much pathos also about the affliction of his niece, who had gone from one fainting fit to another, ever since her uncle was found hanging on the St. Michael's pear-tree with his pockets inside out. The village poet likewise commemorated the young lady's grief in seventeen stanzas of a ballad. The selectmen held a meeting, and in consideration of Mr. Higginbotham's claims on the town, determined to issue handbills, offering a reward of five hundred dollars for the apprehension of his murderers, and the recovery of the stolen property.

Meanwhile, the whole population of Parker's Falls, consisting of shopkeepers, mistresses of boarding-houses, factory-girls, millmen, and school-boys, rushed into the street and kept up such a terrible loquacity, as more than compensated for the silence of the cotton-machines, which refrained from their usual din out of respect to the deceased. Had Mr. Higginbotham cared about posthumous renown, his untimely ghost would have exulted in this tumult. Our friend Dominicus, in his vanity of heart, forgot his intended precautions, and mounting on the town-pump announced himself as the bearer of the authentic intelligence which had caused so wonderful a sensation. He immediately became the great man of the moment, and had just begun a new edition of the narrative, with a voice like a field preacher, when the mail stage drove into the village street. It had travelled all night, and must have shifted horses at Kimballton, at three in the morning.

"Now we shall hear all the particulars," shouted the crowd.

The coach rumbled up to the piazza of the tavern, followed by a thousand people; for if any man had been minding his own business till then, he now left it at sixes and sevens to hear the news. The pedler, foremost in the race, discovered two passengers, both of whom had been startled from a comfortable nap to find themselves in the centre of a mob. Every man assailing them with separate questions, all propounded at once, the couple were struck speechless, though one was a lawyer and the other a young lady.

"Mr. Higginbotham! Mr. Higginbotham! Tell us the particulars about old Mr. Higginbotham!" bawled the mob. "What is the coroner's verdict? Are the murderers apprehended? Is Mr. Higginbotham's niece come out of her fainting fits? Mr. Higginbotham! Mr. Higginbotham!!"

The coachman said not a word, except to swear awfully at the ostler for not bringing him a fresh team of horses. The lawyer inside had generally his wits about him even when asleep; the first thing he did, after learning the cause of the excitement, was to produce a large, red pocket-book. Meantime, Dominicus Pike, being an extremely polite young man, and also suspecting that a female tongue would tell the story as glibly as a lawyer's, had handed the lady out of the coach. She was a fine, smart girl, now wide awake and bright as a button, and had such a sweet pretty mouth, that Dominicus would almost as lief have heard a love-tale from it as a tale of murder.

"Gentleman and ladies," said the lawyer, to the shopkeepers, the mill-men, and the factory-girls, "I can assure you that some unaccountable mistake, or, more probably, a wilful falsehood, maliciously contrived to injure Mr. Higginbotham's credit, has excited this singular uproar. We passed through Kimballton at three o'clock this morning, and most certainly should have been informed of the murder, had any been perpetrated. But I have proof nearly as strong as Mr. Higginbotham's own oral testimony, in the negative. Here is a note, relating to a suit of his in the Connecticut courts, which was delivered me from that gentleman himself. I find it dated at ten o'clock last evening."

So saying, the lawyer exhibited the date and signature of the note, which irrefragably proved, either that this perverse Mr. Higginbotham was alive when he wrote it, or—as some deemed the more probable case, of two doubtful ones—that he was so absorbed in worldly business as to continue to transact it, even after his death. But unexpected evidence was forthcoming. The young lady, after listening to the pedler's explanation, merely seized a moment to smooth her gown and put her curls in order, and then appeared at the tavern door, making a modest signal to be heard.

"Good people," said she, "I am Mr. Higginbotham's niece."

A wondering murmur passed through the crowd, on beholding her so rosy and bright; that same unhappy niece, whom they had supposed, on the authority of the Parker's Falls Gazette, to be lying at death's door in a fainting-fit. But some shrewd fellows had doubted, all along, whether a young lady would be quite so desperate at the hanging of a rich old uncle.

"You see," continued Miss Higginbotham, with a smile, "that this strange story is quite unfounded as to myself; and I believe I may affirm it to be equally so in regard to my dear uncle Higginbotham. He has the kindness to give me a home in his house, though I contribute to my own support by teaching a school. I left Kimballton this morning to spend the vacation of commencement week with a friend, about five miles from Parker's Falls. My generous uncle, when he heard me on the stairs, called me to his bedside, and gave me two dollars and fifty cents to pay my stage fare, and another dollar for my extra expenses. He then laid his pocketbook under his pillow, shook hands with me, and advised me to take some biscuit in my bag, instead of breakfasting on the road. I feel confident, therefore, that I left my beloved relative alive, and trust that I shall find him so on my return."

The young lady courtesied at the close of her speech, which was so sensible, and well worded, and delivered with such grace and propriety, that everybody thought her fit to be preceptress of the best academy in the State. But a stranger would have supposed that Mr. Higginbotham was an object of abhorrence at Parker's Falls, and that a thanksgiving had been proclaimed for his murder; so excessive was the wrath of the inhabitants on learning their mistake. The millmen resolved to bestow public honors on Dominicus Pike, only hesitating whether to tar and feather him, ride him on a rail, or refresh him with an ablution at the town-pump, on the top of which he had declared himself the bearer of the news. The selectmen, by advice of the lawyer, spoke of prosecuting him for a misdemeanor, in circulating unfounded reports, to the great disturbance of the peace of the commonwealth. Nothing saved Dominicus, either from mob law or a court of justice, but an eloquent appeal made by the young lady in his behalf. Addressing a few words of heartfelt gratitude to his benefactress, he mounted the green cart and rode out of town, under a discharge of artillery from the school-boys, who found plenty of ammunition in the neighboring clay-pits and mud-holes. As he turned his head, to exchange a farewell glance at Mr. Higginbotham's niece, a ball, of the consistence of hasty-pudding, hit him slap in the mouth, giving him a most grim aspect. His whole person was so bespattered with the like filthy missiles, that he had almost a mind to ride back, and supplicate for the threatened ablution at the town-pump; for, though not meant in kindness, it would now have been a deed of charity.

However, the sun shone bright on poor Dominicus, and the mud, an emblem of all stains of undeserved opprobium, was easily brushed off when dry. Being a funny rogue, his heart soon cheered up; nor could he refrain from a hearty laugh at the uproar which his story had excited. The handbills of the selectmen would cause the commitment of all the vagabonds in the State; the paragraph in the Parker's Falls Gazette would be reprinted from Maine to Florida, and perhaps form an item in the London newspapers, and many a miser would tremble for his money-bags and life, on learning the catastrophe of Mr.

Higginbotham. The pedler meditated with much fervor on the charms of the young schoolmistress, and swore that Daniel Webster never spoke nor looked so like an angel as Miss Higginbotham, while defending him from the wrathful populace at Parker's Falls.

Dominicus was now on the Kimballton turnpike, having all along determined to visit that place, though business had drawn him out of the most direct road from Morristown. As he approached the scene of the supposed murder, he continued to revolve the circumstances in his mind, and was astonished at the aspect which the whole case assumed. Had nothing occurred to corroborate the story of the first traveller, it might now have been considered as a hoax; but the yellow man was evidently acquainted either with the report or the fact; and there was a mystery in his dismayed and guilty look on being abruptly questioned. When, to this singular combination of incidents, it was added that the rumor tallied exactly with Mr. Higginbotham's character and habits of life; and that he had an orchard, and a St. Michael's pear-tree, near which he always passed at nightfall; the circumstantial evidence appeared so strong that Dominicus doubted whether the autograph produced by the lawyer, or even the niece's direct testimony, ought to be equivalent. Making cautious inquiries along the road, the pedler further learned that Mr. Higginbotham had in his service an Irishman of doubtful character, whom he had hired without a recommendation, on the score of economy.

"May I be hanged myself." exclaimed Dominicus Pike, aloud, on reaching the top of a lonely hill, "if I'll believe old

Higginbotham is unhanged, till I see him with my own eyes, and hear it from his own mouth! And as he's a real shaver, I'll have the minister or some other responsible man for an indorser."

It was growing dusk when he reached the toll-house on Kimballton turnpike, about a quarter of a mile from the village of this name. His little mare was fast bringing him up with a man on horseback, who trotted through the gate a few rods in advance of him, nodded to the toll-gatherer, and kept on towards the village. Dominicus was acquainted with the tollman, and while making change, the usual remarks on the weather passed between them.

"I suppose," said the pedler, throwing back his whiplash, to bring it down like a feather on the mare's flank, "you have not seen anything of old Mr. Higginbotham within a day or two?"

"Yes," answered the toll-gatherer. "He passed the gate just before you drove up, and yonder he rides now, if you can see him through the dusk. He's been to Woodfield this afternoon, attending a sheriff's sale there. The old man generally shakes hands and has a little chat with me; but to-night, he nodded,—as if to say, 'Charge my toll,' —and jogged on; for wherever he goes, he must always be at home by eight o'clock."

"So they tell me," said Dominicus.

"I never saw a man look so yellow and thin as the squire does," continued the toll-gatherer. "Says I to myself, to-night, he's more like a ghost or an old mummy than good flesh and blood."

The pedler strained his eyes through the twilight, and could just discern the horseman now far ahead on the village road. He seemed to recognize the rear of Mr. Higginbotham; but through the evening shadows, and amid the dust from the horse's feet, the figure appeared dim and unsubstantial; as if the shape of the mysterious old man were faintly moulded of darkness and gray light. Dominicus shivered.

"Mr. Higginbotham has come back from the other world, by way of the Kimballton turnpike," thought he.

He shook the reins and rode forward, keeping about the same distance in the rear of the gray old shadow, till the latter was concealed by a bend of the road. On reaching this point, the pedler no longer saw the man on horseback, but found himself at the head of the village street, not far from a number of stores and two taverns clustered round the meeting-house steeple. On his left were a stone wall and a gate, the boundary of a wood-lot, beyond which lay an orchard, farther still, a mowing-field, and last of all, a house. These were the premises of Mr. Higginbotham, whose dwelling stood beside the old highway, but had been left in the background by the Kimballton turnpike. Dominicus knew the place; and the little mare stopped short by instinct; for he was not conscious of tightening the reins.

"For the soul of me I cannot get by this gate!" said he, trembling. "I never shall be my own man again, till I see whether Mr. Higginbotham is hanging on the St. Michael's pear-tree!"

He leaped from the cart, gave the rein a turn round the gate-post, and ran along the green path of the wood-lot as if Old Nick were chasing behind. Just then the village clock tolled eight, and as each deep stroke fell, Dominicus gave a fresh bound and flew faster than before, till, dim in the solitary centre of the orchard, he saw the fated pear-tree. One great branch stretched from the old contorted trunk across the path, and threw the darkest shadow on that one spot. But something seemed to struggle beneath the branch!

The pedler had never pretended to more courage than befits a man of peaceable occupation, nor could he account for his valor on this awful emergency. Certain it is, however, that he rushed forward, prostrated a sturdy Irishman with the butt end of his whip, and found—not indeed hanging on the St. Michael's pear-tree, but trembling beneath it, with a halter round his neck —the old, identical Mr. Higginbotham!

"Mr. Higginbotham," said Dominicus, tremulously, "you're an honest man, and I'll take your word for it. Have you been hanged or not?"

If the riddle be not already guessed, a few words will explain the simple machinery by which this "coming event" was made to "cast its shadow before." Three men had plotted the robbery and murder of Mr. Higginbotham; two of them, successively, lost courage and fled, each delaying the crime one night by their disappearance; the third was in the act of perpetration, when a champion, blindly obeying the call of fate, like the heroes of old romance, appeared in the person of Dominicus Pike.

It only remains to say, that Mr. Higginbotham took the pedler into high favor, sanctioned his addresses to the pretty schoolmistress, and settled his whole property on their children, allowing themselves the interest. In due time, the old gentleman capped the climax of his favors, by dying a Christian death, in bed, since which melancholy event, Dominicus Pike has removed from Kimballton, and established a large tobacco manufactory in my native village.

LITTLE ANNIE'S RAMBLE

DING-DONG! Ding-dong! Ding-dong! The town-crier has rung his bell, at a distant corner, and little Annie stands on her father's door-steps, trying to hear what the man with the loud voice is talking about. Let me listen too. O, he is telling the people that an elephant, and a lion, and a royal tiger, and a horse with horns, and other strange beasts from foreign countries, have come to town, and will receive all visitors who choose to wait upon them. Perhaps little Annie would like to go. Yes; and I can see that the pretty child is weary of this wide and pleasant street, with the green trees flinging their shade across the quiet sunshine, and the pavements and the sidewalks all as clean as if the housemaid had just swept them with her broom. She feels that impulse to go strolling away,—that longing after the mystery of the great world,—which many children feel, and which I felt in my childhood. Little Annie shall take a ramble with me. See! I do but hold out my hand, and, like some bright bird in the sunny air, with her blue silk frock fluttering upwards from her white pantalets, she comes bounding on tiptoe across the street.

Smooth back your brown curls, Annie; and let me tie on your bonnet, and we will set forth! What a strange couple to go on their rambles together! One walks in black attire, with a measured step, and a heavy brow, and his thoughtful eyes bent down, while the gay little girl trips lightly along, as if she were forced to keep hold of my hand, lest her feet should dance away from the earth. Yet there is sympathy between us. If I pride myself on anything, it is because I have a smile that children love; and, on the other hand, there are few grown ladies that could entice me from the side of little Annie; for I delight to let my mind go hand in hand with the mind of a sinless child. So, come, Annie; but if I moralize as we go, do not listen to me; only look about you, and be merry!

Now we turn the corner. Here are hacks with two horses, and stage-coaches with four, thundering to meet each other, and trucks and carts moving at a slower pace, being heavily laden with barrels from the wharves, and here are rattling gigs, which perhaps will be smashed to pieces before our eyes. Hitherward, also, comes a man trundling a wheelbarrow along the pavement. Is not little Annie afraid of such a tumult? No; she does not even shrink closer to my side, but passes on with fearless confidence, a happy child amidst a great throng of grown people, who pay the same reverence to her infancy that they would to extreme old age. Nobody jostles her; all turn aside to make way for little Annie; and what is most singular, she appears conscious of her claim to such respect. Now her

eyes brighten with pleasure! A street musician has seated himself on the steps of yonder church, and pours forth his strains to the busy town, a melody that has gone astray among the tramp of footsteps, the buzz of voices, and the war of passing wheels. Who heeds the poor organ-grinder? None but myself and little Annie, whose feet begin to move in unison with the lively tune, as if she were loath that music should be wasted without a dance. But where would Annie find a partner? Some have the gout in their toes, or the rheumatism in their joints; some are stiff with age; some feeble with disease; some are so lean that their bones would rattle, and others of such ponderous size that their agility would crack the flagstones; but many, many have leaden feet, because their hearts are far heavier than lead. It is a sad thought that I have chanced upon. What a company of dancers should we be! For I, too, am a gentleman of sober footsteps, and therefore, little Annie, let us walk sedately on.

It is a question with me, whether this giddy child, or my sage self, have most pleasure in looking at the shop windows. We love the silks of sunny hue, that glow within the darkened premises of the spruce dry goods' men; we are pleasantly dazzled by the burnished silver, and the chased gold, the rings of wedlock and the costly love ornaments, glistening at the window of the jeweller; but Annie, more than I, seeks for a glimpse of her passing figure in the dusty looking-glasses at the hardware stores. All that is bright and gay attracts us both.

Here is a shop to which the recollections of my boyhood, as well as present partialities, give a peculiar magic. How delightful to let the fancy revel on the dainties of a confectioner; those pies, with such white and flaky paste, their contents being a mystery, whether rich mince, with whole plums intermixed, or piquant apple, delicately rose flavored; those cakes, heart-shaped or round, piled in a lofty pyramid; those sweet little circlets, sweetly named kisses; those dark majestic masses, fit to be bridal loaves at the wedding of an heiress, mountains in size, their summits deeply snow-covered with sugar! Then the mighty treasures of sugar-plums, white, and crimson, and yellow, in large glass vases; and candy of all varieties; and those little cockles, or whatever they are called, much prized by children for their sweetness, and more for the mottoes which they enclose, by love-sick maids and bachelors! O, my mouth waters, little Annie, and so doth yours; but we will not be tempted, except to an imaginary feast; so let us hasten onward, devouring the vision of a plum-cake.

Here are pleasures, as some people would say, of a more exalted kind, in the window of a bookseller. Is Annie a literary lady? Yes; she is deeply read in Peter Parley's tomes, and has an increasing love for fairy-tales, though seldom met with now-a-days, and she will subscribe, next year, to the Juvenile Miscellany. But, truth to tell, she is apt to turn away from the printed page, and keep gazing at the pretty pictures, such as the gay-colored ones which make this shop window the continual loitering-place of children. What would Annie think, if in the book which I mean to send her, on New Year's day, she should find her sweet little self, bound up in silk or morocco with gilt edges, there to remain till she become a woman grown, with children of her own to read about their mother's childhood? That would be very queer.

Little Annie is weary of pictures, and pulls me onward by the hand, till suddenly we pause at the most wondrous shop in all the town. O my stars! Is this a toyshop, or is it fairyland? For here are gilded chariots, in which the king and queen of the fairies might ride side by side, while their courtiers, on these small horses, should gallop in triumphal procession before and behind the royal pair. Here, too, are dishes of china ware, fit to be the dining set of those same princely personages, when they make a regal banquet in the stateliest hall of their palace, full five feet high, and behold their nobles feasting adown the long perspective of the table. Betwixt the king and queen should sit my little Annie, the prettiest fairy of them all. Here stands a turbaned turk, threatening us with his sabre, like an ugly heathen as he is. And next a Chinese mandarin, who nods his head at Annie and myself. Here we may review a whole army of horse and foot, in red and blue uniforms, with drums, fifes, trumpets, and all kinds of noiseless music; they have halted on the shelf of this window, after their weary march from Liliput. But what cares Annie for soldiers? No conquering queen is she, neither a Semiramis nor a Catharine; her whole heart is set upon that doll, who gazes at us with such a fashionable stare. This is the little girl's true plaything. Though made of wood, a doll is a visionary and ethereal personage, endowed by childish fancy with a peculiar life; the mimic lady is a heroine of romance, an actor and a sufferer in a thousand shadowy scenes, the chief inhabitant of that wild world with which children ape the real one. Little Annie does not understand what I am saying, but looks wishfully at the proud lady in the window. We will invite her home with us as we return. Meantime, good-by, Dame Doll! A toy yourself, you look forth from your window upon many ladies that are also toys, though they walk and speak, and upon a crowd in pursuit of toys, though they wear grave visages. O, with your never-closing eyes, had you but an intellect to moralize on all that flits before them, what a wise doll would you be! Come, little Annie, we shall find toys enough, go where we may.

Now we elbow our way among the throng again. It is curious, in the most crowded part of a town, to meet with living creatures that had their birthplace in some far solitude, but have acquired a second nature in the wilderness of men. Look up, Annie, at that canary-bird, hanging out of the window in his cage. Poor little fellow! His golden feathers are all tarnished in this smoky sunshine; he would have glistened twice as brightly among the summer islands; but still he has become a citizen in all his tastes and habits, and would not sing half so well without the uproar that drowns his music. What a pity that he does not know how miserable he is! There is a parrot, too, calling out, "Pretty Poll! Pretty Poll!" as we pass by. Foolish bird, to be talking about her prettiness to strangers, especially as she is not a pretty Poll, though gaudily dressed in green and yellow. If she had said "Pretty Annie," there would

have been some sense in it. See that gray squirrel, at the door of the fruit shop, whirling round and round so merrily within his wire wheel! Being condemned to the treadmill, he makes it an amusement. Admirable philosophy!

Here comes a big, rough dog, a countryman's dog in search of his master; smelling at everybody's heels, and touching little Annie's hand with his cold nose, but hurrying away, though she would fain have patted him. Success to your search, Fidelity! And there sits a great yellow cat upon a window-sill, a very corpulent and comfortable cat, gazing at this transitory world, with owl's eyes, and making pithy comments, doubtless, or what appear such, to the silly beast. O sage puss, make room for me beside you, and we will be a pair of philosophers!

Here we see something to remind us of the town-crier, and his ding-dong bell! Look! look at that great cloth spread out in the air, pictured all over with wild beasts, as if they had met together to choose a king, according to their custom in the days of Æsop. But they are choosing neither a king nor a president; else we should hear a most horrible snarling! They have come from the deep woods, and the wild mountains, and the desert sands, and the polar snows, only to do homage to my little Annie. As we enter among them, the great elephant makes us a bow, in the best style of elephantine courtesy, bending lowly down his mountain bulk, with trunk abased, and leg thrust out behind. Annie returns the salute, much to the gratification of the elephant, who is certainly the best-bred monster in the caravan. The lion and the lioness are busy with two beef-bones. The royal tiger, the beautiful, the untamable, keeps pacing his narrow cage with a haughty step, unmindful of the spectators or recalling the fierce deeds of his former life, when he was wont to leap forth upon such inferior animals, from the jungles of Bengal.

Here we see the very same wolf—do not go near him, Annie!—the selfsame wolf that devoured little Red Riding Hood and her grandmother. In the next cage, a hyena from Egypt, who has doubtless howled around the pyramids, and a black bear from our own forests, are fellow-prisoners, and most excellent friends. Are there any two living creatures who have so few sympathies that they cannot possibly be friends? Here sits a great white bear, whom common observers would call a very stupid beast, though I perceive him to be only absorbed in contemplation; he is thinking of his voyages on an iceberg, and of his comfortable home in the vicinity of the north pole, and of the little cubs whom he left rolling in the eternal snows. In fact, he is a bear of sentiment. But, O, those unsentimental monkeys! the ugly, grinning, aping, chattering, ill-natured, mischievous, and queer little brutes. Annie does not love the monkeys. Their ugliness shocks her pure, instinctive delicacy of taste, and makes her mind unquiet, because it bears a wild and dark resemblance to humanity. But here is a little pony, just big enough for Annie to ride, and round and round he gallops in a circle, keeping time with his trampling hoofs to a band of music. And here,—with a laced coat and a cocked hat, and a riding-whip in his hand,—here comes a little gentleman, small enough to be king

of the fairies, and ugly enough to be king of the gnomes, and takes a flying leap into the saddle. Merrily, merrily, plays the music, and merrily gallops the pony, and merrily rides the little old gentleman. Come, Annie, into the street again; perchance we may see monkeys on horseback there!

Mercy on us, what a noisy world we quiet people live in! Did Annie ever read the Cries of London City? With what lusty lungs doth yonder man proclaim that his wheelbarrow is full of lobsters! Here comes another mounted on a cart, and blowing a hoarse and dreadful blast from a tin horn, as much as to say "Fresh fish!" And hark! a voice on high, like that of a muezzin from the summit of a mosque, announcing that some chimney-sweeper has emerged from smoke and soot, and darksome caverns, into the upper air. What cares the world for that? But, well-a-day! we hear a shrill voice of affliction, the scream of a little child, rising louder with every repetition of that smart, sharp, slapping sound, produced by an open hand on tender flesh. Annie sympathizes, though without experience of such direful woe. Lo! the town-crier again, with some new secret for the public ear. Will he tell us of an auction, or of a lost pocket-book, or a show of beautiful wax figures, or of some monstrous beast more horrible than any in the caravan? I guess the latter. See how he uplifts the bell in his right hand, and shakes it slowly at first, then with a hurried motion, till the clapper seems to strike both sides at once, and the sounds are scattered forth in quick succession, far and near. Ding-dong! Ding-dong! Ding-dong!

Now he raises his clear, loud voice,

above all the din of the town; it drowns the buzzing talk of many tongues, and draws each man's mind from his own business; it rolls up and down the echoing street, and ascends to the hushed chamber of the sick, and penetrates downward to the cellar-kitchen, where the hot cook turns from the fire to listen. Who, of all that address the public ear, whether in church, or courthouse, or hall of state, has such an attentive audience as the town-crier? What saith the people's orator?

"Strayed from her home, a LITTLE GIRL, of five years old, in a blue silk frock and white pantalets, with brown curling hair and hazel eyes. Whoever will bring her back to her afflicted mother—"

Stop, stop, town-crier! The lost is found. O, my pretty Annie, we forgot to tell your mother of our ramble, and she is in despair, and has sent the town-crier to bellow up and down the streets, affrighting old and young, for the loss of a little girl who has not once let go my hand? Well, let us hasten homeward; and as we go, forget not to thank Heaven, my Annie, that, after wandering a little way into the world, you may return at the first summons, with an untainted and unwearied heart, and be a happy child again. But I have gone too far astray for the town-crier to call me back.

Sweet has been the charm of childhood on my spirit, throughout my ramble with little Annie! Say not that it has been a waste of precious moments, an idle matter, a babble of childish talk, and a reverie of childish imaginations, about topics unworthy of a grown man's notice. Has it been merely this? Not so; not so. They are not truly wise who would affirm it. As the pure breath of children revives the life of aged men, so is our moral nature revived by their free and simple thoughts, their native feeling, their airy mirth, for little cause or none, their grief, soon roused and soon allayed. Their influence on us is at least reciprocal with ours on them. When our infancy is almost forgotten, and our boyhood long departed, though it seems but as yesterday; when life settles darkly down upon us, and we doubt whether to call ourselves young any more, then it is good to steal away from the society of bearded men, and even of gentler woman, and spend an hour or two with children. After drinking from those fountains of still fresh existence, we shall return into the crowd, as I do now, to struggle onward and do our part in life, perhaps as fervently as ever, but, for a time, with a kinder and purer heart, and a spirit more lightly wise. All this by thy sweet magic, dear little Annie!

WAKEFIELD

IN some old magazine or newspaper, I recollect a story, told as truth, of a man—let us call him Wakefield—who absented himself for a long time from his wife. The fact, thus abstractedly stated, is not very uncommon, nor--

without a proper distinction of circumstances—to be condemned either as naughty or nonsensical. Howbeit, this, though far from the most aggravated, is perhaps the strangest instance, on record, of marital delinquency; and moreover, as remarkable a freak as may be found in the whole list of human oddities. The wedded couple lived in London. The man, under pretence of going a journey, took lodgings in the next street to his own house, and there, unheard of by his wife or friends, and without the shadow of a reason for such self-banishment, dwelt upwards of twenty years. During that period, he beheld his home every day, and frequently the forlorn Mrs. Wakefield. And after so great a gap in his matrimonial felicity—when his death was reckoned certain, his estate settled, his name dismissed from memory, and his wife, long, long ago, resigned to her autumnal widowhood—he entered the door one evening, quietly, as from a day's absence, and became a loving spouse till death.

This outline is all that I remember. But the incident, though of the purest originality, unexampled and probably never to be repeated, is one, I think, which appeals to the generous sympathies of mankind. We know, each for himself, that none of us would perpetrate such a folly, yet feel as if some other might. To my own contemplations, at least, it has often recurred, always exciting wonder, but with a sense that the story must be true, and a conception of its hero's character. Whenever any subject so forcibly affects the mind, time is well spent in thinking of it. If the reader choose, let him do his own meditation; or if he prefer to ramble with me through the twenty years of

Wakefield's vagary, I bid him welcome; trusting that there will be a pervading spirit and a moral, even should we fail to find them, done up neatly, and condensed into the final sentence. Thought has always its efficacy, and every striking incident its moral?

What sort of a man was Wakefield? We are free to shape out our own idea, and call it by his name. He was now in the meridian of life; his matrimonial affections, never violent, were sobered into a calm, habitual sentiment; of all husbands, he was likely to be the most constant, because a certain sluggishness would keep his heart at rest, wherever it might be placed. He was intellectual, but not actively so; his mind occupied itself in long and lazy musings, that tended to no purpose, or had not vigor to attain it; his thoughts were seldom so energetic as to seize hold of words. Imagination, in the proper meaning of the term, made no part of Wakefield's gifts. With a cold, but not depraved nor wandering heart, and a mind never feverish with riotous thoughts, nor perplexed with originality, who could have anticipated, that our friend would entitle himself to a foremost place among the doers of eccentric deeds? Had his acquaintances been asked, who was the man in London the surest to perform nothing to-day which should be remembered on the morrow, they would have thought of Wakefield. Only the wife of his bosom might have hesitated. She, without having analyzed his character, was partly aware of a quiet selfishness, that had rusted into his inactive mind,—of a peculiar sort of vanity, the most uneasy attribute about him,—of a disposition to craft, which had seldom produced more positive effects than the keeping of petty secrets, hardly worth revealing,—and, lastly, of what she called a little strangeness, sometimes, in the good man. This latter quality is indefinable, and perhaps non-existent.

Let us now imagine Wakefield bidding adieu to his wife. It is the dusk of an October evening. His equipment is a drab great coat, a hat covered with an oilcloth, top boots, an umbrella in one hand and a small portmanteau in the other. He has informed Mrs. Wakefield that he is to take the night coach into the country. She would fain inquire the length of his journey, its object, and the probable time of his return; but, indulgent to his harmless love of mystery, interrogates him only by a look. He tells her not to expect him positively by the return coach, nor to be alarmed should he tarry three or four days; but, at all events, to look for him at supper on Friday evening. Wakefield himself, be it considered, has no suspicion of what is before him. He holds out his hands; she gives her own, and meets his parting kiss, in the matter-of-course way of a ten years' matrimony; and forth goes the middle-aged Mr. Wakefield, almost resolved to perplex his good lady by a whole week's absence. After the door has closed behind him, she perceives it thrust partly open, and a vision of her husband's face, through the aperture, smiling on her, and gone in a moment. For the time, this little incident is dismissed without a thought. But, long afterwards, when she has been more years a widow than a wife, that smile recurs, and flickers across all her reminiscences of Wakefield's visage. In her many musings, she surrounds the original smile with a multitude of fantasies, which make it strange and awful;

as, for instance, if she imagines him in a coffin, that parting look is frozen on his pale features; or, if she dreams of him in heaven, still his blessed spirit wears a quiet and crafty smile. Yet, for its sake, when all others have given him up for dead, she sometimes doubts whether she is a widow.

But our business is with the husband. We must hurry after him, along the street, ere he lose his individuality, and melt into the great mass of London life. It would be vain searching for him there. Let us follow close at his heels, therefore, until, after several superfluous turns and doublings, we find him comfortably established by the fireside of a small apartment, previously bespoken. He is in the next street to his own, and at his journey's end. He can scarcely trust his good fortune in having got thither unperceived,—recollecting that, at one time, he was delayed by the throng, in the very focus of a lighted lantern; and, again, there were footsteps that seemed to tread behind his own, distinct from the multitudinous tramp around him; and, anon, he heard a voice shouting afar, and fancied that it called his name. Doubtless, a dozen busybodies had been watching him, and told his wife the whole affair. Poor Wakefield! Little knowest thou thine own insignificance in this great world! No mortal eye but mine has traced thee. Go quietly to thy bed, foolish man; and, on the morrow, if thou wilt be wise, get thee home to good Mrs. Wakefield, and tell her the truth. Remove not thyself, even for a little week, from thy place in her chaste bosom. Were she, for a single moment, to deem thee dead, or lost, or lastingly divided from her, thou wouldst be wofully conscious of a change in thy true wife, forever after. It is perilous to make a chasm in human affections; not that they gape so long and wide,— but so quickly close again!

Almost repenting of his frolic, or whatever it may be termed, Wakefield lies down betimes, and, starting from his first nap, spreads forth his arms into the wide and solitary waste of the unaccustomed bed. "No,"—thinks he, gathering the bedclothes about him,—"I will not sleep alone another night."

In the morning, he rises earlier than usual, and sets himself to consider what he really means to do. Such are his loose and rambling modes of thought, that he has taken this very singular step, with the consciousness of a purpose, indeed, but without being able to define it sufficiently for his own contemplation. The vagueness of the project, and the convulsive effort with which he plunges into the execution of it, are equally characteristic of a feeble-minded man. Wakefield sifts his ideas, however, as minutely as he may, and finds himself curious to know the progress of matters at home,—how his exemplary wife will endure her widowhood of a week; and, briefly, how the little sphere of creatures and circumstances in which he was a central object will be affected by his removal. A morbid vanity, therefore, lies nearest the bottom of the affair. But how is he to attain his ends? Not, certainly, by keeping close in this comfortable lodging, where, though he slept and awoke in the next street to his home, he is as effectually abroad, as if the stage-coach had been whirling him away all night. Yet, should he reappear, the whole project is knocked in the head. His poor brains being hopelessly puzzled with this dilemma, he at length

ventures out, partly resolving to cross the head of the street, and send one hasty glance towards his forsaken domicile. Habit—for he is a man of habits— takes him by the hand, and guides him, wholly unaware, to his own door, where, just at the critical moment, he is aroused by the scraping of his foot upon the step. Wakefield! whither are you going?

At that instant, his fate was turning on the pivot. Little dreaming of the doom to which his first backward step devotes him, he hurries away, breathless with agitation hitherto unfelt, and hardly dares turn his head, at the distant corner. Can it be, that nobody caught sight of him? Will not the whole household—the decent Mrs. Wakefield, the smart maid-servant, and the dirty little footboy—raise a hue and cry, through London streets, in pursuit of their fugitive lord and master? Wonderful escape! He gathers courage to pause and look homeward, but is perplexed with a sense of change about the familiar edifice, such as affects us all, when, after a separation of months or years, we again see some hill or lake, or work of art, with which we were friends, of old. In ordinary cases, this indescribable impression is caused by the comparison and contrast between our imperfect reminiscences and the reality. In Wakefield, the magic of a single night has wrought a similar transformation, because, in that brief period, a great moral change has been effected. But this is a secret from himself. Before leaving the spot, he catches a far and momentary glimpse of his wife, passing athwart the front window, with her face turned towards the head of the street. The crafty nincompoop takes to his heels, scared with the idea, that, among a thousand such atoms of mortality, her eye must have detected him. Right glad is his heart, though his brain be somewhat dizzy, when he finds himself by the coal-fire of his lodgings.

So much for the commencement of this long whimwham. After the initial conception, and the stirring up of the man's sluggish temperament to put it in practice, the whole matter evolves itself in a natural train. We may suppose him, as the result of deep deliberation, buying a new wig, of reddish hair, and selecting sundry garments, in a fashion unlike his customary suit of brown, from a Jew's old-clothes bag. It is accomplished. Wakefield is another man. The new system being now established, a retrograde movement to the old would be almost as difficult as the step that placed him in his unparalleled position. Furthermore, he is rendered obstinate by a sulkiness, occasionally incident to his temper, and brought on, at present, by the inadequate sensation which he conceives to have been produced in the bosom of Mrs. Wakefield. He will not go back until she be frightened half to death. Well; twice or thrice has she passed before his sight, each time with a heavier step, a paler cheek, and more anxious brow; and in the third week of his nonappearance, he detects a portent of evil entering the house, in the guise of an apothecary. Next day, the knocker is muffled. Towards nightfall comes the chariot of a physician, and deposits its big-wigged and solemn burden at Wakefield's door, whence, after a quarter of an hour's visit, he emerges, perchance the herald of a funeral. Dear woman! Will she die? By this time

Wakefield is excited to something like energy of feeling, but still lingers away from his wife's bedside, pleading with his conscience, that she must not be disturbed at such a juncture. If aught else restrains him, he does not know it. In the course of a few weeks she gradually recovers; the crisis is over; her heart is sad, perhaps, but quiet; and, let him return soon or late, it will never be feverish for him again. Such ideas glimmer through the mist of Wakefield's mind, and render him indistinctly conscious that an almost impassable gulf divides his hired apartment from his former home. "It is but in the next street!" he sometimes says. Fool! it is in another world. Hitherto, he has put off his return from one particular day to another; henceforward, he leaves the precise time undetermined. Not tomorrow,—probably next week,—pretty soon. Poor man! The dead have nearly as much chance of revisiting their earthly homes as the self-banished Wakefield.

Would that I had a folio to write, instead of an article of a dozen pages! Then might I exemplify how an influence, beyond our control, lays its strong hand on every deed which we do, and weaves its consequences into an iron tissue of necessity. Wakefield is spell-bound. We must leave him, for ten years or so, to haunt around his house, without once crossing the threshold, and to be faithful to his wife, with all the affection of which his heart is capable, while he is slowly fading out of hers. Long since, it must be remarked, he has lost the perception of singularity in his conduct.

Now for a scene! Amid the throng of a London street, we distinguish a man, now waxing elderly, with few characteristics to attract careless observers, yet bearing, in his whole aspect, the handwriting of no common fate, for such as have the skill to read it. He is meagre; his low and narrow forehead is deeply wrinkled; his eyes, small and lustreless, sometimes wander apprehensively about him, but oftener seem to look inward. He bends his head, and moves with an indescribable obliquity of gait, as if unwilling to display his full front to the world. Watch him, long enough to see what we have described, and you will allow, that circumstances, —which often produce remarkable men from nature's ordinary handiwork,— have produced one such here. Next, leaving him to sidle along the footwalk, cast your eyes in the opposite direction, where a portly female, considerably in the wane of life, with a prayer-book in her hand, is proceeding to yonder church. She has the placid mien of settled widowhood. Her regrets have either died away, or have become so essential to her heart, that they would be poorly exchanged for joy. Just as the lean man and well-conditioned woman are passing, a slight obstruction occurs, and brings these two figures directly in contact. Their hands touch; the pressure of the crowd forces her bosom against his shoulder; they stand; face to face, staring into each other's eyes. After a ten years' separation, thus Wakefield meets his wife!

The throng eddies away, and carries them asunder. The sober widow, resuming her former pace, proceeds to church, but pauses in the portal, and throws a perplexed glance along the street. She passes in, however, opening her prayer-book as she goes. And the man! with so wild a face, that busy and selfish London stands to gaze after him, he hurries to his lodgings, bolts the door, and throws himself upon the bed. The latent feelings of years break out; his feeble mind acquires a brief energy from their strength; all the miserable strangeness of his life is revealed to him at a glance: and he cries out, passionately, "Wakefield! Wakefield! You are mad!"

Perhaps he was so. The singularity of his situation must have so moulded him to himself, that, considered in regard to his fellow-creatures and the business of life, he could not be said to possess his right mind. He had contrived, or rather he had happened, to dissever himself from the world,—to vanish,—to give up his place and privileges with living men, without being admitted among the dead. The life of a hermit is nowise parallel to his. He was in the bustle of the city, as of old; but the crowd swept by, and saw him not; he was, we may figuratively say, always beside his wife, and at his hearth, yet must never feel the warmth of the one nor the affection of the other. It was Wakefield's unprecedented fate to retain his original share of human sympathies, and to be still involved in human interests, while he had lost his reciprocal influence on them. It would be a most curious speculation to trace out the effect of such circumstances on his heart and intellect, separately, and in unison. Yet, changed as he was, he would seldom be conscious of it, but deem himself the same man as ever; glimpses of the truth, indeed, would come, but only for the moment; and still he would keep saying,—"I shall soon go back!"—nor reflect that he had been saying so for twenty years.

I conceive, also, that these twenty

years would appear, in the retrospect, scarcely longer than the week to which Wakefield had at first limited his absence. He would look on the affair as no more than an interlude in the main business of his life. When, after a little while more, he should deem it time to re-enter his parlor, his wife would clap her hands for joy, on beholding the middle-aged Mr. Wakefield. Alas, what a mistake! Would Time but await the close of our favorite follies, we should be young men, all of us, and till Doomsday.

One evening, in the twentieth year since he vanished, Wakefield is taking his customary walk towards the dwelling which he still calls his own. It is a gusty night of autumn, with frequent showers, that patter down upon the pavement, and are gone before a man can put up his umbrella. Pausing near the house, Wakefield discerns, through the parlor windows on the second floor, the red glow, and the glimmer and fitful flash of a comfortable fire. On the ceiling appears a grotesque shadow of good Mrs. Wakefield. The cap, the nose and chin, and the broad waist, form an admirable caricature, which dances, moreover, with the up-flickering and down-sinking blaze, almost too merrily for the shade of an elderly widow. At this instant, a shower chances to fall, and is driven, by the unmannerly gust, full into Wakefield's face and bosom. He is quite penetrated with its autumnal chill.

Shall he stand wet and shivering here, when his own hearth has a good fire to warm him, and his own wife will run to fetch the gray coat and small-clothes, which, doubtless, she has kept carefully in the closet of their bed-chamber? No! Wakefield is no such fool. He ascends the steps—heavily!—for twenty years have stiffened his legs, since he came down,—but he knows it not. Stay, Wakefield! Would you go to the sole home that is left you? Then step into your grave! The door opens. As he passes in we have a parting glimpse of his visage, and recognize the crafty smile, which was the precursor of the little joke, that he has ever since been playing off at his wife's expense. How unmercifully has he quizzed the woman! Well, a good night's rest to Wakefield!

This happy event—supposing it to be such—could only have occurred at an unpremeditated moment. We will not follow our friend across the threshold. He has left us much food for thought, a portion of which shall lend its wisdom to a moral, and be shaped into a figure. Amid the seeming confusion of our mysterious world, individuals are so nicely adjusted to a system, and systems to one another, and to a whole, that, by stepping aside for a moment, a man exposes himself to a fearful risk of losing his place forever. Like Wakefield, he may become, as it were, the Outcast of the Universe.

A RILL FROM THE TOWN-PUMP

(SCENE,—*the corner of two principal streets.** The TOWN-PUMP *talking through its nose*)

NOON, by the North clock! Noon, by the east! High noon, too, by these hot sunbeams, which fall, scarcely aslope, upon my head, and almost make the water bubble and smoke in the trough under my nose. Truly, we public characters have a tough time of it! And among all the town officers, chosen at March meeting, where is he that sustains, for a single year, the burden of such manifold duties as are imposed, in perpetuity, upon the Town-Pump? The title of "town treasurer" is rightfully mine, as guardian of the best treasure that the town has. The overseers of the poor ought to make me their chairman, since I provide bountifully for the pauper, without expense to him that pays taxes. I am at the head of the fire department, and one of the physicians to the board of health. As a keeper of the peace, all water-drinkers will confess me equal to the constable. I perform some of the duties of the town clerk, by promulgating public notices, when they are posted on my front. To speak within bounds, I am the chief person of the municipality, and exhibit, moreover, an admirable pattern to my brother officers, by the cool, steady, upright, downright, and impartial discharge of my business, and the constancy with which I stand to my post. Summer or winter, nobody seeks me in vain; for, all day long, I am seen at the busiest corner, just above the market, stretching out my arms, to

* Essex and Washington Streets, Salem.

rich and poor alike; and at night, I hold a lantern over my head, both to show where I am, and keep people out of the gutters.

At this sultry noontide I am cup-bearer to the parched populace, for whose benefit an iron goblet is chained to my waist. Like a dram-seller on the mall, at muster-day, I cry aloud to all and sundry, in my plainest accents, and at the very tiptop of my voice. Here it is, gentlemen! Here is the good liquor! Walk up, walk up, gentlemen, walk up, walk up! Here is the superior stuff! Here is the unadulterated ale of father Adam,—better than Cognac, Hoi-lands, Jamaica, strong beer, or wine of any price; here it is, by the hogshead or the single glass, and not a cent to pay! Walk up, gentlemen, walk up, and help yourselves!

It were a pity if all this outcry should draw no customers. Here they come. A hot day, gentlemen! Quaff, and away again, so as to keep yourselves in a nice cool sweat. You, my friend, will need another cupful, to wash the dust out of your throat, if it be as thick there as it is on your cowhide shoes. I see that you have trudged half a score of miles to-day; and, like a wise man, have passed by the taverns, and stopped at the running brooks and well-curbs. Otherwise, betwixt heat without and fire within, you would have been burned to a cinder, or melted down to nothing at all, in the fashion of a jelly-fish. Drink, and make room for that other fellow, who seeks my aid to quench the fiery fever of last night's potations, which he drained from no cup of mine. Welcome, most rubicund sir! You and I have been great strangers, hitherto; nor, to confess the truth, will my nose be anxious for a closer intimacy, till the fumes of your breath be a little less potent. Mercy on you, man! the water absolutely hisses down your red-hot gullet, and is converted quite to steam, in the miniature tophet which you mistake for a stomach. Fill again, and tell me, on the word of an honest toper, did you ever, in cellar, tavern, or any kind of a dram-shop, spend the price of your children's food for a swig half so delicious? Now, for the first time these ten years, you know the flavor of cold water. Good-by; and, whenever you are thirsty, remember that I keep a constant supply, at the old stand. Who next? O, my little friend, you are let loose from school, and come hither to scrub your blooming face, and drown the memory of certain taps of the ferule, and other school-boy troubles, in a draught from the Town-Pump. Take it, pure as the current of your young life. Take it, and may your heart and tongue never be scorched with a fiercer thirst than now! There, my dear child, put down the cup, and yield your place to this elderly gentleman, who treads so tenderly over the paving-stones, that I suspect he is afraid of breaking them. What! he limps by, without so much as thanking me, as if my hospitable offers were meant only for people who have no wine-cellars. Well, well, sir,—no harm done, I hope! Go draw the cork, tip the decanter; but when your great toe shall set you a-roaring, it will be no affair of mine. If gentlemen love the pleasant titillation of the gout, it is all one to the Town-Pump. This thirsty dog, with his red tongue lolling out, does not scorn my

hospitality, but stands on his hind legs, and laps eagerly out of the trough. See how lightly he capers away again! Jowler, did your worship ever have the gout?

Are you all satisfied? Then wipe your mouths, my good friends; and, while my spout has a moment's leisure, I will delight the town with a few historical reminiscences. In far antiquity, beneath a darksome shadow of venerable boughs, a spring bubbled out of the leaf-strewn earth, in the very spot where you now behold me, on the sunny pavement. The water was as bright and clear, and deemed as precious, as liquid diamonds. The Indian sagamores drank of it, from time immemorial, till the fatal deluge of the fire-water burst upon the red-men, and swept their whole race away from the cold fountains. Endicott and his followers came next, and often knelt down to drink, dipping their long beards in the spring. The richest goblet, then, was of birch bark. Governor Winthrop, after a journey afoot from Boston, drank here, out of the hollow of his hand. The elder Higginson here wet his palm, and laid it on the brow of the first town-born child. For many years it was the watering-place, and, as it were, the wash-bowl of the vicinity,— whither all decent folks resorted, to purify their visages, and gaze at them afterwards—at least, the pretty maidens did—in the mirror which it made. On Sabbath days, whenever a babe was to be baptized, the sexton filled his basin here, and placed it on the communion-table of the humble meeting-house, which partly covered the site of yonder stately brick one. Thus, one generation after another was consecrated to Heaven by its waters, and cast their waxing and waning shadows into its glassy bosom.

and vanished from the earth, as if mortal life were but a flitting image in a fountain. Finally, the fountain vanished also. Cellars were dug on all sides, and cart-loads of gravel flung upon its source, whence oozed a turbid stream, forming a mud-puddle, at the corner of two streets. In the hot months, when its refreshment was most needed, the dust flew in clouds over the forgotten birthplace of the waters, now their grave. But, in the course of time, a Town-Pump was sunk into the source of the ancient spring; and when the first decayed, another took its place,— and then another, and still another,— till here stand I, gentlemen and ladies, to serve you with my iron goblet. Drink, and be refreshed! The water is as pure and cold as that which slaked the thirst of the red sagamore, beneath the aged boughs, though now the gem of the wilderness is treasured under these hot stones, where no shadow falls but from the brick buildings. And be it the moral of my story, that, as this wasted and long-lost fountain is now known and prized again, so shall the virtues of cold water, too little valued since your fathers' days, be recognized by all.

Your pardon, good people! I must interrupt my stream of eloquence, and spout forth a stream of water, to replenish the trough for this teamster and his two yoke of oxen, who have come from Topsfield, or somewhere along that way. No part of my business is pleasanter than the watering of cattle. Look! how rapidly they lower the water-mark on the sides of the trough, till their capacious stomachs are moistened with a gallon or two apiece, and they can afford time to breathe it in, with sighs of calm enjoyment. Now they roll their quiet eyes around the brim of their monstrous drinking-vessel. An ox is your true toper.

But I perceive, my dear auditors, that you are impatient for the remainder of my discourse. Impute it, I beseech you, to no defect of modesty, if I insist a little longer on so fruitful a topic as my own multifarious merits. It is altogether for your good. The better you think of me, the better men and women will you find yourselves. I shall say nothing of my all-important aid on washing-days; though, on that account alone, I might call myself the household god of a hundred families. Far be it from me also to hint, my respectable friends, of the show of dirty faces which you would present without my pains to keep you clean. Nor will I remind you how often, when the midnight bells make you tremble for your combustible town, you have fled to the Town-Pump, and found me always at my post, firm, amid the confusion, and ready to drain my vital current in your behalf. Neither is it worth while to lay much stress on my claims to a medical diploma, as the physician, whose simple rule of practice is preferable to all the nauseous lore, which has found men sick or left them so, since the days of Hippocrates. Let us take a broader view of my beneficial influence on mankind.

No; these are trifles, compared with the merits which wise men concede to me—if not in my single self, yet as the representative of a class—of being the grand reformer of the age. From my spout, and such spouts as mine, must flow the stream, that shall cleanse our earth of the vast portion of its crime and anguish, which has gushed from the fiery fountains of the still. In this mighty enterprise, the cow shall be my great confederate. Milk and water! The TOWN-PUMP and the Cow! Such is the glorious copartnership that shall tear down the distilleries and brew-houses, uproot the vineyards, shatter the cider-presses, ruin the tea and coffee trade, and finally monopolize the whole business of quenching thirst. Blessed consummation! Then Poverty shall pass away from the land, finding no hovel so wretched, where her squalid form may shelter itself. Then Disease, for lack of other victims, shall gnaw its own heart, and die. Then Sin, if she do not die, shall lose half her strength. Until now, the frenzy of hereditary fever has raged in the human blood, transmitted from sire to son, and rekindled, in every generation, by fresh draughts of liquid flame. When that inward fire shall be extinguished, the heat of passion cannot but grow cool, and war—the drunkenness of nations—perhaps will cease. At least there will be no war of households. The husband and wife, drinking deep of peaceful joy,—a calm bliss of temperate affections,—shall pass hand in hand through life, and lie down, not reluctantly, at its protracted close. To them, the past will be no turmoil of mad dreams, nor the future an eternity of such moments as follows the delirium of the drunkard. Their dead faces shall express what their spirits were, and are to be, by a lingering smile of memory and hope.

Ahem! Dry work, this speechifying; especially to an unpractised orator. I never conceived, till now, what toil the temperance lecturers undergo for my sake. Hereafter they shall have the business to themselves. Do, some kind Christian, pump a stroke or two, just to wet my whistle. Thank you, sir! My dear hearers, when the world shall have been regenerated, by my instrumentality, you will collect your useless vats and liquor-casks into one great pile, and make a bonfire in honor of the Town-Pump. And when I shall have decayed, like my predecessors, then, if you revere my memory, let a marble fountain, richly sculptured, take my place upon this spot. Such monuments should be erected everywhere, and inscribed with the names of the distinguished champions of my cause. Now listen; for something very important is to come next.

There are two or three honest friend of mine—and true friends, I know, they are—who, nevertheless, by their fiery pugnacity in my behalf, do put me in fearful hazard of a broken nose, or even a total overthrow upon the pavement, and the loss of the treasure which I guard. I pray you, gentlemen, let this fault be amended. Is it decent, think you, to get tipsy with zeal for temperance, and take up the honorable cause of the Town-Pump in the style of a toper fighting for his brandy-bottle? Or can the excellent qualities of cold water be not otherwise exemplified than by plunging, slapdash, into hot water, and wofully scalding yourselves and other people? Trust me they may. In the moral warfare which you are to wage— and, indeed, in the whole conduct of your lives—you cannot choose a better example than myself, who have never permitted the dust and sultry atmosphere, the turbulence and manifold disquietudes of the world around me, to reach that deep, calm well of purity which may be called my soul. And whenever I pour out that soul, it is to cool earth's fever or cleanse its stains.

One o'clock! Nay, then, if the dinner-bell begins to speak, I may as well hold my peace. Here comes a pretty young girl of my acquaintance, with a large stone pitcher for me to fill. May she draw a husband, while drawing her water, as Rachel did of old. Hold out your vessel, my dear! There it is, full to the brim; so now run home, peeping at your sweet image in the pitcher, as you go; and forget not, in a glass of my own liquor, to drink—"SUCCESS TO THE TOWN-PUMP!"

THE GREAT CARBUNCLE *

A MYSTERY OF THE WHITE MOUNTAINS

AT nightfall, once, in the olden time, on the rugged side of one of the Crystal Hills, a party of adventurers were refreshing themselves, after a toilsome and fruitless quest for the Great Carbuncle. They had come thither, not as friends, nor partners in the enterprise, but each, save one youthful pair, impelled by his own selfish and solitary longing for this wondrous gem. Their feeling of brotherhood, however, was strong enough to induce them to contribute a mutual aid in building a rude hut of branches, and kindling a great fire of shattered pines, that had drifted down the headlong current of the Amonoosuck, on the lower bank of which they were to pass the night. There was but one of their number, perhaps, who had become so estranged from natural sympathies, by the absorbing spell of the pursuit, as to acknowledge no satisfaction at the sight of human faces, in the remote and solitary region whither they had as-

cended. A vast extent of wilderness lay between them and the nearest settlement, while scant a mile above their heads was that black verge, where the hills throw off their shaggy mantle of forest trees, and either robe themselves in clouds or tower naked into the sky. The roar of the Amonoosuck would have been too awful for endurance, if only a solitary man had listened, while the mountain stream talked with the wind.

The adventurers, therefore, exchanged hospitable greetings, and welcomed one another to the hut, where each man was the host, and all were the guests of the whole company. They spread their individual supplies of food on the flat surface of a rock, and partook of a general repast; at the close of which, a sentiment of good fellowship was perceptible among the party, though repressed by the idea that the renewed search for the Great Carbuncle must make them strangers again in the morning. Seven men and one young woman, they warmed themselves together at the fire, which extended its bright wall along the whole front of their wigwam. As they observed the various and contrasted figures that made up the assemblage, each man looking like a caricature of

* The Indian tradition, on which this somewhat extravagant tale is founded, is both too wild and too beautiful to be adequately wrought up in prose. Sullivan, in his History of Maine, written since the Revolution, remarks that even then the existence of the Great Carbuncle was not entirely discredited.

himself, in the unsteady light that flickered over him, they came mutually to the conclusion, that an odder society had never met, in city or wilderness, on mountain or plain.

The eldest of the group, a tall, lean, weather-beaten man, some sixty years of age, was clad in the skins of wild animals, whose fashion of dress he did well to imitate, since the deer, the wolf, and the bear had long been his most intimate companions. He was one of those ill-fated mortals, such as the Indians told of, whom, in their early youth, the Great Carbuncle smote with a peculiar madness, and became the passionate dream of their existence. All who visited that region knew him as the Seeker, and by no other name. As none could remember when he first took up the search, there went a fable in the valley of the Saco, that for his inordinate lust after the Great Carbuncle he had been condemned to wander among the mountains till the end of time, still with the same feverish hopes at sunrise,—the same despair at eve. Near this miserable Seeker sat a little elderly personage, wearing a high-crowned hat, shaped somewhat like a crucible. He was from beyond the sea, a Doctor Cacaphodel, who had wilted and dried himself into a mummy, by continually stooping over charcoal furnaces and inhaling unwholesome fumes, during his researches in chemistry and alchemy. It was told of him, whether truly or not, that, at the commencement of his studies, he had drained his body of all its richest blood, and wasted it, with other inestimable ingredients, in an unsuccessful experiment,—and had never been a well man since. Another of the adventurers was Master Ichabod Pigsnort, a weighty merchant and selectman of Boston, and an elder of the famous Mr. Norton's church. His enemies had a ridiculous story, that Master Pigsnort was accustomed to spend a whole hour, after prayer time, every morning and evening, in wallowing naked among an immense quantity of pine-tree shillings, which were the earliest silver coinage of Massachusetts. The fourth whom we shall notice had no name, that his companions knew of, and was chiefly distinguished by a sneer that always contorted his thin visage, and by a prodigious pair of spectacles, which were supposed to deform and discolor the whole face of nature, to this gentleman's perception. The fifth adventurer, likewise lacked a name, which was the greater pity, as he appeared to be a poet. He was a bright-eyed man, but wofully pined away, which was no more than natural, if, as some people affirmed, his ordinary diet was fog, morning mist, and a slice of the densest cloud within his reach, sauced with moonshine, whenever he could get it. Certain it is, that the poetry, which flowed from him, had a smack of all these dainties. The sixth of the party was a young man of haughty mien, and sat somewhat apart from the rest, wearing his plumed hat loftily among his elders, while the fire glittered on the rich embroidery of his dress, and gleamed intensely on the jewelled pommel of his sword. This was the Lord de Vere, who, when at home, was said to spend much of his time in the burial-vault of his dead progenitors, rummaging their mouldy coffins in search of all the earthly pride and vainglory that was hidden among bones and dust; so that, besides his own share, he had the collected haughtiness of his whole line of ancestry.

Lastly, there was a handsome youth in rustic garb, and by his side, a blooming little person, in whom a delicate shade of maiden reserve was just melting into the rich glow of a young wife's affection. Her name was Hannah, and her husband's Matthew; two homely names, yet well enough adapted to the simple pair, who seemed strangely out of place among the whimsical fraternity whose wits had been set agog by the Great Carbuncle.

Beneath the shelter of one hut, in the bright blaze of the same fire, sat this varied group of adventurers, all so intent upon a single object, that, of whatever else they began to speak, their closing words were sure to be illuminated with the Great Carbuncle. Several related the circumstances that brought them thither. One had listened to a traveller's tale of this marvellous stone, in his own distant country, and had immediately been seized with such a thirst for beholding it, as could only be quenched in its intensest lustre. Another, so long ago as when the famous Captain Smith visited these coasts, had seen it blazing far at sea, and had felt no rest in all the intervening years, till now that he took up the search. A third, being encamped on a hunting expedition, full forty miles south of the White Mountains, awoke at midnight, and beheld the Great Carbuncle gleaming, like a meteor, so that the shadows of the trees fell backward from it. They spoke of the innumerable attempts which had been made to reach the spot, and of the singular fatality which had hitherto withheld success from all adventurers, though it might seem so easy to follow

to its source a light that overpowered the moon, and almost matched the sun. It was observable that each smiled scornfully at the madness of every other, in anticipating better fortune than the past, yet nourished a scarcely hidden conviction, that he would himself be the favored one. As if to allay their too sanguine hopes, they recurred to the Indian traditions, that a spirit kept watch about the gem, and bewildered those who sought it, either by removing it from peak to peak of the higher hills, or by calling up a mist from the enchanted lake over which it hung. But these tales were deemed unworthy of credit; all professing to believe, that the search had been baffled by want of sagacity or perseverance in the adventurers, or such other causes as might naturally obstruct the passage to any given point, among the intricacies of forest, valley, and mountain.

In a pause of the conversation, the wearer of the prodigious spectacles looked around upon the party, making each individual, in turn, the object of the sneer which invariably dwelt upon his countenance.

"So, fellow-pilgrims," said he, "here we are, seven wise men and one fair damsel,—who, doubtless, is as wise as any graybeard of the company: here we are, I say, all bound on the same goodly enterprise. Methinks, now, it were not amiss that each of us declare what he proposes to do with the Great Carbuncle, provided he have the good hap to clutch it. What says our friend in the bear-skin? How mean you, good sir, to enjoy the prize which you have been seeking, the Lord knows how long, among the Crystal Hills?"

"How enjoy it!" exclaimed the aged

Seeker, bitterly. "I hope for no enjoyment from it,—that folly has past long ago! I keep up the search for this accursed stone, because the vain ambition of my youth has become a fate upon me, in old age. The pursuit alone is my strength,—the energy of my soul,—the warmth of my blood, and the pith and marrow of my bones! Were I to turn my back upon it, I should fall down dead, on the hither side of the Notch, which is the gateway of this mountain region. Yet, not to have my wasted lifetime back again, would I give up my hopes of the Great Carbuncle! Having found it, I shall bear it to a certain cavern that I wot of, and there, grasping it in my arms, lie down and die, and keep it buried with me forever."

"O wretch, regardless of the interests of science!" cried Doctor Cacaphodel, with philosophic indignation. "Thou art not worthy to behold, even from afar off, the lustre of this most precious gem that ever was concocted in the laboratory of Nature. Mine is the sole purpose for which a wise man may desire the possession of the Great Carbuncle. Immediately on obtaining it,—for I have a presentiment, good people, that the prize is reserved to crown my scientific reputation,—I shall return to Europe, and employ my remaining years in reducing it to its first elements. A portion of the stone will I grind to impalpable powder; other parts shall be dissolved in acids, or whatever solvents will act upon so admirable a composition; and the remainder I design to melt in the crucible, or set on fire with the blowpipe. By these various methods I shall gain an accurate analysis, and finally bestow the result of my labors upon the world, in a folio volume."

"Excellent!" quoth the man with the spectacles. "Nor need you hesitate, learned sir, on account of the necessary destruction of the gem; since the perusal of your folio may teach every mother's son of us to concoct a Great Carbuncle of his own."

"But, verily," said Master Ichabod Pigsnort, "for mine own part I object to the making of these counterfeits, as being calculated to reduce the marketable value of the true gem. I tell ye frankly, sirs, I have an interest in keeping up the price. Here have I quitted my regular traffic, leaving my warehouse in the care of my clerks, and putting my credit to great hazard, and, furthermore, have put myself in peril of death or captivity by the accursed heathen savages,—and all this without daring to ask the prayers of the congregation, because the quest for the Great Carbuncle is deemed little better than a traffic with the Evil One. Now think ye that I would have done this grievous wrong to my soul, body, reputation, and estate, without a reasonable chance of profit?"

"Not I, pious Master Pigsnort," said the man with the spectacles. "I never laid such a great folly to thy charge."

"Truly, I hope not," said the merchant. "Now, as touching this Great Carbuncle, I am free to own that I have never had a glimpse of it; but be it only the hundredth part so bright as people tell, it will surely outvalue the Great Mogul's best diamond, which he holds at an incalculable sum. Wherefore, I am minded to put the Great Carbuncle on shipboard, and voyage with it to England, France, Spain, Italy, or unto Heathendom, if Providence should send me thither, and, in a word, dispose of the gem to the best bidder, mong the potentates of the earth, that e may place it among his crown jewels. f any of ye have a wiser plan, let him xpound it."

"That have I, thou sordid man!" exlaimed the poet. "Dost thou desire othing brighter than gold, that thou ouldst transmute all this ethereal lustre ato such dross as thou wallowest in lready? For myself, hiding the jewel nder my cloak, I shall hie me back ● my attic chamber, in one of the arksome alleys of London. There, ight and day, will I gaze upon it,— ay soul shall drink its radiance,—it aall be diffused throughout my intelctual powers, and gleam brightly in very line of poesy that I indite. Thus, ●ng ages after I am gone, the splenor of the Great Carbuncle will blaze round my name!"

"Well said, Master Poet!" cried he f the spectacles. "Hide it under thy oak, sayest thou? Why, it will gleam arough the holes, and make thee look ke a jack-o'lantern!"

"To think!" ejaculated the Lord de ere, rather to himself than his com-anions, the best of whom he held utrly unworthy of his intercourse,—"to aink that a fellow in a tattered cloak aould talk of conveying the Great Caruncle to a garret in Grub Street! Have ot I resolved within myself, that the hole earth contains no fitter ornament r the great hall of my ancestral castle? here shall it flame for ages, making noonday of midnight, glittering on ae suits of armor, the banners, and scutcheons that hang around the wall, ad keeping bright the memory of eroes. Wherefore have all other adven-trers sought the prize in vain, but aat I might win it, and make it a symbol of the glories of our lofty line? And never, on the diadem of the White Mountains did the Great Carbuncle hold a place half so honored as is reserved for it in the hall of the De Veres!"

"It is a noble thought," said the Cynic, with an obsequious sneer. "Yet, might I presume to say so, the gem would make a rare sepulchral lamp, and would display the glories of your lordship's progenitors more truly in the ancestral vault than in the castle hall."

"Nay, forsooth," observed Matthew, the young rustic, who sat hand in hand with his bride, "the gentleman has bethought himself of a profitable use for this bright stone. Hannah here and I are seeking it for a like purpose."

"How, fellow!" exclaimed his lordship, in surprise. "What castle hall hast thou to hang it in?"

"No castle," replied Matthew, "but as neat a cottage as any within sight of the Crystal Hills. Ye must know, friends, that Hannah and I, being wedded the last week, have taken up the search of the Great Carbuncle, because we shall need its light in the long winter evenings; and it will be such a pretty thing to show the neighbors when they visit us. It will shine through the house, so that we may pick up a pin in any corner, and will set all the windows aglowing, as if there were a great fire of pine-knots in the chimney. And then how pleasant, when we awake in the night, to be able to see one another's faces!"

There was a general smile among the adventurers at the simplicity of the young couple's project, in regard to this wondrous and invaluable stone, with which the greatest monarch on earth might have been proud to adorn his palace. Especially the man with spectacles, who had sneered at all the company in turn, now twisted his visage into such an expression of ill-natured mirth, that Matthew asked him, rather peevishly, what he himself meant to do with the Great Carbuncle.

"The Great Carbuncle!" answered the Cynic, with ineffable scorn. "Why, you blockhead, there is no such thing, in *rerum natura*. I have come three thousand miles, and am resolved to set my foot on every peak of these mountains, and poke my head into every chasm, for the sole purpose of demonstrating to the satisfaction of any man, one whit less an ass than thyself, that the Great Carbuncle is all a humbug!"

Vain and foolish were the motives that had brought most of the adventurers to the Crystal Hills, but none so vain, so foolish, and so impious too, as that of the scoffer with the prodigious spectacles. He was one of those wretched and evil men whose yearnings are downward to the darkness, instead of heavenward, and who, could they but extinguish the lights which God hath kindled for us, would count the midnight gloom their chiefest glory. As the Cynic spoke, several of the party were startled by a gleam of red splendor, that showed the huge shapes of the surrounding mountains, and the rock-bestrewn bed of the turbulent river, with an illumination unlike that of their fire, on the trunks and black boughs of the forest-trees. They listened for the roll of thunder, but heard nothing, and were glad that the tempest came not near them. The stars, those dial-points of heaven, now warned the adventurers to close their eyes on the blazing logs, and open them, in dreams, to the glow of the Great Carbuncle.

The young married couple had taken their lodgings in the farthest corner of the wigwam, and were separated from the rest of the party by a curtain of curiously-woven twigs, such as might have hung, in deep festoons, around the bridal bower of Eve. The modest little wife had wrought this piece of tapestry while the other guests were talking. She and her husband fell asleep with hands tenderly clasped, and awoke, from visions of unearthly radiance, to meet the more blessed light of one another's eyes. They awoke at the same instant, and with one happy smile beaming over their two faces, which grew brighter with their consciousness of the reality of life and love. But no sooner did she recollect where they were, than the bride peeped through the interstices of the leafy curtain, and saw that the outer room of the hut was deserted.

"Up, dear Matthew!" cried she, in haste. "The strange folk are all gone. Up, this very minute, or we shall lose the Great Carbuncle!"

In truth, so little did these poor young people deserve the mighty prize which had lured them thither, that they had slept peacefully all night, and till the summits of the hills were glittering with sunshine; while the other adventurers had tossed their limbs in feverish wakefulness, or dreamed of climbing precipices, and set off to realize their dreams with the earliest peep of dawn. But Matthew and Hannah, after their calm rest, were as light as two young deer, and merely stopped to say their prayers, and wash themselves in a cold pool of the Amonoosuck, and then to taste a morsel of food, ere they turned their faces to the mountain-side. It was a sweet emblem of conjugal affection, as they toiled up the difficult ascent, gathering strength from the mutual aid which they afforded. After several little accidents, such as a torn robe, a lost shoe, and the entanglement of Hannah's hair in a bough, they reached the upper verge of the forest, and were now to pursue a more adventurous course. The innumerable trunks and heavy foliage of the trees had hitherto shut in their thoughts, which now shrank affrighted from the region of wind, and cloud, and naked rocks, and desolate sunshine, that rose immeasurably above them. They gazed back at the obscure wilderness which they had traversed, and longed to be buried again in its depths, rather than trust themselves to so vast and visible a solitude.

"Shall we go on?" said Matthew, throwing his arm round Hannah's waist, both to protect her, and to comfort his heart by drawing her close to it.

But the little bride, simple as she was, had a woman's love of jewels, and could not forego the hope of possessing the very brightest in the world, in spite of the perils with which it must be won. "Let us climb a little higher," whispered she, yet tremulously, as she turned her face upward to the lonely sky.

"Come, then," said Matthew, mustering his manly courage, and drawing her along with him; for she became timid again the moment that he grew bold.

And upward, accordingly, went the pilgrims of the Great Carbuncle, now treading upon the tops and thickly-interwoven branches of dwarf pines, which by the growth of centuries, though mossy with age, had barely reached three feet in altitude. Next, they came to masses and fragments of naked rock, heaped confusedly together, like a cairn reared by giants, in memory of a giant chief. In this bleak realm of upper air nothing breathed, nothing grew; there was no life but what was concentrated in their two hearts; they had climbed so high that Nature herself seemed no longer to keep them company. She lingered beneath them, within the verge of the forest-trees, and sent a farewell glance after her children, as they strayed where her own green footprints had never been. But soon they were to be hidden from her eye. Densely and dark the mists began to gather below, casting black spots of shadow on the vast landscape, and sailing heavily to one centre, as if the loftiest mountain-peak had summoned a council of its kindred clouds. Finally the vapors welded themselves, as it were, into a mass, presenting the appearance of a pavement over which the wanderers might have trodden, but where they would vainly have sought an avenue to the blessed earth which they had lost. And the lovers yearned to behold that green earth again, more intensely, alas! than, beneath a clouded sky, they had ever desired a glimpse of heaven. They even felt it a relief to their desolation, when the mists, creeping gradually up the mountain, concealed its lonely peak, and thus annihilated, at least for them, the whole region of visible space. But they drew closer together, with a fond and melancholy gaze, dreading lest the universal cloud should snatch them from each other's sight.

Still, perhaps, they would have been resolute to climb as far and as high, between earth and heaven, as they could find foothold, if Hannah's strength had not begun to fail, and with that her courage also. Her breath grew short. She refused to burden her husband with her weight, but often tottered against his side, and recovered herself each time by a feebler effort. At last she sank down on one of the rocky steps of the acclivity.

"We are lost, dear Matthew," said she, mournfully. "We shall never find our way to the earth again. And O, how happy we might have been in our cottage!"

"Dear heart!—we will yet be happy there," answered Matthew. "Look! In this direction the sunshine penetrates the dismal mist. By its aid I can direct our course to the passage of the Notch. Let us go back, love, and dream no more of the Great Carbuncle!"

"The sun cannot be yonder," said Hannah, with despondence. "By this time it must be noon. If there could ever be any sunshine here, it would come from above our heads."

"But look!" repeated Matthew, in a somewhat altered tone. "It is brightening every moment. If not sunshine, what can it be?"

Nor could the young bride any longer deny that a radiance was breaking through the mist, and changing its dim hue to a dusky red, which continually grew more vivid, as if brilliant particles were interfused with the gloom. Now, also, the cloud began to roll away from the mountain, while, as it heavily withdrew, one object after another started out of its impenetrable obscurity into sight, with precisely the effect of a new creation, before the indistinctness of the old chaos had been completely swallowed up. As the process

went on, they saw the gleaming of water close at their feet, and found themselves on the very border of a mountain lake, deep, bright, clear, and calmly beautiful, spreading from brim to brim of a basin that had been scooped out of the solid rock. A ray of glory flashed across its surface. The pilgrims looked whence it should proceed, but closed their eyes with a thrill of awful admiration, to exclude the fervid splendor that glowed from the brow of a cliff, impending over the enchanted lake. For the simple pair had reached that lake of mystery, and found the long-sought shrine of the Great Carbuncle!

They threw their arms around each other, and trembled at their own success; for as the legends of this wondrous gem rushed thick upon their memory, they felt themselves marked out by fate,—and the consciousness was fearful. Often, from childhood upward, they had seen it shining like a distant star. And now that star was throwing its intensest lustre on their hearts. They seemed changed to one another's eyes, in the red brilliancy that flamed upon their cheeks, while it lent the same fire to the lake, the rocks, and sky, and to the mists which had rolled back before its power. But, with their next glance, they beheld an object that drew their attention even from the mighty stone. At the base of the cliff directly beneath the Great Carbuncle appeared the figure of a man, with his arms extended in the act of climbing, and his face turned upward, as if to drink the full gush of splendor. But he stirred not, no more than if changed to marble.

"It is the Seeker," whispered Hanah, convulsively grasping her husband's rm. "Matthew, he is dead."

"The joy of success has killed him," eplied Matthew, trembling violently. Or, perhaps the very light of the Great 'arbuncle was death!"

"The Great Carbuncle," cried a peeish voice behind them. "The Great Humbug! If you have found it, prithee oint it out to me."

They turned their heads, and there as the Cynic, with his prodigious specacles set carefully on his nose, staring ow at the lake, now at the rocks, now t the distant masses of vapor, now ght at the Great Carbuncle itself, yet eemingly as unconscious of its light, s if all the scattered clouds were conensed about his person. Though its diance actually threw the shadow of e unbeliever at his own feet, as he urned his back upon the glorious jewel, e would not be convinced that there as the least glimmer there.

"Where is your Great Humbug?" he peated. "I challenge you to make me e it!"

"There," said Matthew, incensed at ch perverse blindness, and turning e Cynic round towards the illuminated iff. "Take off those abominable speccles, and you cannot help seeing it!"

Now these colored spectacles probly darkened the Cynic's sight, in at ast as great a degree as the smoked asses through which people gaze at eclipse. With resolute bravado, hower, he snatched them from his nose, d fixed a bold stare full upon the ddy blaze of the Great Carbuncle. at, scarcely had he encountered it, en, with a deep, shuddering groan, dropped his head, and pressed both nds across his miserable eyes. Thence-

forth there was, in very truth, no light of the Great Carbuncle, nor any other light on earth, nor light of heaven itself, for the poor Cynic. So long accustomed to view all objects through a medium that deprived them of every glimpse of brightness, a single flash of so glorious a phenomenon, striking upon his naked vision, had blinded him forever.

"Matthew," said Hannah, clinging to him, "let us go hence!"

Matthew saw that she was faint, and kneeling down supported her in his arms, while he threw some of the thrillingly cold water of the enchanted lake upon her face and bosom. It revived her, but could not renovate her courage.

"Yes, dearest!" cried Matthew, pressing her tremulous form to his breast, —"we will go hence, and return to our humble cottage. The blessed sunshine, and the quiet moonlight, shall come through our window. We will kindle the cheerful glow of our hearth, at eventide, and be happy in its light. But never again will we desire more light than all the world may share with us."

"No," said his bride, "for how could we live by day, or sleep by night in this awful blaze of the Great Carbuncle!"

Out of the hollow of their hands they drank each a draught from the lake, which presented them its waters uncontaminated by an earthly lip. Then, lending their guidance to the blinded Cynic, who uttered not a word, and even stifled his groans in his own most wretched heart, they began to descend the mountain. Yet, as they left the shore, till then untrodden, of the spirit's lake, they threw a farewell glance towards the cliff, and beheld the vapors gathering in dense volumes, through which the gem burned duskily.

As touching the other pilgrims of the Great Carbuncle, the legend goes on to tell, that the worshipful Master Ichabod Pigsnort soon gave up the quest, as a desperate speculation, and wisely resolved to betake himself again to his warehouse, near the town dock, in Boston. But, as he passed through the Notch of the mountains, a war party of Indians captured our unlucky merchant, and carried him to Montreal, there holding him in bondage, till, by the payment of a heavy ransom, he had wofully subtracted from his hoard of pine-tree shillings. By his long absence, moreover, his affairs had become so disordered, that, for the rest of his life, instead of wallowing in silver, he had seldom a sixpence-worth of copper. Doctor Cacaphodel, the alchemist, returned to his laboratory with a prodigious fragment of granite, which he ground to powder, dissolved in acids, melted in the crucible, and burned with the blowpipe, and published the result of his experiments in one of the heaviest folios of the day. And, for all these purposes, the gem itself could not have answered better than the granite. The poet, by a somewhat similar mistake, made prize of a great piece of ice, which he found in a sunless chasm of the mountains, and swore that it corresponded, in all points, with his idea of the Great Carbuncle. The critics say, that, if his poetry lacked the splendor of the gem, it retained all the coldness of the ice. The Lord de Vere went back to his ancestral hall, where he contented himself with a wax-lighted chandelier, and filled,

in due course of time, another coffin in the ancestral vault. As the funeral torches gleamed within that dark receptacle, there was no need of the Great Carbuncle to show the vanity of earthly pomp.

The Cynic, having cast aside his spectacles, wandered about the world, a miserable object, and was punished with an agonizing desire of light, for the wilful blindness of his former life. The whole night long, he would lift his splendor-blasted orbs to the moon and stars; he turned his face eastward, at sunrise, as duly as a Persian idolater; he made a pilgrimage to Rome, to witness the magnificent illumination of St. Peter's Church; and finally perished in the great fire of London, into the midst of which he had thrust himself, with the desperate idea of catching one feeble ray from the blaze that was kindling earth and heaven.

Matthew and his bride spent many peaceful years, and were fond of telling the legend of the Great Carbuncle. The tale, however, towards the close of their lengthened lives, did not meet with the full credence that had been accorded to it by those who remembered the ancient lustre of the gem. For it is affirmed, that, from the hour when two mortals had shown themselves so simply wise as to reject a jewel which would have dimmed all earthly things, its splendor waned. When other pilgrims reached the cliff, they found only an opaque stone, with particles of mica glittering on its surface. There is also a tradition that, as the youthful pair departed, the gem was loosened from the forehead of the cliff, and fell into the enchanted lake, and that, at noontide, the Seeker's form may still

e seen to bend over its quenchless
leam.

Some few believe that this inesti-
nable stone is blazing, as of old, and
y that they have caught its radiance,
ke a flash of summer lightning, far
down the valley of the Saco. And be
it owned, that, many a mile from the
Crystal Hills, I saw a wondrous light
around their summits, and was lured,
by the faith of poesy, to be the latest
pilgrim of the GREAT CARBUNCLE.

THE PROPHETIC PICTURES *

"BUT this painter," cried Walter Lud-
w, with animation, "he not only excels
. his peculiar art, but possesses vast
:quirements in all other learning and
ience. He talks Hebrew with Dr.
:ather, and gives lectures in anatomy
Dr. Boylston. In a word, he will
eet the best-instructed man among us,
his own ground. Moreover, he is a
lished gentleman,—a citizen of the
orld,—yes, a true cosmopolite; for he
ll speak like a native of each clime
d country on the globe, except our
vn forests, whither he is now going.
or is all this what I most admire in
m."

"Indeed!" said Elinor, who had lis-
ned with a woman's interest to the
scription of such a man. "Yet this
admirable enough."

"Surely it is," replied her lover, "but
less so than his natural gift of adapt-
g himself to every variety of charter, insomuch that all men—and all
men, too, Elinor—shall find a mirror
themselves in this wonderful painter.
t the greatest wonder is yet to be
d."

This story was suggested by an anecdote of
art, related in Dunlap's History of the Arts
Design,—a most entertaining book to the
eral reader, and a deeply interesting one,
should think, to the artist.

"Nay, if he have more wonderful attributes than these," said Elinor, laughing, "Boston is a perilous abode for the
poor gentleman. Are you telling me of
a painter, or a wizard?"

"In truth," answered he, "that question might be asked much more seriously than you suppose. They say that
he paints not merely a man's features,
but his mind and heart. He catches the
secret sentiments and passions, and
throws them upon the canvas, like sunshine,—or perhaps, in the portraits of
dark-souled men, like a gleam of infernal fire. It is an awful gift," added
Walter, lowering his voice from its tone
of enthusiasm; "I shall be almost afraid
to sit to him."

"Walter, are you in earnest?" exclaimed Elinor.

"For Heaven's sake, dearest Elinor,
do not let him paint the look which you
now wear," said her lover, smiling,
though rather perplexed. "There: it is
passing away now, but when you spoke,
you seemed frightened to death, and
very sad besides. What were you thinking of?"

"Nothing, nothing," answered Elinor,
hastily. "You paint my face with your
own fantasies. Well, come for me to-
morrow, and we will visit this wonder-

ful artist."

But when the young man had departed, it cannot be denied that a remarkable expression was again visible on the fair and youthful face of his mistress. It was a sad and anxious look, little in accordance with what should have been the feelings of a maiden on the eve of wedlock. Yet Walter Ludlow was the chosen of her heart.

"A look!" said Elinor to herself. "No wonder that it startled him, if it expressed what I sometimes feel. I know, by my own experience, how frightful a look may be. But it was all fancy. I thought nothing of it at the time, —I have seen nothing of it since,—I did but dream it."

And she busied herself about the embroidery of a ruff, in which she meant that her portrait should be taken.

The painter, of whom they had been speaking, was not one of those native artists, who, at a later period than this, borrowed their colors from the Indians, and manufactured their pencils of the furs of wild beasts. Perhaps, if he could have revoked his life and prearranged his destiny, he might have chosen to belong to that school without a master, in the hope of being at least original, since there were no works of art to imitate nor rules to follow. But he had been born and educated in Europe. People said, that he had studied the grandeur or beauty of conception, and every touch of the master hand, in all the most famous pictures, in cabinets and galleries, and on the walls of churches, till there was nothing more for his powerful mind to learn. Art could add nothing to its lessons, but Nature might. He had therefore visited a world whither none of his professional brethren had preceded him, to feast his eyes on visible images, that were noble and picturesque, yet had never been transferred to canvas. America was too poor to afford other temptations to an artist of eminence, though many of the colonial gentry, on the painter's arrival, had expressed a wish to transmit their lineaments to posterity by means of his skill. Whenever such proposals were made, he fixed his piercing eyes on the applicant, and seemed to look him through and through. If he beheld only a sleek and comfortable visage, though there were a gold-laced coat to adorn the picture, and golden guineas to pay for it, he civilly rejected the task and the reward. But if the face were the index of anything uncommon, in thought, sentiment, or experience; or if he met a beggar in the street, with a white beard and a furrowed brow; or if sometimes a child happened to look up and smile; he would exhaust all the art on them that he denied to wealth.

Pictorial skill being so rare in the colonies, the painter became an object of general curiosity. If few or none could appreciate the technical merit of his productions, yet there were points in regard to which the opinion of the crowd was as valuable as the refined judgment of the amateur. He watched the effect that each picture produced on such untutored beholders, and derived profit from their remarks, while they would as soon have thought of instructing Nature herself as him who seemed to rival her. Their admiration, it must be owned, was tinctured with the prejudices of the age and country. Some deemed it an offence against the Mosaic law, and even a presumptuous mockery of the Creator, to bring into

istence such lively images of his crea-
res. Others, frightened at the art
iich could raise phantoms at will, and
ep the form of the dead among the
ing, were inclined to consider the
inter as a magician, or perhaps the
mous Black Man of old witch times,
tting mischief in a new guise. These
olish fancies were more than half be-
ved among the mob. Even in superior
cles his character was invested with
vague awe, partly rising like smoke-
eaths from the popular superstitions,
t chiefly caused by the varied knowl-
ge and talents which he made sub-
vient to his profession.

Being on the eve of marriage, Wal-
Ludlow and Elinor were eager to
tain their portraits, as the first of
at, they doubtless hoped, would be
ong series of family pictures. The day
er the conversation above recorded
ey visited the painter's rooms. A ser-
nt ushered them into an apartment,
ere, though the artist himself was
t visble, there were personages whom
ey could hardly forbear greeting with
erence. They knew, indeed, that the
ole assembly were but pictures, yet
t it impossible to separate the idea
life and intellect from such striking
interfeits. Several of the portraits
re known to them, either as dis-
guished characters of the day, or
eir private acquaintances. There was
vernor Burnett, looking as if he had
t received an undutiful communica-
n from the House of Representa-
es, and were inditing a most sharp
ponse. Mr. Cooke hung beside the
er whom he opposed, sturdy, and
newhat puritanical, as befitted a pop-
r leader. The ancient lady of Sir
lliam Phipps eyed them from the
wall, in ruff and farthingale, an imperious old dame, not unsuspected of
witchcraft. John Winslow, then a very
young man, wore the expression of warlike enterprise, which long afterwards
made him a distinguished general. Their
personal friends were recognized at a
glance. In most of the pictures, the
whole mind and character were brought
out on the countenance, and concentrated into a single look, so that, to
speak paradoxically, the originals hardly
resembled themselves so strikingly as
the portraits did.

Among these modern worthies, there
were two old bearded Saints, who had
almost vanished into the darkening canvas. There was also a pale, but unfaded
Madonna, who had perhaps been worshipped in Rome, and now regarded
the lovers with such a mild and holy
look, that they longed to worship too.

"How singular a thought," observed
Walter Ludlow, "that this beautiful
face has been beautiful for above two
hundred years! O, if all beauty would
endure so well! Do you not envy her,
Elinor?"

"If earth were Heaven, I might,"
she replied. "But where all things fade,
how miserable to be the one that could
not fade!"

"This dark old St. Peter has a fierce
and ugly scowl, saint though he be,"
continued Walter. "He troubles me. But
the virgin looks kindly at us."

"Yes; but very sorrowfully, methinks," said Elinor.

The easel stood beneath these three
old pictures, sustaining one that had
been recently commenced. After a little
inspection they began to recognize the
features of their own minister, the Rev.
Dr. Colman, growing into shape and

life, as it were, out of a cloud.

"Kind old man!" exclaimed Elinor. "He gazes at me as if he were about to utter a word of paternal advice."

"And at me," said Walter, "as if he were about to shake his head and rebuke me for some suspected iniquity. But so does the original. I sha'l never feel quite comfortable under his eye till we stand before him to be married."

They now heard a footstep on the floor, and turning, beheld the painter, who had been some moments in the room, and had listened to a few of their remarks. He was a middle-aged man, with a countenance well worthy of his own pencil. Indeed, by the picturesque, though careless arrangement of his rich dress, and, perhaps, because his soul dwelt always among painted shapes, he looked somewhat like a portrait himself. His visitors were sensible of a kindred between the artist and his works, and felt as if one of the pictures had stepped from the canvas to salute them.

Walter Ludlow, who was slightly known to the painter, explained the object of their visit. While he spoke, a sunbeam was falling athwart his figure and Elinor's, with so happy an effect, that they also seemed living pictures of youth and beauty, gladdened by bright fortune. The artist was evidently struck.

"My easel is occupied for several ensuing days, and my stay in Boston must be brief," said he thoughtfully; then, after an observant glance, he added: "but your wishes shall be gratified, though I disappoint the Chief Justice and Madame Oliver. I must not lose this opportunity, for the sake of painting a few ells of broadcloth and brocade."

The painter expressed a desire to introduce both their portraits into one picture, and represent them engaged in some appropriate action. This plan would have delighted the lovers, but was necessarily rejected, because so large a space of canvas would have been unfit for the room which it was intended to decorate. Two half-length portraits were therefore fixed upon. After they had taken leave, Walter Ludlow asked Elinor, with a smile, whether she knew what an influence over their fates the painter was about to acquire.

"The old women of Boston affirm," continued he, "that after he has once got possession of a person's face and figure, he may paint him in any act or situation whatever,—and the picture will be prophetic. Do you believe it?"

"Not quite," said Elinor, smiling. "Yet, if he has such magic, there is something so gentle in his manner that I am sure he will use it well."

It was the painter's choice to proceed with both the portraits at the same time, assigning as a reason, in the mystical language which he sometimes used, that the faces threw light upon each other. Accordingly, he gave now a touch to Walter, and now to Elinor, and the features of one and the other began to start forth so vividly that it appeared as if his triumphant art would actually disengage them from the canvas. Amid the rich light and deep shade, they beheld their phantom selves. But, though the likeness promised to be perfect, they were not quite satisfied with the expression; it seemed more vague than in most of the painter's works. He, however, was satis-

d with the prospect of success, and
ing much interested in the lovers,
iployed his leisure moments, unknown
them, in making a crayon sketch of
eir two figures. During their sittings
engaged them in conversation, and
idled up their faces with characteris-
: traits, which, though continually
rying, it was his purpose to combine
d fix. At length he announced, that
their next visit both the portraits
uld be ready for delivery.

"If my pencil will but be true to
y conception, in the few last touches
ich I meditate," observed he, "these
o pictures will be my very best per-
rmances. Seldom, indeed, has an artist
ch subjects."

While speaking he still bent his pene-
tive eye upon them, nor withdrew it
they had reached the bottom of the
irs.

Nothing, in the whole circle of human
nities takes stronger hold of the imag-
tion than this affair of having a
rtrait painted. Yet why should it be
? The looking-glass, the polished
bes of the andirons, the mirror-like
ter, and all other reflecting surfaces,
ntinually present us with portraits,
rather ghosts, of ourselves, which
glance at and straightway forget
m. But we forget them only because
ey vanish. It is the idea of duration,
of earthly immortality,—that gives
ch a mysterious interest to our own
rtraits. Walter and Elinor were not
ensible to this feeling, and hastened
the painter's room, punctually at the
pointed hour, to meet those pictured
apes which were to be their repre-
atatives with posterity. The sunshine
shed after them into the apartment,
t left it somewhat gloomy as they
closed the door.

Their eyes were immediately attracted to their portraits, which rested
against the farthest wall of the room.
At the first glance, through the dim
light and the distance, seeing themselves
in precisely their natural attitudes, and
with all the air that they recognized so
well, they uttered a simultaneous exclamation of delight.

"There we stand," cried Walter, enthusiastically, "fixed in sunshine forever! No dark passions can gather on
our faces!"

"No," said Elinor, more calmly; "no
dreary change can sadden us."

This was said while they were approaching, and had yet gained only an
imperfect view of the pictures. The
painter, after saluting them, busied himself at a table in completing a crayon
sketch, leaving his visitors to form their
own judgment as to his perfected labors.
At intervals, he sent a glance from beneath his deep eyebrows, watching their
countenances in profile, with his pencil
suspended over the sketch. They had
now stood some moments, each in front
of the other's picture, contemplating it
with entranced attention, but without
uttering a word. At length, Walter
stepped forward,—then back,—viewing
Elinor's portrait in various lights, and
finally spoke.

"Is there not a change?" said he, in
a doubtful and meditative tone. "Yes;
the perception of it grows more vivid
the longer I look. It is certainly the
same picture that I saw yesterday; the
dress,—the features,—all are the same;
and yet something is altered."

"Is, then, the picture less like than
it was yesterday?" inquired the painter.

now drawing near, with irrepressible interest.

"The features are perfect, Elinor," answered Walter; "and, at the first glance, the expression seemed also hers. But I could fancy that the portrait has changed countenance, while I have been looking at it. The eyes are fixed on mine with a strangely sad and anxious expression. Nay, it is grief and terror! Is this like Elinor?"

"Compare the living face with the pictured one," said the painter.

Walter glanced sidelong at his mistress, and started. Motionless and absorbed—fascinated, as it were—in contemplation of Walter's portrait, Elinor's face had assumed precisely the expression of which he had just been complaining. Had she practised for whole hours before a mirror, she could not have caught the look so successfully. Had the picture itself been a mirror, it could not have thrown back her present aspect with stronger and more melancholy truth. She appeared quite unconscious of the dialogue between the artist and her lover.

"Elinor," exclaimed Walter, in amazement, "what change has come over you?"

She did not hear him, nor desist from her fixed gaze, till he seized her hand, and thus attracted her notice; then, with a sudden tremor, she looked from the picture to the face of the original.

"Do you see no change in your portrait?" asked she.

"In mine?—None!" replied Walter, examining it. "But let me see! Yes! there is a slight change,—an improvement, I think, in the picture, though none in the likeness. It has a livelier expression than yesterday, as if some

bright thought were flashing from the eyes, and about to be uttered from the lips. Now that I have caught the look it becomes very decided."

While he was intent on these observations, Elinor turned to the painter. She regarded him with grief and awe, and felt that he repaid her with sympathy and commiseration, though wherefore she could but vaguely guess.

"That look!" whispered she, and shuddered. "How came it there?"

"Madam," said the painter, sadly, taking her hand, and leading her apart, "in both these pictures, I have painted what I saw. The artist—the true artist—must look beneath the exterior. It is his gift—his proudest, but often a melancholy one—to see the inmost soul, and, by a power indefinable even to himself, to make it glow or darken upon the canvas, in glances that express the thought and sentiment of years. Would that I might convince myself of error in the present instance!"

They had now approached the table, on which were heads in chalk, hands almost as expressive as ordinary faces, ivied church-towers, thatched cottages, old thunder-stricken trees, Oriental and antique costume, and all such picturesque vagaries of an artist's idle moments. Turning them over, with seeming carelessness, a crayon sketch of two figures was disclosed.

"If I have failed," continued he, "if your heart does not see itself reflected in your own portrait,—if you have no secret cause to trust my delineation of the other,—it is not yet too late to alter them. I might change the action of these figures too. But would it influence the event?"

He directed her notice to the sketch.

thrill ran through Elinor's frame;
shriek was upon her lips; but she
fled it, with the self-command that
comes habitual to all who hide
oughts of fear and anguish within
eir bosoms. Turning from the table,
e perceived that Walter had advanced
ar enough to have seen the sketch,
ough she could not determine whether
had caught his eye.

"We will not have the pictures al-
ed," said she, hastily. "If mine is sad,
shall but look the gayer for the con-
st."

"Be it so," answered the painter,
wing. "May your griefs be such fan-
ul ones, that only your picture may
ourn for them! For your joys,—may
ey be true and deep, and paint them-
lves upon this lovely face, till it quite
lie my art!"

After the marriage of Walter and
inor, the pictures formed the two
ost splendid ornaments of their abode.
ey hung side by side, separated by
narrow panel, appearing to eye each
her constantly, yet always returning
e gaze of the spectator. Travelled
ntlemen, who professed a knowledge
such subjects, reckoned these among
e most admirable specimens of mod-
n portraiture; while common observ-
s compared them with the originals,
ature by feature, and were rapturous
praise of the likeness. But, it was
a third class—neither travelled con-
isseurs nor common observers, but
ople of natural sensibility—that the
ctures wrought their strongest effect.
ich persons might gaze carelessly at
st, but, becoming interested, would
turn day after day, and study these
inted faces like the pages of a mystic
olume. Walter Ludlow's portrait at-

tracted their earliest notice. In the absence of himself and his bride, they
sometimes disputed as to the expression
which the painter had intended to throw
upon the features; all agreeing that
there was a look of earnest import,
though no two explained it alike. There
was less diversity of opinion in regard
to Elinor's picture. They differed indeed, in their attempts to estimate the
nature and depth of the gloom that
dwelt upon her face, but agreed that
it was gloom, and alien from the natural
temperament of their youthful friend.
A certain fanciful person annnounced,
as the result of much scrutiny, that
both these pictures were parts of one
design, and that the melancholy strength
of feeling in Elinor's countenance bore
reference to the more vivid emotion,
or, as he termed it, the wild passion,
in that of Walter. Though unskilled
in the art, he even began a sketch,
in which the action of the two figures
was to correspond with their mutual
expression.

It was whispered among friends, that,
day by day, Elinor's face was assuming a deeper shade of pensiveness, which
threatened soon to render her too true
a counterpart of her melancholy picture. Walter, on the other hand, instead of acquiring the vivid look which
the painter had given him on the canvas, became reserved and downcast,
with no outward flashes of emotion,
however it might be smouldering within. In course of time, Elinor hung a
gorgeous curtain of purple silk, wrought
with flowers, and fringed with heavy
golden tassels, before the pictures, under pretence that the dust would tarnish their hues, or the light dim them.
It was enough. Her visitors felt that

the massive folds of the silk must never be withdrawn, nor the portraits mentioned in her presence.

Time wore on; and the painter came again. He had been far enough to the north to see the silver cascade of the Crystal Hills, and to look over the vast round of cloud and forest, from the summit of New England's loftiest mountain. But he did not profane that scene by the mockery of his art. He had also lain in a canoe on the bosom of Lake George, making his soul the mirror of its loveliness and grandeur, till not a picture in the Vatican was more vivid than his recollection. He had gone with the Indian hunters to Niagara, and there, again, had flung his hopeless pencil down the precipice, feeling that he could as soon paint the roar, as aught else that goes to make up the wondrous cataract. In truth, it was seldom his impulse to copy natural scenery, except as a framework for the delineations of the human form and face, instinct with thought, passion, or suffering. With store of such his adventurous ramble had enriched him: the stern dignity of Indian chiefs; the dusky loveliness of Indian girls; the domestic life of wigwams; the stealthy march; the battle beneath gloomy pine-trees; the frontier fortress with its garrison; the anomaly of the old French partisan, bred in courts, but grown gray in shaggy deserts; such were the scenes and portraits that he had sketched. The glow of perilous moments; flashes of wild feeling; struggles of fierce power, —love, hate, grief, frenzy,—in a word, all the worn-out heart of the old earth had been revealed to him under a new form. His portfolio was filled with graphic illustrations of the volume of his memory, which genius would tra mute into its own substance, and iml with immortality. He felt that the de wisdom in his art which he had sou; so far was found.

But, amid stern or lovely nature, the perils of the forest, or its ov whelming peacefulness, still there h been two phantoms, the companions his way. Like all other men arou whom an engrossing purpose wreath itself, he was insulated from the m of human kind. He had no aim, pleasure, no sympathies, but what w ultimately connected with his a Though gentle in manner, and upri; in intent and action, he did not poss kindly feelings; his heart was cold; living creature could be brought n enough to keep him warm. For th two beings, however, he had felt, its greatest intensity, the sort of terest which always allied him to subjects of his pencil. He had pried i their souls with his keenest insight, a pictured the result upon their featu with his utmost skill, so as barely fall short of that standard which genius ever reached,—his own sev conception. He had caught from duskiness of the future—at least, so fancied—a fearful secret, and had scurely revealed it on the portraits. much of himself—of his imaginat and all other powers—had been lavisl on the study of Walter and Elinor, tl he almost regarded them as creations his own, like the thousands with wh he had peopled the realms of Pictu Therefore did they flit through the t light of the woods, hover on the n of waterfalls, look forth from mirror of the lake, nor melt away the noontide sun. They haunted

torial fancy, not as mockeries of
e, nor pale goblins of the dead, but
the guise of portraits, each with the
alterable expression which his magic
d evoked from the caverns of the
al. He could not recross the Atlantic,
he had again beheld the originals
those airy pictures.

"O glorious art!" thus mused the en-
usiastic painter, as he trod the street.
hou art the image of the Creator's
n. The innumerable forms that wan-
c in nothingness start into being at
y beck. The dead live again. Thou
callest them to their old scenes, and
est their gray shadows the lustre of
better life, at once earthly and im-
ortal. Thou snatchest back the fleet-
g moments of History. With thee
ere is no Past; for at thy touch all
at is great becomes forever present;
d illustrious men live through long
es, in the visible performance of the
ry deeds which made them what they
e. O potent Art! as thou bringest the
ntly revealed Past to stand in that
rrow strip of sunlight which we call
w, canst thou summon the shrouded
ture to meet her there? Have I not
hieved it? Am I not thy Prophet?"

Thus, with a proud yet melancholy
vor did he almost cry aloud, as he
ssed through the toilsome street,
nong people that knew not of his rev-
es, nor could understand nor care
r them. It is not good for man to
erish a solitary ambition. Unless there
those around him by whose example
may regulate himself, his thoughts,
sires, and hopes will become extrava-
nt, and he the semblance, perhaps the
ality, of a madman. Reading other
soms with an acuteness almost pre-
natural, the painter failed to see the

disorder of his own.

"And this should be the house," said
he, looking up and down the front before he knocked. "Heaven help my
brains! That picture! Methinks it will
never vanish. Whether I look at the
windows or the door, there it is framed
within them, painted strongly, and glowing in the richest tints,—the faces of
the portraits,—the figures and action
of the sketch!"

He knocked.

"The Portraits! Are they within?"
inquired he, of the domestic; then recollecting himself,—"your master and
mistress! Are they at home?"

"They are, sir," said the servant,
adding, as he noticed that picturesque
aspect of which the painter could never
divest himself,—"and the Portraits
too!"

The guest was admitted into a parlor,
communicating by a central door with
an interior room of the same size. As
the first apartment was empty, he
passed to the entrance of the second,
within which his eyes were greeted by
those living personages—as well as their
pictured representatives—who had long
been the objects of so singular an interest. He involuntarily paused on the
threshold.

They had not perceived his approach.
Walter and Elinor were standing before the portraits, whence the former
had just flung back the rich and voluminous folds of the silken curtain, holding
its golden tassel with one hand, while
the other grasped that of his bride.
The pictures, concealed for months,
gleamed forth again in undiminished
splendor, appearing to throw a sombre
light across the room, rather than to
be disclosed by a borrowed radiance.

That of Elinor had been almost prophetic. A pensiveness, and next a gentle sorrow, had successively dwelt upon her countenance, deepening, with the lapse of time, into a quiet anguish. A mixture of affright would now have made it the very expression of the portrait. Walter's face was moody and dull, or animated only by fitful flashes, which left a heavier darkness for their momentary illumination. He looked from Elinor to her portrait, and thence to his own, in the contemplation of which he finally stood absorbed.

The painter seemed to hear the step of Destiny approaching behind him, on its progress towards its victims. A strange thought darted into his mind. Was not his own the form in which that destiny had embodied itself, and he a chief agent of the coming evil which he had foreshadowed?

Still Walter remained silent before the picture, communing with it, as with his own heart, and abandoning himself to the spell of evil influence that the painter had cast upon the features. Gradually his eyes kindled; while as Elinor watched the increasing wildness of his face, her own assumed a look of terror; and when at last he turned upon her, the resemblance of both to their portraits was complete.

"Our fate is upon us!" howled Wal-

ter. "Die!"

Drawing a knife, he sustained her she was sinking to the ground, a aimed it at her bosom. In the actio and in the look and attitude of eac the painter beheld the figures of h sketch. The picture, with all its tr mendous coloring, was finished.

"Hold, madman!" cried he, sternly.

He had advanced from the door, a interposed himself between the wretch beings, with the same sense of pow to regulate their destiny as to alter scene upon the canvas. He stood lil a magician, controlling the phantom which he had evoked.

"What!" muttered Walter Ludlow, he relapsed from fierce excitement in silent gloom. "Does Fate impede own decree?"

"Wretched lady!" said the painte "Did I not warn you?"

"You did," replied Elinor, calmly, her terror gave place to the quiet gri which it had disturbed. "But—I lov him!"

Is there not a deep moral in tl tale? Could the result of one, or our deeds, be shadowed forth and s before us, some would call it Fa and hurry onward, others be swej along by their passionate desires, an none be turned aside by the PROPHET PICTURES.

DAVID SWAN

A FANTASY

WE can be but partially acquainted even with the events which actually in-

fluence our course through life, and o final destiny. There are innumerab other events —if such they may called—which come close upon us, y ass away without actual results, or ven betraying their near approach, by ae reflection of any light or shadow cross our minds. Could we know all ae vicissitudes of our fortunes, life ould be too full of hope and fear, xultation or disappointment, to afford s a single hour of true serenity. This lea may be illustrated by a page from ae secret history of David Swan.

We have nothing to do with David ntil we find him, at the age of twenty, a the high road from his native place the city of Boston, where his uncle, small dealer in the grocery line, was take him behind the counter. Be it lough to say, that he was a native f New Hampshire, born of respectable arents, and had received an ordinary hool education, with a classic finish y a year at Gilmanton Academy. After urneying on foot, from sunrise till arly noon of a summer's day, his eariness and the increasing heat de-rmined him to sit down in the first nvenient shade, and await the coming of the stage-coach. As if planted on urpose for him, there soon appeared little tuft of maples, with a delightful cess in the midst, and such a fresh bbling spring, that it seemed never have sparkled for any wayfarer but avid Swan. Virgin or not, he kissed with his thirsty lips, and then flung mself along the brink, pillowing his ad upon some skirts and a pair of ntaloons, tied up in a striped cotton andkerchief. The sunbeams could not ach him; the dust did not yet rise om the road, after the heavy rain yesterday; and his grassy lair suited e young man better than a bed of wn. The spring murmured drowsily side him; the branches waved dream-

ily across the blue sky overhead; and a deep sleep, perchance hiding dreams within its depths, fell upon David Swan. But we are to relate events which he did not dream of.

While he lay sound asleep in the shade, other people were wide awake, and passed to and fro, afoot, on horse-back, and in all sorts of vehicles, along the sunny road by his bed-chamber. Some looked neither to the right hand nor the left, and knew not that he was there; some merely glanced that way, without admitting the slumberer among their busy thoughts; some laughed to see how soundly he slept; and several, whose hearts were brimming full of scorn, ejected their venomous superflu-ity on David Swan. A middle-aged widow, when nobody else was near, thrust her head a little way into the recess, and vowed that the young fellow looked charming in his sleep. A temper-ance lecturer saw him, and wrought poor David into the texture of his eve-ning's discourse, as an awful instance of dead drunkenness by the roadside. But censure, praise, merriment, scorn, and indifference were all one, or rather all nothing, to David Swan.

He had slept only a few moments when a brown carriage, drawn by a handsome pair of horses, bowled easily along, and was brought to a standstill nearly in front of David's resting-place. A linchpin had fallen out, and permitted one of the wheels to slide off. The damage was slight, and oc-casioned merely a momentary alarm to an elderly merchant and his wife, who were returning to Boston in the car-riage. While the coachman and a ser-vant were replacing the wheel, the lady and gentleman sheltered themselves beneath the maple trees, and there espied the bubbling fountain and David Swan asleep beside it. Impressed with the awe which the humblest sleeper usually sheds around him, the merchant trod as lightly as the gout would allow; and his spouse took good heed not to rustle her silk gown, lest David should start up, all of a sudden.

"How soundly he sleeps!" whispered the old gentleman. "From what a depth he draws that easy breath! Such sleep as that, brought on without an opiate, would be worth more to me than half my income; for it would suppose health and an untroubled mind."

"And youth, besides," said the lady. "Healthy and quiet age does not sleep thus. Our slumber is no more like his than our wakefulness."

The longer they looked, the more did this elderly couple feel interested in the unknown youth, to whom the wayside and the maple shade were as a secret chamber, with the rich gloom of damask curtains brooding over him. Perceiving that a stray sunbeam glimmered down upon his face, the lady contrived to twist a branch aside, so as to intercept it. And having done this little act of kindness, she began to feel like a mother to him.

"Providence seems to have laid him here," whispered she to her husband, "and to have brought us hither to find him, after our disappointment in our cousin's son. Methinks I can see a likeness to our departed Henry. Shall we waken him?"

"To what purpose?" said the merchant, hesitating. "We know nothing of the youth's character."

"That open countenance!" replied his wife, in the same hushed voice, yet earnestly. "This innocent sleep!"

While these whispers were passing, the sleeper's heart did not throb, nor his breath become agitated, nor his features betray the least token of interest. Yet Fortune was bending over him, just ready to let fall a burden of gold. The old merchant had lost his only son, and had no heir to his wealth, except a distant relative, with whose conduct he was dissatisfied. In such cases, people sometimes do stranger things than to act the magician, and awaken a young man to splendor who fell asleep in poverty.

"Shall we not waken him?" repeated the lady, persuasively.

"The coach is ready, sir," said the servant, behind.

The old couple started, reddened, and hurried away, mutually wondering that they should ever have dreamed of doing anything so very ridiculous. The merchant threw himself back in the carriage, and occupied his mind with the plan of a magnificent asylum for unfortunate men of business. Meanwhile David Swan enjoyed his nap.

The carriage could not have gone above a mile or two, when a pretty young girl came along, with a tripping pace, which showed precisely how her little heart was dancing in her bosom. Perhaps it was this merry kind of motion that caused—is there any harm in saying it?—her garter to slip its knot. Conscious that the silken girth—if silk it were—was relaxing its hold, she turned aside into the shelter of the maple trees, and there found a young man asleep by the spring! Blushing as red as any rose that she should have intruded into a gentleman's bed-chamber, and for such a purpose, to he was about to make her escape on ptoe. But there was peril near the leeper. A monster of a bee had been andering overhead—buzz, buzz, buzz —now among the leaves, now flashing through the strips of sunshine, and now ost in the dark shade, till finally he ppeared to be settling on the eyelid f David Swan. The sting of a bee is ometimes deadly. As free-hearted as he was innocent, the girl attacked the intruder with her handkerchief, rushed him soundly, and drove him from beneath the maple shade. How sweet a picture! This good deed accomplished, with quickened breath, and a eeper blush, she stole a glance at the outhful stranger for whom she had een battling with a dragon in the air.

"He is handsome!" thought she, and lushed redder yet.

How could it be that no dream of liss grew so strong within him, that, hattered by its very strength, it should art asunder, and allow him to perseive the girl among its phantoms? Why, at least, did no smile of welcome righten upon his face? She was come, he maid whose soul, according to the ld and beautiful idea, had been severed from his own, and whom, in all is vague but passionate desires, he earned to meet. Her only could he ove with a perfect love,—him only ould she receive into the depths of her heart,—and now her image was aintly blushing in the fountain, by his ide; should it pass away, its happy ustre would never gleam upon his life gain.

"How sound he sleeps!" murmured the girl.

She departed, but did not trip along the road so lightly as when she came.

Now, this girl's father was a thriving country merchant in the neighborhood, and happened, at that identical time, to be looking out for just such a young man as David Swan. Had David formed a wayside acquaintance with the daughter, he would have became the father's clerk,_ and all else in natural succession. So here, again, had good fortune—the best of fortunes —stolen so near, that her garments brushed against him; and he knew nothing of the matter.

The girl was hardly out of sight, when two men turned aside beneath the maple shade. Both had dark faces, set off by cloth caps, which were drawn down aslant over their brows. Their dresses were shabby, yet had a certain smartness. These were a couple of rascals, who got their living by whatever the Devil sent them; and now, in the interim of other business, had staked the joint profits of their next piece of villainy on a game of cards, which was to have been decided here under the trees. But finding David asleep by the spring, one of the rogues whispered to his fellow,—

"Hist!—Do you see that bundle under his head?"

The other villain nodded, winked, and leered.

"I'll bet you a horn of brandy," said the first, "that the chap has either a pocket-book, or a snug little hoard of small change, stowed away amongst his shirts. And if not there, we shall find it in his pantaloons pocket."

"But how if he wakes?" said the other.

His companion thrust aside his waistcoat, pointed to the handle of a dirk, and nodded.

"So be it!" muttered the second villain.

They approached the unconscious David, and while one pointed the dagger towards his heart, the other began to search the bundle beneath his head. Their two faces, grim, wrinkled, and ghastly with guilt and fear, bent over their victim, looking horrible enough to be mistaken for fiends, should he suddenly awake. Nay, had the villains glanced aside into the spring, even they would hardly have known themselves, as reflected there. But David Swan had never worn a more tranquil aspect, even when asleep on his mother's breast.

"I must take away the bundle," whispered one.

"If he stirs, I'll strike," muttered the other.

But, at this moment, a dog, scenting along the ground, came in beneath the maple trees, and gazed alternately at each of these wicked men, and then at the quiet sleeper. He then lapped out of the fountain.

"Pshaw!" said one villain. "We can do nothing now. The dog's master must be close behind."

"Let's take a drink and be off," said the other.

The man, with the dagger, thrust back the weapon into his bosom, and drew forth a pocket-pistol, but not of that kind which kills by a single discharge. It was a flask of liquor, with a block-tin tumbler screwed upon the mouth. Each drank a comfortable dram, and left the spot, with so many jests, and such laughter at their unaccomplished wickedness, that they might be said to have gone on their way rejoicing. In a few hours, they had forgotten the whole affair, nor once imagined that the recording angel had written down the crime of murder against their souls in letters as durable as eternity. As for David Swan, he still slept quietly, neither conscious of the shadow of death when it hung over him, nor of the glow of renewed life, when that shadow was withdrawn.

He slept, but no longer so quietly as at first. An hour's repose had snatched from his elastic frame the weariness with which many hours of toil had burdened it. Now he stirred,—now moved his lips, without a sound,—now talked, in an inward tone, to the noonday spectres of his dream. But a noise of wheels came rattling louder and louder along the road, until it dashed through the dispersing mist of David's slumber—and there was the stage-coach. He started up, with all his ideas about him.

"Halloo, driver!—Take a passenger?" shouted he.

"Room on top!" answered the driver.

Up mounted David, and bowled away merrily towards Boston, without so much as a parting glance at that fountain of dreamlike vicissitude. He knew not that a phantom of Wealth had thrown a golden hue upon its waters —nor that one of Love had sighed softly to their murmur,—nor that one of Death had threatened to crimson them with his blood,—all, in the brief hour since he lay down to sleep. Sleeping or waking, we hear not the airy footsteps of the strange things that almost happen. Does it not argue a superintending Providence, that while viewless and unexpected events thrust themselves continually athwart our path, there should still be regularity enough in mortal life to render foresight even partially available?

SIGHTS FROM A STEEPLE

So! I have climbed high, and my reward is small. Here I stand, with wearied knees, earth, indeed, at a dizzy depth below, but heaven far, far beyond me still. O that I could soar up into the very zenith, where man never breathed nor eagle ever flew, and where the ethereal azure melts away from the eye, and appears only a deepened shade of nothingness! And yet I shiver at that cold and solitary thought. What clouds are gathering in the golden west, with direful intent against the brightness and the warmth of this summer afternoon! They are ponderous air ships, black as death, and freighted with the tempest; and at intervals their thunder, the signal-guns of that unearthly squadron, rolls distant along the deep of heaven. These nearer heaps of fleecy vapor—methinks I could roll and toss upon them the whole day long!—seem scattered here and there, for the repose of tired pilgrims through the sky. Perhaps—for who can tell?—beautiful spirits are disporting themselves there, and will bless my mortal eye with the brief appearance of their curly locks of golden light, and laughing faces, fair and faint as the people of a rosy dream. Or, where the floating mass so imperfectly obstructs the color of the firmament, a slender foot and fairy limb, resting too heavily upon the frail support, may be thrust through, and suddenly withdrawn, while longing fancy follows them in vain. Yonder again is an airy archipelago, where the sunbeams love to linger in their journeyings through space. Every one of those little clouds has been dipped and steeped in radiance, which the slightest pressure might disengage in silvery profusion, like water wrung from a sea-maid's hair. Bright they are as a young man's visions, and, like them, would be realized in chillness, obscurity, and tears. I will look on them no more.

In three parts of the visible circle, whose centre is this spire, I discern cultivated fields, villages, white country-seats, the waving lines of rivulets, little placid lakes, and here and there a rising ground, that would fain be termed a hill. On the fourth side is the sea, stretching away towards a viewless boundary, blue and calm, except where the passing anger of a shadow flits across its surface, and is gone. Hitherward, a broad inlet penetrates far into the land; on the verge of the harbor, formed by its extremity, is a town; and over it am I, a watchman, all-heeding and unheeded. O that the multitude of chimneys could speak, like those of Madrid, and betray, in smoky whispers, the secrets of all who, since their first foundation, have assembled at the hearths within! O that the Limping Devil of Le Sage would perch beside me here, extend his wand over this contiguity of roofs, uncover every chamber, and make me familiar with their inhabitants! The most desirable mode of existence might be that of a spiritualized Paul Pry, hovering invisible round man and woman, witnessing their deeds, searching into their hearts, borrowing brightness from their felicity, and shade from their sorrow, and retaining no emotion peculiar to himself. But none of these things are possible; and if I would know the interior of brick walls, or the mystery of human bosoms, I can but guess.

Yonder is a fair street, extending north and south. The stately mansions are placed each on its carpet of verdant grass, and a long flight of steps descends from every door to the pavement. Ornamental trees, the broad-leafed horse-chestnut, the elm so lofty and bending, the graceful but infrequent willow, and others whereof I know not the names, grow thrivingly among brick and stone. The oblique rays of the sun are intercepted by these green citizens, and by the houses, so that one side of the street is a shaded and pleasant walk. On its whole extent there is now but a single passenger, advancing from the upper end; and he, unless distance and the medium of a pocket spyglass do him more than justice, is a fine young man of twenty. He saunters slowly forward, slapping his left hand with his folded gloves, bending his eyes upon the pavement, and sometimes raising them to throw a glance before him. Certainly, he has a pensive air. Is he in doubt, or in debt? Is he, if the question be allowable, in love? Does he strive to be melancholy and gentleman-like?—Or, is he merely overcome by the heat? But I bid him farewell, for the present. The door of one of the houses—an aristocratic edifice, with curtains of purple and gold waving from the windows, is now opened, and down the steps come two ladies, swinging their parasols, and lightly arrayed for a summer ramble. Both are young, both are pretty; but methinks the left-hand lass is the fairer of the twain; and, though she be so serious at this moment, I could swear that there is a treasure of gentle fun within her. They stand talking a little while upon the steps, and finally proceed up the street. Meantime, as their faces are now turned from me, I may look elsewhere.

Upon that wharf, and down the corresponding street, is a busy contrast to the quiet scene which I have just noticed. Business evidently has its centre there, and many a man is wasting the summer afternoon in labor and anxiety in losing riches, or in gaining them, when he would be wiser to flee away to some pleasant country village, or shaded lake in the forest, or wild and cool sea-beach. I see vessels unlading at the wharf, and precious merchandise strewn upon the ground, abundantly as at the bottom of the sea, that market whence no goods return, and where there is no captain nor supercargo to render an account of sales. Here the clerks are diligent with their paper and pencils, and sailors ply the block and tackle that hang over the hold, accompanying their toil with cries, long drawn and roughly melodious, till the bales and puncheons ascend to upper air. At a little distance, a group of gentlemen are assembled round the door of a warehouse. Grave seniors be they, and would wager—if it were safe, in these times to be responsible for any one—that the least eminent among them might vie with old Vicentio, that incomparable trafficker of Pisa. I can even select the wealthiest of the company. It is the elderly personage, in somewhat rusty black, with powdered hair, the superfluous whiteness of which is visible upon the cape of his coat. His twenty ships are wafted on some of their many courses by every breeze that blows, and his name—I will venture to say, though I know it not—is a familiar sound among the far-separated merchants of Europe and the Indies.

But I bestow too much of my attention in this quarter. On looking again to the long and shady walk, I perceive that the two fair girls have encountered the young man. After a sort of shyness in the recognition, he turns back with them. Moreover he has sanctioned my taste in regard to his companions by placing himself on the inner side of the pavement, nearest the Venus to whom I—enacting on a steeple top the part of Paris on the top of Ida—adjudged the golden apple.

In two streets, converging at right angles towards my watchtower, I distinguished three different processions. One is a proud array of voluntary soldiers, in bright uniform, resembling, from the height whence I look down, the painted veterans that garrison the windows of a toyshop. And yet, it stirs my heart; their regular advance, their nodding plumes, the sunflash on their bayonets and musket-barrels, the roll of their drums ascending past me, and the fife ever and anon piercing through, —these things have wakened a war-like fire, peaceful though I be. Close to their rear marches a battalion of school-boys, ranged in crooked and irregular platoons, shouldering sticks, thumping a harsh and unripe clatter from an instrument of tin, and ridiculously aping the intricate manœuvres of the foremost band. Nevertheless, as slight differences are scarcely perceptible from a church spire, one might be tempted to ask, "Which are the boys?"—or rather, "Which the men?" But, leaving these, let us turn to the third procession, which, though sadder in outward show, may excite identical reflections in the thoughtful mind. It is a funeral. A hearse, drawn by a black and bony steed, and covered by a dusty pall; two or three coaches rumbling over the stones, their drivers half asleep; a dozen couple of careless mourners in their every-day attire; such was not the fashion of our fathers, when they carried a friend to his grave. There is now no doleful clang of the bell to proclaim sorrow to the town. Was the King of Terrors more awful in those days than in our own, that wisdom and philosophy have been able to produce this change? Not so. Here is a proof that he retains his proper majesty. The military men and the military boys, are wheeling round the corner, and meet the funeral full in the face. Immediately the drum is silent, all but the tap that regulates each simultaneous footfall. The soldiers yield the path to the dusty hearse and unpretending train, and the children quit their ranks, and cluster on the sidewalks, with timorous and instinctive curiosity. The mourners enter the churchyard at the base of the steeple, and pause by an open grave among the burial-stones; the lightning glimmers on them as they lower down the coffin, and the thunder rattles heavily while they throw the earth upon its lid. Verily, the shower is near, and I tremble for the young man and the girls, who have now disappeared from the long and shady street.

How various are the situations of the people covered by the roofs beneath me, and how diversified are the events at this moment befalling them! The new born, the aged, the dying, the strong in life, and the recent dead, are in the chambers of these many mansions. The full of hope, the happy, the miserable, and the desperate dwell together within the circle of my glance. In some of the houses over which my eyes roam so coldly, guilt is entering into hearts that are still tenanted by a debased and trodden virtue,—guilt is on the very edge of commission, and the impending deed might be averted; guilt is done, and the criminal wonders if it be irrevocable. There are broad thoughts struggling in my mind, and, were I able to give them distinctness, they would make their way in eloquence. Lo! the rain-drops are descending.

The clouds, within a little time, have gathered over all the sky, hanging heavily, as if about to drop in one unbroken mass upon the earth. At intervals, the lightning flashes from their brooding hearts, quivers, disappears, and then comes the thunder, travelling slowly after its twin-born flame. A strong wind has sprung up, howls through the darkened streets, and raises the dust in dense bodies, to rebel against the approaching storm. The disbanded soldiers fly, the funeral has already vanished like its dead, and all people hurry homeward,—all that have a home; while a few lounge by the corners, or trudge on desperately, at their leisure. In a narrow lane, which communicates with the shady street, I discern the rich old merchant, putting himself to the top of his speed, lest the rain should convert his hair-powder to a paste. Unhappy gentleman! By the slow vehemence, and painful moderation wherewith he journeys, it is but too evident that Podagra has left its thrilling tenderness in his great toe. But yonder, at a far more rapid

pace, come three other of my acquaintance,—the two pretty girls and the young man, unseasonably interrupted in their walk. Their footsteps are supported by the risen dust,—the wind lends them its velocity,—they fly like three sea-birds driven landward by the tempestuous breeze. The ladies would not thus rival Atalanta if they but knew that any one were at leisure to observe them. Ah! as they hasten onward, laughing in the angry face of nature, a sudden catastrophe has chanced. At the corner where the narrow lane enters into the street, they come plump against the old merchant whose tortoise motion has just brought him to that point. He likes not the sweet encounter; the darkness of the whole air gathers speedily upon his visage, and there is a pause on both sides. Finally, he thrusts aside the youth with little courtesy, seizes an arm of each of the two girls, and plods onward, like a magician with a prize of captive fairies. All this is easy to be understood. How disconsolate the poor lover stands! regardless of the rain that threatens an exceeding damage to his well-fashioned habiliments, till he catches a backward glance of mirth from a bright eye, and turns away with whatever comfort it conveys.

The old man and his daughters are safely housed, and now the storm lets loose its fury. In every dwelling I perceive the faces of the chambermaids as they shut down the windows, excluding the impetuous shower, and shrinking away from the quick fiery glare. The large drops descend with force upon the slated roofs, and rise again in smoke. There is a rush and roar, as of a river through the air, and muddy streams ubble majestically along the pavement, whirl their dusky foam into the kennel, and disappear beneath iron grates. Thus did Arethusa sink. I love not my station here aloft, in the midst of the tumult which I am powerless to direct or quell, with the blue lightning wrinkling on my brow, and the thunder muttering its first awful syllables in my ear. I will descend. Yet let me give another glance to the sea, where the foam breaks out in long white lines upon a broad expanse of blackness, or boils up in far distant points, like snowy mountain-tops in the eddies of a flood; and let me look once more at the green plain, and little hills of the country, over which the giant of the storm is striding in robes of mist, and at the town, whose obscured and desolate streets might beseem a city of the dead; and turning a single moment to the sky, now gloomy as an author's prospects, I prepare to resume my station on lower earth. But stay! A little speck of azure has widened in the western heavens; the sunbeams find a passage, and go rejoicing through the tempest; and on yonder darkest cloud, born, like hallowed hopes, of the glory of another world, and the trouble and tears of this, brightens forth the Rainbow.

THE HOLLOW OF THE THREE HILLS

In those strange old times, when fantastic dreams and madmen's reveries were realized among the actual circumstances of life, two persons met together at an appointed hour and place. One was a lady, graceful in form and fair of feature, though pale and troubled, and smitten with an untimely blight in what should have been the fullest bloom of her years; the other was an ancient and meanly-dressed woman, of ill-favored aspect, and so withered, shrunken, and decrepit, that even the space since she began to decay must have exceeded the ordinary term of human existence. In the spot where they encountered, no mortal could observe them. Three little hills stood near each other, and down in the midst of them sunk a hollow basin, almost mathematically circular, two or three hundred feet in breadth, and of such depth that a stately cedar might but just be visible above the sides. Dwarf pines were numerous upon the hills, and partly fringed the outer verge of the intermediate hollow; within which there was nothing but the brown grass of October, and here and there a tree trunk, that had fallen long ago, and lay mouldering with no green successor from its roots. One of these masses of decaying wood, formerly a majestic oak, rested close beside a pool of green and sluggish water at the bottom of the basin. Such scenes as this (so gray tradition tells) were once the resort of the Power of Evil and his plighted subjects; and here, at midnight or on the dim verge of evening, they were said to stand round the mantling pool, disturbing its putrid waters in the performance of an impious baptismal rite. The chill beauty of an autumnal sunset was now gilding the three hilltops, whence a paler tint stole down their sides into the hollow.

"Here is our pleasant meeting come to pass," said the aged crone, "according as thou hast desired. Say quickly what thou wouldst have of me, for there is but a short hour that we may tarry here."

As the old withered woman spoke, a smile glimmered on her countenance, like lamplight on the wall of a sepulchre. The lady trembled, and cast her eyes upward to the verge of the basin, as if meditating to return with her purpose unaccomplished. But it was not so ordained.

"I am a stranger in this land, as you know," said she at length. "Whence I come it matters not; but I have left those behind me with whom my fate was intimately bound, and from whom I am cut off forever. There is a weight in my bosom that I cannot away with, and I have come hither to inquire of their welfare."

"And who is there by this green pool that can bring thee news from the ends of the earth?" cried the old woman, peering into the lady's face. "Not from my lips mayst thou hear these tidings; yet be thou bold, and the daylight shall not pass away from yonder hill-top, before thy wish be granted."

"I will do your bidding, though I die," replied the lady, desperately.

The old woman seated herself on the trunk of the fallen tree, threw aside the hood that shrouded her gray locks, and beckoned her companion to draw near.

"Kneel down," she said, "and lay your forehead on my knees."

She hesitated a moment, but the anxiety that had long been kindling burned fiercely up within her. As she knelt down, the border of her garment was dipped into the pool; she laid her forehead on the old woman's knees, and the latter drew a cloak about the lady's face, so that she was in darkness. Then she heard the muttered words of prayer, in the midst of which she started, and would have arisen.

"Let me flee,—let me flee and hide myself, that they may not look upon me!" she cried. But, with returning recollection, she hushed herself, and was still as death.

For it seemed as if other voices—familiar in infancy, and unforgotten through many wanderings, and in all the vicissitudes of her heart and fortune—were mingling with the accents of the prayer. At first the words were faint and indistinct, not rendered so by distance, but rather resembling the dim pages of a book which we strive to read by an imperfect and gradually brightening light. In such a manner, as the prayer proceeded, did those voices strengthen upon the ear; till at length the petition ended, and the conversation of an aged man, and of a woman broken and decayed like himself, became distinctly audible to the lady as she knelt. But those strangers appeared not to stand in the hollow depth between the three hills. Their voices were encompassed and re-echoed by the walls of a chamber, the windows of which were rattling in the breeze; the regular vibration of a clock, the crackling of a fire, and the tinkling of the embers as they fell among the ashes, rendered the scene almost as vivid as if painted to the eye. By a melancholy hearth sat these two old people, the man calmly despondent, the woman querulous and tearful, and their words were all of sorrow.

They spoke of a daughter, a wanderer they knew not where, bearing dishonor along with her, and leaving shame and affliction to bring their gray heads to the grave. They alluded also to other and more recent woe, but in the midst of their talk, their voices seemed to melt into the sound of the wind sweeping mournfully among the autumn leaves; and when the lady lifted her eyes, there was she kneeling in the hollow between three hills.

"A weary and lonesome time yonder old couple have of it," remarked the old woman, smiling in the lady's face.

"And did you also hear them?" exclaimed she, a sense of intolerable humiliation triumphing over her agony and fear.

"Yea; and we have yet more to hear," replied the old woman. "Wherefore, cover thy face quickly."

Again the withered hag poured forth the monotonous words of a prayer that was not meant to be acceptable in Heaven; and soon, in the pauses of her breath, strange murmurings began to thicken, gradually increasing so as to drown and overpower the charm by which they grew. Shrieks pierced through the obscurity of sound, and were succeeded by the singing of sweet female voices, which in their turn gave way to a wild roar of laughter, broken suddenly by groanings and sobs, forming altogether a ghastly confusion of terror and mourning and mirth. Chains were rattling, fierce and stern voices uttered threats, and the scourge resounded at their command. All these noises deepened and became substantial to the listener's ear, till she could distinguish every soft and dreamy accent of the love songs, that died causelessly into

funeral hymns. She shuddered at the unprovoked wrath which blazed up like the spontaneous kindling of flame, and she grew faint at the fearful merriment, raging miserably around her. In the midst of this wild scene, where unbound passions jostled each other in a drunken career, there was one solemn voice of a man, and a manly and melodious voice it might once have been. He went to and fro continually, and his feet sounded upon the floor. In each member of that frenzied company, whose own burning thoughts had become their exclusive world, he sought an auditor for the story of his individual wrong, and interpreted their laughter and tears as his reward of scorn or pity. He spoke of woman's perfidy, of a wife who had broken her holiest vows, of a home and heart made desolate. Even as he went on, the shout, the laugh, the shriek, the sob, rose up in unison, till they changed into the hollow, fitful, and uneven sound of the wind, as it fought among the pine-trees on those three lonely hills. The lady looked up, and there was the withered woman smiling in her face.

"Couldst thou have thought there were such merry times in a madhouse?" inquired the latter.

"True, true," said the lady to herself; "there is mirth within its walls, but misery, misery, without."

"Wouldst thou hear more?" demanded the old woman.

"There is one other voice I would fain listen to again," replied the lady, faintly.

"Then, lay down thy head speedily upon my knees, that thou mayst get thee hence before the hour be passed."

The golden skirts of day were yet

lingering upon the hills, but deep shades obscured the hollow and the pool, as if sombre night were rising thence to overspread the world. Again that evil woman began to weave her spell. Long did it proceed unanswered, till the knolling of a bell stole in among the intervals of her words, like a clang that had travelled far over valley and rising ground, and was just ready to die in the air. The lady shook upon her companion's knees, as she heard that boding sound. Stronger it grew and sadder, and deepened into the tone of a death-bell, knolling dolefully from some ivy-mantled tower, and bearing tidings of mortality and woe to the cottage, to the hall, and to the solitary wayfarer, that all might weep for the doom appointed in turn to them. Then came a measured tread, passing slowly, slowly on, as of mourners with a coffin, their garments trailing on the ground, so that the ear could measure the length of their melancholy array. Before them went the priest, reading the burial service, while the leaves of his book were rustling in the breeze. And though no voice but his was heard to speak aloud, still there were revilings and anathemas, whispered but distinct, from women and from men, breathed against the daughter who had wrung the aged hearts of her parents,—the wife who had betrayed the trusting fondness of her husband, —the mother who had sinned against natural affection, and left her child to die. The sweeping sound of the funeral train faded away like a thin vapor, and the wind that just before had seemed to shake the coffin pall moaned sadly round the verge of the Hollow between three Hills. But when the old woman stirred the kneeling lady, she lifted not her head.

"Here has been a sweet hour's sport!" said the withered crone, chuckling to herself.

THE TOLL-GATHERER'S DAY

A SKETCH OF TRANSITORY LIFE

METHINKS, for a person whose instinct bids him rather to pore over the current of life than to plunge into its tumultuous waves, no undesirable retreat were a toll-house beside some thronged thoroughfare of the land. In youth, perhaps, it is good for the observer to run about the earth,—to leave the track of his footsteps far and wide, —to mingle himself with the action of numberless vicissitudes,—and, finally, in some calm solitude, to feed a musing spirit on all that he has seen and felt. But there are natures too indolent, or too sensitive, to endure the dust, the sunshine, or the rain, the turmoil of moral and physical elements, to which all the wayfarers of the world expose themselves. For such a man, how pleasant a miracle, could life be made to roll its variegated length by the threshold of his own hermitage, and the great globe, as it were, perform its revolutions and shift its thousand scenes before his eyes without whirling him onward in its course. If any mortal be favored with a lot analogous to this, it is the toll-gatherer. So, at least, have I often fancied, while lounging on a bench at the door of a small square edifice, which stands between shore and shore in the midst of a long bridge. Beneath the timbers ebbs and flows an arm of the sea; while above, like the life-blood through a great artery, the travel of the north and east is continually throbbing. Sitting on the aforesaid bench, I amuse myself with a conception, illustrated by numerous pencil-sketches in the air, of the toll-gatherer's day.

In the morning—dim, gray, dewy summer's morn—the distant roll of ponderous wheels begins to mingle with my old friend's slumbers, creaking more and more harshly through the midst of his dream, and gradually replacing it with realities. Hardly conscious of the change from sleep to wakefulness, he finds himself partly clad and throwing wide the toll-gates for the passage of a fragrant load of hay. The timbers groan beneath the slow-revolving wheels; one sturdy yeoman stalks beside the oxen, and, peering from the summit of the hay, by the glimmer of the half-extinguished lantern over the toll-house, is seen the drowsy visage of his comrade, who has enjoyed a nap some ten miles long. The toll is paid,—creak, creak again go the wheels, and the huge haymow vanishes into the morning mist. As yet, nature is but half awake, and familiar objects appear visionary. But yonder, dashing from the shore with a rattling thunder of the wheels and a confused clatter of hoofs, comes the never-tiring mail, which has hurried onward at the same headlong, restless rate, all through the quiet night. The bridge resounds in one continued peal as the coach rolls on without a pause, merely affording the toll-gatherer a glimpse at the sleepy passengers, who now bestir their torpid limbs, and snuff a cordial in the briny air. The morn breathes upon them and blushes, and they forget how wearily the darkness toiled away. And behold now the fervid day, in his bright chariot, glittering aslant over the waves, now scorning to throw a tribute of his golden beams on the toll-gatherer's little hermitage. The old man looks eastward, and (for he is a moralizer) frames a simile of the stage-coach and the sun.

While the world is rousing itself, we may glance slightly at the scene of our sketch. It sits above the bosom of the broad flood, a spot not of earth, but in the midst of waters, which rush with a murmuring sound among the massive beams beneath. Over the door is a weather-beaten board, inscribed with the rates of toll, in letters so nearly effaced that the gilding of the sunshine can hardly make them legible. Beneath the window is a wooden bench, on which a long succession of weary wayfarers have reposed themselves. Peeping within doors, we perceive the whitewashed walls bedecked with sundry lithographic prints and advertisements of various import, and the immense showbill of a wandering caravan. And there sits our good old toll-gatherer, glorified by the early sunbeams. He is a man, as his aspect may announce, of quiet soul, and thoughtful, shrewd, yet simple mind, who of the wisdom which the passing world scatters along the wayside has gathered a reasonable store.

Now the sun smiles upon the landscape, and earth smiles back again upon the sky. Frequent, now, are the travellers. The toll-gatherer's practised ear can distinguish the weight of every vehicle, the number of its wheels, and how many horses beat the resounding timbers with their iron tramp. Here, in a substantial family chaise, setting forth betimes to take advantage of the dewy road, come a gentleman and his wife, with their rosy-cheeked little girl sitting gladsomely between them. The bottom of the chaise is heaped with multifarious bandboxes, and carpet-bags, and beneath the axle swings a leathern trunk, dusty with yesterday's journey. Next appears a four-wheeled carryall, peopled with a round half-dozen of pretty girls, all drawn by a single horse, and driven by a single gentleman. Luckless wight, doomed, through a whole summer day, to be the butt of mirth and mischief among the frolicsome maidens! Bolt upright in a sulky rides a thin, sour-visaged man, who, as he pays his toll, hands the toll-gatherer a printed card to stick upon the wall. The vinegar-faced traveller proves to be a manufacturer of pickles. Now paces slowly from timber to timber a horseman clad in black, with a meditative brow, as of one who, whithersoever his steed might bear him, would still journey through a mist of brooding thought. He is a country preacher, going to labor at a protracted meeting. The next object passing townward is a butcher's cart, canopied with its arch of snow-white cotton. Behind comes a "sauceman," driving a wagon full of new potatoes, green ears of corn, beets, carrots, turnips, and summer squashes; and next, two wrinkled, withered, witch-looking old gossips, in an antediluvian chaise, drawn by a horse of former generations, and going to peddle out a lot of huckleberries. See

there, a man trundling a wheelbarrow-load of lobsters. And now a milk-cart rattles briskly onward, covered with green canvas, and conveying the contributions of a whole herd of cows, in large tin canisters. But let all these pay their toll and pass. Here comes a spectacle that causes the old toll-gatherer to smile benignantly, as if the travellers brought sunshine with them and lavished its gladsome influence all along the road.

It is a barouche of the newest style, the varnished panels of which reflect the whole moving panorama of the landscape, and show a picture, likewise, of our friend, with his visage broadened, so that his meditative smile is transformed to grotesque merriment. Within, sits a youth, fresh as the summer morn, and beside him a young lady in white, with white gloves upon her slender hands and a white veil flowing down over her face. But methinks her blushing cheek burns through the snowy veil. Another white-robed virgin sits in front. And who are these, on whom, and on all that appertains to them, the dust of earth seems never to have settled? Two lovers, whom the priest has blessed, this blessed morn, and sent them forth, with one of the bridemaids, on the matrimonial tour. Take my blessing too, ye happy ones! May the sky not frown upon you, nor clouds bedew you with their chill and sullen rain! May the hot sun kindle no fever in your hearts! May your whole life's pilgrimage be as blissful as this first day's journey, and its close be gladdened with even brighter anticipations than those which hallow your bridal night!

They pass; and ere the reflection of their joy has faded from his face, another spectacle throws a melancholy shadow over the spirit of the observing man. In a close carriage sits a fragile figure, muffled carefully, and shrinking even from the mild breath of summer. She leans against a manly form, and his arm enfolds hers, as if to guard his treasure from some enemy. Let but a few weeks pass, and when he shall strive to embrace that loved one, he will press only desolation to his heart.

And now has morning gathered up her dewy pearls, and fled away. The sun rolls blazing through the sky, and cannot find a cloud to cool his face with. The horses toil sluggishly along the bridge, and heave their glistening sides in short quick pantings, when the reins are tightened at the toll-house. Glisten, too, the faces of the travellers. Their garments are thickly bestrewn with dust; their whiskers and hair look hoary; their throats are choked with the dusty atmosphere which they have left behind them. No air is stirring on the road. Nature dares draw no breath, lest she should inhale a stifling cloud of dust. "A hot and dusty day!" cry the poor pilgrims, as they wipe their begrimed foreheads, and woo the doubtful breeze which the river bears along with it. "Awful hot! Dreadful dusty!" answers the sympathetic toll-gatherer. They start again, to pass through the fiery furnace, while he re-enters his cool hermitage, and besprinkles it with a pail of briny water from the stream beneath. He thinks within himself, that the sun is not so fierce here as elsewhere, and that the gentle air does not forget him in these sultry days. Yes, old friend; and a quiet heart will make a dog-day temperate. He hears a weary footstep, and perceives a traveller with pack and staff, who sits down upon the hospitable bench, and removes the hat from his wet brow. The toll-gatherer administers a cup of cold water, and discovering his guest to be a man of homely sense, he engages him in profitable talk, uttering the maxims of a philosophy which he has found in his own soul, but knows not how it came there. And as the wayfarer makes ready to resume his journey, he tells him a sovereign remedy for blistered feet.

Now comes the noontide hour,—of all the hours, nearest akin to midnight; for each has its own calmness and repose. Soon, however, the world begins to turn again upon its axis, and it seems the busiest epoch of the day; when an accident impedes the march of sublunary things. The draw being lifted to permit the passage of a schooner, laden with wood from the Eastern forests, she sticks immovably, right athwart the bridge! Meanwhile, on both sides of the chasm, a throng of impatient travellers fret and fume. Here are two sailors in a gig, with the top thrown back, both puffing cigars, and swearing all sorts of forecastle oaths; there, in a smart chaise, a dashingly-dressed gentleman and lady, he from a tailor's shopboard, and she from a milliner's backroom,—the aristocrats of a summer afternoon. And what are the haughtiest of us, but the ephemeral aristocrats of a summer's day. Here is a tin-pedler, whose glittering ware bedazzles all beholders, like a travelling meteor, or opposition sun; and on the other side a seller of spruce beer, which brisk liquor is confined in several dozen of stone bottles. Here comes a party of ladies on horseback, in green riding-habits, and gentlemen attendant; and there a flock of sheep for the market, pattering over the bridge with a multitudinous clatter of their little hoofs. Here a Frenchman, with a hand-organ on his shoulder; and there an itinerant Swiss jeweller. On this side, heralded by a blast of clarions and bugles, appears a train of wagons, conveying all the wild beasts of a caravan; and on that, a company of summer soldiers, marching from village to village on a festival campaign, attended by the "Brass band." Now look at the scene, and it presents an emblem of the mysterious confusion, the apparently insolvable riddle, in which individuals, or the great world itself, seem often to be involved. What miracle shall set all things right again?

But see! the schooner has thrust her bulky carcass through the chasm; the draw descends; horse and foot pass onward, and leave the bridge vacant from end to end. "And thus," muses the toll-gatherer, "have I found it with all stoppages, even though the universe seemed to be at a stand." The sage old man!

Far westward now, the reddening sun throws a broad sheet of splendor across the flood, and to the eyes of distant boatmen gleams brightly among the timbers of the bridge. Strollers come from the town to quaff the freshening breeze. One or two let down long lines, and haul up flapping flounders, or cunners, or small cod, or perhaps an eel. Others, and fair girls among them, with the flush of the hot day still on their cheeks, bend over the railing and watch the heaps of seaweed floating upward with the flowing tide. The horses now tramp heavily along the bridge, and wistfully bethink them of their stables. Rest, rest, thou weary world! for to-morrow's round of toil and pleasure will be as wearisome as to-day's has been; yet both shall bear thee onward a day's march of eternity. Now the old toll-gatherer looks seaward, and discerns the lighthouse kindling on a far island, and the stars, too, kindling in the sky, as if but a little way beyond; and mingling reveries of Heaven with remembrances of Earth, the whole procession of mortal travellers, all the dusty pilgrimage which he has witnessed, seems like a flitting show of phantoms for his thoughtful soul to muse upon.

THE VISION OF THE FOUNTAIN

AT fifteen, I became a resident in a country village, more than a hundred miles from home. The morning after my arrival—a September morning, but warm and bright as any in July—I rambled into a wood of oaks, with a few walnut-trees intermixed, forming the closest shade above my head. The ground was rocky, uneven, overgrown with bushes and clumps of young saplings, and traversed only by cattle-paths. The track, which I chanced to follow, led me to a crystal spring, with a border of grass, as freshly green as on May morning, and overshadowed by the limb of a great oak. One solitary sunbeam found its way down, and played like a goldfish in the water.

From my childhood, I have loved to gaze into a spring. The water filled a circular basin, small but deep, and set round with stones, some of which were covered with slimy moss, the others naked, and of variegated hue, reddish, white and brown. The bottom was covered with coarse sand, which sparkled in the lonely sunbeam, and seemed to illuminate the spring with an unborrowed light. In one spot, the gush of the water violently agitated the sand, but without obscuring the fountain, or breaking the glassiness of its surface. It appeared as if some living creature were about to emerge—the Naiad of the spring, perhaps—in the shape of a beautiful young woman, with a gown of filmy water-moss, a belt of rainbow drops, and a cold, pure, passionless countenance. How would the beholder shiver, pleasantly, yet fearfully, to see her sitting on one of the stones, paddling her white feet in the ripples, and throwing up water, to sparkle in the sun! Wherever she laid her hands on grass and flowers, they would immediately be moist as with morning dew. Then would she set about her labors, like a careful housewife, to clear the fountain of withered leaves, and bits of slimy wood, and old acorns from the oaks above, and grains of corn left by cattle in drinking, till the bright sand, in the bright water, were like a treasury of diamonds. But should the intruder approach too near, he would find only the drops of a summer shower glistening about the spot where he had seen her.

Reclining on the border of grass, where the dewy goddess should have been, I bent forward, and a pair of eyes met mine within the watery mirror. They were the reflection of my own. I looked again, and lo! another face, deeper in the fountain than my own image, more distinct in all the features, yet faint as thought. The vision had the aspect of a fair young girl, with locks of paly gold. A mirthful expression laughed in the eyes and dimpled over the whole shadowy countenance, till it seemed just what a fountain would be, if, while dancing merrily into the sunshine, it should assume the shape of a woman. Through the dim rosiness of the cheeks, I could see the brown leaves, the slimy twigs, the acorns, and the sparkling sand. The solitary sunbeam was diffused among the golden hair, which melted into its faint brightness, and became a glory round that head so beautiful.

My description can give no idea how suddenly the fountain was thus tenanted, and how soon it was left desolate. I breathed; and there was the face! I held my breath; and it was gone! Had it passed away, or faded into nothing? I doubted whether it had ever been.

My sweet readers, what a dreamy and delicious hour did I spend, where that vision found and left me! For a long time I sat perfectly still, waiting till it should reappear, and fearful that the slightest motion, or even the flutter of my breath, might frighten it away. Thus have I often started from a pleasant dream, and then kept quiet, in hopes to wile it back. Deep were my musings, as to the race and attributes of that ethereal being. Had I created her? Was she the daughter of my fancy, akin to those strange shapes which peep under the lids of children's eyes? And did her beauty gladden me, for that one moment, and then die? Or was she a water-nymph within the fountain, or fairy, or woodland goddess, peeping over my shoulder, or the ghost of some forsaken maid, who had drowned herself for love? Or, in good truth, had a lovely girl, with a warm heart, and lips that would bear pressure, stolen softly behind me, and thrown her image into the spring?

I watched and waited, but no vision came again. I departed, but with a spell upon me, which drew me back, that same afternoon, to the haunted spring. There was the water gushing, the sand sparkling, and the sunbeam glittering. There the vision was not, but only a great frog, the hermit of that solitude, who immediately withdrew his speckled snout and made himself invisible, all except a pair of long legs, beneath a stone. Methought he had a devilish look! I could have slain him as an enchanter, who kept the mysterious beauty imprisoned in the fountain.

Sad and heavy, I was returning to the village. Between me and the church-spire rose a little hill, and on its summit a group of trees, insulated from all the rest of the wood, with their own share of radiance hovering on them from the west, and their own solitary shadow falling to the east. The afternoon being far declined, the sunshine was almost pensive, and the shade almost cheerful; glory and gloom were mingled in the placid light; as if the spirits of the Day and Evening had met in friendship under those trees, and

found themselves akin. I was admiring the picture, when the shape of a young girl emerged from behind the clump of oaks. My heart knew her; it was the Vision; but so distant and ethereal did she seem, so unmixed with earth, so imbued with the pensive glory of the spot where she was standing, that my spirit sunk within me, sadder than before. How could I ever reach her?

While I gazed, a sudden shower came pattering down upon the leaves. In a moment the air was full of brightness, each rain-drop catching a portion of sunlight as it fell, and the whole gentle shower appearing like a mist, just substantial enough to bear the burden of radiance. A rainbow, vivid as Niagara's, was painted in the air. Its southern limb came down before the group of trees, and enveloped the fair Vision, as if the hues of Heaven were the only garment for her beauty. When the rainbow vanished, she who had seemed a part of it was no longer there. Was her existence absorbed in nature's loveliest phenomenon, and did her pure frame dissolve away in the varied light? Yet I would not despair of her return; for, robed in the rainbow, she was the emblem of Hope.

Thus did the vision leave me; and many a doleful day succeeded to the parting moment. By the spring, and in the wood, and on the hill, and through the village; at dewy sunrise, burning noon, and at that magic hour of sunset, when she had vanished from my sight, I sought her, but in vain. Weeks came and went, months rolled away, and she appeared not in them. I imparted my mystery to none, but wandered to and fro, or sat in solitude, like one that had caught a glimpse of

Heaven, and could take no more joy on earth. I withdrew into an inner world, where my thoughts lived and breathed, and the Vision in the midst of them. Without intending it, I became at once the author and hero of a romance, conjuring up rivals, imagining events, the actions of others and my own, and experiencing every change of passion, till jealousy and despair had their end in bliss. O, had I the burning fancy of my early youth, with manhood's colder gift, the power of expression, your hearts, sweet ladies, should flutter at my tale!

In the middle of January, I was summoned home. The day before my departure, visiting the spots which had been hallowed by the Vision, I found that the spring had a frozen bosom, and nothing but the snow and a glare of winter sunshine, on the hill of the rainbow. "Let me hope," thought I, "or my heart will be as icy as the fountain, and the whole world as desolate as this snowy hill." Most of the day was spent in preparing for the journey, which was to commence at four o'clock the next morning. About an hour after supper, when all was in readiness, I descended from my chamber to the sitting-room, to take leave of the old clergyman and his family, with whom I had been an inmate. A gust of wind blew out my lamp as I passed through the entry.

According to their invariable custom, so pleasant a one when the fire blazes cheerfully, the family were sitting in the parlor, with no other light than what came from the hearth. As the good clergyman's scanty stipend compelled him to use all sorts of economy, the foundation of his fires was always a large heap of tan, or ground bark, which would smoulder away, from morning till night, with a dull warmth and no flame. This evening the heap of tan was newly put on, and surmounted with three sticks of red oak, full of moisture, and a few pieces of dry pine, that had not yet kindled. There was no light, except the little that came sullenly from two half-burned brands, without even glimmering on the andirons. But I knew the position of the old minister's arm-chair, and also where his wife sat, with her knitting-work, and how to avoid his two daughters, one a stout country lass, and the other a consumptive girl. Groping through the gloom, I found my own place next to that of the son, a learned collegian, who had come home to keep school in the village during the winter vacation. I noticed that there was less room than usual, to-night, between the collegian's chair and mine.

As people are always taciturn in the dark, not a word was said for some time after my entrance. Nothing broke the stillness but the regular click of the matron's knitting-needles. At times, the fire threw out a brief and dusky gleam, which twinkled on the old man's glasses, and hovered doubtfully round our circle, but was far too faint to portray the individuals who composed it. Were we not like ghosts? Dreamy as the scene was, might it not be a type of the mode in which departed people, who had known and loved each other here, would hold communion in eternity? We were aware of each other's presence, not by sight, nor sound, nor touch, but by an inward consciousness. Would it not be so among the dead?

The silence was interrupted by the

consumptive daughter addressing a remark to some one in the circle, whom she called Rachel. Her tremulous and decayed accents were answered by a single word, but in a voice that made me start, and bend towards the spot whence it had proceeded. Had I ever heard that sweet, low tone? If not, why did it rouse up so many old recollections, or mockeries of such, the shadows of things familiar, yet unknown, and fill my mind with confused images of her features who had spoken, though buried in the gloom of the parlor? Whom had my heart recognized, that it throbbed so? I listened, to catch her gentle breathing, and strove, by the intensity of my gaze, to picture forth a shape where none was visible.

Suddenly, the dry pine caught; the fire blazed up with a ruddy glow; and where the darkness had been, there was she—the Vision of the Fountain! A spirit of radiance only, she had vanished with the rainbow, and appeared again in the firelight, perhaps to flicker with the blaze, and be gone. Yet her cheek was rosy and lifelike, and her features, in the bright warmth of the room, were even sweeter and tenderer than my recollection of them. She knew me! The mirthful expression that had laughed in her eyes and dimpled over her countenance, when I beheld her faint beauty in the fountain, was laughing and dimpling there now. One moment, our glance mingled,—the next, down rolled the heap of tan upon the kindled wood,—and darkness snatched away that Daughter of the Light, and gave her back to me no more!

Fair ladies, there is nothing more to tell. Must the simple mystery be revealed, then, that Rachel was the daughter of the village squire, and had left home for a boarding-school the morning after I arrived, and returned the day before my departure? If I transformed her to an angel, it is what every youthful lover does for his mistress. Therein consists the essence of my story. But slight the change, sweet maids, to make angels of yourselves!

FANCY'S SHOW-BOX

A MORALITY

What is guilt? A stain upon the soul. And it is a point of vast interest whether the soul may contract such stains, in all their depth and flagrancy, from deeds which may have been plotted and resolved upon, but which, physically, have never had existence. Must the fleshly hand and visible frame of man set its seal to the evil designs of the soul, in order to give them their entire validity against the sinner? Or, while none but crimes perpetrated are cognizable before an earthly tribunal, will guilty thoughts—of which guilty deeds are no more than shadows—will these draw down the full weight of a condemning sentence in the supreme court of eternity? In the solitude of a midnight chamber, or in a desert afar from men, or in a church, while the body is kneeling the soul may pollute itself even with those crimes which we are accustomed to deem altogether carnal. If this be true, it is a fearful truth.

Let us illustrate the subject by an imaginary example. A venerable gentleman, one Mr. Smith, who had long been regarded as a pattern of moral excellence, was warming his aged blood with a glass or two of generous wine. His children being gone forth about their worldly business, and his grandchildren at school, he sat alone in a deep, luxurious arm-chair, with his feet beneath a richly-carved mahogany table. Some old people have a dread of solitude, and when better company may not be had, rejoice even to hear the quiet breathing of a babe asleep upon the carpet. But Mr. Smith, whose silver hair was the bright symbol of a life unstained, except by such spots as are inseparable from human nature, he had no need of a babe to protect him by its purity, nor of a grown person, to stand between him and his own soul. Nevertheless, either Manhood must converse with Age, or Womanhood must soothe him with gentle cares, or Infancy must sport around his chair, or his thoughts will stray into the misty region of the past, and the old man be chill and sad. Wine will not always cheer him. Such might have been the case with Mr. Smith, when, through the brilliant medium of his glass of old Madeira, he beheld three figures entering the room. These were Fancy, who had assumed the garb and aspect of an itinerant showman, with a box of pictures on her back; and Memory, in the likeness of a clerk, with a pen behind her ear, an inkhorn at her buttonhole, and a huge manuscript volume

beneath her arm; and lastly, behind the other two, a person shrouded in a dusky mantle, which concealed both face and form. But Mr. Smith had a shrewd idea that it was Conscience.

How kind of Fancy, Memory, and Conscience to visit the old gentleman, just as he was beginning to imagine that the wine had neither so bright a sparkle, nor so excellent a flavor, as when himself and the liquor were less aged! Through the dim length of the apartment, where crimson curtains muffled the glare of sunshine, and created a rich obscurity, the three guests drew near the silver-haired old man. Memory, with a finger between the leaves of her huge volume, placed herself at his right hand. Conscience, with her face still hidden in the dusky mantle, took her station on the left, so as to be next his heart; while Fancy set down her picture-box upon the table, with the magnifying glass convenient to his eye. We can sketch merely the outlines of two or three out of the many pictures, which, at the pulling of a string, successively peopled the box with the semblances of living scenes.

One was a moonlight picture; in the background, a lowly dwelling; and in front, partly shadowed by a tree, yet besprinkled with flakes of radiance, two youthful figures, male and female. The young man stood with folded arms, a haughty smile upon his lip and a gleam of triumph in his eye, as he glanced downward at the kneeling girl. She was almost prostrate at his feet, evidently sinking under a weight of shame and anguish, which hardly allowed her to lift her clasped hands in supplication. Her eyes she could not lift. But neither her agony nor the lovely features on which it was depicted, nor the slender grace of the form which it convulsed, appeared to soften the obduracy of the young man. He was the personification of triumphant scorn. Now, strange to say, as old Mr. Smith peeped through the magnifying glass, which made the objects start out from the canvas with magical deception, he began to recognize the farmhouse, the tree, and both the figures of the picture. The young man, in times, long past, had often met his gaze within the looking-glass; the girl was the very image of his first love,—his cottage love,—his Martha Burroughs! Mr. Smith was scandalized. "O, vile and slanderous picture!" he exclaims. "When have I triumphed over ruined innocence? Was not Martha wedded, in her teens, to David Tomkins, who won her girlish love and long enjoyed her affection as a wife? And ever since his death she has lived a reputable widow!" Meantime, Memory was turning over the leaves of her volume, rustling them to and fro with uncertain fingers, until, among the earlier pages, she found one which had reference to this picture. She reads it, close to the old gentleman's ear; it is a record merely of sinful thought, which never was embodied in an act; but, while Memory is reading Conscience unveils her face, and strikes a dagger to the heart of Mr. Smith. Though not a death-blow, the torture was extreme.

The exhibition proceeded. One after another, Fancy displayed her pictures, all of which appeared to have been painted by some malicious artist, on purpose to vex Mr. Smith. Not a shadow of proof could have been adduced, in any earthly court, that he

was guilty of the slightest of those sins which were thus made to stare him in the face. In one scene there was a table set out, with several bottles, and glasses half filled with wine, which threw back the dull ray of an expiring lamp. There had been mirth and revelry, until the hand of the clock stood just at midnight, when murder stepped between the boon companions. A young man had fallen on the floor, and lay stone dead, with a ghastly wound crushed into his temple, while over him, with a delirium of mingled rage and horror in his countenance, stood the youthful likeness of Mr. Smith. The murdered youth wore the features of Edward Spencer! "What does this rascal of a painter mean?" cries Mr. Smith, provoked beyond all patience. "Edward Spencer was my earliest and dearest friend, true to me as I to him, through more than half a century. Neither I, nor any other, ever murdered him. Was he not alive within five years, and did he not, in token of our long friendship, bequeath me his gold-headed cane, and a mourning ring?" Again had Memory been turning over her volume, and fixed at length upon so confused a page, that she surely must have scribbled it when she was tipsy. The purport was, however, that, while Mr. Smith and Edward Spencer were heating their young blood with wine, a quarrel had flashed up between them, and Mr. Smith, in deadly wrath, had flung a bottle at Spencer's head. True, it missed its aim, and merely smashed a looking-glass; and the next morning, when the incident was imperfectly remembered, they had shaken hands with a hearty laugh. Yet, again, while Memory was reading, Conscience unveiled her face, struck a dagger to the heart of Mr. Smith, and quelled his remonstrance with her iron frown. The pain was quite excruciating.

Some of the pictures had been painted with so doubtful a touch, and in colors so faint and pale, that the subjects could barely be conjectured. A dull, semi-transparent mist had been thrown over the surface of the canvas, into which the figures seemed to vanish, while the eye sought most earnestly to fix them. But, in every scene, however dubiously portrayed, Mr. Smith was invariably haunted by his own lineaments, at various ages, as in a dusty mirror. After poring several minutes over one of these blurred and almost indistinguishable pictures, he began to see that the painter had intended to represent him, now in the decline of life, as stripping the clothes from the backs of three half-starved children. "Really, this puzzles me!" quoth Mr. Smith, with the irony of conscious rectitude. "Asking pardon of the painter, I pronounce him a fool, as well as a scandalous knave. A man of my standing in the world, to be robbing little children of their clothes! Ridiculous!" But while he spoke, Memory had searched her fatal volume, and found a page, which, with her sad, calm voice, she poured into his ear. It was not altogether inapplicable to the misty scene. It told how Mr. Smith had been grievously tempted by many devilish sophistries, on the ground of a legal quibble, to commence a lawsuit against three orphan children, joint heirs to a considerable estate. Fortunately, before he was quite decided, his claims had turned out nearly as devoid of law as justice. As Memory ceased to read, Conscience

again thrust aside her mantle, and would have struck her victim with the envenomed dagger, only that he struggled, and clasped his hands before his heart. Even then, however, he sustained an ugly gash.

Why should we follow Fancy through the whole series of those awful pictures? Painted by an artist of wondrous power, and terrible acquaintance with the secret soul, they embodied the ghosts of all the never perpetrated sins that had glided through the lifetime of Mr. Smith. And could such beings of cloudy fantasy, so near akin to nothingness, give valid evidence against him, at the day of judgment? Be that the case or not, there is reason to believe that one truly penitential tear would have washed away each hateful picture, and left the canvas white as snow. But Mr. Smith, at a prick of Conscience too keen to be endured, bellowed aloud, with impatient agony, and suddenly discovered that his three guests were gone. There he sat alone, a silver-haired and highly venerated old man, in the rich gloom of the crimson-curtained room, with no box of pictures on the table, but only a decanter of most excellent Madeira. Yet his heart still seemed to fester with the venom of the dagger.

Nevertheless, the unfortunate old gentleman might have argued the matter with Conscience, and alleged many reasons wherefore she should not smite him so pitilessly. Were we to take up his cause, it should be somewhat in the following fashion: A scheme of guilt, till it be put in execution, greatly resembles a train of incidents in a projected tale. The latter, in order to produce a sense of reality in the reader's mind, must be conceived with such proportionate strength by the author as to seem, in the glow of fancy, more like truth past, present, or to come, than purely fiction. The prospective sinner, on the other hand, weaves his plot of crime, but seldom or never feels a perfect certainty that it will be executed. There is a dreaminess diffused about his thoughts; in a dream, as it were, he strikes the death-blow into his victim's heart, and starts to find an indelible bloodstain on his hand. Thus a novel-writer, or a dramatist, in creating a villain of romance, and fitting him with evil deeds, and the villain of actual life, in projecting crimes that will be perpetrated, may almost meet each other, half-way between reality and fancy. It is not until the crime is accomplished, that guilt clinches its gripe upon the guilty heart, and claims it for its own. Then, and not before, sin is actually felt and acknowledged, and, if unaccompanied by repentance, grows a thousand-fold more virulent by its self-consciousness. Be it considered, also, that men often over-estimate their capacity for evil. At a distance, while its attendant circumstances do not press upon their notice, and its results are dimly seen, they can bear to contemplate it. They may take the steps which lead to crime, impelled by the same sort of mental action as in working out a mathematical problem, yet be powerless with compunction at the final moment. They knew not what deed it was that they deemed themselves resolved to do. In truth, there is no such thing in man's nature as a settled and full resolve, either for good or evil, except at the very moment of execution. Let us hope, therefore, that all the dreadful consequences of sin will not be incurred, unless the act have set its seal upon the thought.

Yet, with the slight fancy work which we have framed, some sad and awful truths are interwoven. Man must not disclaim his brotherhood, even with the guiltiest, since, though his hand be clean, his heart has surely been polluted by the flitting phantoms of iniquity. He must feel that, when he shall knock at the gate of Heaven, no semblance of an unspotted life can entitle him to entrance there. Penitence must kneel, and Mercy come from the footstool of the throne, or that golden gate will never open!

TWICE-TOLD TALES

DR. HEIDEGGER'S EXPERIMENT

THAT very singular man, old Dr. Heidegger, once invited four venerable friends to meet him in his study. There were three white-bearded gentlemen, Mr. Medbourne, Colonel Killigrew, and Mr. Gascoigne, and a withered gentlewoman, whose name was the Widow Wycherly. They were all melancholy old creatures, who had been unfortunate in life, and whose greatest misfortune it was, that they were not long ago in their graves. Mr. Medbourne, in the vigor of his age, had been a prosperous merchant, but had lost his all by a frantic speculation, and was now little better than a mendicant. Colonel Killigrew had wasted his best years, and his health and substance, in the pursuit of sinful pleasures, which had given birth to a brood of pains, such as the gout, and divers other torments of soul and body. Mr. Gascoigne was a ruined politician, a man of evil fame, or at least had been so, till time had buried him from the knowledge of the present generation, and made him obscure instead of infamous. As for the Widow Wycherly, tradition tells us that she was a great beauty in her day; but, for a long while past, she had lived in deep seclusion, on account of certain scandalous stories which had prejudiced the gentry of the town against her. It is a circumstance worth mentioning, that each of these three old gentlemen, Mr. Medbourne, Colonel Killigrew, and Mr. Gascoigne, were early lovers of the Widow Wycherly, and had once been on the point of cutting each other's throats for her sake. And, before proceeding further, I will merely hint that Dr. Heidegger and all his four guests were sometimes thought to be a little beside themselves; as is not unfrequently the case with old people, when worried either by present troubles or woful recollections.

"My dear old friends," said Dr. Heidegger, motioning them to be seated, "I am desirous of your assistance in one of those little experiments with which I amuse myself here in my study."

If all stories were true, Dr. Heidegger's study must have been a very curious place. It was a dim, old-fashioned chamber, festooned with cobwebs and besprinkled with antique dust. Around the walls stood several oaken bookcases, the lower shelves of which were filled with rows of gigantic folios and black-letter quartos, and the upper with little parchment-covered duodecimos. Over the central bookcase was a bronze bust of Hippocrates, with which, according to some authorities, Dr. Heidegger was accustomed to hold consultations in all difficult cases of his practice. In the obscurest corner of the room stood a tall and narrow oaken closet, with its door ajar, within which doubtfully appeared a skeleton. Between two of the bookcases hung a looking-glass, presenting its high and dusty plate within a tarnished gilt frame. Among many wonderful stories related of this mirror, it was fabled that the spirits of all the doctor's deceased patients dwelt within its verge, and would stare him in the face whenever he looked thitherward. The opposite side of the chamber was ornamented with the full-length portrait of a young lady, arrayed in the faded magnificence of silk, satin, and brocade, and with a visage as faded as her dress. Above half a century ago, Dr. Heidegger had been on the point of marriage with this young lady; but, being affected with some slight disorder, she had swallowed one of her lover's prescriptions, and died on the bridal evening. The greatest curiosity of the study remains to be mentioned; it was a ponderous folio volume, bound in black leather, with massive silver clasps. There were no letters on the back, and nobody could tell the title of the book. But it was well known to be a book of magic; and once, when a chambermaid had lifted it merely to brush away the dust, the skeleton had rattled in its closet, the picture of the young lady had stepped one foot upon the floor, and several ghastly faces had peeped forth from the mirror; while the brazen head of Hippocrates frowned, and said—"Forbear!"

Such was Dr. Heidegger's study. On the summer afternoon of our tale, a small round table, as black as ebony, stood in the centre of the room, sustaining a cut-glass vase of beautiful form and elaborate workmanship. The sunshine came through the window, between the heavy festoons of two faded damask curtains, and fell directly across this vase; so that a mild splendor was reflected from it on the ashen visages of the five old people who sat around. Four champagne glasses were also on the table.

"My dear old friends," repeated Dr. Heidegger, "may I reckon on your aid in performing an exceedingly curious experiment?"

Now Dr. Heidegger was a very strange old gentleman, whose eccentricity had become the nucleus for a thousand fantastic stories. Some of these fables, to my shame be it spoken, might possibly be traced back to mine own veracious self; and if any passages of the present tale should startle the reader's faith, I must be content to bear the stigma of a fiction-monger.

When the doctor's four guests heard him talk of his proposed experiment, they anticipated nothing more wonderful than the murder of a mouse in an air-pump, or the examination of a cobweb by the microscope, or some similar nonsense, with which he was constantly in the habit of pestering his intimates. But without waiting for a reply, Dr. Heidegger hobbled across the chamber, and returned with the same ponderous folio, bound in black leather, which common report affirmed to be a book of magic. Undoing the silver clasps he opened the volume, and took from among its black-letter pages a rose, or what was once a rose, though now the green leaves and crimson petals had assumed one brownish hue, and the ancient flower seemed ready to crumble to dust in the doctor's hands.

"This rose," said Dr. Heidegger, with a sigh, "this same withered and crumbling flower, blossomed five and fifty years ago. It was given me by Sylvia

Ward, whose portrait hangs yonder; and I meant to wear it in my bosom at our wedding. Five and fifty years it has been treasured between the leaves of this old volume. Now, would you deem it possible that this rose of half a century could ever bloom again?"

"Nonsense!" said the Widow Wycherly, with a peevish toss of her head. "You might as well ask whether an old woman's wrinkled face could ever bloom again."

"See!" answered Dr. Heidegger.

He uncovered the vase, and threw the faded rose into the water which it contained. At first it lay lightly on the surface of the fluid, appearing to imbibe none of its moisture. Soon, however, a singular change began to be visible. The crushed and dried petals stirred, and assumed a deepening tinge of crimson, as if the flower were reviving from a deathlike slumber; the slender stalk and twigs of foliage became green; and there was the rose of half a century, looking as fresh as when Sylvia Ward had first given it to her lover. It was scarcely full blown; for some of its delicate red leaves curled modestly around its moist bosom, within which two or three dew-drops were sparkling.

"That is certainly a very pretty deception," said the doctor's friends; carelessly, however, for they had witnessed greater miracles at a conjurer's show; "pray how was it effected?"

"Did you never hear of the 'Fountain of Youth'?" asked Dr. Heidegger, "which Ponce de Leon, the Spanish adventurer, went in search of two or three centuries ago?"

"But did Ponce de Leon ever find it?" said the Widow Wycherly.

"No," answered Dr. Heidegger, "for he never sought it in the right place. The famous Fountain of Youth, if I am rightly informed, is situated in the southern part of the Floridian peninsula, not far from Lake Macaco. Its source is overshadowed by several gigantic magnolias, which, though numberless centuries old, have been kept as fresh as violets by the virtues of this wonderful water. An acquaintance of mine, knowing my curiosity in such matters, has sent me what you see in the vase."

"Ahem!" said Colonel Killigrew, who believed not a word of the doctor's story; "and what may be the effect of this fluid on the human frame?"

"You shall judge for yourself, my dear colonel," replied Dr. Heidegger; "and all of you, my respected friends, are welcome to so much of this admirable fluid as may restore to you the bloom of youth. For my own part, having had much trouble in growing old I am in no hurry to grow young again. With your permission, therefore, I will merely watch the progress of the experiment."

While he spoke, Dr. Heidegger had been filling the four champagne glasses with the water of the Fountain of Youth. It was apparently impregnated with an effervescent gas, for little bubbles were continually ascending from the depths of the glasses and bursting in silvery spray at the surface. As the liquor diffused a pleasant perfume, the old people doubted not that it possessed cordial and comfortable properties; and though utter sceptics as to its rejuvenescent power, they were inclined to swallow it at once. But Dr. Heidegger besought them to stay a moment.

"Before you drink, my respectable old friends," said he, "it would be well that, with the experience of a lifetime to direct you, you should draw up a few general rules for your guidance, in passing a second time through the perils of youth. Think what a sin and shame it would be, if, with your peculiar advantages, you should not become patterns of virtue and wisdom to all the young people of the age!"

The doctor's four venerable friends made him no answer, except by a feeble and tremulous laugh; so very ridiculous was the idea, that, knowing how closely repentance treads behind the steps of error, they should ever go astray again.

"Drink, then," said the doctor, bowing: "I rejoice that I have so well selected the subjects of my experiment."

With palsied hands, they raised the glasses to their lips. The liquor, if it really possessed such virtues as Dr. Heidegger imputed to it, could not have been bestowed on four human beings who needed it more wofully. They looked as if they had never known what youth or pleasure was, but had been the offspring of Nature's dotage, and always the gray, decrepit, sapless, miserable creatures who now sat stooping round the doctor's table, without life enough in their souls or bodies to be animated even by the prospect of growing young again. They drank off the water, and replaced their glasses on the table.

Assuredly there was an almost immediate improvement in the aspect of the party, not unlike what might have been produced by a glass of generous wine together with a sudden glow of cheerful sunshine, brightening over all their visages at once. There was a healthful suffusion on their cheeks, instead of the ashen hue that had made them look so corpse-like. They gazed at one another, and fancied that some magic power had really begun to smooth away the deep and sad inscriptions which Father Time had been so long engraving on their brows. The Widow Wycherly adjusted her cap, for she felt almost like a woman again.

"Give us more of this wondrous water!" cried they eagerly. "We are younger,—but we are still too old! Quick,—give us more!"

"Patience, patience!" quoth Dr. Heidegger, who sat watching the experiment, with philosophic coolness. "You have been a long time growing old. Surely, you might be content to grow young in half an hour! But the water is at your service."

Again he filled their glasses with the liquor of youth, enough of which still remained in the vase to turn half the old people in the city to the age of their own grandchildren. While the bubbles were yet sparkling on the brim the doctor's four guests snatched their glasses from the table, and swallowed the contents at a single gulp. Was it delusion? even while the draught was passing down their throats, it seemed to have wrought a change on their whole systems. Their eyes grew clear and bright; a dark shade deepened among their silvery locks; they sat around the table, three gentlemen of middle age, and a woman hardly beyond her buxom prime.

"My dear widow, you are charming!" cried Colonel Killigrew, whose eyes had been fixed upon her face, while the shadows of age were flitting from it like darkness from the crimson day-break.

The fair widow knew, of old, that Colonel Killigrew's compliments were not always measured by sober truth; so she started up and ran to the mirror, still dreading that the ugly visage of an old woman would meet her gaze. Meanwhile, the three gentlemen behaved in such a manner, as proved that the water of the Fountain of Youth possessed some intoxicating qualities; unless, indeed, their exhilaration of spirits were merely a lightsome dizziness, caused by the sudden removal of the weight of years. Mr. Gascoigne's mind seemed to run on political topics, but whether relating to the past, present, or future could not easily be determined, since the same ideas and phrases have been in vogue these fifty years. Now he rattled forth full-throated sentences about patriotism, national glory, and the people's right; now he muttered some perilous stuff or other, in a sly and doubtful whisper, so cautiously that even his own conscience could scarcely catch the secret; and now, again, he spoke in measured accents, and a deeply deferential tone, as if a royal ear were listening to his well-turned periods. Colonel Killigrew all this time had been trolling forth a jolly bottle-song, and ringing his glass in symphony with the chorus, while his eyes wandered toward the buxom figure of the Widow Wycherly. On the other side of the table, Mr. Medbourne was involved in a calculation of dollars and cents, with which was strangely intermingled a project for supplying the East Indies with ice, by harnessing a team of whales to the polar icebergs.

As for the Widow Wycherly, she stood before the mirror courtesying and simpering to her own image, and greeting it as the friend whom she loved better than all the world beside. She thrust her face close to the glass, to see whether some long-remembered wrinkle or crow's foot had indeed vanished. She examined whether the snow had so entirely melted from her hair, that the venerable cap could be safely thrown aside. At last, turning briskly away, she came with a sort of dancing step to the table.

"My dear old doctor," cried she, "pray favor me with another glass!"

"Certainly, my dear madam, certainly!" replied the complaisant doctor; "see! I have already filled the glasses."

There, in fact, stood the four glasses, brimful of this wonderful water, the delicate spray of which, as it effervesced from the surface, resembled the tremulous glitter of diamonds. It was now so nearly sunset, that the chamber had grown duskier than ever; but a mild and moonlike splendor gleamed from within the vase, and rested alike on the four guests, and on the doctor's venerable figure. He sat in a high-backed, elaborately-carved, oaken arm-chair, with a gray dignity of aspect that might have well befitted that very Father Time whose power had never been disputed, save by this fortunate company. Even while quaffing the third draught of the Fountain of Youth, they were almost awed by the expression of his mysterious visage.

But the next moment the exhilarating gush of young life shot through their veins. They were now in the happy prime of youth. Age, with its miserable train of cares and sorrows and diseases, was remembered only as the trouble of a dream, from which they had joyously awoke. The fresh gloss of the soul, so early lost, and without which the world's successive scenes had been but a gallery of faded pictures, again threw its enchantment over all their prospects. They felt like new-created beings, in a new-created universe.

"We are young! We are young!" they cried exultingly.

Youth, like the extremity of age, had effaced the strongly-marked characteristics of middle life, and mutually assimilated them all. They were a group of merry youngsters, almost maddened with the exuberant frolicsomeness of their years. The most singular effect of their gayety was an impulse to mock the infirmity and decrepitude of which they had so lately been the victims. They laughed loudly at their old-fashioned attire, the wide-skirted coats and flapped waistcoats of the young men, and the ancient cap and gown of the blooming girl. One limped across the floor, like a gouty grandfather; one set a pair of spectacles astride of his nose, and pretended to pore over the black-letter pages of the book of magic; a third seated himself in an arm-chair, and strove to imitate the venerable dignity of Dr. Heidegger. Then all shouted mirthfully, and leaped about the room. The Widow Wycherly—if so fresh a damsel could be called a widow—tripped up to the doctor's chair, with a mischievous merriment in her rosy face.

"Doctor, you dear old soul," cried she, "get up and dance with me!" And then the four young people laughed louder than ever, to think what a queer figure the poor old doctor would cut.

"Pray excuse me," answered the doctor quietly. "I am old and rheumatic and my dancing days were over long ago. But either of these gay young gentlemen will be glad of so pretty a partner."

"Dance with me, Clara," cried Colonel Killigrew.

"No, no, I will be her partner!" shouted Mr. Gascoigne.

"She promised me her hand, fifty years ago!" exclaimed Mr. Medbourne.

They all gathered round her. One caught both her hands in his passionate grasp,—another threw his arm about her waist,—the third buried his hand among the glossy curls that clustered beneath the widow's cap. Blushing, panting, struggling, chiding, laughing, her warm breath fanning each of their faces by turns, she strove to disengage herself yet still remained in their triple embrace. Never was there a livelier picture of youthful rivalship, with bewitching beauty for the prize. Yet, by a strange deception, owing to the duskiness of the chamber, and the antique dresses which they still wore, the tall mirror is said to have reflected the figures of the three old, gray, withered grandsires, ridiculously contending for the skinny ugliness of a shrivelled grandam.

But they were young: their burning passions proved them so. Inflamed to madness by the coquetry of the girl widow, who neither granted nor quite withheld her favors, the three rivals began to interchange threatening glances. Still keeping hold of the fair prize they grappled fiercely at one another's throats. As they struggled to and fro the table was overturned, and the vase dashed into a thousand fragments. The precious Water of Youth flowed in a bright stream across the floor, moistening the wings of a butterfly, which grown old in the decline of summer, had alighted there to die. The insect fluttered lightly through the chamber, and settled on the snowy head of Dr. Heidegger.

"Come, come, gentlemen!—come, Madame Wycherly," exclaimed the doctor, "I really must protest against this riot."

They stood still, and shivered; for it seemed as if gray Time were calling them back from their sunny youth, far down into the chill and darksome vale of years. They looked at old Dr. Heidegger, who sat in his carved arm-chair holding the rose of half a century, which he had rescued from among the fragments of the shattered vase. At the motion of his hand the four rioters resumed their seats; the more readily, because their violent exertions had wearied them, youthful though they were.

"My poor Sylvia's rose!" ejaculated Dr. Heidegger, holding it in the light of the sunset clouds; "it appears to be fading again."

And so it was. Even while the party were looking at it the flower continued to shrivel up, till it became as dry and fragile as when the doctor had first thrown it into the vase. He shook off the few drops of moisture which clung to its petals.

"I love it as well thus as in its dewy freshness," observed he, pressing the withered rose to his withered lips. While he spoke, the butterfly fluttered down from the doctor's snowy head and fell upon the floor.

His guests shivered again. A strange chillness, whether of the body or spirit they could not tell, was creeping gradually over them all. They gazed at one another, and fancied that each fleeting moment snatched away a charm, and left a deepening furrow where none had

been before. Was it an illusion? Had the changes of a lifetime been crowded into so brief a space, and were they now four aged people, sitting with their old friend, Dr. Heidegger?

"Are we grown old again so soon?" cried they, dolefully.

In truth they had. The Water of Youth possessed merely a virtue more transient than that of wine. The delirium which it created had effervesced away. Yes! they were old again. With a shuddering impulse that showed her a woman still, the widow clasped her skinny hands before her face, and wished that the coffin-lid were over it since it could be no longer beautiful.

"Yes, friends, ye are old again," said Dr. Heidegger; "and lo! the Water of Youth is all lavished on the ground. Well—I bemoan it not; for if the fountain gushed at my very doorstep I would not stoop to bathe my lips in it,—no, though its delirium were for years instead of moments. Such is the lesson ye have taught me!"

But the doctor's four friends had taught no such lesson to themselves. They resolved forthwith to make a pilgrimage to Florida, and quaff at morning, noon, and night from the Fountain of Youth.

NOTE.—In an English Review, not long since, I have been accused of plagiarizing the idea of this story from a chapter in one of the novels of Alexandre Dumas. There has undoubtedly been a plagiarism on one side or the other; but as my story was written a good deal more than twenty years ago, and as the novel is of considerably more recent date, I take pleasure in thinking that M. Dumas has done me the honor to appropriate one of the fanciful conceptions of my earlier days. He is heartily welcome to it; nor is it the only instance by many in which the great French Romancer has exercised the privilege of commanding genius by confiscating the intellectual property of less famous people to his own use and behoof.

September, 1860.

LEGENDS OF THE PROVINCE HOUSE

I. HOWE'S MASQUERADE

ONE afternoon last summer, while walking along Washington Street, my eye was attracted by a signboard protruding over a narrow archway, nearly opposite the Old South Church. The sign represented the front of a stately edifice, which was designated as the "OLD PROVINCE HOUSE, kept by Thomas Waite." I was glad to be thus reminded of a purpose, long entertained, of visiting and rambling over the mansion of the old royal governors of Massachusetts; and entering the arched passage, which penetrated through the middle of a brick row of shops, a few steps transported me from the busy heart of modern Boston into a small and secluded court-yard. One side of this space was occupied by the square front of the Province House, three stories high, and surmounted by a cupola, on the top of which a gilded Indian was discernible, with his bow bent and his arrow on the string, as if aiming at the weathercock on the spire of the Old South. The figure has kept this attitude for seventy years or more, ever since good Deacon Drowne, a cunning carver of wood, first stationed him on his long sentinel's watch over the city.

The Province House is constructed of brick, which seems recently to have been overlaid with a coat of light-colored paint. A flight of red freestone steps, fenced in by a balustrade of curiously wrought iron ascends from the court-yard to the spacious porch, over which is a balcony, with an iron balustrade of similar pattern and workmanship to that beneath. These letters and figures—16 P. S. 79—are wrought into the iron-work of the balcony, and probably express the date of the edifice, with the initials of its founder's name. A wide door with double leaves admitted me into the hall or entry, on the right of which is the entrance to the bar-room.

It was in this apartment, I presume, that the ancient governors held their levees, with vice-regal pomp, surrounded by the military men, the councillors, the judges, and other officers of the crown, while all the loyalty of the province thronged to do them honor. But the room, in its present condition, cannot boast even of faded magnificence. The panelled wainscot is covered with dingy paint, and acquires a duskier hue from the deep shadow into which the Province House is thrown by the brick block that shuts it in from Washington Street. A ray of sunshine never visits this apartment any more than the glare of the festal torches, which have been extinguished from the era of the Revolution. The most venerable and ornamental object is a chimney-piece set round with Dutch tiles of blue-figured China, representing scenes from Scripture; and, for aught I know, the lady of Pownall or Bernard may have sat beside this fireplace and told her children the story of each blue tile. A bar in modern style, well replenished with decanters, bottles, cigar-boxes, and net-work bags of lemons, and provided with a beer-pump and a soda-fount, extends along one side of the room. At my entrance, an elderly person was smacking his lips with a zest which satisfied me that the cellars of the Province House still hold good liquor, though doubtless of other vintages than were quaffed by the old governors. After sipping a glass of port sangaree, prepared by the skilful hands of Mr. Thomas Waite, I besought that worthy successor and representative of so many historic personages to conduct me over their time-honored mansion.

He readily complied; but, to confess the truth, I was forced to draw strenuously upon my imagination, in order to find aught that was interesting in a house which, without its historic associations, would have seemed merely such a tavern as is usually favored by the custom of decent city boarders, and old-fashioned country gentlemen. The chambers, which were probably spacious in former times, are now cut up by partitions, and subdivided into little nooks, each affording scanty room for the narrow bed, and chair, and dressing-table of a single lodger. The great staircase, however, may be termed, without much hyperbole, a feature of grandeur and magnificence. It winds through the midst of the house by flights of broad steps, each flight terminating in a square landing-place, whence the ascent is continued towards the cupola. A carved balustrade, freshly painted in the lower stories, but growing dingier as we ascend, borders the staircase with its quaintly twisted and intertwined pillars, from top to bottom. Up these stairs the military boots, or perchance the gouty shoes, of many a governor have trodden, as the wearers mounted to the cupola, which afforded them so wide a view

over their metropolis and the surrounding country. The cupola is an octagon, with several windows, and a door opening upon the roof. From this station, as I pleased myself with imagining, Gage may have beheld his disastrous victory on Bunker Hill, (unless one of the tri-mountains intervened,) and Howe have marked the approaches of Washington's besieging army; although the buildings since erected in the vicinity, have shut out almost every object, save the steeple of the Old South, which seems almost within arm's length. Descending from the cupola, I paused in the garret to observe the ponderous white-oak framework, so much more massive than the frames of modern houses, and thereby resembling an antique skeleton. The brick walls, the materials of which were imported from Holland, and the timbers of the mansion, are still as sound as ever; but the floors and other interior parts being greatly decayed, it is contemplated to gut the whole, and build a new house within the ancient frame and brick work. Among other inconveniences of the present edifice, mine host mentioned that any jar or motion was apt to shake down the dust of ages out of the ceiling of one chamber upon the floor of that beneath it.

We stepped forth from the great front window into the balcony, where, in old times, it was doubtless the custom of the king's representative to show himself to a loyal populace, requiting their huzzas and tossed-up hats with stately bendings of his dignified person. In those days, the front of the Province House looked upon the street; and the whole site now occupied by the brick range of stores, as well as the present courtyard, was laid out in grass plats, overshadowed by trees and bordered by a wrought-iron fence. Now, the old aristocratic edifice hides its time-worn visage behind an upstart modern building; at one of the back windows I observed some pretty tailoresses, sewing, and chatting, and laughing, with now and then a careless glance towards the balcony. Descending thence, we again entered the bar-room, where the elderly gentleman above mentioned, the smack of whose lips had spoken so favorably for Mr. Waite's good liquor, was still lounging in his chair. He seemed to be, if not a lodger, at least a familiar visitor of the house, who might be supposed to have his regular score at the bar, his summer seat at the open window, and his prescriptive corner at the winter's fireside. Being of a sociable aspect, I ventured to address him with a remark, calculated to draw forth his historical reminiscences, if any such were in his mind; and it gratified me to discover, that, between memory and tradition, the old gentleman was really possessed of some very pleasant gossip about the Province House. The portion of his talk which chiefly interested me, was the outline of the following legend. He professed to have received it at one or two removes from an eyewitness; but this derivation, together with the lapse of time, must have afforded opportunities for many variations of the narrative; so that, despairing of literal and absolute truth, I have not scrupled to make such further changes as seemed conducive to the reader's profit and delight.

At one of the entertainments given at the Province House, during the latter part of the siege of Boston, there passed a scene which has never yet been satisfactorily explained. The officers of the British army, and the loyal gentry of the province, most of whom were collected within the beleaguered town, had been invited to a masked ball; for it was the policy of Sir William Howe to hide the distress and danger of the period, and the desperate aspect of the siege under an ostentation of festivity. The spectacle of this evening, if the oldest members of the provincial court circle might be believed, was the most gay and gorgeous affair that had occurred in the annals of the government. The brilliantly-lighted apartments were thronged with figures that seemed to have stepped from the dark canvas of historic portraits, or to have flitted forth from the magic pages of romance, or at least to have flown hither from one of the London theatres, without a change of garments. Steeled knights of the Conquest, bearded statesmen of Queen Elizabeth, and high-ruffled ladies of her court, were mingled with characters of comedy, such as a party-colored Merry Andrew, jingling his cap and bells; a Falstaff, almost as provocative of laughter as his prototype; and a Don Quixote, with a bean-pole for a lance and a potlid for a shield.

But the broadest merriment was excited by a group of figures ridiculously dressed in old regimentals, which seemed to have been purchased at a military rag-fair, or pilfered from some receptacle of the cast-off clothes of both the French and British armies. Portions of their attire had probably been worn at the siege of Louisburg, and the coats of most recent cut might have been rent and tattered by sword, ball, or bayonet as long ago as Wolfe's victory. One of these worthies—a tall, lank figure, brandishing a rusty sword of immense longitude—purported to be no less a personage than General George Washington; and the other principal officers of the American army, such as Gates, Lee, Putnam, Schuyler, Ward, and Heath, were represented by similar scarecrows. An interview in the mock heroic style, between the rebel warriors and the British commander-in-chief, was received with immense applause, which came loudest of all from the loyalists of the colony. There was one of the guests, however, who stood apart, eying these antics sternly and scornfully, at once with a frown and a bitter smile.

It was an old man, formerly of high station and great repute in the province, and who had been a very famous soldier in his day. Some surprise had been expressed, that a person of Colonel Joliffe's known whig principles, though now too old to take an active part in the contest, should have remained in Boston during the siege, and especially that he should consent to show himself in the mansion of Sir William Howe. But thither he had come, with a fair granddaughter under his arm; and here, amid all the mirth and buffoonery, stood his stern old figure, the best sustained character in the masquerade, because so well representing the antique spirit of his native land. The other guests affirmed that Colonel Joliffe's black puritanical scowl threw a shadow round about him; although in spite of his sombre influence, their gayety continued to blaze higher, like—(an ominous comparison)—the flickering brilliancy of a lamp which has but a little while to burn. Eleven strokes, full half

an hour ago, had pealed from the clock of the Old South, when a rumor was circulated among the company that some new spectacle or pageant was about to be exhibited, which should put a fitting close to the splendid festivities of the night.

"What new jest has your Excellency in hand?" asked the Rev. Mather Byles, whose Presbyterian scruples had not kept him from the entertainment. "Trust me, sir, I have already laughed more than beseems my cloth, at your Homeric confabulation with yonder ragamuffin General of the rebels. One other such fit of merriment, and I must throw off my clerical wig and band."

"Not so, good Doctor Byles," answered Sir William Howe; "if mirth were a crime, you had never gained your doctorate in divinity. As to this new foolery, I know no more about it than yourself; perhaps not so much. Honestly now, Doctor, have you not stirred up the sober brains of some of your countrymen to enact a scene in our masquerade?"

"Perhaps," slyly remarked the granddaughter of Colonel Joliffe, whose high spirit had been stung by many taunts against New England,—"perhaps we are to have a mask of allegorical figures. Victory, with trophies from Lexington and Bunker Hill,—Plenty, with her overflowing horn, to typify the present abundance in this good town,—and Glory, with a wreath for his Excellency's brow."

Sir William Howe smiled at words which he would have answered with one of his darkest frowns, had they been uttered by lips that wore a beard. He was spared the necessity of a retort, by a singular interruption. A sound of music was heard without the house, as if proceeding from a full band of military instruments stationed in the street, playing not such a festal strain as was suited to the occasion; but a slow funeral march. The drums appeared to be muffled, and the trumpets poured forth a wailing breath, which at once hushed the merriment of the auditors, filling all with wonder, and some with apprehension. The idea occurred to many, that either the funeral procession of some great personage had halted in front of the Province House, or that a corpse, in a velvet-covered and gorgeously-decorated coffin, was about to be borne from the portal. After listening a moment, Sir William Howe called, in a stern voice, to the leader of the musicians, who had hitherto enlivened the entertainment with gay and lightsome melodies. The man was drummajor to one of the British regiments.

"Dighton," demanded the general, "what means this foolery? Bid your band silence that dead march—or, by my word, they shall have sufficient cause for their lugubrious strains! Silence it, sirrah!"

"Please your honor," answered the drum-major, whose rubicund visage had lost all its color, "the fault is none of mine. I and my band are all here together; and I question whether there be a man of us that could play that march without book. I never heard it but once before, and that was at the funeral of his late Majesty, King George the Second."

"Well, well!" said Sir William Howe, recovering his composure,—"it is the prelude to some masquerading antic. Let it pass."

A figure now presented itself, but among the many fantastic masks that were dispersed through the apartments, none could tell precisely from whence it came. It was a man in an old-fashioned dress of black serge, and having the aspect of a steward, or principal domestic in the household of a nobleman, or great English landholder. This figure advanced to the outer door of the mansion, and throwing both its leaves wide open, withdrew a little to one side and looked back towards the grand staircase, as if expecting some person to descend. At the same time, the music in the street sounded a loud and doleful summons. The eyes of Sir William Howe and his guests being directed to the staircase, there appeared on the uppermost landing-place that was discernible from the bottom, several personages descending towards the door. The foremost was a man of stern visage, wearing a steeple-crowned hat and a skullcap beneath it; a dark cloak, and huge wrinkled boots that came half-way up his legs. Under his arm was a rolled-up banner, which seemed to be the banner of England, but strangely rent and torn; he had a sword in his right hand, and grasped a Bible in his left. The next figure was of milder aspect, yet full of dignity, wearing a broad ruff over which descended a beard, a gown of wrought velvet, and a doublet and hose of black satin. He carried a roll of manuscript in his hand. Close behind these two came a young man of very striking countenance and demeanor, with deep thought and contemplation on his brow, and perhaps a flash of enthusiasm in his eye. His garb, like that of his predecessors, was of an antique fashion, and there was a stain of blood upon his ruff. In the same group with these were three or four others, all men of dignity and evident command, and bearing themselves like personages who were accustomed to the gaze of the multitude. It was the idea of the beholder, that these figures went to join the mysterious funeral that had halted in front of the Province House; yet that supposition seemed to be contradicted by the air of triumph with which they waved their hands, as they crossed the threshold and vanished through the portal.

"In the Devil's name, what is this?" muttered Sir William Howe to a gentleman beside him; "a procession of the regicide judges of King Charles the martyr?"

"These," said Colonel Joliffe, breaking silence almost for the first time that evening,—"these, if I interpret them right, are the Puritan governors—the rulers of the old, original Democracy of Massachusetts. Endicott, with the banner from which he had torn the symbol of subjection, and Winthrop, and Sir Henry Vane, and Dudley, Haynes, Bellingham, and Leverett."

"Why had that young man a stain of blood upon his ruff?" asked Miss Joliffe.

"Because, in after years," answered her grandfather, "he laid down the wisest head in England upon the block, for the principles of liberty."

"Will not your Excellency order out the guard?" whispered Lord Percy, who, with other British officers, had now assembled round the General. "There may be a plot under this mummery."

"Tush! we have nothing to fear," carelessly replied Sir William Howe. "There can be no worse treason in the matter than a jest, and that somewhat of the dullest. Even were it a sharp and bitter one, our best policy would be to laugh it off. See—here come more of these gentry."

Another group of characters had now partly descended the staircase. The first was a venerable and white-bearded patriarch, who cautiously felt his way downward with a staff. Treading hastily behind him, and stretching forth his gauntleted hand as if to grasp the old man's shoulder, came a tall, soldier-like figure, equipped with a plumed cap of steel, a bright breastplate, and a long sword, which rattled against the stairs. Next was seen a stout man, dressed in rich and courtly attire, but not of courtly demeanor; his gait had the swinging motion of a seaman's walk; and chancing to stumble on the staircase, he suddenly grew wrathful, and was heard to mutter an oath. He was followed by a noble-looking personage in a curled wig, such as are represented in the portraits of Queen Anne's time and earlier; and the breast of his coat was decorated with an embroidered star. While advancing to the door, he bowed to the right hand and to the left, in a very gracious and insinuating style; but as he crossed the threshold, unlike the early Puritan governors, he seemed to wring his hands with sorrow.

"Prithee, play the part of a chorus, good Doctor Byles," said Sir William Howe. "What worthies are these?"

"If it please your Excellency, they lived somewhat before my day," answered the Doctor; "but doubtless our friend, the Colonel, has been hand in glove with them."

"Their living faces I never looked upon," said Colonel Joliffe, gravely; "although I have spoken face to face with many rulers of this land, and shall greet yet another with an old man's blessing ere I die. But we talk of these figures. I take the venerable patriarch to be Bradstreet, the last of the Puritans, who was governor at ninety, or thereabouts. The next is Sir Edmund Andros, a tyrant, as any New England school-boy will tell you; and therefore the people cast him down from his high seat into a dungeon. Then comes Sir William Phipps, shepherd, cooper, sea-captain, and governor,—may many of his countrymen rise as high from as low an origin! Lastly, you saw the gracious Earl of Bellamont, who ruled us under King William."

"But what is the meaning of it all?" asked Lord Percy.

"Now, were I a rebel," said Miss Joliffe, half aloud, "I might fancy that the ghosts of these ancient governors had been summoned to form the funeral procession of royal authority in New England."

Several other figures were now seen at the turn of the staircase. The one in advance had a thoughtful, anxious, and somewhat crafty expression of face; and in spite of his loftiness of manner, which was evidently the result both of an ambitious spirit and of long continuance in high stations, he seemed not incapable of cringing to a greater than himself. A few steps behind came an officer in a scarlet and embroidered uniform, cut in a fashion old enough to have been worn by the Duke of Marlborough. His nose had a rubicund tinge, which, together with the twinkle of his eye, might have marked him as a lover of the wine-cup and good fellowship; notwithstanding which tokens, he appeared ill at ease, and often glanced

around him, as if apprehensive of some secret mischief. Next came a portly gentleman, wearing a coat of shaggy cloth, lined with silken velvet; he had sense, shrewdness, and humor in his face, and a folio volume under his arm; but his aspect was that of a man vexed and tormented beyond all patience, and harassed almost to death. He went hastily down, and was followed by a dignified person, dressed in a purple velvet suit, with very rich embroidery; his demeanor would have possessed much stateliness, only that a grievous fit of the gout compelled him to hobble from stair to stair, with contortions of face and body. When Doctor Byles beheld this figure on the staircase, he shivered as with an ague, but continued to watch him steadfastly, until the gouty gentleman had reached the threshold, made a gesture of anguish and despair, and vanished into the outer gloom, whither the funeral music summoned him.

"Governor Belcher!—my old patron! —in his very shape and dress!" gasped Doctor Byles. "This is an awful mockery!"

"A tedious foolery, rather," said Sir William Howe, with an air of indifference. "But who were the three that preceded him?"

"Governor Dudley, a cunning politician,—yet his craft once brought him to a prison," replied Colonel Joliffe. "Governor Shute, formerly a Colonel under Marlborough, and whom the people frightened out of the province; and learned Governor Burnet, whom the legislature tormented into a mortal fever."

"Methinks they were miserable men, these royal governors of Massachusetts," observed Miss Joliffe. "Heavens, how dim the light grows!"

It was certainly a fact that the large lamp which illuminated the staircase now burned dim and duskily: so that several figures, which passed hastily down the stairs and went forth from the porch appeared rather like shadows than persons of fleshly substance. Sir William Howe and his guests stood at the doors of the contiguous apartments, watching the progress of this singular pageant, with various emotions of anger, contempt, or half-acknowledged fear, but still with an anxious curiosity. The shapes which now seemed hastening to join the mysterious procession were recognized rather by striking peculiarities of dress, or broad characteristics of manner, than by any perceptible resemblance of features to their prototypes. Their faces, indeed, were invariably kept in deep shadow. But Doctor Byles, and other gentlemen who had long been familiar with the successive rulers of the province, were heard to whisper the names of Shirley, of Pownall, of Sir Francis Bernard, and of the well-remembered Hutchinson; thereby confessing that the actors, whoever they might be, in this spectral march of governors, had succeeded in putting on some distant portraiture of the real personages. As they vanished from the door, still did these shadows toss their arms into the gloom of night, with a dread expression of woe. Following the mimic representative of Hutchinson came a military figure, holding before his face the cocked hat which he had taken from his powdered head; but his epaulettes and other insignia of rank were those of a general officer; and something in his mien reminded the

beholders of one who had recently been master of the Province House, and chief of all the land.

"The shape of Gage, as true as in a looking-glass," exclaimed Lord Percy, turning pale.

"No, surely," cried Miss Joliffe, laughing hysterically; "it could not be Gage, or Sir William would have greeted his old comrade in arms! Perhaps he will not suffer the next to pass unchallenged."

"Of that be assured, young lady," answered Sir William Howe, fixing his eyes, with a very marked expression, upon the immovable visage of her grandfather. "I have long enough delayed to pay the ceremonies of a host to these departing guests. The next that takes his leave shall receive due courtesy."

A wild and dreary burst of music came through the open door. It seemed as if the procession, which had been gradually filling up its ranks, were now about to move, and that this loud peal of the wailing trumpets and roll of the muffled drums were a call to some loiterer to make haste. Many eyes, by an irresistible impulse, were turned upon Sir William Howe, as if it were he whom the dreary music summoned to the funeral of departed power.

"See!—here comes the last!" whispered Miss Joliffe, pointing her tremulous finger to the staircase.

A figure had come into view as if descending the stairs; although so dusky was the region whence it emerged, some of the spectators fancied that they had seen this human shape suddenly moulding itself amid the gloom. Downward the figure came, with a stately and marshal tread, and reaching the lowest stair was observed to be a tall man, booted and wrapped in a military cloak, which was drawn up around the face so as to meet the flapped brim of a laced hat. The features, therefore, were completely hidden. But the British officers deemed that they had seen that military cloak before, and even recognized the frayed embroidery on the collar, as well as the gilded scabbard of a sword which protruded from the folds of the cloak, and glittered in a vivid gleam of light. Apart from these trifling particulars, there were characteristics of gait and bearing which impelled the wondering guests to glance from the shrouded figure to Sir William Howe, as if to satisfy themselves that their host had not suddenly vanished from the midst of them.

With a dark flush of wrath upon his brow, they saw the General draw his sword and advance to meet the figure in the cloak before the latter had stepped one pace upon the floor. "Villain, unmuffle yourself!" cried he. "You pass no farther!"

The figure, without blenching a hair's breadth from the sword which was pointed at his breast, made a solemn pause and lowered the cape of the cloak from about his face, yet not sufficiently for the spectators to catch a glimpse of it. But Sir William Howe had evidently seen enough. The sternness of his countenance gave place to a look of wild amazement, if not horror, while he recoiled several steps from the figure, and let fall his sword upon the floor. The martial shape again drew the cloak about his features and passed on; but reaching the threshold, with his back towards the spectators, he was seen to stamp his foot and shake his clinched

hands in the air. It was afterwards affirmed that Sir William Howe had repeated that selfsame gesture of rage and sorrow when, for the last time, and as the last royal governor, he passed through the portal of the Province House.

"Hark!—the procession moves," said Miss Joliffe.

The music was dying away along the street, and its dismal strains were mingled with the knell of midnight from the steeple of the Old South, and with the roar of artillery, which announced that the beleaguering army of Washington had intrenched itself upon a nearer height than before. As the deep boom of the cannon smote upon his ear, Colonel Joliffe raised himself to the full height of his aged form, and smiled sternly on the British General.

"Would your Excellency inquire further into the mystery of the pageant?" said he.

"Take care of your gray head," cried Sir William Howe, fiercely, though with a quivering lip. "It has stood too long on a traitor's shoulders!"

"You must make haste to chop it off, then," calmly replied the Colonel; "for a few hours longer and not all the power of Sir William Howe, nor of his master, shall cause one of these gray hairs to fall. The empire of Britain, in this ancient province, is at its last gasp to-night;—almost while I speak it is a dead corpse;—and methinks the shadows of the old governors are fit mourners at its funeral!"

With these words Colonel Joliffe threw on his cloak, and drawing his granddaughter's arm within his own, retired from the last festival that a British ruler ever held in the old province of

Massachusetts Bay. It was supposed that the Colonel and the young lady possessed some secret intelligence in regard to the mysterious pageant of that night. However this might be, such knowledge has never become general. The actors in the scene have vanished into deeper obscurity than even that wild Indian band who scattered the cargoes of the tea-ships on the waves, and gained a place in history, yet left no names. But superstition among other legends of this mansion, repeats the wondrous tale, that on the anniversary night of Britain's discomfiture, the ghosts of the ancient governors of Massachusetts still glide through the portal of the Province House. And, last of all, comes a figure shrouded in a military cloak, tossing his clinched hands into the air, and stamping his iron-shod boots upon the broad freestone steps, with a semblance of feverish despair, but without the sound of a foot-tramp.

When the truth-telling accents of the elderly gentleman were hushed, I drew a long breath and looked round the room, striving, with the best energy of my imagination, to throw a tinge of romance and historic grandeur over the realities of the scene. But my nostrils snuffed up a scent of cigar-smoke, clouds of which the narrator had emitted by way of visible emblem, I suppose, of the nebulous obscurity of his tale. Moreover, my gorgeous fantasies were wofully disturbed by the rattling of the spoon in a tumbler of whiskey-punch, which Mr. Thomas Waite was mingling for a customer. Nor did it add to the picturesque appearance of the panelled walls, that the slate of the Brookline stage was suspended against them, instead of the armorial escutcheon of some far-descended governor. A stage-driver sat at one of the windows, reading a penny-paper of the day—the Boston Times—and presenting a figure which could nowise be brought into any picture of "Times in Boston" seventy or a hundred years ago. On the window-seat lay a bundle, neatly done up in brown paper, the direction of which I had the idle curiosity to read. "MISS SUSAN HUGGINS, at the PROVINCE HOUSE." A pretty chambermaid, no doubt. In truth, it is desperately hard work when we attempt to throw the spell of hoar antiquity over localities with which the living world, and the day that is passing over us, have aught to do. Yet, as I glanced at the stately staircase, down which the procession of the old governors had descended, and as I emerged through the venerable portal whence their figures had preceded me, it gladdened me to be conscious of a thrill of awe. Then diving through the narrow archway, a few strides transported me into the densest throng of Washington Street.

II. EDWARD RANDOLPH'S PORTRAIT

THE old legendary guest of the Province House abode in my remembrance from midsummer till January. One idle evening, last winter, confident that he would be found in the snuggest corner of the bar-room, I resolved to pay him another visit, hoping to deserve well of my country, by snatching from oblivion some else unheard-of fact of history. The night was chill and raw, and rendered boisterous by almost a gale of wind, which whistled along Washington Street, causing the gaslights to flare and flicker within the lamps. As I hurried onward my fancy was busy with a comparison between the present aspect of the street and that which it probably wore when the British governors inhabited the mansion whither I was now going. Brick edifices in those times were few, till a succession of destructive fires had swept, and swept again, the wooden dwellings and warehouses from the most populous quarters of the town. The buildings stood insulated and independent, not, as now, merging their separate existences into connected ranges, with a front of tiresome identity,—but each possessing features of its own, as if the owner's individual taste had shaped it,—and the whole presenting a picturesque irregularity, the absence of which is hardly compensated by any beauties of our modern architecture. Such a scene, dimly vanishing from the eye by the ray of here and there a tallow candle, glimmering through the small panes of scattered windows, would form a sombre contrast to the street as I beheld it, with the gaslights blazing from corner to corner, flaming within the shops, and throwing a noonday brightness through the huge plates of glass.

But the black, lowering sky, as I turned my eyes upward, wore, doubtless, the same visage as when it frowned upon the ante-Revolutionary New Englanders. The wintry blast had the same shriek that was familiar to their ears. The Old South Church, too, still pointed its antique spire into the darkness, and was lost between earth and heaven; and as I passed, its clock, which had warned so many generations how transitory was their lifetime, spoke heavily and slow the same unregarded moral to myself. "Only seven o'clock," thought I. "My old friend's legends will scarcely kill the hours 'twixt this and bedtime."

Passing through the narrow arch, I crossed the court-yard, the confined precincts of which were made visible by a lantern over the portal of the Province House. On entering the bar-room I found, as I expected, the old tradition-monger seated by a special good fire of anthracite, compelling clouds of smoke from a corpulent cigar. He recognized me with evident pleasure; for my rare properties as a patient listener invariably make me a favorite with elderly gentlemen and ladies of narrative propensities. Drawing a chair to the fire, I desired mine host to favor us with a glass apiece of whiskey-punch, which was speedily prepared, steaming hot, with a slice of lemon at the bottom, a dark-red stratum of port wine upon the surface, and a sprinkling of nutmeg strewn over all. As we touched our glasses together, my legendary friend made himself known to me as Mr. Bela Tiffany; and I rejoiced at the oddity of the name, because it gave his image and character a sort of individuality in my conception. The old gentleman's draught acted as a solvent upon his memory, so that it overflowed with tales, traditions, anecdotes of famous dead people, and traits of ancient manners, some of which were childish as a nurse's lullaby, while others might have been worth the notice of the grave historian. Nothing impressed me more than a story of a black, mysterious picture, which used to hang in one of the chambers of the Province House, directly above the room where we were now sitting. The following is as correct a version of the fact as the reader would be likely to obtain from any other source, although, assuredly, it has a tinge of romance approaching the marvellous.

In one of the apartments of the Province House there was long preserved an ancient picture, the frame of which was as black as ebony, and the canvas itself so dark with age, damp, and smoke, that not a touch of the painter's art could be discerned. Time had thrown an impenetrable veil over it, and left to tradition, and fable, and conjecture to say what had once been there portrayed. During the rule of many successive governors it had hung, by prescriptive and undisputed right, over the mantel-piece of the same chamber; and it still kept its place when Lieutenant-Governor Hutchinson assumed the administration of the province, on the departure of Sir Francis Bernard.

The Lieutenant-Governor sat, one afternoon, resting his head against the carved back of his stately arm-chair, and gazing up thoughtfully at the void blackness of the picture. It was scarcely a time for such inactive musing, when affairs of the deepest moment required the ruler's decision; for within that very hour Hutchinson had received intelligence of the arrival of a British fleet, bringing three regiments from Halifax to overawe the insubordination of the people. These troops awaited his permission to occupy the fortress of Castle William, and the town itself. Yet, instead of affixing his signature to an official order, there sat the Lieutenant-Governor, so carefully scrutinizing the black waste of canvas, that his demeanor attracted the notice of two young persons who attended him. One, wearing a military dress of buff, was his kinsman, Francis Lincoln, the Provincial Captain of Castle William; the other, who sat on a low stool beside his chair, was Alice Vane, his favorite niece.

She was clad entirely in white, a pale, ethereal creature, who, though a native of New England, had been educated abroad, and seemed not merely a stranger from another clime, but almost a being from another world. For several years, until left an orphan, she had dwelt with her father in sunny Italy, and there had acquired a taste and enthusiasm for sculpture and painting which she found few opportunities of gratifying in the undecorated dwellings of the colonial gentry. It was said that the early productions of her own pencil exhibited no inferior genius, though, perhaps, the rude atmosphere of New England had cramped her hand and dimmed the glowing colors of her fancy. But observing her uncle's steadfast gaze, which appeared to search through the mist of years to discover the subject of the picture, her curiosity was excited.

"Is it known, my dear uncle," inquired she, "what this old picture once represented? Possibly, could it be made visible, it might prove a masterpiece of some great artist,—else, why has it so long held such a conspicuous place?"

As her uncle, contrary to his usual custom, (for he was as attentive to all the humors and caprices of Alice as if she had been his own best-beloved child,) did not immediately reply, the young Captain of Castle William took that office upon himself.

"This dark old square of canvas, my fair cousin," said he, "has been an heirloom in the Province House from time immemorial. As to the painter, I can tell you nothing; but if half the stories told of it be true, not one of the great Italian masters has ever produced so marvellous a piece of work as that before you."

Captain Lincoln proceeded to relate some of the strange fables and fantasies which, as it was impossible to refute them by ocular demonstration, had grown to be articles of popular belief in reference to this old picture. One of the wildest, and at the same time the best accredited accounts, stated it to be an original and authentic portrait of the Evil One, taken at a witch-meeting near Salem; and that its strong and terrible resemblance had been confirmed by several of the confessing wizards and witches, at their trial, in open court. It was likewise affirmed that a familiar spirit, or demon, abode behind the blackness of the picture, and had shown himself at seasons of public calamity to more than one of the royal governors. Shirley, for instance, had beheld this ominous apparition on the eve of General Abercrombie's shameful and bloody defeat under the walls of Ticonderoga. Many of the servants of the Province House had caught glimpses of a visage frowning down upon them, at morning or evening twilight,—or in the depths of night, while raking up the fire that glimmered on the hearth beneath; although, if any were bold enough to hold a torch before the picture, it would appear as black and undistinguishable as ever. The oldest inhabitant of Boston recollected that his father, in whose days the portrait had not wholly faded out of sight, had once looked upon it, but would never suffer himself to be questioned as to the face which was there represented. In connection with such stories, it was remarkable that over the top of the frame there were some ragged remnants of black silk, indicating that a veil had formerly hung down before the picture, until the duskiness of time had so effectually concealed it. But, after all, it was the most singular part of the affair, that so many of the pompous governors of Massachusetts had allowed the obliterated picture to remain in the state-chamber of the Province House.

"Some of these fables are really awful," observed Alice Vane, who had occasionally shuddered, as well as smiled, while her cousin spoke. "It would be almost worth while to wipe away the black surface of the canvas, since the original picture can hardly be so formidable as those which fancy paints instead of it."

"But would it be possible," inquired her cousin, "to restore this dark picture to its pristine hues?"

"Such arts are known in Italy," said Alice.

The Lieutenant-Governor had roused himself from his abstracted mood, and listened with a smile to the conversation of his young relatives. Yet his voice had something peculiar in its tones, when he undertook the explanation of the mystery.

"I am sorry, Alice, to destroy your faith in the legends of which you are so fond," remarked he; "but my antiquarian researches have long since made me acquainted with the subject of this picture—if picture it can be called—which is no more visible, nor ever will be, than the face of the long-buried man whom it once represented. It was the portrait of Edward Randolph, the founder of this house, a person famous in the history of New England."

"Of that Edward Randolph," exclaimed Captain Lincoln, "who obtained the repeal of the first provincial charter, under which our forefathers had enjoyed almost democratic privileges! He that was styled the arch-enemy of New England, and whose memory is still held in detestation as the destroyer of our liberties!"

"It was the same Randolph," answered Hutchinson, moving uneasily in his chair. "It was his lot to taste the bitterness of popular odium."

"Our annals tell us," continued the Captain of Castle William, "that the curse of the people followed this Randolph where he went, and wrought evil in all the subsequent events of his life, and that its effect was seen likewise in the manner of his death. They say, too, that the inward misery of that curse worked itself outward, and was visible on the wretched man's countenance, making it too horrible to be looked upon. If so, and if this picture truly represented his aspect, it was in mercy that the cloud of blackness has gathered over it."

"These traditions are folly, to one who has proved, as I have, how little of historic truth lies at the bottom," said the Lieutenant-Governor. "As regards the life and character of Edward Randolph, too implicit credence has been given to Dr. Cotton Mather, who —I must say it, though some of his blood runs in my veins—has filled our early history with old women's tales, as fanciful and extravagant as those of Greece or Rome."

"And yet," whispered Alice Vane, "may not such fables have a moral? And, methinks, if the visage of this portrait be so dreadful, it is not without a cause that it has hung so long in a chamber of the Province House. When the rulers feel themselves irresponsible, it were well that they should be reminded of the awful weight of a people's curse."

The Lieutenant-Governor started, and gazed for a moment at his niece, as if her girlish fantasies had struck upon some feeling in his own breast, which all his policy or principles could not entirely subdue. He knew, indeed, that Alice, in spite of her foreign education, retained the native sympathies of a New England girl.

"Peace, silly child," cried he, at last, more harshly than he had ever before addressed the gentle Alice. "The rebuke of a king is more to be dreaded than the clamor of a wild, misguided multitude. Captain Lincoln, it is decided. The fortress of Castle William must be occupied by the Royal troops. The two remaining regiments shall be billeted in the town, or encamped upon the Common. It is time, after years of tumult, and almost rebellion, that his majesty's government should have a wall of strength about it."

"Trust, sir,—trust yet a while to the loyalty of the people," said Captain Lincoln; "nor teach them that they can ever be on other terms with British soldiers than those of brotherhood, as when they fought side by side through the French war. Do not convert the streets of your native town into a camp. Think twice before you give up old Castle William, the key of the province, into other keeping than that of true-born New-Englanders."

"Young man, it is decided," repeated Hutchinson, rising from his chair. "A British officer will be in attendance this evening, to receive the necessary instructions for the disposal of the troops. Your presence also will be required. Till then, farewell."

With these words the Lieutenant-Governor hastily left the room, while Alice and her cousin more slowly followed, whispering together, and once pausing to glance back at the mysterious picture. The Captain of Castle William fancied that the girl's air and mien were such as might have belonged to one of those spirits of fable—fairies, or creatures of a more antique mythology—who sometimes mingled their agency with mortal affairs, half in caprice, yet with a sensibility to human weal or woe. As he held the door for her to pass, Alice beckoned to the picture and smiled.

"Come forth, dark and evil Shape!" cried she. "It is thine hour!"

In the evening, Lieutenant-Governor Hutchinson sat in the same chamber where the foregoing scene had occurred, surrounded by several persons whose various interests had summoned them together. There were the Selectmen of Boston, plain, patriarchal fathers of the people, excellent representatives of the old puritanical founders, whose sombre strength had stamped so deep an impress upon the New England character. Contrasting with these were one or two members of Council, richly dressed in the white wigs, the embroidered waistcoats and other magnificence of the time, and making a somewhat ostentatious display of courtier-like ceremonial. In attendance, likewise, was a major of the British army, awaiting the Lieutenant-Governor's orders for the landing of the troops, which still remained on board the transports. The Captain of Castle William stood beside Hutchinson's chair, with folded arms, glancing rather haughtily at the British officer, by whom he was soon to be superseded in his command. On a table, in the centre of the chamber, stood a branched silver candlestick, throwing down the glow of half a dozen wax lights upon a paper apparently ready for the Lieutenant-Governor's signature.

Partly shrouded in the voluminous folds of one of the window-curtains, which fell from the ceiling to the floor, was seen the white drapery of a lady's robe. It may appear strange that Alice Vane should have been there, at such a time; but there was something so child-like, so wayward, in her singular character, so apart from ordinary rules, that her presence did not surprise the few who noticed it. Meantime, the chairman of the Selectmen was addressing to the Lieutenant-Governor a long and solemn protest against the reception of the British troops into the town.

"And if your Honor," concluded this excellent, but somewhat prosy old gentleman, "shall see fit to persist in bringing these mercenary sworders and musketeers into our quiet streets, not on our heads be the responsibility. Think, sir, while there is yet time, that if one drop of blood be shed, that blood shall be an eternal stain upon your Honor's memory. You, sir, have written with an able pen the deeds of our forefathers. The more to be desired is it, therefore, that yourself should deserve honorable mention, as a true patriot and upright ruler, when your own doings shall be written down in history."

"I am not insensible, my good sir, to the natural desire to stand well in the annals of my country," replied Hutchinson, controlling his impatience into courtesy, "nor know I any better method of attaining that end than by withstanding the merely temporary spirit of mischief, which, with your pardon, seems to have infected elder men than myself. Would you have me wait till the mob shall sack the Province House, as they did my private mansion? Trust me, sir, the time may come when you will be glad to flee for protection to the King's banner, the raising of which is now so distasteful to you."

"Yes," said the British major, who was impatiently expecting the Lieutenant-Governor's orders. "The demagogues of this Province have raised the Devil, and cannot lay him again. We will exorcise him in God's name and the King's."

"If you meddle with the Devil, take care of his claws!" answered the Captain of Castle William, stirred by the taunt against his countrymen.

"Craving your pardon, young sir," said the venerable Selectman, "let not an evil spirit enter into your words. We will strive against the oppressor with prayer and fasting, as our forefathers would have done. Like them, moreover, we will submit to whatever lot a wise Providence may send us,— always, after our own best exertions to amend it."

"And there peep forth the Devil's claws!" muttered Hutchinson, who well understood the nature of Puritan submission. "This matter shall be expedited forthwith. When there shall be a sentinel at every corner, and a court of guard before the town-house, a loyal gentleman may venture to walk abroad. What to me is the outcry of a mob, in this remote province of the realm? The King is my master, and England is my country! Upheld by their armed strength, I set my foot upon the rabble, and defy them!"

He snatched a pen, and was about to affix his signature to the paper that lay on the table, when the Captain of Castle William placed his hand upon his shoulder. The freedom of the action, so contrary to the ceremonious respect which was then considered due to rank and dignity, awakened general surprise, and in none more than in the Lieutenant-Governor himself. Looking angrily up, he perceived that his young relative was pointing his finger to the opposite wall. Hutchinson's eye followed the signal; and he saw, what had hitherto been unobserved, that a black silk curtain was suspended before the mysterious picture, so as completely to conceal it. His thoughts immediately recurred to the scene of the preceding afternoon; and, in his surprise, confused by indistinct emotions, yet sensible that his niece must have had an agency in this phenomenon, he called loudly upon her.

"Alice!—Come hither, Alice!"

No sooner had he spoken than Alice Vane glided from her station, and pressing one hand across her eyes, with the other snatched away the sable curtain that concealed the portrait. An exclamation of surprise burst from every beholder; but the Lieutenant-Governor's voice had a tone of horror.

"By heaven," said he, in a low, inward murmur, speaking rather to himself than to those around him, "if the spirit of Edward Randolph were to appear among us from the place of torment, he could not wear more of the terrors of hell upon his face!"

"For some wise end," said the aged Selectman, solemnly, "hath Providence scattered away the mist of years that had so long hid this dreadful effigy. Until this hour no living man hath seen what we behold!"

Within the antique frame, which so recently had enclosed a sable waste of canvas, now appeared a visible picture, still dark, indeed, in its hues and shadings, but thrown forward in strong relief. It was a half-length figure of a gentleman in a rich, but very old-fashioned dress of embroidered velvet, with a broad ruff and a beard, and wearing a hat, the brim of which overshadowed his forehead. Beneath this cloud the eyes had a peculiar glare, which was almost lifelike. The whole portrait started so distinctly out of the background, that it had the effect of a person looking down from the wall at the astonished and awe-stricken spectators. The expression of the face, if any words can convey an idea of it, was that of a wretch detected in some hideous guilt, and exposed to the bitter hatred and laughter and withering scorn of a vast surrounding multitude. There was the struggle of defiance, beaten down and overwhelmed by the crushing weight of ignominy. The torture of the soul had come forth upon his countenance. It seemed as if the picture while hidden behind the cloud of immemorial years, had been all the time acquiring an intenser depth and darkness of expression, till now it gloomed forth again and threw its evil omen over the present hour. Such, if the wild legend may be credited, was the portrait of Edward Randolph, as he appeared when a people's curse had wrought its influence upon his nature.

" 'Twould drive me mad,--that awful face!" said Hutchinson, who seemed fascinated by the contemplation of it.

"Be warned, then!" whispered Alice. "He trampled on a people's rights. Behold his punishment,—and avoid a crime like his!"

The Lieutenant-Governor actually trembled for an instant; but, exerting his energy—which was not, however, his most characteristic feature—he strove to shake off the spell of Randolph's countenance.

"Girl!" cried he, laughing bitterly, as he turned to Alice, "have you brought hither your painter's art,—your Italian spirit of intrigue,—your tricks of stage effect,—and think to influence the councils of rulers and the affairs of nations by such shallow contrivances? See here!"

"Stay yet awhile," said the Select-man, as Hutchinson again snatched the pen; "for if ever mortal man received a warning from a tormented soul, your Honor is that man!"

"Away!' answered Hutchinson, fierce-ly. "Though yonder senseless picture cried 'Forbear!' it should not move me!"

Casting a scowl of defiance at the pictured face, (which seemed, at that moment, to intensify the horror of its miserable and wicked look,) he scrawled on the paper, in characters that betok-ened it a deed of desperation, the name of Thomas Hutchinson. Then, it is said, he shuddered, as if that signature had granted away his salvation.

"It is done," said he; and placed his hand upon his brow.

"May Heaven forgive the deed," said the soft, sad accents of Alice Vane, like the voice of a good spirit flitting away.

When morning came there was a stifled whisper through the household, and spreading thence about the town, that the dark, mysterious picture had started from the wall, and spoken face to face with Lieutenant - Governor Hutchinson. If such a miracle had been wrought, however, no traces of it re-mained behind; for within the antique frame nothing could be discerned save the impenetrable cloud which had cov-ered the canvas since the memory of man. If the figure had, indeed, stepped forth, it had fled back, spirit-like, at the daydawn, and hidden itself behind a century's obscurity. The truth probably was, that Alice Vane's secret for re-storing the hues of the picture had merely effected a temporary renovation. But those who, in that brief interval, had beheld the awful visage of Edward

Randolph desired no second glance, and ever afterwards trembled at the recol-lection of the scene, as if an evil spirit had appeared visibly among them. And as for Hutchinson, when, far over the ocean, his dying hour drew on, he gasped for breath, and complained that he was choking with the blood of the Boston Massacre; and Francis Lincoln, the former Captain of Castle William, who was standing at his bedside, per-ceived a likeness in his frenzied look to that of Edward Randolph. Did his broken spirit feel, at that dre d hour, the tremendous burden of a people's curse?

At the conclusion of this miraculous legend, I inquired of mine host whether the picture still remained in the cham-ber over our heads; but Mr. Tiffany informed me that it had long since been removed, and was supposed to be hid-den in some out-of-the-way corner of the New England Museum. Perchance some curious antiquary may light upon it there, and, with the assistance of Mr. Howorth, the picture-cleaner, may supply a not unnecessary proof of the authen-ticity of the facts here set down. Dur-ing the progress of the story a storm had been gathering abroad, and raging and rattling so loudly in the upper regions of the Province House, that it seemed as if all the old governors and great men were running riot above stairs, while Mr. Bela Tiffany babbled of them below. In the course of gen-erations, when many people have lived and died in an ancient house, the whis-tling of the wind through its crannies, and the creaking of its beams and rafters, become strangely like the tones of the human voice, or thundering laughter, or heavy footsteps treading the deserted chambers. It is as if the echoes of half a century were revived. Such were the ghostly sounds that roared and murmured in our ears, when I took leave of the circle round the fireside of the Province House, and, plunging down the door-steps, fought my way homeward against a drifting snow-storm.

III. LADY ELEANORE'S MANTLE

MINE excellent friend, the landlord of the Province House, was pleased, the other evening, to invite Mr. Tiffany and myself to an oyster-supper. This slight mark of respect and gratitude, as he handsomely observed, was far less than the ingenious tale-teller, and I, the humble note-taker of his narratives, had fairly earned, by the public notice which our joint lucubrations had attracted to his establishment. Many a cigar had been smoked within his premises,—many a glass of wine, or more potent aqua vitæ, had been quaffed,—many a dinner had been eaten by curious strangers, who, save for the fortunate conjunction of Mr. Tiffany and me, would never have ventured through that darksome avenue, which gives access to the historic precincts of the Province House. In short, if any credit be due to the courteous assurances of Mr. Thomas Waite, we had brought his forgotten mansion almost as effectually into public view as if we had thrown down the vulgar range of shoe-shops and drygoods stores, which hides its aristocratic front from Washington Street. It may be unadvisable, however, to speak too loudly of the increased custom of the house, lest Mr. Waite should find it difficult to renew the lease on so favorable terms as heretofore.

Being thus welcomed as benefactors, neither Mr. Tiffany nor myself felt any scruple in doing full justice to the good things that were set before us. If the feast were less magnificent than those same panelled walls had witnessed in a bygone century,—if mine host presided with somewhat less of state than might have befitted a successor of the royal governors,—if the guests made a less imposing show than the bewigged and powdered and embroidered dignitaries, who erst banqueted at the gubernatorial table, and now sleep within their armorial tombs on Copp's Hill, or round King's Chapel,—yet never, I may boldly say, did a more comfortable little party assemble in the Province House from Queen Anne's days to the Revolution. The occasion was rendered more interesting by the presence of a venerable personage, whose own actual reminiscences went back to the epoch of Gage and Howe, and even supplied him with a doubtful anecdote or two of Hutchinson. He was one of that small and now all but extinguished class, whose attachment to royalty, and to the colonial institutions and customs that were connected with it, had never yielded to the democratic heresies of after times. The young queen of Britain has not a more loyal subject in her realm,—perhaps not one who would kneel before her throne with such reverential love,—as this old grandsire, whose head has whitened beneath the mild sway of the Republic, which still, in his mellower moments, he terms a usurpation. Yet prejudices so obstinate have not made him an ungentle or impracticable companion. If the truth must be told, the life of the aged loyalist has been of such a scrambling and unsettled character,—he has had so little choice of friends, and been so often destitute of any,—that I doubt whether he would refuse a cup of kindness with either Oliver Cromwell or John Hancock; to say nothing of any democrat now upon the stage. In another paper of this series I may perhaps give the reader a closer glimpse of his portrait.

Our host, in due season, uncorked a bottle of Madeira, of such exquisite perfume and admirable flavor, that he surely must have discovered it in an ancient bin, down deep beneath the deepest cellar, where some jolly old butler stored away the Governor's choicest wine, and forgot to reveal the secret on his death-bed. Peace to his red-nosed ghost, and a libation to his memory! This precious liquor was imbibed by Mr. Tiffany with peculiar zest; and after sipping the third glass, it was his pleasure to give us one of the oddest legends which he had yet raked from the storehouse where he keeps such matters. With some suitable adornments from my own fancy, it ran pretty much as follows.

Not long after Colonel Shute had assumed the government of Massachusetts Bay, now nearly a hundred and twenty years ago, a young lady of rank and fortune arrived from England to claim his protection as her guardian. He was her distant relative, but the nearest who had survived the gradual extinction of her family; so that no more eligible shelter could be found for the rich and high-born lady Eleanore Rochcliffe than within the Province House of a Transatlantic colony. The consort of Governor Shute, moreover, had been as a mother to her childhood, and was now anxious to receive her, in the hope that a beautiful young woman would be exposed to infinitely less peril from the primitive society of New England than amid the artifices and corruptions of a court. If either the Governor or his lady had especially consulted their own comfort, they would probably have sought to devolve the responsibility on other hands; since, with some noble and splendid traits of character, Lady Eleanore was remarkable for a harsh, unyielding pride, a haughty consciousness of her hereditary and personal advantages, which made her almost incapable of control. Judging from many traditionary anecdotes, this peculiar temper was hardly less than a monomania; or, if the acts which it inspired were those of a sane person, it seemed due from Providence that pride so sinful should be followed by as severe a retribution. That tinge of the marvellous which is thrown over so many of these half-forgotten legends has probably imparted an additional wildness to the strange story of Lady Eleanore Rochcliffe.

The ship in which she came passenger had arrived at Newport, whence Lady Eleanore was conveyed to Boston in the Governor's coach, attended by a small escort of gentlemen on horseback. The ponderous equipage, with its four black horses, attracted much notice as it rumbled through Cornhill, surrounded by the prancing steeds of half a dozen cavaliers, with swords dangling to their stirrups and pistols at their holsters. Through the large glass windows of the coach, as it rolled along, the people could discern the figure of Lady Eleanore, strangely combining an almost queenly stateliness with the grace and beauty of a maiden in her teens. A singular tale had gone abroad among the ladies of the province, that their fair rival was indebted for much of the irresistible charm of her appearance to a certain article of dress—an embroidered mantle—which had been wrought by the most skilful artist in London, and possessed even magical properties of adornment. On the present occasion, however, she owed nothing to the witchery of dress, being clad in a riding-habit of velvet, which would have appeared stiff and ungraceful on any other form.

The coachman reined in his four black steeds, and the whole cavalcade came to a pause in front of the contorted iron balustrade that fenced the Province House from the public street. It was an awkward coincidence, that the bell of the Old South was just then tolling for a funeral; so that, instead of a gladsome peal with which it was customary to announce the arrival of distinguished strangers, Lady Eleanore Rochcliffe was ushered by a doleful clang, as if calamity had come embodied in her beautiful person.

"A very great disrespect!" exclaimed Captain Langford, an English officer, who had recently brought despatches to Governor Shute. "The funeral should have been deferred, lest Lady Eleanore's spirits be affected by such a dismal welcome."

"With your pardon, sir," replied Dr. Clarke, a physician, and a famous champion of the popular party, "whatever the heralds may pretend, a dead beggar must have precedence of a living queen. King Death confers high privileges."

These remarks were interchanged while the speakers waited a passage through the crowd which had gathered on each side of the gateway, leaving an open avenue to the portal of the Province House. A black slave in livery now leaped from behind the coach, and threw open the door; while at the same moment Governor Shute descended the flight of steps from his mansion to assist Lady Eleanore in alighting. But the Governor's stately approach was anticipated in a manner that excited general astonishment. A pale young man, with his black hair all in disorder, rushed from the throng and prostrated himself beside the coach, thus offering his person as a footstool for Lady Eleanore Rochcliffe to tread upon. She held back an instant; yet with an expression as if doubting whether the young man were worthy to bear the weight of her footstep, rather than dissatisfied to receive such awful reverence from a fellow-mortal.

"Up, sir," said the Governor, sternly, at the same time lifting his cane over the intruder. "What means the Bedlamite by this freak?"

"Nay," answered Lady Eleanore playfully, but with more scorn than pity in her tone, "your Excellency shall not strike him. When men seek only to be trampled upon, it were a pity to deny them a favor so easily granted,—and so well deserved!"

Then, though as lightly as a sunbeam on a cloud, she placed her foot upon the cowering form, and extended her hand to meet that of the Governor. There was a brief interval, during which Lady Eleanore retained this attitude; and never, surely, was there an apter emblem of aristocracy and hereditary pride, trampling on human sympathies and the kindred of nature, than these two figures presented at that moment. Yet the spectators were so smitten with her beauty, and so essential did pride seem to the existence of such a creature, that they gave a simultaneous acclamation of applause.

"Who is this insolent young fellow?" inquired Captain Langford, who still remained beside Doctor Clarke. "If he be in his senses, his impertinence demands the bastinado. If mad, Lady Eleanore should be secured from further inconvenience by his confinement."

"His name is Jervase Helwyse," answered the Doctor,—"a youth of no birth or fortune, or other advantages, save the mind and soul that nature gave him; and being secretary to our colonial agent in London, it was his misfortune to meet this Lady Eleanore Rochcliffe. He loved her,—and her scorn has driven him mad."

"He was mad so to aspire," observed the English officer.

"It may be so," said Doctor Clarke, frowning as he spoke. "But I tell you, sir, I could wellnigh doubt the justice of Heaven above us, if no signal humiliation overtake this lady who now treads so haughtily into yonder mansion. She seeks to place herself above the sympathies of our common nature, which envelops all human souls. See if that nature do not assert its claim over her in some mode that shall bring her level with the lowest!"

"Never!" cried Captain Langford, indignantly,—"neither in life, nor when they lay her with her ancestors."

Not many days afterwards the Governor gave a ball in honor of Lady Eleanore Rochcliffe. The principal gentry of the colony received invitations, which were distributed to their residences, far and near, by messengers on horseback, bearing missives sealed with all the formality of official despatches. In obedience to the summons, there was a general gathering of rank, wealth, and beauty; and the wide door of the Province House had seldom given admittance to more numerous and honorable guests than on the evening of Lady Eleanore's ball. Without much extravagance of eulogy, the spectacle might even be termed splendid; for, according to the fashion of the times, the ladies shone in rich silks and satins, outspread over wide-projecting hoops; and the gentlemen glittered in gold embroidery, laid unsparingly upon the purple, or scarlet, or sky-blue velvet, which was the material of their coats and waistcoats. The latter article of dress was of great importance, since it enveloped the wearer's body nearly to the knees, and was perhaps bedizened with the amount of his whole year's income, in golden flowers and foliage. The altered taste of the present day,—a taste symbolic of a deep change in the whole system of society,—would look upon almost any of those gorgeous figures as ridiculous; although that evening the guests sought their reflections in the pier-glasses, and rejoiced to catch their own glitter amid the glittering crowd. What a pity that one of the stately mirrors has not preserved a picture of the scene, which, by the very traits that were so transitory, might have taught us much that would be worth knowing and remembering!

Would, at least, that either painter or mirror could convey to us some faint idea of a garment, already noticed in this legend,—the Lady Eleanore's embroidered mantle,—which the gossips whispered was invested with magic properties, so as to lend a new and untried grace to her figure each time that she put it on! Idle fancy as it is, this mysterious mantle has thrown an awe around my image of her, partly from its fabled virtues, and partly because it was the handiwork of a dying woman, and, perchance, owed the fantastic grace of its conception to the delirium of approaching death.

After the ceremonial greetings had been paid, Lady Eleanore Rochcliffe stood apart from the mob of guests, insulating herself within a small and distinguished circle, to whom she accorded a more cordial favor than to the general throng. The waxen torches threw their radiance vividly over the scene, bringing out its brilliant points in strong relief; but she gazed carelessly, and with now and then an expression of weariness or scorn, tempered with such feminine grace, that her auditors scarcely perceived the moral deformity of which it was the utterance. She beheld the spectacle not with vulgar ridicule, as disdaining to be pleased with the provincial mockery of a court festival, but with the deeper scorn of one whose spirit held itself too high to participate in the enjoyment of other human souls. Whether or no the recollections of those who saw her that evening were influenced by the strange events with which she was subsequently connected, so it was, that her figure ever after recurred to them as marked by something wild and unnatural; although, at the time, the general whisper was of her exceeding beauty, and of the indescribable charm which her mantle threw around her. Some close observers, indeed, detected a feverish flush and alternate paleness of countenance, with a corresponding flow and revulsion of spirits, and once or twice a painful and helpless betrayal of lassitude, as if she were on the point of sinking to the ground. Then, with a nervous shudder, she seemed to arouse her energies, and threw some bright and playful, yet half-wicked sarcasm into the conversation. There was so strange a characteristic in her manners and sentiments, that it astonished every right-minded listener; till looking in her face, a lurking and incomprehensible glance and smile perplexed them with doubts both as to her seriousness and sanity. Gradually, Lady Eleanore Rochcliffe's circle grew smaller, till only four gentlemen remained in it. These were Captain Langford, the English officer before mentioned; a Virginian planter, who had come to Massachusetts on some political errand; a young Episcopal clergyman, the grandson of a British earl; and lastly, the private secretary of Governor Shute, whose obsequiousness had won a sort of tolerance from Lady Eleanore.

At different periods of the evening the liveried servants of the Province House passed among the guests, bearing huge trays of refreshments, and French and Spanish wines. Lady Eleanore Rochcliffe, who refused to wet her beautiful lips even with a bubble of champagne, had sunk back into a large damask chair, apparently overwearied either with the excitement of the scene or its tedium; and while, for an instant, she was unconscious of voices, laughter, and music, a young man stole forward, and knelt down at her feet. He bore a salver in his hand, on which was a chased silver goblet, filled to the brim with wine, which he offered as reverentially as to a crowned queen, or rather with the awful devotion of a priest doing sacrifice to his idol. Conscious that some one touched her robe, Lady Eleanore started, and unclosed her eyes upon the pale, wild features and disheveled hair of Jervase Helwyse.

"Why do you haunt me thus?" said she, in a languid tone, but with a kinder feeling than she ordinarily permitted herself to express. "They tell me that I have done you harm."

"Heaven knows if that be so," replied the young man, solemnly. "But, Lady Eleanore, in requital of that harm, if such there be, and for your own earthly and heavenly welfare, I pray you to take one sip of this holy wine, and then to pass the goblet round among the guests. And this shall be a symbol that you have not sought to withdraw yourself from the chain of human sympathies,—which whoso would shake off must keep company with fallen angels."

"Where has this mad fellow stolen that sacramental vessel?" exclaimed the Episcopal clergyman.

This question drew the notice of the guests to the silver cup, which was recognized as appertaining to the communion plate of the Old South Church; and, for aught that could be known, it was brimming over with the consecrated wine.

"Perhaps it is poisoned," half whispered the Governor's secretary.

"Pour it down the villain's throat!" cried the Virginian, fiercely.

"Turn him out of the house!" cried Captain Langford, seizing Jervase Helwyse so roughly by the shoulder that the sacramental cup was overturned, and its contents sprinkled upon Lady Eleanore's mantle. "Whether knave, fool, or Bedlamite, it is intolerable that the fellow should go at large."

"Pray, gentlemen, do my poor admirer no harm," said Lady Eleanore, with a faint and weary smile. "Take him out of my sight, if such be your pleasure; for I can find in my heart to do nothing but laugh at him,—whereas, in all decency and conscience, it would become me to weep for the mischief I have wrought!"

But while the bystanders were attempting to lead away the unfortunate young man, he broke from them, and with a wild, impassioned earnestness, offered a new and equally strange petition to Lady Eleanore. It was no other than that she should throw off the mantel, which, while he pressed the silver cup of wine upon her, she had drawn more closely around her form, so as almost to shroud herself within it.

"Cast it from you!" exclaimed Jervase Helwyse, clasping his hands in an agony of entreaty. "It may not yet be too late! Give the accursed garment to the flames!"

But Lady Eleanore, with a laugh of scorn, drew the rich folds of the em broidered mantle over her head, in such a fashion as to give a completely new aspect to her beautiful face, which—half hidden, half revealed—seemed to belong to some being of mysterious character and purposes.

"Farewell, Jervase Helwyse!" said she. "Keep my image in your remembrance, as you behold it now."

"Alas, lady!" he replied, in a tone no longer wild, but sad as a funeral bell. "We must meet shortly, when your face may wear another aspect, and that shall be the image that must abide within me."

He made no more resistance to the violent efforts of the gentlemen and servants, who almost dragged him out of the apartment, and dismissed him roughly from the iron gate of the Province House. Captain Langford, who had been very active in this affair, was returning to the presence of Lady Eleanore Rochcliffe, when he encountered the physician, Dr. Clarke, with whom he had held some casual talk on the day of her arrival. The Doctor stood apart, separated from Lady Eleanore by the width of the room, but eying her with such keen sagacity, that Captain Langford involuntarily gave him credit for the discovery of some deep secret.

"You appear to be smitten, after all, with the charms of this queenly maiden," said he, hoping thus to draw forth the physician's hidden knowledge.

"God forbid!" answered Doctor Clarke, with a grave smile; "and if you be wise, you will put up the same prayer for yourself. Woe to those who shall be smitten by this beautiful Lady Eleanore! But yonder stands the Governor,—and I have a word or two for

his private ear. Good night!"

He accordingly advanced to Governor Shute, and addressed him in so low a tone that none of the bystanders could catch a word of what he said, although the sudden change of his Excellency's hitherto cheerful visage betokened that the communication could be of no agreeable import. A very few moments afterwards, it was announced to the guests that an unforeseen circumstance rendered it necessary to put a premature close to the festival.

The ball at the Province House supplied a topic of conversation for the colonial metropolis for some days after its occurrence, and might still longer have been the general theme, only that a subject of all-engrossing interest thrust it, for a time, from the public recollection. This was the appearance of a dreadful epidemic, which, in that age, and long before and afterwards, was wont to slay its hundreds and thousands on both sides of the Atlantic. On the occasion of which we speak, it was distinguished by a peculiar virulence, insomuch that it has left its trace—its pit-marks, to use an appropriate figure—on the history of the country, the affairs of which were thrown into confusion by its ravages. At first, unlike its ordinary course, the disease seemed to confine itself to the higher circles of society, selecting its victims from among the proud, the well-born, and the wealthy, entering unabashed into stately chambers, and lying down with the slumberers in silken beds. Some of the most distinguished guests of the Province House,—even those whom the haughty Lady Eleanore Rochcliffe had deemed not unworthy of her favor,—were stricken by this fatal scourge. It was noticed, with an un-generous bitterness of feeling, that the four gentlemen,—the Virginian, the British officer, the young clergyman, and the Governor's secretary,—who had been her most devoted attendants on the evening of the ball, were the fore-most on whom the plague-stroke fell. But the disease, pursuing its onward progress, soon ceased to be exclusively a prerogative of aristocracy. Its red brand was no longer conferred, like a noble's star or an order of knighthood. It threaded its way through the narrow and crooked streets, and entered the low, mean, darksome dwellings, and laid its hand of death upon the artisans and laboring classes of the town. It compelled rich and poor to feel them-selves brethren, then; and stalking to and fro across the Three Hills, with a fierceness which made it almost a new pestilence, there was that mighty conqueror,—that scourge and horror of our forefathers,—the Small Pox!

We cannot estimate the affright which this plague inspired of yore, by contemplating it as the fangless mon-ster of the present day. We must re-member, rather, with what awe we watched the gigantic footsteps of the Asiatic cholera, striding from shore to shore of the Atlantic, and marching like destiny upon cities far remote, which light had already half depopulated. There is no other fear so horrible and inhumanizing, as that which makes man dread to breathe Heaven's vital air, lest it be poison, or to grasp the hand of a brother or friend, lest the gripe of the pestilence should clutch him. Such was the dismay that now followed in the track of the disease, or ran be-ore it throughout the town. Graves

were hastily dug, and the pestilential relics as hastily covered, because the dead were enemies of the living, and strove to draw them headlong, as it were, into their own dismal pit. The public councils were suspended, as if mortal wisdom might relinquish its de-vices, now that an unearthly usurper had found his way into the ruler's man-sion. Had an enemy's fleet been hover-ing on the coast, or his armies trampling on our soil, the people would probably have committed their defence to that same direful conqueror who had wrought their own calamity, and would permit no interference with his sway. This conqueror had a symbol of his triumphs. It was a blood-red flag, that fluttered in the tainted air over the door of every dwelling into which the Small Pox had entered.

Such a banner was long since wav-ing over the portal of the Province House; for thence, as was proved by tracking its footsteps back, had all this dreadful mischief issued. It had been traced back to a lady's luxurious cham-ber,—to the proudest of the proud,—to her that was so delicate, and hardly owned herself of earthly mould,—to the haughty one, who took her stand above human sympathies,—to Lady Eleanore! There remained no room for doubt that the contagion had lurked in that gorgeous mantle which threw so strange a grace around her at the fes-tival. Its fantastic splendor had been conceived in the delirious brain of a woman on her death-bed, and was the last toil of her stiffening fingers, which had interwoven fate and misery with its golden threads. This dark tale, whis-pered at first, was now bruited far and wide. The people raved against the

Lady Eleanore, and cried out that her pride and scorn had evoked a fiend, and that, between them both, this monstrous evil had been born. At times their rage and despair took the semblance of grinning mirth; and whenever the red flag of the pestilence was hoisted over another, and yet another door, they clapped their hands and shouted through the street, in bitter mockery: "Behold a new triumph for the Lady Eleanore!"

One day, in the midst of these dismal times, a wild figure approached the portal of the Province House, and, folding his arms, stood contemplating the scarlet banner, which a passing breeze shook fitfully, as if to fling abroad the contagion that it typified. At length, climbing one of the pillars by means of the iron balustrade, he took down the flag, and entered the mansion, waving it above his head. At the foot of the staircase he met the Governor, booted and spurred, with his cloak drawn around him, evidently on the point of setting forth upon a journey.

"Wretched lunatic, what do you seek here?" exclaimed Shute, extending his cane to guard himself from contact. "There is nothing here but Death. Back,—or you will meet him!"

"Death will not touch me, the banner-bearer of the pestilence!" cried Jervase Helwyse, shaking the red flag aloft. "Death, and the Pestilence, who wears the aspect of the Lady Eleanore, will walk through the streets to-night, and I must march before them with this banner!"

"Why do I waste words on the fellow?" muttered the Governor, drawing his cloak across his mouth. "What matters his miserable life, when none of us are sure of twelve hours' breath? On,

fool, to your own destruction!"

He made way for Jervase Helwyse, who immediately ascended the staircase, but, on the first landing-place, was arrested by the firm grasp of a hand upon his shoulder. Looking fiercely up, with a madman's impulse to struggle with and rend asunder his opponent, he found himself powerless beneath a calm, stern eye, which possessed the mysterious property of quelling frenzy at its height. The person whom he had now encountered was the physician, Doctor Clarke, the duties of whose sad profession had led him to the Province House, where he was an infrequent guest in more prosperous times.

"Young man, what is your purpose?" demanded he.

"I seek the Lady Eleanore," answered Jervase Helwyse, submissively.

"All have fled from her," said the physician. "Why do you seek her now? I tell you, youth, her nurse fell death-stricken on the threshold of that fatal chamber. Know ye not, that never came such a curse to our shores as this lovely Lady Eleanore?—that her breath has filled the air with poison?—that she has shaken pestilence and death upon the land from the folds of her accursed mantle?"

"Let me look upon her!" rejoined the mad youth, more wildly. "Let me behold her, in her awful beauty, clad in the regal garments of the pestilence! She and Death sit on a throne together. Let me kneel down before them!"

"Poor youth!" said Doctor Clarke; and, moved by a deep sense of human weakness, a smile of caustic humor curled his lip even then. "Wilt thou still worship the destroyer, and surround her image with fantasies the more magnificent the more evil she has wrought? Thus man doth ever to his tyrants! Approach, then! Madness, as I have noted, has that good efficacy, that it will guard you from contagion, —and perchance its own cure may be found in yonder chamber."

Ascending another flight of stairs, he threw open a door, and signed to Jervase Helwyse that he should enter. The poor lunatic, it seems probable, had cherished a delusion that his haughty mistress sat in state, unharmed herself by the pestilential influence which, as by enchantment, she scattered round about her. He dreamed, no doubt, that her beauty was not dimmed, but brightened into superhuman splendor. With such anticipations, he stole reverentially to the door at which the physician stood, but paused upon the threshold, gazing fearfully into the gloom of the darkened chamber.

"Where is the Lady Eleanore?" whispered he.

"Call her," replied the physician.

"Lady Eleanore!—Princess!—Queen of Death!" cried Jervase Helwyse, advancing three steps into the chamber. "She is not here! There, on yonder table, I behold the sparkle of a diamond which once she wore upon her bosom. There,"—and he shuddered,—"there hangs her mantle, on which a dead woman embroidered a spell of dreadful potency. But where is the Lady Eleanore?"

Something stirred within the silken curtains of a canopied bed; and a low moan was uttered, which, listening intently, Jervase Helwyse began to distinguish as a woman's voice, complaining dolefully of thirst. He fancied, even, that he recognized its tones.

"My throat! — my throat is scorched!" murmured the voice. "A drop of water!"

"What thing art thou?" said the brain-stricken youth, drawing near the bed and tearing asunder its curtains. "Whose voice hast thou stolen for thy murmurs and miserable petitions, as if Lady Eleanore could be conscious of mortal infirmity? Fie! Heap of diseased mortality, why lurkest thou in my lady's chamber?"

"O Jervase Helwyse," said the voice, —and as it spoke, the figure contorted itself, struggling to hide its blasted face, —"look not now on the woman you once loved! The curse of Heaven hath stricken me, because I would not call man my brother, nor woman sister. I wrapped myself in PRIDE as in a MANTLE, and scorned the sympathies of nature; and therefore has nature made this wretched body the medium of a dreadful sympathy. You are avenged,—they are all avenged,—Nature is avenged,—for I am Eleanore Rochcliffe!"

The malice of his mental disease, the bitterness lurking at the bottom of his heart, mad as he was, for a blighted and ruined life, and love that had been paid with cruel scorn, awoke within the breast of Jervase Helwyse. He shook his finger at the wretched girl, and the chamber echoed, the curtains of the bed were shaken, with his outburst of insane merriment.

"Another triumph for the Lady Eleanore!" he cried. "All have been her victims! Who so worthy to be the final victim as herself?"

Impelled by some new fantasy of his crazed intellect, he snatched the fatal mantle, and rushed from the chamber and the house. That night, a procession passed, by torchlight, through the streets, bearing in the midst the figure of a woman, enveloped with a richly-embroidered mantle; while in advance stalked Jervase Helwyse, waving the red flag of the pestilence. Arriving opposite the Province House, the mob burned the effigy, and a strong wind came and swept away the ashes. It was said, that, from that very hour, the pestilence abated, as if its sway had some mysterious connection, from the first plague-stroke to the last, with Lady Eleanore's Mantle. A remarkable uncertainty broods over that unhappy lady's fate. There is a belief, however, that, in a certain chamber of this mansion, a female form may sometimes be duskily discerned, shrinking into the darkest corner, and muffling her face within an embroidered mantle. Supposing the legend true, can this be other than the once proud Lady Eleanore?

Mine host, and the old loyalist, and I, bestowed no little warmth of applause upon this narrative, in which we had all been deeply interested; for the reader can scarcely conceive how unspeakably the effect of such a tale is heightened, when, as in the present case, we may repose confidence in the veracity of him who tells it. For my own part, knowing how scrupulous is Mr. Tiffany to settle the foundation of his facts, I could not have believed him one whit the more faithfully, had he professed himself an eyewitness of the doings and sufferings of poor Lady Eleanore. Some sceptics, it is true, might demand documentary evidence, or even require him to produce the embroidered mantle, forgetting that—Heaven be praised!—it was consumed to ashes. But now the old loyalist, whose blood was warmed by the good cheer, began to talk, in his turn, about the traditions of the Province House, and hinted that he, if it were agreeable, might add a few reminiscences to our legendary stock. Mr. Tiffany, having no cause to dread a rival, immediately besought him to favor us with a specimen; my own entreaties, of course, were urged to the same effect; and our venerable guest, well pleased to find willing auditors, awaited only the return of Mr. Thomas Waite, who had been summoned forth to provide accommodations for several new arrivals. Perchance the public—but be this as its own caprice and ours shall settle the matter—may read the result in another Tale of the Province House.

IV. OLD ESTHER DUDLEY

OUR host having resumed the chair, he, as well as Mr. Tiffany and myself, expressed much eagerness to be made acquainted with the story to which the loyalist had alluded. That venerable man first of all saw fit to moisten his throat with another glass of wine, and then, turning his face towards our coal fire, looked steadfastly for a few moments into the depths of its cheerful glow. Finally, he poured forth a great fluency of speech. The generous liquid that he had imbibed, while it warmed his age-chilled blood, likewise took off the chill from his heart and mind, and gave him an energy to think and feel which we could hardly have expected to find beneath the snows of fourscore winters. His feelings, indeed, appeared to me more excitable than those of a younger man; or, at least, the same degree of feeling manifested itself by more visible effects, than if his judgment and will had possessed the potency of meridian life. At the pathetic passages of his narrative he readily melted into tears. When a breath of indignation swept across his spirit, the blood flushed his withered visage even to the roots of his white hair; and he shook his clinched fist at the trio of peaceful auditors, seeming to fancy enemies in those who felt very kindly towards the desolate old soul. But ever and anon, sometimes in the midst of his most earnest talk, this ancient person's intellect would wander vaguely, losing its hold of the matter in hand, and groping for it amid misty shadows. Then would he cackle forth a feeble laugh, and express a doubt whether his wits—for by that phrase it pleased our ancient friend to signify his mental powers—were not getting a little the worse for wear.

Under these disadvantages, the old loyalist's story required more revision to render it fit for the public eye than those of the series which have preceded it; nor should it be concealed, that the sentiment and tone of the affair may have undergone some slight, or perchance more than slight metamorphosis, in its transmission to the reader through the medium of a thoroughgoing democrat. The tale itself is a mere sketch, with no involution of plot, nor any great interest of events, yet possessing, if I have rehearsed it aright, that pensive influence over the mind which the shadow of the old Province House flings upon the loiterer in its court-yard.

The hour had come—the hour of defeat and humiliation—when Sir William Howe was to pass over the threshold of the Province House, and embark, with no such triumphal ceremonies as he once promised himself, on board the British fleet. He bade his servants and military attendants go before him, and lingered a moment in the loneliness of the mansion, to quell the fierce emotions that struggled in his bosom as with a death throb. Preferable, then, would be have deemed his fate, had a warrior's death left him a claim to the narrow territory of a grave within the soil which the King had given him to defend. With an ominous perception that, as his departing footsteps echoed adown the staircase, the sway of Britain was passing forever from New England, he smote his clinched hand on his brow, and cursed the destiny that had flung the shame of a dismembered empire upon him.

"Would to God," cried he, hardly repressing his tears of rage, "that the rebels were even now at the doorstep! A blood-stain upon the floor should then bear testimony that the last British ruler was faithful to his trust."

The tremulous voice of a woman replied to his exclamation.

"Heaven's cause and the King's are one," it said. "Go forth, Sir William Howe, and trust in Heaven to bring back a royal governor in triumph."

Subduing at once the passion to which

he had yielded only in the faith that it was unwitnessed, Sir William Howe became conscious that an aged woman, leaning on a gold-headed staff, was standing betwixt him and the door. It was old Esther Dudley, who had dwelt almost immemorial years in this mansion, until her presence seemed as inseparable from it as the recollections of its history. She was the daughter of an ancient and once eminent family, which had fallen into poverty and decay, and left its last descendant no resource save the bounty of the King, nor any shelter except within the walls of the Province House. An office in the household, with merely nominal duties, had been assigned to her as a pretext for the payment of a small pension. the greater part of which she expended in adorning herself with an antique magnificence of attire. The claims of Esther Dudley's gentle blood were acknowledged by all the successive governors; and they treated her with the punctilious courtesy which it was her foible to demand, not always with success, from a neglectful world. The only actual share which she assumed in the business of the mansion, was to glide through its passages and public chambers, late at night, to see that the servants had dropped no fire from their flaring torches, nor left embers crackling and blazing on the hearths. Perhaps it was this invariable custom of walking her rounds in the hush of midnight that caused the superstition of the times to invest the old woman with attributes of awe and mystery; fabling that she had entered the portal of the Province House, none knew whence, in the train of the first royal governor, and that it was her fate to dwell there till the last should have departed. But Sir William Howe, if he ever heard this legend, had forgotten it.

"Mistress Dudley, why are you loitering here?" asked he, with some severity of tone. "It is my pleasure to be the last in this mansion of the King."

"Not so, if it please your Excellency," answered the time-stricken woman. "This roof has sheltered me long. I will not pass from it until they bear me to the tomb of my forefathers. What other shelter is there for old Esther Dudley, save the Province House or the grave?"

"Now Heaven forgive me!" said Sir William Howe to himself. "I was about to leave this wretched old creature to starve or beg. Take this, good Mistress Dudley," he added, putting a purse into her hands. "King George's head on these golden guineas is sterling yet, and will continue so, I warrant you, even should the rebels crown John Hancock their king. That purse will buy a better shelter than the Province House can now afford."

"While the burden of life remains upon me, I will have no other shelter than this roof," persisted Esther Dudley, striking her staff upon the floor, with a gesture that expressed immovable resolve. "And when your Excellency returns in triumph, I will totter into the porch to welcome you."

"My poor old friend!" answered the British general,—and all his manly and martial pride could no longer restrain a gush of bitter tears. "This is an evil hour for you and me. The province which the King intrusted to my charge is lost. I go hence in misfortune,—perchance in disgrace,—to return no more. And you, whose present being is incorporated with the past,—who have seen governor after governor, in stately pageantry, ascend these steps,—whose whole life has been an observance of majestic ceremonies, and a worship of the King,—how will you endure the change? Come with us! Bid farewell to a land that has shaken off its allegiance, and live still under a royal government, at Halifax."

"Never, never!" said the pertinacious old dame. "Here will I abide; and King George shall still have one true subject in his disloyal province."

"Beshrew the old fool!" muttered Sir William Howe, growing impatient of her obstinacy, and ashamed of the emotion into which he had been betrayed. "She is the very moral of old-fashioned prejudice, and could exist nowhere but in this musty edifice. Well, then, Mistress Dudley, since you will needs tarry, I give the Province House in charge to you. Take this key, and keep it safe until myself, or some other royal governor, shall demand it of you."

Smiling bitterly at himself and her, he took the heavy key of the Province House, and delivering it into the old lady's hands, drew his cloak around him for departure. As the General glanced back at Esther Dudley's antique figure, he deemed her well fitted for such a charge, as being so perfect a representative of the decayed past,— of an age gone by, with its manners, opinions, faith, and feelings all fallen into oblivion or scorn,—of what had once been a reality, but was now merely a vision of faded magnificence. Then Sir William Howe strode forth, smiting his clinched hands together, in the fierce anguish of his spirit; and old Esther Dudley was left to keep watch in the lonely Province House, dwelling there with Memory; and if Hope ever seemed to flit around her, still it was Memory in disguise.

The total change of affairs that ensued on the departure of the British troops did not drive the venerable lady from her stronghold. There was not, for many years afterwards, a governor of Massachusetts; and the magistrates, who had charge of such matters, saw no objection to Esther Dudley's residence in the Province House, especially as they must otherwise have paid a hireling for taking care of the premises, which with her was a labor of love. And so they left her the undisturbed mistress of the old historic edifice. Many and strange were the fables which the gossips whispered about her, in all the chimney-corners of the town. Among the time-worn articles of furniture that had been left in the mansion there was a tall, antique mirror, which was well worthy of a tale by itself, and perhaps may hereafter be the theme of one. The gold of its heavily-wrought frame was tarnished, and its surface so blurred, that the old woman's figure, whenever she paused before it, looked indistinct and ghost-like. But it was the general belief that Esther could cause the governors of the overthrown dynasty, with the beautiful ladies who had once adorned their festivals, the Indian chiefs who had come up to the Province House to hold council or swear allegiance, the grim Provincial warriors, the severe clergymen,—in short, all the pageantry of gone days,—all the figures that ever swept across the broad plate of glass in former times,—she could cause the whole to reappear, and people the inner world of the mirror with shadows of old life. Such legends as these, together with the singularity of her isolated existence, her age, and the infirmity that each added winter flung upon her, made Mistress Dudley the object both of fear and pity; and it was partly the result of either sentiment, that, amid all the angry license of the times, neither wrong nor insult ever fell upon her unprotected head. Indeed, there was so much haughtiness in her demeanor towards intruders, among whom she reckoned all persons acting under the new authorities, that it was really an affair of no small nerve to look her in the face. And to do the people justice, stern republicans as they had now become, they were well content that the old gentlewoman, in her hoop petticoat and faded embroidery, should still haunt the palace of ruined pride and overthrown power, the symbol of a departed system, embodying a history in her person. So Esther Dudley dwelt, year after year, in the Province House, still reverencing all that others had flung aside, still faithful to her King, who, so long as the venerable dame yet held her post, might be said to retain one true subject in New England, and one spot of the empire that had been wrested from him.

And did she dwell there in utter loneliness? Rumor said, not so. Whenever her chill and withered heart desired warmth, she was wont to summon a black slave of Governor Shirley's from the blurred mirror, and send him in search of guests who had long ago been familiar in those deserted chambers. Forth went the sable messenger, with the starlight or the moonshine gleaming through him, and did his errand in the burial-ground, knocking at the iron doors of tombs, or upon the marble slabs that covered them, and whispering to those within, "My mistress, old Esther Dudley, bids you to the Province House at midnight." And punctually as the clock of the Old South told twelve came the shadows of the Olivers, the Hutchinsons, the Dudleys, all the grandees of a bygone generation, gliding beneath the portal into the well-known mansion, where Esther mingled with them as if she likewise were a shade. Without vouching for the truth of such traditions, it is certain that Mistress Dudley sometimes assembled a few of the staunch though crestfallen old tories who had lingered in the rebel town during those days of wrath and tribulation. Out of a cob-webbed bottle containing liquor that a royal governor might have smacked his lips over they quaffed healths to the King, and babbled treason to the Republic, feeling as if the protecting shadow of the throne were still flung around them. But, draining the last drops of their liquor, they stole timorously homeward, and answered not again, if the rude mob reviled them in the street.

Yet Esther Dudley's most frequent and favored guests were the children of the town. Towards them she was never stern. A kindly and loving nature, hindered elsewhere from its free course by a thousand rocky prejudices, lavished itself upon these little ones. By bribes of gingerbread of her own making, stamped with a royal crown, she tempted their sunny sportiveness beneath the gloomy portal of the Province House, and would often beguile them to spend a whole playday there, sitting in a circle round the verge of her hoop petticoat, greedily attentive to her stories of a dead world. And when these little boys and girls stole forth again from the dark mysterious mansion, they went bewildered, full of old feelings that graver people had long ago forgotten, rubbing their eyes at the world around them, as if they had gone astray into ancient times, and become children of the past. At home, when their parents asked where they had loitered such a weary while, and with whom they had been at play, the children would talk of all the departed worthies of the Province, as far back as Governor Belcher, and the haughty dame of Sir William Phipps. It would seem as though they had been sitting on the knees of these famous personages, whom the grave had hidden for half a century, and had toyed with the embroidery of their rich waistcoats, or roguishly pulled the long curls of their flowing wigs. "But Governor Belcher has been dead this many a year," would the mother say to her little boy. "And did you really see him at the Province House?" "Oh yes, dear mother! yes!" the half-dreaming child would answer. "But when old Esther had done speaking about him, he faded away out of his chair." Thus, without affrighting her little guests, she led them by the hand into the chambers of her own desolate heart, and made childhood's fancy discern the ghosts that haunted there.

Living so continually in her own circle of ideas, and never regulating her mind by a proper reference to present things, Esther Dudley appears to have grown partially crazed. It was found that she had no right sense of the progress and true state of the Revolutionary war, but held a constant faith that the armies of Britain were victorious on every field, and destined to be ultimately triumphant. Whenever the town rejoiced for a battle won by Washington, or Gates, or Morgan, or Greene, the news, in passing through the door of the Province House, as through the ivory gate of dreams, became metamorphosed into a strange tale of the prowess of Howe, Clinton, or Cornwallis. Sooner or later, it was her invincible belief, the colonies would be prostrate at the footstool of the King. Sometimes she seemed to take for granted that such was already the case. On one occasion, she startled the town's people by a brilliant illumination of the Province House, with candles at every pane of glass, and a transparency of the King's initials and a crown of light in the great balcony window. The figure of the aged woman, in the most gorgeous of her mildewed velvets and brocades, was seen passing from casement to casement, until she paused before the balcony, and flourished a huge key above her head. Her wrinkled visage actually gleamed with triumph, as if the soul within her were a festal lamp.

"What means this blaze of light? What does old Esther's joy portend?" whispered a spectator. "It is frightful to see her gliding about the chambers, and rejoicing there without a soul to bear her company."

"It is as if she were making merry in a tomb," said another.

"Pshaw! It is no such mystery," observed an old man, after some brief exercise of memory. "Mistress Dudley is keeping jubilee for the King of England's birthday."

Then the people laughed aloud, and would have thrown mud against the blazing transparency of the King's crown and initials, only that they pitied the poor old dame, who was so dismally triumphant amid the wreck and ruin of the system to which she appertained.

Oftentimes it was her custom to climb the weary staircase that wound upward to the cupola, and thence strain her dimmed eyesight seaward and countryward, watching for a British fleet, or for the march of a grand procession, with the King's banner floating over it. The passengers in the street below would discern her anxious visage, and send up a shout: "When the golden Indian on the Province House shall shoot his arrow, and when the cock on the Old South spire shall crow, then look for a royal governor again!"—for this had grown a byword through the town. And at last, after long, long years, old Esther Dudley knew, or perchance she only dreamed, that a royal governor was on the eve of returning to the Province House, to receive the heavy key which Sir William Howe had committed to her charge. Now it was the fact, that intelligence bearing some faint analogy to Esther's version of it was current among the town's people. She set the mansion in the best order that her means allowed, and, arraying herself in silks and tarnished gold, stood long before the blurred mirror to admire her own magnificence. As she gazed, the gray and withered lady moved her ashen lips, murmuring half aloud, talking to shapes that she saw within the mirror, to shadows of her own fantasies, to the household friends of memory, and bidding them rejoice with her, and come forth to meet the governor. And while absorbed in this communion, Mistress Dudley heard the tramp of many footsteps in the street, and, looking out at the window, beheld what she construed as the royal governor's arrival.

"O happy day! O blessed, blessed hour!" she exclaimed. "Let me but bid him welcome within the portal, and my task in the Province House, and on earth is done!"

Then with tottering feet, which age and tremulous joy caused to tread amiss, she hurried down the grand staircase, her silks sweeping and rustling as she went, so that the sound was as if the train of spectral courtiers were thronging from the dim mirror. And Esther Dudley fancied, that, as soon as the wide door should be flung open, all the pomp and splendor of bygone times would pace majestically into the Province House, and the gilded tapestry of the past would be brightened by the sunshine of the present. She turned the key, withdrew it from the lock, unclosed the door, and stepped across the threshold. Advancing up the court-yard appeared a person of most dignified mien, with tokens, as Esther interpreted them, of gentle blood, high rank, and long-accustomed authority, even in his walk and every gesture. He was richly dressed, but wore a gouty shoe, which, however, did not lessen the stateliness of his gait. Around and behind him were people in plain civic dresses, and two or three war-worn veterans, evidently officers of rank, arrayed in a uniform of blue and buff. But Esther Dudley, firm in the belief that had fastened its roots about her heart, beheld only the principal personage, and never doubted that this was the long-looked-for governor, to whom she was to surrender up her charge. As he approached, she involuntarily sank down on her knees, and tremblingly held forth the heavy key.

"Receive my trust! take it quickly!" cried she; "for methinks Death is striving to snatch away my triumph. But he comes too late. Thank Heaven for this blessed hour! God save King George!"

"That, Madam, is a strange prayer to be offered up at such a moment," replied the unknown guest of the Province House, and courteously removing his hat he offered his arm to raise the aged woman. "Yet, in reverence for your gray hairs and long-kept faith, Heaven forbid that any here should say you nay. Over the realms which still acknowledge his sceptre, God save King George!"

Esther Dudley started to her feet, and hastily clutching back the key, gazed with fearful earnestness at the stranger; and dimly and doubtfully, as if suddenly awakened from a dream, her bewildered eyes half recognized his face. Years ago she had known him among the gentry of the province. But the ban of the King had fallen upon him! How, then, came the doomed victim here? Proscribed, excluded from mercy, the monarch's most dreaded and hated foe, this New England merchant had stood triumphantly against a kingdom's strength; and his foot now trod upon humbled Royalty, as he ascended the steps of the Province House, the people's chosen Governor of Massachusetts.

"Wretch, wretch that I am!" muttered the old woman, with such a heartbroken expression that the tears gushed from the stranger's eyes. "Have I bidden a traitor welcome? Come, Death! come quickly!"

"Alas, venerable lady!" said Governor Hancock, lending her his support with all the reverence that a courtier would have shown to a queen. "Your life has been prolonged until the world has changed around you. You have treasured up all that time has rendered worthless,—the principles, feelings, manners, modes of being and acting, which another generation has flung aside,—and you are a symbol of the past. And I, and these around me,—we represent a new race of men,—living no longer in the past, scarcely in the present,—but projecting our lives forward into the future. Ceasing to model ourselves on ancestral superstitions, it is our faith and principle to press onward, onward! Yet," continued he, turning to his attendants, "let us reverence, for the last time, the stately and gorgeous prejudices of the tottering Past!"

While the republican governor spoke, he had continued to support the helpless form of Esther Dudley; her weight grew heavier against his arm; but at last, with a sudden effort to free herself, the ancient woman sank down beside one of the pillars of the portal. The key of the Province House fell from her grasp, and clanked against the stone.

"I have been faithful unto death," murmured she. "God save the King!"

"She hath done her office!" said Hancock, solemnly. "We will follow her reverently to the tomb of her ancestors; and then, my fellow-citizens, onward, onward! We are no longer children of the Past!"

As the old loyalist concluded his narrative, the enthusiasm which had been fitfully flashing within his sunken eyes and quivering across his wrinkled visage, faded away, as if all the lingering fire of his soul were extinguished. Just then, too, a lamp upon the mantelpiece threw out a dying gleam, which vanished as speedily as it shot upward, compelling our eyes to grope for one another's features by the dim glow of the hearth. With such a lingering fire, methought, with such a dying dream, had the glory of the ancient system vanished from the Province House, when the spirit of old Esther Dudley took its flight. And now, again, the clock of the Old South threw its voice of ages on the breeze, knolling the hourly knell of the Past, crying out far and wide through the multitudinous city, and filling our ears, as we sat in the dusky chamber, with its reverberating depth of tone. In that same mansion,—in that very chamber,—what a volume of history had been told off into hours by the

same voice that was now trembling in the air. Many a governor had heard those midnight accents, and longed to exchange his stately cares for slumber. And as for mine host, and Mr. Bela Tiffany, and the old loyalist, and me, we had babbled about dreams of the past until we almost fancied that the clock was still striking in a bygone century. Neither of us would have wondered had a hoop-petticoated phantom of Esther Dudley tottered into the chamber, walking her rounds in the hush of midnight, as of yore, and motioned us to quench the fading embers of the fire, and leave the historic precincts to herself and her kindred shades. But as no such vision was vouchsafed, I retired unbidden, and would advise Mr. Tiffany to lay hold of another auditor, being resolved not to show my face in the Province House for a good while hence, if ever.

THE HAUNTED MIND

WHAT a singular moment is the first one, when you have hardly begun to recollect yourself, after starting from midnight slumber! By unclosing your eyes so suddenly, you seem to have surprised the personages of your dream in full convocation round your bed, and catch one broad glance at them before they can flit into obscurity. Or, to vary the metaphor, you find yourself, for a single instant, wide awake in that realm of illusions, whither sleep has been the passport, and behold its ghostly inhabitants and wondrous scenery, with a perception of their strangeness such as you

never attain while the dream is undisturbed. The distant sound of a church-clock is borne faintly on the wind. You question with yourself, half seriously, whether it has stolen to your waking ear from some gray tower that stood within the precincts of your dream. While yet in suspense, another clock flings its heavy clang over the slumbering town with so full and distinct a sound, and such a long murmur in the neighboring air, that you are certain it must proceed from the steeple at the nearest corner. You count the strokes, one—two, and there they cease, with a booming sound, like the gathering of a third stroke within the bell.

If you could choose an hour of wakefulness out of the whole night, it would be this. Since your sober bedtime, at eleven, you have had rest enough to take off the pressure of yesterday's fatigue; while before you, till the sun comes from "far Cathay" to brighten your window, there is almost the space of a summer night; one hour to be spent in thought, with the mind's eye half shut, and two in pleasant dreams, and two in that strangest of enjoyments, —the forgetfulness alike of joy and woe. The moment of rising belongs to another period of time, and appears so distant that the plunge out of a warm bed into the frosty air cannot yet be anticipated with dismay. Yesterday has already vanished among the shadows of the past; to-morrow has not yet emerged from the future. You have found an intermediate space, where the business of life does not intrude; where the passing moment lingers, and becomes truly the present; a spot where Father Time, when he thinks nobody is watching him, sits down by the wayside to take breath. O that he would fall asleep, and let mortals live on without growing older!

Hitherto you have lain perfectly still, because the slightest motion would dissipate the fragments of your slumber. Now, being irrevocably awake, you peep through the half-drawn window-curtain, and observe that the glass is ornamented with fanciful devices in frostwork, and that each pane presents something like a frozen dream. There will be time enough to trace out the analogy, while waiting the summons to breakfast. Seen through the clear portion of the glass, where the silvery mountain-peaks of the frost scenery do not ascend, the most conspicuous object is the steeple; the white spire of which directs you to the wintry lustre of the firmament. You may almost distinguish the figures on the clock that has just told the hour. Such a frosty sky, and the snow-covered roofs, and the long vista of the frozen street, all white, and the distant water hardened into rock, might make you shiver, even under four blankets and a woolen comforter. Yet look at that one glorious star! Its beams are distinguishable from all the rest, and actually cast the shadow of the casement on the bed with a radiance of deeper hue than moonlight, though not so accurate an outline.

You sink down and muffle your head in the clothes, shivering all the while, but less from bodily chill than the bare idea of a polar atmosphere. It is too cold even for the thoughts to venture abroad. You speculate on the luxury of wearing out a whole existence in bed, like an oyster in its shell, content with the sluggish ecstasy of inaction, and drowsily conscious of nothing but delicious warmth, such as you now feel again. Ah! that idea has brought a hideous one in its train. You think how the dead are lying in their cold shrouds and narrow coffins, through the drear winter of the grave, and cannot persuade your fancy that they neither shrink nor shiver, when the snow is drifting over their little hillocks, and the bitter blast howls against the door of the tomb. That gloomy thought will collect a gloomy multitude, and throw its complexion over your wakeful hour.

In the depths of every heart there is a tomb and a dungeon, though the lights, the music, and revelry above may cause us to forget their existence, and the buried ones, or prisoners whom they hide. But sometimes, and oftenest at midnight, these dark receptacles are flung wide open. In an hour like this, when the mind has a passive sensibility, but no active strength; when the imagination is a mirror, imparting vividness to all ideas, without the power of selecting or controlling them; then pray that your griefs may slumber, and the brotherhood of remorse not break their chain. It is too late! A funeral train comes gliding by your bed, in which Passion and Feeling assume bodily shape, and things of the mind become dim spectres to the eye. There is your earliest Sorrow, a pale young mourner, wearing a sister's likeness to first love, sadly beautiful, with a hallowed sweetness in her melancholy features, and grace in the flow of her sable robe. Next appears a shade of ruined loveliness, with dust among her golden hair, and her bright garments all faded and defaced, stealing from your glance with drooping head, as fearful of reproach; she was your fondest Hope, but a delusive one; so call her Disappointment now. A sterner form succeeds, with a brow of wrinkles, a look and gesture of iron authority; there is no name for him unless it be Fatality, an emblem of the evil influence that rules your fortunes; a demon to whom you subjected yourself by some error at the outset of life, and were bound his slave forever, by once obeying him. See! those fiendish lineaments graven on the darkness, the writhed lip of scorn, the mockery of that living eye, the pointed finger, touching the sore place in your heart! Do you remember any act of enormous folly at which you would blush even in the remotest cavern of the earth? Then recognize your Shame.

Pass, wretched band! Well for the wakeful one, if, riotously miserable, a fiercer tribe do not surround him,—the devils of a guilty heart, that holds its hell within itself. What if Remorse should assume the features of an injured friend? What if the fiend should come in woman's garments, with a pale beauty amid sin and desolation, and lie down by your side? What if he should stand at your bed's foot, in the likeness of a corpse, with a bloody stain upon the shroud? Sufficient, without such guilt, is this nightmare of the soul; this heavy, heavy sinking of the spirits; this wintry gloom about the heart; this indistinct horror of the mind, blending itself with the darkness of the chamber.

By a desperate effort, you start upright, breaking from a sort of conscious sleep, and gazing wildly round the bed, as if the fiends were anywhere but in your haunted mind. At the same moment, the slumbering embers on the hearth send forth a gleam which palely illuminates the whole outer room, and flickers through the door of the bed-chamber, but cannot quite dispel its obscurity. Your eye searches for whatever may remind you of the living world. With eager minuteness, you take note of the table near the fireplace, the book with an ivory knife between its leaves, the unfolded letter, the hat and the fallen glove. Soon the flame vanishes, and with it the whole scene is gone, though its image remains an instant in your mind's eye, when darkness has swallowed the reality. Throughout the chamber, there is the same obscurity as before, but not the same gloom within your breast. As your head falls back upon the pillow, you think—in a whisper be it spoken—how pleasant, in these night solitudes, would be the rise and fall of a softer breathing than your own, the slight pressure of a tenderer bosom, the quiet throb of a purer heart, imparting its peacefulness to your troubled one, as if the fond sleeper were involving you in her dream.

Her influence is over you, though she have no existence but in that momentary image. You sink down in a flowery spot, on the borders of sleep and wakefulness, while your thoughts rise before you in pictures, all disconnected, yet all assimilated by a pervading gladsomeness and beauty. The wheeling of gorgeous squadrons, that glitter in the sun, is succeeded by the merriment of children round the door of a schoolhouse, beneath the glimmering shadow of old trees, at the corner of a rustic lane. You stand in the sunny rain of a summer shower, and wander among the sunny trees of an autumnal wood, and look upward at the brightest of all rainbows, over-arching the unbroken sheet of snow, on the American side of Niagara. Your mind struggles pleasantly between the dancing radiance round the hearth of a young man and his recent bride, and the twittering flight of birds in spring about their new-made nest. You feel the merry bounding of a ship before the breeze; and watch the tuneful feet of rosy girls, as they twine their last and merriest dance, in a splendid ball-room; and find yourself in the brilliant circle of a crowded theatre, as the curtain falls over a light and airy scene.

With an involuntary start, you seize hold on consciousness, and prove yourself but half awake, by running a doubtful parallel between human life and the hour which has now elapsed. In both you emerge from mystery, pass through a vicissitude that you can but imperfectly control, and are borne onward to another mystery. Now comes the peal of the distant clock, with fainter and fainter strokes as you plunge farther into the wilderness of sleep. It is the knell of a temporary death. Your spirit has departed, and strays like a free citizen among the people of a shadowy world, beholding strange sights, yet without wonder or dismay. So calm, perhaps, will be the final change; so undisturbed, as if among familiar things, the entrance of the soul to its eternal home!

THE VILLAGE UNCLE

AN IMAGINARY RETROSPECT

COME! another log upon the hearth. True, our little parlor is comfortable, especially here, where the old man sits in his old arm-chair; but on Thanksgiving night the blaze should dance higher up the chimney, and send a shower of sparks into the outer darkness. Toss on an armful of those dry oak chips, the last relics of the Mermaid's knee-timbers, the bones of your namesake, Susan. Higher yet, and clearer be the blaze, till our cottage windows glow the ruddiest in the village, and the light of our household mirth flash far across the bay to Nahant. And now, come, Susan, come, my children, draw your chairs round me, all of you. There is a dimness over your figures! You sit quivering indistinctly with each motion of the blaze, which eddies about you like a flood, so that you all have the look of visions, or people that dwell only in the firelight, and will vanish from existence as completely as your own shadows when the flame shall sink among the embers. Hark! let me listen for the swell of the surf; it should be audible a mile inland on a night like this. Yes; there I catch the sound, but only an uncertain murmur, as if a good way down over the beach; though, by the almanac, it is high tide at eight o'clock, and the billows must now be dashing within thirty yards of our door. Ah! the old man's ears are failing him; and so is his eyesight, and perhaps his mind; else you would not all be so shadowy, in the blaze of his Thanksgiving fire.

How strangely the past is peeping over the shoulders of the present! To judge by my recollections, it is but a few moments since I sat in another room; yonder model of a vessel was not there, nor the old chest of drawers, nor Susan's profile and mine, in that gilt frame; nothing, in short, except this same fire, which glimmered on books, papers, and a picture, and half discovered my solitary figure in a looking-glass. But it was paler than my rugged old self, and younger, too, by almost half a century. Speak to me, Susan; speak, my beloved ones; for the scene is glimmering on my sight again, and as it brightens you fade away. O, I should be loath to lose my treasure of past happiness, and become once more what I was then,—a hermit in the depths of my own mind; sometimes yawning over drowsy volumes, and anon a scribbler of wearier trash than what I read; a man who had wandered out of the real world and got into its shadow, where his troubles, joys, and vicissitudes were of such slight stuff that he hardly knew whether he lived or only dreamed of living. Thank Heaven, I am an old man now, and have done with all such vanities.

Still this dimness of mine eyes! Come nearer, Susan, and stand before the fullest blaze of the hearth. Now I behold you illuminated from head to foot, in your clean cap and decent gown, with the dear lock of gray hair across your forehead, and a quiet smile about your mouth, while the eyes alone are concealed by the red gleam of the fire upon your spectacles. There, you made me tremble again! When the flame quivered, my sweet Susan, you quivered with it, and grew indistinct, as if melting into the warm light, that my last glimpse of you might be as visionary as the first was, full many a year since. Do you remember it? You stood on the little bridge over the brook that runs across King's Beach into the sea. It was twilight; the waves rolling in, the wind sweeping by, the crimson clouds fading in the west, and the silver moon brightening above the hill; and on the bridge were you, fluttering in the breeze like a sea-bird that might skim away at your pleasure. You seemed a daughter of the viewless wind, a creature of the ocean foam and the crimson light, whose merry life was spent in dancing on the crests of the billows that threw up their spray to support your footsteps. As I drew nearer, I fancied you akin to the race of mermaids, and thought how pleasant it would be to dwell with you among the quiet coves, in the shadow of the cliffs, and to roam along secluded beaches of the purest sand, and when our northern shores grew bleak, to haunt the islands, green and lonely, far amid summer seas. And yet it gladdened me, after all this nonsense, to find you nothing but a pretty young girl, sadly perplexed with the rude behavior of the wind about your petticoats.

Thus I did with Susan as with most other things in my earlier days, dipping her image into my mind and coloring it of a thousand fantastic hues, before I could see her as she really was. Now, Susan, for a sober picture of our village! It was a small collection of dwellings that seemed to have been cast up by the sea, with the rockweed and marine plants that it vomits after a storm, or to have come ashore among the pipe-staves and other lumber which had been washed from the deck of an Eastern schooner. There was just space for the narrow and sandy street between the beach in front and a precipitous hill that lifted its rocky forehead in the rear, among a waste of juniper-bushes and the wild growth of a broken pasture. The village was picturesque, in the variety of its edifices, though all were rude. Here stood a little old hovel, built, perhaps, of driftwood, there a row of boathouses, and beyond them a two-story dwelling, of dark and weather-beaten aspect, the whole intermixed with one or two snug cottages, painted white, a sufficiency of pigsties,

and a shoemaker's shop. Two grocery stores stand opposite each other, in the centre of the village. These were the places of resort, at their idle hours, of a hardy throng of fishermen, in red baize shirts, oilcloth trousers, and boots of brown leather covering the whole leg,—true seven-league boots, but fitter to wade the ocean than walk the earth. The wearers seemed amphibious, as if they did but creep out of salt water to sun themselves; nor would it have been wonderful to see their lower limbs covered with clusters of little shellfish, such as cling to rocks and old ship-timber over which the tide ebbs and flows. When their fleet of boats was weather-bound, the butchers raised their price, and the spit was busier than the frying-pan; for this was a place of fish, and known as such to all the country round about; the very air was fishy, being perfumed with dead sculpins, hard-heads, and dog-fish, strewn plentifully on the beach. You see, children, the village is but little changed since your mother and I were young.

How like a dream it was, when I bent over a pool of water, one pleasant morning, and saw that the ocean had dashed its spray over me and made me a fisherman! There were the tarpauling, the baize shirt, the oilcloth trousers and seven-league boots, and there my own features, but so reddened with sunburn and sea-breezes that methought I had another face, and on other shoulders too. The seagulls and the loons, and I, had now all one trade; we skimmed the crested waves and sought our prey beneath them, the man with as keen enjoyment as the birds. Always, when the east grew purple, I launched my dory, my little flat-bottomed skiff, and rowed cross-handed to Point Ledge, the Middle Ledge, or, perhaps, beyond Egg Rock; often, too, did I anchor off Dread Ledge, a spot of peril to ships unpiloted; and sometimes spread an adventurous sail and tracked across the bay to South Shore, casting my lines in sight of Scituate. Ere nightfall I hauled my skiff high and dry on the beach, laden with red rock-cod, or the white-bellied ones of deep water; haddock, bearing the black marks of Saint Peter's fingers near the gills; the long-bearded hake, whose liver holds oil enough for a midnight lamp; and now and then a mighty halibut, with a back broad as my boat. In the autumn I tolled and caught those lovely fish, the mackerel. When the wind was high,—when the whale-boats, anchored off the Point, nodded their slender masts at each other, and the dories pitched and tossed in the surf,—when Nahant Beach was thundering three miles off, and the spray broke a hundred feet in air round the distant base of Egg Rock,—when the brimful and boisterous sea threatened to tumble over the street of our village, —then I made a holiday on shore.

Many such a day did I sit snugly in Mr. Bartlett's store, attentive to the yarns of Uncle Parker,—uncle to the whole village, by right of seniority, but of southern blood, with no kindred in New England. His figure is before me now, enthroned upon a mackerel-barrel; a lean old man, of great height, but bent with years, and twisted into an uncouth shape by seven broken limbs; furrowed also, and weather-worn, as if every gale, for the better part of a century, had caught him somewhere on the sea. He looked like a harbinger of tempest; a shipmate of the Flying Dutchman. After innumerable voyages aboard men-of-war and merchantmen, fishing schooners and chebacco boats, the old salt had become master of a handcart, which he daily trundled about the vicinity, and sometimes blew his fish-horn through the streets of Salem. One of Uncle Parker's eyes had been blown out with gunpowder, and the other did but glimmer in its socket. Turning it upward as he spoke, it was his delight to tell of cruises against the French, and battles with his own shipmates, when he and an antagonist used to be seated astride of a sailor's chest, each fastened down by a spike-nail through his trousers, and there to fight it out. Sometimes he expatiated on the delicious flavor of the hagden, a greasy and goose-like fowl, which the sailors catch with hook and line on the Grand Banks. He dwelt with rapture on an interminable winter at the Isle of Sables, where he had gladdened himself, amid polar snows, with the rum and sugar saved from the wreck of a West India schooner. And wrathfully did he shake his fist as he related how a party of Cape Cod men had robbed him and his companions of their lawful spoil, and sailed away with every keg of old Jamaica, leaving him not a drop to drown his sorrow. Villains they were, and of that wicked brotherhood who are said to tie lanterns to horses' tails to mislead the mariner along the dangerous shores of the Cape.

Even now, I seem to see the group of fishermen, with that old salt in the midst. One fellow sits on the counter, a second bestrides an oil barrel, a third lolls at his length on a parcel of new cod-lines, and another has planted the tarry seat of his trousers on a heap of salt, which will shortly be sprinkled over a lot of fish. They are a likely set of men. Some have voyaged to the East Indies or the Pacific, and most of them have sailed in Marblehead schooners to Newfoundland; a few have been no farther than the Middle Banks, and one or two have always fished along the shore; but, as Uncle Parker used to say, they have all been christened in salt water, and know more than men ever learn in the bushes. A curious figure, by way of contrast, is a fish-dealer from far-up country, listening with eyes wide open to narratives that might startle Sinbad the sailor. Be it well with you, my brethren! Ye are all gone, some to your graves ashore, and others to the depths of ocean; but my faith is strong that ye are happy; for whenever I behold your forms, whether in dream or vision, each departed friend is puffing his long nine, and a mug of the right black-strap goes round from lip to lip.

But where was the mermaid in those delightful times? At a certain window near the centre of the village appeared a pretty display of gingerbread men and horses, picture-books and ballads, small fishhooks, pins, needles, sugar-plums, and brass thimbles,—articles on which the young fishermen used to expend their money from pure gallantry. What a picture was Susan behind the counter! A slender maiden, though the child of rugged parents, she had the slimmest of all waists, brown hair curling on her neck, and a complexion rather pale, except when the sea-breeze flushed it. A few freckles became beauty spots beneath her eyelids. How was it, Susan, that you talked and acted so carelessly, yet always for the best, doing whatever was right in your own eyes, and never

once doing wrong in mine, nor shocked a taste that had been morbidly sensitive till now? And whence had you that happiest gift, of brightening every topic with an unsought gayety, quiet but irresistible, so that even gloomy spirits felt your sunshine, and did not shrink from it? Nature wrought the charm. She made you a frank, simple, kind-hearted, sensible, and mirthful girl. Obeying nature, you did free things without indelicacy, displayed a maiden's thoughts to every eye, and proved yourself as innocent as naked Eve.

It was beautiful to observe how her simple and happy nature mingled itself with mine. She kindled a domestic fire within my heart, and took up her dwelling there, even in that chill and lonesome cavern, hung round with glittering icicles of fancy. She gave me warmth of feeling, while the influence of my mind made her contemplative. I taught her to love the moonlight hour, when the expanse of the encircled bay was smooth as a great mirror, and slept in a transparent shadow; while beyond Nahant the wind rippled the dim ocean into a dreamy brightness, which grew faint afar off, without becoming gloomier. I held her hand and pointed to the long surf wave, as it rolled calmly on the beach, in an unbroken line of silver; we were silent together till its deep and peaceful murmur had swept by us. When the Sabbath sun shone down into the recesses of the cliffs, I led the mermaid thither, and told her that those huge, gray, shattered rocks, and her native sea, that raged forever like a storm against them, and her own slender beauty, in so stern a scene, were all combined into a strain of poetry. But on the Sabbath eve, when her mother had gone early to bed, and her gentle sister had smiled and left us, as we sat alone by the quiet hearth, with household things around, it was her turn to make me feel that here was a deeper poetry, and that this was the dearest hour of all. Thus went on our wooing, till I had shot wild-fowl enough to feather our bridal bed, and the Daughter of the Sea was mine.

I built a cottage for Susan and myself, and made a gateway in the form of a Gothic arch, by setting up a whale's jaw-bones. We bought a heifer with her first calf, and had a little garden on the hillside, to supply us with potatoes and green sauce for our fish. Our parlor, small and neat, was ornamented with our two profiles in one gilt frame, and with shells and pretty pebbles on the mantel-piece, selected from the sea's treasury of such things, on Nahant Beach. On the desk, beneath the looking-glass, lay the Bible, which I had begun to read aloud at the book of Genesis, and the singing-book that Susan used for her evening psalm. Except the almanac, we had no other literature. All that I heard of books, was when an Indian history or tale of shipwreck was sold by a peddler or wandering subscription man to some one in the village, and read through its owner's nose to a slumberous auditory. Like my brother fishermen, I grew into the belief that all human erudition was collected in our pedagogue, whose green spectacles and solemn phiz, as he passed to his little school-house, amid a waste of sand, might have gained him a diploma from any college in New England. In truth I dreaded him. When our children were old enough to claim his care, you remember, Susan, how I frowned, though

you were pleased, at this learned man's encomiums on their proficiency. I feared to trust them even with the alphabet; it was the key to a fatal treasure.

But I loved to lead them by their little hands along the beach, and point to nature in the vast and the minute, the sky, the sea, the green earth, the pebbles, and the shells. Then did I discourse of the mighty works and coextensive goodness of the Deity, with the simple wisdom of a man whose mind had profited by lonely days upon the deep, and his heart by the strong and pure affections of his evening home. Sometimes my voice lost itself in a tremulous depth; for I felt His eye upon me as I spoke. Once, while my wife and all of us were gazing at ourselves, in the mirror left by the tide in a hollow of the sand, I pointed to the pictured heaven below, and bade her observe how religion was strewn everywhere in our path; since even a casual pool of water recalled the idea of that home whither we were travelling, to rest forever with our children. Suddenly your image, Susan, and all the little faces made up of yours and mine, seemed to fade away and vanish around me, leaving a pale visage like my own of former days within the frame of a large looking-glass. Strange illusion!

My life glided on, the past appearing to mingle with the present and absorb the future, till the whole lies before me at a glance. My manhood has long been waning with a stanch decay; my earlier contemporaries, after lives of unbroken health, are all at rest, without having known the weariness of late age; and now, with a wrinkled forehead and thin white hair as badges of my dignity, I have become the patriarch, the Uncle of the village. I love that name; it widens the circle of my sympathies; it joins all the youthful to my household, in the kindred of affection.

Like Uncle Parker, whose rheumatic bones were dashed against Egg Rock full forty years ago, I am a spinner of long yarns. Seated on the gunwale of a dory, or on the sunny side of a boat-house, where the warmth is grateful to my limbs, or by my own hearth, when a friend or two are there, I overflow with talk, and yet am never tedious. With a broken voice I give utterance to much wisdom. Such, Heaven be praised! is the vigor of my faculties, that many a forgotten usage, and traditions ancient in my youth, and early adventures of myself or others, hitherto effaced by things more recent, acquire new distinctness in my memory. I remember the happy days when the haddock were more numerous on all the fishing-grounds than sculpins in the surf; when the deep-water cod swam close in shore, and the dogfish, with his poisonous horn, had not learned to take the hook. I can number every equinoctial storm in which the sea has overwhelmed the street, flooded the cellars of the village, and hissed upon our kitchen hearth. I give the history of the great whale that was landed on Whale Beach, and whose jaws, being now my gate-way, will last for ages after my coffin shall have passed beneath them. Thence it is an easy digression to the halibut, scarcely smaller than the whale, which ran out six cod-lines, and hauled my dory to the mouth of Boston Harbor, before I could touch him with the gaff.

If melancholy accidents be the theme of conversation, I tell how a friend of mine was taken out of his boat by an enormous shark; and the sad, true tale of a young man on the eve of marriage, who had been nine days missing, when his drowned body floated into the very pathway, on Marblehead Neck, that had often led him to the dwelling of his bride; as if the dripping corpse would have come where the mourner was. With such awful fidelity did that lover return to fulfil his vows! Another favorite story is of a crazy maiden, who conversed with angels and had the gift of prophecy, and whom all the village loved and pitied, though she went from door to door accusing us of sin, exhorting to repentance, and foretelling our destruction by flood or earthquake. If the young men boast their knowledge of the ledges and sunken rocks, I speak of pilots who knew the wind by its scent and the wave by its taste, and could have steered blindfold to any port between Boston and Mount Desert, guided only by the rote of the shore,—the peculiar sound of the surf on each island, beach, and line of rocks along the coast. Thus do I talk, and all my auditors grow wise, while they deem it pastime.

I recollect no happier portion of my life than this, my calm old age. It is like the sunny and sheltered slope of a valley, where, late in the autumn, the grass is greener than in August, and intermixed with golden dandelions, that have not been seen till now since the first warmth of the year. But with me, the verdure and the flowers are not frost-bitten in the midst of winter. A playfulness has revisited my mind; a sympathy with the young and gay; an unpainful interest in the business of others; a light and wandering curiosity; arising, perhaps, from the sense that my toil on earth is ended, and the brief hour till bedtime may be spent in play. Still, I have fancied that there is a depth of feeling and reflection, under this superficial levity, peculiar to one who has lived long and is soon to die.

Show me anything that would make an infant smile, and you shall behold a gleam of mirth over the hoary ruin of my visage. I can spend a pleasant hour in the sun, watching the sports of the village children on the edge of the surf; now they chase the retreating wave far down over the wet sand; now it steals softly up to kiss their naked feet; now it comes onward with threatening front, and roars after the laughing crew as they scamper beyond its reach. Why should not an old man be merry too, when the great sea is at play with those little children? I delight, also, to follow in the wake of a pleasure-party of young men and girls, strolling along the beach after an early supper at the Point. Here, with handkerchiefs at nose, they bend over a heap of eel-grass, entangled in which is a dead skate, so oddly accoutred with two legs and a long tail that they mistake him for a drowned animal. A few steps farther the ladies scream, and the gentlemen make ready to protect them against a young shark of the dogfish kind, rolling with a life-like motion in the tide that has thrown him up. Next, they are smit with wonder at the black shells of a wagon-load of live lobsters, packed in rockweed for the country market. And when they reach the fleet of dories, just hauled ashore after the day's fishing, how do I laugh in my sleeve, and sometimes roar outright, at the simplicity of these young folks and the sly humor of the fishermen! In winter, when our village is

thrown into a bustle by the arrival of perhaps a score of country dealers, bargaining for frozen fish, to be transported hundreds of miles, and eaten fresh in Vermont or Canada, I am a pleased but idle spectator in the throng. For I launch my boat no more.

When the shore was solitary, I have found a pleasure that seemed even to exalt my mind, in observing the sports or contentions of two gulls, as they wheeled and hovered about each other, with hoarse screams, one moment flapping on the foam of the wave, and then soaring aloft till their white bosoms melted into the upper sunshine. In the calm of the summer sunset I drag my aged limbs, with a little ostentation of activity, because I am so old, up to the rocky brow of the hill. There I see the white sails of many a vessel outward bound or homeward from afar, and the black trail of a vapor behind the eastern steamboat; there, too, is the sun, going down, but not in gloom, and there the illimitable ocean mingling with the sky, to remind me of eternity.

But sweetest of all is the hour of cheerful musing and pleasant talk, that comes between the dusk and the lighted candle, by my glowing fireside. And never, even on the first Thanksgiving night, when Susan and I sat alone with our hopes, nor the second, when a stranger had been sent to gladden us, and be the visible image of our affection, did I feel such joy as now. All that belong to me are here; Death has taken none, nor Disease kept them away, nor Strife divided them from their parents or each other; with neither poverty nor riches to disturb them, nor the misery of desires beyond their lot, they have kept New England's festival round the patriarch's board. For I am a patriarch! Here I sit among my descendants, in my old arm-chair and immemorial corner, while the firelight throws an appropriate glory round my venerable frame. Susan! My children! Something whispers me that this happiest hour must be the final one, and that nothing remains but to bless you all and depart with a treasure of recollected joys to Heaven. Will you meet me there? Alas! your figures grow indistinct, fading into pictures on the air, and now to fainter outlines, while the fire is glimmering on the walls of a familiar room, and shows the book that I flung down, and the sheet that I left half written, some fifty years ago. I lift my eyes to the looking-glass and perceive myself alone, unless those be the mermaid's features retiring into the depths of the mirror, with a tender and melancholy smile.

Ah! one feels a chillness, not bodily, but about the heart, and, moreover, a foolish dread of looking behind him, after these pastimes. I can imagine precisely how a magician would sit down in gloom and terror, after dismissing the shadows that had personated dead or distant people, and stripping his cavern of the unreal splendor which had changed it to a palace. And now for a moral to my reverie. Shall it be, that, since fancy can create so bright a dream of happiness, it were better to dream on from youth to age, than to awake and strive doubtfully for something real! O, the slight tissue of a dream can no more preserve us from the stern reality of misfortune, than a robe of cobweb could repel the wintry blast. Be this the moral, then. In chaste and warm affections, humble wishes, and honest toil for some useful end, there is health for the mind, and quiet for the heart, the prospect of a happy life, and the fairest hope of Heaven.

THE AMBITIOUS GUEST

ONE September night a family had gathered round their hearth, and piled it high with the driftwood of mountain streams, the dry cones of the pine, and the splintered ruins of great trees, that had come crashing down the precipice. Up the chimney roared the fire, and brightened the room with its broad blaze. The faces of the father and mother had a sober gladness; the children laughed; the eldest daughter was the image of Happiness at seventeen; and the aged grandmother, who sat knitting in the warmest place, was the image of Happiness grown old. They had found the "herb, heart's-ease," in the bleakest spot of all New England. This family were situated in the Notch of the White Hills, where the wind was sharp throughout the year, and pitilessly cold in the winter,—giving their cottage all its fresh inclemency before it descended on the valley of the Saco. They dwelt in a cold spot and a dangerous one; for a mountain towered above their heads, so steep that the stones would often rumble down its sides, and startle them at midnight.

The daughter had just uttered some simple jest that filled them all with mirth, when the wind came through the Notch and seemed to pause before their cottage,—rattling the door, with a sound of wailing and lamentation, before it passed into the valley. For a moment it saddened them, though there was nothing unusual in the tones. But the family were glad again, when they perceived that the latch was lifted by some traveller whose footsteps had been unheard amid the dreary blast which heralded his approach, and wailed as he was entering, and went moaning away from the door.

Though they dwelt in such a solitude, these people held daily converse with the world. The romantic pass of the Notch is a great artery, through which the life-blood of internal commerce is continually throbbing, between Maine on one side, and the Green Mountains and the shores of the St. Lawrence on the other. The stage-coach always drew up before the door of the cottage. The wayfarer, with no companion but his staff, paused here to exchange a word, that the sense of loneliness might not utterly overcome him ere he could pass through the cleft of the mountain, or reach the first house in the valley. And here the teamster, on his way to Portland market, would put up for the night; and, if a bachelor, might sit an hour beyond the usual bedtime, and steal a kiss from the mountain maid at parting. It was one of those primitive taverns where the traveller pays only for food and lodging, but meets with a homely kindness beyond all price. When the footsteps were heard, therefore, between the outer door and the inner one, the whole family rose up, grandmother, children, and all, as if about to welcome some one who belonged to them, and whose fate was linked with theirs.

The door was opened by a young man. His face at first wore the melancholy expression, almost despondency, of one who travels a wild and bleak road at nightfall and alone, but soon brightened up when he saw the kindly warmth of his reception. He felt his heart spring forward to meet them all, from the old woman, who wiped a chair with her apron, to the little child that held out its arms to him. One glance and smile placed the stranger on a footing of innocent familiarity with the eldest daughter.

"Ah, this fire is the right thing!" cried he; "especially when there is such a pleasant circle round it. I am quite benumbed; for the Notch is just like the pipe of a great pair of bellows; it has blown a terrible blast in my face, all the way from Bartlett."

"Then you are going towards Vermont?" said the master of the house, as he helped to take a light knapsack off the young man's shoulders.

"Yes; to Burlington, and far enough beyond," replied he. "I meant to have been at Ethan Crawford's to-night; but a pedestrian lingers along such a road as this. It is no matter; for, when I saw this good fire, and all your cheerful faces, I felt as if you had kindled it on purpose for me, and were waiting my arrival. So I shall sit down among you, and make myself at home."

The frank-hearted stranger had just drawn his chair to the fire, when something like a heavy footstep was heard without, rushing down the steep side of the mountain, as with long and rapid strides, and taking such a leap, in passing the cottage, as to strike the opposite precipice. The family held their breath, because they knew the sound, and their guest held his by instinct.

"The old mountain has thrown a stone at us, for fear we should forget him," said the landlord, recovering himself. "He sometimes nods his head, and threatens to come down; but we are old neighbors, and agree together pretty well, upon the whole. Besides, we have a sure place of refuge, hard by, if he should be coming in good earnest."

Let us now suppose the stranger to have finished his supper of bear's meat; and, by his natural felicity of manner, to have placed himself on a footing of kindness with the whole family, so that they talked as freely together as if he belonged to their mountain brood. He was of a proud, yet gentle spirit,—haughty and reserved among the rich and great; but ever ready to stoop his head to the lowly cottage door, and be like a brother or a son at the poor man's fireside. In the household of the Notch, he found warmth and simplicity of feeling, the pervading intelligence of New England, and a poetry of native growth, which they had gathered, when they little thought of it, from the mountain peaks and chasms, and at the very threshold of their romantic and dangerous abode. He had travelled far and alone; his whole life, indeed, had been a solitary path; for, with the lofty caution of his nature, he had kept himself apart from those who might otherwise have been his companions. The family, too, though so kind and hospitable, had that consciousness of unity among themselves, and separation from the world at large, which, in every domestic circle,

should still keep a holy place where no stranger may intrude. But, this evening, a prophetic sympathy impelled the refined and educated youth to pour out his heart before the simple mountaineers, and constrained them to answer him with the same free confidence. And thus it should have been. Is not the kindred of a common fate a closer tie than that of birth?

The secret of the young man's character was a high and abstracted ambition. He could have borne to live an undistinguished life, but not to be forgotten in the grave. Yearning desire had been transformed to hope; and hope, long cherished, had become like certainty, that, obscurely as he journeyed now, a glory was to beam on all his pathway,—though not, perhaps, while he was treading it. But, when posterity should gaze back into the gloom of what was now the present, they would trace the brightness of his footsteps, brightening as meaner glories faded, and confess, that a gifted one had passed from his cradle to his tomb, with none to recognize him.

"As yet," cried the stranger,—his cheek glowing and his eye flashing with enthusiasm,—"as yet, I have done nothing. Were I to vanish from the earth to-morrow, none would know so much of me as you; that a nameless youth came up, at nightfall, from the valley of the Saco, and opened his heart to you in the evening, and passed through the Notch, by sunrise, and was seen no more. Not a soul would ask,—'Who was he?—Whither did the wanderer go?' But, I cannot die till I have achieved my destiny. Then, let Death come! I shall have built my monument!"

There was a continual flow of natural

emotion, gushing forth amid abstracted reverie, which enabled the family to understand this young man's sentiments, though so foreign from their own. With quick sensibility of the ludicrous, he blushed at the ardor into which he had been betrayed.

"You laugh at me," said he, taking the eldest daughter's hand and laughing himself. "You think my ambition as nonsensical as if I were to freeze myself to death on the top of Mount Washington, only that people might spy at me from the country round about. And truly, that would be a noble pedestal for a man's statue!"

"It is better to sit here by this fire," answered the girl, blushing, "and be comfortable and contented, though nobody thinks about us."

"I suppose," said her father, after a fit of musing, "there is something natural in what the young man says; and if my mind had been turned that way, I might have felt just the same. It is strange, wife, how his talk has set my head running on things, that are pretty certain never to come to pass."

"Perhaps they may," observed the wife. "Is the man thinking what he will do when he is a widower?"

"No, no!" cried he, repelling the idea with reproachful kindness. "When I think of your death, Esther, I think of mine, too. But I was wishing we had a good farm in Bartlett, or Bethlehem, or Littleton, or some other township round the White Mountains; but not where they could tumble on our heads. I should want to stand well with my neighbors, and be called Squire, and sent to General Court for a term or two; for a plain, honest man may do as much good there as a lawyer. And when I

should be grown quite an old man, and you an old woman, so as not to be long apart, I might die happy enough in my bed, and leave you all crying round me. A slate gravestone would suit me as well as a marble one,—with just my name and age, and a verse of a hymn, and something to let people know that I lived an honest man and died a Christian."

"There now," exclaimed the stranger; "it is our nature to desire a monument, be it slate, or marble, or a pillar of granite, or a glorious memory in the universal heart of man."

"We're in a strange way, to-night," said the wife, with tears in her eyes. "They say it's a sign of something, when folks' minds go a wandering so. Hark to the children!"

They listened accordingly. The younger children had been put to bed in another room, but with an open door between, so that they could be heard talking busily among themselves. One and all seemed to have caught the infection from the fireside circle, and were outvying each other, in wild wishes, and childish projects of what they would do, when they came to be men and women. At length, a little boy, instead of addressing his brothers and sisters, called out to his mother.

"I'll tell you what I wish, mother," cried he. "I want you and father, and grandma'm, and all of us, and the stranger too, to start right away, and go and take a drink out of the basin of the Flume!"

Nobody could help laughing at the child's notion of leaving a warm bed, and dragging them from a cheerful fire, to visit the basin of the Flume,—a brook, which tumbles over the precipice, deep within the Notch. The boy had hardly spoken, when a wagon rattled along the road, and stopped a moment before the door. It appeared to contain two or three men, who were cheering their hearts with the rough chorus of a song, which resounded, in broken notes, between the cliffs, while the singers hesitated whether to continue their journey, or put up here for the night.

"Father," said the girl, "they are calling you by name."

But the good man doubted whether they had really called him, and was unwilling to show himself too solicitous of gain, by inviting people to patronize his house. He therefore did not hurry to the door; and the lash being soon applied, the travellers plunged into the Notch, still singing and laughing, though their music and mirth came back drearily from the heart of the mountain.

"There, mother!" cried the boy, again. "They'd have given us a ride to the Flume."

Again they laughed at the child's pertinacious fancy for a night ramble. But it happened, that a light cloud passed over the daughter's spirit; she looked gravely into the fire, and drew a breath that was almost a sigh. It forced its way, in spite of a little struggle to repress it. Then starting and blushing, she looked quickly round the circle, as if they had caught a glimpse into her bosom. The stranger asked what she had been thinking of.

"Nothing," answered she, with a downcast smile. "Only I felt lonesome just then."

"O, I have always had a gift of feeling what is in other people's hearts," said he, half seriously. "Shall I tell the secrets of yours? For I know what to think when a young girl shivers by a warm hearth, and complains of lonesomeness at her mother's side. Shall I put these feelings into words?"

"They would not be a girl's feelings any longer, if they could be put into words," replied the mountain nymph laughing, but avoiding his eye.

All this was said apart. Perhaps a germ of love was springing in their hearts, so pure that it might blossom in Paradise, since it could not be matured on earth; for women worship such gentle dignity as his; and the proud, contemplative, yet kindly soul is oftenest captivated by simplicity like hers. But, while they spoke softly, and he was watching the happy sadness, the lightsome shadows, the shy yearnings of a maiden's nature, the wind, through the Notch, took a deeper and drearier sound. It seemed, as the fanciful stranger said, like the choral strain of the spirits of the blast, who, in old Indian times, had their dwelling among these mountains, and made their heights and recesses a sacred region. There was a wail along the road as if a funeral were passing. To chase away the gloom, the family threw pine-branches on their fire, till the dry leaves crackled and the flame arose, discovering once again a scene of peace and humble happiness. The light hovered about them fondly, and caressed them all. There were the little faces of the children, peeping from their bed apart, and here the father's frame of strength, the mother's subdued and careful mien, the high-browed youth, the budding girl, and the good old grandam, still knitting in the warmest place. The aged woman looked up from her task, and, with fingers ever busy, was the next to speak.

"Old folks have their notions," said she, "as well as young ones. You've been wishing and planning; and letting your heads run on one thing and another till you've set my mind a wandering too. Now what should an old woman wish for when she can go but a step or two before she comes to her grave? Children, it will haunt me night and day till I tell you.

"What is it, mother?" cried the husband and wife, at once.

Then the old woman, with an air of mystery, which drew the circle closer round the fire, informed them that she had provided her grave-clothes some years before,—a nice linen shroud, a cap with a muslin ruff, and everything of a finer sort than she had worn since her wedding-day. But, this evening, an old superstition had strangely recurred to her. It used to be said, in her younger days, that, if anything were amiss with a corpse, if only the ruff were not smooth, or the cap did not set right, the corpse, in the coffin and beneath the clods, would strive to put up its cold hands and arrange it. The bare thought made her nervous.

"Don't talk so, grandmother!" said the girl, shuddering.

"Now,"—continued the old woman, with singular earnestness, yet smiling strangely at her own folly,—"I want one of you, my children,—when your mother is dressed and in the coffin,—I want one of you to hold a looking-glass over my face. Who knows but I may take a glimpse at myself, and see whether all's right?"

"Old and young, we dream of graves and monuments," murmured the stranger youth. "I wonder how mariners feel when the ship is sinking, and they, un-known and undistinguished, are to be buried together in the ocean,—that wide and nameless sepulchre?"

For a moment the old woman's ghastly conception so engrossed the minds of her hearers, that a sound, abroad in the night, rising like the roar of a blast, had grown broad, deep, and terrible, before the fated group were conscious of it. The house, and all within it, trembled; the foundations of the earth seemed to be shaken, as if this awful sound were the peal of the last trump. Young and old exchanged one wild glance, and remained an instant, pale, affrighted, without utterance or power to move. Then the same shriek burst simultaneously from all their lips.

"The Slide! The Slide!"

The simplest words must intimate, but not portray, the unutterable horror of the catastrophe. The victims rushed from their cottage, and sought refuge in what they deemed a safer spot,—where, in contemplation of such an emergency, a sort of barrier had been reared. Alas! they had quitted their security, and fled right into the pathway of destruction. Down came the whole side of the mountain in a cataract of ruin. Just before it reached the house, the stream broke into two branches,—shivered not a window there, but overwhelmed the whole vicinity, blocked up the road, and annihilated everything in its dreadful course. Long ere the thunder of that great Slide had ceased to roar among the mountains, the mortal agony had been endured, and the victims were at peace. Their bodies were never found.

The next morning the light smoke was seen stealing from the cottage chimney up the mountain side. Within, the fire was yet smouldering on the hearth, and the chairs in a circle round it, as if the inhabitants had but gone forth to view the devastation of the Slide and would shortly return to thank Heaven for their miraculous escape. All had left separate tokens, by which those who had known the family were made to shed a tear for each. Who has not heard their name? The story has been told far and wide, and will forever be a legend of these mountains. Poets have sung their fate.

There were circumstances which led some to suppose that a stranger had been received into the cottage on this awful night, and had shared the catastrophe of all its inmates. Others denied that there were sufficient grounds for such a conjecture. Woe for the high-souled youth, with his dream of Earthly Immortality! His name and person utterly unknown; his history, his way of life, his plans, a mystery never to be solved; his death and his existence equally a doubt! Whose was the agony of that death-moment?

THE SISTER YEARS

Last night, between eleven and twelve o'clock, when the Old Year was leaving her final footprints on the borders of Time's empire, she found herself in possession of a few spare moments, and sat down—of all places in the world—on the steps of our new City Hall. The wintry moonlight showed that she looked weary of body and sad of heart, like many another wayfarer of earth. Her garments, having been exposed to much foul weather and rough usage, were in very ill condition; and as the hurry of her journey had never before allowed her to take an instant's rest, her shoes were so worn as to be scarcely worth the mending. But, after trudging only a little distance farther, this poor Old Year was destined to enjoy a long long sleep. I forgot to mention, that when she seated herself on the steps she deposited by her side a very capacious bandbox, in which, as is the custom among travellers of her sex, she carried a great deal of valuable property. Be-

sides this luggage there was a folio book under her arm, very much resembling the annual volume of a newspaper. Placing this volume across her knees, and resting her elbows upon it, with her forehead in her hands, the weary, bedraggled, world-worn Old Year heaved a heavy sigh, and appeared to be taking no very pleasant retrospect of her past existence.

While she thus awaited the midnight knell that was to summon her to the innumerable sisterhood of departed Years, there came a young maiden treading lightsomely on tiptoe along the street, from the direction of the Railroad Depot. She was evidently a stranger, and perhaps had come to town by the evening train of cars. There was a smiling cheerfulness in this fair maiden's face, which bespoke her fully confident of a kind reception from the multitude of people with whom she was soon to form acquaintance. Her dress was rather too airy for the season, and was bedizened with fluttering ribbons and other vanities, which were likely soon to be rent away by the fierce storms, or to fade in the hot sunshine, amid which she was to pursue her changeful course. But still she was a wonderfully pleasant-looking figure, and had so much promise and such an indescribable hopefulness in her aspect that hardly anybody could meet her without anticipating some very desirable thing,—the consummation of some long-sought good,—from her kind offices. A few dismal characters there may be, here and there about the world, who have so often been trifled with by young maidens as promising as she, that they have now ceased to pin any faith upon the skirts of the New Year. But, for my own part, I have great faith in her; and should I live to see fifty more such, still, from each of those successive sisters, I shall reckon upon receiving something that will be worth living for.

The New Year—for this young maiden was no less a personage—carried all her goods and chattels in a basket of no great size or weight, which hung upon her arm. She greeted the disconsolate Old Year with great affection, and sat down beside her on the steps of the City Hall, waiting for the signal to begin her rambles through the world. The two were own sisters, being both granddaughters of Time; and though one looked so much older than the other, it was rather owing to hardships and trouble than to age, since there was but a twelvemonth's difference between them.

"Well, my dear sister," said the New Year, after the first salutations, "you look almost tired to death. What have you been about during your sojourn in this part of Infinite Space?"

"O, I have it all recorded here in my Book of Chronicles," answered the Old Year, in a heavy tone. "There is nothing that would amuse you; and you will soon get sufficient knowledge of such matters from your own personal experience. It is but tiresome reading."

Nevertheless, she turned over the leaves of the folio, and glanced at them by the light of the moon, feeling an irresistible spell of interest in her own biography, although its incidents were remembered without pleasure. The volume, though she termed it her Book of Chronicles, seemed to be neither more nor less than the Salem Gazette for 1838; in the accuracy of which journal the sagacious Old Year had so much confidence, that she deemed it needless to record her history with her own pen.

"What have you been doing in the political way?" asked the New Year.

"Why, my course here in the United States," said the Old Year,—"though perhaps I ought to blush at the confession,—my political course, I must acknowledge, has been rather vacillatory, sometimes inclining towards the Whigs,—then causing the Administration party to shout for triumph,—and now again uplifting what seemed the almost prostrate banner of the Opposition; so that historians will hardly know what to make of me, in this respect. But the Loco Focos—"

"I do not like these party nicknames," interrupted her sister, who seemed remarkably touchy about some points. "Perhaps we shall part in better humor, if we avoid any political discussion."

"With all my heart," replied the Old Year, who had already been tormented half to death with squabbles of this kind. "I care not if the names of Whig or Tory, with their interminable brawls about Banks and the Sub-Treasury, Abolition, Texas, the Florida War, and a million of other topics,—which you will learn soon enough for your own comfort,—I care not, I say, if no whisper of these matters ever reaches my ears again. Yet they have occupied so large a share of my attention, that I scarcely know what else to tell you. There has indeed been a curious sort of war on the Canada border, where blood has streamed in the names of Liberty and Patriotism; but it must remain for some future, perhaps far distant Year, to tell whether or no those holy names have been rightfully invoked. Nothing so much depresses me, in my view of mortal affairs, as to see high energies wasted, and human life and happiness thrown away, for ends that appear oftentimes unwise, and still oftener remain unaccomplished. But the wisest people and the best keep a steadfast faith that the progress of Mankind is onward and upward, and that the toil and anguish of the path serve to wear away the imperfections of the Immortal Pilgrim, and will be felt no more, when they have done their office."

"Perhaps," cried the hopeful New Year, "perhaps I shall see that happy day!"

"I doubt whether it be so close at hand," answered the Old Year, gravely smiling. "You will soon grow weary of looking for that blessed consummation, and will turn for amusement (as has frequently been my own practice) to the affairs of some sober little city, like this of Salem. Here we sit on the steps of the new City Hall, which has been completed under my administration; and it would make you laugh to see how the game of politics, of which the Capitol at Washington is the great chessboard, is here played in miniature. Burning Ambition finds its fuel here; here Patriotism speaks boldly in the people's behalf, and virtuous Economy demands retrenchment in the emoluments of a lamplighter; here the Aldermen range their senatorial dignity around the Mayor's chair of state, and the Common Council feel that they have liberty in charge. In short, human weakness and strength, passion and policy, Man's tendencies, his aims and modes of pursuing them, his individual character, and his character in the mass, may be studied almost as well here as on the theatre of nations; and with this great advantage, that, be the lesson ever so disastrous, its Lilliputian scope still makes the beholder smile."

"Have you done much for the improvement of the City?" asked the New Year. "Judging from what little I have seen, it appears to be ancient and time-worn."

"I have opened the Railroad," said the elder Year, "and half a dozen times a day, you will hear the bell (which once summoned the Monks of a Spanish Convent to their devotions) announcing the arrival or departure of the cars. Old Salem now wears a much livelier expression than when I first beheld her. Strangers rumble down from Boston by hundreds at a time. New faces throng in Essex Street. Railroad hacks and omnibuses rattle over the pavements. There is a perceptible increase of oyster-shops, and other establishments for the accommodation of a transitory diurnal multitude. But a more important change awaits the venerable town. An immense accumulation of musty prejudices will be carried off by the free circulation of society. A peculiarity of character, of which the inhabitants themselves are hardly sensible, will be rubbed down and worn away by the attrition of foreign substances. Much of the result will be good; there will likewise be a few things not so good. Whether for better or worse, there will be a probable diminution of the moral influence of wealth, and the sway of an aristocratic class, which, from an era far beyond my memory, has held firmer dominion here than in any other New England town."

The Old Year having talked away nearly all of her little remaining breath, now closed her Book of Chronicles, and was about to take her departure. But her sister detained her a while longer, by inquiring the contents of the huge bandbox, which she was so painfully lugging along with her.

"These are merely a few trifles," replied the Old Year, "which I have picked up in my rambles, and am going to deposit, in the receptacle of things past and forgotten. We sisterhood of Years never carry anything really valuable out of the world with us. Here are patterns of most of the fashions which I brought into vogue, and which have already lived out their allotted term. You will supply their place, with others equally ephemeral. Here, put up in little China pots, like rouge, is a considerable lot of beautiful women's bloom, which the disconsolate fair ones owe me a bitter grudge for stealing. I have likewise a quantity of men's dark hair, instead of which, I have left gray locks, or none at all. The tears of

widows and other afflicted mortals, who have received comfort during the last twelve months, are preserved in some dozens of essence bottles, well corked and sealed. I have several bundles of love-letters, eloquently breathing an eternity of burning passion, which grew cold and perished, almost before the ink was dry. Moreover, here is an assortment of many thousand broken promises, and other broken ware, all very light and packed into little space. The heaviest articles in my possession are a large parcel of disappointed hopes, which, a little while ago, were buoyant enough to have inflated Mr. Lauriat's balloon."

"I have a fine lot of hopes here in my basket," remarked the New Year. "They are a sweet-smelling flower,—a species of rose."

"They soon lose their perfume," replied the sombre Old Year. "What else have you brought to insure a welcome from the discontented race of mortals?"

"Why, to say the truth, little or nothing else," said her sister, with a smile,—"save a few new Annuals and Almanacs, and some New Year's gifts for the children. But I heartily wish well to poor mortals, and mean to do all I can for their improvement and happiness."

"It is a good resolution," rejoined the Old Year; "and, by the way, I have a plentiful assortment of good resolutions, which have now grown so stale and musty, that I am ashamed to carry them any further. Only for fear that the City authorities would send Constable Mansfield with a warrant after me, I should toss them into the street at once. Many other matters go to make up the contents of my bandbox; but the whole lot would not fetch a single id, even at an auction of worn-out furniture; and as they are worth nothing either to you or anybody else, I need not trouble you with a longer catalogue."

"And must I also pick up such worthless luggage in my travels?" asked the New Year.

"Most certainly,—and well, if you have no heavier load to bear," replied the other. "And now, my dear sister, I must bid you farewell, earnestly advising and exhorting you to expect no gratitude nor good will from this peevish, unreasonable, inconsiderate, ill-intending, and worse-behaving world. However warmly its inhabitants may seem to welcome you, yet, do what you may, and lavish on them what means of happiness you please, they will still be complaining, still craving what it is not in your power to give, still looking forward to some other Year for the accomplishment of projects which ought never to have been formed, and which, if successful, would only provide new occasions of discontent. If these ridiculous people ever seen anything tolerable in you, it will be after you are gone forever."

"But I," cried the fresh-hearted New Year, "I shall try to leave men wiser than I find them. I will offer them freely whatever good gifts Providence permits me to distribute, and will tell them to be thankful for what they have, and humbly hopeful for more; and surely, if they are not absolute fools, they will condescend to be happy, and will allow me to be a happy Year. For my happiness must depend on them."

"Alas for you, then, my poor sister!" said the Old Year, sighing, as she uplifted her burden. "We grandchildren of Time are born to trouble. Happiness, they say, dwells in the mansions of Eternity; but we can only lead mortals thither, step by step, with reluctant murmurings, and ourselves must perish on the threshold. But hark! my task is done."

The clock in the tall steeple of Dr. Emerson's church struck twelve; there was a response from Dr. Flint's, in the opposite quarter of the city; and while the strokes were yet dropping into the air, the Old Year either flitted or faded away,—and not the wisdom and might of Angels, to say nothing of the remorseful yearnings of the millions who had used her ill, could have prevailed with that departed Year to return one step. But she, in the company of Time and all her kindred, must hereafter hold a reckoning with Mankind. So shall it be, likewise, with the maidenly New Year, who, as the clock ceased to strike, arose from the steps of the City Hall and set out rather timorously on her earthly course.

"A happy New Year!" cried a watchman, eying her figure very questionably, but without the least suspicion that he was addressing the New Year in person.

"Thank you kindly!" said the New Year; and she gave the watchman one of the roses of hope from her basket. "May this flower keep a sweet smell long after I have bidden you good-by."

Then she stepped on more briskly through the silent streets; and such as were awake at the moment heard her footfall, and said, "The New Year is come!" Wherever there was a knot of midnight roisterers they quaffed her health. She sighed, however, to perceive that the air was tainted—as the atmosphere of this world must continually be—with the dying breaths of mortals who had lingered just long enough for her to bury them. But there were millions left alive to rejoice at her coming; and so she pursued her way with confidence, strewing emblematic flowers on the doorstep of almost every dwelling, which some persons will gather up and wear in their bosoms, and others will trample under foot. The Carrier Boy can only say further, that, early this morning, she filled his basket with New Year's Addresses, assuring him that the whole City, with our new Mayor, and the Aldermen and Common Council at its head, would make a general rush to secure copies. Kind Patrons, will not you redeem the pledge of the NEW YEAR?

SNOW-FLAKES

THERE is snow in yonder cold gray sky of the morning!—and, through the partially frosted window-panes, I love to watch the gradual beginning of the storm. A few feathery flakes are scattered widely through the air, and hover downward with uncertain flight, now almost alighting on the earth, now whirled again aloft into remote regions of the atmosphere. These are not the big flakes, heavy with moisture, which melt as they touch the ground, and are portentous of a soaking rain. It is to be, in good earnest, a wintry storm. The two or three people visible on the sidewalks have an aspect of endurance, a blue-nosed, frosty fortitude, which is evidently assumed in anticipation of a comfortless and blustering day. By nightfall, or at least before the sun sheds another glimmering smile upon us, the street and our little garden will be heaped with mountain snow-drifts. The soil, already frozen for weeks past, is prepared to sustain whatever burden may be laid upon it; and, to a Northern eye, the landscape will lose its melancholy bleakness and acquire a beauty of its own, when Mother Earth, like her children, shall have put on the fleecy garb of her winter's wear. The cloud spirits are slowly weaving her white mantle. As yet, indeed, there is barely a rime like hoarfrost over the brown surface of the street; the withered green of the grass plat is still discernible; and the slated roofs of the houses do but begin to look gray, instead of black. All the snow that has yet fallen within the circumference of my view, were it heaped up together, would hardly equal the hillock of a grave. Thus gradually by silent and stealthy influences, are great changes wrought. These little snow particles, which the storm spirit flings by handfuls through the air, will bury the great earth under their accumulated mass, nor permit her to behold her sister sky again for dreary months. We likewise, shall lose sight of our mother's familiar visage, and must content ourselves with looking heavenward the oftener.

Now, leaving the storm to do his appointed office, let us sit down, pen in hand, by our fireside. Gloomy as it may

m, there is an influence productive of
eerfulness, and favorable to imagina-
e thought, in the atmosphere of a
owy day. The native of a southern
me may woo the muse beneath the
vy shade of summer foliage, reclining
banks of turf, while the sound of
ging birds and warbling rivulets
imes in with the music of his soul.
our brief summer, I do not think, but
ly exist in the vague enjoyment of a
eam. My hour of inspiration—if that
ur ever comes—is when the green log
sses upon the hearth, and the bright
me, brighter for the gloom of the
amber, rustles high up the chimney,
d the coals drop tinkling down among
e growing heaps of ashes. When the
sement rattles in the gust, and the
ow-flakes or the sleety rain-drops pelt
rd against the window-panes, then I
read out my sheet of paper, with the
rtainty that thoughts and fancies will
eam forth upon it, like stars at twi-
ht, or like violets in May,—perhaps
fade as soon. However transitory
eir glow, they at least shine amid the
rksome shadow which the clouds of
e outward sky fling through the room.
lessed, therefore, and reverently wei-
med by me, her true-born son, be
ew England's winter, which makes us,
e and all, the nurslings of the storm,
d sings a familiar lullaby even in the
ildest shriek of the December blast.
ow look we forth again, and see how
uch of his task the storm spirit has
one.

Slow and sure! He has the day, per-
nance the week, before him, and may
ke his own time to accomplish Na-
re's burial in snow. A smooth mantle
scarcely yet thrown over the withered
rass plat, and the dry stalks of an-

nuals still thrust themselves through the
white surface in all parts of the garden.
The leafless rose-bushes stand shivering
in a shallow snow-drift, looking, poor
things! as disconsolate as if they possessed a human consciousness of the
dreary scene. This is a sad time for the
shrubs that do not perish with the summer; they neither live nor die; what
they retain of life seems but the chilling sense of death. Very sad are the
flower-shrubs in midwinter! The roofs
of the houses are now all white, save
where the eddying wind has kept them
bare at the bleak corners. To discern
the real intensity of the storm, we must
fix upon some distant object,—as yonder spire,—and observe how the riotous
gust fights with the descending snow
throughout the intervening space. Sometimes the entire prospect is obscured;
then, again, we have a distinct, but
transient glimpse of the tall steeple,
like a giant's ghost; and now the dense
wreaths sweep between, as if demons
were flinging snow-drifts at each other
in mid-air. Look next into the street,
where we have an amusing parallel to
the combat of those fancied demons in
the upper regions. It is a snow battle
of school-boys. What a pretty satire on
war and military glory might be written,
in the form of a child's story, by describing the snowball fights of two rival
schools, the alternate defeats and victories of each, and the final triumph of
one party, or perhaps of neither! What
pitched battles, worthy to be chanted in
Homeric strains! What storming of for-
tresses, built all of massive snow-blocks!
What feats of individual prowess, and
embodied onsets of martial enthusiasm!
And when some well-contested and decisive victory had put a period to the

war, both armies should unite to build a lofty monument of snow upon the battle-field, and crown it with the victor's statue, hewn of the same frozen marble. In a few days or weeks thereafter, the passer-by would observe a shapeless mound upon the level common; and, unmindful of the famous victory, would ask, "How came it there? Who reared it? And what means it?" The shattered pedestal of many a battle monument has provoked these questions, when none could answer.

Turn we again to the fireside, and sit musing there, lending our ears to the wind, till perhaps it shall seem like an articulate voice, and dictate wild and airy matter for the pen. Would it might inspire me to sketch out the personification of a New England winter! And that idea, if I can seize the snow-wreathed figures that flit before my fancy, shall be the theme of the next page.

How does Winter herald his approach? By the shrieking blast of latter autumn, which is Nature's cry of lamentation, as the destroyer rushes among the shivering groves where she has lingered, and scatters the sear leaves upon the tempest. When that cry is heard, the people wrap themselves in cloaks, and shake their heads disconsolately, saying, "Winter is at hand!" Then the axe of the woodcutter echoes sharp and diligently in the forest, then the coal merchants rejoice, because each shriek of Nature in her agony adds something to the price of coal per ton, —then the peat smoke spreads its aromatic fragrance through the atmosphere. A few days more; and at eventide, the children look out of the window, and dimly perceive the flaunting of a snowy

mantle in the air. It is stern Winter's vesture. They crowd around the hearth and cling to their mother's gown, press between their father's knees, a frightened by the hollow roaring voice that bellows adown the wide flue of the chimney. It is the voice of Winter; and when parents and children hear it, the shudder and exclaim, "Winter is come Cold Winter has begun his reign already!" Now, throughout New England, each hearth becomes an altar sending up the smoke of a continual sacrifice to the immitigable deity who tyrannizes over forest, country side and town. Wrapped in his white mantle his staff a huge icicle, his beard and hair a wind-tossed snow-drift, he travels over the land in the midst of the northern blast; and woe to the homeless wanderer whom he finds upon his path There he lies stark and stiff, a human shape of ice, on the spot where Winter overtook him. On strides the tyrant over the rushing rivers and broad lakes which turn to rock beneath his footstep His dreary empire is established; and around stretches the desolation of the Pole. Yet not ungrateful be his New England children,—for Winter is our sire, though a stern and rough one,— not ungrateful even for the severities which have nourished our unyielding strength of character. And let us thank him, too, for the sleigh-rides, cheered by the music of merry bells,—for the crackling and rustling hearth, when the ruddy firelight gleams on hardy Manhood and the blooming cheek of Woman —for all the home enjoyments, and the kindred virtues which flourish in frozen soil. Not that we grieve, when after some seven months of storm and bitter frost, Spring, in the guise of

wer-crowned virgin, is seen driving
vay the hoary despot, pelting him with
olets by the handful, and strewing
een grass on the path behind him.
ften, ere he will give up his empire,
d Winter rushes fiercely back and
rls a snow-drift at the shrinking form
 Spring; yet, step by step, he is com-
lled to retreat northward, and spends
e summer months within the Arctic
rcle.

Such fantasies, intermixed among
aver toils of mind, have made the
nter's day pass pleasantly. Meanwhile,
e storm has raged without abatement,
d now, as the brief afternoon de-
ines, is tossing denser volumes to and
o about the atmosphere. On the win-
ow-sill there is a layer of snow, reach-
g half-way up the lowest pane of
ass. The garden is one unbroken bed.
long the street are two or three spots
  uncovered earth, where the gust has
hirled away the snow, heaping it else-
here to the fence-tops, or piling huge
nks against the doors of houses. A
litary passenger is seen, now striding
id-leg deep across a drift, now scud-
ng over the bare ground, while his
oak is swollen with the wind. And
ow the jingling of bells, a sluggish
und, responsive to the horse's toil-
me progress through the unbroken
ifts, announces the passage of a sleigh,
ith a boy clinging behind, and duck-
g his head to escape detection by

the driver. Next comes a sledge, laden
with wood for some unthrifty housekeeper, whom winter has surprised at
a cold hearth. But what dismal equipage
now struggles along the uneven street?
A sable hearse, bestrewn with snow, is
bearing a dead man through the storm
to his frozen bed. O how dreary is a
burial in winter, when the bosom of
Mother Earth has no warmth for her
poor child!

Evening—the early eve of December
—begins to spread its deepening veil
over the comfortless scene; the firelight
gradually brightens, and throws my
flickering shadow upon the walls and
ceiling of the chamber; but still the
storm rages and rattles against the windows. Alas! I shiver, and think it time to
be disconsolate. But, taking a farewell
glance at dead nature in her shroud,
I perceive a flock of snow-birds, skim-
ming lightsomely through the tempest,
and flitting from drift to drift as spor-
tively as swallows in the delightful prime
of summer. Whence come they? Where
do they build their nests, and seek their
food? Why, having airy wings, do they
not follow summer around the earth
instead of making themselves the play
mates of the storm, and fluttering on
the dreary verge of the winter's eve?
I know not whence they come, nor
why; yet my spirit has been cheered
by that wandering flock of snow-birds.

THE SEVEN VAGABONDS

RAMBLING on foot in the spring of
y life and the summer of the year,
 came one afternoon to a point which

gave me the choice of three directions.
Straight before me, the main road extended its dusty length to Boston; on

the left a branch went towards the sea, and would have lengthened my journey a trifle, of twenty or thirty miles; while, by the right-hand path, I might have gone over hills and lakes to Canada, visiting in my way the celebrated town of Stamford. On a level spot of grass, at the foot of the guide-post, appeared an object, which, though locomotive on a different principle, reminded me of Gulliver's portable mansion among the Brobdignags. It was a huge covered wagon, or more properly, a small house on wheels, with a door on one side and a window shaded by green blinds on the other. Two horses, munching provender out of the baskets which muzzled them, were fastened near the vehicle: a delectable sound of music proceeded from the interior; and I immediately conjectured that this was some itinerant show, halting at the confluence of the roads to intercept such idle travellers as myself. A shower had long been climbing up the western sky, and now hung so blackly over my onward path that it was a point of wisdom to seek shelter here.

"Halloo! Who stands guard here? Is the doorkeeper asleep?" cried I, approaching a ladder of two or three steps which was let down from the wagon.

The music ceased at my summons, and there appeared at the door, not the sort of figure that I had mentally assigned to the wandering showman, but a most respectable old personage, whom I was sorry to have addressed in so free a style. He wore a snuff-colored coat and smallclothes, with white-top boots, and exhibited the mild dignity of aspect and manner which may often be noticed in aged schoolmasters, and sometimes in deacons, selectmen, or other poten-

tates of that kind. A small piece of s[il]ver was my passport within his pre[m]ises, where I found only one other pe[r]son, hereafter to be described.

"This is a dull day for busines[s]" said the old gentleman, as he usher[ed] me in; "but I merely tarry here to r[e]fresh the cattle, being bound for t[he] camp-meeting at Stamford."

Perhaps the movable scene of th[is] narrative is still peregrinating New En[g]land, and may enable the reader to te[st] the accuracy of my description. T[he] spectacle—for I will not use the u[n]worthy term of puppet-show—consist[ed] of a multitude of little people assemble[d] on a miniature stage. Among them we[re] artisans of every kind, in the attitud[e] of their toil, and a group of fair ladi[es] and gay gentlemen standing ready f[or] the dance; a company of foot soldie[rs] formed a line across the stage, looki[ng] stern, grim, and terrible enough, [to] make it a pleasant consideration th[at] they were but three inches high; an[d] conspicuous above the whole was se[en] a Merry Andrew, in the pointed cap an[d] motley coat of his profession. All th[e] inhabitants of this mimic world we[re] motionless, like the figures in a pictur[e], or like that people who one mome[nt] were alive in the midst of their busine[ss] and delights, and the next were tran[s]formed to statues, preserving an etern[al] semblance of labor that was ended, an[d] pleasure that could be felt no mor[e]. Anon, however, the old gentlema[n] turned the handle of a barrel orga[n] the first note of which produced [a] most enlivening effect upon the figure[s] and awoke them all to their proper o[c]cupations and amusements. By the sel[f] same impulse the tailor plied his needl[e] the blacksmith's hammer descende[d] on the anvil, and the dancers whirled away on feathery tiptoes; the company of soldiers broke into platoons, retreated from the stage, and were succeeded by a troop of horse, who came prancing forward with such a sound of trumpets and trampling of hoofs, as might have startled Don Quixote himself; while an old toper, of inveterate ill habits, uplifted his black bottle and took off a hearty swig. Meantime the Merry Andrew began to caper and turn somersets, shaking his sides, nodding his head, and winking his eyes in as lifelike a manner as if he were ridiculing the nonsense of all human affairs, and making fun of the whole multitude beneath him. At length the old magician (for I compared the showman to Prospero, entertaining his guests with a mask of shadows) paused that I might give utterance to my wonder.

"What an admirable piece of work is this!" exclaimed I, lifting up my hands in astonishment.

Indeed, I liked the spectacle, and was tickled with the old man's gravity as he presided at it, for I had none of that foolish wisdom which reproves every occupation that is not useful in this world of vanities. If there be a faculty which I possess more perfectly than most men, it is that of throwing myself mentally into situations foreign to my own, and detecting, with a cheerful eye, the desirable circumstances of each. I could have envied the life of this gray-headed showman, spent as it had been in a course of safe and pleasurable adventure, in driving his huge vehicle sometimes through the sands of Cape Cod, and sometimes over the rough forest roads of the north and east, and halting now on the green before a vil-

lage meeting-house, and now in a paved square of the metropolis. How often must his heart have been gladdened by the delight of children, as they viewed these animated figures! or his pride indulged, by haranguing learnedly to grown men on the mechanical powers which produced such wonderful effects! or his gallantry brought into play (for this is an attribute which such grave men do not lack) by the visits of pretty maidens! And then with how fresh a feeling must he return, at intervals, to his own peculiar home!

"I would I were assured of as happy a life as his," thought I.

Though the showman's wagon might have accommodated fifteen or twenty spectators, it now contained only himself and me, and a third person at whom I threw a glance on entering. He was a neat and trim young man of two or three and twenty; his drab hat, and green frock-coat with velvet collar, were smart, though no longer new; while a pair of green spectacles, that seemed needless to his brisk little eyes, gave him something of a scholar-like and literary air. After allowing me a sufficient time to inspect the puppets, he advanced with a bow, and drew my attention to some books in a corner of the wagon. These he forthwith began to extol, with an amazing volubility of well-sounding words, and an ingenuity of praise that won him my heart, as being myself one of the most merciful of critics. Indeed, his stock required some considerable powers of commendation in the salesman; there were several ancient friends of mine, the novels of those happy days when my affections wavered between the Scottish Chiefs and Thomas Thumb; besides a few of later date, whose merits had not been acknowledged by the public. I was glad to find that dear little venerable volume, the New England Primer, looking as antique as ever, though in its thousandth new edition; a bundle of superannuated gilt picture-books made such a child of me, that, partly for the glittering covers, and partly for the fairytales within, I bought the whole; and an assortment of ballads and popular theatrical songs drew largely on my purse. To balance these expenditures, I meddled neither with sermons, nor science, nor morality, though volumes of each were there; nor with a Life of Franklin in the coarsest of paper, but so showily bound that it was emblematical of the Doctor himself, in the court dress which he refused to wear at Paris; nor with Webster's Spelling-Book, nor some of Byron's minor poems, nor half a dozen little Testaments at twenty-five cents each.

Thus far the collection might have been swept from some great bookstore, or picked up at an evening auction-room; but there was one small blue-covered pamphlet, which the pedler handed me with so peculiar an air that I purchased it immediately at his own price; and then, for the first time, the thought struck me, that I had spoken face to face with the veritable author of a printed book. The literary man now evinced a great kindness for me, and I ventured to inquire which way he was travelling.

"O," said he, "I keep company with this old gentleman here, and we are moving now towards the camp-meeting at Stamford."

He then explained to me, that for the present season he had rented a cor-

ner of the wagon as a book-store, whi as he wittily observed, was a true C culating Library, since there were f parts of the country where it had n gone its rounds. I approved of the pl exceedingly, and began to sum up wit in my mind the many uncommon feli ties in the life of a book-pedler, esp cially when his character resembled th of the individual before me. At a hi rate was to be reckoned the daily a hourly enjoyment of such interviews the present, in which he seized up the admiration of a passing strang and made him aware that a man literary taste, and even of litera achievement, was travelling the count in a showman's wagon. A more valuab yet not infrequent triumph, might won in his conversations with son elderly clergyman, long vegetating in rocky, woody, watery back settleme of New England, who, as he recruit his library from the pedler's stock sermons, would exhort him to seek college education and become the fir scholar in his class. Sweeter and proud yet would be his sensations, when, tal ing poetry while he sold spelling-book he should charm the mind, and hap touch the heart of a fair country scho mistress, herself an unhonored poetes a wearer of blue stockings which nor but himself took pains to look at. B the scene of his completest glory, wou be when the wagon had halted for t night, and his stock of books was tran ferred to some crowded bar-room. Th would he recommend to the multifa ous company, whether traveller fro the city, or teamster from the hills, neighboring squire, or the landlord hin self, or his loutish hostler, works suit to each particular taste and capacit

oving, all the while, by acute criticism
and profound remark, that the lore in
his books was even exceeded by that
his brain.

Thus happily would he traverse the
land; sometimes a herald before the
march of Mind; sometimes walking arm
arm with awful Literature; and reap-
g everywhere a harvest of real and
nsible popularity, which the secluded
bookworms, by whose toil he lived could
ever hope for.

"If ever I meddle with literature,"
thought I, fixing myself with adaman-
ne resolution, "it shall be as a trav-
ling bookseller."

Though it was still mid-afternoon, the
r had now grown dark about us, and
few drops of rain came down upon
the roof of our vehicle, pattering like
the feet of birds that had flown thither
rest. A sound of pleasant voices made
listen, and there soon appeared half-
ay up the ladder the pretty person
a young damsel, whose rosy face was
cheerful, that even amid the gloomy
ght it seemed as if the sunbeams were
eeping under her bonnet. We next saw
the dark and handsome features of a
young man, who, with easier gallantry
an might have been expected in the
art of Yankee-land, was assisting her
to the wagon. It became immediately
vident to us, when the two strangers
ood within the door, that they were
a profession kindred to those of my
mpanions; and I was delighted with
e more than hospitable, the even pa-
rnal kindness, of the old showman's
anner, as he welcomed them; while
e man of literature hastened to lead
e merry-eyed girl to a seat on the
ng bench.

"You are housed but just in time, my

young friends," said the master of the
wagon. "The sky would have been down
upon you within five minutes."

The young man's reply marked him
as a foreigner, not by any variation
from the idiom and accent of good
English, but because he spoke with more
caution and accuracy, than if perfectly
familiar with the language.

"We knew that a shower was hanging
over us," said he, "and consulted
whether it were best to enter the house
on the top of yonder hill, but seeing
your wagon in the road—"

"We agreed to come hither," interrupted the girl, with a smile, "because
we should be more at home in a wandering house like this."

I, meanwhile, with many a wild and
undetermined fantasy, was narrowly in-
specting these two doves that had flown
into our ark. The young man, tall, agile,
and athletic, wore a mass of black shining curls clustering round a dark and
vivacious countenance, which, if it had
not greater expression, was at least more
active, and attracted readier notice, than
the quiet faces of our countrymen. At
his first appearance, he had been laden
with a neat mahogany box, of about
two feet square, but very light in proportion to its size, which he had immediately unstrapped from his shoulders
and deposited on the floor of the wagon.

The girl had nearly as fair a complexion as our own beauties, and a
brighter one than most of them; the
lightness of her figure, which seemed
calculated to traverse the whole world
without weariness, suited well with the
glowing cheerfulness of her face; and
her gay attire, combining the rainbow
hues of crimson, green, and a deep
orange, was as proper to her lightsome

aspect as if she had been born in it. This gay stranger was appropriately burdened with that mirth-inspiring instrument, the fiddle, which her companion took from her hands, and shortly began the process of tuning. Neither of us—the previous company of the wagon —needed to inquire their trade; for this could be no mystery to frequenters of brigade musters, ordinations, cattle-shows, commencements, and other festal meetings in our sober land; and there is a dear friend of mine, who will smile when this page recalls to his memory a chivalrous deed performed by us in rescuing the show-box of such a couple from a mob of great double-fisted countrymen.

"Come," said I to the damsel of gay attire, "shall we visit all the wonders of the world together?"

She understood the metaphor at once; though indeed it would not much have troubled me, if she had assented to the literal meaning of my words. The mahogany box was placed in a proper position, and I peeped in through its small round magnifying window, while the girl sat by my side, and gave short descriptive sketches, as one after another the pictures were unfolded to my view. We visited together, at least our imaginations did, full many a famous city, in the streets of which I had long yearned to tread; once, I remember, we were in the harbor of Barcelona, gazing townwards; next, she bore me through the air to Sicily, and bade me look up at blazing Ætna; then we took wings to Venice, and sat in a gondola beneath the arch of the Rialto; and anon she sat me down among the thronged spectators at the coronation of Napoleon. But there was one scene, its locality she could not

tell, which charmed my attention long than all those gorgeous palaces a churches, because the fancy haunt me, that I myself, the preceding sum mer, had beheld just such a humb meeting-house, in just such a pine-su rounded nook, among our own gre mountains. All these pictures were to erably executed, though far inferior the girl's touches of description; n was it easy to comprehend, how in few sentences, and these, as I suppose in a language foreign to her, she co trived to present an airy copy of eac varied scene. When we had travelle through the vast extent of the mahogar box, I looked into my guide's face.

"Where are you going, my pret maid?" inquired I, in the words of a old song.

"Ah," said the gay damsel, "yo might as well ask where the summe wind is going. We are wanderers her and there, and everywhere. Whereve there is mirth, our merry hearts ar drawn to it. To-day, indeed, the peopl have told us of a great frolic and fe tival in these parts; so perhaps we ma be needed at what you call the camp meeting at Stamford."

Then in my happy youth, and whil her pleasant voice yet sounded in m ears, I sighed; for none but myself, thought, should have been her compan ion in a life which seemed to realiz my own wild fancies, cherished a through visionary boyhood to that hou To these two strangers, the world wa in its golden age, not that indeed it wa less dark and sad than ever, but be cause its weariness and sorrow had n community with their ethereal natur Wherever they might appear in thei pilgrimage of bliss, Youth would ech ack their gladness. care-stricken Maturity would rest a moment from its toil, and Age, tottering among the graves, would smile in withered joy for their sakes. The lonely cot, the narrow and gloomy street, the sombre shade, would catch a passing gleam like that now shining on ourselves, as these bright spirits wandered by. Blessed pair, whose happy home was throughout all the earth! I looked at my shoulders, and thought them broad enough to sustain those pictured towns and mountains; mine, too, was an elastic foot, as tireless as the wing of the bird of paradise; mine was then an untroubled heart, that would have gone singing on its delightful way.

"O maiden!" said I aloud, "why did you not come hither alone?"

While the merry girl and myself were busy with the showbox, the unceasing rain had driven another wayfarer into the wagon. He seemed pretty nearly of the old showman's age, but much smaller, leaner, and more withered than he, and less respectably clad in a patched suit of gray; withal, he had a thin, shrewd countenance, and a pair of diminutive gray eyes, which peeped rather too keenly out of their puckered sockets. This old fellow had been joking with the showman, in a manner which intimated previous acquaintance; but perceiving that the damsel and I had terminated our affairs, he drew forth a folded document, and presented it to me. As I had anticipated, it proved to be a circular, written in a very fair and legible hand, and signed by several distinguished gentlemen whom I had never heard of, stating that the bearer had encountered every variety of misfortune. and recommending him to the

notice of all charitable people. Previous disbursements had left me no more than a five-dollar bill, out of which, however, I offered to make the beggar a donation, provided he would give me change for it. The object of my beneficence looked keenly in my face, and discerned that I had none of that abominable spirit, characteristic though it be of a full-blooded Yankee, which takes pleasure in detecting every little harmless piece of knavery.

"Why, perhaps," said the ragged old mendicant, "if the bank is in good standing, I can't say but I may have enough about me to change your bill."

"It is a bill of the Suffolk Bank," said I, "and better than the specie."

As the beggar had nothing to object, he now produced a small buff-leather bag, tied up carefully with a shoestring. When this was opened, there appeared a very comfortable treasure of silver coins, of all sorts and sizes; and I even fancied that I saw, gleaming among them, the golden plumage of that rare bird in our currency, the American Eagle. In this precious heap was my bank-note deposited, the rate of exchange being considerably against me. His wants being thus relieved, the destitute man pulled out of his pocket an old pack of greasy cards, which had probably contributed to fill the buff-leather bag, in more ways than one.

"Come," said he, "I spy a rare fortune in your face, and for twenty-five cents more, I'll tell you what it is."

I never refuse to take a glimpse into futurity; so, after shuffling the cards, and when the fair damsel had cut them, I dealt a portion to the prophetic beggar. Like others of his profession, before predicting the shadowy events that were moving on to meet me, he gave proof of his preternatural science, by describing scenes through which I had already passed. Here let me have credit for a sober fact. When the old man had read a page in his book of fate, he bent his keen gray eyes on mine, and proceeded to relate, in all its minute particulars, what was then the most singular event of my life. It was one which I had no purpose to disclose, till the general unfolding of all secrets; nor would it be a much stranger instance of inscrutable knowledge, or fortunate conjecture, if the beggar were to meet me in the street to-day, and repeat, word for word, the page which I have here written. The fortune-teller, after predicting a destiny which time seems loath to make good, put up his cards, secreted his treasure-bag, and began to converse with the other occupants of the wagon.

"Well, old friend," said the showman, "you have not yet told us which way your face is turned this afternoon."

"I am taking a trip northward, this warm weather," replied the conjurer, "across the Connecticut first, and then up through Vermont, and may be into Canada before the fall. But I must stop and see the breaking up of the camp-meeting at Stamford."

I began to think that all the vagrants in New England were converging to the camp-meeting, and had made this wagon their rendezvous by the way. The showman now proposed, that, when the shower was over, they should pursue the road to Stamford together, it being sometimes the policy of these people to form a sort of league or confederacy.

"And the young lady too," observed the gallant bibliopolist, bowing to her profoundly, "and this foreign gentleman, as I understand, are on a jaunt of pleasure to the same spot. It would add incalculably to my own enjoyment and I presume to that of my colleague and his friend, if they could be prevailed upon to join our party."

This arrangement met with approbation on all hands, nor were any of those concerned more sensible of its advantages than myself, who had no title to be included in it. Having already satisfied myself as to the several modes in which the four others attained felicity, I next set my mind at work to discover what enjoyments were peculiar to the old "Straggler," as the people of the country would have termed the wandering mendicant and prophet. As he pretended to familiarity with the Devil, so I fancied that he was fitted to pursue and take delight in his way of life, by possessing some of the mental and moral characteristics, the lighter and more comic ones, of the Devil in popular stories. Among them might be reckoned a love of deception for its own sake, a shrewd eye and keen relish for human weakness and ridiculous infirmity, and the talent of petty fraud. Thus to this old man there would be pleasure even in the consciousness, so insupportable to some minds, that his whole life was a cheat upon the world, and that, so far as he was concerned with the public, his little cunning had the upper hand of its united wisdom. Every day would furnish him with a succession of minute and pungent triumphs; as when, for instance, his importunity wrung a pittance out of the heart of a miser, or when my silly good nature transferred a part of my slender purse to his plump leather bag; or when ome ostentatious gentleman should hrow a coin to the ragged beggar who vas richer than himself; or when, hough he would not always be so de-cidedly diabolical, his pretended wants hould make him a sharer in the scanty iving of real indigence. And then what in inexhaustible field of enjoyment, both as enabling him to discern so much folly and achieve such quantities of minor mischief, was opened to his sneer-ng spirit by his pretensions to prophetic knowledge.

All this was a sort of happiness which I could conceive of, though I had little sympathy with it. Perhaps, had I been hen inclined to admit it, I might have found that the roving life was more proper to him than to either of his companions; for Satan, to whom I had compared the poor man, has delighted, ever since the time of Job, in "wander-ng up and down upon the earth"; and indeed a crafty disposition, which op-erates not in deep-laid plans, but in disconnected tricks, could not have an adequate scope, unless naturally im-pelled to a continual change of scene and society. My reflections were here interrupted.

"Another visitor!" exclaimed the old showman.

The door of the wagon had been closed against the tempest, which was roaring and blustering with prodigious fury and commotion, and beating vio-ently against our shelter, as if it claimed all those homeless people for its law-ful prey, while we, caring little for the displeasure of the elements, sat com-fortably talking. There was now an at-tempt to open the door, succeeded by a voice, uttering some strange, unin-telligible gibberish, which my compan-ions mistook for Greek, and I suspected to be thieves' Latin. However, the show-man stepped forward, and gave admit-tance to a figure which made me im-agine, either that our wagon had rolled back two hundred years into past ages, or that the forest and its old inhabitants had sprung up around us by enchant-ment.

It was a red Indian, armed with his bow and arrow. His dress was a sort of cap, adorned with a single feather of some wild bird, and a frock of blue cotton, girded tight about him; on his breast, like orders of knighthood, hung a crescent and a circle, and other orna-ments of silver; while a small crucifix betokened that our Father the Pope had interposed between the Indian and the Great Spirit, whom he had worshipped in his simplicity. This son of the wilder-ness, and pilgrim of the storm, took his place silently in the midst of us. When the first surprise was over, I rightly conjectured him to be one of the Penob-scot tribe, parties of which I had often seen, in their summer excursions down our Eastern rivers. There they paddle their birch canoes among the coasting schooners, and build their wigwam be-side some roaring milldam, and drive a little trade in basket-work where their fathers hunted deer. Our new visitor was probably wandering through the country towards Boston, subsisting on the careless charity of the people, while he turned his archery to profitable ac-count by shooting at cents, which were to be the prize of his successful aim.

The Indian had not long been seated, ere our merry damsel sought to draw him into conversation. She, indeed, seemed all made up of sunshine in the month of May; for there was nothing so dark and dismal that her pleasant mind could not cast a glow over it; and the wild man, like a fir-tree in his native forest, soon began to brighten into a sort of sombre cheerfulness. At length, she inquired whether his journey had any particular end or purpose.

"I go shoot at the camp-meeting at Stamford," replied the Indian.

"And here are five more," said the girl, "all aiming at the camp-meeting too. You shall be one of us, for we travel with light hearts; and as for me, I sing merry songs, and tell merry tales; and am full of merry thoughts, and I dance merrily along the road, so that there is never any sadness among them that keep me company. But O, you would find it very dull indeed to go all the way to Stamford alone!"

My ideas of the aboriginal character led me to fear that the Indian would prefer his own solitary musings to the gay society thus offered him; on the contrary, the girl's proposal met with immediate acceptance, and seemed to animate him with a misty expectation of enjoyment. I now gave myself up to a course of thought which, whether it flowed naturally from this combination of events, or was drawn forth by a wayward fancy, caused my mind to thrill as if I were listening to deep music. I saw mankind, in this weary old age of the world, either enduring a sluggish existence amid the smoke and dust of cities, or, if they breathed a purer air, still lying down at night with no hope but to wear out to-morrow, and all the to-morrows which make up life, among the same dull scenes and in the same wretched toil that had darkened the sunshine of to-day. But there were some, full of the primeval

instinct, who preserved the freshness of youth to their latest years by the continual excitement of new objects, new pursuits, and new associates; and cared little, though their birthplace might have been here in New England, if the grave should close over them in Central Asia. Fate was summoning a parliament of these free spirits; unconscious of the impulse which directed them to a common centre, they had come hither from far and near; and last of all appeared the representative of those mighty vagrants who had chased the deer during thousands of years, and were chasing it now in the Spirit Land. Wandering down through the waste of ages, the woods had vanished around his path; his arm had lost somewhat of its strength, his foot of its fleetness, his mien of its wild regality, his heart and mind of their savage virtue and uncultured force; but here, untamable to the routine of artificial life, roving now along the dusty road, as of old over the forest leaves, here was the Indian still.

"Well," said the old showman, in the midst of my meditations, "here is an honest company of us—one, two, three, four, five, six—all going to the camp-meeting at Stamford. Now, hoping no offence, I should like to know where this young gentleman may be going?"

I started. How came I among these wanderers? The free mind that preferred its own folly to another's wisdom; the open spirit, that found companions everywhere; above all, the restless impulse, that had so often made me wretched in the midst of enjoyments; these were my claims to be of their society.

"My friends!" cried I, stepping into the centre of the wagon, "I am going with you to the camp-meeting at Stamford."

"But in what capacity?" asked the old showman, after a moment's silence. "All of us here can get our bread in some creditable way. Every honest man should have his livelihood. You, sir, as I take it, are a mere strolling gentleman."

I proceeded to inform the company, that, when Nature gave me a propensity to their way of life, she had not left me altogether destitute of qualifications for it; though I could not deny that my talent was less respectable, and might be less profitable than the meanest of theirs. My design, in short, was to imitate the story-tellers of whom Oriental travellers have told us, and become an itinerant novelist, reciting my own extemporaneous fictions to such audiences as I could collect.

"Either this," said I, "is my vocation, or I have been born in vain."

The fortune-teller, with a sly wink to the company, proposed to take me as an apprentice to one or the other of his professions, either of which, undoubtedly, would have given full scope to whatever inventive talent I might possess. The bibliopolist spoke a few words in opposition to my plan, influenced partly, I suspect, by the jealousy of authorship, and partly by an apprehension that the *viva voce* practice would become general among novelists, to the infinite detriment of the book-trade. Dreading a rejection, I solicited the interest of the merry damsel.

"Mirth," cried I, most aptly appropriating the words of L'Allegro, "to thee I sue! Mirth, admit me of thy crew!"

"Let us indulge the poor youth," said Mirth, with a kindness which made me love her dearly, though I was no such coxcomb as to misinterpret her motives. "I have espied much promise in him. True, a shadow sometimes flits across his brow, but the sunshine is sure to follow in a moment. He is never guilty of a sad thought, but a merry one is twin born with it. We will take him with us; and you shall see that he will set us all a-laughing before we reach the camp-meeting at Stamford."

Her voice silenced the scruples of the rest, and gained me admittance into the league; according to the terms of which, without community of goods or profits, we were to lend each other all the aid, and avert all the harm, that might be in our power. This affair settled, a marvellous jollity entered into the whole tribe of us, manifesting itself characteristically in each individual. The old showman, sitting down to his barrel-organ, stirred up the souls of the pygmy people with one of the quickest tunes in the music-book; tailors, blacksmiths, gentlemen, and ladies, all seemed to share in the spirit of the occasion; and the Merry Andrew played his part more facetiously than ever, nodding and winking particularly at me. The young foreigner flourished his fiddle-bow with a master's hand, and gave an inspiring echo to the showman's melody. The bookish man and the merry damsel started up simultaneously to dance, the former enacting the double shuffle in a style which everybody must have witnessed, ere Election week was blotted out of time; while the girl, setting her arms akimbo with both hands at her slim waist, displayed such light rapidity of foot, and harmony of varying attitude and motion, that I could not conceive how she ever was to stop; imagining, at the moment, that Nature had made her, as the old showman had made his puppets, for no earthly purpose but to dance jigs. The Indian bellowed forth a succession of most hideous outcries, somewhat affrighting us, till we interpreted them as the war song, with which, in imitation of his ancestors, he was prefacing the assault on Stamford. The conjurer, meanwhile, sat demurely in a corner, extracting a sly enjoyment from the whole scene, and, like the facetious Merry Andrew, directing his queer glance particularly at me.

As for myself, with great exhilaration of fancy, I began to arrange and color the incidents of a tale, wherewith I proposed to amuse an audience that very evening; for I saw my associates were a little ashamed of me, and that no time was to be lost in obtaining a public acknowledgment of my abilities.

"Come, fellow-laborers," at last said the old showman, whom we had elected President; "the shower is over, and we must be doing our duty by these poor souls at Stamford."

"We'll come among them in procession, with music and dancing," cried the merry damsel.

Accordingly—for it must be understood that our pilgrimage was to be performed on foot—we sallied joyously out of the wagon, each of us, even the old gentleman in his white-top boots, giving a great skip as we came down the ladder. Above our heads there was such a glory of sunshine and splendor of clouds, and such brightness of verdure below, that, as I modestly remarked at the time, Nature seemed to have washed her face, and put on the best of her jewelry and a fresh green gown, in honor of our confederation. Casting our eyes northward, we beheld a horseman approaching leisurely, and splashing through the little puddles on the Stamford road. Onward he came, sticking up in his saddle with rigid perpendicularity, a tall, thin figure in rusty black, whom the showman and the conjurer shortly recognized to be, what his aspect sufficiently indicated, a travelling preacher of great fame among the Methodists. What puzzled us was the fact, that his face appeared turned from, instead of to, the camp-meeting at Stamford. However, as this new votary of the wandering life drew near the little green space, where the guide-post and our wagon were situated, my six fellow-vagabonds and myself rushed forward and surrounded him, crying out with united voices:

"What news, what news, from the camp-meeting at Stamford?"

The missionary looked down, in surprise, at as singular a knot of people as could have been selected from all his heterogeneous auditors. Indeed, considering that we might all be classified under the general head of Vagabond, there was great diversity of character among the grave old showman, the sly, prophetic beggar, the fiddling foreigner and his merry damsel, the smart bibliopolist, the sombre Indian, and myself, the itinerant novelist, a slender youth of eighteen. I even fancied that a smile was endeavoring to disturb the iron gravity of the preacher's mouth.

"Good people," answered he, "the camp-meeting is broke up."

So saying, the Methodist minister switched his steed, and rode westward. Our union being thus nullified, by the removal of its object, we were sundered at once to the four winds of Heaven. The fortune-teller, giving a nod to all, and a peculiar wink to me, departed on his northern tour, chuckling within himself as he took the Stamford road. The old showman and his literary co-adjutor were already tackling their horses to the wagon, with a design to peregrinate southwest along the sea-coast. The foreigner and the merry damsel took their laughing leave, and pursued the eastern road, which I had that day trodden; as they passed away, the young man played a lively strain, and the girl's happy spirit broke into a dance: and thus dissolving, as it were, into sunbeams and gay music, that pleasant pair departed from my view. Finally, with a pensive shadow thrown across my mind, yet emulous of the light philosophy of my late companions, I joined myself to the Penobscot Indian and set forth towards the distant city.

THE WHITE OLD MAID

THE moonbeams came through two deep and narrow windows, and showed a spacious chamber richly furnished in an antique fashion. From one lattice, the shadow of the diamond panes was thrown upon the floor; the ghostly light, through the other, slept upon a bed, falling between the heavy silken curtains, and illuminating the face of a young man. But, how quietly the slumberer lay! how pale his features! and how like a shroud the sheet was wound about his frame! Yes; it was a corpse, in its burial clothes.

Suddenly the fixed features seemed to move with dark emotion. Strange fantasy! It was but the shadow of the fringed curtain, waving betwixt the dead face and the moonlight, as the door of the chamber opened, and a girl stole softly to the bedside. Was there delusion in the moonbeams, or did her gesture and her eye betray a gleam of triumph, as she bent over the pale corpse—pale as itself—and pressed her living lips to the cold ones of the dead? As she drew back from that long kiss, her features writhed as if a proud heart were fighting with its anguish. Again it seemed that the features of the corpse had moved, responsive to her own. Still an illusion! The silken curtain had waved a second time betwixt the dead face and the moonlight, as another fair young girl unclosed the door and glided, ghost-like, to the bedside. There the two maidens stood, both beautiful, with the pale beauty of the dead between them. But she who had first entered was proud and stately; and the other, a soft and fragile thing.

"Away!" cried the lofty one. "Thou hadst him living! The dead is mine!"

"Thine!" returned the other, shuddering. "Well hast thou spoken! The dead is thine!"

The proud girl started, and stared into her face. with a ghastly look. But a wild and mournful expression passed across the features of the gentle one; and, weak and helpless, she sank down on the bed, her head pillowed beside that of the corpse, and her hair mingling with his dark locks. A creature of hope and joy, the first draught of sorrow had bewildered her.

"Edith!" cried her rival.

Edith groaned, as with a sudden compression of the heart; and removing her cheek from the dead youth's pillow, she stood upright, fearfully encountering the eyes of the lofty girl.

"Wilt thou betray me?" said the latter, calmly.

"Till the dead bid me speak, I will be silent," answered Edith. "Leave us alone together! Go, and live many years, and then return, and tell me of thy life. He, too, will be here! Then, if thou tellest of sufferings more than death, we will both forgive thee."

"And what shall be the token?" asked the proud girl, as if her heart acknowledged a meaning in these wild words.

"This lock of hair," said Edith, lifting one of the dark, clustering curls that lay heavily on the dead man's brow.

The two maidens joined their hands over the bosom of the corpse, and appointed a day and hour, far, far in time to come, for their next meeting in that chamber. The statelier girl gave one deep look at the motionless countenance, and departed,—yet turned again and trembled, ere she closed the door, almost believing that her dead lover frowned upon her. And Edith, too! Was not her white form fading into the moonlight? Scorning her own weakness, she went forth, and perceived that a negro slave was waiting in the passage, with a wax light, which he held between her face and his own, and regarded her, as she thought, with an ugly expression of merriment. Lifting his torch on high, the slave lighted her down the staircase, and undid the portal of the mansion. The young clergyman of the town had just ascended the steps, and bowing to the lady, passed in without a word.

Years, many years rolled on; the world seemed new again, so much older was it grown since the night when those pale girls had clasped their hands across the bosom of the corpse. In the interval, a lonely woman had passed from youth to extreme age, and was known by all the town as the "Old Maid in the Winding Sheet." A taint of insanity had affected her whole life, but so quiet, sad, and gentle, so utterly free from violence, that she was suffered to pursue her harmless fantasies, unmolested by the world, with whose business or pleasures she had naught to do. She dwelt alone, and never came into the daylight, except to follow funerals. Whenever a corpse was borne along the street, in sunshine, rain, or snow, whether a pompous train, of the rich and proud, thronged after it, or few and humble were the mourners, behind them came the lonely woman, in a long, white garment, which the people called her shroud. She took no place among the kindred or the friends, but stood at the door to hear the funeral prayer, and walked in the rear of the procession, as one whose earthly charge it was to haunt the house of mourning, and be the shadow of affliction, and see that the dead were duly buried. So long had this been her custom, that the inhabitants of the town deemed her a part of every funeral, as much as the coffin-pall or the very corpse itself, and augured ill of the sinner's destiny, unless the "Old Maid in the Winding Sheet" came gliding, like a ghost, behind. Once, it is said, she affrighted a bridal party with her pale presence, appearing suddenly in the illuminated hall, just as the priest was uniting a false maid to a wealthy man, before her lover had been dead a year. Evil was the omen to that marriage! Sometimes she stole forth by moonlight, and visited the graves of venerable Integrity, and wedded Love, and virgin Innocence, and every spot where the ashes of a kind and faithful heart were mouldering. Over the hillocks of those favored dead would she stretch out her arms, with a gesture, as if she were scattering seeds; and many believed that she brought them from the garden of Paradise; for the graves, which she had visited, were green beneath the snow, and covered with sweet flowers from April to November. Her blessing was better than a holy verse upon the tombstone. Thus wore away her long, sad, peaceful, and fantastic life, till few were so old as she, and the people of later generations wondered how the dead had ever been buried, or mourners had endured their grief, without the "Old Maid in the Winding Sheet."

Still, years went on, and still she followed funerals, and was not yet summoned to her own festival of death. One afternoon the great street of the town was all alive with business and bustle, though the sun now gilded only the upper half of the church-spire, having left the housetops and loftiest trees in shadow. The scene was cheerful and animated, in spite of the sombre shade between the high brick buildings. Here were pompous merchants, in white wigs and laced velvet; the bronzed faces of sea captains; the foreign garb and air of Spanish creoles; and the disdainful port of natives of Old England; all contrasted with the rough aspect of one or two back settlers, negotiating sales of timber, from forests where axe had never sounded. Sometimes a lady passed, swelling roundly forth in an embroidered petticoat, balancing her steps in highheeled shoes, and courtesying, with lofty grace, to the punctilious obeisances of the gentlemen. The life of the town seemed to have its very centre not far from an old mansion, that stood somewhat back from the pavement, surrounded by neglected grass, with a strange air of loneliness, rather deepened than dispelled by the throng so near it. Its site would have been suitably occupied by a magnificent Exchange, or a brick block, lettered all over with various signs; or the large house itself might have made a noble tavern, with the "King's Arms" swinging before it, and guests in every chamber, instead of the present solitude. But, owing to some dispute about the right of inheritance, the mansion had been long without a tenant, decaying from year to year, and throwing the stately gloom of its shadow over the busiest part of the town. Such was the scene, and such the time, when a figure, unlike any that have been described, was observed at a distance down the street.

"I espy a strange sail, yonder," remarked a Liverpool captain; "that woman in the long, white garment!"

The sailor seemed much struck by the object, as were several others, who at the same moment, caught a glimpse of the figure that had attracted his notice. Almost immediately, the various topics of conversation gave place to speculations, in an undertone, on this unwonted occurrence.

"Can there be a funeral so late this afternoon?" inquired some.

They looked for the signs of death at every door,—the sexton, the hearse, the assemblage of black-clad relatives, —all that makes up the woful pomp of funerals. They raised their eyes, also, to the sun-gilt spire of the church, and wondered that no clang proceeded from its bell, which had always tolled till now, when this figure appeared in the light of day. But none had heard that a corpse was to be borne to its home that afternoon, nor was there any token of a funeral, except the apparition of the "Old Maid in the Winding Sheet."

"What may this portend?" asked each man of his neighbor.

All smiled as they put the question, yet with a certain trouble in their eyes, as if pestilence, or some other wide calamity, were prognosticated by the untimely intrusion among the living of one whose presence had always been associated with death and woe. What a comet is to the earth was that sad woman to the town. Still she moved on, while the hum of surprise was hushed at her approach, and the proud and the humble stood aside that her white garment might not wave against them. It was a long, loose robe, of spotless purity. Its wearer appeared very old, pale, emaciated, and feeble, yet glided onward, without the unsteady pace of extreme age. At one point of her course, a little rosy boy burst forth from a door, and ran, with open arms,

towards the ghostly woman, seeming to expect a kiss from her bloodless lips. She made a slight pause, fixing her eye upon him with an expression of no earthly sweetness, so that the child shivered and stood awestruck, rather than affrighted, while the Old Maid passed on. Perhaps her garment might have been polluted even by an infant's touch; perhaps her kiss would have been death to the sweet boy within a year.

"She is but a shadow," whispered the superstitious. "The child put forth his arms and could not grasp her robe!"

The wonder was increased when the Old Maid passed beneath the porch of the deserted mansion, ascended the moss-covered steps, lifted the iron knocker, and gave three raps. The people could only conjecture that some old remembrance, troubling her bewildered brain, had impelled the poor woman hither to visit the friends of her youth; all gone from their home, long since and forever, unless their ghosts still haunted it,—fit company for the "Old Maid in the Winding Sheet." An elderly man approached the steps, and reverently uncovering his gray locks, essayed to explain the matter.

"None, Madam," said he, "have dwelt in this house these fifteen years agone, —no, not since the death of old Colonel Fenwicke, whose funeral you may remember to have followed. His heirs, being ill agreed among themselves, have let the mansion house go to ruin."

The Old Maid looked slowly round, with a slight gesture of one hand, and a finger of the other upon her lip, appearing more shadow-like than ever, in the obscurity of the porch. But again she lifted the hammer, and gave, this time, a single rap. Could it be that a footstep was now heard coming down the staircase of the old mansion, which all conceived to have been so long untenanted? Slowly, feebly, yet heavily, like the pace of an aged and infirm person, the step approached, more distinct on every downward stair, till it reached the portal. The bar fell on the inside; the door was opened. One upward glance towards the church-spire, whence the sunshine had just faded, was the last that the people saw of the "Old Maid in the Winding Sheet."

"Who undid the door?" asked many. This question, owing to the depth of shadow beneath the porch, no one could satisfactorily answer. Two or three aged men, while protesting against an inference, which might be drawn, affirmed that the person within was a negro, and bore a singular resemblance to old Cæsar, formerly a slave in the house, but freed by death some thirty years before.

"Her summons has waked up a servant of the old family," said one, half seriously.

"Let us wait here," replied another. "More guests will knock at the door, anon. But, the gate of the graveyard should be thrown open!"

Twilight had overspread the town before the crowd began to separate, or the comments on this incident were exhausted. One after another was wending his way homeward, when a coach —no common spectacle in those days— drove slowly into the street. It was an old-fashioned equipage, hanging close to the ground, with arms on the panels, a footman behind, and a grave, corpulent coachman seated high in front,— the whole giving an idea of solemn state

and dignity. There was something awful in the heavy rumbling of the wheels. The coach rolled down the street, till, coming to the gateway of the deserted mansion, it drew up, and the footman sprang to the ground.

"Whose grand coach is this?" asked a very inquisitive body.

The footman made no reply, but ascended the steps of the old house, gave three raps with the iron hammer, and returned to open the coach-door. An old man, possessed of the heraldic lore so common in that day, examined the shield of arms on the panel.

"Azure, a lion's head erased, between three flower-de-luces," said he; then whispered the name of the family to whom these bearings belonged. The last inheritor of its honors was recently dead, after a long residence amid the splendor of the British court, where his birth and wealth had given him no mean station. "He left no child," continued the herald, "and these arms, being in a lozenge, betoken that the coach appertains to his widow."

Further disclosures, perhaps, might have been made had not the speaker suddenly been struck dumb by the stern eye of an ancient lady, who thrust forth her head from the coach, preparing to descend. As she emerged the people saw that her dress was magnificent, and her figure dignified, in spite of age and infirmity,—a stately ruin, but with a look, at once, of pride and wretchedness. Her strong and rigid features had an awe about them unlike that of the white Old Maid, but as of something evil. She passed up the steps, leaning on a gold-headed cane; the door swung open as she ascended,—and the light of a torch glittered on the embroidery of her dress, and gleamed on the pillars of the porch. After a momentary pause,—a glance backwards, and then a desperate effort,—she went in. The decipherer of the coat-of-arms had ventured up the lowest step, and shrinking back immediately, pale and tremulous, affirmed that the torch was held by the very image of old Cæsar.

"But such a hideous grin," added he. "was never seen on the face of mortal man, black or white! It will haunt me till my dying day."

Meantime, the coach had wheeled round, with a prodigious clatter on the pavement, and rumbled up the street disappearing in the twilight, while the ear still tracked its course. Scarcely was it gone when the people began to question whether the coach and attendants, the ancient lady, the spectre of old Cæsar, and the Old Maid herself, were not all a strangely combined delusion, with some dark purport in its mystery. The whole town was astir, so that, instead of dispersing, the crowd continually increased, and stood gazing up at the windows of the mansion, now silvered by the brightening moon. The elders, glad to indulge the narrative propensity of age, told of the long-faded splendor of the family, the entertainments they had given, and the guests, the greatest of the land, and even titled and noble ones from abroad, who had passed beneath that portal. These graphic reminiscences seemed to call up the ghosts of those to whom they referred. So strong was the impression, on some of the more imaginative hearers, that two or three were seized with trembling fits, at one and the same moment, protesting that they had distinctly heard three other raps

of the iron knocker.

"Impossible!" exclaimed others. "See! The moon shines beneath the porch, and shows every part of it, except in the narrow shade of that pillar. There is no one there!"

"Did not the door open?" whispered one of these fanciful persons.

"Didst thou see it, too?" said his companion, in a startled tone.

But the general sentiment was opposed to the idea, that a third visitant had made application at the door of the deserted house. A few, however, adhered to this new marvel, and even declared that a red gleam, like that of a torch, had shone through the great front window, as if the negro were lighting a guest up the staircase. This, too, was pronounced a mere fantasy. But, at once, the whole multitude started, and each man beheld his own terror painted in the faces of all the rest.

"What an awful thing is this!" cried they.

A shriek, too fearfully distinct for doubt, had been heard within the mansion, breaking forth suddenly. and succeeded by a deep stillness, as if a heart had burst in giving it utterance. The people knew not whether to fly from the very sight of the house, or to rush trembling in, and search out the strange mystery. Amid their confusion and affright, they were somewhat reassured by the appearance of their clergyman, a venerable patriarch, and equally a saint, who had taught them and their fathers the way to Heaven for more than the space of an ordinary lifetime. He was a reverend figure, with long, white hair upon his shoulders, a white beard upon his breast, and a back so bent over his staff, that he seemed to be looking downward, continually, as if to choose a proper grave for his weary frame. It was some time before the good old man, being deaf, and of impaired intellect, could be made to comprehend such portions of the affair as were comprehensible at all. But, when possessed of the facts, his energies assumed unexpected vigor.

"Verily," said the old gentleman, "it will be fitting that I enter the mansion house of the worthy Colonel Fenwicke, lest any harm should have befallen that true Christian woman, whom ye call the 'Old Maid in the Winding Sheet.'"

Behold, then, the venerable clergyman ascending the steps of the mansion, with a torch-bearer behind him. It was the elderly man who had spoken to the Old Maid, and the same who had afterwards explained the shield of arms, and recognized the features of the negro. Like their predecessors, they gave three raps, with the iron hammer.

"Old Cæsar cometh not," observed the priest. "Well I wot he no longer doth service in this mansion."

"Assuredly, then, it was something worse, in old Cæsar's likeness!" said the other adventurer.

"Be it as God wills," answered the clergyman. "See! my strength, though it be much decayed, hath sufficed to open this heavy door. Let us enter, and pass up the staircase."

Here occurred a singular exemplification of the dreamy state of a very old man's mind. As they ascended the wide flight of stairs, the aged clergyman appeared to move with caution, occasionally standing aside, and oftener bending his head, as it were in salutation, thus practising all the gestures of one who makes his way through a throng. Reaching the head of the staircase, he looked around, with sad and solemn benignity, laid aside his staff, bared his hoary locks, and was evidently on the point of commencing a prayer.

"Reverend Sir," said his attendant, who conceived this a very suitable prelude to their further search, "would it not be well that the people join with us in prayer?"

"Welladay!" cried the old clergyman, staring strangely around him. "Art thou here with me, and none other? Verily, past times were present to me, and I deemed that I was to make a funeral prayer, as many a time heretofore, from the head of this staircase. Of a truth, I saw the shades of many that are gone. Yea, I have prayed at their burials, one after another, and the 'Old Maid in the Winding Sheet' hath seen them to their graves!"

Being now more thoroughly awake to their present purpose, he took his staff, and struck forcibly on the floor, till there came an echo from each deserted chamber, but no menial, to answer their summons. They therefore walked along the passage, and again paused, opposite to the great front window, through which was seen the crowd, in the shadow and partial moonlight of the street beneath. On their right hand was the open door of a chamber, and a closed one on their left. The clergyman pointed his cane to the carved oak panel of the latter.

"Within that chamber," observed he, "a whole lifetime since, did I sit by the death-bed of a goodly young man, who being now at the last gasp—"

Apparently there was some powerful excitement in the ideas which had now flashed across his mind. He snatched the torch from his companion's hand, and threw open the door with such sudden violence, that the flame was extinguished, leaving them no other light than the moonbeams, which fell through two windows into the spacious chamber. It was sufficient to discover all that could be known. In a high-backed, oaken arm-chair, upright, with her hands clasped across her breast, and her head thrown back, sat the "Old Maid in the Winding Sheet." The stately dame had fallen on her knees, with her forehead on the holy knees of the Old Maid, one hand upon the floor, and the other pressed convulsively against her heart.

It clutched a lock of hair, once sable, now discolored with a greenish mould. As the priest and layman advanced into the chamber, the Old Maid's features assumed such a semblance of shifting expression, that they trusted to hear the whole mystery explained, by a single word. But it was only the shadow of a tattered curtain, waving betwixt the dead face and the moonlight.

"Both dead!" said the venerable man. "Then who shall divulge the secret? Methinks it glimmers to and fro in my mind, like the light and shadow across the Old Maid's face. And now 't is gone!"

PETER GOLDTHWAITE'S TREASURE

"AND so, Peter, you won't even consider of the business?" said Mr. John Brown, buttoning his surtout over the snug rotundity of his person, and drawing on his gloves. "You positively refuse to let me have this crazy old house, and the land under and adjoining, at the price named?"

"Neither at that, nor treble the sum," responded the gaunt, grizzled, and threadbare Peter Goldthwaite. "The fact is, Mr. Brown, you must find another site for your brick block, and be content to leave my estate with the present owner. Next summer, I intend to put a splendid new mansion over the cellar of the old house."

"Pho, Peter!" cried Mr. Brown, as he opened the kitchen door; "content yourself with building castles in the air, where house-lots are cheaper than on earth, to say nothing of the cost of bricks and mortar. Such foundations are solid enough for your edifices; while this underneath us is just the thing for mine; and so we may both be suited. What say you, again?"

"Precisely what I said before, Mr. Brown," answered Peter Goldthwaite. "And, as for castles in the air, mine may not be as magnificent as that sort of architecture, but perhaps as substantial, Mr. Brown, as the very respectable brick block with dry-goods stores, tailors' shops, and banking-rooms on the lower floor, and lawyers' offices in the second story, which you are so anxious to substitute."

"And the cost, Peter, eh?" said Mr. Brown, as he withdrew, in something of a pet. "That, I suppose, will be provided for, offhand, by drawing a check on Bubble Bank!"

John Brown and Peter Goldthwaite had been jointly known to the commercial world between twenty and thirty years before, under the firm of Goldthwaite & Brown; which copartnership, however, was speedily dissolved, by the natural incongruity of its constituent parts. Since that event, John Brown, with exactly the qualities of a thousand other John Browns, and by just such plodding methods as they used, had prospered wonderfully, and become one of the wealthiest John Browns on earth. Peter Goldthwaite, on the contrary, after innumerable schemes, which ought to have collected all the coin and paper currency of the country into his coffers, was as needy a gentleman as ever wore a patch upon his elbow. The contract between him and his former partner may be briefly marked: for Brown never reckoned upon luck, yet always had it; while Peter made luck the main condition of his projects, and always missed it. While the means held out, his speculations had been magnificent, but were chiefly confined, of late years, to such small business as adventures in the lottery. Once, he had gone on a gold-gathering expedition, somewhere to the South, and ingeniously contrived to empty his pockets more thoroughly than ever; while others, doubtless, were filling theirs with native bullion by the handful. More recently, he had expended a legacy of a thousand or two of dollars in purchasing Mexican scrip, and thereby became the proprietor of a province; which, however, so far as Peter could find out, was situated where he might have had an empire for the same money,—in the clouds. From a search after this valuable real estate, Peter re-

turned so gaunt and threadbare, that, on reaching New England, the scarecrows in the cornfields beckoned to him as he passed by. "They did but flutter in the wind," quoth Peter Goldthwaite. No, Peter, they beckoned, for the scarecrows knew their brother!

At the period of our story, his whole visible income would not have paid the tax of the old mansion in which we find him. It was one of those rusty, moss-grown, many-peaked wooden houses, which are scattered about the streets of our elder towns, with a beetle-browed second story projecting over the foundation, as if it frowned at the novelty around it. This old paternal edifice, needy as he was, and though being centrally situated on the principal street of the town, it would have brought him a handsome sum, the sagacious Peter had his own reasons for never parting with, either by auction or private sale. There seemed, indeed, to be a fatality that connected him with his birthplace; for, often as he had stood on the verge of ruin, and standing there even now, he had not yet taken the step beyond it, which would have compelled him to surrender the house to his creditors. So here he dwelt with bad luck till good should come.

Here, then, in his kitchen, the only room where a spark of fire took off the chill of a November evening, poor Peter Goldthwaite had just been visited by his rich old partner. At the close of their interview, Peter, with rather a mortified look, glanced downwards at his dress, parts of which appeared as ancient as the days of Goldthwaite & Brown. His upper garment was a mixed surtout, wofully faded, and patched with newer stuff on each elbow; beneath this, he wore a threadbare black coat, some of the silk buttons of which had been replaced with others of a different pattern; and lastly, though he lacked not a pair of gray pantaloons, they were very shabby ones, and had been partially turned brown, by the frequent toasting of Peter's shins before a scanty fire. Peter's person was in keeping with his goodly apparel. Gray-headed, hollow-eyed, pale-cheeked, and lean-bodied, he was the perfect picture of a man who had fed on windy schemes and empty hopes, till he could neither live on such unwholesome trash, nor stomach more substantial food. But withal, this Peter Goldthwaite, crack-brained simpleton as, perhaps, he was, might have cut a very brilliant figure in the world, had he employed his imagination in the airy business of poetry, instead of making it a demon of mischief in mercantile pursuits. After all, he was no bad fellow, but as harmless as a child, and as honest and honorable, and as much of the gentleman which nature meant him for, as an irregular life and depressed circumstances will permit any man to be.

As Peter stood on the uneven bricks of his hearth, looking round at the disconsolate old kitchen, his eyes began to kindle with the illumination of an enthusiasm that never long deserted him. He raised his hand, clinched it, and smote it energetically against the smoky panel over the fireplace.

"The time is come!" said he. "With such a treasure at command, it were folly to be a poor man any longer. To-morrow morning I will begin with the garret, nor desist till I have torn the house down!"

Deep in the chimney-corner, like a witch in a dark cavern, sat a little old woman, mending one of the two pairs of stockings wherewith Peter Goldthwaite kept his toes from being frostbitten. As the feet were ragged past all darning, she had cut pieces out of a cast-off flannel petticoat, to make new soles. Tabitha Porter was an old maid, upwards of sixty years of age, fifty-five of which she had sat in that same chimney-corner, such being the length of time since Peter's grandfather had taken her from the almshouse. She had no friend but Peter, nor Peter any friend but Tabitha; so long as Peter might have a shelter for his own head, Tabitha would know where to shelter hers; or, being homeless elsewhere, she would take her master by the hand, and bring him to her native home, the almshouse. Should it ever be necessary, she loved him well enough to feed him with her last morsel and clothe him with her under petticoat. But Tabitha was a queer old woman, and, though never infected with Peter's flightiness, had become so accustomed to his freaks and follies, that she viewed them all as matters of course. Hearing him threaten to tear the house down, she looked quietly up from her work.

"Best leave the kitchen till the last, Mr. Peter," said she.

"The sooner we have it all down the better," said Peter Goldthwaite. "I am tired to death of living in this cold, dark, windy, smoky, creaking, groaning, dismal old house. I shall feel like a younger man, when we get into my splendid brick mansion, as, please Heaven, we shall, by this time next autumn. You shall have a room on the sunny side, old Tabby, finished and furnished as best may suit your own notions."

"I should like it pretty much such a room as this kitchen," answered Tabitha. "It will never be like home to me, till the chimney-corner gets as black with smoke as this; and that won't be these hundred years. How much do you mean to lay out on the house, Mr. Peter?"

"What is that to the purpose?" exclaimed Peter, loftily. "Did not my great-granduncle, Peter Goldthwaite, who died seventy years ago, and whose namesake I am, leave treasure enough to build twenty such?"

"I can't say but he did, Mr. Peter," said Tabitha, threading her needle.

Tabitha well understood that Peter had reference to an immense hoard of the precious metals, which was said to exist somewhere in the cellar or walls, or under the floors, or in some concealed closet, or other out-of-the way nook of the house. This wealth, according to tradition, had been accumulated by a former Peter Goldthwaite, whose character seems to have borne a remarkable similitude to that of the Peter of our story. Like him he was a wild projector, seeking to heap up gold by the bushel and the cart-load, instead of scraping it together, coin by coin. Like Peter the second, too, his projects had almost invariably failed, and, but for the magnificent success of the final one, would have left him with hardly a coat and pair of breeches to his gaunt and grizzled person. Reports were various, as to the nature of his fortunate speculation; one intimating that the ancient Peter had made the gold by alchemy; another, that he had conjured it out of people's pockets by the black art; and a third, still more unaccountable, that the Devil had given him free access to the old provincial treasury. It was affirmed, however, that some secret impediment had debarred him from the enjoyment of his riches, and that he had a motive for concealing them from his heir, or, at any rate, had died without disclosing the place of deposit. The present Peter's father had faith enough in the story to cause the cellar to be dug over. Peter himself chose to consider the legend as an indisputable truth, and, amid his many troubles, had this one consolation, that, should all other resources fail, he might build up his fortunes by tearing his house down. Yet, unless he felt a lurking distrust of the golden tale, it is difficult to account for his permitting the paternal roof to stand so long, since he had never yet seen the moment when his predecessor's treasure would not have found plenty of room in his own strong box. But now was the crisis. Should he delay the search a little longer, the house would pass from the lineal heir, and with it the vast heap of gold, to remain in its burial-place till the ruin of the aged walls should discover it to strangers of a future generation.

"Yes!" cried Peter Goldthwaite again; "to-morrow I will set about it."

The deeper he looked at the matter, the more certain of success grew Peter. His spirits were naturally so elastic, that even now, in the blasted autumn of his age, he could often compete with the spring-time gayety of other people. Enlivened by his brightening prospects, he began to caper about the kitchen like a hob-goblin, with the queerest antics of his lean limbs, and gesticulations of his starved features Nay, in the exuberance of his feelings, he seized both of

Tabitha's hands, and danced the old lady across the floor, till the oddity of her rheumatic motions set him into a roar of laughter, which was echoed back from the rooms and chambers, as if Peter Goldthwaite were laughing in every one. Finally, he bounded upward, almost out of sight, into the smoke that clouded the roof of the kitchen, and alighting safely on the floor again, endeavored to resume his customary gravity.

"To-morrow, at sunrise," he repeated, taking his lamp, to retire to bed, "I'll see whether this treasure be hid in the wall of the garret."

"And, as we're out of wood, Mr. Peter," said Tabitha, puffing and panting with her late gymnastics, "as fast as you tear the house down, I'll make a fire with the pieces."

Gorgeous, that night, were the dreams of Peter Goldthwaite! At one time, he was turning a ponderous key in an iron door, not unlike the door of a sepulchre, but which, being opened, disclosed a vault, heaped up with gold coin, as plentifully as golden corn in a granary. There were chased goblets, also, and tureens, salvers, dinner-dishes, and dish-covers, of gold, or silver gilt, besides chains and other jewels, incalculably rich, though tarnished with the damps of the vault; for, of all the wealth that was irrevocably lost to man, whether buried in the earth or sunken in the sea, Peter Goldthwaite had found it in this one treasure-place. Anon, he had returned to the old house, as poor as ever, and was received at the door, by the gaunt and grizzled figure of a man, whom he might have mistaken for himself, only that his garments were of a much elder fashion. But the house, with-

out losing its former aspect, had been changed into a palace of the precious metals. The floors, walls, and ceilings were of burnished silver; the doors, the window-frames, the cornices, the balustrades, and the steps of the staircase, of pure gold; and silver, with gold bottoms, were the chairs, and gold, standing on silver legs, the high chests of drawers, and silver the bedsteads, with blankets of woven gold, and sheets of silver tissue. The house had evidently been transmuted by a single touch; for it retained all the marks that Peter remembered, but in gold or silver, instead of wood; and the initials of his name, which, when a boy, he had cut in the wooden doorpost, remained as deep in the pillar of gold. A happy man would have been Peter Goldthwaite, except for a certain ocular deception, which, whenever he glanced backward, caused the house to darken from its glittering magnificence into the sordid gloom of yesterday.

Up, betimes, rose Peter, seized an axe, hammer, and saw, which he had placed by his bedside, and hied him to the garret. It was but scantily lighted up, as yet, by the frosty fragments of a sunbeam, which began to glimmer through the almost opaque bull's eyes of the window. A moralizer might find abundant themes for his speculative and impracticable wisdom in a garret. There is the limbo of departed fashions, aged trifles of a day, and whatever was valuable only to one generation of men, and which passed to the garret when that generation passed to the grave, not for safe keeping, but to be out of the way. Peter saw piles of yellow and musty account-books, in parchment covers, wherein creditors, long dead and buried, had written the names of dead and buried debtors, in ink now so faded, that their moss-grown tombstones were more legible. He found old moth-eaten garments all in rags and tatters, or Peter would have put them on. Here was a naked and rusty sword, not a sword of service, but a gentleman's small French rapier, which had never left its scabbard till it lost it. Here were canes of twenty different sorts, but no gold-headed ones, and shoe-buckles of various pattern and material, but not silver, nor set with precious stones. Here was a large box full of shoes, with high heels and peaked toes. Here, on a shelf, were a multitude of phials, half filled with old apothecaries' stuff, which, when the other half had done its business on Peter's ancestors, had been brought hither from the death chamber. Here—not to give a longer inventory of articles that will never be put up at auction—was the fragment of a full-length looking-glass, which, by the dust and dimness of its surface, made the picture of these old things look older than the reality. When Peter, not knowing that there was a mirror there, caught the faint traces of his own figure, he partly imagined that the former Peter Goldthwaite had come back either to assist or impede his search for the hidden wealth. And at that moment a strange notion glimmered through his brain, that he was the identical Peter who had concealed the gold, and ought to know whereabout it lay. This, however, he had unaccountably forgotten.

"Well, Mr. Peter!" cried Tabitha, on the garret stairs. "Have you torn the house down enough to heat the tea-kettle?"

"Not yet, old Tabby," answered Peter; "but that's soon done—as you shall see."

With the word in his mouth, he uplifted the axe, and laid about him so vigorously, that the dust flew, the boards crashed, and, in a twinkling, the old woman had an apronful of broken rubbish.

"We shall get our winter's wood cheap," quoth Tabitha.

The good work being thus commenced, Peter beat down all before him, smiting and hewing at the joists and timbers, unclinching spike-nails, ripping and tearing away boards, with a tremendous racket, from morning till night. He took care, however, to leave the outside shell of the house untouched, so that the neighbors might not suspect what was going on.

Never, in any of his vagaries, though each had made him happy while it lasted, had Peter been happier than now. Perhaps, after all, there was something in Peter Goldthwaite's turn of mind, which brought him an inward recompense for all the external evil that it caused. If he were poor, ill clad, even hungry, and exposed, as it were, to be utterly annihilated by a precipice of impending ruin, yet only his body remained in these miserable circumstances, while his aspiring soul enjoyed the sunshine of a bright futurity. It was his nature to be always young, and the tendency of his mode of life to keep him so. Gray hairs were nothing, no, nor wrinkles, nor infirmity; he might look old, indeed, and be somewhat disagreeably connected with a gaunt old figure, much the worse for wear; but the true, the essential Peter, was a young man of high hopes, just entering on the world. At the kindling of each new fire, his burnt-out youth rose afresh from the old embers and ashes. It rose exulting now. Having lived thus long—not too long, but just to the right age—a susceptible bachelor, with warm and tender dreams, he resolved, so soon as the hidden gold should flash to light, to go a-wooing, and win the love of the fairest maid in town. What heart could resist him? Happy Peter Goldthwaite!

Every evening—as Peter had long absented himself from his former lounging-places, at insurance-offices, newsrooms, and bookstores, and as the honor of his company was seldom requested in private circles—he and Tabitha used to sit down sociably by the kitchen hearth. This was always heaped plentifully with the rubbish of his day's labor. As the foundation of the fire, there would be a goodly-sized backlog of red oak, which, after being sheltered from rain or damp above a century, still hissed with the heat, and distilled streams of water from each end, as if the tree had been cut down within a week or two. Next, there were large sticks, sound, black, and heavy, which had lost the principle of decay, and were indestructible except by fire, wherein they glowed like red-hot bars of iron. On this solid basis, Tabitha would rear a lighter structure composed of the splinters of door-panels, ornamented mouldings, and such quick combustibles, which caught like straw, and threw a brilliant blaze high up the spacious flue, making its sooty sides visible almost to the chimney-top. Meantime, the gleam of the old kitchen would be chased out of the cobwebbed corners, and away from the dusky crossbeams overhead, and driven nobody could tell whither, while Peter smiled like a gladsome man, and Tabitha seemed a picture of comfortable age. All this, of course, was but an emblem of the bright fortune which the destruction of the house would shed upon its occupants.

While the dry pine was flaming and crackling, like an irregular discharge of fairy musketry, Peter sat looking and listening, in a pleasant state of excitement. But, when the brief blaze and uproar were succeeded by the dark-red glow, the substantial heat, and the deep singing sound, which were to last throughout the evening, his humor became talkative. One night, the hundredth time, he teased Tabitha to tell him something new about his great-granduncle.

"You have been sitting in that chimney-corner fifty-five years, old Tabby, and must have heard many a tradition about him," said Peter. "Did not you tell me, that, when you first came to the house, there was an old woman sitting where you sit now, who had been housekeeper to the famous Peter Goldthwaite?"

"So there was, Mr. Peter," answered Tabitha; "and she was near about a hundred years old. She used to say, that she and old Peter Goldthwaite had often spent a sociable evening by the kitchen fire,—pretty much as you and I am doing now, Mr. Peter."

"The old fellow must have resembled me in more points than one," said Peter, complacently, "or he never would have grown so rich. But, methinks, he might have invested the money better than he did—no interest!—nothing but good security!—and the house to be torn down to come at it! What made him hide it so snug, Tabby?"

"Because he could not spend it," said

Tabitha; "for, as often as he went to unlock the chest, the Old Scratch came behind and caught his arm. The money, they say, was paid Peter out of his purse; and he wanted Peter to give him a deed of this house and land, which Peter swore he would not do."

"Just as I swore to John Brown, my old partner," remarked Peter. "But this is all nonsense, Tabby! I don't believe the story."

"Well, it may not be just the truth," said Tabitha; "for some folks say, that Peter did make over the house to the Old Scratch; and that's the reason it has always been so unlucky to them that lived in it. And as soon as Peter had given him the deed, the chest flew open, and Peter caught up a handful of the gold. But, lo and behold!—there was nothing in his fist but a parcel of old rags."

"Hold your tongue, you silly old Tabby!" cried Peter in great wrath. "They were as good golden guineas as ever bore the effigies of the king of England. It seems as if I could recollect the whole circumstance, and how I, or old Peter, or whoever it was, thrust in my hand, or his hand, and drew it out, all of a blaze with gold. Old rags, indeed!"

But it was not an old woman's legend that would discourage Peter Goldthwaite. All night long, he slept among pleasant dreams, and awoke at daylight with a joyous throb of the heart, which few are fortunate enough to feel beyond their boyhood. Day after day, he labored hard, without wasting a moment, except at meal-times, when Tabitha summoned him to the pork and cabbage, or such other sustenance as she had picked up, or Providence had sent them. Being a truly pious man, Peter never failed to ask a blessing; if the food were none of the best, then so much the more earnestly, as it was more needed;—nor to return thanks, if the dinner had been scanty, yet for the good appetite, which was better than a sick stomach at a feast. Then did he hurry back to his toil, and, in a moment, was lost to sight in a cloud of dust from the old walls, though sufficiently perceptible to the ear, by the clatter which he raised in the midst of it. How enviable is the consciousness of being usefully employed! Nothing troubled Peter; or nothing but those phantoms of the mind, which seem like vague recollections, yet have also the aspect of presentiments. He often paused, with his axe uplifted in the air, and said to himself,—"Peter Goldthwaite, did you never strike this blow before?"—or, "Peter, what need of tearing the whole house down? Think, a little while, and you will remember where the gold is hidden." Days and weeks passed on, however, without any remarkable discovery. Sometimes, indeed, a lean gray rat peeped forth at the lean, gray man, wondering what devil had got into the old house, which had always been so peaceable till now. And, occasionally, Peter sympathized with the sorrows of a female mouse, who had brought five or six pretty, little, soft, and delicate young ones into the world, just in time to see them crushed by its ruin. But, as yet, no treasure!

By this time, Peter, being as determined as Fate, and as diligent as Time, had made an end with the uppermost regions, and got down to the second story, where he was busy in one of the front chambers. It had formerly been the state bed-chamber, and was honored by tradition as the sleeping apartment of Governor Dudley, and many other eminent guests. The furniture was gone. There were remnants of faded and tattered paper-hangings, but larger spaces of bare wall, ornamented with charcoal-sketches, chiefly of people's heads in profile. These being specimens of Peter's youthful genius, it went more to his heart to obliterate them, than if they had been pictures on a church wall by Michael Angelo. One sketch, however, and that the best one, affected him differently. It represented a ragged man, partly supporting himself on a spade, and bending his lean body over a hole in the earth, with one hand extended to grasp something that he had found. But, close behind him, with a fiendish laugh on his features, appeared a figure with horns, a tufted tail, and a cloven hoof.

"Avaunt, Satan!" cried Peter. "The man shall have his gold!"

Uplifting his axe, he hit the horned gentleman such a blow on the head, as not only demolished him, but the treasure-seeker also, and caused the whole scene to vanish like magic. Moreover, his axe broke quite through the plaster and laths, and discovered a cavity.

"Mercy on us, Mr. Peter, are you quarrelling with the Old Scratch?" said Tabitha, who was seeking some fuel to put under the dinner-pot.

Without answering the old woman, Peter broke down a further space of the wall, and laid open a small closet or cupboard, on one side of the fireplace, about breast high from the ground. It contained nothing but a brass lamp, covered with verdigris, and a dusty piece of parchment. While Peter inspected the latter, Tabitha seized the lamp, and began to rub it with her apron.

"There is no use in rubbing it, Tabitha," said Peter. "It is not Aladdin's lamp, though I take it to be a token of as much luck. Look here, Tabby!"

Tabitha took the parchment, and held it close to her nose, which was saddled with a pair of iron-bound spectacles. But no sooner had she begun to puzzle over it, than she burst into a chuckling laugh, holding both her hands against her sides.

"You can't make a fool of the old woman!" cried she. "This is your own handwriting, Mr. Peter! the same as in the letter you sent me from Mexico."

"There is certainly a considerable resemblance," said Peter, again examining the parchment. "But you know yourself, Tabby, that this closet must have been plastered up before you came to the house, or I came into the world. No, this is old Peter Goldthwaite's writing; these columns of pounds, shillings, and pence are his figures denoting the amount of the treasure; and this at the bottom, is doubtless a reference to the place of concealment. But the ink has either faded or peeled off, so that it is absolutely illegible. What a pity!"

"Well, this lamp is as good as new. That's some comfort," said Tabitha.

"A lamp!" thought Peter. "That indicates light on my researches."

For the present, Peter felt more inclined to ponder on this discovery than to resume his labors. After Tabitha had gone down stairs, he stood poring over the parchment, at one of the front windows, which was so obscured with dust that the sun could barely throw an uncertain shadow of the casement across the floor. Peter forced it open, and looked out upon the great street of the town, while the sun looked in at his old house. The air, though mild, and even warm, thrilled Peter as with a dash of water.

It was the first day of the January thaw. The snow lay deep upon the housetops, but was rapidly dissolving into millions of water-drops, which sparkled downwards through the sunshine, with the noise of a summer shower beneath the eaves. Along the street, the trodden snow was as hard and solid as a pavement of white marble, and had not yet grown moist in the spring-like temperature. But, when Peter thrust forth his head, he saw that the inhabitants, if not the town, were already thawed out by this warm day, after two or three weeks of winter weather. It gladdened him,—a gladness with a sigh breathing through it,—to see the stream of ladies, gliding along the slippery sidewalks, with their red cheeks set off by quilted hoods, boas, and sable capes, like roses amidst a new kind of foliage. The sleigh-bells jingled to and fro continually, sometimes announcing the arrival of a sleigh from Vermont, laden with the frozen bodies of porkers, or sheep, and perhaps a deer or two; sometimes of a regular market man, with chickens, geese, and turkeys, comprising the whole colony of a barnyard; and sometimes of a farmer and his dame, who had come to town partly for the ride, partly to go a-shopping, and partly for the sale of some eggs and butter. This couple rode in an old-fashioned square sleigh, which had served them twenty winters, and stood twenty summers in the sun beside their door. Now, a gentleman and lady skimmed the snow, in an elegant car, shaped somewhat like a cockle-shell. Now, a stage-sleigh, with its cloth curtains thrust aside to admit the sun, dashed rapidly down the street, whirling in and out among the vehicles that obstructed its passage. Now came, round a corner, the similitude of Noah's ark, on runners, being an immense open sleigh, with seats for fifty people, and drawn by a dozen horses. This spacious receptacle was populous with merry maids and merry bachelors, merry girls and boys, and merry old folks, all alive with fun, and grinning to the full width of their mouths. They kept up a buzz of babbling voices and low laughter, and sometimes burst into a deep, joyous shout, which the spectators answered with three cheers, while a gang of roguish boys let drive their snowballs right among the pleasure party. The sleigh passed on, and, when concealed by a bend of the street, was still audible by a distant cry of merriment.

Never had Peter beheld a livelier scene than was constituted by all these accessories: the bright sun; the flashing water-drops; the gleaming snow; the cheerful multitude; the variety of rapid vehicles; and the jingle-jangle of merry bells, which made the heart dance to their music. Nothing dismal was to be seen, except that peaked piece of antiquity, Peter Goldthwaite's house, which might well look sad externally, since such a terrible consumption was preying on its insides. And Peter's gaunt figure, half visible in the projecting second story, was worthy of his house.

"Peter! How goes it, friend Peter?" cried a voice across the street, as Peter was drawing in his head. "Look out here, Peter!"

Peter looked, and saw his old partner, Mr. John Brown, on the opposite sidewalk, portly and comfortable, with his furred cloak thrown open, disclosing a handsome surtout beneath. His voice had directed the attention of the whole town to Peter Goldthwaite's window, and to the dusty scarecrow which appeared at it.

"I say, Peter," cried Mr. Brown again, "what the devil are you about there, that I hear such a racket, whenever I pass by? You are repairing the old house, I suppose,—making a new one of it,—eh?"

"To late for that, I am afraid, Mr. Brown," replied Peter. "If I make it new, it will be new inside and out, from the cellar upwards."

"Had not you better let me take the job?" said Mr. Brown, significantly.

"Not yet," answered Peter, hastily shutting the window; for, ever since he had been in search of the treasure, he hated to have people stare at him.

As he drew back, ashamed of his outward poverty, yet proud of the secret wealth within his grasp, a haughty smile shone out on Peter's visage, with precisely the effect of the dim sunbeams in the squalid chamber. He endeavored to assume such a mien as his ancestor had probably worn, when he gloried in the building of a strong house for a home to many generations of his posterity. But the chamber was very dark to his snow-dazzled eyes, and very dismal, too, in contrast with the living scene that he had just looked upon. His brief glimpse into the street had given him a forcible impression of the manner in which the world kept itself cheerful and prosperous, by social pleasures and

an intercourse of business, while he, in seclusion, was pursuing an object that might possibly be a phantasm, by a method which most people would call madness. It is one great advantage of a gregarious mode of life, that each person rectifies his mind by other minds, and squares his conduct to that of his neighbors, so as seldom to be lost in eccentricity. Peter Goldthwaite had exposed himself to this influence, by merely looking out of the window. For a while, he doubted whether there were any hidden chest of gold, and, in that case, whether it was so exceedingly wise to tear the house down, only to be convinced of its non-existence.

But this was momentary. Peter, the Destroyer, resumed the task which fate had assigned him, nor faltered again, till it was accomplished. In the course of his search, he met with many things that are usually found in the ruins of an old house, and also with some that are not. What seemed most to the purpose, was a rusty key, which had been thrust into a chink of the wall, with a wooden label appended to the handle, bearing the initials, P. G. Another singular discovery was that of a bottle of wine, walled up in an old oven. A tradition ran in the family, that Peter's grandfather, a jovial officer in the old French war, had set aside many dozens of the precious liquor, for the benefit of topers then unborn. Peter needed no cordial to sustain his hopes, and therefore kept the wine to gladden his success. Many halfpence did he pick up, that had been lost through the cracks of the floor, and some few Spanish coins, and the half of a broken sixpence, which had doubtless been a love token. There was likewise a silver coronation medal of George the Third. But, old Peter Goldthwaite's strong box fled from one dark corner to another, or otherwise eluded the second Peter's clutches, till, should he seek much farther, he must burrow into the earth.

We will not follow him in his triumphant progress, step by step. Suffice it, that Peter worked like a steam-engine, and finished, in that one winter, the job, which all the former inhabitants of the house, with the time and the elements to aid them, had only half done in a century. Except the kitchen, every room and chamber was now gutted. The house was nothing but a shell,—the apparition of a house,—as unreal as the painted edifices of a theatre. It was like the perfect rind of a great cheese, in which a mouse had dwelt and nibbled, till it was a cheese no more. And Peter was the mouse.

What Peter had torn down, Tabitha had burned up: for she wisely considered that, without a house, they should need no wood to warm it; and therefore economy was nonsense. Thus the whole house might be said to have dissolved in smoke, and flown up among the clouds, through the great black flue of the kitchen chimney. It was an admirable parallel to the feat of the man who jumped down his own throat.

On the night between the last day of winter and the first of spring, every chink and cranny had been ransacked, except within the precincts of the kitchen. This fated evening was an ugly one. A snow-storm had set in some hours before, and was still driven and tossed about the atmosphere by a real hurricane, which fought against the house, as if the prince of the air, in person, were putting the final stroke to Peter's labors. The framework being so much weakened, and the inward props removed, it would have been no marvel, if, in some stronger wrestle of the blast, the rotten walls of the edifice, and all the peaked roofs, had come crashing down upon the owner's head. He, however, was careless of the peril, but as wild and restless as the night itself, or as the flame that quivered up the chimney, at each roar of the tempestuous wind.

"The wine, Tabitha!" he cried. "My grandfather's rich old wine! We will drink it now!"

Tabitha arose from her smoke-blackened bench in the chimney-corner, and placed the bottle before Peter, close beside the old brass lamp, which had likewise been the prize of his researches. Peter held it before his eyes, and looking through the liquid medium, beheld the kitchen illuminated with a golden glory, which also enveloped Tabitha, and gilded her silver hair, and converted her mean garments into robes of queenly splendor. It reminded him of his golden dream.

"Mr. Peter," remarked Tabitha, "must the wine be drunk before the money is found?"

"The money *is* found!" exclaimed Peter, with a sort of fierceness. "The chest is within my reach. I will not sleep, till I have turned this key in the rusty lock. But, first of all, let us drink!"

There being no corkscrew in the house, he smote the neck of the bottle with old Peter Goldthwaite's rusty key, and decapitated the sealed cork at a single blow. He then filled two little china teacups, which Tabitha had brought from the cupboard. So clear and brilliant was this aged wine, that it shone within the cups, and rendered the sprig of scarlet flowers, at the bottom of each, more distinctly visible than when there had been no wine there. Its rich and delicate perfume wasted itself round the kitchen.

"Drink, Tabitha!" cried Peter. "Blessings on the honest old fellow who set aside this good liquor for you and me! And here's to Peter Goldthwaite's memory!"

"And good cause have we to remember him," quoth Tabitha, as she drank.

How many years, and through what changes of fortune, and various calamity, had that bottle hoarded up its effervescent joy, to be quaffed at last by two such boon companions! A portion of the happiness of a former age had been kept for them, and was now set free, in a crowd of rejoicing visions, to sport amid the storm and desolation of the present time. Until they have finished the bottle, we must turn our eyes elsewhere.

It so chanced, that, on this stormy night, Mr. John Brown found himself ill at ease, in his wire-cushioned armchair, by the glowing grate of anthracite, which heated his handsome parlor. He was naturally a good sort of a man, and kind and pitiful, whenever the misfortunes of others happened to reach his heart through the padded vest of his own prosperity. This evening, he had thought much about his old partner, Peter Goldthwaite, his strange vagaries, and continual ill luck, the poverty of his dwelling at Mr. Brown's last visit, and Peter's crazed and haggard aspect, when he had talked with him at the window.

"Poor fellow!" thought Mr. John Brown. "Poor, crack-brained Peter Goldthwaite! For old acquaintance' sake I ought to have taken care that he was comfortable, this rough winter."

These feelings grew so powerful, that in spite of the inclement weather, he resolved to visit Peter Goldthwaite immediately. The strength of the impulse was really singular. Every shriek of the blast seemed a summons, or would have seemed so, had Mr. Brown been accustomed to hear the echoes of his own fancy in the wind. Much amazed at such active benevolence, he huddled himself in his cloak, muffled his throat and ears in comforters and handkerchiefs, and thus fortified bade defiance to the tempest. But the powers of the air had rather the best of the battle. Mr. Brown was just weathering the corner, by Peter Goldthwaite's house, when the hurricane caught him off his feet, tossed him face downward into a snow-bank, and proceeded to bury his protuberant part beneath fresh drifts. There seemed little hope of his reappearance, earlier than the next thaw. At the same moment his hat was snatched away, and whirled aloft into some far distant region, whence no tidings have as yet returned.

Nevertheless, Mr. Brown contrived to burrow a passage through the snow-drift, and, with his bare head bent against the storm, floundered onward to Peter's door. There was such a creaking, and groaning, and rattling, and such an ominous shaking throughout the crazy edifice, that the loudest rap would have been inaudible to those within. He therefore entered, without ceremony, and groped his way to the kitchen.

His intrusion, even there, was unnoticed. Peter and Tabitha stood with heir backs to the door, stooping over large chest, which, apparently, they ad just dragged from a cavity, or concealed closet, on the left side of the himney. By the lamp in the old oman's hand, Mr. Brown saw that the hest was barred and clamped with iron, trengthened with iron plates, and tudded with iron nails, so as to be a t receptacle in which the wealth of ne century might be hoarded up for he wants of another. Peter Goldhwaite was inserting a key into the ock.

"O Tabitha!" cried he, with tremuous rapture, "how shall I endure the ffulgence? The gold!—the bright, bright old! Methinks I can remember my last lance at it, just as the iron-plated lid ell down. And ever since, being seventy ears, it has been blazing in secret, and athering its splendor against this glorius moment! It will flash upon us like he noonday sun!"

"Then shade your eyes, Mr. Peter!" aid Tabitha, with somewhat less paience than usual. "But, for mercy's ake, do turn the key!"

And, with a strong effort of both ands, Peter did force the rusty key hrough the intricacies of the rusty lock. Ir. Brown, in the mean time, had rawn near, and thrust his eager visage etween those of the other two, at the nstant that Peter threw up the lid. No udden blaze illuminated the kitchen.

"What's here?" exclaimed Tabitha, djusting her spectacles, and holding he lamp over the open chest. "Old 'eter Goldthwaite's hoard of old rags."

"Pretty much so, Tabby," said Mr. Irown, lifting a handful of the treasure. O what a ghost of dead and buried vealth had Peter Goldthwaite raised,

to scare himself out of his scanty wits withal! Here was the semblance of an incalculable sum, enough to purchase the whole town, and build every street anew, but which, vast as it was, no sane man would have given a solid sixpence for. What then, in sober earnest, were the delusive treasures of the chest? Why, here were old provincial bills of credit, and treasury-notes, and bills of land banks, and all other bubbles of the sort, from the first issue, above a century and a half ago, down nearly to the Revolution. Bills of a thousand pounds were intermixed with parchment pennies, and worth no more than they.

"And this, then, is old Peter Goldthwaite's treasure!" said John Brown. "Your namesake, Peter, was something like yourself; and, when the provincial currency had depreciated fifty or seventy-five per cent, he bought it up, in expectation of a rise. I have heard my grandfather say, that old Peter gave his father a mortgage of this very house and land, to raise cash for his silly project. But the currency kept sinking, till nobody would take it as a gift; and there was old Peter Goldthwaite, like Peter the second, with thousands in his strong box, and hardly a coat to his back. He went mad upon the strength of it. But, never mind, Peter! It is just the sort of capital for building castles in the air."

"The house will be down about our ears!" cried Tabitha, as the wind shook it with increasing violence.

"Let it fall!" said Peter, folding his arms, as he seated himself upon the chest.

"No. no, my old friend Peter," said John Brown. "I have house-room for you and Tabby, and a safe vault for the chest of treasure. To-morrow we will try to come to an agreement about the sale of this old house. Real estate is well up, and I could afford you a pretty handsome price."

"And I," observed Peter Goldthwaite, with reviving spirits, "have a plan for laying out the cash to great advantage."

"Why, as to that," muttered John Brown to himself, "we must apply to the next court for a guardian to take care of the solid cash; and if Peter insists upon speculating, he may do it to his heart's content, with old PETER GOLDTHWAITE'S TREASURE."

TWICE-TOLD TALES

—

THE SNOW-IMAGE

A CHILDISH MIRACLE

ONE afternoon of a cold winter's day, when the sun shone forth with chilly brightness, after a long storm, two children asked leave of their mother to run out and play in the new-fallen snow. The elder child was a little girl, whom, because she was of a tender and modest disposition, and was thought to be very beautiful, her parents, and other people who were familiar with her, used to call Violet. But her brother was known by the style and title of Peony, on account of the ruddiness of his broad and round little phiz, which made everybody think of sunshine and great scarlet flowers. The father of these two children, a certain Mr. Lindsey, it is important to say, was an excellent but exceedingly matter-of-fact sort of man, a dealer in hardware, and was sturdily accustomed to take what is called the common-sense view of all matters that came under his consideration. With a heart about as tender as other people's, he had a head as hard and impenetrable, and therefore, perhaps, as empty, as one of the iron pots which it was part of his business to sell. The mother's character, on the other hand, had a strain of poetry in it, a trait of unworldly beauty,—a delicate and dewy flower, as it were, that had survived out of her imaginative youth, and still kept itself alive amid the dusty realities of matrimony and motherhood.

So, Violet and Peony, as I began with saying, besought their mother to let them run out and play in the new snow; for, though it had looked so dreary and dismal, drifting downward out of the gray sky, it had a very cheerful aspect, now that the sun was shining on it. The children dwelt in a city, and had no wider play-place than a little garden before the house, divided by a white fence from the street, and with a pear-tree and two or three plum-trees overshadowing it, and some rose-bushes just in front of the parlor windows. The trees and shrubs, however, were now leafless, and their twigs were enveloped in the light snow, which thus made a kind of wintry foliage, with here and there a pendent icicle for the fruit.

"Yes, Violet,—yes, my little Peony," said their kind mother, "you may go out and play in the new snow."

Accordingly, the good lady bundled up her darlings in woolen jackets and wadded sacks, and put comforters round their necks, and a pair of striped gaiters on each little pair of legs, and worsted mittens on their hands, and gave them a kiss apiece, by way of a spell to keep away Jack Frost. Forth sallied the two children, with a hop-skip-and-jump, that carried them at once into the very heart of a huge snow-drift, whence Violet emerged like a snow-bunting, while little Peony floundered out with his round face in full bloom. Then what a merry time had they! To look at them, frolicking in the wintry garden, you would have thought that the dark and pitiless storm had been sent for no other purpose but to provide a new plaything for Violet and Peony, and that they themselves had been created, as the snow-birds were, to take delight only in the tempest, and in the white mantle which it spread over the earth.

At last, when they had frosted one another all over with handfuls of snow, Violet, after laughing heartily at little Peony's figure, was struck with a new idea.

"You look exactly like a snow-image, Peony," said she, "if your cheeks were not so red. And that puts me in mind! Let us make an image out of snow,—an image of a little girl,—and it shall be our sister, and shall run about and play with us all winter long. Won't it be nice?"

"O yes!" cried Peony, as plainly as he could speak, for he was but a little boy. "That will be nice! And mamma shall see it!"

"Yes," answered Violet, "mamma shall see the new little girl. But she must not make her come into the warm parlor; for, you know, our little snow-sister will not love the warmth."

And forthwith the children began this great business of making a snow-image that should run about; while their mother, who was sitting at the window and overheard some of their talk, could not help smiling at the gravity with which they set about it. They really seemed to imagine that there would be no difficulty whatever in creating a live little girl out of the snow. And, to say the truth, if miracles are ever to be

wrought, it will be by putting our hand to the work in precisely such a simple and undoubting frame of mind as that in which Violet and Peony now undertook to perform one, without so much as knowing that it was a miracle. So thought the mother; and thought, likewise, that the new snow, just fallen from Heaven, would be excellent material to make new beings of, if it were not so very cold. She gazed at the children a moment longer, delighting to watch their little figures,—the girl, tall for her age, graceful and agile, and so delicately colored that she looked like a cheerful thought more than a physical reality,—while Peony expanded in breadth rather than height, and rolled along on his short and sturdy legs, as substantial as an elephant, though not quite so big. Then the mother resumed her work. What it was I forget; but she was either trimming a silken bonnet for Violet, or darning a pair of stockings for little Peony's short legs. Again, however, and again, and yet other agains, she could not help turning her head to the window, to see how the children got on with their snow-image.

Indeed, it was an exceedingly pleasant sight, those bright little souls at their tasks! Moreover, it was really wonderful to observe how knowingly and skilfully they managed the matter. Violet assumed the chief direction, and told Peony what to do, while, with her own delicate fingers, she shaped out all the nicer parts of the snow-figure. It seemed, in fact, not so much to be made by the children, as to grow up under their hands, while they were playing and prattling about it. Their mother was quite surprised at this; and the longer she looked, the more and more surprised she grew.

"What remarkable children mine are!" thought she, smiling with a mother's pride; and smiling at herself, too, for being so proud of them. "What other children could have made anything so like a little girl's figure out of snow, at the first trial? Well;—but now I must finish Peony's new frock, for his grandfather is coming to-morrow, and I want the little fellow to look handsome."

So she took up the frock, and was soon as busily at work again with her needle as the two children with their snow-image. But still, as the needle travelled hither and thither through the seams of the dress, the mother made her toil light and happy by listening to the airy voices of Violet and Peony. They kept talking to one another all the time, their tongues being quite as active as their feet and hands. Except at intervals, she could not distinctly hear what was said, but had merely a sweet impression that they were in a most loving mood, and were enjoying themselves highly, and that the business of making the snow-image went prosperously on. Now and then, however, when Violet and Peony happened to raise their voices, the words were as audible as if they had been spoken in the very parlor where the mother sat. O, how delightfully those words echoed in her heart, even though they meant nothing so very wise or wonderful, after all!

But you must know a mother listens with her heart, much more than with her ears; and thus she is often delighted with the trills of celestial music, when other people can hear nothing of the kind.

"Peony, Peony!" cried Violet to her brother, who had gone to another part of the garden. "bring me some of that fresh snow, Peony from the very farthest corner, where we have not been trampling. I want it to shape our little snow-sister's bosom with. You know that part must be quite pure, just as it came out of the sky!"

"Here it is, Violet!" answered Peony, in his bluff tone,—but a very sweet tone, too,—as he came floundering through the half-trodden drifts. "Here is the snow for her little bosom. O Violet, how beau-ti-ful she begins to look!"

"Yes," said Violet, thoughtfully and quietly, "our snow-sister does look very lovely. I did not quite know, Peony, that we could make such a sweet little girl as this!"

The mother, as she listened, thought how fit and delightful an incident it would be, if fairies, or, still better, if angel-children were to come from Paradise, and play invisibly with her own darlings, and help them to make their snow-image, giving it the features of celestial babyhood! Violet and Peony would not be aware of their immortal playmates,—only they would see that the image grew very beautiful while they worked at it, and would think that they themselves had done it all.

"My little girl and boy deserve such playmates, if mortal children ever did!" said the mother to herself; and then she smiled again at her own motherly pride.

Nevertheless, the idea seized upon her imagination; and, ever and anon, she took a glimpse out of the window, half dreaming that she might see the golden-haired children of Paradise sporting with her own golden-haired Violet and bright-cheeked Peony.

Now, for a few moments, there was

a busy and earnest, but indistinct hum of the two children's voices, as Violet and Peony wrought together with one happy consent. Violet still seemed to be the guiding spirit, while Peony acted rather as a laborer, and brought her the snow from far and near. And yet the little urchin evidently had a proper understanding of the matter, too!

"Peony, Peony!" cried Violet; for her brother was again at the other side of the garden. "Bring me those light wreaths of snow that have rested on the lower branches of the pear-tree. You can clamber on the snow-drift, Peony, and reach them easily. I must have them to make some ringlets for our snow-sister's head!"

"Here they are, Violet!" answered the little boy. "Take care you do not break them. Well done! Well done! How pretty!"

"Does she not look sweetly?" said Violet, with a very satisfied tone; "and now we must have some little shining bits of ice, to make the brightness of her eyes. She is not finished yet. Mamma will see how very beautiful she is; but papa will say, 'Tush! nonsense!— come in out of the cold!'"

"Let us call mamma to look out," said Peony; and then he shouted lustily, "Mamma! mamma!! mamma!!! Look out, and see what a nice 'ittle girl we are making!"

The mother put down her work for an instant, and looked out of the window. But it so happened that the sun—for this was one of the shortest days of the whole year—had sunken so nearly to the edge of the world that his setting shine came obliquely into the lady's eyes. So she was dazzled, you must understand, and could not very distinctly observe what was in the garden. Still, however, through all that bright, blinding dazzle of the sun and the new snow, she beheld a small white figure in the garden, that seemed to have a wonderful deal of human likeness about it. And she saw Violet and Peony,—indeed, she looked more at them than at the image, —she saw the two children still at work; Peony bringing fresh snow, and Violet applying it to the figure as scientifically as a sculptor adds clay to his model. Indistinctly as she discerned the snow-child, the mother thought to herself that never before was there a snow-figure so cunningly made, nor ever such a dear little girl and boy to make it.

"They do everything better than other children," said she, very complacently. "No wonder they make better snow-images!"

She sat down again to her work, and made as much haste with it as possible, because twilight would soon come, and Peony's frock was not yet finished, and grandfather was expected, by railroad, pretty early in the morning. Faster and faster, therefore, went her flying fingers. The children, likewise, kept busily at work in the garden, and still the mother listened, whenever she could catch a word. She was amused to observe how their little imaginations had got mixed up with what they were doing, and were carried away by it. They seemed positively to think that the snow-child would run about and play with them.

"What a nice playmate she will be for us, all winter long!" said Violet. "I hope papa will not be afraid of her giving us a cold! Shan't you love her dearly, Peony?"

"O yes!" cried Peony. "And I will hug her, and she shall sit down close by me, and drink some of my warm milk!"

"O no, Peony!" answered Violet, with grave wisdom. "That will not do at all. Warm milk will not be wholesome for our little snow-sister. Little snow-people, like her, eat nothing but icicles. No, no, Peony; we must not give her anything warm to drink!"

There was a minute or two of silence; for Peony, whose short legs were never weary, had gone on a pilgrimage again to the other side of the garden. All of a sudden, Violet cried out, loudly and joyfully,—

"Look here, Peony! Come quickly! A light has been shining on her cheek out of that rose-colored cloud! and the color does not go away! Is not that beautiful!"

"Yes; it is beau-ti-ful," answered Peony, pronouncing the three syllables with deliberate accuracy. "O Violet, only look at her hair! It is all like gold!"

"O, certainly," said Violet, with tranquillity, as if it were very much a matter of course. "That color, you know, comes from the golden clouds, that we see up there in the sky. She is almost finished now. But her lips must be made very red,—redder than her cheeks. Perhaps, Peony, it will make them red, if we both kiss them!"

Accordingly, the mother heard two smart little smacks, as if both her children were kissing the snow-image on its frozen mouth. But as this did not seem to make the lips quite red enough, Violet next proposed that the snow-child should be invited to kiss Peony's scarlet cheek.

"Come, 'ittle snow-sister, kiss me!" cried Peony.

"There! she has kissed you," added Violet, "and now her lips are very red. And she blushed a little, too!"

"O, what a cold kiss!" cried Peony.

Just then, there came a breeze of the pure west wind, sweeping through the garden and rattling the parlor windows. It sounded so wintry cold, that the mother was about to tap on the window-pane with her thimbled finger, to summon the two children in, when they both cried out to her with one voice. The tone was not a tone of surprise, although they were evidently a good deal excited; it appeared rather as if they were very much rejoiced at some event that had now happened, but which they had been looking for, and had reckoned upon all along.

"Mamma! mamma! We have finished our little snow-sister, and she is running about the garden with us!"

"What imaginative little beings my children are!" thought the mother, putting the last few stitches into Peony's frock. "And it is strange, too, that they make me almost as much a child as they themselves are! I can hardly help believing, now, that the snow-image has really come to life!"

"Dear mamma!" cried Violet, "pray look out, and see what a sweet playmate we have!"

The mother, being thus entreated, could no longer delay to look forth from the window. The sun was now gone out of the sky, leaving, however, a rich inheritance of his brightness among those purple and golden clouds which make the sunsets of winter so magnificent. But there was not the slightest gleam or dazzle, either on the window or on the snow; so that the good lady could look all over the garden, and see everything and everybody in it. And what do you think she saw there? Violet and Peony, of course, her own two darling children. Ah, but whom or what did she besides? Why, if you will believe me, there was a small figure of a girl, dressed all in white, with rose-tinged cheeks and ringlets of golden hue, playing about the garden with the two children! A stranger though she was, the child seemed to be on as familiar terms with Violet and Peony, and they with her, as if all the three had been playmates during the whole of their little lives. The mother thought to herself that it must certainly be the daughter of one of the neighbors, and that, seeing Violet and Peony in the garden, the child had run across the street to play with them. So this kind lady went to the door, intending to invite the little runaway into her comfortable parlor; for, now that the sunshine was withdrawn, the atmosphere, out of doors, was already growing very cold.

But, after opening the house-door, she stood an instant on the threshold, hesitating whether she ought to ask the child to come in, or whether she should even speak to her. Indeed, she almost doubted whether it were a real child, after all, or only a light wreath of the new-fallen snow, blown hither and thither about the garden by the intensely cold west-wind. There was certainly something very singular in the aspect of the little stranger. Among all the children of the neighborhood, the lady could remember no such face, with its pure white, and delicate rose-color, and the golden ringlets tossing about the forehead and cheeks. And as for her dress, which was entirely of white, and fluttering in the breeze, it was such as

no reasonable woman would put upon a little girl, when sending her out to play, in the depth of winter. It made this kind and careful mother shiver only to look at those small feet, with nothing in the world on them except a very thin pair of white slippers. Nevertheless, airily as she was clad, the child seemed to feel not the slightest inconvenience from the cold, but danced so lightly over the snow that the tips of her toes left hardly a print in its surface; while Violet could but just keep pace with her, and Peony's short legs compelled him to lag behind.

Once, in the course of their play, the strange child placed herself between Violet and Peony, and taking a hand of each, skipped merrily forward, and they along with her. Almost immediately, however, Peony pulled away his little fist, and began to rub it as if the fingers were tingling with cold; while Violet also released herself, though with less abruptness, gravely remarking that it was better not to take hold of hands. The white-robed damsel said not a word, but danced about, just as merrily as before. If Violet and Peony did not choose to play with her, she could make just as good a playmate of the brisk and cold west-wind, which kept blowing her all about the garden, and took such liberties with her, that they seemed to have been friends for a long time. All this while, the mother stood on the threshold, wondering how a little girl could look so much like a flying snow-drift, or how a snow-drift could look so very like a little girl.

She called Violet, and whispered to her.

"Violet, my darling, what is this child's name?" asked she. "Does she live ear us?"

"Why, dearest mamma," answered Violet, laughing to think that her mother did not comprehend so very plain an affair, "this is our little snow-sister, whom we have just been making!"

"Yes, dear mamma," cried Peony, running to his mother, and looking up simply into her face. "This is our snow-image! Is it not a nice 'ittle child?"

At this instant a flock of snow-birds came flittering through the air. As was very natural, they avoided Violet and Peony. But—and this looked strange—they flew at once to the white-robed child, fluttered eagerly about her head, alighted on her shoulders, and seemed to claim her as an old acquaintance. She, on her part, was evidently as glad to see these little birds, old Winter's grandchildren, as they were to see her, and welcomed them by holding out both her hands. Hereupon, they each and all tried to alight on her two palms and ten small fingers and thumbs, crowding one another off, with an immense fluttering of their tiny wings. One dear little bird nestled tenderly in her bosom; another put its bill to her lips. They were as joyous, all the while, and seemed as much in their element, as you may have seen them when sporting with a snow-storm.

Violet and Peony stood laughing at this pretty sight; for they enjoyed the merry time which their new playmate was having with these small-winged visitants almost as much as if they themselves took part in it.

"Violet," said her mother, greatly perplexed, "tell me the truth, without any jest. Who is this little girl?"

"My darling mamma," answered Violet, looking seriously into her mother's face, and apparently surprised that she should need any further explanation, "I have told you truly who she is. It is our little snow-image which Peony and I have been making. Peony will tell you so, as well as I."

"Yes, mamma," asseverated Peony, with much gravity in his crimson little phiz; "this is 'ittle snow-child. Is not she a nice one? But, mamma, her hand is, oh! so very cold!"

While mamma still hesitated what to think and what to do, the street-gate was thrown open, and the father of Violet and Peony appeared, wrapped in a pilot-cloth sack, with a fur cup drawn down over his ears, and the thickest of gloves upon his hands. Mr. Lindsey was a middle-aged man, with a weary and yet a happy look in his wind-flushed and frost-pinched face, as if he had been busy all the day long, and was glad to get back to his quiet home. His eyes brightened at the sight of his wife and children, although he could not help uttering a word or two of surprise, at finding the whole family in the open air, on so bleak a day and after sunset too. He soon perceived the little white stranger, sporting to and fro in the garden, like a dancing snow-wreath, and the flock of snow-birds fluttering about her head.

"Pray, what little girl may that be?" inquired this very sensible man. "Surely her mother must be crazy, to let her go out in such bitter weather as it has been to-day, with only that flimsy white gown, and those thin slippers!"

"My dear husband," said his wife, "I know no more about the little thing than you do. Some neighbor's child, I suppose. Our Violet and Peony," she added, laughing at herself for repeating so absurd a story, "insist that she is nothing but a snow-image, which they have been busy about in the garden, almost all the afternoon."

As she said this, the mother glanced her eyes toward the spot where the children's snow-image had been made. What was her surprise, on perceiving that there was not the slightest trace of so much labor!—no image at all,—no piled-up heap of snow!—nothing whatever, save the prints of little footsteps around a vacant space!

"This is very strange!" said she.

"What is strange, dear mother?" asked Violet. "Dear father, do not you see how it is? This is our snow-image, which Peony and I have made, because we wanted another playmate. Did not we, Peony?"

"Yes, papa," said crimson Peony. "This be our 'ittle snow-sister. Is she not beau-ti-ful? But she gave me such a cold kiss!"

"Poh, nonsense, children!" cried their good, honest father, who, as we have already intimated, had an exceedingly common-sensible way of looking at matters. "Do not tell me of making live figures out of snow? Come, wife; this little stranger must not stay out in the bleak air a moment longer. We will bring her into the parlor; and you shall give her a supper of warm bread and milk, and make her as comfortable as you can. Meanwhile, I will inquire among the neighbors; or, if necessary, send the city-crier about the streets, to give notice of a lost child."

So saying, this honest and very kind-hearted man was going toward the little white damsel, with the best intentions in the world. But Violet and Peony, each seizing their father by the hand, earnestly besought him not to make her come in.

"Dear father," cried Violet, putting herself before him, "it is true what I have been telling you! This is our little snow-girl, and she cannot live any longer than while she breathes the cold west-wind. Do not make her come into the hot room!"

"Yes, father," shouted Peony, stamping his little foot, so mightily was he in earnest, "this be nothing but our 'ittle snow-child! She will not love the hot fire!"

"Nonsense, children, nonsense, nonsense!" cried the father, half vexed, half laughing at what he considered their foolish obstinacy. "Run into the house, this moment! It is too late to play any longer, now. I must take care of this little girl immediately, or she will catch her death-a-cold!"

"Husband! dear husband!" said his wife, in a low voice,—for she had been looking narrowly at the snow-child, and was more perplexed than ever,—"there is something very singular in all this. You will think me foolish,—but—but—may it not be that some invisible angel has been attracted by the simplicity and good faith with which our children set about their undertaking? May he not have spent an hour of his immortality in playing with those dear little souls? and so the result is what we call a miracle. No, no! Do not laugh at me; I see what a foolish thought it is!"

"My dear wife," replied the husband laughing heartily, "you are as much a child as Violet and Peony."

And in one sense so she was, for all through life she had kept her heart full of childlike simplicity and faith, which was as pure and clear as crystal; and

ooking at all matters through this transparent medium, she sometimes saw
truths so profound, that other people
laughed at them as nonsense and absurdity.

But now kind Mr. Lindsey had entered the garden, breaking away from
his two children, who still sent their
shrill voices after him, beseeching him
to let the snow-child stay and enjoy herself in the cold west-wind. As he approached, the snow-birds took to flight.
The little white damsel, also, fled backward, shaking her head, as if to say,
"Pray, do not touch me!" and roguishly,
as it appeared, leading him through the
deepest of the snow. Once, the good man
stumbled, and floundered down upon
his face, so that, gathering himself up
again, with the snow sticking to his
rough pilot-cloth sack, he looked as
white and wintry as a snow-image of
the largest size. Some of the neighbors,
meanwhile, seeing him from their windows, wondered what could possess poor
Mr. Lindsey to be running about his
garden in pursuit of a snow-drift, which
the west-wind was driving hither and
thither! At length, after a vast deal of
trouble, he chased the little stranger
into a corner, where she could not possibly escape him. His wife had been looking on, and, it being nearly twilight, was
wonder-struck to observe how the snow-
child gleamed and sparkled, and how
she seemed to shed a glow all round
about her; and when driven into the
corner, she positively glittered like a
star! It was a frosty kind of brightness,
too, like that of an icicle in the moonlight. The wife thought it strange that
good Mr. Lindsey should see nothing
remarkable in the snow-child's appearance.

"Come, you odd little thing!" cried
the honest man, seizing her by the hand,
"I have caught you at last, and will
make you comfortable in spite of yourself. We will put a nice warm pair of
worsted stockings on your frozen little
feet, and you shall have a good thick
shawl to wrap yourself in. Your poor
white nose, I am afraid, is actually
frost-bitten. But we will make it all
right. Come along in."

And so, with a most benevolent smile
on his sagacious visage, all purple as it
was with the cold, this very well-meaning gentleman took the snow-child by
the hand and led her towards the house.
She followed him, droopingly and reluctant; for all the glow and sparkle was
gone out of her figure; and whereas just
before she had resembled a bright,
frosty, star-gemmed evening, with a
crimson gleam on the cold horizon, she
now looked as dull and languid as a
thaw. As kind Mr. Lindsey led her up
the steps of the door, Violet and Peony
looked into his face,—their eyes full of
tears, which froze before they could run
down their cheeks,—and again entreated
him not to bring their snow-image into
the house.

"Not bring her in!" exclaimed the
kind-hearted man. "Why, you are crazy,
my little Violet!—quite crazy, my small
Peony! She is so cold already, that her
hand has almost frozen mine, in spite
of my thick gloves. Would you have
her freeze to death?"

His wife, as he came up the steps,
had been taking another long, earnest,
almost awe-stricken gaze at the little
white stranger. She hardly knew whether
it was a dream or no: but she could not
help fancying that she saw the delicate
print of Violet's fingers on the child's

neck. It looked just as if, while Violet was shaping out the image, she had given it a gentle pat with her hand, and had neglected to smooth the impression quite away.

"After all, husband," said the mother, recurring to her idea that the angels would be as much delighted to play with Violet and Peony as she herself was,—"after all, she does look strangely like a snow-image! I do believe she is made of snow!"

A puff of the west-wind blew against the snow-child, and again she sparkled like a star.

"Snow!" repeated good Mr. Lindsey, drawing the reluctant guest over his hospitable threshold. "No wonder she looks like snow. She is half frozen, poor little thing! But a good fire will put everything to rights."

Without further talk, and always with the same best intentions, this highly benevolent and common-sensible individual led the little white damsel—drooping, drooping, drooping, more and more—out of the frosty air, and into his comfortable parlor. A Heidenberg stove, filled to the brim with intensely burning anthracite, was sending a bright gleam through the isinglass of its iron door, and causing the vase of water on its top to fume and bubble with excitement. A warm, sultry smell was diffused throughout the room. A thermometer on the wall farthest from the stove stood at eighty degrees. The parlor was hung with red curtains, and covered with a red carpet, and looked just as warm as it felt. The difference betwixt the atmosphere here and the cold, wintry twilight out of doors was like stepping at once from Nova Zembla to the hottest part of India, or from the North Pole

into an oven. O, this was a fine place for the little white stranger!

The common-sensible man placed the snow-child on the hearth-rug, right in front of the hissing and fuming stove.

"Now she will be comfortable!" cried Mr. Lindsey, rubbing his hands and looking about him, with the pleasantest smile you ever saw. "Make yourself at home, my child."

Sad, sad and drooping looked the little white maiden, as she stood on the hearth-rug, with the hot blast of the stove striking through her like a pestilence. Once, she threw a glance wistfully toward the windows, and caught a glimpse, through its red curtains, of the snow-covered roofs, and the stars glimmering frostily, and all the delicious intensity of the cold night. The bleak wind rattled the window-panes, as if it were summoning her to come forth. But there stood the snow-child, drooping, before the hot stove!

But the common-sensible man saw nothing amiss.

"Come, wife," said he, "let her have a pair of thick stockings and a woollen shawl or blanket directly; and tell Dora to give her some warm supper as soon as the milk boils. You, Violet and Peony, amuse your little friend. She is out of spirits, you see, at finding herself in a strange place. For my part, I will go around among the neighbors, and find out where she belongs."

The mother, meanwhile, had gone in search of the shawl and stockings; for her own view of the matter, however subtle and delicate, had given away, as it always did, to the stubborn materialism of her husband. Without heeding the remonstrances of his two children, who still kept murmuring that their little snow-sister did not love the warmth, good Mr. Lindsey took his departure, shutting the parlor door carefully behind him. Turning up the collar of his sack over his ears, he emerged from the house, and had barely reached the street-gate, when he was recalled by the screams of Violet and Peony, and the rapping of a thimbled finger against the parlor window.

"Husband! husband!" cried his wife, showing her horror-stricken face through the window-panes. "There is no need of going for the child's parents!"

"We told you so, father!" screamed Violet and Peony, as he re-entered the parlor. "You would bring her in; and now our poor—dear—beau-ti-ful little snow-sister is thawed!"

And their own sweet little faces were already dissolved in tears; so that their father, seeing what strange things occasionally happen in this every-day world, felt not a little anxious lest his children might be going to thaw too! In the utmost perplexity, he demanded an explanation of his wife. She could only reply, that, being summoned to the parlor by the cries of Violet and Peony, she found no trace of the little white maiden, unless it were the remains of a heap of snow, which, while she was gazing at it, melted quite away upon the hearth-rug.

"And there you see all that is left of it!" added she, pointing to a pool of water, in front of the stove.

"Yes, father," said Violet, looking reproachfully at him, through her tears, "there is all that is left of our dear little snow-sister!"

"Naughty father," cried Peony, stamping his foot, and—I shudder to say—shaking his little fist at the com-

mon-sensible man. "We told you how it would be. What for did you bring her in?"

And the Heidenberg stove, through the isinglass of its door, seemed to glare at good Mr. Lindsey, like a red-eyed demon, triumphing in the mischief which it had done!

This, you will observe, was one of those rare cases, which yet will occasionally happen, where common-sense finds itself at fault. The remarkable story of the snow-image, though to that sagacious class of people to whom good Mr. Lindsey belongs it may seem but a childish affair, is, nevertheless, capable of being moralized in various methods, greatly for their edification. One of its lessons, for instance, might be, that it behooves men, and especially men of benevolence, to consider well what they are about, and, before acting on their philanthropic purposes, to be quite sure that they comprehend the nature and all the relations of the business in hand. What has been established as an element of good to one being may prove absolute mischief to another; even as the warmth of the parlor was proper enough for children of flesh and blood, like Violet and Peony,—though by no means very wholesome, even for them,—but involved nothing short of annihilation to the unfortunate snow-image.

But, after all, there is no teaching anything to wise men of good Mr. Lindsey's stamp. They know everything—oh, to be sure!—everything that has been, and everything that is, and everything that, by any future possibility, can be. And, should some phenomenon of nature or Providence transcend their system, they will not recognize it, even if it come to pass under their very noses.

"Wife," said Mr. Lindsey, after a fit of silence, "see what a quantity of snow the children have brought in on their feet! It has made quite a puddle here before the stove. Pray tell Dora to bring some towels and sop it up!"

THE GREAT STONE FACE

ONE afternoon, when the sun was going down, a mother and her little boy sat at the door of their cottage, talking about the Great Stone Face. They had but to lift their eyes, and there it was plainly to be seen, though miles away, with the sunshine brightening all its features.

And what was the Great Stone Face?

Embosomed amongst a family of lofty mountains, there was a valley so spacious that it contained many thousand inhabitants. Some of these good people dwelt in log-huts, with the black forest all around them, on the steep and difficult hillsides. Others had their homes in comfortable farm-houses, and cultivated the rich soil on the gentle slopes or level surfaces of the valley. Others, again, were congregated into populous villages, where some wild, highland rivulet, tumbling down from its birthplace in the upper mountain region, had been caught and tamed by human cunning, and compelled to turn the machinery of cotton-factories. The inhabitants of this valley, in short, were numerous, and of many modes of life. But all of them, grown people and children, had a kind of familiarity with the Great Stone Face, although some possessed the gift of distinguishing this grand natural phenomenon more perfectly than many of their neighbors.

The Great Stone Face, then, was a work of Nature in her mood of majestic playfulness, formed on the perpendicular side of a mountain by some immense rocks, which had been thrown together in such a position as, when viewed at a proper distance, precisely to resemble the features of the human countenance. It seemed as if an enormous giant, or a Titan, had sculptured his own likeness on the precipice. There was the broad arch of the forehead, a hundred feet in height; the nose, with its long bridge; and the vast lips, which, if they could have spoken, would have rolled their thunder accents from one end of the valley to the other. True, it is, that if the spectator approached too near, he lost the outline of the gigantic visage, and could discern only a heap of ponderous and gigantic rocks, piled in chaotic ruin one upon another. Retracing his steps, however, the wondrous features would again be seen; and the farther he withdrew from them, the more like a human face, with all its original divinity intact, did they appear; until, as it grew dim in the distance, with the clouds and glorified vapor of the mountains clustering about it, the Great Stone Face seemed positively to be alive.

It was a happy lot for children to grow up to manhood or womanhood with the Great Stone Face before their eyes, for all the features were noble, and the expression was at once grand and sweet, as if it were the glow of a vast, warm heart, that embraced all mankind in its affections, and had room for more. It was an education only to look at it. According to the belief of many people, the valley owed much of its fertility to this benign aspect that was continually beaming over it, illuminating the clouds, and infusing tenderness into the sunshine.

As we began with saying, a mother and her little boy sat at their cottage door, gazing at the Great Stone Face, and talking about it. The child's name was Ernest.

"Mother," said he, while the Titanic visage smiled on him, "I wish that it could speak, for it looks so very kindly that its voice must needs be pleasant. If I were to see a man with such a face, I should love him dearly."

"If an old prophecy should come to pass," answered his mother, "we may see a man, some time or other, with exactly such a face as that."

"What prophecy do you mean, dear mother?" eagerly inquired Ernest. "Pray tell me all about it!"

So his mother told him a story that her own mother had told to her, when she herself was younger than little Ernest; a story, not of things that were past, but of what was yet to come; a story, nevertheless, so very old, that even the Indians, who formerly inhabited this valley, had heard it from their forefathers, to whom, as they affirmed, it had been murmured by the mountain streams, and whispered by the wind among the tree-tops. The purport was, that, at some future day, a child should be born hereabouts, who was destined to become the greatest and

noblest personage of his time, and whose countenance in manhood should bear an exact resemblance to the Great Stone Face. Not a few old-fashioned people, and young ones likewise, in the ardor of their hopes, still cherished an enduring faith in this old prophecy. But others, who had seen more of the world, had watched and waited till they were weary, and had beheld no man with such a face, nor any man that proved to be much greater or nobler than his neighbors, concluded it to be nothing but an idle tale. At all events, the great man of the prophecy had not yet appeared.

"O mother, dear mother!" cried Ernest, clapping his hands above his head, "I do hope that I shall live to see him!"

His mother was an affectionate and thoughtful woman, and felt that it was wisest not to discourage the generous hopes of her little boy. So she only said to him, "Perhaps you may."

And Ernest never forgot the story that his mother told him. It was always in his mind, whenever he looked upon the Great Stone Face. He spent his childhood in the log-cottage where he was born, and was dutiful to his mother, and helpful to her in many things, assisting her much with his little hands, and more with his loving heart. In this manner, from a happy yet often pensive child, he grew up to be a mild, quiet, unobtrusive boy, and sun-browned with labor in the fields, but with more intelligence brightening his aspects than is seen in many lads who have been taught at famous schools. Yet Ernest had had no teacher, save only that the Great Stone Face became one to him. When the toil of the day was over, he would gaze at it for hours, until he began to imagine that those vast features recognized him, and gave him a smile of kindness and encouragement, responsive to his own look of veneration. We must not take upon us to affirm that this was a mistake, although the Face may have looked no more kindly at Ernest than at all the world besides. But the secret was, that the boy's tender and confiding simplicity discerned what other people could not see; and thus the love, which was meant for all, became his peculiar portion.

About this time, there went a rumor throughout the valley, that the great man, foretold from ages long ago, who was to bear a resemblance to the Great Stone Face, had appeared at last. It seems that, many years before, a young man had migrated from the valley and settled at a distant seaport, where, after getting together a little money, he had set up as a shopkeeper. His name—but I could never learn whether it was his real one, or a nickname that had grown out of his habits and success in life— was Gathergold. Being shrewd and active, and endowed by Providence with that inscrutable faculty which develops itself in what the world calls luck, he became an exceedingly rich merchant, and owner of a whole fleet of bulky-bottomed ships. All the countries of the globe appeared to join hands for the mere purpose of adding heap after heap to the mountainous accumulation of this one man's wealth. The cold regions of the North, almost within the gloom and shadow of the Arctic Circle, sent him their tribute in the shape of furs; hot Africa sifted for him the golden sands of her rivers, and gathered up the ivory tusks of her great elephants out of the forests; the East came bringing him the

rich shawls, and spices, and teas, and the effulgence of diamonds, and the gleaming purity of large pearls. The ocean, not to be behindhand with the earth, yielded up her mighty whales, that Mr. Gathergold might sell their oil, and make a profit on it. Be the original commodity what it might, it was gold within his grasp. It might be said of him, as of Midas in the fable, that whatever he touched with his finger immediately glistened, and grew yellow, and was changed at once into sterling metal, or, which suited him still better, into piles of coin. And, when Mr. Gathergold had become so very rich that it would have taken him a hundred years only to count his wealth, he bethought himself of his native valley, and resolved to go back thither, and end his days where he was born. With this purpose in view, he sent a skilful architect to build him such a palace as should be fit for a man of his vast wealth to live in.

As I have said above, it had already been rumored in the valley that Mr. Gathergold had turned out to be the prophetic personage so long and vainly looked for, and that his visage was the perfect and undeniable similitude of the Great Stone Face. People were the more ready to believe that this must needs be the fact, when they beheld the splendid edifice that rose, as if by enchantment, on the site of his father's old weather-beaten farm-house. The exterior was of marble, so dazzling white that it seemed as though the whole structure might melt away in the sunshine, like those humbler ones which Mr. Gathergold, in his young play-days, before his fingers were gifted with the touch of transmutation, had been accustomed to

build of snow. It had a richly ornamented portico, supported by tall pillars,
beneath which was a lofty door, studded
with silver knobs, and made of a kind
of variegated wood that had been
brought from beyond the sea. The windows, from the floor to the ceiling of
each stately apartment, were composed,
respectively, of but one enormous pane
of glass, so transparently pure that it
was said to be a finer medium than
even the vacant atmosphere. Hardly
anybody had been permitted to see the
interior of this palace; but it was reported, and with good semblance of
truth, to be far more gorgeous than the
outside, insomuch that whatever was
iron or brass in other houses was silver
or gold in this; and Mr. Gathergold's
bed-chamber, especially, made such a
glittering appearance that no ordinary
man would have been able to close his
eyes there. But, on the other hand, Mr.
Gathergold was now so inured to wealth,
that perhaps he could not have closed
his eyes unless where the gleam of it
was certain to find its way beneath his
eyelids.

In due time the mansion was finished;
next came the upholsterers, with magnificent furniture; then, a whole troop
of black and white servants, the harbingers of Mr. Gathergold, who, in his
own majestic person, was expected to
arrive at sunset. Our friend Ernest,
meanwhile, had been deeply stirred by
the idea that the great man, the noble
man, the man of prophecy, after so
many ages of delay, was at length to be
made manifest to his native valley. He
knew, boy as he was, that there were a
thousand ways in which Mr. Gathergold,
with his vast wealth, might transform
himself into an angel of beneficence, and

assume a control over human affairs as
wide and benignant as the smile of the
Great Stone Face. Full of faith and
hope, Ernest doubted not that what the
people said was true, and that now he
was to behold the living likeness of
those wondrous features on the mountain-side. While the boy was still gazing
up the valley, and fancying, as he always
did, that the Great Stone Face returned
his gaze and looked kindly at him, the
rumbling of wheels was heard, approaching swiftly along the winding road.

"Here he comes!" cried a group of
people who were assembled to witness
the arrival. "Here comes the great Mr.
Gathergold!"

A carriage, drawn by four horses,
dashed round the turn of the road.
Within it, thrust partly out of the window, appeared the physiognomy of a
little old man, with a skin as yellow as
if his own Midas-hand had transmuted
it. He had a low forehead, small, sharp
eyes, puckered about with innumerable
wrinkles, and very thin lips, which he
made still thinner by pressing them
forcibly together.

"The very image of the Great Stone
Face!" shouted the people. "Sure
enough, the old prophecy is true; and
here we have the great man come, at
last!"

And, what greatly perplexed Ernest,
they seemed actually to believe that
here was the likeness which they spoke
of. By the roadside there chanced to be
an old beggar-woman and two little
beggar-children, stragglers from some
far-off region, who, as the carriage rolled
onward, held out their hands and lifted
up their doleful voices, most piteously
beseeching charity. A yellow claw—the
very same that had clawed together so

much wealth—poked itself out of the coach-window, and dropped some copper coins upon the ground; so that, though the great man's name seems to have been Gathergold, he might just as suitably have been nicknamed Scattercopper. Still, nevertheless, with an earnest shout, and evidently with as much good faith as ever, the people bellowed,—

"He is the very image of the Great Stone Face!"

But Ernest turned sadly from the wrinkled shrewdness of that sordid visage, and gazed up the valley, where, amid a gathering mist, gilded by the last sunbeams, he could still distinguish those glorious features which had impressed themselves into his soul. Their aspect cheered him. What did the benign lips seem to say?

"He will come! Fear not, Ernest; the man will come!"

The years went on, and Ernest ceased to be a boy. He had grown to be a young man now. He attracted little notice from the other inhabitants of the valley; for they saw nothing remarkable in his way of life, save that, when the labor of the day was over, he still loved to go apart and gaze and meditate upon the Great Stone Face. According to their idea of the matter, it was a folly indeed, but pardonable, inasmuch as Ernest was industrious, kind, and neighborly, and neglected no duty for the sake of indulging this idle habit. They knew not that the Great Stone Face had become a teacher to him, and that the sentiment which was expressed in it would enlarge the young man's heart, and fill it with wider and deeper sympathies than other hearts. They knew not that thence

would come a better wisdom than could be learned from books, and a better life than could be moulded on the defaced example of other human lives. Neither did Ernest know that the thoughts and affections which came to him so naturally, in the fields and at the fireside, and wherever he communed with himself, were of a higher tone than those which all men shared with him. A simple soul,—simple as when his mother first taught him the old prophecy,—he beheld the marvellous features beaming adown the valley, and still wondered that their human counterpart was so long in making his appearance.

By this time poor Mr. Gathergold was dead and buried; and the oddest part of the matter was, that his wealth, which was the body and spirit of his existence, had disappeared before his death, leaving nothing of him but a living skeleton, covered over with a wrinkled, yellow skin. Since the melting away of his gold, it had been very generally conceded that there was no such striking resemblance, after all, betwixt the ignoble features of the ruined merchant and that majestic face upon the mountain-side. So the people ceased to honor him during his lifetime, and quietly consigned him to forgetfulness after his decease. Once in a while, it is true his memory was brought up in connection with the magnificent palace which he had built, and which had long ago been turned into a hotel for the accommodation of strangers, multitudes of whom came, every summer, to visit that famous natural curiosity, the Great Stone Face. Thus, Mr. Gathergold being discredited and thrown into the shade, the man of prophecy was yet to come.

It so happened that a native-born son of the valley, many years before, had enlisted as a soldier, and, after a great deal of hard fighting, had now become an illustrious commander. Whatever he may be called in history, he was known in camps and on the battlefield under the nickname of Old Blood-and-Thunder. This war-worn veteran, being now infirm with age and wounds, and weary of the turmoil of a military life, and of the roll of the drum and the clangor of the trumpet, that had so long been ringing in his ears, had lately signified a purpose of returning to his native valley, hoping to find repose where he remembered to have left it. The inhabitants, his old neighbors and their grown-up children, were resolved to welcome the renowned warrior with a salute of cannon and a public dinner; and all the more enthusiastically, it being affirmed that now, at last, the likeness of the Great Stone Face had actually appeared. An aide-de-camp of old Blood-and-Thunder, travelling through the valley, was said to have been struck with the resemblance. Moreover, the schoolmates and early acquaintances of the general were ready to testify, on oath, that, to the best of their recollection, the aforesaid general had been exceedingly like the majestic image, even when a boy, only that the idea had never occurred to them at that period. Great, therefore, was the excitement throughout the valley; and many people, who had never once thought of glancing at the Great Stone Face for years before, now spent their time in gazing at it, for the sake of knowing exactly how General Blood-and-Thunder looked.

On the day of the great festival,

Ernest, with all the other people of the valley, left their work, and proceeded to the spot where the sylvan banquet was prepared. As he approached, the loud voice of the Reverend Doctor Battleblast was heard, beseeching a blessing on the good things set before them, and on the distinguished friend of peace in whose honor they were assembled. The tables were arranged in a cleared space of the woods, shut in by the surrounding trees, except where a vista opened eastward, and afforded a distant view of the Great Stone Face. Over the general's chair, which was a relic from the home of Washington, there was an arch of verdant boughs, with the laurel profusely intermixed, and surmounted by his country's banner, beneath which he had won his victories. Our friend Ernest raised himself on his tip-toes, in hopes to get a glimpse of the celebrated guest; but there was a mighty crowd about the tables anxious to hear the toasts and speeches, and to catch any word that might fall from the general in reply; and a volunteer company, doing duty as a guard, pricked ruthlessly with their bayonets at any particularly quiet person among the throng. So Ernest, being of an unobtrusive character, was thrust quite into the background, where he could see no more of Old Blood-and-Thunder's physiognomy than if it had been still blazing on the battle-field. To console himself, he turned towards the Great Stone Face, which, like a faithful and long-remembered friend, looked back and smiled upon him through the vista of the forest. Meantime, however, he could overhear the remarks of various individuals, who were comparing the features of the hero with the face on the distant mountain-side.

"'T is the same face, to a hair!" cried one man, cutting a caper for joy.

"Wonderfully like, that's a fact!" responded another.

"Like! why, I call it Old Blood-and-Thunder himself, in a monstrous looking-glass!" cried a third. "And why not? He's the greatest man of this or any other age, beyond a doubt."

And then all three of the speakers gave a great shout, which communicated electricity to the crowd, and called forth a roar from a thousand voices, that went reverberating for miles among the mountains, until you might have supposed that the Great Stone Face had poured its thunder-breath into the cry. All these comments, and this vast enthusiasm, served the more to interest our friend; nor did he think of questioning that now, at length, the mountain-visage had found its human counterpart. It is true, Ernest had imagined that this long-looked-for personage would appear in the character of a man of peace, uttering wisdom, and doing good, and making people happy. But, taking an habitual breadth of view, with all his simplicity, he contended that Providence should choose its own method of blessing mankind, and could conceive that this great end might be effected even by a warrior and a bloody sword, should inscrutable wisdom see fit to order matters so.

"The general! the general!" was now the cry. "Hush! silence! Old Blood-and-Thunder's going to make a speech."

Even so; for, the cloth being removed, the general's health had been drunk amid shouts of applause, and

he now stood upon his feet to thank the company. Ernest saw him. There he was, over the shoulders of the crowd, from the two glittering epaulets and embroidered collar upward, beneath the arch of green boughs with intertwined laurel, and the banner drooping as if to shade his brow! And there, too, visible in the same glance, through the vista of the forest, appeared the Great Stone Face! And was there, indeed, such a resemblance as the crowd had testified? Alas, Ernest could not recognize it! He beheld a war-worn and weather-beaten countenance, full of energy, and expressive of an iron will; but the gentle wisdom, the deep, broad, tender sympathies were altogether wanting in Old Blood-and-Thunder's visage; and even if the Great Stone Face had assumed his look of stern command, the milder traits would still have tempered it.

"This is not the man of prophecy," sighed Ernest to himself, as he made his way out of the throng. "And must the world wait longer yet?"

The mists had congregated about the distant mountain-side, and there were seen the grand and awful features of the Great Stone Face, awful but benignant, as if a mighty angel were sitting among the hills, and enrobing himself in a cloud-vesture of gold and purple. As he looked, Ernest could hardly believe but that a smile beamed over the whole visage, with a radiance still brightening, although without motion of the lips. It was probably the effect of the western sunshine, melting through the thinly diffused vapors that had swept between him and the object that he gazed at. But—as it always did—the aspect of his marvellous friend made Ernest as hopeful as if he had never hoped in vain.

"Fear not, Ernest," said his heart, even as if the Great Face were whispering him,—"fear not, Ernest; he will come."

More years sped swiftly and tranquilly away. Ernest still dwelt in his native valley, and was now a man of middle age. By imperceptible degrees, he had become known among the people. Now, as heretofore, he labored for his bread, and was the same simple-hearted man that he had always been. But he had thought and felt so much, he had given so many of the best hours of his life to unworldly hopes for some great good to mankind, that it seemed as though he had been talking with the angels, and had imbibed a portion of their wisdom unawares. It was visible in the calm and well-considered beneficence of his daily life, the quiet stream of which had made a wide green margin all along its course. Not a day passed by, that the world was not the better because this man, humble as he was, had lived. He never stepped aside from his own path, yet would always reach a blessing to his neighbor. Almost involuntarily, too, he had become a preacher. The pure and high simplicity of his thought, which, as one of its manifestations, took shape in the good deeds that dropped silently from his hand, flowed also forth in speech. He uttered truths that wrought upon and moulded the lives of those who heard him. His auditors, it may be, never suspected that Ernest, their own neighbor and familiar friend, was more than an ordinary man; least of all did Ernest himself suspect it; but, inevitably as the murmur of a rivulet, came thoughts out of his mouth that no other human lips had spoken.

When the people's minds had had a little time to cool, they were ready enough to acknowledge their mistake in imagining a similarity between General Blood-and-Thunder's truculent physiognomy and the benign visage on the mountain-side. But now, again, there were reports and many paragraphs in the newspapers, affirming that the likeness of the Great Stone Face had appeared upon the broad shoulders of a certain eminent statesman. He, like Mr. Gathergold and Old Blood-and-Thunder, was a native of the valley, but had left it in his early days, and taken up the trades of law and politics. Instead of the rich man's wealth and the warrior's sword, he had but a tongue, and it was mightier than both together. So wonderfully eloquent was he, that whatever he might choose to say, his auditors had no choice but to believe him; wrong looked like right, and right like wrong; for when it pleased him he could make a kind of illuminated fog with his mere breath, and obscure the natural daylight with it. His tongue, indeed, was a magic instrument: sometimes it rumbled like the thunder; sometimes it warbled like the sweetest music. It was the blast of war,—the song of peace; and it seemed to have a heart in it, when there was no such matter. In good truth he was a wondrous man; and when his tongue had acquired him all other imaginable success,—when it had been heard in halls of state, and in the courts of princes and potentates, —after it had made him known all over the world, even as a voice crying from shore to shore,—it finally persuaded his countrymen to select him for the presidency. Before this time,—indeed, as soon as he began to grow celebrated,—his admirers had found out the resemblance between him and the Great Stone Face; and so much were they struck by it, that throughout the country this distinguished gentleman was known by the name of Old Stony Phiz. The phrase was considered as giving a highly favorable aspect to his political prospects; for, as is likewise the case with the Popedom, nobody ever becomes president without taking a name other than his own.

While his friends were doing their best to make him president, Old Stony Phiz, as he was called, set out on a visit to the valley where he was born. Of course, he had no other object than to shake hands with his fellow-citizens, and neither thought nor cared about any effect which his progress through the country might have upon the election. Magnificent preparations were made to receive the illustrious statesman; a cavalcade of horsemen set forth to meet him at the boundary line of the State, and all the people left their business and gathered along the wayside to see him pass. Among these was Ernest. Though more than once disappointed, as we have seen, he had such a hopeful and confiding nature, that he was always ready to believe in whatever seemed beautiful and good. He kept his heart continually open, and thus was sure to catch the blessing from on high, when it should come. So now again, as buoyantly as ever, he went forth to behold the likeness of the Great Stone Face.

The cavalcade came prancing along the road, with a great clattering of hoofs and a mighty cloud of dust, which rose up so dense and high that the visage of the mountain-side was completely hidden from Ernest's eyes. All the great men of the neighborhood were there on horseback: militia officers in uniform; the member of Congress; the sheriff of the county; the editors of newspapers; and many a farmer too had mounted his patient steed, with his Sunday coat upon his back. It really was a very brilliant spectacle, especially as there were numerous banners flaunting over the cavalcade, on some of which were gorgeous portraits of the illustrious statesman and the Great Stone Face, smiling familiarly at one another, like two brothers. If the pictures were to be trusted, the mutual resemblance, it must be confessed, was marvellous. We must not forget to mention that there was a band of music, which made the echoes of the mountains ring and reverberate with the loud triumph of its strains; so that airy and soul-thrilling melodies broke out among all the heights and hollows, as if every nook of his native valley had found a voice, to welcome the distinguished guest. But the grandest effect was when the far-off mountain precipice flung back the music; for then the Great Stone Face itself seemed to be swelling the triumphant chorus, in acknowledgment that, at length, the man of prophecy was come.

All this while the people were throwing up their hats and shouting, with enthusiasm so contagious that the heart of Ernest kindled up, and he likewise threw up his hat, and shouted, as loudly as the loudest, "Huzza for the great man! Huzza for Old Stony Phiz!" But as yet he had not seen him.

"Here he is, now!" cried those who

stood near Ernest. "There! There! Look at Old Stony Phiz and then at the Old Man of the Mountain, and see if they are not as like as two twin-brothers!"

In the midst of all this gallant array came an open barouche, drawn by four white horses; and in the barouche, with his massive head uncovered, sat the illustrious statesman, Old Stony Phiz himself.

"Confess it," said one of Ernest's neighbors to him, "the Great Stone Face has met its match at last."

Now, it must be owned that, at his first glimpse of the countenance which was bowing and smiling from the barouche, Ernest did fancy that there was a resemblance between it and the old familiar face upon the mountain-side. The brow, with its massive depth and loftiness, and all the other features, indeed, were boldly and strongly hewn, as if in emulation of a more than heroic, of a Titanic model. But the sublimity and stateliness, the grand expression of a divine sympathy, that illuminated the mountain visage, and ethe-realized its ponderous granite substance into spirit, might here be sought in vain. Something had been originally left out, or had departed. And therefore the marvellously gifted statesman had always a weary gloom in the deep caverns of his eyes, as of a child that has outgrown its playthings, or a man of mighty faculties and little aims, whose life, with all its high performances, was vague and empty, because no high purpose had endowed it with reality.

Still, Ernest's neighbor was thrusting his elbow into his side, and pressing him for an answer.

"Confess! confess! Is not he the very picture of your Old Man of the Mountain?"

"No!" said Ernest, bluntly, "I see little or no likeness."

"Then so much the worse for the Great Stone Face!" answered his neighbor; and again he set up a shout for Old Stony Phiz.

But Ernest turned away, melancholy, and almost despondent; for this was the saddest of his disappointments, to behold a man who might have fulfilled the prophecy, and had not willed to do so. Meantime, the cavalcade, the banners, the music, and the barouches swept past him, with the vociferous crowd in the rear, leaving the dust to settle down, and the Great Stone Face to be revealed again, with the grandeur that it had worn for untold centuries.

"Lo, here I am, Ernest!" the benign lips seemed to say. "I have waited longer than thou, and am not yet weary. Fear not; the man will come."

The years hurried onward, treading in their haste on one another's heels. And now they began to bring white hairs, and scatter them over the head of Ernest; they made reverend wrinkles across his forehead, and furrows in his cheeks. He was an aged man. But not in vain had he grown old: more than the white hairs on his head were the sage thoughts in his mind; his wrinkles and furrows were inscriptions that Time had graved, and in which he had written legends of wisdom that had been tested by the tenor of a life. And Ernest had ceased to be obscure. Unsought for, undesired, had come the fame which so many seek, and made him known in the great world, beyond the limits of the valley in which he had dwelt so quietly. College professors, and even the active men of cities, came from far to see and converse with Ernest; for the report had gone abroad that this simple husbandman had ideas unlike those of other men, not gained from books, but of a higher tone,—a tranquil and familiar majesty, as if he had been talking with the angels as his daily friends. Whether it were sage, statesman, or philanthropist, Ernest received these visitors with the gentle sincerity that had characterized him from boyhood, and spoke freely with them of whatever came uppermost, or lay deepest in his heart or their own. While they talked together, his face would kindle, unawares, and shine upon them, as with a mild evening light. Pensive with the fulness of such discourse, his guests took leave and went their way; and, passing up the valley, paused to look at the Great Stone Face, imagining that they had seen its likeness in a human countenance, but could not remember where.

While Ernest had been growing up and growing old, a bountiful Providence had granted a new poet to this earth. He, likewise, was a native of the valley, but had spent the greater part of his life at a distance from that romantic region, pouring out his sweet music amid the bustle and din of cities. Often, however, did the mountains which had been familiar to him in his childhood lift their snowy peaks into the clear atmosphere of his poetry. Neither was the Great Stone Face forgotten, for the poet had celebrated it in an ode, which was grand enough to have been uttered by its own majestic lips. This man of genius, we may say, had come down from heaven with wonderful endowments. If he sang of a mountain, the eyes of all mankind beheld a mightier grandeur reposing on its breast, or soaring to its summit, than had before been seen there. If his theme were a lovely lake, a celestial smile had now been thrown over it, to gleam forever on its surface. If it were the vast old sea, even the deep immensity of its dread bosom seemed to swell the higher, as if moved by the emotions of the song. Thus the world assumed another and a better aspect from the hour that the poet blessed it with his happy eyes. The Creator had bestowed him, as the last, best touch to his own handiwork. Creation was not finished till the poet came to interpret, and so complete it.

The effect was no less high and beautiful, when his human brethren were the subject of his verse. The man or woman, sordid with the common dust of life, who crossed his daily path, and the little child who played in it, were glorified if he beheld them in his mood of poetic faith. He showed the golden links of the great chain that intertwined them with an angelic kindred; he brought out the hidden traits of a celestial birth that made them worthy of such kin. Some, indeed, there were, who thought to show the soundness of their judgment by affirming that all the beauty and dignity of the natural world existed only in the poet's fancy. Let such men speak for themselves, who undoubtedly appear to have been spawned forth by Nature with a contemptuous bitterness; she having plastered them up out of her refuse stuff, after all the swine were made. As respects all things else, the poet's ideal was the truest truth.

The songs of this poet found their

way to Ernest. He read them, after his customary toil, seated on the bench before his cottage door, where, for such a length of time, he had filled his repose with thought, by gazing at the Great Stone Face. And now, as he read stanzas that caused the soul to thrill within him, he lifted his eyes to the vast countenance beaming on him so benignantly.

"O majestic friend," he murmured, addressing the Great Stone Face, "is not this man worthy to resemble thee?"

The Face seemed to smile, but answered not a word.

Now it happened that the poet, though he dwelt so far away, had not only heard of Ernest, but had meditated much upon his character, until he deemed nothing so desirable as to meet this man, whose untaught wisdom walked hand in hand with the noble simplicity of his life. One summer morning, therefore, he took passage by the railroad, and, in the decline of the afternoon, alighted from the cars at no great distance from Ernest's cottage. The great hotel, which had formerly been the palace of Mr. Gathergold, was close at hand, but the poet, with his carpet-bag on his arm, inquired at once where Ernest dwelt, and was resolved to be accepted as his guest.

Approaching the door, he there found the good old man, holding a volume in his hand, which alternately he read, and then, with a finger between the leaves, looked lovingly at the Great Stone Face.

"Good evening," said the poet. "Can you give a traveller a night's lodging?"

"Willingly," answered Ernest; and then he added, smiling, "Methinks I never saw the Great Stone Face look so

hospitably at a stranger."

The poet sat down on the bench beside him, and he and Ernest talked together. Often had the poet held intercourse with the wittiest and the wisest, but never before with a man like Ernest, whose thoughts and feelings gushed up with such a natural freedom, and who made great truths so familiar by his simple utterance of them. Angels, as had been so often said, seemed to have wrought with him at his labor in the fields; angels seemed to have sat with him by the fireside; and, dwelling with angels as friend with friends, he had imbibed the sublimity of their ideas, and imbued it with the sweet and lowly charm of household words. So thought the poet. And Ernest, on the other hand, was moved and agitated by the living images which the poet flung out of his mind, and which peopled all the air about the cottage door with shapes of beauty, both gay and pensive. The sympathies of these two men instructed them with a profounder sense than either could have attained alone. Their minds accorded into one strain, and made delightful music which neither of them could have claimed as all his own, nor distinguished his own share from the other's. They led one another, as it were, into a high pavilion of their thoughts, so remote, and hitherto so dim, that they had never entered it before, and so beautiful that they desired to be there always.

As Ernest listened to the poet, he imagined that the Great Stone Face was bending forward to listen too. He gazed earnestly into the poet's glowing eyes.

"Who are you, my strangely gifted

guest?" he said.

The poet laid his finger on the volume that Ernest had been reading.

"You have read these poems," said he. "You know me, then,—for I wrote them."

Again, and still more earnestly than before, Ernest examined the poet's features; then turned towards the Great Stone Face; then back, with an uncertain aspect, to his guest. But his countenance fell; he shook his head, and sighed.

"Wherefore are you sad?" inquired the poet.

"Because," replied Ernest, "all through life I have awaited the fulfilment of a prophecy; and, when I read these poems, I hoped that it might be fulfilled in you."

"You hoped," answered the poet, faintly smiling, "to find in me the likeness of the Great Stone Face. And you are disappointed, as formerly with Mr. Gathergold, and Old Blood-and-Thunder, and Old Stony Phiz. Yes, Ernest, it is my doom. You must add my name to the illustrious three, and record another failure of your hopes. For—in shame and sadness do I speak it, Ernest —I am not worthy to be typified by yonder benign and majestic image."

"And why?" asked Ernest. He pointed to the volume. "Are not those thoughts divine?"

"They have a strain of the Divinity," replied the poet. "You can hear in them the far-off echo of a heavenly song. But my life, dear Ernest, has not corresponded with my thought. I have had grand dreams, but they have been only dreams, because I have lived—and that, too, by my own choice—among poor and mean realities. Sometimes even—

shall I dare to say it?—I lack faith in the grandeur, the beauty, and the goodness which my own works are said to have made more evident in nature and in human life. Why, then, pure seeker of the good and true, shouldst thou hope to find me in yonder image of the divine!"

The poet spoke sadly, and his eyes were dim with tears. So, likewise, were those of Ernest.

At the hour of sunset, as had long been his frequent custom, Ernest was to discourse to an assemblage of the neighboring inhabitants, in the open air. He and the poet, arm in arm, still talking together as they went along, proceeded to the spot. It was a small nook among the hills, with a gray precipice behind, the stern front of which was relieved by the pleasant foliage of many creeping plants, that made a tapestry for the naked rock, by hanging their festoons from all its rugged angles. At a small elevation above the ground, set in a rich framework of verdure, there appeared a niche, spacious enough to admit a human figure, with freedom for such gestures as spontaneously accompany earnest thought and genuine emotion. Into this natural pulpit Ernest ascended, and threw a look of familiar kindness around upon his audience. They stood, or sat, or reclined upon the grass, as seemed good to each, with the departing sunshine falling obliquely over them, and mingling its subdued cheerfulness with the solemnity of a grove of ancient trees, beneath and amid the boughs of which the golden rays were constrained to pass. In another direction was seen the Great Stone Face, with the same cheer, combined with the same solemnity, in its benignant aspect.

Ernest began to speak, giving to the people of what was in his heart and mind. His words had power, because they accorded with his thoughts; and his thoughts had reality and depth, because they harmonized with the life which he had always lived. It was not mere breath that this preacher uttered; they were the words of life, because a life of good deeds and holy love was melted into them. Pearls, pure and rich, had been dissolved into this precious draught. The poet, as he listened, felt that the being and character of Ernest were a nobler strain of poetry than he had ever written. His eyes glistening with tears, he gazed reverentially at the venerable man, and said within himself that never was there an aspect so worthy of a prophet and a sage as that mild, sweet, thoughtful countenance, with the glory of white hair diffused about it. At a distance, but distinctly to be seen, high up in the golden light of the setting sun, appeared the Great Stone Face, with hoary mists around it, like the white hairs around the brow of Ernest. Its look of grand beneficence seemed to embrace the world.

At that moment, in sympathy with a thought which he was about to utter, the face of Ernest assumed a grandeur of expression, so imbued with benevolence, that the poet, by an irresistible impulse, threw his arms aloft, and shouted,—

"Behold! Behold! Ernest is himself the likeness of the Great Stone Face!"

Then all the people looked, and saw that what the deep-sighted poet said was true. The prophecy was fulfilled. But Ernest, having finished what he had to say, took the poet's arm, and walked slowly homeward, still hoping that some wiser and better man than himself would by and by appear, bearing a resemblance to the GREAT STONE FACE.

MAIN-STREET

A RESPECTABLE-LOOKING individual makes his bow, and addresses the public. In my daily walks along the principal street of my native town, it has often occurred to me, that, if its growth from infancy upward, and the vicissitude of characteristic scenes that have passed along this thoroughfare during the more than two centuries of its existence, could be presented to the eye in a shifting panorama, it would be an exceedingly effective method of illustrating the march of time. Acting on this idea, I have contrived a certain pictorial exhibition, somewhat in the nature of a puppet-show, by means of which I propose to call up the multiform and many-colored Past before the spectator, and show him the ghosts of his forefathers, amid a succession of historic incidents, with no greater trouble than the turning of a crank. Be pleased, therefore, my indulgent patrons, to walk into the show-room, and take your seats before yonder mysterious curtain. The little wheels and springs of my machinery have been well oiled; a multitude of puppets are dressed in character, representing all varieties of fashion, from the Puritan cloak and jerkin to the latest Oak Hall coat; the lamps are trimmed, and shall brighten into noontide sunshine, or fade away in moonlight, or muffle their brilliancy in a November cloud, as the nature of the scene may require; and, in short, the exhibition is just ready to commence. Unless something should go wrong,—as, for instance, the misplacing of a picture, whereby the people and events of one century might be thrust into the middle of another; or the breaking of a wire, which would bring the course of time to a sudden period, —barring, I say, the casualties to which such a complicated piece of mechanism is liable,—I flatter myself, ladies and gentlemen, that the performance will elicit your generous approbation.

Ting-a-ting-ting! goes the bell; the curtain rises; and we behold—not, indeed, the Main-street—but the track of leaf-strewn forest-land over which its dusty pavement is hereafter to extend.

You perceive, at a glance, that this is the ancient and primitive wood,—the ever-youthful and venerably old,—verdant with new twigs, yet hoary, as it were, with the snowfall of innumerable years, that have accumulated upon its intermingled branches. The white man's axe has never smitten a single tree; his footstep has never crumpled a single one of the withered leaves, which all the autumns since the flood have been harvesting beneath. Yet, see! along through the vista of impending boughs there is already a faintly-traced path, running nearly east and west, as if a

prophecy or foreboding of the future street had stolen into the heart of the solemn old wood. Onward goes this hardly perceptible track, now ascending over a natural swell of land, now subsiding gently into a hollow; traversed here by a little streamlet, which glitters like a snake through the gleam of sunshine, and quickly hides itself among the underbrush, in its quest for the neighboring cove; and impeded there by the massy corpse of a giant of the forest, which had lived out its incalculable term of life, and been overthrown by mere old age, and lies buried in the new vegetation that is born of its decay. What footsteps can have worn this half-seen path? Hark! Do we not hear them now rustling softly over the leaves? We discern an Indian woman,—a majestic and queenly woman, or else her spectral image does not represent her truly,—for this is the great Squaw Sachem, whose rule, with that of her sons, extends from Mystic to Agawam. That red chief, who stalks by her side, is Wappacowet, her second husband, the priest and magician, whose incantations shall hereafter affright the pale-faced settlers with grisly phantoms, dancing and shrieking in the woods, at midnight. But greater would be the affright of the Indian necromancer, if, mirrored in the pool of water at his feet, he could catch a prophetic glimpse of the noonday marvels which the white man is destined to achieve; if he could see, as in a dream, the stone-front of the stately hall, which will cast its shadow over this very spot; if he could be aware that the future edifice will contain a noble Museum, where, among countless curiosities of earth and sea, a few In dian arrow-heads shall be treasured up as memorials of a vanished race!

No such forebodings disturb the Squaw Sachem and Wappacowet. They pass on, beneath the tangled shade, holding high talk on matters of state and religion, and imagine, doubtless, that their own system of affairs will endure forever. Meanwhile, how full of its own proper life is the scene that lies around them! The gray squirrel runs up the trees, and rustles among the upper branches. Was not that the leap of a deer? And there is the whir of a partridge! Methinks, too, I catch the cruel and stealthy eye of a wolf, as he draws back into yonder impervious density of underbrush. So, there, amid the murmur of boughs, go the Indian queen and the Indian priest; while the gloom of the broad wilderness impends over them, and its sombre mystery invests them as with something preternatural; and only momentary streaks of quivering sunlight, once in a great while, find their way down, and glimmer among the feathers in their dusky hair. Can it be that the thronged street of a city will ever pass into this twilight solitude,—over those soft heaps of the decaying tree-trunks, and through the swampy places, green with water-moss, and penetrate that hopeless entanglement of great trees, which have been uprooted and tossed together by a whirlwind? It has been a wilderness from the creation. Must it not be a wilderness forever?

Here an acidulous-looking gentleman in blue glasses, with bows of Berlin steel, who has taken a seat at the extremity of the front row, begins, at this early stage of the exhibition, to criticise. "The whole affair is a manifest catch-penny!" observes he, scarcely under his breath. "The trees look more like weeds in a garden than a primitive forest; the Squaw Sachem and Wappacowet are stiff in their pasteboard joints; and the squirrels, the deer, and the wolf move with all the grace of a child's wooden monkey, sliding up and down a stick."

"I am obliged to you, sir, for the candor of your remarks," replies the showman, with a bow. "Perhaps they are just. Human art has its limits, and we must now and then ask a little aid from the spectator's imagination."

"You will get no such aid from mine," responds the critic. "I make it a point to see things precisely as they are. But come! go ahead! the stage is waiting!"

The showman proceeds.

Casting our eyes again over the scene, we perceive that strangers have found their way into the solitary place. In more than one spot, among the trees, an upheaved axe is glittering in the sunshine. Roger Conant, the first settler in Naumkeag, has built his dwelling, months ago, on the border of the forest-path; and at this moment he comes eastward through the vista of woods, with his gun over his shoulder, bringing home the choice portions of a deer. His stalwart figure, clad in a leather jerkin and breeches of the same, strides sturdily onward, with such an air of physical force and energy that we might almost expect the very trees to stand aside, and give him room to pass. And so, indeed, they must; for, humble as is his name in history, Roger Conant still is of that class of men who do not merely find, but make, their place in the system of human affairs; a man of thoughtful strength, he has planted the germ of a city. There stands his habitation, showing in its rough architecture some features of the Indian wigwam, and some of the log-cabin, and somewhat, too, of the straw-thatched cottage in Old England, where this good yeoman had his birth and breeding. The dwelling is surrounded by a cleared space of a few acres, where Indian corn grows thrivingly among the stumps of the trees; while the dark forest hems it in, and seems to gaze silently and solemnly, as if wondering at the breadth of sunshine which the white man spreads around him. An Indian, half hidden in the dusky shade, is gazing and wondering too.

Within the door of the cottage you discern the wife, with her ruddy English cheek. She is singing, doubtless, a psalm tune, at her household work; or, perhaps she sighs at the remembrance of the cheerful gossip, and all the merry social life, of her native village beyond the vast and melancholy sea. Yet the next moment she laughs, with sympathetic glee, at the sports of her little tribe of children; and soon turns round, with the home-look in her face, as her husband's foot is heard approaching the rough-hewn threshold. How sweet must it be for those who have an Eden in their hearts, like Roger Conant and his wife, to find a new world to project it into, as they have, instead of dwelling among old haunts of men, where so many household fires have been kindled and burnt out, that the very glow of happiness has something dreary in it! Not that this pair are alone in their wild Eden, for here comes Goodwife Massey, the young spouse of Jeffrey Massey, from her home hard by, with an infant at her breast. Dame Conant has another of like age; and it shall hereafter be one of the disputed points of history which of these two babies was the first town-born child.

But see! Roger Conant has other neighbors within view. Peter Palfrey likewise has built himself a house, and so has Balch, and Norman, and Woodbury. Their dwellings, indeed,—such is the ingenious contrivance of this piece of pictorial mechanism,—seem to have arisen, at various points of the scene, even while we have been looking at it. The forest-track, trodden more and more by the hob-nailed shoes of these sturdy and ponderous Englishmen, has now a distinctness which it never could have acquired from the light tread of a hundred times as many Indian moccasons. It will be a street, anon. As we observe it now, it goes onward from one clearing to another, here plunging into a shadowy strip of woods, there open to the sunshine, but everywhere showing a decided line, along which human interests have begun to hold their career. Over yonder swampy spot, two trees have been felled, and laid side by side, to make a causeway. In another place, the axe has cleared away a confused intricacy of fallen trees and clustered boughs, which had been tossed together by a hurricane. So now the little children, just beginning to run alone, may trip along the path, and not often stumble over an impediment, unless they stray from it to gather wood-berries beneath the trees. And, besides the feet of grown people and children, there are the cloven hoofs of a small herd of cows, who seek their subsistence from the native grasses, and help to deepen the track of the future thoroughfare. Goats also browse along it, and nibble at the twigs that thrust themselves across the way. Not seldom, in its more secluded portions, where the black shadow of the forest strives to hide the trace of human footsteps, stalks a gaunt wolf, on the watch for a kid or a young calf; or fixes his hungry gaze on the group of children gathering berries, and can hardly forbear to rush upon them. And the Indians, coming from their distant wigwams to view the white man's settlement, marvel at the deep track which he makes, and perhaps are saddened by a flitting presentiment that this heavy tread will find its way over all the land, and that the wild woods, the wild wolf, and the wild Indian will alike be trampled beneath it. Even so shall it be. The pavements of the Main-street must be laid over the red man's grave.

Behold! here is a spectacle which should be ushered in by the peal of trumpets, if Naumkeag had ever yet heard that cheery music, and by the roar of cannon, echoing among the woods. A procession,—for, by its dignity, as marking an epoch in the history of the street, it deserves that name,— a procession advances along the pathway. The good ship Abigail has arrived from England, bringing wares and merchandise, for the comfort of the inhabitants, and traffic with the Indians; bringing passengers too, and, more important than all, a governor for the new settlement. Roger Conant and Peter Palfrey, with their companions, have been to the shore to welcome them; and now, with such honor and triumph as their rude way of life permits, are escorting the sea-flushed voyagers to their habitations. At the point where Endicott enters upon the scene two venerable trees unite their branches high above his head; thus forming a triumphal arch of living verdure, beneath which he pauses, with his wife leaning on his arm, to catch the first impression of their new-found home. The old settlers gaze not less earnestly at him than he at the hoary woods and the rough surface of the clearings. They like his bearded face, under the shadow of the broad-brimmed and steeple-crowned Puritan hat;—a visage resolute, grave, and thoughtful, yet apt to kindle with that glow of a cheerful spirit by which men of strong character are enabled to go joyfully on their proper tasks. His form, too, as you see it, in a doublet and hose of sad-colored cloth, is of a manly make, fit for toil and hardship, and fit to wield the heavy sword that hangs from his leathern belt. His aspect is a better warrant for the ruler's office than the parchment commission which he bears, however fortified it may be with the broad seal of the London council. Peter Palfrey nods to Roger Conant. "The worshipful Court of Assistants have done wisely," say they between themselves. "They have chosen for our governor a man out of a thousand." Then they toss up their hats,—they and all the uncouth figures of their company, most of whom are clad in skins, inasmuch as their old kersey and linsey-woolsey garments have been torn and tattered by many a long month's wear, —they all toss up their hats, and salute their new governor and captain with a hearty English shout of welcome. We seem to hear it with our own ears, so perfectly is the action represented in this life-like, this almost magic picture!

But have you observed the lady who leans upon the arm of Endicott?—a rose of beauty from an English garden, now to be transplanted to a fresher soil. It may be that, long years—centuries, indeed—after this fair flower shall have decayed, other flowers of the same race will appear in the same soil, and gladden other generations with hereditary beauty. Does not the vision haunt us yet? Has not Nature kept the mould unbroken, deeming it a pity that the idea should vanish from mortal sight forever, after only once assuming earthly substance? Do we not recognize in that fair woman's face the model of features which still beam, at happy moments, on what was then the woodland pathway, but has long since grown into a busy street?

"This is too ridiculous!—positively insufferable!" mutters the same critic who had before expressed his disapprobation. "Here is a pasteboard figure, such as a child would cut out of a card with a pair of very dull scissors; and the fellow modestly requests us to see in it the prototype of hereditary beauty!"

"But, sir, you have not the proper point of view," remarks the showman. "You sit altogether too near to get the best effect of my pictorial exhibition. Pray oblige me by removing to this other bench, and I venture to assure you the proper light and shadow will transform the spectacle into quite another thing."

"Pshaw!" replies the critic: "I want no other light and shade. I have already told you that it is my business to see things just as they are."

"I would suggest to the author of this ingenious exhibition," observes a gentlemanly person, who has shown signs of being much interested,—"I would suggest that Anna Gower, the first wife of Governor Endicott, and who came with him from England, left no posterity; and that, consequently, we cannot be indebted to that honorable lady for any specimens of feminine loveliness now extant among us."

Having nothing to allege against this genealogical objection, the showman points again to the scene.

During this little interruption, you perceive that the Anglo-Saxon energy —as the phrase now goes—has been at work in the spectacle before us. So many chimneys now send up their smoke that it begins to have the aspect of a village street; although everything is so inartificial and inceptive, that it seems as if one returning wave of the wild nature might overwhelm it all. But the one edifice which gives the pledge of permanence to this bold enterprise is seen at the central point of the picture. There stands the meeting-house, a small structure, low-roofed, without a spire, and built of rough timber, newly hewn, with the sap still in the logs, and here and there a strip of bark adhering to them. A meaner temple was never consecrated to the worship of the Deity. With the alternative of kneeling beneath the awful vault of the firmament, it is strange that men should creep into this pent-up nook, and expect God's presence there. Such, at least, one would imagine, might be the feeling of these forest-settlers, accustomed as they had been to stand under the dim arches of vast cathedrals, and to offer up their hereditary worship in the old, ivy-covered churches of rural England, around which lay the bones of many generations of their forefathers. How could they dispense with the carved altar-work?—how, with the pictured windows, where the light of common day was hallowed by being transmitted through the glorified figures of saints? —how, with the lofty roof, imbued, as it must have been, with the prayers that had gone upward for centuries?— how, with the rich peal of the solemn organ, rolling along the aisles, pervading the whole church, and sweeping the soul away on a flood of audible religion? They needed nothing of all this. Their house of worship, like their ceremonial, was naked, simple, and severe. But the zeal of a recovered faith burned like a lamp within their hearts, enriching everything around them with its radiance; making of these new walls, and this narrow compass, its own cathedral; and being, in itself, that spiritual mystery and experience of which sacred architecture, pictured windows, and the organ's grand solemnity are remote and imperfect symbols. All was well, so long as their lamps were freshly kindled at the heavenly flame. After a while, however, whether in their time or their children's, these lamps began to burn more dimly, or with a less genuine lustre; and then it might be seen how hard, cold, and confined was their system,—how like an iron cage was that which they called Liberty.

Too much of this. Look again at the picture, and observe how the aforesaid Anglo-Saxon energy is now trampling along the street, and raising a positive cloud of dust beneath its sturdy footsteps. For there the carpenters are building a new house, the frame of which was hewn and fitted in England, of English oak, and sent hither on shipboard; and here a blacksmith makes huge clang and clatter on his anvil, shaping out tools and weapons; and yonder a wheelwright, who boasts himself a London workman, regularly bred to his handicraft, is fashioning a set of wagon-wheels, the track of which shall soon be visible. The wild forest is shrinking back; the street has lost the aromatic odor of the pine-trees, and of the sweet-fern that grew beneath them. The tender and modest wild-flowers, those gentle children of savage nature that grew pale beneath the ever-brooding shade, have shrunk away and disappeared, like stars that vanish in the breadth of light. Gardens are fenced in, and display pumpkin-beds and rows of cabbages and beans; and, though the governor and the minister both view them with a disapproving eye, plants of broad-leaved tobacco, which the cultivators are enjoined to use privily, or not at all. No wolf, for a year past, has been heard to bark, or known to range among the dwellings, except that single one, whose grisly head, with a plash of blood beneath it, is now affixed to the portal of the meeting-house. The partridge has ceased to run across the too-frequented path. Of all the wild life that used to throng here, only the Indians still come into the settlement, bringing the skins of beaver and otter, bear and elk, which they sell to Endicott for the wares of England. And there is little John Massey, the son of Jeffrey Massey and the first-born of Naumkeag, playing beside his father's threshold, a child six or seven years old. Which is the better grown infant,— the town or the boy?

The red men have become aware that the street is no longer free to them. save by the sufferance and permission of the settlers. Often, to impress them with an awe of English power, there is a muster and training of the town-forces, and a stately march of the mail-clad band, like this which we now see advancing up the street. There they come, fifty of them, or more; all with their iron breastplates and steel caps well burnished, and glimmering bravely against the sun; their ponderous muskets on their shoulders, their bandoliers about their waists, their lighted matches in their hands, and the drum and fife playing cheerily before them. See! do they not step like martial men? Do they not manœuvre like soldiers who have seen stricken fields? And well they may; for this band is composed of precisely such materials as those with which Cromwell is preparing to beat down the strength of a kingdom; and his famous regiment of Ironsides might be recruited from just such men. In everything, at this period, New England was the essential spirit and flower of that which was about to become uppermost in the mother-country. Many a bold and wise man lost the fame which would have accrued to him in English history by crossing the Atlantic with our forefathers. Many a valiant captain, who might have been foremost at Marston Moor or Naseby, exhausted his martial ardor in the command of a log-built fortress like that which you observe on the gently rising ground at the right of the pathway,—its banner fluttering in the breeze, and the culverins and sakers showing their deadly muzzles over the rampart.

A multitude of people were now thronging to New England: some, because the ancient and ponderous framework of Church and State threatened to tumble down upon their heads; others, because they despaired of such a downfall. Among those who came to Naumkeag were men of history and legend, whose feet leave a track of brightness along any pathway which they have trodden. You shall behold their life-like images,—their spectres, if you choose so to call them,—passing, encountering with a familiar nod, stopping to converse together, praying, bearing weapons, laboring or resting from their labors, in the Main-street. Here, now, comes Hugh Peters, an earnest, restless man, walking swiftly, as being impelled by that fiery activity of nature which shall hereafter thrust him into the conflict of dangerous affairs, make him the chaplain and counsellor of Cromwell, and finally bring him to a bloody end. He pauses, by the meeting-house, to exchange a greeting with Roger Williams, whose face indicates, methinks, a gentler spirit, kinder and more expansive, than that of Peters; yet not less active for what he discerns to be the will of God, or the welfare of mankind. And look! here is a guest for Endicott, coming forth out of the forest, through which he has been journeying from Boston, and which with its rude branches has caught hold of his attire, and has wet his feet with its swamps and streams. Still there is something in his mild and venerable, though not aged presence,—a propriety, an equilibrium, in Governor Winthrop's nature,—that causes the disarray of his costume to be unnoticed, and gives us the same impression as if he were clad in such grave and rich attire as we may suppose him to have worn in the Council-chamber of the colony. Is not this characteristic wonderfully perceptible in our spectral representative of his person? But what dignitary is this crossing from the other side to greet the governor? A stately personage, in a dark velvet cloak, with a hoary beard, and a gold chain across his breast; he has the authoritative port of one who has filled the highest civic station in the first of cities. Of all men in the world, we should least expect to meet the Lord Mayor of London—as Sir Richard Saltonstall has been, once and again—in a forest-bordered settlement of the western wilderness.

Farther down the street, we see Emanuel Downing, a grave and worthy citizen, with his son George, a stripling who has a career before him; his shrewd and quick capacity and pliant conscience shall not only exalt him high, but secure him from a downfall. Here is another figure, on whose characteristic make and expressive action I will stake the credit of my pictorial puppet-show. Have you not already detected a quaint, sly humor in that face,—an eccentricity in the manner,—a certain indescribable waywardness,—all the marks, in short, of an original man, unmistakably impressed, yet kept down by a sense of clerical restraint? That is Nathaniel Ward, the minister of Ipswich, but better remembered as the simple cobbler of Agawam. He hammered his sole so faithfully, and stitched his upper-leather so well, that the shoe is hardly yet worn out, though thrown aside for some two centuries past. And next, among these Puritans and Roundheads, we observe the very model of a Cavalier, with the curling lovelock, the fantastically trimmed beard, the embroidery, the ornamented rapier, the gilded dagger, and all other foppishnesses that

distinguish the wild gallants who rode headlong to their overthrow in the cause of King Charles. This is Morton of Merry Mount, who has come hither to hold a council with Endicott, but will shortly be his prisoner. Yonder pale, decaying figure of a white-robed woman, who glides slowly along the street, is the Lady Arabella, looking for her own grave in the virgin soil. That other female form, who seems to be talking—we might almost say preaching or expounding—in the centre of a group of profoundly attentive auditors, is Ann Hutchinson. And here comes Vane—

"But, my dear sir," interrupts the same gentleman who before questioned the showman's genealogical accuracy, "allow me to observe that these historical personages could not possibly have met together in the Main-street. They might, and probably did, all visit our old town, at one time or another, but not simultaneously; and you have fallen into anachronisms that I postively shudder to think of!"

"The fellow," adds the scarcely civil critic, "has learned a bead-roll of historic names, whom he lugs into his pictorial puppet-show, as he calls it, helter-skelter, without caring whether they were contemporaries or not,—and sets them all by the ears together. But was there ever such a fund of impudence? To hear his running commentary, you would suppose that these miserable slips of painted pasteboard, with hardly the remotest outlines of the human figure, had all the character and expression of Michael Angelo's pictures. Well! go on, sir!"

"Sir, you break the illusion of the

scene," mildly remonstrates the show-man.

"Illusion! What illusion?" rejoins the critic, with a contemptuous snort. "On the word of a gentleman, I see nothing illusive in the wretchedly bedaubed sheet of canvas that forms your back-ground, or in these pasteboard slips that hitch and jerk along the front. The only illusion, permit me to say, is in the puppet-showman's tongue,—and that but a wretched one, into the bargain!"

"We public men," replies the show-man, meekly, "must lay our account, sometimes, to meet an uncandid sever-ity of criticism. But—merely for your own pleasure, sir—let me entreat you to take another point of view. Sit far-ther back, by that young lady, in whose face I have watched the reflection of every changing scene; only oblige me by sitting there; and, take my word for it, the slips of pasteboard shall assume spiritual life, and the bedaubed canvas become an airy and changeable reflex of what it purports to represent."

"I know better," retorts the critic, settling himself in his seat, with sullen but self-complacent immovableness. "And, as for my own pleasure, I shall best consult it by remaining precisely where I am."

The showman bows, and waves his hand; and at the signal, as if time and vicissitude had been awaiting his per-mission to move onward, the mimic street becomes alive again.

Years have rolled over our scene, and converted the forest-track into a dusty thoroughfare, which, being inter-sected with lanes and cross-paths, may fairly be designated as the Main-street. On the ground-sites of many of the log-built sheds, into which the first settlers crept for shelter, houses of quaint archi-tecture have now risen. These later edifices are built, as you see, in one gen-erally accordant style, though with such subordinate variety as keeps the be-holder's curiosity excited, and causes each structure, like its owner's character, to produce its own peculiar impression. Most of them have one huge chimney in the centre, with flues so vast that it must have been easy for the witches to fly out of them, as they were wont to do, when bound on an aerial visit to the Black Man in the forest. Around this great chimney the wooden house clusters itself, in a whole community of gable-ends, each ascending into its own separate peak; the second story, with its lattice-windows, projecting over the first; and the door, which is per-haps arched, provided on the outside with an iron hammer, wherewith the visitor's hand may give a thundering rat-a-tat. The timber framework of these houses, as compared with those of recent date, is like the skeleton of an old giant, beside the frail bones of a modern man of fashion. Many of them, by the vast strength and sound-ness of their oaken substance, have been preserved through a length of time which would have tried the stability of brick and stone; so that, in all the progressive decay and continual recon-struction of the street, down to our own days, we shall still behold these old edifices occupying their long-accus-tomed sites. For instance, on the upper corner of that green lane which shall hereafter be North-street, we see the Curwen House, newly built, with the carpenters still at work on the roof, nailing down the last sheaf of shingles. On the lower corner stands another dwelling,—destined, at some period of its existence, to be the abode of an unsuccessful alchemist,—which shall likewise survive to our own generation, and perhaps long outlive it. Thus through the medium of these patriarchal edifices, we have now established a sort of kindred and hereditary acquaintance with the Main-street.

Great as is the transformation produced by a short term of years, each single day creeps through the Puritan settlement sluggishly enough. It shall pass before your eyes, condensed into the space of a few moments. The gray light of early morning is slowly diffusing itself over the scene; and the bell-man, whose office it is to cry the hour at the street-corners, rings the last peal upon his hand-bell, and goes wearily homewards, with the owls, the bats, and other creatures of the night. Lattices are thrust back on their hinges, as if the town were opening its eyes, in the summer morning. Forth stumbles the still drowsy cow-herd, with his horn; putting which to his lips, it emits a bellowing bray, impossible to be represented in the picture, but which reaches the pricked-up ears of every cow in the settlement, and tells her that the dewy pasture-hour is come. House after house awakes, and sends the smoke up curling from its chimney, like frosty breath from living nostrils; and as those white wreaths of smoke, though impregnated with earthy admixtures, climb skyward, so, from each dwelling, does the morning worship—its spiritual essence bearing up its human imperfection—find its way to the Heavenly Father's throne.

The breakfast-hour being passed, the inhabitants do not, as usual, go to their fields or workshops, but remain within doors; or perhaps walk the street, with a grave sobriety, yet a disengaged and unburdened aspect, that belongs neither to a holiday nor a Sabbath. And, indeed, this passing day is neither, nor is it a common week-day, although partaking of all the three. It is the Thursday Lecture; an institution which New England has long ago relinquished, and almost forgotten, yet which it would have been better to retain, as bearing relations to both the spiritual and ordinary life, and bringing each acquainted with the other. The tokens of its observance, however, which here meet our eyes, are of rather a questionable cast. It is, in one sense, a day of public shame; the day on which transgressors, who have made themselves liable to the minor severities of the Puritan law, receive their reward of ignominy. At this very moment, the constable has bound an idle fellow to the whipping-post, and is giving him his deserts with a cat-o'-nine-tails. Ever since sunrise, Daniel Fairfield has been standing on the steps of the meeting-house, with a halter about his neck, which he is condemned to wear visibly throughout his lifetime; Dorothy Talby is chained to a post at the corner of Prison-lane, with the hot sun blazing on her matronly face, and all for no other offence than lifting her hand against her husband; while, through the bars of that great wooden cage, in the centre of the scene, we discern either a human being or a wild beast, or both in one, whom this public infamy causes to roar, and gnash his teeth, and shake the strong oaken bars, as if he would break forth, and tear in pieces the little children who have been peeping at him.

Such are the profitable sights that serve the good people to while away the earlier part of lecture-day. Betimes in the forenoon, a traveller—the first traveller that has come hitherward this morning—rides slowly into the street, on his patient steed. He seems a clergyman; and, as he draws near, we recognize the minister of Lynn, who was pre-engaged to lecture here, and has been revolving his discourse as he rode through the hoary wilderness. Behold, now, the whole town thronging into the meeting-house, mostly with such sombre visages that the sunshine becomes little better than a shadow when it falls upon them. There go the Thirteen Men, grim rulers of a grim community! There goes John Massey, the first town-born child, now a youth of twenty, whose eye wanders with peculiar interest towards that buxom damsel who comes up the steps at the same instant. There hobbles Goody Foster, a sour and bitter old beldam, looking as if she went to curse, and not to pray, and whom many of her neighbors suspect of taking an occasional airing on a broomstick. There, too, slinking shamefacedly in, you observe that same poor do-nothing and good-for-nothing whom we saw castigated just now at the whipping-post. Last of all, there goes the tithing-man, lugging in a couple of small boys, whom he has caught at play beneath God's blessed sunshine, in a back lane. What native of Naumkeag, whose recollections go back more than thirty years, does not still shudder at that dark ogre of his infancy, who perhaps had long ceased to have an actual existence, but still lived in his childish belief, in a horrible idea, and in the nurse's threat, as the Tidy Man!

It will be hardly worth our while to wait two, or it may be three, turnings of the hour-glass, for the conclusion of the lecture. Therefore, by my control over light and darkness, I cause the dusk, and then the starless night, to brood over the street; and summon forth again the bellman, with his lantern casting a gleam about his footsteps, to pace wearily from corner to corner, and shout drowsily the hour to drowsy or dreaming ears. Happy are we, if for nothing else, yet because we did not live in those days. In truth, when the first novelty and stir of spirit had subsided, —when the new settlement, between the forest-border and the sea, had become actually a little town,—its daily life must have trudged onward with hardly anything to diversify and enliven it, while also its rigidity could not fail to cause miserable distortions of the moral nature. Such a life was sinister to the intellect, and sinister to the heart; especially when one generation had bequeathed its religious gloom, and the counterfeit of its religious ardor, to the next; for these characteristics, as was inevitable, assumed the form both of hypocrisy and exaggeration, by being inherited from the example and precept of other human beings, and not from an original and spiritual source. The sons and grandchildren of the first settlers were a race of lower and narrower souls than their progenitors had been. The latter were stern, severe, intolerant, but not superstitious, not even fanatical; and endowed, if any men of that age were, with a far-seeing worldly sagacity. But it was impossible for the succeeding race to grow up, in heaven's freedom, beneath the discipline which their gloomy energy of character had established; nor, it may be, have we even yet thrown off all the unfavorable influences which, among many good ones, were bequeathed to us by our Puritan forefathers. Let us thank God for having given us such ancestors; and let each successive generation thank him, not less fervently, for being one step farther from them in the march of ages.

"What is all this?" cries the critic. "A sermon? If so, it is not in the bill."

"Very true," replies the showman; "and I ask pardon of the audience."

Look now at the street, and observe a strange people entering it. Their garments are torn and disordered, their faces haggard, their figures emaciated; for they have made their way hither through pathless deserts, suffering hunger and hardship, with no other shelter than a hollow tree, the lair of a wild beast, or an Indian wigwam. Nor, in the most inhospitable and dangerous of such lodging-places, was there half the peril that awaits them in this thoroughfare of Christian men, with those secure dwellings and warm hearths on either side of it, and yonder meeting-house as the central object of the scene. These wanderers have received from Heaven a gift that, in all epochs of the world, has brought with it the penalties of mortal suffering and persecution, scorn, enmity, and death itself;—a gift that, thus terrible to its possessors, has ever been most hateful to all other men, since its very existence seems to threaten the overthrow of whatever else the toilsome ages have built up;—the gift of a new idea. You can discern it in them, illuminating their faces—their whole persons, indeed, however earthly and cloddish—with a light that inevitably shines through, and makes the startled community aware that these men are not as they themselves are,—not brethren nor neighbors of their thought. Forthwith, it is as if an earthquake rumbled through the town, making its vibrations felt at every hearth-stone, and especially causing the spire of the meeting-house to totter. The Quakers have come. We are in peril! See! they trample upon our wise and well-established laws in the person of our chief magistrate; for Governor Endicott is passing, now an aged man, and dignified with long habits of authority,—and not one of the irreverent vagabonds has moved his hat. Did you note the ominous frown of the white-bearded Puritan governor, as he turned himself about, and, in his anger, half-uplifted the staff that has become a needful support to his old age? Here comes old Mr. Norris, our venerable minister. Will they doff their hats, and pay reverence to him? No: their hats stick fast to their ungracious heads, as if they grew there; and—impious varlets that they are, and worse than the heathen Indians!—they eye our reverend pastor with a peculiar scorn, distrust, unbelief, and utter denial of his sanctified pretensions, of which he himself immediately becomes conscious; the more bitterly conscious, as he never knew nor dreamed of the like before.

But look yonder! Can we believe our eyes? A Quaker woman, clad in sackcloth, and with ashes on her head, has mounted the steps of the meeting-house. She addresses the people in a wild, shrill voice,—wild and shrill it must be, to suit such a figure,—which makes them tremble and turn pale, although they crowd open-mouthed to hear her. She is bold against established authority; she denounces the priest and his steeple-house. Many of her hearers are appalled; some weep; and others listen with a rapt attention, as if a living truth had now, for the first time, forced its way through the crust of habit, reached their hearts, and awakened them to life. This matter must be looked to; else we have brought our faith across the seas with us in vain; and it had been better that the old forest were still standing here, waving its tangled boughs, and murmuring to the sky out of its desolate recesses, instead of this goodly street, if such blasphemies be spoken in it.

So thought the old Puritans. What was their mode of action may be partly judged from the spectacles which now pass before your eyes. Joshua Buffum is standing in the pillory. Cassandra Southwick is led to prison. And there a woman,—it is Ann Coleman,—naked from the waist upward, and bound to the tail of a cart, is dragged through the Main-street at the pace of a brisk walk, while the constable follows with a whip of knotted cords. A strong-armed fellow is that constable; and each time that he flourishes his lash in the air, you see a frown wrinkling and twisting his brow, and, at the same instant, a smile upon his lips. He loves his business, faithful officer that he is, and puts his soul into every stroke, zealous to fulfil the injunction of Major Hawthorne's warrant, in the spirit and to the letter. There came down a stroke that has drawn blood! Ten such stripes are to be given in Salem, ten in Boston, and ten in Dedham; and, with those thirty stripes of blood upon her, she is to be driven into the forest. The crimson trail goes wavering along the Main-street; but

Heaven grant that, as the rain of so many years has wept upon it, time after time, and washed it all away, so there may have been a dew of mercy, to cleanse this cruel blood-stain out of the record of the persecutor's life!

Pass on, thou spectral constable, and betake thee to thine own place of torment. Meanwhile, by the silent operation of the mechanism behind the scenes, a considerable space of time would seem to have lapsed over the street. The older dwellings now begin to look weather-beaten, through the effect of the many eastern storms that have moistened their unpainted shingles and clapboards, for not less than forty years. Such is the age we would assign to the town, judging by the aspect of John Massey, the first town-born child, whom his neighbors now call Goodman Massey, and whom we see yonder, a grave, almost autumnal-looking man, with children of his own about him. To the patriarchs of the settlement, no doubt, the Main-street is still but an affair of yesterday, hardly more antique, even if destined to be more permanent, than a path shovelled through the snow. But to the middle-aged and elderly men who came hither in childhood or early youth, it presents the aspect of a long and well-established work, on which they have expended the strength and ardor of their life. And the younger people, native to the street, whose earliest recollections are of creeping over the paternal threshold, and rolling on the grassy margin of the track, look at it as one of the perdurable things of our mortal state,—as old as the hills of the great pasture, or the headland at the harbor's mouth. Their fathers and grandsires tell them how, within a few years past, the forest stood here, with but a lonely track beneath its tangled shade. Vain legend! They cannot make it true and real to their conceptions. With them, moreover, the Main-street is a street indeed, worthy to hold its way with the thronged and stately avenues of cities beyond the sea. The old Puritans tell them of the crowds that hurry along Cheapside and Fleet-street and the Strand, and of the rush of tumultuous life at Temple Bar. They describe London Bridge, itself a street, with a row of houses on each side. They speak of the vast structure of the Tower, and the solemn grandeur of Westminster Abbey. The children listen, and still inquire if the streets of London are longer and broader than the one before their father's door; if the Tower is bigger than the jail in Prison-lane; if the old Abbey will hold a larger congregation than our meeting-house. Nothing impresses them, except their own experience.

It seems all a fable, too, that wolves have ever prowled here; and not less so, that the Squaw Sachem, and the Sagamore her son, once ruled over this region, and treated as sovereign potentates with the English settlers, then so few and storm-beaten, now so powerful. There stand some school-boys, you observe, in a little group around a drunken Indian, himself a prince of the Squaw Sachem's lineage. He brought hither some beaver-skins for sale, and has already swallowed the larger portion of their price in deadly draughts of fire-water. Is there not a touch of pathos in that picture? and does it not go far towards telling the whole story of the vast growth and prosperity of one race, and the fated decay of another?—the

children of the stranger making game of the great Squaw Sachem's grandson!

But the whole race of red men have not vanished with that wild princess and her posterity. This march of soldiers along the street betokens the breaking out of King Philip's war; and these young men, the flower of Essex, are on their way to defend the villages on the Connecticut; where, at Bloody Brook, a terrible blow shall be smitten, and hardly one of that gallant band be left alive. And there, at that stately mansion, with its three peaks in front, and its two little peaked towers, one on either side of the door, we see brave Captain Gardner issuing forth, clad in his embroidered buff-coat, and his plumed cap upon his head. His trusty sword, in its steel scabbard, strikes clanking on the door-step. See how the people throng to their doors and windows, as the cavalier rides past, reining his mettled steed so gallantly, and looking so like the very soul and emblem of martial achievement,—destined, too, to meet a warrior's fate, at the desperate assault on the fortress of the Narragansetts!

"The mettled steed looks like a pig," interrupts the critic, "and Captain Gardner himself like the Devil, though a very tame one, and on a most diminutive scale."

"Sir, sir!" cries the persecuted showman, losing all patience,—for, indeed, he had particularly prided himself on these figures of Captain Gardner and his horse,—"I see that there is no hope of pleasing you. Pray, sir, do me the favor to take back your money, and withdraw!"

"Not I!" answers the unconscionable critic. "I am just beginning to get interested in the matter. Come! turn your crank, and grind out a few more of these fooleries!"

The showman rubs his brow impulsively, whisks the little rod with which he points out the notabilities of the scene,—but, finally, with the inevitable acquiescence of all public servants, resumes his composure, and goes on.

Pass onward, onward, Time! Build up new houses here, and tear down thy works of yesterday, that have already the rusty moss upon them! Summon forth the minister to the abode of the young maiden, and bid him unite her to the joyful bridegroom! Let the youthful parents carry their first-born to the meeting-house, to receive the baptismal rite! Knock at the door, whence the sable line of the funeral is next to issue! Provide other successive generations of men, to trade, talk, quarrel, or walk in friendly intercourse along the street, as their fathers did before them! Do all thy daily and accustomed business, Father Time, in this thoroughfare, which thy footsteps, for so many years, have now made dusty! But here, at last, thou leadest along a procession which, once witnessed, shall appear no more, and be remembered only as a hideous dream of thine, or a frenzy of thy old brain.

"Turn your crank, I say," bellows the remorseless critic, "and grind it out, whatever it be, without further preface!"

The showman deems it best to comply.

Then, here comes the worshipful Captain Curwen, sheriff of Essex, on horseback, at the head of an armed guard, escorting a company of condemned prisoners from the jail to their place of execution on Gallows Hill. The witches! There is no mistaking them! The witches! As they approach up Prison-lane, and turn into the Main-street, let us watch their faces, as if we made a part of the pale crowd that presses so eagerly about them, yet shrinks back with such shuddering dread, leaving an open passage betwixt a dense throng on either side. Listen to what the people say.

There is old George Jacobs, known hereabouts these sixty years, as a man whom we thought upright in all his way of life, quiet, blameless, a good husband before his pious wife was summoned from the evil to come, and a good father to the children whom she left him. Ah! but when that blessed woman went to heaven, George Jacob's heart was empty, his hearth lonely, his life broken up; his children were married, and betook themselves to habitations of their own; and Satan, in his wanderings up and down, beheld this forlorn old man, to whom life was a sameness and a weariness, and found the way to tempt him. So the miserable sinner was prevailed with to mount into the air, and career among the clouds; and he is proved to have been present at a witch-meeting as far off as Falmouth, on the very same night that his next neighbors saw him, with his rheumatic stoop, going in at his own door. There is John Willard, too; an honest man we thought him, and so shrewd and active in his business, so practical, so intent on every-day affairs, so constant at his little place of trade, where he bartered English goods for Indian corn and all kinds of country produce! How could such a man find time, or what could put it into his mind, to leave his proper calling, and become a wizard? It is a mystery, unless the Black Man tempted him with great heaps of gold. See that aged couple,—a sad sight, truly,—John Proctor, and his wife Elizabeth. If there were two old people in all the County of Essex who seemed to have led a true Christian life, and to be treading hopefully the little remnant of their earthly path, it was this very pair. Yet have we heard it sworn, to the satisfaction of the worshipful Chief-justice Sewell, and all the court and jury, that Proctor and his wife have shown their withered faces at children's bedsides, mocking, making mouths, and affrighting the poor little innocents in the night-time. They, or their spectral appearances, have stuck pins into the afflicted ones, and thrown them into deadly fainting-fits with a touch, or but a look. And, while we supposed the old man to be reading the Bible to his old wife,—she meanwhile knitting in the chimney-corner,—the pair of hoary reprobates have whisked up the chimney, both on one broomstick, and flown away to a witch-communion, far into the depths of the chill, dark forest. How foolish! Were it only for fear of rheumatic pains in their old bones, they had better have stayed at home. But away they went; and the laughter of their decayed, cackling voices has been heard at midnight, aloft in the air. Now, in the sunny noontide, as they go tottering to the gallows, it is the Devil's turn to laugh.

Behind these two,—who help one another along, and seem to be comforting and encouraging each other, in a manner truly pitiful, if it were not a sin to pity the old witch and wizard,—behind them comes a woman, with a dark, proud face that has been beautiful, and a figure that is still majestic. Do you know her? It is Martha Carrier, whom the Devil found in a humble cottage, and looked into her discontented heart, and saw pride there, and tempted her with his promise that she should be Queen of Hell. And now, with that lofty demeanor, she is passing to her kingdom, and, by her unquenchable pride, transforms this escort of shame into a triumphal procession, that shall attend her to the gates of her infernal palace, and seat her upon the fiery throne. Within this hour, she shall assume her royal dignity.

Last of the miserable train comes a man clad in black, of small stature and a dark complexion, with a clerical band about his neck. Many a time, in the years gone by, that face has been uplifted heavenward from the pulpit of the East Meeting-house, when the Rev. Mr. Burroughs seemed to worship God. What!—he? The holy man!—the learned!—the wise! How has the Devil tempted him? His fellow-criminals, for the most part, are obtuse, uncultivated creatures, some of them scarcely half-witted by nature, and others greatly decayed in their intellects through age. They were an easy prey for the destroyer. Not so with this George Burroughs, as we judge by the inward light which glows through his dark countenance, and, we might almost say, glorifies his figure, in spite of the soil and haggardness of long imprisonment,—in spite of the heavy shadow that must fall on him, while death is walking by his side. What bribe could Satan offer rich enough to tempt and overcome this man? Alas! it may have been in the very strength of his high and searching intellect that the Tempter found the weakness which betrayed him. He yearned for knowledge; he went groping onward into a world of mystery; at first, as the witnesses have sworn, he summoned up the ghosts of his two dead wives, and talked with them of matters beyond the grave; and, when their responses failed to satisfy the intense and sinful craving of his spirit, he called on Satan, and was heard. Yet, —to look at him,—who, that had not known the proof, could believe him guilty? Who would not say, while we see him offering comfort to the weak and aged partners of his horrible crime, —while we hear his ejaculations of prayer, that seem to bubble up out of the depths of his heart, and fly heavenward, unawares,—while we behold a radiance brightening on his features as from the other world, which is but a few steps off,—who would not say, that, over the dusty track of the Main-street, a Christian saint is now going to a martyr's death? May not the Arch Fiend have been too subtle for the court and jury, and betrayed them—laughing in his sleeves the while—into the awful error of pouring out sanctified blood as an acceptable sacrifice upon God's altar? Ah no! for listen to wise Cotton Mather, who, as he sits there on his horse, speaks comfortably to the perplexed multitude, and tells them that all has been religiously and justly done, and that Satan's power shall this day receive its death-blow in New England. Heaven grant it be so!—the great scholar must be right; so lead the poor creatures to their death! Do you see that group of children and half-grown girls, and, among them, an old, hag-like Indian woman, Tituba by name? Those are the Afflicted Ones. Behold, at this very instant, a proof of Satan's power

and malice! Mercy Parris, the minister's daughter, has been smitten by a flash of Martha Carrier's eye, and falls down in the street, writhing with horrible spasms and foaming at the mouth, like the possessed one spoken of in Scripture. Hurry on the accursed witches to the gallows, ere they do more mischief! —ere they fling out their withered arms, and scatter pestilence by handfuls among the crowd!—ere, as their parting legacy, they cast a blight over the land, so that henceforth it may bear no fruit nor blade of grass, and be fit for nothing but a sepulchre for their unhallowed carcasses! So, on they go; and old George Jacobs has stumbled, by reason of his infirmity; but Goodman Proctor and his wife lean on one another, and walk at a reasonably steady pace, considering their age. Mr. Burroughs seems to administer counsel to Martha Carrier, whose face and mien, methinks, are milder and humbler than they were. Among the multitude, meanwhile, there is horror, fear, and distrust; and friend looks askance at friend, and the husband at his wife, and the wife at him, and even the mother at her little child; as if in every creature that God has made they suspected a witch, or dreaded an accuser. Never, never again, whether in this or any other shape, may Universal Madness riot in the Main-street!

I perceive in your eyes, my indulgent spectators, the criticism which you are too kind to utter. These scenes, you think, are all too sombre. So, indeed, they are; but the blame must rest on the sombre spirit of our forefathers, who wove their web of life with hardly a single thread of rose-color or gold, and not on me, who have a tropic-love of sunshine, and would gladly gild all the world with it, if I knew where to find so much. That you may believe me, I will exhibit one of the only class of scenes, so far as my investigation has taught me, in which our ancestors were wont to steep their tough old hearts in wine and strong drink, and indulge an outbreak of grisly jollity.

Here it comes, out of the same house whence we saw brave Captain Gardner go forth to the wars. What! A coffin borne on men's shoulders, and six aged gentlemen as pall-bearers, and a long train of mourners, with black gloves and black hat-bands, and everything black, save a white handkerchief in each mourner's hand, to wipe away his tears withal. Now, my kind patrons, you are angry with me. You were bidden to a bridal-dance, and find yourselves walking in a funeral procession. Even so; but look back through all the social customs of New England, in the first century of her existence, and read all her traits of character; and if you find one occasion, other than a funeral feast, where jollity was sanctioned by universal practice, I will set fire to my puppet-show without another word. These are the obsequies of old Governor Bradstreet, the patriarch and survivor of the first settlers, who, having intermarried with the Widow Gardner, is now resting from his labors, at the great age of ninety-four. The white-bearded corpse, which was his spirit's earthly garniture, now lies beneath yonder coffin-lid. Many a cask of ale and cider is on tap, and many a draught of spiced wine and aquavitæ has been quaffed. Else why should the bearers stagger, as they tremulously uphold the coffin?—and the aged pall-bearers, too, as they strive to walk

solemnly beside it?—and wherefore do the mourners tread on one another's heels?—and why, if we may ask without offence, should the nose of the Reverend Mr. Noyes, through which he has just been delivering the funeral discourse, glow like a ruddy coal of fire? Well, well, old friends! Pass on, with your burden of mortality, and lay it in the tomb with jolly hearts. People should be permitted to enjoy themselves in their own fashion; every man to his taste; but New England must have been a dismal abode for the man of pleasure, when the only boon-companion was Death!

Under cover of a mist that has settled over the scene, a few years flit by, and escape our notice. As the atmosphere becomes transparent, we perceive a decrepit grandsire, hobbling along the street. Do you recognize him? We saw him, first, as the baby in Goodwife Massey's arms, when the primeval trees were flinging their shadow over Roger Conant's cabin; we have seen him, as the boy, the youth, the man, bearing his humble part in all the successive scenes, and forming the index-figure whereby to note the age of his coeval town. And here he is, old Goodman Massey, taking his last walk,—often pausing,—often leaning over his staff,—and calling to mind whose dwelling stood at such and such a spot, and whose field or garden occupied the site of those more recent houses. He can render a reason for all the bends and deviations of the thoroughfare, which, in its flexible and plastic infancy, was made to swerve aside from a straight line, in order to visit every settler's door. The Main-street is still youthful; the coeval man is in his last age. Soon he will be gone.

a patriarch of fourscore, yet shall retain a sort of infantine life in our local history, as the first town-born child.

Behold here a change, wrought in the twinkling of an eye, like an incident in a tale of magic, even while your observation has been fixed upon the scene. The Main-street has vanished out of sight. In its stead appears a wintry waste of snow, with the sun just peeping over it, cold and bright, and tinging the white expanse with the faintest and most ethereal rose-color. This is the great Snow of 1717, famous for the mountain-drifts in which it buried the whole country. It would seem as if the street, the growth of which we have noted so attentively, following it from its first phase, as an Indian track, until it reached the dignity of sidewalks, were all at once obliterated and resolved into a drearier pathlessness than when the forest covered it. The gigantic swells and billows of the snow have swept over each man's metes and bounds, and annihilated all the visible distinctions of human property. So that now, the traces of former times and hitherto accomplished deeds being done away, mankind should be at liberty to enter on new paths, and guide themselves by other laws than heretofore; if, indeed, the race be not extinct, and it be worth our while to go on with the march of life, over the cold and desolate expanse that lies before us. It may be, however, that matters are not so desperate as they appear. That vast icicle, glittering so cheerlessly in the sunshine, must be the spire of the meeting-house, incrusted with frozen sleet. Those great heaps, too, which we mistook for drifts, are houses, buried up to their eaves, and with their peaked roofs rounded by the

depth of snow upon them. There, now, comes a gush of smoke from what I judge to be the chimney of the Ship Tavern;—and another—another—and another—from the chimneys of other dwellings, where fireside comfort, domestic peace, the sports of children, and the quietude of age, are living yet, in spite of the frozen crust above them.

But it is time to change the scene. Its dreary monotony shall not test your fortitude like one of our actual New England winters, which leaves so large a blank,—so melancholy a death-spot,—in lives so brief that they ought to be all summer-time. Here, at least, I may claim to be ruler of the seasons. One turn of the crank shall melt away the snow from the Main-street, and show the trees in their full foliage, the rosebushes in bloom, and a border of green grass along the sidewalk. There! But what! How! The scene will not move. A wire is broken. The street continues buried beneath the snow, and the fate of Herculaneum and Pompeii has its parallel in this catastrophe.

Alas! my kind and gentle audience, you know not the extent of your misfortune. The scenes to come were far better than the past. The street itself would have been more worthy of pictorial exhibition; the deeds of its inhabitants, not less so. And how would your interest have deepened, as, passing out of the cold shadow of antiquity, in my long and weary course, I should arrive within the limits of man's memory, and, leading you at last into the sunshine of the present, should give a reflex of the very life that is flitting past us! Your own beauty, my fair townswoman, would have beamed upon you out of my scene. Not a gentleman that walks the street but should have beheld his own face and figure, his gait, the peculiar swing of his arm, and the coat that he put on yesterday. Then, too,—and it is what I chiefly regret,— I had expended a vast deal of light and brilliancy on a representation of the street in its whole length, from Buffum's Corner downward, on the night of the grand illumination for General Taylor's triumph. Lastly, I should have given the crank one other turn, and have brought out the future, showing you who shall walk the Main-street to-mor-row, and, perchance, whose funeral shall pass through it!

But these, like most other human purposes, lie unaccomplished; and I have only further to say, that any lady or gentleman who may feel dissatisfied with the evening's entertainment shall receive back the admission fee at the door.

"Then give me mine," cries the critic, stretching out his palm. "I said that your exhibition would prove a humbug, and so it has turned out. So, hand over my quarter!"

ETHAN BRAND

A CHAPTER FROM AN ABORTIVE ROMANCE

BARTRAM, the lime-burner, a rough, heavy-looking man, begrimed with charcoal, sat watching his kiln, at nightfall, while his little son played at building houses with the scattered fragments of marble, when, on the hillside below them, they heard a roar of laughter, not mirthful, but slow, and even solemn, like a wind shaking the boughs of the forest.

"Father, what is that?" asked the little boy, leaving his play, and pressing betwixt his father's knees.

"O, some drunken man, I suppose," answered the lime-burner; "some merry fellow from the bar-room in the village, who dared not laugh loud enough within doors, lest he should blow the roof of the house off. So here he is, shaking his jolly sides at the foot of Graylock."

"But, father," said the child, more sensitive than the obtuse, middle-aged clown, "he does not laugh like a man that is glad. So the noise frightens me!"

"Don't be a fool, child!" cried his father, gruffly. "You will never make a man, I do believe; there is too much of your mother in you. I have known the rustling of a leaf startle you. Hark! Here comes the merry fellow, now. You shall see that there is no harm in him."

Bartram and his little son, while they were talking thus, sat watching the same lime-kiln that had been the scene of Ethan Brand's solitary and meditative life, before he began his search for the Unpardonable Sin. Many years, as we have seen, had now elapsed since that portentous night when the IDEA was first developed. The kiln, however, on the mountain-side, stood unimpaired, and was in nothing changed since he had thrown his dark thoughts into the intense glow of its furnace, and melted them, as it were, into the one thought that took possession of his life. It was a rude, round, tower-like structure, about twenty feet high, heavily built of rough stones, and with a hillock of earth heaped about the larger part of its circumference; so that the blocks and fragments of marble might be drawn by cart-loads, and thrown in at the top. There was an opening at the bottom of the tower, like an oven-mouth, but large enough to admit a man in a stooping posture, and provided with a massive iron door. With the smoke and jets of flame issuing from the chinks and crevices of this door, which seemed to give admittance into the hillside, it resembled nothing so much as the private entrance to the infernal regions, which the shepherds of the Delectable Mountains were accustomed to show to pilgrims.

There are many such lime-kilns in that tract of country, for the purpose of burning the white marble which composes a large part of the substance of the hills. Some of them, built years ago, and long deserted, with weeds growing in the vacant round of the interior, which is open to the sky, and grass and wild-flowers rooting themselves into the chinks of the stones, look already like relics of antiquity, and may yet be over-spread with the lichens of centuries to come. Others, where the lime-burner still feeds his daily and night-long fire, afford points of interest to the wanderer among the hills, who seats himself on a log of wood or a fragment of marble, to hold a chat with the solitary man. It is a lonesome, and, when the character is inclined to thought, may be an intensely thoughtful occupation; as it proved in the case of Ethan Brand, who had mused to such strange purpose, in days gone by, while the fire in this very kiln was burning.

The man who now watched the fire was of a different order, and troubled himself with no thoughts save the very few that were requisite to his business. At frequent intervals, he flung back the clashing weight of the iron door, and, turning his face from the insufferable glare, thrust in huge logs of oak, or stirred the immense brands with a long pole. Within the furnace were seen the curling and riotous flames, and the burning marble, almost molten with the intensity of heat; while without, the reflection of the fire quivered on the dark intricacy of the surrounding forest, and showed in the foreground a bright and ruddy little picture of the hut, the spring beside its door, the athletic and coal-begrimed figure of the lime-burner, and the half-frightened child, shrinking into the protection of his father's shadow. And when again the iron door was closed, then reappeared the tender light of the half-full moon, which vainly strove to trace out the indistinct shapes of the neighboring mountains; and, in the upper sky, there was a flitting congregation of clouds, still faintly tinged with the rosy sunset, though thus far down into the valley the sunshine had vanished long and long ago.

The little boy now crept still closer to his father, as footsteps were heard ascending the hillside, and a human form thrust aside the bushes that clustered beneath the trees.

"Halloo! who is it?" cried the lime-burner, vexed at his son's timidity, yet half infected by it. "Come forward, and show yourself, like a man, or I'll fling this chunk of marble at your head!"

"You offer me a rough welcome," said a gloomy voice, as the unknown man drew nigh. "Yet I neither claim nor desire a kinder one, even at my own fireside."

To obtain a distincter view, Bartram threw open the iron door of the kiln, whence immediately issued a gush of fierce light, that smote full upon the stranger's face and figure. To a careless eye there appeared nothing very remarkable in his aspect, which was that of a man in a coarse, brown, country-made suit of clothes, tall and thin, with the staff and heavy shoes of a wayfarer. As he advanced, he fixed his eyes— which were very bright—intently upon the brightness of the furnace, as if he beheld, or expected to behold, some object worthy of note within it.

"Good evening, stranger," said the lime-burner; "whence come you, so late in the day?"

"I come from my search," answered the wayfarer; "for, at last, it is finished."

"Drunk!—or crazy!" muttered Bartram to himself. "I shall have trouble with the fellow. The sooner I drive him away, the better."

The little boy, all in a tremble, whispered to his father, and begged him to shut the door of the kiln, so that there might not be so much light; for that there was something in the man's face which he was afraid to look at, yet could not look away from. And, indeed, even the lime-burner's dull and torpid sense began to be impressed by an indescribable something in that thin, rugged, thoughtful visage, with the grizzled hair hanging wildly about it, and those deeply-sunken eyes, which gleamed like fires within the entrance of a mysterious cavern. But, as he closed the door, the stranger turned towards him, and spoke in a quiet, familiar way, that made Bartram feel as if he were a sane and sensible man, after all.

"Your task draws to an end, I see," said he. "This marble has already been burning three days. A few hours more will convert the stone to lime."

"Why, who are you?" exclaimed the lime-burner. "You seem as well acquainted with my business as I am myself."

"And well I may be," said the stranger; "for I followed the same craft many a long year, and here, too, on this very spot. But you are a new-comer in these parts. Did you never hear of Ethan Brand?"

"The man that went in search of the Unpardonable Sin?" asked Bartram, with a laugh.

"The same," answered the stranger. "He has found what he sought, and therefore he comes back again."

"What! then you are Ethan Brand himself?" cried the lime-burner, in amazement. "I am a new-comer here, as you say, and they call it eighteen years since you left the foot of Graylock. But, I can tell you, the good folks still talk about Ethan Brand, in the village yonder, and what a strange errand took him away from his lime-kiln. Well, and so you have found the Unpardonable Sin?"

"Even so!" said the stranger, calmly.

"If the question is a fair one," proceeded Bartram, "where might it be?"

Ethan Brand laid his finger on his own heart.

"Here!" replied he.

And then, without mirth in his countenance, but as if moved by an involuntary recognition of the infinite absurdity of seeking throughout the world for what was the closest of all things to himself, and looking into every heart, save his own, for what was hidden in no other breast, he broke into a laugh of scorn. It was the same slow, heavy laugh, that had almost appalled the lime-burner when it heralded the wayfarer's approach.

The solitary mountain-side was made dismal by it. Laughter, when out of place, mistimed, or bursting forth from a disordered state of feeling, may be the most terrible modulation of the human voice. The laughter of one asleep, even if it be a little child,—the madman's laugh,—the wild, screaming laugh of a born idiot,—are sounds that we sometimes tremble to hear, and would always willingly forget. Poets have imagined no utterance of fiends or hobgoblins so fearfully appropriate as a laugh. And even the obtuse lime-burner felt his nerves shaken, as this strange man looked inward at his own heart, and burst into laughter that rolled away into the night, and was indistinctly reverberated among the hills.

"Joe," said he to his little son, "scamper down to the tavern in the village, and tell the jolly fellows there that Ethan Brand has come back, and that he has found the Unpardonable Sin!"

The boy darted away on his errand, to which Ethan Brand made no objection, nor seemed hardly to notice it. He sat on a log of wood, looking steadfastly at the iron door of the kiln. When the child was out of sight, and his swift and light footsteps ceased to be heard treading first on the fallen leaves, and then on the rocky mountain-path, the lime-burner began to regret his departure. He felt that the little fellow's presence had been a barrier between his guest and himself, and that he must now deal, heart to heart, with a man who, on his own confession, had committed the one only crime for which Heaven could afford no mercy. That crime, in its indistinct blackness, seemed to overshadow him. The lime-burner's own sins rose up within him, and made his memory riotous with a throng of evil shapes that asserted their kindred with the Master Sin, whatever it might be, which it was within the scope of man's corrupted nature to conceive and cherish. They were all of one family; they went to and fro between his breast and Ethan Brand's, and carried dark greetings from one to the other.

Then Bartram remembered the stories which had grown traditionary in reference to this strange man, who had come upon him like a shadow of the night, and was making himself at home in his old place, after so long absence that the dead people, dead and buried for years, would have had more right to be at home, in any familiar spot, than he. Ethan Brand, it was said, had conversed with Satan himself in the lurid blaze of this very kiln. The legend had been matter of mirth heretofore, but looked grisly now. According to this tale, before Ethan Brand departed on his search, he had been accustomed to evoke a fiend from the hot furnace of the lime-kiln, night after night, in order to confer with him about the Unpardonable Sin; the man and the fiend each laboring to frame the image of some mode of guilt which could neither be atoned for nor forgiven. And, with the first gleam of light upon the mountain-top, the fiend crept in at the iron door, there to abide the intensest element of fire, until again summoned forth to share in the dreadful task of extending man's possible guilt beyond the scope of Heaven's else infinite mercy.

While the lime-burner was struggling with the horror of these thoughts, Ethan Brand rose from the log, and flung open the door of the kiln. The action was in such accordance with the idea in Bartram's mind, that he almost expected to see the Evil One issue forth, red-hot from the raging furnace.

"Hold! hold!" cried he, with a tremulous attempt to laugh; for he was ashamed of his fears, although they overmastered him. "Don't, for mercy's sake, bring out your devil now!"

"Man!" sternly replied Ethan Brand, "what need have I of the devil? I have left him behind me, on my track. It is with such half-way sinners as you that he busies himself. Fear not, because I open the door. I do but act by old custom, and am going to trim your fire, like a lime-burner, as I was once."

He stirred the vast coals, thrust in more wood, and bent forward to gaze into the hollow prison-house of the fire, regardless of the fierce glow that reddened upon his face. The lime-burner sat watching him, and half suspected his strange guest of a purpose, if not to evoke a fiend, at least to plunge bodily into the flames, and thus vanish from the sight of man. Ethan Brand, however, drew quietly back, and closed the door of the kiln.

"I have looked," said he, "into many a human heart that was seven times hotter with sinful passions than yonder furnace is with fire. But I found not there what I sought. No, not the Unpardonable Sin!"

"What is the Unpardonable Sin?" asked the lime-burner; and then he shrank farther from his companion, trembling lest his question should be answered.

"It is a sin that grew within my own breast," replied Ethan Brand, standing erect, with a pride that distinguishes all enthusiasts of his stamp. "A sin that grew nowhere else! The sin of an intellect that triumphed over the sense of brotherhood with man and reverence for God, and sacrificed everything to its own mighty claims! The only sin that deserves a recompense of immortal agony! Freely, were it to do again, would I incur the guilt. Unshrinkingly I accept the retribution!"

"The man's head is turned," muttered the lime-burner to himself. "He may be a sinner, like the rest of us,—nothing more likely,—but, I'll be sworn, he is a madman too."

Nevertheless he felt uncomfortable at his situation, alone with Ethan Brand on the wild mountain-side, and was right glad to hear the rough murmur of tongues, and the footsteps of what seemed a pretty numerous party, stumbling over the stones and rustling through the underbrush. Soon appeared the whole lazy regiment that was wont to infest the village tavern, comprehending three or four individuals who had drunk flip beside the bar-room fire through all the winters, and smoked their pipes beneath the stoop through all the summers, since Ethan Brand's departure. Laughing boisterously, and mingling all their voices together in unceremonious talk, they now burst into the moonshine and narrow streaks of firelight that illuminated the open space before the lime-kiln. Bartram set the door ajar again, flooding the spot with light, that the whole company might get a fair view of Ethan Brand, and he of them.

There, among other old acquaintances, was a once ubiquitous man, now almost extinct, but whom we were formerly sure to encounter at the hotel of every thriving village throughout the country. It was the stage-agent. The present specimen of the genus was a wilted and smoke-dried man, wrinkled and red-nosed, in a smartly-cut, brown, bob-tailed coat, with brass buttons, who, for a length of time unknown, had kept his desk and corner in the bar-room, and was still puffing what seemed to be the same cigar that he had lighted twenty years before. He had great fame as a dry joker, though, perhaps, less on account of any intrinsic humor than from a certain flavor of brandy-toddy and tobacco-smoke, which impregnated all his ideas and expressions, as well as his person. Another well-remembered though strangely-altered face was that of Lawyer Giles, as people still called him in courtesy; an elderly ragamuffin, in his soiled shirt-sleeves and tow-cloth trousers. This poor fellow had been an attorney, in what he called his better days, a sharp practitioner, and in great vogue among the village litigants; but flip, and sling, and toddy, and cock-tails, imbibed at all hours, morning, noon, and night, had caused him to slide from intellectual to various kinds and de-grees of bodily labor, till at last, to adopt his own phrase, he slid into a soap-vat. In other words, Giles was now a soap-boiler, in a small way. He had come to be but the fragment of a human being, a part of one foot having been chopped off by an axe, and an en-tire hand torn away by the devilish

grip of a steam-engine. Yet, though the corporeal hand was gone, a spiritual member remained; for, stretching forth the stump, Giles steadfastly averred that he felt an invisible thumb and fingers with as vivid a sensation as before the real ones were amputated. A maimed and miserable wretch he was; but one, nevertheless, whom the world could not trample on, and had no right to scorn, either in this or any previous stage of his misfortunes, since he had still kept up the courage and spirit of a man, asked nothing in charity, and with his one hand—and that the left one—fought a stern battle against want and hostile circumstances.

Among the throng, too, came another personage, who, with certain points of similarity to Lawyer Giles, had many more of difference. It was the village doctor; a man of some fifty years, whom, at an earlier period of his life, we introduced as paying a professional visit to Ethan Brand during the latter's supposed insanity. He was now a purple-visaged, rude, and brutal, yet half-gentlemanly figure, with something wild, ruined, and desperate in his talk, and in all the details of his gesture and man-ners. Brandy possessed this man like an evil spirit, and made him as surly and savage as a wild beast, and as miserable as a lost soul; but there was supposed to be in him such wonderful skill, such native gifts of healing, beyond any which medical science could impart, that society caught hold of him, and would not let him sink out of its reach. So, swaying to and fro upon his horse, and grumbling thick accents at the bed-side, he visited all the sick-chambers for miles about among the mountain towns, and sometimes raised a dying man, as it were, by miracle, or quite as often, no doubt, sent his patient to a grave that was dug many a year too soon. The doctor had an everlasting pipe in his mouth, and, as somebody said, in allusion to his habit of swearing, it was always alight with hell-fire.

These three worthies pressed forward, and greeted Ethan Brand each after his own fashion, earnestly inviting him to partake of the contents of a certain black bottle, in which, as they averred, he would find something far better worth seeking for than the Unpardonable Sin. No mind, which has wrought itself by intense and solitary meditation into a high state of enthusiasm, can endure the kind of contact with low and vulgar modes of thought and feeling to which Ethan Brand was now subjected. It made him doubt—and, strange to say, it was a painful doubt—whether he had indeed found the Unpardonable Sin, and found it within himself. The whole question on which he had exhausted life, and more than life, looked like a delusion.

"Leave me," he said, bitterly, "ye brute beasts, that have made yourselves so, shrivelling up your souls with fiery liquors! I have done with you. Years and years ago, I groped into your hearts, and found nothing there for my purpose. Get ye gone!"

"Why, you uncivil scoundrel," cried the fierce doctor, "is that the way you respond to the kindness of your best friends? Then let me tell you the truth. You have no more found the Unpardonable Sin than yonder boy Joe has. You are but a crazy fellow,—I told you so twenty years ago,—neither better nor worse than a crazy fellow, and the fit companion of old Humphrey, here!"

He pointed to an old man, shabbily dressed, with long white hair, thin visage, and unsteady eyes. For some years past this aged person had been wandering about among the hills, inquiring of all travellers whom he met for his daughter. The girl, it seemed, had gone off with a company of circus-performers; and occasionally tidings of her came to the village, and fine stories were told of her glittering appearance as she rode on horse-back in the ring, or performed marvellous feats on the tight-rope.

The white-haired father now approached Ethan Brand, and gazed unsteadily into his face.

"They tell me you have been all over the earth," said he, wringing his hands with earnestness. "You must have seen my daughter, for she makes a grand figure in the world, and everybody goes to see her. Did she send any word to her old father, or say when she was coming back?"

Ethan Brand's eye quailed beneath the old man's. That daughter, from whom he so earnestly desired a word of greeting, was the Esther of our tale, the very girl whom, with such cold and remorseless purpose, Ethan Brand had made the subject of a psychological experiment, and wasted, absorbed, and perhaps annihilated her soul, in the process.

"Yes," murmured he, turning away from the hoary wanderer; "it is no delusion. There is an Unpardonable Sin!"

While these things were passing, a merry scene was going forward in the area of cheerful light, beside the spring and before the door of the hut. A number of the youth of the village, young men and girls, had hurried up the hillside, impelled by curiosity to see Ethan

Brand, the hero of so many a legend familiar to their childhood. Finding nothing, however, very remarkable in his aspect,—nothing but a sun-burnt wayfarer, in plain garb and dusty shoes, who sat looking into the fire, as if he fancied pictures among the coals,—these young people speedily grew tired of observing him. As it happened, there was other amusement at hand. An old German Jew, travelling with a diorama on his back, was passing down the mountain-road towards the village just as the party turned aside from it, and, in hopes of eking out the profits of the day, the showman had kept them company to the lime-kiln.

"Come, old Dutchman," cried one of the young men, "let us see your pictures, if you can swear they are worth looking at!"

"O yes, Captain," answered the Jew, —whether as a matter of courtesy or craft, he styled everybody Captain,—"I shall show you, indeed, some very superb pictures!"

So, placing his box in a proper position, he invited the young men and girls to look through the glass orifices of the machine, and proceed to exhibit a series of the most outrageous scratchings and daubings, as specimens of the fine arts, that ever an itinerant showman had the face to impose upon his circle of spectators. The pictures were worn out, moreover, tattered, full of cracks and wrinkles, dingy with tobacco-smoke, and otherwise in a most pitiable condition. Some purported to be cities, public edifices, and ruined castles in Europe; others represented Napoleon's battles and Nelson's sea-fight; and in the midst of these would be seen a gigantic, brown, hairy hand,—which might have been mistaken for the Hand of Destiny though, in truth, it was only the show man's,—pointing its forefinger to various scenes of the conflict, while it owner gave historical illustrations When, with much merriment at it abominable deficiency of merit, the ex hibition was concluded, the German bade little Joe put his head into the box. Viewed through the magnifying glasses, the boy's round, rosy visage assumed the strangest imaginable aspect of an immense Titanic child, the mouth grinning broadly, and the eyes and every other feature overflowing with fun at the joke. Suddenly, however, that merry face turned pale, and its expression changed to horror, for this easily impressed and excitable child had become sensible that the eye of Ethan Brand was fixed upon him through the glass.

"You make the little man to be afraid, Captain," said the German Jew, turning up the dark and strong outline of his visage, from his stooping posture. "But look again, and, by chance, I shall cause you to see somewhat that is very fine, upon my word!"

Ethan Brand gazed into the box for an instant, and then starting back looked fixedly at the German. What had he seen? Nothing apparently; for a curious youth, who had peeped in almost at the same moment, beheld only a vacant space of canvas.

"I remember you now," muttered Ethan Brand to the showman.

"Ah, Captain," whispered the Jew of Nuremberg, with a dark smile, "I find it to be a heavy matter in my show-box,—this Unpardonable Sin! By my faith, Captain, it has wearied my shoulders, this long day, to carry it over the mountain "

"Peace," answered Ethan Brand, sternly, "or get thee into the furnace yonder!"

The Jew's exhibition had scarcely concluded, when a great, elderly dog,—who seemed to be his own master, as no person in the company laid claim to him,—saw fit to render himself the object of public notice. Hitherto, he had shown himself a very quiet, well-disposed old dog, going round from one to another, and, by way of being sociable, offering his rough head to be patted by any kindly hand that would take so much trouble. But now, all of a sudden, this grave and venerable quadruped, of his own mere motion, and without the slightest suggestion from anybody else, began to run round after his tail, which, to heighten the absurdity of the proceeding, was a great deal shorter than it should have been. Never was seen such headlong eagerness in pursuit of an object that could not possibly be attained; never was heard such a tremendous outbreak of growling, snarling, barking, and snapping,—as if one end of the ridiculous brute's body were at deadly and most unforgivable enmity with the other. Faster and faster, round about went the cur; and faster and still faster fled the unapproachable brevity of his tail; and louder and fiercer grew his yells of rage and animosity; until, utterly exhausted, and as far from the goal as ever, the foolish old dog ceased his performance as suddenly as he had begun it. The next moment, he was as mild, quiet, sensible, and respectable in his deportment as when he first scraped acquaintance with the company.

As may be supposed, the exhibition was greeted with universal laughter, clapping of hands, and shouts of encore, to which the canine performer responded by wagging all that there was to wag of his tail, but appeared totally unable to repeat his very successful effort to amuse the spectators.

Meanwhile, Ethan Brand had resumed his seat upon the log, and moved, it might be, by a perception of some remote analogy between his own case and that of this self-pursuing cur, he broke into the awful laugh, which, more than any other token, expressed the condition of his inward being. From that moment, the merriment of the party was at an end; they stood aghast, dreading lest the inauspicious sound should be reverberated around the horizon, and that mountain would thunder it to mountain, and so the horror be prolonged upon their ears. Then, whispering one to another that it was late,—that the moon was almost down,—that the August night was growing chill,—they hurried homewards, leaving the lime-burner and little Joe to deal as they might with their unwelcome guest. Save for these three human beings, the open space on the hillside was a solitude, set in a vast gloom of forest. Beyond that darksome verge, the fire-light glimmered on the stately trunks and almost black foliage of pines, intermixed with the lighter verdure of sapling oaks, maples, and poplars, while here and there lay the gigantic corpses of dead trees, decaying on the leaf-strewn soil. And it seemed to little Joe—a timorous and imaginative child—that the silent forest was holding its breath, until some fearful thing should happen.

Ethan Brand thrust more wood into the fire, and closed the door of the kiln; then looking over his shoulder at the lime-burner and his son, he bade, rather than advised, them to retire to rest.

"For myself, I cannot sleep," said he. "I have matters that it concerns me to meditate upon. I will watch the fire, as I used to do in the old time."

"And call the devil out of the furnace to keep you company, I suppose," muttered Bartram, who had been making intimate acquaintance with the black bottle above mentioned. "But watch, if you like, and call as many devils as you like! For my part, I shall be all the better for a snooze. Come, Joe!"

As the boy followed his father into the hut, he looked back at the wayfarer, and the tears came into his eyes, for his tender spirit had an intuition of the bleak and terrible loneliness in which this man had enveloped himself.

When they had gone, Ethan Brand sat listening to the crackling of the kindled wood, and looking at the little spirts of fire that issued through the chinks of the door. These trifles, however, once so familiar, had but the slightest hold of his attention, while deep within his mind he was reviewing the gradual but marvellous change that had been wrought upon him by the search to which he had devoted himself. He remembered how the night dew had fallen upon him,—how the dark forest had whispered to him,—how the stars had gleamed upon him,—a simple and loving man, watching his fire in the years gone by, and ever musing as it burned. He remembered with what tenderness, with what love and sympathy for mankind, and what pity for human guilt and woe, he had first begun to contemplate those ideas which afterwards became the inspiration of his life; with what reverence he had then

looked into the heart of man, viewing it as a temple originally divine, and, however, desecrated, still to be held sacred by a brother; with what awful fear he had deprecated the success of his pursuit, and prayed that the Unpardonable Sin might never be revealed to him. Then ensued that vast intellectual development, which, in its progress, disturbed the counterpoise between his mind and heart. The Idea that possessed his life had operated as a means of education; it had gone on cultivating his powers to the highest point of which they were susceptible; it had raised him from the level of an unlettered laborer to stand on a star-lit eminence, whither the philosophers of the earth, laden with the lore of universities, might vainly strive to clamber after him. So much for the intellect! But where was the heart? That, indeed, had withered,— had contracted,—had hardened,—had perished! It had ceased to partake of the universal throb. He had lost his hold of the magnetic chain of humanity. He was no longer a brother-man, opening the chambers or the dungeons of our common nature by the key of holy sympathy, which gave him a right to share in all its secrets; he was now a cold observer, looking on mankind as the subject of his experiment, and, at length, converting man and woman to be his puppets, and pulling the wires that moved them to such degrees of crime as were demanded for his study.

Thus Ethan Brand became a fiend. He began to be so from the moment that his moral nature had ceased to keep the pace of improvement with his intellect. And now, as his highest effort and inevitable development,—as the bright and gorgeous flower, and rich delicious fruit of his life's labor,—he had produced the Unpardonable Sin!

"What more have I to seek? What more to achieve?" said Ethan Brand to himself. "My task is done, and well done!"

Starting from the log with a certain alacrity in his gait, and ascending the hillock of earth that was raised against the stone circumference of the lime-kiln, he thus reached the top of the structure. It was a space of perhaps ten feet across, from edge to edge, presenting a view of the upper surface of the immense mass of broken marble with which the kiln was heaped. All these innumerable blocks and fragments of marble were red-hot and vividly on fire, sending up great spouts of blue flame, which quivered aloft and danced madly, as within a magic circle, and sank and rose again, with continual and multitudinous activity. As the lonely man bent forward over this terrible body of fire, the blasting heat smote up against his person with a breath that, it might be supposed, would have scorched and shrivelled him up in a moment.

Ethan Brand stood erect, and raised his arms on high. The blue flames played upon his face, and imparted the wild and ghastly light which alone could have suited its expression; it was that of a fiend on the verge of plunging into his gulf of intensest torment.

"O Mother Earth," cried he, "who art no more my mother, and into whose bosom this frame shall never be resolved! O mankind, whose brotherhood I have cast off, and trampled thy great heart beneath my feet! O stars of heaven, that shone on me of old, as if to light me onward and upward!—farewell all, and forever. Come, deadly element of Fire,—henceforth my familiar friend! Embrace me, as I do thee!"

That night the sound of a fearful peal of laughter rolled heavily through the sleep of the lime-burner and his little son; dim shapes of horror and anguish haunted their dreams, and seemed still present in the rude hovel, when they opened their eyes to the daylight.

"Up, boy, up!" cried the lime-burner, staring about him. "Thank Heaven, the night is gone, at last; and rather than pass such another, I would watch my lime-kiln, wide awake, for a twelve-month. This Ethan Brand, with his humbug of an Unpardonable Sin, has done me no such mighty favor, in taking my place!"

He issued from the hut, followed by little Joe, who kept fast hold of his father's hand. The early sunshine was already pouring its gold upon the mountain-tops; and though the valleys were still in shadow, they smiled cheerfully in the promise of the bright day that was hastening onward. The village, completely shut in by hills, which swelled away gently about it, looked as if it had rested peacefully in the hollow of the great hand of Providence. Every dwelling was distinctly visible; the little spires of the two churches pointed upwards, and caught a fore-glimmering of brightness from the sun-gilt skies upon their gilded weathercocks. The tavern was astir, and the figure of the old, smoke-dried stage-agent, cigar in mouth, was seen beneath the stoop. Old Graylock was glorified with a golden cloud upon his head. Scattered likewise over the breasts of the surrounding mountains there were heaps of hoary mist, in fantastic shapes, some of them far down into the valley, others high up towards the summits, and still others, of the same family of midst or cloud, hovering in the gold radiance of the upper atmosphere. Stepping from one to another of the clouds that rested on the hills, and thence to the loftier brotherhood that sailed in air, it seemed almost as if a mortal man might thus ascend into the heavenly regions. Earth was so mingled with sky that it was a day-dream to look at it.

To supply that charm of the familiar and homely, which Nature so readily adopts into a scene like this, the stage-coach was rattling down the mountain-road, and the driver sounded his horn, while echo caught up the notes, and intertwined them into a rich and varied and elaborate harmony, of which the original performer could lay claim to little share. The great hills played a concert among themselves, each contributing a strain of airy sweetness.

Little Joe's face brightened at once.

"Dear father," cried he, skipping cheerily to and fro, "that strange man is gone, and the sky and the mountains all seem glad of it!"

"Yes," growled the lime-burner, with an oath, "but he has let the fire go down, and no thanks to him if five hundred bushels of lime are not spoiled. If I catch the fellow hereabouts again, I shall feel like tossing him into the furnace!"

With his long pole in his hand, he ascended to the top of the kiln. After a moment's pause, he called to his son.

"Come up here, Joe!" said he.

So little Joe ran up the hillock, and stood by his father's side. The marble was all burnt into perfect, snow-white lime. But on its surface, in the midst of the circle,—snow-white too, and thoroughly converted into lime,—lay a human skeleton, in the attitude of a person who, after long toil, lies down to long repose. Within the ribs—strange to say—was the shape of a human heart.

"Was the fellow's heart made of marble?" cried Bartram, in some perplexity at this phenomenon. "At any rate, it is burnt into what looks like special good lime, and, taking all the bones together, my kiln is half a bushel the richer for him.

So saying, the rude lime-burner lifted his pole, and, letting it fall upon the skeleton, the relics of Ethan Brand were crumbled into fragments.

———

A BELL'S BIOGRAPHY

HEARKEN to our neighbor with the iron tongue! While I sit musing over my sheet of foolscap, he emphatically tells the hour, in tones loud enough for all the town to hear, though doubtless intended only as a gentle hint to myself, that I may begin his biography before the evening shall be further wasted. Unquestionably, a personage in such an elevated position, and making so great a noise in the world, has a fair claim to the services of a biographer. He is the representative and most illustrious member of that innumerable class whose characteristic feature is the tongue, and whose sole business to clamor for the public good. If any of his noisy brethren, in our tongue-governed democracy, be envious of the superiority which I have assigned him, they have my free consent to hang themselves as high as he. And, for his history, let not the reader apprehend an empty repetition of ding-dong-bell. He has been the passive hero of wonderful vicissitudes, with which I have chanced to become acquainted, possibly from his own mouth; while the careless multitude supposed him to be talking merely of the time of the day, or calling them to dinner or to church, or bidding drowsy people go bedward, or the dead to their graves. Many a revolution has it been his fate to go through, and invariably with a prodigious uproar. And whether or no he have told me his reminiscences, this at least is true, that the more I study his deep-toned language, the more sense and sentiment and soul do I discover in it.

This bell—for we may as well drop our quaint personification—is of antique French manufacture, and the symbol of the cross betokens that it was meant to be suspended in the belfry of a Romish place of worship. The old people hereabout have a tradition, that a considerable part of the metal was supplied by a brass cannon, captured in one of the victories of Louis the Fourteenth over the Spaniards, and that a Bourbon princess threw her golden crucifix into the molten mass. It is said, likewise, that a bishop baptized and blessed the bell, and prayed that a heavenly influence might mingle with its tones. When all due ceremonies had been performed, the Grand Monarque bestowed the gift—than which none could resound his beneficence more loudly—on the Jesuits, who were then converting the American Indians to the spiritual dominion of the Pope. So the bell,—our selfsame bell, whose familiar voice we may hear at all hours, in the streets,—this very bell sent forth its first-born accents from the tower of a log-built chapel, westward of Lake Champlain, and near the mighty stream of the Saint Lawrence. It was called Our Lady's Chapel of the Forest. The peal went forth as if to redeem and consecrate the heathen wilderness. The wolf growled at the sound, as he prowled stealthily through the underbrush; the grim bear turned his back, and stalked sullenly away; the startled doe leaped up, and led her fawn into a deeper solitude. The red men wondered what awful voice was speaking amid the wind that roared through the tree-tops; and following reverentially its summons, the dark-robed fathers blessed them, as they drew near the cross-crowned chapel. In a little time, there was a crucifix on every dusky bosom. The Indians knelt beneath the lowly roof, worshipping in the same forms that were observed under the vast dome of Saint Peter's, when the Pope performed high mass in the presence of kneeling princes. All the religious festivals, that awoke the chiming bells of lofty cathedrals, called forth a peal from Our Lady's Chapel of the Forest. Loudly rang the bell of the wilderness while the streets of Paris echoed with rejoicings for the birthday of the Bourbon, or whenever France had triumphed on some European battle-field. And the solemn woods were saddened with a melancholy knell, as often as the thick-strewn leaves were swept away from the virgin soil for the burial of an Indian chief.

Meantime, the bells of a hostile people and a hostile faith were ringing on Sabbaths and lecture-days, at Boston and other Puritan towns. Their echoes died away hundreds of miles southeastward of Our Lady's Chapel. But scouts had threaded the pathless desert that lay between, and, from behind the huge tree-trunks, perceived the Indians assembling at the summons of the bell. Some bore flaxen-haired scalps at their girdles, as if to lay those bloody trophies on Our Lady's altar. It was reported, and believed, all through England, that the Pope of Rome and the King of France had established this little chapel in the forest for the purpose of stirring up the red men to a crusade against the English settlers. The latter took energetic measures to secure their religion and their lives. On the eve of an especial fast of the Romish Church, while the bell tolled dismally, and the priests were chanting a doleful stave, a band of New England rangers rushed from the surrounding woods. Fierce shouts, and the report of musketry, pealed suddenly within the chapel. The ministering priests threw themselves before the altar, and were slain even on its steps. If, as antique traditions tell us, no grass will grow where the blood of martyrs has been shed, there should be a barren spot, to this very day, on the site of that desecrated altar.

While the blood was still plashing from step to step, the leader of the rangers seized a torch, and applied it to the drapery of the shrine. The flame and smoke arose, as from a burnt-sacrifice, at once illuminating and obscuring the whole interior of the chapel, —now hiding the dead priests in a sable shroud, now revealing them and their slayers in one terrific glare. Some already wished that the altar-smoke could cover the deed from the sight of Heaven. But one of the rangers—a man of sanctified aspect, though his hands were bloody—approached the captain.

"Sir," said he, "our village meeting-house lacks a bell, and hitherto we have been fain to summon the good people to worship by beat of drum. Give me, I pray you, the bell of this popish chapel, for the sake of the godly Mr. Rogers, who doubtless hath remembered us in the prayers of the congregation ever since we began our march. Who can tell what share of this night's good success we owe to that holy man's wrestling with the Lord?"

"Nay, then," answered the captain "if good Mr. Rogers hath holpen our enterprise, it is right that he should share the spoil. Take the bell and welcome, Deacon Lawson, if you will be at the trouble of carrying it home. Hitherto it hath spoken nothing but papistry, and that too in the French or Indian gibberish; but I warrant me, if Mr. Rogers consecrate it anew, it will talk like a good English and Protestant bell."

So Deacon Lawson and half a score of his townsmen took down the bell suspended it on a pole, and bore it away on their sturdy shoulders, meaning to carry it to the shore of Lake Champlain and thence homeward by water. Far through the woods gleamed the flame of Our Lady's Chapel, flinging fantastic shadows from the clustered foliage, and glancing on brooks that had never caught the sunlight. As the rangers traversed the midnight forest, staggering under their heavy burden, the ongue of the bell gave many a tremendous stroke,—clang, clang, clang!—a most doleful sound, as if it were tolling for the slaughter of the priests and the ruin of the chapel. Little dreamed Deacon Lawson and his townsmen that it was their own funeral knell. A war-party of Indians had heard the report of musketry, and seen the blaze of the chapel, and now were on the track of the rangers, summoned to vengeance by the bell's dismal murmurs. In the midst of a deep swamp they made a sudden onset on the retreating foe. Good Deacon Lawson battled stoutly, but had his skull cloven by a tomahawk, and sank into the depths of the morass, with the ponderous bell above him. And, for many a year thereafter, our hero's voice was heard no more on earth, neither at the hour of worship, nor at festivals, nor funerals.

And is he still buried in that unknown grave? Scarcely so, dear reader. Hark! How plainly we hear him at this moment, the spokesman of Time, proclaiming that it is nine o'clock at night! We may therefore conclude that some happy chance has restored him to upper air.

But there lay the bell, for many silent years; and the wonder is, that he did not lie silent there a century, or perhaps a dozen centuries, till the world should have forgotten, not only his voice, but the voices of the whole brotherhood of bells. How would the first accent of his iron tongue have startled his resurrectionists! But he was not fated to be a subject of discussion among the antiquaries of far posterity. Near the close of the Old French War, a party of New England axe-men, who preceded the march of Colonel Bradstreet toward Lake Ontario, were building a bridge of logs through a swamp. Plunging down a stake, one of these pioneers felt it graze against some hard, smooth substance. He called his comrades, and, by their united efforts, the top of the bell was raised to the surface, a rope made fast to it, and thence passed over the horizontal limb of a tree. Heave-oh! up they hoisted their prize, dripping with moisture, and festooned with verdant water-moss. As the base of the bell emerged from the swamp, the pioneers perceived that a skeleton was clinging with its bony fingers to the clapper, but immediately relaxing its nerveless grasp, sank back into the stagnant water. The bell then gave forth a sullen clang. No wonder that he was in haste to speak, after holding his tongue for such a length of time! The pioneers shoved the bell to and fro, thus ringing a loud and heavy peal, which echoed widely through the forest, and reached the ears of Colonel Bradstreet, and his three thousand men. The soldiers paused on their march; a feeling of religion, mingled with home-tenderness, overpowered their rude hearts; each seemed to hear the clangor of the old church-bell, which had been familiar to him from infancy, and had tolled at the funerals of all his fore-fathers. By what magic had that holy sound strayed over the wide-murmuring ocean, and become audible amid the clash of arms, the loud crashing of the artillery over the rough wilderness-path, and the melancholy roar of the wind among the boughs?

The New-Englanders hid their prize in a shadowy nook, betwixt a large gray stone and the earthy roots of an overthrown tree; and when the campaign was ended, they conveyed our friend to

Boston, and put him up at auction on the sidewalk of King Street. He was suspended, for the nonce, by a block and tackle, and being swung backward and forward, gave such loud and clear testimony to his own merits, that the auctioneer had no need to say a word. The highest bidder was a rich old representative from our town, who piously bestowed the bell on the meeting-house where he had been a worshipper for half a century. The good man had his reward. By a strange coincidence, the very first duty of the sexton, after the bell had been hoisted into the belfry, was to toll the funeral knell of the donor. Soon, however, those doleful echoes were drowned by a triumphant peal for the surrender of Quebec.

Ever since that period, our hero has occupied the same elevated station, and has put in his word on all matters of public importance, civil, military, or religious. On the day when Independence was first proclaimed in the street beneath, he uttered a peal which many deemed ominous and fearful, rather than triumphant. But he has told the same story these sixty years, and none mistake his meaning now. When Washington, in the fulness of his glory, rode through our flower-strewn streets, this was the tongue that bade the Father of his Country welcome! Again the same voice was heard, when La Fayette came to gather in his half-century's harvest of gratitude. Meantime, vast changes have been going on below. His voice, which once floated over a little provincial seaport, is now reverberated between brick edifices, and strikes the ear amid the buzz and tumult of a city. On the Sabbaths of olden time, the summons of the bell was obeyed by a pic-turesque and varied throng; stately gentlemen in purple velvet coats, embroidered waistcoats, white wigs and gold-laced hats, stepping with grave courtesy beside ladies in flowered satin gowns, and hoop-petticoats of majestic circumference; while behind followed liveried slave or bondsman, bearing the psalm-book, and a stove for his mistress' feet. The commonalty, clad in homely garb, gave precedence to their betters at the door of the meeting-house, as if admitting that there were distinctions between them, even in the sight of God. Yet, as their coffins were borne one after another through the street, the bell has tolled a requiem for all alike. What mattered it, whether or no there were a silver scutcheon on the coffin-lid? "Open thy bosom, Mother Earth!" Thus spake the bell. "Another of thy children is coming to his long rest. Take him to thy bosom, and let him slumber in peace." Thus spake the bell, and Mother Earth received her child. With the selfsame tones will the present generation be ushered to the embraces of their mother; and Mother Earth will still receive her children. Is not thy tongue a-weary, mournful talker of two centuries? O funeral bell! wilt thou never be shattered with thine own melancholy strokes? Yea, and a trumpet-call shall arouse the sleepers, whom thy heavy clang could awake no more.

Again,—again, thy voice, reminding me that I am wasting the "midnight oil." In my lonely fantasy, I can scarce believe that other mortals have caught the sound, or that it vibrates elsewhere than in my secret soul. But to many hast thou spoken. Anxious men have heard thee on their sleepless pillows and bethought themselves anew of to-morrow's care. In a brief interval of wakefulness, the sons of toil have heard thee, and say, "Is so much of our quiet slumber spent?—is the morning so near at hand?" Crime has heard thee, and mutters, "Now is the very hour!" Despair answers thee, "Thus much of this weary life is gone!" The young mother, on her bed of pain and ecstasy, has counted thy echoing strokes, and dates from them her first-born's share of life and immortality. The bridegroom and the bride have listened, and feel that their night of rapture flits like a dream away. Thine accents have fallen faintly on the ear of the dying man, and warned him that, ere thou speakest again, his spirit shall have passed whither no voice of time can ever reach. Alas for the departing traveller, if thy voice—the voice of fleeting time—have taught him no lessons for Eternity!

SYLPH ETHEREGE

On a bright summer evening, two persons stood among the shrubbery of a garden, stealthily watching a young girl, who sat in the window-seat of a neighboring mansion. One of these unseen observers, a gentleman, was youthful, and had an air of high breeding and refinement, and a face marked with intellect, though otherwise of unprepossessing aspect. His features wore even an ominous, though somewhat mirthful expression, while he pointed his long forefinger at the girl, and seemed to regard her as a creature completely within the scope of his influence.

"The charm works!" said he, in a low, but emphatic whisper.

"Do you know, Edward Hamilton,—since so you choose to be named,—do you know," said the lady beside him, "that I have almost a mind to break the spell at once? What if the lesson should prove too severe! True, if my ward could be thus laughed out of her fantastic nonsense, she might be the better for it through life. But then, she is such a delicate creature! And, besides,

are you not ruining your own chance, by putting forward this shadow of a rival?"

"But will he not vanish into thin air, at my bidding?" rejoined Edward Hamilton. "Let the charm work!"

The girl's slender and sylph-like figure, tinged with radiance from the sunset clouds, and overhung with the rich drapery of the silken curtains, and set within the deep frame of the window, was a perfect picture; or, rather, it was like the original loveliness in a painter's fancy, from which the most finished picture is but an imperfect copy. Though her occupation excited so much interest in the two spectators, she was merely gazing at a miniature which she held in her hand, encased in white satin and red morocco; nor did there appear to be any other cause for the smile of mockery and malice with which Hamilton regarded her.

"The charm works!" muttered he again. "Our pretty Sylvia's scorn will have a dear retribution!"

At this moment the girl raised her

eyes, and, instead of the life-like semblance of the miniature, beheld the ill-omened shape of Edward Hamilton, who now stepped forth from his concealment in the shrubbery.

Sylvia Etherege was an orphan girl, who had spent her life, till within a few months past, under the guardianship, and in the secluded dwelling of an old bachelor uncle. While yet in her cradle, she had been the destined bride of a cousin, who was no less passive in the betrothal than herself. Their future union had been projected, as the means of uniting two rich estates, and was rendered highly expedient, if not indispensable, by the testamentary dispositions of the parents on both sides. Edgar Vaughan, the promised bridegroom, had been bred from infancy in Europe, and had never seen the beautiful girl whose heart he was to claim as his inheritance. But already, for several years, a correspondence had been kept up between the cousins, and had produced an intellectual intimacy, though it could but imperfectly acquaint them with each other's character.

Sylvia was shy, sensitive, and fanciful; and her guardian's secluded habits had shut her out from even so much of the world as is generally open to maidens of her age. She had been left to seek associates and friends for herself in the haunts of imagination, and to converse with them, sometimes in the language of dead poets, oftener in the poetry of her own mind. The companion whom she chiefly summoned up was the cousin with whose idea her earliest thoughts had been connected. She made a vision of Edgar Vaughan, and tinted it with stronger hues than a mere fancy-picture, yet graced it with

so many bright and delicate perfections, that her cousin could nowhere have encountered so dangerous a rival. To this shadow she cherished a romantic fidelity. With its airy presence sitting by her side, or gliding along her favorite paths, the loneliness of her young life was blissful; her heart was satisfied with love, while yet its virgin purity was untainted by the earthliness that the touch of a real lover would have left there. Edgar Vaughan seemed to be conscious of her character; for, in his letters, he gave her a name that was happily appropriate to the sensitiveness of her disposition, the delicate peculiarity of her manners, and the ethereal beauty both of her mind and person. Instead of Sylvia, he called her Sylph,—with the prerogative of a cousin and a lover,—his dear Sylph Etherege.

When Sylvia was seventeen, her guardian died, and she passed under the care of Mrs. Grosvenor, a lady of wealth and fashion, and Sylvia's nearest relative, though a distant one. While an inmate of Mrs. Grosvenor's family, she still preserved somewhat of her life-long habits of seclusion, and shrank from a too familiar intercourse with those around her. Still, too, she was faithful to her cousin, or to the shadow which bore his name.

The time drew near when Edgar Vaughan, whose education had been completed by an extensive range of travel, was to revisit the soil of his nativity. Edward Hamilton, a young gentleman, who had been Vaughan's companion, both in his studies and rambles, had already recrossed the Atlantic, bringing letters to Mrs. Grosvenor and Sylvia Etherege. These credentials insured him an earnest welcome, which, however, on Sylvia's part, was not followed by personal partiality, or even the regard that seemed due to her cousin's most intimate friend. As she herself could have assigned no cause for her repugnance, it might be termed instinctive. Hamilton's person, it is true, was the reverse of attractive, especially when beheld for the first time. Yet, in the eyes of the most fastidious judges, the defect of natural grace was compensated by the polish of his manners, and by the intellect which so often gleamed through his dark features. Mrs. Grosvenor, with whom he immediately became a prodigious favorite, exerted herself to overcome Sylvia's dislike. But, in this matter, her ward could neither be reasoned with nor persuaded. The presence of Edward Hamilton was sure to render her cold, shy, and distant, abstracting all the vivacity from her deportment, as if a cloud had come betwixt her and the sunshine.

The simplicity of Sylvia's demeanor rendered it easy for so keen an observer as Hamilton to detect her feelings. Whenever any slight circumstance made him sensible of them, a smile might be seen to flit over the young man's sallow visage. None, that had once beheld this smile, were in any danger of forgetting it; whenever they recalled to memory the features of Edward Hamilton, they were always duskily illuminated by this expression of mockery and malice.

In a few weeks after Hamilton's arrival, he presented to Sylvia Etherege a miniature of her cousin, which, as he informed her, would have been delivered sooner, but was detained with a portion of his baggage. This was the miniature in the contemplation of which we beheld Sylvia so absorbed, at the commencement of our story. Such, in truth, was too often the habit of the shy and musing girl. The beauty of the pictured countenance was almost too perfect to represent a human creature, that had been born of a fallen and world-worn race, and had lived to manhood amid ordinary troubles and enjoyments, and must become wrinkled with age and care. It seemed too bright for a thing formed of dust, and doomed to crumble into dust again. Sylvia feared that such a being would be too refined and delicate to love a simple girl like her. Yet, even while her spirit drooped with that apprehension, the picture was but the masculine counterpart of Sylph Etherege's sylph-like beauty. There was that resemblance between her own face and the miniature which is said often to exist between lovers whom Heaven has destined for each other, and which, in this instance, might be owing to the kindred blood of the two parties. Sylvia felt, indeed, that there was something familiar in the countenance, so like a friend did the eyes smile upon her, and seem to imply a knowledge of her thoughts. She could account for this impression only by supposing that, in some of her day-dreams, imagination had conjured up the true similitude of her distant and unseen lover.

But now could Sylvia give a brighter semblance of reality to those daydreams. Clasping the miniature to her heart, she could summon forth, from that haunted cell of pure and blissful fantasies, the life-like shadow, to roam with her in the moonlight garden. Even at noontide it sat with her in the arbor, when the sunshine threw its broken flakes of gold into the clustering shade. The effect upon her mind was hardly less powerful than if she had actually listened to, and reciprocated, the vows of Edgar Vaughan; for, though the illusion never quite deceived her, yet the remembrance was as distinct as of a remembered interview. Those heavenly eyes gazed forever into her soul, which drank at them as at a fountain, and was disquieted if reality threw a momentary cloud between. She heard the melody of a voice breathing sentiments with which her own chimed in like music. O, happy, yet hapless girl! Thus to create the being whom she loves, to endow him with all the attributes that were most fascinating to her heart, and then to flit with the airy creature into the realm of fantasy and moonlight, where dwelt his dreamy kindred! For her lover wiled Sylvia away from earth, which seemed strange, and dull, and darksome, and lured her to a country where her spirit roamed in peaceful rapture, deeming that it had found its home. Many, in their youth, have visited that land of dreams, and wandered so long in its enchanted groves, that, when banished thence, they feel like exiles everywhere.

The dark-browed Edward Hamilton, like the villain of a tale, would often glide through the romance wherein poor Sylvia walked. Sometimes, at the most blissful moment of her ecstasy, when the features of the miniature were pictured brightest in the air, they would suddenly change, and darken, and be transformed into his visage. And always, when such change occurred, the intrusive visage wore that peculiar smile with which Hamilton had glanced at Sylvia.

Before the close of summer, it was told Sylvia Etherege that Vaughan had arrived from France, and that she would meet him—would meet, for the first

time, the loved of years—that very evening. We will not tell how often and how earnestly she gazed upon the miniature, thus endeavoring to prepare herself for the approaching interview, lest the throbbing of her timorous heart should stifle the words of welcome. While the twilight grew deeper and duskier, she sat with Mrs. Grosvenor in an inner apartment, lighted only by the softened gleam from an alabaster lamp, which was burning at a distance on the centre-table of the drawing-room. Never before had Sylph Etherege looked so sylph-like. She had communed with a creature of imagination, till her own loveliness seemed but the creation of a delicate and dreamy fancy. Every vibration of her spirit was visible in her frame, as she listened to the rattling of wheels and the tramp upon the pavement, and deemed that even the breeze bore the sound of her lover's footsteps, as if he trode upon the viewless air. Mrs. Grosvenor, too, while she watched the tremulous flow of Sylvia's feelings, was deeply moved; she looked uneasily at the agitated girl, and was about to speak, when the opening of the street door arrested the words upon her lips.

Footsteps ascended the staircase, with a confident and familiar tread, and some one entered the drawing-room. From the sofa where they sat, in the inner apartment, Mrs. Grosvenor and Sylvia could not discern the visitor.

"Sylph!" cried a voice. "Dearest Sylph! Where are you, sweet Sylph Etherege? Here is your Edgar Vaughan!"

But instead of answering, or rising to meet her lover,—who had greeted her by the sweet and fanciful name, which, appropriate as it was to her character, was known only to him.—Sylvia grasped Mrs. Grosvenor's arm, while her whole frame shook with the throbbing of her heart.

"Who is it?" gasped she. "Who calls me Sylph?"

Before Mrs. Grosvenor could reply, the stranger entered the room, bearing the lamp in his hand. Approaching the sofa, he displayed to Sylvia the features of Edward Hamilton, illuminated by that evil smile, from which his face derived so marked an individuality.

"Is not the miniature an admirable likeness?" inquired he.

Sylvia shuddered, but had not power to turn away her white face from his gaze. The miniature, which she had been holding in her hand, fell down upon the floor, where Hamilton, or Vaughan, set his foot upon it, and crushed the ivory counterfeit to fragments.

"There, my sweet Sylph!" he exclaimed. "It was I that created your phantom-lover, and now I annihilate him! Your dream is rudely broken. Awake, Sylph Etherege, awake to truth! I am the only Edgar Vaughan!"

"We have gone too far, Edgar Vaughan," said Mrs. Grosvenor, catching Sylvia in her arms. The revengeful freak, which Vaughan's wounded vanity had suggested, had been countenanced by this lady, in the hope of curing Sylvia of her romantic notions, and reconciling her to the truths and realities of life. "Look at the poor child!" she continued. "I protest I tremble for the consequences!"

"Indeed, madam!" replied Vaughan, sneeringly, as he threw the light of the lamp on Sylvia's closed eyes and marble features. "Well, my conscience is clear. I did but look into this delicate creature's heart; and with the pure fantasies that I found there, I made what seemed a man,—and the delusive shadow has wiled her away to Shadow-land, and vanished there! It is no new tale. Many a sweet maid has shared the lot of poor Sylph Etherege!"

"And now, Edgar Vaughan," said Mrs. Grosvenor, as Sylvia's heart began faintly to throb again, "now try, in good earnest, to win back her love from the phantom which you conjured up. If you succeed, she will be the better, her whole life long, for the lesson we have given her."

Whether the result of the lesson corresponded with Mrs. Grosvenor's hopes, may be gathered from the closing scene of our story. It had been made known to the fashionable world that Edgar Vaughan had returned from France, and, under the assumed name of Edward Hamilton, had won the affections of the lovely girl to whom he had been affianced in his boyhood. The nuptials were to take place at an early date. One evening, before the day of anticipated bliss arrived, Edgar Vaughan entered Mrs. Grosvenor's drawing-room, where he found that lady and Sylph Etherege.

"Only that Sylvia makes no complaint," remarked Mrs. Grosvenor, "I should apprehend that the town air is ill-suited to her constitution. She was always, indeed, a delicate creature; but now she is a mere gossamer. Do but look at her! Did you ever imagine anything so fragile?"

Vaughan was already attentively observing his mistress, who sat in a shadowy and moon-lighted recess of the room, with her dreamy eyes fixed steadfastly upon his own. The bough of a tree was waving before the window, and sometimes enveloped her in the gloom of its shadow, into which she seemed to vanish.

"Yes," he said, to Mrs. Grosvenor. "I can scarcely deem her 'of the earth, earthy.' No wonder that I call her Sylph! Methinks she will fade into the moonlight, which falls upon her through the window. Or, in the open air, she might flit away upon the breeze, like a wreath of mist!"

Sylvia's eyes grew brighter. She waved her hand to Edgar Vaughan, with a ges-ture of ethereal triumph.

"Farewell!" she said. "I will neither fade into the moonlight, nor flit away upon the breeze. Yet you cannot keep me here!"

There was something in Sylvia's look and tones that startled Mrs. Grosvenor, with a terrible apprehension. But as she was rushing towards the girl, Vaughan held her back.

"Stay!" cried he, with a strange smile of mockery and anguish. "Can our sweet Sylph be going to heaven, to seek the original of the miniature?"

THE CANTERBURY PILGRIMS

THE summer moon, which shines in so many a tale, was beaming over a broad extent of uneven country. Some of its brightest rays were flung into a spring of water, where no traveller, toiling as the writer has, up the hilly road beside which it gushes, ever failed to quench his thirst. The work of neat hands and considerate art was visible about this blessed fountain. An open cistern, hewn and hollowed out of solid stone, was placed above the waters, which filled it to the brim, but, by some invisible outlet, were conveyed away without dripping down its sides. Though the basin had not room for another drop, and the continual gush of water made a tremor on the surface, there was a secret charm that forbade it to overflow. I remember, that when I had slaked my summer thirst, and sat panting by the cistern, it was my fanciful theory, that Nature could not afford to lavish so pure a liquid, as she does the waters of all meaner fountains.

While the moon was hanging almost perpendicularly over this spot, two figures appeared on the summit of the hill, and came with noiseless footsteps down towards the spring. They were then in the first freshness of youth; nor is there a wrinkle now on either of their brows, and yet they wore a strange, old-fashioned garb. One, a young man with ruddy cheeks, walked beneath the canopy of a broad-brimmed gray hat; he seemed to have inherited his great-grandsire's square-skirted coat, and a waistcoat that extended its immense flaps to his knees; his brown locks, also, hung down behind, in a mode unknown to our times. By his side was a sweet young damsel, her fair features sheltered by a prim little bonnet, within which appeared the vestal muslin of a cap; her close, long-waisted gown, and indeed her whole attire, might have been worn by some rustic beauty who had faded half a century before. But that there was something too warm and life-like in them, I would here have compared this couple to the ghosts of two young lovers, who had died long since in the glow of passion, and now were straying out of their graves, to renew the old vows, and shadow forth the unforgotten kiss of their earthly lips, beside the moonlit spring.

"Thee and I will rest here a moment, Miriam," said the young man, as they drew near the stone cistern, "for there is no fear that the elders know what we have done; and this may be the last time we shall ever taste this water."

Thus speaking, with a little sadness in his face, which was also visible in that of his companion, he made her sit down on a stone, and was about to place himself very close to her side; she, however, repelled him, though not unkindly.

"Nay, Josiah," said she, giving him a timid push with her maiden hand, "thee must sit farther off, on that other stone, with the spring between us. What would the sisters say, if thee were to sit so close to me?"

"But we are of the world's people now, Miriam," answered Josiah.

The girl persisted in her prudery, nor did the youth, in fact, seem altogether free from a similar sort of shyness; so they sat apart from each other, gazing up the hill, where the moonlight discovered the tops of a group of buildings. While their attention was thus occupied, a party of travellers, who had come wearily up the long ascent, made a halt to refresh themselves at the spring. There were three men, a woman, and a little girl and boy. Their attire was mean, covered with the dust

of the summer's day, and damp with the night-dew; they all looked woebegone, as if the cares and sorrows of the world had made their steps heavier as they climbed the hill; even the two little children appeared older in evil days than the young man and maiden who had first approached the spring.

"Good-evening to you, young folks," was the salutation of the travellers; and "Good-evening, friends," replied the youth and damsel.

"Is that white building the Shaker meeting-house?" asked one of the strangers. "And are those the red roofs of the Shaker village?"

"Friend, it is the Shaker village," answered Josiah, after some hesitation.

The travellers, who, from the first, had looked suspiciously at the garb of these young people, now taxed them with an intention which all the circumstances, indeed, rendered too obvious to be mistaken.

"It is true, friends," replied the young man, summoning up his courage. "Miriam and I have a gift to love each other, and we are going among the world's people, to live after their fashion. And ye know that we do not transgress the law of the land; and neither ye, nor the elders themselves, have a right to hinder us."

"Yet you think it expedient to depart without leave-taking," remarked one of the travellers.

"Yea, ye-a," said Josiah, reluctantly, "because father Job is a very awful man to speak with; and being aged himself, he has but little charity for what he calls the iniquities of the flesh."

"Well," said the stranger, "we will neither use force to bring you back to the village, nor will we betray you to the elders. But sit you here awhile, and when you have heard what we shall tell you of the world which we have left, and into which you are going, perhaps you will turn back with us of your own accord. What say you?" added he, turning to his companions. "We have travelled thus far without becoming known to each other. Shall we tell our stories, here by this pleasant spring, for our own pastime, and the benefit of these misguided young lovers?"

In accordance with this proposal, the whole party stationed themselves round the stone cistern; the two children, being very weary, fell asleep upon the damp earth, and the pretty Shaker girl, whose feelings were those of a nun or a Turkish lady, crept as close as possible to the female traveller, and as far as she well could from the unknown men. The same person who had hitherto been the chief spokesman now stood up, waving his hat in his hand, and suffered the moonlight to fall full upon his front.

"In me," said he, with a certain majesty of utterance, "in me, you behold a poet."

Though a lithographic print of this gentleman is extant, it may be well to notice that he was now nearly forty, a thin and stooping figure, in a black coat, out at elbows; notwithstanding the ill condition of his attire, there were about him several tokens of a peculiar sort of foppery, unworthy of a mature man, particularly in the arrangement of his hair, which was so disposed as to give all possible loftiness and breadth to his forehead. However, he had an intelligent eye, and, on the whole, a marked countenance.

"A poet!" repeated the young Shaker, a little puzzled how to understand such a designation, seldom heard in the utilitarian community where he had spent his life. "O, ay, Miriam, he means a varse-maker, thee must know."

This remark jarred upon the susceptible nerves of the poet; nor could he help wondering what strange fatality had put into this young man's mouth an epithet which ill-natured people had affirmed to be more proper to his merit than the one assumed by himself.

"True, I am a verse-maker," he resumed, "but my verse is no more than the material body into which I breathe the celestial soul of thought. Alas! how many a pang has it cost me, this same insensibility to the ethereal essence of poetry, with which you have here tortured me again, at the moment when I am to relinquish my profession forever! O Fate! why hast thou warred with Nature, turning all her higher and more perfect gifts to the ruin of me, their possessor? What is the voice of song, when the world lacks the ear of taste? How can I rejoice in my strength and delicacy of feeling, when they have but made great sorrows out of little ones? Have I dreaded scorn like death, and yearned for fame as others pant for vital air, only to find myself in a middle state between obscurity and infamy? But I have my revenge! I could have given existence to a thousand bright creations. I crush them into my heart, and there let them putrefy! I shake off the dust of my feet against my countrymen! But posterity, tracing my footsteps up this weary hill, will cry shame upon the unworthy age that drove one of the fathers of American song to end his days in a Shaker village!"

During this harangue, the speaker gesticulated with great energy; and, as poetry is the natural language of passion, there appeared reason to apprehend his final explosion into an ode extempore. The reader must understand that, for all these bitter words, he was a kind, gentle, harmless, poor fellow enough, whom Nature, tossing her ingredients together without looking at her recipe, had sent into the world with too much of one sort of brain, and hardly any of another.

"Friend," said the young Shaker, in some perplexity, "thee seemest to have met with great troubles; and, doubtless, I should pity them, if—if I could but understand what they were."

"Happy in your ignorance!" replied the poet, with an air of sublime superiority. "To your coarser mind, perhaps, I may seem to speak of more important griefs, when I add, what I had wellnigh forgotten, that I am out at elbows, and almost starved to death. At any rate, you have the advice and example of one individual to warn you back; for I am come hither, a disappointed man, flinging aside the fragments of my hopes, and seeking shelter in the calm retreat which you are so anxious to leave."

"I thank thee, friend," rejoined the youth, "but I do not mean to be a poet, nor, Heaven be praised! do I think Miriam ever made a varse in her life. So we need not fear thy disappointments. But, Miriam," he added, with real concern, "thee knowest that the elders admit nobody that has not a gift to be useful. Now, what under the sun can they do with this poor varsemaker?"

"Nay, Josiah, do not thee discourage the poor man," said the girl, in all simplicity and kindness. "Our hymns are very rough, and perhaps they may trust him to smooth them."

Without noticing this hint of professional employment, the poet turned away, and gave himself up to a sort of vague reverie, which he called thought. Sometimes he watched the moon, pouring a silvery liquid on the clouds, through which it slowly melted till they became all bright; then he saw the same sweet radiance dancing on the leafy trees which rustled as if to shake it off, or sleeping on the high tops of hills, or hovering down in distant valleys, like the material of unshaped dreams; lastly, he looked into the spring, and there the light was mingling with the water. In its crystal bosom, too, beholding all heaven reflected there, he found an emblem of a pure and tranquil breast. He listened to that most ethereal of all sounds, the song of crickets, coming in full choir upon the wind, and fancied that, if moonlight could be heard, it would sound just like that. Finally, he took a draught at the Shaker spring, and, as if it were the true Castalia, was forthwith moved to compose a lyric, a Farewell to his Harp, which he swore should be its closing strain, the last verse that an ungrateful world should have from him. This effusion, with two or three other little pieces, subsequently written, he took the first opportunity to send, by one of the Shaker brethren, to Concord, where they were published in the New Hampshire Patriot.

Meantime, another of the Canterbury pilgrims, one so different from the poet that the delicate fancy of the latter could hardly have conceived of him, began to relate his sad experience. He was a small man of quick and unquiet gestures, about fifty years old, with a narrow forehead, all wrinkled and drawn together. He held in his hand a pencil, and a card of some commission-merchant in foreign parts, on the back of which, for there was light enough to read or write by, he seemed ready to figure out a calculation.

"Young man," said he, abruptly, "what quantity of land do the Shakers own here, in Canterbury?"

"That is more than I can tell thee, friend," answered Josiah, "but it is a very rich establishment, and for a long way by the roadside thee may guess the land to be ours, by the neatness of the fences."

"And what may be the value of the whole," continued the stranger, "with all the buildings and improvements, pretty nearly, in round numbers?"

"O, a monstrous sum,—more than I can reckon," replied the young Shaker.

"Well, sir," said the pilgrim, "there was a day, and not very long ago, neither, when I stood at my counting-room window, and watched the signal-flags of three of my own ships entering the harbor, from the East Indies, from Liverpool, and from up the Straits; and I would not have given the invoice of the least of them for the title-deeds of this whole Shaker settlement. You stare. Perhaps, now, you won't believe that I could have put more value on a little piece of paper, no bigger than the palm of your hand, than all these solid acres of grain, grass, and pasture-land would sell for?"

"I won't dispute it, friend," answered Josiah, "but I know I had rather have fifty acres of this good land than a whole sheet of thy paper."

"You may say so now," said the ruined merchant, bitterly, "for my name would not be worth the paper I should write it on. Of course, you must have heard of my failure?"

And the stranger mentioned his name, which, however mighty it might have been in the commercial world, the young Shaker had never heard of among the Canterbury hills.

"Not heard of my failure!" exclaimed the merchant, considerably piqued. "Why, it was spoken of on 'Change in London, and from Boston to New Orleans men trembled in their shoes. At all events, I did fail, and you see me here on my road to the Shaker village, where, doubtless (for the Shakers are a shrewd sect), they will have a due respect for my experience, and give me the management of the trading part of the concern, in which case, I think I can pledge myself to double their capital in four or five years. Turn back with me, young man; for though you will never meet with my good luck, you can hardly escape my bad."

"I will not turn back for this," replied Josiah, calmly, "any more than for the advice of the varse-maker, between whom and thee, friend, I see a sort of likeness, though I can't justly say where it lies. But Miriam and I can earn our daily bread among the world's people, as well as in the Shaker village. And do we want anything more, Miriam?"

"Nothing more, Josiah," said the girl, quietly.

"Yea, Miriam, and daily bread for some other little mouths, if God send them," observed the simple Shaker lad.

Miriam did not reply, but looked down into the spring, where she encountered the image of her own pretty face, blushing within the prim little bonnet. The third pilgrim now took up the conversation. He was a sunburnt countryman, of tall frame and bony strength, on whose rude and manly face there appeared a darker, more sullen and obstinate despondency, than on those of either the poet or the merchant.

"Well, now, youngster," he began, "these folks have had their say, so I'll take my turn. My story will cut but a poor figure by the side of theirs; for I never supposed that I could have a right to meat and drink, and great praise besides, only for tagging rhymes together, as it seems this man does; nor ever tried to get the substance of hundreds into my own hands, like the trader there. When I was about of your years, I married me a wife,—just such a neat and pretty young woman as Miriam, if that's her name,—and all I asked of Providence was an ordinary blessing on the sweat of my brow, so that we might be decent and comfortable, and have daily bread for ourselves, and for some other little mouths that we soon had to feed. We had no great prospects before us; but I never wanted to be idle; and I thought it a matter of course that the Lord would help me, because I was willing to help myself."

"And didn't he help thee, friend?" demanded Josiah, with some eagerness.

"No," said the yeoman, sullenly; "for then you would not have seen me here. I have labored hard for years; and my means have been growing narrower, and my living poorer, and my heart colder and heavier, all the time; till at last I could bear it no longer. I set myself down to calculate whether I had best go on the Oregon expedition, or come here to the Shaker village; but I had not hope enough left in me to begin the world over again; and, to make my story short, here I am. And now, youngster, take my advice, and turn back; or else, some few years hence, you'll have to climb this hill, with as heavy a heart as mine."

This simple story had a strong effect on the young fugitives. The misfortunes of the poet and merchant had won little sympathy from their plain good sense and unworldly feelings, qualities which made them such unprejudiced and inflexible judges, that few men would have chosen to take the opinion of this youth and maiden as to the wisdom or folly of their pursuits. But here was one whose simple wishes had resembled their own, and who, after efforts which almost gave him a right to claim success from fate, had failed in accomplishing them.

"But thy wife, friend?" exclaimed the young man, "what became of the pretty girl, like Miriam? O, I am afraid she is dead!"

"Yea, poor man, she must be dead, —she and the children, too," sobbed Miriam.

The female pilgrim had been leaning over the spring, wherein latterly a tear or two might have been seen to fall, and form its little circle on the surface of the water. She now looked up, disclosing features still comely, but which had acquired an expression of fretfulness, in the same long course of evil fortune that had thrown a sullen gloom over the temper of the unprosperous yeoman.

"I am his wife," said she, a shade of irritability just perceptible in the sadness of her tone. "These poor little things, asleep on the ground, are two of our children. We had two more, but God has provided better for them than we could, by taking them to himself."

"And what would thee advise Josiah and me to do?" asked Miriam, this being the first question which she had put to either of the strangers.

"'T is a thing almost against nature for a woman to try to part true lovers," answered the yeoman's wife, after a pause; "but I'll speak as truly to you as if these were my dying words. Though my husband told you some of our troubles, he didn't mention the greatest, and that which makes all the rest so hard to bear. If you and your sweetheart marry, you'll be kind and pleasant to each other for a year or two, and while that's the case, you never will repent; but, by and by, he'll grow gloomy, rough, and hard to please, and you'll be peevish, and full of little angry fits, and apt to be complaining by the fireside, when he comes to rest himself from his troubles out of doors; so your love will wear away by little and little, and leave you miserable at last. It has been so with us; and yet my husband and I were true lovers once; if ever two young folks were."

As she ceased, the yeoman and his wife exchanged a glance, in which there was more and warmer affection than they had supposed to have escaped the frost of a wintry fate, in either of their breasts. At that moment, when they stood on the utmost verge of married life, one word fitly spoken, or perhaps one peculiar look, had they had mutual confidence enough to reciprocate it, might have renewed all their old feelings, and sent them back, resolved to sustain each other amid the struggles of the world. But the crisis passed, and never came again. Just then, also, the children, roused by their mother's voice, looked up, and added their willing accents to the testimony borne by all the Canterbury pilgrims against the world from which they fled.

"We are tired and hungry!" cried they. "Is it far to the Shaker village?"

The Shaker youth and maiden looked mournfully into each other's eyes. They had but stepped across the threshold of their homes, when lo! the dark array of cares and sorrows that rose up to warn them back. The varied narratives of the strangers had arranged themselves into a parable; they seemed not merely instances of woful fate that had befallen others, but shadowy omens of disappointed hope, and unavailing toil, domestic grief, and estranged affection, that would cloud the onward path of these poor fugitives. But after one instant's hesitation, they opened their arms, and sealed their resolve with as pure and fond an embrace as ever youthful love had hallowed.

"We will not go back," said they. "The world never can be dark to us, for we will always love one another."

Then the Canterbury pilgrims went up the hill, while the poet chanted a drear and desperate stanza of the Farewell to his Harp, fitting music for that melancholy band. They sought a home where all former ties of nature or society would be sundered, and all old distinctions levelled, and a cold and passionless security be substituted for mortal hope and fear, as in that other refuge of the world's weary outcasts, the grave. The lovers drank at the Shaker spring, and then, with chastened hopes, but more confiding affections, went on to mingle in an untried life.

OLD NEWS

I. THE COLONIAL NEWSPAPER

HERE is a volume of what were once newspapers, each on a small half-sheet, yellow and time-stained, of a coarse fabric, and imprinted with a rude old type. Their aspect conveys a singular impression of antiquity, in a species of literature which we are accustomed to consider as connected only with the present moment. Ephemeral as they were intended and supposed to be, they have long outlived the printer in his whole subscription-list, and have proved more durable, as to their physical existence, than most of the timber, bricks, and stone of the town where they were issued. These are but the least of their triumphs. The government, the interests, the opinions, in short, all the moral circumstances that were contemporary with their publication, have passed away, and left no better record of what they were than may be found in these frail leaves. Happy are the editors of newspapers! Their productions excel all others in immediate popularity, and are certain to acquire another sort of value with the lapse of time. They scatter their leaves to the wind, as the sibyl did, and posterity collects them, to be treasured up among the best materials of its wisdom. With hasty pens they write for immortality.

It is pleasant to take one of these little dingy half-sheets between the thumb and finger, and picture forth the personage who, above ninety years ago, held it, wet from the press, and steaming, before the fire. Many of the numbers bear the name of an old colonial dignitary. There he sits, a major, a member of the council, and a weighty merchant, in his high-backed arm-chair, wearing a solemn wig and grave attire, such as befits his imposing gravity of mien, and displaying but little finery, except a huge pair of silver shoe-buckles curiously carved. Observe the awful reverence of his visage, as he reads His Majesty's most gracious speech; and the deliberate wisdom with which he ponders over some paragraph of provincial politics, and the keener intelligence with which he glances at the ship-news and commercial advertisements. Observe, and smile! He may have been a wise man in his day; but, to us, the wisdom of the politician appears like folly, because we can compare its prognostics with actual results; and the old merchant seems to have busied himself about vanities, because we know that the expected ships have been lost at sea, or mouldered at the wharves; that his imported broadcloths were long ago worn to tatters, and his cargoes of wine quaffed to the lees; and that the most precious leaves of his ledger have become waste-paper. Yet his avocations were not so vain as our philosophic moralizing. In this world, we are the things of a moment, and are made to pursue momentary things, with here and there a thought that stretches mistily towards eternity, and perhaps may endure as long. All philosophy that would abstract mankind from the present is no more than words.

The first pages of most of these old papers are as soporific as a bed of poppies. Here we have an erudite clergyman, or perhaps a Cambridge professor, occupying several successive weeks with a criticism on Tate and Brady, as compared with the New England version of the Psalms. Of course, the preference is given to the native article. Here are doctors disagreeing about the treatment of a putrid fever then prevalent, and blackguarding each other with a characteristic virulence that renders the controversy not altogether unreadable. Here are President Wigglesworth and the Rev. Dr. Colman, endeavoring to raise a fund for the support of missionaries among the Indians of Massachusetts Bay. Easy would be the duties of such a mission now! Here—for there is nothing new under the sun—are frequent complaints of the disordered state of the currency, and the project of a bank with a capital of five hundred thousand pounds, secured on lands. Here are literary essays, from the Gentleman's Magazine; and squibs against the Pretender, from the London newspapers. And here, occasionally, are specimens of New England humor, laboriously light and lamentably mirthful, as if some very sober person, in his zeal to be merry, were dancing a jig to the tune of a funeral-psalm. All this is wearisome, and we must turn the leaf.

There is a good deal of amusement, and some profit, in the perusal of those little items which characterize the manners and circumstances of the country. New England was then in a state incomparably more picturesque than at present, or than it has been within the memory of man; there being, as yet, only a narrow strip of civilization along the edge of a vast forest, peopled with enough of its original race to contrast the savage life with the old customs of another world. The white population, also, was diversified by the influx of all sorts of expatriated vagabonds, and by the continual importation of bond-servants from Ireland and elsewhere, so that there was a wild and unsettled multitude, forming a strong minority to the sober descendants of the Puritans. Then, there were the slaves, contributing their dark shade to the picture of society. The consequence of all this was a great variety and singularity of action and incident, many instances of which might be selected from these columns, where they are told with a simplicity and quaintness of style that bring the striking points into very strong relief. It is natural to suppose, too, that these circumstances affected the body of the people, and made their course of life generally less regular than that of their descendants. There is no evidence that the moral standard was higher than now; or, indeed, that morality was so well defined as it has since become. There seem to have been quite as many frauds and robberies, in proportion to the number of honest deeds; there were murders, in hot-blood and in malice; and bloody quarrels over liquor. Some of our fathers also appear to have been yoked to unfaithful wives, if we may trust the frequent notices of elopements from bed and board. The pillory, the whipping-post, the prison, and the gallows, each had their use in those old times; and, in short, as often as our imagination lives in the past, we find it a ruder and rougher age than our own, with hardly any perceptible advantages, and much that gave life a gloomier tinge.

In vain we endeavor to throw a sunny and joyous air over our picture of this period; nothing passes before our fancy but a crowd of sad-visaged people, moving duskily through a dull gray atmosphere. It is certain that winter rushed upon them with fiercer storms than now, blocking up the narrow forest-paths, and overwhelming the roads along the sea-coast with mountain snowdrifts; so that weeks elapsed before the newspaper could announce how many travellers had perished, or what wrecks had strewn the shore. The cold was more piercing then, and lingered further into the spring, making the chimney-corner a comfortable seat till long past May-day. By the number of such accidents on record, we might suppose that the thunder-stone, as they termed it, fell oftener and deadlier, on steeples, dwellings, and unsheltered wretches. In fine, our fathers bore the brunt of more raging and pitiless elements than we. There were forebodings, also, of a more fearful tempest than those of the elements. At two or three dates, we have stories of drums, trumpets, and all sorts of martial music, passing athwart the midnight sky, accompanied with the roar of cannon and rattle of musketry, prophetic echoes of the sounds that were soon to shake the land. Besides these airy prognostics, there were rumors of French fleets on the coast, and of the march of French and Indians through the wilderness, along the borders of the settlements. The country was saddened, moreover, with grievous sickness. The small-pox raged in many of the towns, and seems, though so familiar a scourge, to have been regarded with as much affright as that which drove the throng from Wall Street and Broadway at the approach of a new pestilence. There were autumnal fevers too, and a contagious and destructive throat-distemper,—diseases unwritten in medical books. The dark superstition of former days had not yet been so far dispelled as not to heighten the gloom of the present times. There is an advertisement, indeed, by a committee of the Legislature, calling for information as to the circumstances of sufferers in the "late calamity of 1692," with a view to reparation of their losses and misfortunes. But the tenderness with which, after above forty years, it was thought expedient to allude to the witch-craft delusion, indicates a good deal of lingering error, as well as the advance of more enlightened opinions. The rigid hand of Puritanism might yet be felt upon the reins of government, while some of the ordinances intimate a disorderly spirit on the part of the people. The Suffolk justices, after a preamble that great disturbances have been committed by persons entering town and leaving it in coaches, chaises, calashes, and other wheel-carriages, on the evening before the Sabbath, give notice that a watch will hereafter be set at the "fortification-gate," to prevent these outrages. It is amusing to see Boston assuming the aspect of a walled city, guarded. probably, by a detachment of church-members, with a deacon at their head. Governor Belcher makes proclamation against certain "loose and dissolute people" who have been wont to stop passengers in the streets, on the 5th of November, "otherwise called Pope's Day," and levy contributions for the building of bonfires. In this instance, the populace are more puritanic than the magistrate.

The elaborate solemnities of funerals were in accordance with the sombre character of the times. In cases of ordinary death, the printer seldom fails to notice that the corpse was "very decently interred." But when some mightier mortal has yielded to his fate, the decease of the "worshipful" such-a-one is announced, with all his titles of deacon, justice, counsellor, and colonel; then follows an heraldic sketch of his honorable ancestors, and lastly an account of the black pomp of his funeral, and the liberal expenditure of scarfs, gloves, and mourning-rings. The burial train glides slowly before us, as we have seen it represented in the wood-cuts of that day, the coffin, and the bearers, and the lamentable friends, trailing their long black garments, while grim death, a most misshapen skeleton, with all kinds of doleful emblems, stalks hideously in front. There was a coach-maker at this period, one John Lucas, who seems to have gained the chief of his living by letting out a sable coach to funerals.

It would not be fair, however, to leave quite so dismal an impression on the reader's mind; nor should it be forgotten that happiness may walk soberly in dark attire, as well as dance lightsomely in a gala-dress. And this reminds us that there is an incidental notice of the "dancing-school near the Orange-Tree," whence we may infer that the saltatory art was occasionally practised, though perhaps chastened into a characteristic gravity of movement. This pastime was probably confined to the aristocratic circle, of which the royal governor was the centre. But we are scandalized at the attempt of Jonathan Furness to introduce a more reprehensible amusement: he challenges the whole country to match his black gelding in a race for a hundred pounds, to be decided on Metonomy Common or Chelsea Beach. Nothing as to the manners of the times can be inferred from this freak of an individual. There were no daily and continual opportunities of being merry; but sometimes the people rejoiced, in their own peculiar fashion, oftener with a calm, religious smile than with a broad laugh, as when they feasted, like one great family, at Thanksgiving time, or indulged a livelier mirth throughout the pleasant days of Election-week. This latter was the true holiday-season of New England. Military musters were too seriously important in that warlike time to be classed among amusements; but they stirred up and enlivened the public mind, and were occasions of solemn festival to the governor and great men of the province, at the expense of the field-officers. The Revolution blotted a feast-day out of our calendar; for the anniversary of the king's birth appears to have been celebrated with most imposing pomp, by salutes from Castle William, a military parade, a grand dinner at the townhouse, and a brilliant illumination in the evening. There was nothing forced nor feigned in these testimonials of loyalty to George the Second So long as they dreaded the re-establishment of a popish dynasty, the people were fervent for the house of Hanover: and, besides, the immediate magistracy of the country was a barrier between the monarch and the occasional discontents of the colonies; the waves of faction sometimes reached the governor's chair, but never swelled against the throne. Thus, until oppression was felt to proceed from the king's own hand, New England rejoiced with her whole heart on his Majesty's birthday.

But the slaves, we suspect, were the merriest part of the population, since it was their gift to be merry in the worst of circumstances; and they endured, comparatively, few hardships, under the domestic sway of our fathers. There seems to have been a great trade in these human commodities. No advertisements are more frequent than those of "a negro fellow, fit for almost any household work"; "a negro woman, honest, healthy, and capable"; "a young negro wench, of many desirable qualities"; "a negro man, very fit for a taylor." We know not in what this natural fitness for a tailor consisted, unless it were some peculiarity of conformation that enabled him to sit cross-legged. When the slaves of a family were inconveniently prolific,—it being not quite orthodox to drown the superfluous offspring, like a litter of kittens,—notice was promulgated of "a negro child to be given away." Sometimes the slaves assumed the property of their own persons, and made their escape; among many such instances, the governor raises a hue-and-cry after his negro Juba. But, without venturing a word in extenuation of the general system, we confess our opinion that Cæsar, Pompey, Scipio, and all such great Roman namesakes, would have been better advised had they stayed at home, foddering the cattle, cleaning dishes,—in fine, performing their moderate share of the labors of life, without being harassed by its cares. The sable inmates of the mansion were not excluded from the domestic affections: in families in middling rank, they had their places at the board; and when the circle closed round the evening hearth, its blaze glowed on their dark shining faces, intermixed familiarly with their master's children. It must have contributed to reconcile them to their lot, that they saw white men and women imported from Europe as they had been from Africa, and sold, though only for a term of years, yet as actual slaves to the highest bidder. Slave labor being but a small part of the industry of the country, it did not change the character of the people; the latter, on the contrary, modified and softened the institution, making it a patriarchal, and almost a beautiful, peculiarity of the times.

Ah! We had forgotten the good old merchant, over whose shoulder we were peeping, while he read the newspaper. Let us now suppose him putting on his three-cornered gold-laced hat, grasping his cane, with a head inlaid of ebony and mother-of-pearl, and setting forth, through the crooked streets of Boston, on various errands, suggested by the advertisements of the day. Thus he communes with himself: I must be mindful, says he, to call at Captain Scut's, in Creek Lane, and examine his rich velvet, whether it be fit for my apparel on Election-day,—that I may wear a stately aspect in presence of the governor and my brethren of the council. I will look in also, at the shop of Michael Cario, the jeweller: he has silver buckles of a new fashion; and mine have lasted me some half-score years. My fair daughter Miriam shall have an apron of gold brocade, and a velvet mask,—though it would be a pity the wench should hide her comely visage; and also a French cap, from Robert Jenkins's, on the north side of the town-house. He hath beads, too, and ear-rings, and necklaces, of all sorts; these are but vanities,—nevertheless, they would please the silly maiden well. My dame desireth another female in the kitchen; wherefore, I must inspect the lot of Irish lasses, for sale by Samuel Waldo, aboard the schooner Endeavor; as also the likely negro wench, at Captain Bulfinch's. It were not amiss that I took my daughter Miriam to see the royal wax-work, near the town-dock, that she may learn to honor our most gracious King and Queen, and their royal progeny, even in their waxen images; not that I would approve of image-worship. The camel, too, that strange beast from Africa, with two great humps, to be seen near the common; methinks I would fain go thither, and see how the old patriarchs were wont to ride. I will tarry awhile in Queen Street, at the bookstore of my good friends Kneeland and Green, and purchase Doctor Colman's new sermon, and the volume of discourses by Mr. Henry Flynt; and look over the controversy on baptism, between the Reverend Peter Clarke and an unknown adversary; and see whether this George Whitefield be as great in print as he is famed to be in the pulpit. By that time, the auction will have commenced

at the Royal Exchange, in King Street. Moreover, I must look to the disposal of my last cargo of West India rum and muscovado sugar; and also the lot of choice Cheshire cheese, lest it grow mouldy. It were well that I ordered a cask of good English beer, at the lower end of Milk Street. Then am I to speak with certain dealers about the lot of stout old Vidonia, rich Canary, and Oporto wines, which I have now lying in the cellar of the Old South meeting-house. But, a pipe or two of the rich Canary shall be reserved that it may grow mellow in mine own wine-cellar, and gladden my heart when it begins to droop with old age.

Provident old gentleman! But, was he mindful of his sepulchre? Did he bethink him to call at the work-shop of Timothy Sheaffe, in Cold Lane, and select such a gravestone as would best please him? There wrought the man whose handiwork, or that of his fellow-craftsmen, was ultimately in demand by all the busy multitude who have left a record of their earthly toil in these old time-stained papers. And now, as we turn over the volume, we seem to be wandering among the mossy stones of a burial-ground.

II. THE OLD FRENCH WAR

At a period about twenty years subsequent to that of our former sketch, we again attempt a delineation of some of the characteristics of life and manners in New England. Our text-book, as before, is a file of antique newspapers. The volume which serves us for a writing-desk is a folio of larger dimensions than the one before described; and the papers are generally printed on a whole sheet, sometimes with a supplemental leaf of news and advertisements. They have a venerable appearance, being overspread with the duskiness of more than seventy years, and discolored, here and there, with the deeper stains of some liquid, as if the contents of a wine-glass had long since been splashed upon the page. Still, the old book conveys an impression that, when the separate numbers were flying about town, in the first day or two of their respective existences, they might have been fit reading for very stylish people. Such newspapers could have been issued nowhere but in a metropolis the centre, not only of public and private affairs, but of fashion and gayety. Without any discredit to the colonial press, these might have been, and probably were, spread out on the tables of the British coffee-house, in King Street, for the perusal of the throng of officers who then drank their wine at that celebrated establishment. To interest these military gentlemen, there were bulletins of the war between Prussia and Austria; between England and France, on the old battle-plains of Flanders, and between the same antagonists in the newer fields of the East Indies,—and in our own trackless woods, where white men never trod until they came to fight there. Or, the travelled American, the petit-maitre of the colonies,—the ape of London foppery, as the newspaper was the semblance of the London journals,—he, with his gray powdered periwig, his embroidered coat, lace ruffles, and glossy silk stockings, golden-clocked,—his buckles, of glittering paste, at knee-band and shoe-strap, —his scented handkerchief, and chapeau beneath his arm,—even such a dainty figure need not have disdained to glance at these old yellow pages, while they were the mirror of passing times. For his amusement, there were essays of wit and humor, the light literature of the day, which, for breadth and license, might have proceeded from the pen of Fielding or Smollett; while, in other columns, he would delight his imagination with the enumerated items of all sorts of finery, and with the rival advertisements of half a dozen perukemakers. In short, newer manners and customs had almost entirely superseded those of the Puritans, even in their own city of refuge.

It was natural that, with the lapse of time and increase of wealth and population, the peculiarities of the early settlers should have waxed fainter and fainter through the generations of their descendants, who also had been alloyed by a continual accession of emigrants from many countries and of all characters. It tended to assimilate the colonial manners to those of the mother country, that the commercial intercourse was great, and that the merchants often went thither in their own ships. Indeed, almost every man of adequate fortune felt a yearning desire, and even judged it a filial duty, at least once in his life, to visit the home of his ancestors. They still called it their own home, as if New England were to them, what many of the old Puritans had considered it, not a permanent abiding-place, but merely a lodge in the wilderness, until the trouble of the times should be passed. The example of the royal governors must have had much influence on the manners of the colonists; for these rulers assumed a degree of state and splendor which had never been practised by their predecessors, who differed in nothing from republican chief-magistrates, under the old charter. The officers of the crown, the public characters in the interest of the administration, and the gentlemen of wealth and good descent, generally noted for their loyalty, would constitute a dignified circle, with the governor in the centre, bearing a very passable resemblance to a court. Their ideas, their habits, their code of courtesy, and their dress, would have all the fresh glitter of fashions immediately derived from the fountain-head, in England. To prevent their modes of life from becoming the standard with all who had the ability to imitate them, there was no longer an undue severity of religion, nor as yet any disaffection to British supremacy, nor democratic prejudices against pomp. Thus, while the colonies were attaining that strength which was soon to render them an independent republic, it might have been supposed that the wealthier classes were growing into an aristocracy, and ripening for hereditary rank, while the poor were to be stationary in their abasement, and the country, perhaps, to be a sister monarchy with England. Such, doubtless, were the plausible conjectures deduced from the superficial phenomena of our connection with a monarchical government, until the prospective nobility were levelled with the mob, by the mere gathering of winds that preceded the storm of the Revolution. The portents of that storm were not yet visible in the air. A true picture of society, therefore, would have the rich effect produced by distinctions of rank that seemed permanent, and by appropriate habits of splendor on the part of the gentry.

The people at large had been somewhat changed in character, since the period of our last sketch, by their great exploit, the conquest of Louisburg. After that event, the New-Englanders never settled into precisely the same quiet race which all the world had imagined them to be. They had done a deed of history, and were anxious to add new ones to the record. They had proved themselves powerful enough to influence the result of a war, and were thenceforth called upon, and willingly consented, to join their strength against the enemies of England; on those fields, at least, where victory would redound to their peculiar advantage. And now, in the heat of the Old French War, they might well be termed a martial people. Every man was a soldier, or the father or brother of a soldier; and the whole land literally echoed with the roll of the drum, either beating up for recruits among the towns and villages, or striking the march towards the frontiers. Besides the provincial troops, there were twenty-three British regiments in the northern colonies. The country has never known a period of such excitement and warlike life, except during the Revolution,—perhaps scarcely then; for that was a lingering war, and this a stirring and eventful one.

One would think that no very wonderful talent was requisite for an historical novel, when the rough and hurried paragraphs of these newspapers can recall the past so magically. We seem to be waiting in the street for the arrival of the post-rider—who is seldom more than twelve hours beyond his time—with letters, by way of Albany, from the various departments of the army. Or, we may fancy ourselves in the circle of listeners, all with necks stretched out towards an old gentleman in the centre, who deliberately puts on his spectacles, unfolds the wet newspaper, and gives us the details of the broken and contradictory reports, which have been flying from mouth to mouth, ever since the courier alighted at Secretary Oliver's office. Sometimes we have an account of the Indian skirmishes near Lake George, and how a ranging party of provincials were so closely pursued, that they drew away their arms, and eke their shoes, stockings, and breeches, barely reaching the camp in their shirts, which also were terribly tattered by the bushes. Then, there is a journal of the siege of Fort Niagara, so minute that it almost numbers the cannon-shot and bombs, and describes the effect of the latter missiles on the French commandant's stone mansion, within the fortress. In the letters of the provincial officers, it is amusing to observe how some of them endeavor to catch the careless and jovial turn of old campaigners. One gentleman tells us that he holds a brimming glass in his hand, intending to drink the health of his correspondent, unless a cannon-ball should dash the liquor from his lips; in the midst of his letter, he hears the bells of the French churches ringing, in Quebec, and recollects that it is Sunday; whereupon, like a good Protestant, he resolves to disturb the Catholic worship by a few thirty-two pound shot. While this wicked man of war was thus making a jest of religion, his pious mother had probably put up a note, that very Sabbath-day, desiring the "prayers of the congregation for a son gone a soldiering." We trust, however, that there were some stout old worthies

who were not ashamed to do as their fathers did, but went to prayer, with their soldiers, before leading them to battle; and doubtless fought none the worse for that. If we had enlisted in the Old French War, it should have been under such a captain; for we love to see a man keep the characteristics of his country.*

These letters, and other intelligence from the army, are pleasant and lively reading, and stir up the mind like the music of a drum and fife. It is less agreeable to meet with the accounts of women slain and scalped, and infants dashed against trees, by the Indians on the frontiers. It is a striking circumstance, that innumerable bears, driven from the woods by the uproar of contending armies in their accustomed haunts, broke into the settlements, and committed great ravages among children, as well as sheep and swine. Some of them prowled where bears had never been for a century, penetrating within a mile or two of Boston; a fact that gives a strong and gloomy impression of something very terrific going on in the forest, since these savage beasts fled townward to avoid it. But it is impossible to moralize about such trifles, when every newspaper contains tales of military enterprise, and often a huzza for victory; as, for instance, the taking of Ticonderoga, long a place of awe to

---

* The contemptuous jealousy of the British army, from the general downwards, was very galling to the provincial troops. In one of the newspapers there is an admirable letter of a New England man, copied from the London Chronicle, defending the provincials with an ability worthy of Franklin, and somewhat in his style. The letter is remarkable, also, because it takes up the cause of the whole range of colonies, as if the writer looked upon them all as constituting one country, and that his own. Colonial patriotism had not hitherto been so broad a sentiment.

the provincials, and one of the bloodiest spots in the present war. Nor is it unpleasant, among whole pages of exultation, to find a note of sorrow for the fall of some brave officer; it comes wailing in, like a funeral strain amidst a peal of triumph, itself triumphant too. Such was the lamentation over Wolfe. Somewhere, in this volume of newspapers, though we cannot now lay our finger upon the passage, we recollect a report, that General Wolfe was slain, not by the enemy, but by a shot from his own soldiers.

In the advertising columns, also, we are continually reminded that the country was in a state of war. Governor Pownal. makes proclamation for the enlisting of soldiers, and directs the militia colonels to attend to the discipline of their regiments, and the selectmen of every town to replenish their stocks of ammunition. The magazine, by the way, was generally kept in the upper loft of the village meeting-house. The provincial captains are drumming up for soldiers, in every newspaper. Sir Jeffrey Amherst advertises for batteauxmen, to be employed on the lakes; and gives notice to the officers of seven British regiments, dispersed on the recruiting service, to rendezvous in Boston. Captain Hallowell, of the province ship-of-war King George, invites ablebodied seamen to serve his Majesty, for fifteen pounds, old tenor, per month. By the rewards offered, there would appear to have been frequent desertions from the New England forces; we applaud their wisdom, if not their valor or integrity. Cannon of all calibres, gunpowder and balls, firelocks, pistols, swords, and hangers, were common articles of merchandise. Daniel Jones,

at the sign of the hat and helmet, offers to supply officers with scarlet broadcloth, gold lace for hats and waistcoats, cockades, and other military foppery, allowing credit until the pay-rolls shall be made up. This advertisement gives us quite a gorgeous idea of a provincial captain in full dress.

At the commencement of the campaign of 1759, the British general informs the farmers of New England that a regular market will be established at Lake George, whither they are invited to bring provisions and refreshments of all sorts, for the use of the army. Hence, we may form a singular picture of petty traffic, far away from any permanent settlements, among the hills which border that romantic lake, with the solemn woods over-shadowing the scene. Carcasses of bullocks and fat porkers are placed upright against the huge trunks of the trees; fowls hang from the lower branches, bobbing against the heads of those beneath; butter-firkins, great cheeses, and brown loaves of household bread, baked in distant ovens, are collected under temporary shelters of pine-boughs, with gingerbread and pumpkin-pies, perhaps, and other toothsome dainties. Barrels of cider and spruce-beer are running freely into the wooden canteens of the soldiers. Imagine such a scene, beneath the dark forest canopy, with here and there a few struggling sunbeams to dissipate the gloom. See the shrewd yeomen, haggling with their scarlet-coated customers, abating somewhat in their prices, but still dealing at monstrous profit; and then complete the picture with circumstances that bespeak war and danger. A cannon shall be seen to belch its smoke from among the trees, against some distant canoes on the lake; the traffickers shall pause, and seem to hearken, at intervals, as if they heard the rattle of musketry or the shout of Indians; a scouting-party shall be driven in, with two or three faint and bloody men among them. And, in spite of these disturbances, business goes on briskly in the market of the wilderness.

It must not be supposed that the martial character of the times interrupted all pursuits except those connected with war. On the contrary, there appears to have been a general vigor and vivacity diffused into the whole round of colonial life. During the winter of 1759, it was computed that about a thousand sled-loads of country produce were daily brought into Boston market. It was a symptom of an irregular and unquiet course of affairs, that innumerable lotteries were projected, ostensibly for the purpose of public improvements, such as roads and bridges. Many females seized the opportunity to engage in business as, among others, Alice Quirk, who dealt in crockery and hosiery, next door to Deacon Beautineau's; Mary Jackson, who sold butter, at the Brazen-Head, in Cornhill; Abigail Hiller, who taught ornamental work, near the Orange-Tree, where also were to be seen the King and Queen, in waxwork; Sarah Morehead, an instructor in glass-painting, drawing, and japanning; Mary Salmon, who shod horses, at the south-end; Harriet Pain, at the Buck and Glove, and Mrs. Henrietta Maria Caine, at the Golden Fan, both fashionable milliners; Anna Adams, who advertises Quebec and Garrick bonnets, Prussian cloaks, and scarlet cardinals, opposite the old brick meeting-house; besides a lady at the head of a wine and spirit establishment. Little did these good dames expect to reappear before the public, so long after they had made their last courtesies behind the counter. Our great-grandmothers were a stirring sisterhood, and seem not to have been utterly despised by the gentlemen at the British coffee-house; at least, some gracious bachelor, there resident, gives public notice of his willingness to take a wife, provided she be not above twenty-three, and possess brown hair, regular features, a brisk eye, and a fortune. Now, this was a great condescension towards the ladies of Massachusetts Bay, in a threadbare lieutenant of foot.

Polite literature was beginning to make its appearance. Few native works were advertised, it is true, except sermons and treatises of controversial divinity; nor were the English authors of the day much known on this side of the Atlantic. But catalogues were frequently offered at auction or private sale, comprising the standard English books, history, essays, and poetry, of Queen Anne's age, and the preceding century. We see nothing in the nature of a novel, unless it be "The Two Mothers, price four coppers." There was an American poet, however, of whom Mr. Kettell has preserved no specimen,—the author of "War, an Heroic Poem"; he publishes by subscription, and threatens to prosecute his patrons for not taking their books. We have discovered a periodical, also, and one that has a peculiar claim to be recorded here, since it bore the title of "THE NEW ENGLAND MAGAZINE," a forgotten predecessor, for which we should have a filial respect, and take its excellence on trust. The fine arts, too, were budding into existence. At the "old glass and picture shop," in Cornhill, various maps, plates, and views are advertised, and among them a "Prospect of Boston," a copper-plate engraving of Quebec, and the effigies of all the New England ministers ever done in mezzotinto. All these must have been very salable articles. Other ornamental wares were to be found at the same shop; such as violins, flutes, hautboys, musical books, English and Dutch toys, and London babies. About this period, Mr. Dipper gives notice of a concert of vocal and instrumental music. There had already been an attempt at theatrical exhibitions.

There are tokens, in every newspaper, of a style of luxury and magnificence which we do not usually associate with our ideas of the times. When the property of a deceased person was to be sold, we find, among the household furniture, silk beds and hangings, damask table-cloths, Turkey carpets, pictures, pier-glasses, massive plate, and all things proper for a noble mansion. Wine was more generally drunk than now, though by no means to the neglect of ardent spirits. For the apparel of both sexes, the mercers and milliners imported good store of fine broadcloths, especially scarlet, crimson, and skyblue, silks, satins, lawns, and velvets, gold brocade, and gold and silver lace, and silver tassels, and silver spangles, until Cornhill shone and sparkled with their merchandise. The gaudiest dress permissible by modern taste fades into a Quaker-like sobriety, compared with the deep, rich, glowing splendor of our ancestors. Such figures were almost too fine to go about town on foot; accordingly, carriages were so numerous as

to require a tax; and it is recorded that, when Governor Bernard came to the province, he was met between Dedham and Boston, by a multitude of gentlemen in their coaches and chariots.

Take my arm, gentle reader, and come with me into some street, perhaps trodden by your daily footsteps, but which now has such an aspect of half-familiar strangeness, that you suspect yourself to be walking abroad in a dream. True, there are some brick edifices which you remember from childhood, and which your father and grandfather remembered as well; but you are perplexed by the absence of many that were here only an hour or two since; and still more amazing is the presence of whole rows of wooden and plastered houses, projecting over the sidewalks, and bearing iron figures on their fronts, which prove them to have stood on the same sites above a century. Where have your eyes been, that you never saw them before? Along the ghostly street—for, at length, you conclude that all is unsubstantial, though it be so good a mockery of an antique town,—along the ghostly street there are ghostly people too. Every gentleman has his three-cornered hat, either on his head or under his arm; and all wear wigs, in infinite variety,—the Tie, the Brigadier, the Spencer, the Albemarle, the Major, the Ramillies, the grave Fullbottom, or the giddy Feather-top. Look at the elaborate lace ruffles, and the square-skirted coat of gorgeous hues, bedizened with silver and gold! Make way for the phantom-ladies, whose hoops require such breadth of passage, as they pace majestically along, in silken gowns, blue, green, or yellow, brilliantly embroidered, and with small satin hats, surmounting their powdered hair. Make way; for the whole spectral show will vanish, if your earthly garments brush against their robes. Now that the scene is brightest, and the whole street glitters with imaginary sunshine,—now hark to the bells of the Old South and the Old North, ringing out with a sudden and merry peal, while the cannon of Castle William thunder below the town, and those of the Diana frigate repeat the sound, and the Charlestown batteries reply with a nearer roar! You see the crowd toss up their hats, in visionary joy. You hear of illuminations and fireworks, and of bonfires, built on scaffolds, raised several stories above the ground, that are to blaze all night, in King Street, and on Beacon Hill. And here come the trumpets and kettledrums, and the tramping hoofs of the Boston troop of horse-guards, escorting the governor to King's Chapel, where he is to return solemn thanks for the surrender of Quebec. March on, thou shadowy troop! and vanish, ghostly crowd; and change again, old street! for those stirring times are gone.

Opportunely for the conclusion of our sketch, a fire broke out, on the twentieth of March, 1760, at the Brazen-Head, in Cornhill, and consumed nearly four hundred buildings. Similar disasters have always been epochs in the chronology of Boston. That of 1711 had hitherto been termed the Great Fire, but now resigned its baleful dignity to one which has ever since retained it. Did we desire to move the reader's sympathies on this subject, we would not be grandiloquent about the sea of billowy flame, the glowing and crumbling streets, the broad, black firmament of smoke, and the blast of wind that sprang up

with the conflagration and roared behind it. It would be more effective to mark out a single family, at the moment when the flames caught upon an angle of their dwelling: then would ensue the removal of the bed-ridden grandmother, the cradle with the sleeping infant, and, most dismal of all, the dying man just at the extremity of a lingering disease. Do but imagine the confused agony of one thus awfully disturbed in his last hour; his fearful glance behind at the consuming fire, raging after him, from house to house, as its devoted victim; and, finally, the almost eagerness with which he would seize some calmer interval to die! The Great Fire must have realized many such a scene.

Doubtless posterity has acquired a better city by the calamity of that generation. None will be inclined to lament it at this late day, except the lover of antiquity, who would have been glad to walk among those streets of venerable houses, fancying the old inhabitants still there, that he might commune with their shadows, and paint a more vivid picture of their times.

III. THE OLD TORY

Again we take a leap of about twenty years, and alight in the midst of the Revolution. Indeed, having just closed a volume of colonial newspapers, which represented a period when monarchical and aristocratic sentiments were at the highest,—and now opening another volume printed in the same metropolis, after such sentiments had long been deemed a sin and shame,—we feel as if the leap were more than figurative. Our late course of reading has tinctured us, for the moment, with antique prejudices; and we shrink from the strangely-contrasted times into which we emerge, like one of those immutable old Tories, who acknowledge no oppression in the Stamp-Act. It may be the most effective method of going through the present file of papers, to follow out this idea, and transform ourself, perchance, from a modern Tory, into such a sturdy King-man as once wore that pliable nickname.

Well, then, here we sit, an old, gray, withered, sour-visaged, threadbare sort of gentleman, erect enough, here in our solitude, but marked out by a depressed and distrustful mien abroad, as one conscious of a stigma upon his forehead, though for no crime. We were already in the decline of life when the first tremors of the earthquake that has convulsed the continent were felt. Our mind had grown too rigid to change any of its opinions, when the voice of the people demanded that all should be changed. We are an Episcopalian, and sat under the high-church doctrines of Doctor Caner; we have been a captain of the provincial forces, and love our king the better for the blood that we shed in his cause on the Plains of Abraham. Among all the refugees, there is not one more loyal to the backbone than we. Still we lingered behind when the British army evacuated Boston, sweeping in its train most of those with whom we held communion; the old, loyal gentlemen, the aristocracy of the colonies, the hereditary Englishman, imbued with more than native zeal and admiration for the glorious island and its monarch, because the far intervening ocean threw a dim reverence around them. When our brethren departed, we

could not tear our aged roots out of the soil. We have remained, therefore, enduring to be outwardly a freeman, but idolizing King George in secrecy and silence,—one true old heart amongst a host of enemies. We watch, with a weary hope, for the moment when all this turmoil shall subside, and the impious novelty that has distracted our latter years, like a wild dream, give place to the blessed quietude of royal sway, with the king's name in every ordinance, his prayer in the church, his health at the board, and his love in the people's heart. Meantime, our old age finds little honor. Hustled have we been, till driven from town-meetings; dirty water has been cast upon our ruffles by a Whig chambermaid; John Hancock's coachman seizes every opportunity to bespatter us with mud; daily are we hooted by the unbreeched rebel brats; and narrowly, once, did our gray hairs escape the ignominy of tar and feathers. Alas! only that we cannot bear to die till the next royal governor comes over, we would fain be in our quiet grave.

Such an old man among new things are we who now hold at arm's length the rebel newspaper of the day. The very figure-head, for the thousandth time, elicits a groan of spiteful lamentation. Where are the united heart and crown, the loyal emblem, that used to hallow the sheet on which it was impressed, in our younger days? In its stead we find a continental officer, with the Declaration of Independence in one hand, a drawn sword in the other, and above his head a scroll, bearing the motto, "We appeal to Heaven." Then say we, with a prospective triumph, let Heaven judge, in its own good time! The material of the sheet attracts our scorn. It is a fair specimen of rebel manufacture, thick and coarse, like wrapping-paper, all overspread with little knobs; and of such a deep, dingy blue color, that we wipe our spectacles thrice before we can distinguish a letter of the wretched print. Thus, in all points, the newspaper is a type of the times, far more fit for the rough hands of a democratic mob, than for our own delicate, though bony fingers. Nay; we will not handle it without our gloves!

Glancing down the page, our eyes are greeted everywhere by the offer of lands at auction, for sale or to be leased, not by the rightful owners, but a rebel committee; notices of the town constable, that he is authorized to receive the taxes on such an estate, in default of which, that also is to be knocked down to the highest bidder; and notifications of complaints filed by the Attorney-general against certain traitorous absentees, and of confiscations that are to ensue. And who are these traitors? Our own best friends; names as old, once as honored, as any in the land where they are no longer to have a patrimony, nor to be remembered as good men who have passed away. We are ashamed of not relinquishing our little property, too; but comfort ourselves because we still keep our principles, without gratifying the rebels with our plunder. Plunder, indeed, they are seizing everywhere,—by the strong hand at sea, as well as by legal forms on shore. Here are prize-vessels for sale; no French nor Spanish merchantmen, whose wealth is the birthright of British subjects, but hulls of British oak, from Liverpool, Bristol, and the Thames, laden with the king's own stores, for his army in New York. And what a fleet of privateers—

pirates, say we—are fitting out for new ravages, with rebellion in their very names! The Free Yankee, the General Green, the Saratoga, the Lafayette, and the Grand Monarch! Yes, the Grand Monarch; so is a French king styled, by the sons of Englishmen. And here we have an ordinance from the Court of Versailles, with the Bourbon's own signature affixed, as it New England were already a French province. Everything is French,—French soldiers, French sailors, French surgeons, and French diseases too, I trow; besides French dancing-masters and French milliners, to debauch our daughters with French fashions! Everything in America is French, except the Canadas, the loyal Canadas, which we helped to wrest from France. And to that old French province the Englishman of the colonies must go to find his country!

O the misery of seeing the whole system of things changed in my old days, when I would be loath to change even a pair of buckles! The British coffee-house, where oft we sat, brimful of wine and loyalty, with the gallant gentlemen of Amherst's army, when we wore a red-coat too,—the British coffee-house, forsooth, must now be styled the American, with a golden eagle instead of the royal arms above the door. Even the street it stands in is no longer King Street! Nothing is the king's, except this heavy heart in my old bosom. Wherever I glance my eyes, they meet something that pricks them like a needle. This soap-maker, for instance, this Robert Hewes, has conspired against my peace, by notifying that his shop is situated near Liberty Stump. But when will their misnamed Liberty have its true emblem in that Stump, hewn down by British steel.

Where shall we buy our next year's almanac? Not this of Weatherwise's, certainly; for it contains a likeness of George Washington, the upright rebel, whom we most hate, though reverentially, as a fallen angel, with his heavenly brightness undiminished, evincing pure fame in an unhallowed cause. And here is a new book for my evening's recreation,—a History of the War till the close of the year 1779, with the heads of thirteen distinguished officers, engraved on copperplate. A plague upon their heads! We desire not to see them till they grin at us from the balcony before the town-house, fixed on spikes as the heads of traitors. How bloody-minded the villains make a peaceable old man! What next? An Oration, on the Horrid Massacre of 1770. When that blood was shed,—the first that the British soldier ever drew from the bosoms of our countrymen,—we turned sick at heart, and do so still, as often as they make it reek anew from among the stones in King Street. The pool that we saw that night has swelled into a lake,— English blood and American,—no! all British, all blood of my brethren. And here come down tears. Shame on me, since half of them are shed for rebels! Who are not rebels now! Even the women art thrusting their white hands into the war, and come out in this very paper with proposals to form a society —the lady of George Washington at their head—for clothing the continental troops. They will strip off their stiff petticoats to cover the ragged rascals, and then enlist in the ranks themselves.

What have we here? Burgoyne's proclamation turned into Hudibrastic rhyme! And here, some verses against the king, in which the scribbler leaves a blank for the name of George, as if his doggerel might yet exalt him to the pillory. Such, after years of rebellion, is the heart's unconquerable reverence for the Lord's anointed! In the next column, we have Scripture parodied in a squib against his sacred Majesty. What would our Puritan great-grandsires have said to that? They never laughed at God's word, though they cut off a king's head.

Yes; it was for us to prove how disloyalty goes hand in hand with irreligion, and all other vices come trooping in the train. Now-a-days men commit robbery and sacrilege for the mere luxury of wickedness, as this advertisement testifies. Three hundred pounds reward for the detection of the villains who stole and destroyed the cushions and pulpit drapery of the Brattle Street and Old South churches. Was it a crime? I can scarcely think our temples hallowed, since the king ceased to be prayed for. But it is not temples only that they rob. Here a man offers a thousand dollars— a thousand dollars, in Continental rags! —for the recovery of his stolen cloak; and other articles of clothing. Horse-thieves are innumerable. Now is the day when every beggar gets on horseback. And is not the whole land like a beggar on horseback riding post to the Devil? Ha! here is a murder, too. A woman slain at midnight, by an unknown ruffian, and found cold, stiff, and bloody in her violated bed! Let the hue and cry follow hard after the man in the uniform of blue and buff who last went by that way. My life on it, he is the blood-stained ravisher! These deserters whom we see proclaimed in every column,—proof that the banditti are as false to their stars and stripes as to the Holy Red-cross,—they bring the crimes of a rebel camp into a soil well suited to them; the bosom of a people, without the heart that kept them virtuous,—their king!

Here, flaunting down a whole column, with official seal and signature, here comes a proclamation. By whose authority? Ah! the United States,—these thirteen little anarchies, assembled in that one grand anarchy, their Congress. And what the import? A general Fast. By Heaven! for once the traitorous blockheads have legislated wisely! Yea: let a misguided people kneel down in sackcloth and ashes, from end to end, from border to border, of their wasted country. Well may they fast where there is no food, and cry aloud for whatever remnant of God's mercy their sins may not have exhausted. We too will fast, even at a rebel summons. Pray others as they will, there shall be at least an old man kneeling for the righteous cause. Lord, put down the rebels! God save the king!

Peace to the good old Tory! One of our objects has been to exemplify, without softening a single prejudice proper to the character which we assumed, that the Americans who clung to the losing side in the Revolution were men greatly to be pitied, and often worthy of our sympathy. It would be difficult to say whose lot was most lamentable, that of the active Tories, who gave up their patrimonies for a pittance from the British pension-roll, and their native land for a cold reception in their miscalled home, or the passive ones who remained behind to endure the coldness of former friends, and the public oppro-

brium, as despised citizens, under a government which they abhorred. In justice to the old gentleman who has favored us with his discontented musings, we must remark that the state of the country, so far as can be gathered from these papers, was of dismal augury for the tendencies of democratic rule. It was pardonable in the conservative of that day to mistake the temporary evils of a change for permanent diseases of the system which that change was to establish. A revolution, or anything that interrupts social order, may afford opportunities for the individual display of eminent virtues, but its effects are pernicious to general morality. Most people are so constituted that they can be virtuous only in a certain routine; and an irregular course of public affairs demoralizes them. One great source of disorder was the multitude of disbanded troops, who were continually returning home, after terms of service just long enough to give them a distaste to peaceable occupations; neither citizens nor soldiers, they were very liable to become ruffians. Almost all our impressions in regard to this period are unpleasant, whether referring to the state of civil society, or to the character of the contest, which, especially where native Americans were opposed to each other, was waged with the deadly hatred of fraternal enemies. It is the beauty of war, for men to commit mutual havoc with undisturbed good humor.

The present volume of newspapers contains fewer characteristic traits than any which we have looked over. Except for the peculiarities attendant on the passing struggle, manners seem to have taken a modern cast. Whatever antique fashions lingered into the war of the

Revolution, or beyond it, they were not so strongly marked as to leave their traces in the public journals. Moreover, the old newspapers had an indescribable picturesqueness, not to be found in the later ones. Whether it be something in the literary execution, or the ancient print and paper, and the idea that those same musty pages have been handled by people once alive and bustling amid the scenes there recorded, yet now in their graves beyond the memory of man; so it is, that in those elder volumes we seem to find the life of a past age preserved between the leaves, like a dry specimen of foliage. It is so difficult to discover what touches are really picturesque, that we doubt whether our attempts have produced any similar effect.

THE MAN OF ADAMANT

AN APOLOGUE

IN the old times of religious gloom and intolerance lived Richard Digby, the gloomiest and most intolerant of a stern brotherhood. His plan of salvation was so narrow, that, like a plank in a tempestuous sea, it could avail no sinner but himself, who bestrode it triumphantly, and hurled anathemas against the wretches whom he saw struggling with the billows of eternal death. In his view of the matter, it was a most abominable crime,—as, indeed, it is a great folly,— for men to trust to their own strength, or even to grapple to any other fragment of the wreck, save this narrow plank, which, moreover, he took special care to keep out of their reach. In other words, as his creed was like no man's else, and being well pleased that Providence had intrusted him alone, of mortals, with the treasure of a true faith, Richard Digby determined to seclude himself to the sole and constant enjoyment of his happy fortune.

"And verily," thought he, "I deem it a chief condition of Heaven's mercy to myself, that I hold no communion with those abominable myriads which it hath cast off to perish. Peradventure, were I to tarry longer in the tents of Kedar, the gracious boon would be revoked, and I also be swallowed up in the deluge of wrath, or consumed in the storm of fire and brimstone, or involved in whatever new kind of ruin is ordained for the horrible perversity of this generation."

So Richard Digby took an axe, to hew space enough for a tabernacle in the wilderness, and some few other necessaries, especially a sword and gun, to smite and slay any intruder upon his hallowed seclusion; and plunged into the dreariest depths of the forest. On its verge, however, he paused a moment, to shake off the dust of his feet against the village where he had dwelt, and to invoke a curse on the meeting-house which he regarded as a temple of heathen idolatry. He felt a curiosity, also, to see whether the fire and brimstone would not rush down from Heaven at once, now that the one righteous man had provided for his own safety. But, as the sunshine continued to fall peacefully n the cottages and fields, and the husbandmen labored and children played, and as there were many tokens of present happiness, and nothing ominous of a speedy judgment, he turned away, somewhat disappointed. The farther he went, however, and the lonelier he felt himself, and the thicker the trees stood along his path, and the darker the shadow overhead, so much the more did Richard Digby exult. He talked to himself, as he strode onward; he read his Bible to himself, as he sat beneath the trees; and, as the gloom of the forest hid the blessed sky, I had almost added, that, at morning, noon, and eventide, he prayed to himself. So congenial was this mode of life to his disposition, that he often laughed to himself, but was displeased when an echo tossed him back the long, loud roar.

In this manner, he journeyed onward three days and two nights, and came, on the third evening, to the mouth of a cave, which, at first sight, reminded him of Elijah's cave at Horeb, though perhaps it more resembled Abraham's sepulchral cave, at Machpelah. It entered into the heart of a rocky hill. There was so dense a veil of tangled foliage about it, that none but a sworn lover of gloomy recesses would have discovered the low arch of its entrance, or have dared to step within its vaulted chamber, where the burning eyes of a panther might encounter him. If Nature meant this remote and dismal cavern for the use of man, it could only be to bury in its gloom the victims of a pestilence, and then to block up its mouth with stones, and avoid the spot forever after. There was nothing bright nor cheerful near it, except a bubbling fountain, some twenty paces off, at which Richard Digby hardly threw away a glance. But he thrust his head into the cave, shivered, and congratulated himself.

"The finger of Providence hath pointed my way!" cried he, aloud, while the tomb-like den returned a strange echo, as if some one within were mocking him. "Here my soul will be at peace; for the wicked will not find me. Here I can read the Scriptures, and be no more provoked with lying interpretations. Here I can offer up acceptable prayers, because my voice will not be mingled with the sinful supplications of the multitude. Of a truth, the only way to heaven leadeth through the narrow entrance of this cave,—and I alone have found it!"

In regard to this cave, it was observable that the roof, so far as the imperfect light permitted it to be seen, was hung with substances resembling opaque icicles; for the damps of unknown centuries, dripping down continually, had become as hard as adamant; and wherever that moisture fell, it seemed to possess the power of converting what it bathed to stone. The fallen leaves and sprigs of foliage, which the wind had swept into the cave, and the little feathery shrubs, rooted near the threshold, were not wet with a natural dew, but had been embalmed by this wondrous process. And here I am put in mind that Richard Digby, before he withdrew himself from the world, was supposed by skilful physicians to have contracted a disease for which no remedy was written in their medical books. It was a deposition of calculous particles within his heart, caused by an obstructed circulation of the blood; and, unless a miracle should be wrought for him, there was danger that the malady might act on the entire substance of the organ, and change his fleshy heart to stone. Many, indeed, affirmed that the process was already near its consummation. Richard Digby, however, could never be convinced that any such direful work was going on within him; nor when he saw the sprigs of marble foliage, did his heart even throb the quicker, at the similitude suggested by these tender herbs. It may be that this same insensibility was a symptom of the disease.

Be that as it might, Richard Digby was well contented with his sepulchral cave. So dearly did he love this congenial spot, that instead of going a few paces to the bubbling spring for water, he allayed his thirst with now and then a drop of moisture from the roof, which, had it fallen anywhere but on his tongue, would have been congealed into a pebble. For a man predisposed to stoniness of the heart, this surely was unwholesome liquor. But there he dwelt, for three days more, eating herbs and roots, drinking his own destruction, sleeping, as it were, in a tomb, and awaking to the solitude of death, yet esteeming this horrible mode of life as hardly inferior to celestial bliss. Perhaps superior; for, above the sky, there would be angels to disturb him. At the close of the third day, he sat in the portal of his mansion reading the Bible aloud, because no other ear could profit by it, and reading it amiss, because the rays of the setting sun did not penetrate the dismal depth of shadow round about him, nor fall upon the sacred page. Suddenly, however, a faint gleam of light was thrown over the volume, and, raising his eyes, Richard Digby saw that a young woman stood before the mouth of the cave, and that the sunbeams bathed her white garment, which thus seemed to possess a radiance of its own.

"Good evening, Richard," said the girl; "I have come from afar to find thee."

The slender grace and gentle loveliness of this young woman were at once recognized by Richard Digby. Her name was Mary Goffe. She had been a convert to his preaching of the word in England, before he yielded himself to that exclusive bigotry which now enfolded him with such an iron grasp that no other sentiment could reach his bosom. When he came a pilgrim to America, she had remained in her father's hall; but now, as it appeared, had crossed the ocean after him, impelled by the same faith that led other exiles hither, and perhaps by love almost as holy. What else but faith and love united could have sustained so delicate a creature, wandering thus far into the forest, with her golden hair dishevelled by the boughs and her feet wounded by the thorns? Yet, weary and faint though she must have been, and affrighted at the dreariness of the cave, she looked on the lonely man with a mild and pitying expression, such as might beam from an angel's eyes towards an afflicted mortal. But the recluse, frowning sternly upon her, and keeping his finger between the leaves of his half-closed Bible, motioned her away with his hand.

"Off!" cried he. "I am sanctified, and thou art sinful. Away!"

"O Richard," said she, earnestly, "I have come this weary way because I heard that a grievous distemper had seized upon thy heart; and a great Physician had given me the skill to cure it. There is no other remedy than his which I have brought thee. Turn me not away, therefore, nor refuse my medicine; for then must this dismal cave be thy sepulchre."

"Away!" replied Richard Digby, still with a dark frown. "My heart is in better condition than thine own. Leave me, earthly one; for the sun is almost set; and when no light reaches the door of he cave, then is my prayer-time."

Now, great as was her need, Mary Goffe did not plead with this stony-hearted man for shelter and protection, nor ask anything whatever for her own sake. All her zeal was for his welfare.

"Come back with me!" she exclaimed, clasping her hands,—"come back to thy fellow-men; for they need thee, Richard, and thou hast tenfold need of them. Stay not in this evil den; for the air is chill, and the damps are fatal; nor will any that perish within it ever find the path to heaven. Hasten hence, I entreat thee, for thine own soul's sake; for either the roof will fall upon thy head, or some other speedy destruction is at hand."

"Perverse woman!" answered Richard Digby, laughing aloud,—for he was moved to bitter mirth by her foolish vehemence,—"I tell thee that the path to heaven leadeth straight through this narrow portal where I sit. And, moreover, the destruction thou speakest of is ordained, not for this blessed cave, but for all other habitations of mankind, throughout the earth. Get thee hence speedily, that thou mayest have thy share!"

So saying, he opened his Bible again, and fixed his eyes intently on the page, being resolved to withdraw his thoughts from this child of sin and wrath, and to waste no more of his holy breath upon

her. The shadow had now grown so deep where he was sitting that he made continual mistakes in what he read, converting all that was gracious and merciful to denunciations of vengeance and unutterable woe on every created being but himself. Mary Goffe, meanwhile, was leaning against a tree, beside the sepulchral cave, very sad, yet with something heavenly and ethereal in her unselfish sorrow. The light from the setting sun still glorified her form, and was reflected a little way within the darksome den, discovering so terrible a gloom that the maiden shuddered for its self-doomed inhabitant. Espying the bright fountain near at hand, she hastened thither, and scooped up a portion of its water in a cup of birchen bark. A few tears mingled with the draught, and perhaps gave it all its efficacy. She then returned to the mouth of the cave, and knelt down at Richard Digby's feet.

"Richard," she said, with passionate fervor, yet a gentleness in all her passion, "I pray thee, by thy hope of heaven, and as thou wouldst not dwell in this tomb forever, drink of this hallowed water, be it but a single drop! Then, make room for me by thy side, and let us read together one page of that blessed volume,—and, lastly, kneel down with me and pray! Do this, and thy stony heart shall become softer than a babe's, and all will be well."

But Richard Digby, in utter abhorrence of the proposal, cast the Bible at his feet, and eyed her with such a fixed and evil frown, that he looked less like a living man than a marble statue, wrought by some dark-imagined sculptor to express the most repulsive mood that human features could assume. And, as his look grew even devilish, so, with an equal change, did Mary Goffe become more sad, more mild, more pitiful, more like a sorrowing angel. But the more heavenly she was the more hateful did she seem to Richard Digby, who at length raised his hand, and smote down the cup of hallowed water upon the threshold of the cave, thus rejecting the only medicine that could have cured his stony heart. A sweet perfume lingered in the air for a moment, and then was gone.

"Tempt me no more, accursed woman," exclaimed he, still with his marble frown, "lest I smite thee down also! What hast thou to do with my Bible?—what with my prayers?—what with my heaven?"

No sooner had he spoken these dreadful words, than Richard Digby's heart ceased to beat; while—so the legend says—the form of Mary Goffe melted into the last sunbeams, and returned from the sepulchral cave to heaven. For Mary Goffe had been buried in an English churchyard months before; and either it was her ghost that haunted the wild forest, or else a dreamlike spirit, typifying pure Religion.

About a century afterwards, when the trackless forest of Richard Digby's day had long been interspersed with settlements, the children of a neighboring farmer were playing at the foot of a hill. The trees, on account of the rude and broken surface of this acclivity, had never been felled, and were crowded so densely together as to hide all but a few rocky prominences, wherever their roots could grapple with the soil. A little boy and girl, to conceal themselves from their playmates, had crept into the deepest shade, where not only the darksome pines, but a thick veil of creeping plants, suspended from an overhanging rock, combined to make a twilight at noonday, and almost a midnight at all other seasons. There the children hid themselves, and shouted, repeating the cry at intervals, till the whole party of pursuers were drawn thither, and, pulling aside the matted foliage, let in a doubtful glimpse of daylight. But scarcely was this accomplished, when the little group uttered a simultaneous shriek, and tumbled headlong down the hill, making the best of their way homeward, without a second glance into the gloomy recess. Their father, unable to comprehend what had so startled them, took his axe, and, by felling one or two trees, and tearing away the creeping plants, laid the mystery open to the day. He had discovered the entrance of a cave, closely resembling the mouth of a sepulchre, within which sat the figure of a man, whose gesture and attitude warned the father and children to stand back, while his visage wore a most forbidding frown. This repulsive personage seemed to have been carved in the same gray stone that formed the walls and portal of the cave. On minuter inspection, indeed, such blemishes were observed as made it doubtful whether the figure were really a statue, chiselled by human art, and somewhat worn and defaced by the lapse of ages, or a freak of Nature, who might have chosen to imitate, in stone, her usual handiwork of flesh. Perhaps it was the least unreasonable idea, suggested by this strange spectacle, that the moisture of the cave possessed a petrifying quality, which had thus awfully embalmed a human corpse.

There was something so frightful in the aspect of this Man of Adamant.

hat the farmer, the moment that he recovered from the fascination of his first gaze, began to heap stones into the mouth of the cavern. His wife, who had followed him to the hill, assisted her husband's efforts. The children, also, approached as near as they durst, with their little hands full of pebbles, and cast them on the pile. Earth was then thrown into the crevices, and the whole fabric overlaid with sods. Thus all traces of the discovery were obliterated, leaving only a marvellous legend, which grew wilder from one generation to another, as the children told it to their grandchildren, and they to their posterity, till few believed that there had ever been a cavern or a statue where now they saw but a grassy patch on the shadowy hillside. Yet grown people avoid the spot, nor do children play there. Friendship, and Love, and Piety, all human and celestial sympathies, should keep aloof from that hidden cave; for there still sits, and, unless an earthquake crumble down the roof upon his head, shall sit forever, the shape of Richard Digby, in the attitude of repelling the whole race of mortals,—not from heaven,—but from the horrible loneliness of his dark, cold sepulchre!

THE HOUSE OF THE SEVEN GABLES

——

CHAPTER I

THE OLD PYNCHEON FAMILY

HALF-WAY down a by-street of one of our New England towns, stands a rusty wooden house, with seven acutely-peaked gables, facing towards various points of the compass, and a huge, clustered chimney in the midst. The street is Pyncheon-street; the house is the old Pyncheon-house; and an elm-tree, of wide circumference, rooted before the door, is familiar to every town-born child by the title of the Pyncheon-elm. On my occasional visits to the town aforesaid, I seldom fail to turn down Pyncheon-street, for the sake of passing through the shadow of these two antiquities,—the great elm-tree, and the weather-beaten edifice.

The aspect of the venerable mansion has always affected me like a human countenance, bearing the traces not merely of outward storm and sunshine, but expressive, also, of the long lapse of mortal life, and accompanying vicissitudes that have passed within. Were these to be worthily recounted, they would form a narrative of no small interest and instruction, and possessing, moreover, a certain remarkable unity, which might almost seem the result of artistic arrangement. But the story would include a chain of events extending over the better part of two centuries, and, written out with reasonable amplitude, would fill a bigger folio volume, or a longer series of duodecimos, than could prudently be appropriated to the annals of all New England during a similar period. It consequently becomes imperative to make short work with most of the traditionary lore of which the old Pyncheon-house, otherwise known as the House of the Seven Gables, has been the theme. With a brief sketch, therefore, of the circumstances amid which the foundation of the house was laid, and a rapid glimpse at its quaint exterior, as it grew black in the prevalent east wind,—pointing, too, here and there, at some spot of more verdant mossiness on its roof and walls,—we shall commence the real action of our tale at an epoch not very remote from the present day. Still, there will be a connection with the long past —a reference to forgotten events and personages, and to manners, feelings, and opinions, almost or wholly obsolete —which, if adequately translated to the reader, would serve to illustrate how much of old material goes to make up the freshest novelty of human life. Hence, too, might be drawn a weighty lesson from the little-regarded truth, that the act of the passing generation is the germ which may and must produce good or evil fruit, in a far distant time; that, together with the seed of the merely temporary crop, which mortals term expediency, they inevitably sow the acorns of a more enduring growth, which may darkly overshadow their posterity.

The House of the Seven Gables, antique as it now looks, was not the first habitation erected by civilized man on precisely the same spot of ground. Pyncheon-street formerly bore the humbler appellation of Maule's-lane, from the name of the original occupant of the soil, before whose cottage-door it was a cow-path. A natural spring of soft and pleasant water—a rare treasure on the sea-girt peninsula, where the Puritan settlement was made—had early induced Matthew Maule to build a hut, shaggy with thatch, at this point, although somewhat too remote from what was then the centre of the village. In the growth of the town, however, after some thirty or forty years, the site covered by this rude hovel had become exceedingly desirable in the eyes of a prominent and powerful personage, who asserted plausible claims to the proprietorship of this, and a large adjacent tract of land, on the strength of a grant from the legislature. Colonel Pyncheon, the claimant, as we gather from whatever traits of him are preserved, was characterized by an iron energy of purpose. Matthew Maule, on the other hand, though an obscure man, was stubborn in the defence of what he considered his right; and, for several years, he succeeded in protecting the acre or two of earth, which, with his own toil, he had hewn out of the primeval forest, to be his garden-ground and homestead. No written record of this dispute is known to be in existence. Our acquaintance with the whole subject is derived chiefly from tradition. It would be bold,

therefore, and possibly unjust, to venture a decisive opinion as to its merits; although it appears to have been at least a matter of doubt, whether Colonel Pyncheon's claim were not unduly stretched, in order to make it cover the small metes and bounds of Matthew Maule. What greatly strengthens such a suspicion is the fact that this controversy between two ill-matched antagonists—at a period, moreover, laud it as we may, when personal influence had far more weight than now—remained for years undecided, and came to a close only with the death of the party occupying the disputed soil. The mode of his death, too, affects the mind differently, in our day, from what it did a century and a half ago. It was a death that blasted with strange horror the humble name of the dweller in the cottage, and made it seem almost a religious act to drive the plough over the little area of his habitation, and obliterate his place and memory from among men.

Old Matthew Maule, in a word, was executed for the crime of witchcraft. He was one of the martyrs to that terrible delusion, which should teach us, among its other morals, that the influential classes, and those who take upon themselves to be leaders of the people, are fully liable to all the passionate error that has ever characterized the maddest mob. Clergymen, judges, statesmen,—the wisest, calmest, holiest persons of their day,—stood in the inner circle round about the gallows, loudest to applaud the work of blood, latest to confess themselves miserably deceived. If any one part of their proceedings can be said to deserve less blame than another, it was the singular indiscrimination with which they persecuted, not merely the poor and aged, as in former judicial massacres, but people of all ranks; their own equals, brethren, and wives. Amid the disorder of such various ruin, it is not strange that a man of inconsiderable note, like Maule, should have trodden a martyr's path to the hill of execution almost unremarked in the throng of his fellow-sufferers. But, in after days, when the frenzy of that hideous epoch had subsided, it was remembered how loudly Colonel Pyncheon had joined in the general cry, to purge the land from witchcraft; nor did it fail to be whispered, that there was an invidious acrimony in the zeal with which he had sought the condemnation of Matthew Maule. It was well known that the victim had recognized the bitterness of personal enmity in his persecutor's conduct towards him, and that he declared himself hunted to death for his spoil. At the moment of execution—with the halter about his neck, and while Colonel Pyncheon sat on horseback, grimly gazing at the scene—Maule had addressed him from the scaffold, and uttered a prophecy, of which history, as well as fireside tradition, has preserved the very words. "God," said the dying man, pointing his finger, with a ghastly look, at the undismayed countenance of his enemy, "God will give him blood to drink!"

After the reputed wizard's death, his humble homestead had fallen an easy spoil into Colonel Pyncheon's grasp. When it was understood, however, that the colonel intended to erect a family mansion—spacious, ponderously framed of oaken timber, and calculated to endure for many generations of his posterity—over the spot first covered by the log-built hut of Matthew Maule,

there was much shaking of the head among the village gossips. Without absolutely expressing a doubt whether the stalwart Puritan had acted as a man of conscience and integrity, throughout the proceedings which have been sketched, they, nevertheless, hinted that he was about to build his house over an unquiet grave. His home would include the home of the dead and buried wizard, and would thus afford the ghost of the latter a kind of privilege to haunt its new apartments, and the chambers into which future bridegrooms were to lead their brides, and where children of the Pyncheon blood were to be born. The terror and ugliness of Maule's crime, and the wretchedness of his punishment, would darken the freshly-plastered walls and infect them early with the scent of an old and melancholy house. Why, then,—while so much of the soil around him was bestrewn with the virgin forest-leaves,—why should Colonel Pyncheon prefer a site that had already been accurst?

But the Puritan soldier and magistrate was not a man to be turned aside from his well-considered scheme, either by dread of the wizard's ghost, or by flimsy sentimentalities of any kind, however specious. Had he been told of a bad air, it might have moved him somewhat; but he was ready to encounter an evil spirit on his own ground. Endowed with common sense, as massive and hard as blocks of granite, fastened together by stern rigidity of purpose, as with iron clamps, he followed out his original design, probably without so much as imagining an objection to it. On the score of delicacy, or any scrupulousness which a finer sensibility might have taught him, the colonel, like most of his breed and generation, was impenetrable. He, therefore, dug his cellar, and laid the deep foundations of his mansion, on the square of earth whence Matthew Maule, forty years before, had first swept away the fallen leaves. It was a curious, and, as some people thought, an ominous fact, that, very soon after the workmen began their operations, the spring of water, above mentioned, entirely lost the deliciousness of its pristine quality. Whether its sources were disturbed by the depth of the new cellar, or whatever subtler cause might lurk at the bottom, it is certain that the water of Maule's Well, as it continued to be called, grew hard and brackish. Even such we find it now; and any old woman of the neighborhood will certify that it is productive of intestinal mischief to those who quench their thirst there.

The reader may deem it singular that the head carpenter of the new edifice was no other than the son of the very man from whose dead gripe the property of the soil had been wrested. Not improbably he was the best workman of his time; or, perhaps, the colonel thought it expedient, or was impelled by some better feeling, thus openly to cast aside all animosity against the race of his fallen antagonist. Nor was it out of keeping with the general coarseness and matter-of-fact character of the age, that the son should be willing to earn an honest penny, or, rather, a weighty amount of sterling pounds, from the purse of his father's deadly enemy. At all events, Thomas Maule became the architect of the House of the Seven Gables and performed his duty so faithfully that the timber frame-work, fastened by his hands, still holds together.

Thus the great house was built. Familiar as it stands in the writer's recollection,—for it has been an object of curiosity with him from boyhood, both as a specimen of the best and stateliest architecture of a long-past epoch, and as the scene of events more full of human interest, perhaps, than those of a gray feudal castle,—familiar as it stands, in its rusty old age, it is therefore only the more difficult to imagine the bright novelty with which it first caught the sunshine. The impression of its actual state, at this distance of a hundred and sixty years, darkens, inevitably, through the picture which we would fain give of its appearance on the morning when the Puritan magnate bade all the town to be his guests. A ceremony of consecration, festive as well as religious, was now to be performed. A prayer and discourse from the Rev. Mr. Higginson, and the outpouring of a psalm from the general throat of the community, was to be made acceptable to the grosser sense by ale, cider, wine, and brandy, in copious effusion, and, as some authorities aver, by an ox, roasted whole, or, at least, by the weight and substance of an ox, in more manageable joints and sirloins. The carcass of a deer, shot within twenty miles, had supplied material for the vast circumference of a pasty. A cod-fish, of sixty pounds, caught in the bay, had been dissolved into the rich liquid of a chowder. The chimney of the new house, in short, belching forth its kitchen-smoke, impregnated the whole air with the scent of meats, fowls, and fishes, spicily concocted with odoriferous herbs, and onions in abundance. The mere smell of such festivity, making its way to everybody's nostrils, was at once an invitation and an appetite.

Maule's-lane, or Pyncheon-street, as it were now more decorous to call it, was thronged, at the appointed hour, as with a congregation on its way to church. All, as they approached, looked upward at the imposing edifice, which was henceforth to assume its rank among the habitations of mankind. There it rose, a little withdrawn from the line of the street, but in pride, not modesty. Its whole visible exterior was ornamented with quaint figures, conceived in the grotesqueness of a gothic fancy, and drawn or stamped in the glittering plaster, composed of lime, pebbles, and bits of glass, with which the wood-work of the walls was overspread. On every side, the seven gables pointed sharply towards the sky, and presented the aspect of a whole sisterhood of edifices, breathing through the spiracles of one great chimney. The many lattices, with their small, diamond-shaped panes, admitted the sunlight into the hall and chamber, while, nevertheless, the second story, projecting far over the base, and itself retiring beneath the third, threw a shadow and thoughtful gloom into the lower rooms. Carved globes of wood were affixed under the jutting stories. Little spiral rods of iron beautified each of the seven peaks. On the triangular portion of the gable, that fronted next the street, was a dial, put up that very morning, and on which the sun was still marking the passage of the first bright hour in a history that was not destined to be all so bright. All around were scattered shavings, chips, shingles, and broken halves of bricks; these, together with the lately-turned earth, on which the grass had not begun to grow, contributed to the impression of strangeness and novelty proper to a house that had yet its place to make among men's daily interests.

The principal entrance, which had almost the breadth of a church-door, was in the angle between the two front gables, and was covered by an open porch, with benches beneath its shelter. Under this arched doorway, scraping their feet on the unworn threshold, now trod the clergymen, the elders, the magistrates, the deacons, and whatever of aristocracy there was in town or county. Thither, too, thronged the plebeian classes, as freely as their betters, and in larger number. Just within the entrance, however, stood two serving-men, pointing some of the guests to the neighborhood of the kitchen, and ushering others into the statelier rooms,—hospitable alike to all, but still with a scrutinizing regard to the high or low degree of each. Velvet garments, sombre but rich, stiffly-plaited ruffs and bands, embroidered gloves, venerable beards, the mien and countenance of authority, made it easy to distinguish the gentlemen of worship, at that period, from the tradesman, with his plodding air, or the laborer, in his leathern jerkin, stealing awe-stricken into the house which he had perhaps helped to build.

One inauspicious circumstance there was, which awakened a hardly-concealed displeasure in the breasts of a few of the more punctilious visitors. The founder of this stately mansion—a gentleman noted for the square and ponderous courtesy of his demeanor—ought surely to have stood in his own hall, and to have offered the first welcome to so many eminent personages as here presented themselves in honor of his solemn festival. He was as yet invisible; the most favored of the guests had not beheld him. This sluggishness on Colonel Pyncheon's part became still more unaccountable, when the second dignitary of the province made his appearance, and found no more ceremonious a reception. The lieutenant-governor, although his visit was one of the anticipated glories of the day, had alighted from his horse, and assisted his lady from her side-saddle, and crossed the colonel's threshold, without other greeting than that of the principal domestic.

This person—a gray-headed man, of quiet and most respectful deportment— found it necessary to explain that his master still remained in his study, or private apartment; on entering which, an hour before, he had expressed a wish on no account to be disturbed.

"Do not you see, fellow," said the high sheriff of the county, taking the servant aside, "that this is no less a man than the lieutenant-governor? Summon Colonel Pyncheon at once! I know that he received letters from England, this morning; and, in the perusal and consideration of them, an hour may have passed away, without his noticing it. But he will be ill-pleased, I judge, if you suffer him to neglect the courtesy due to one of our chief rulers, and who may be said to represent King William, in the absence of the governor himself. Call your master instantly!"

"Nay, please your worship," answered the man, in much perplexity, but with a backwardness that strikingly indicated the hard and severe character of Colonel Pyncheon's domestic rule; "my master's orders were exceeding strict; and, as your worship knows, he permits of no discretion in the obedience of those who owe him service. Let who list open yonder door; I dare not, though the governor's own voice should bid me do it!"

"Pooh, pooh, master high sheriff!" cried the lieutenant-governor, who had overheard the foregoing discussion, and felt himself high enough in station to play a little with his dignity. "I will take the matter into my own hands. It is time that the good colonel came forth to greet his friends; else we shall be apt to suspect that he has taken a sip too much of his Canary wine, in his extreme deliberation which cask it were best to broach, in honor of the day! But since he is so much behindhand, I will give him a remembrancer myself!"

Accordingly, with such a tramp of his ponderous riding-boots as might of itself have been audible in the remotest of the seven gables, he advanced to the door, which the servant pointed out, and made its new panels reëcho with a loud, free knock. Then, looking round with a smile, to the spectators, he awaited a response. As none came, however, he knocked again, but with the same unsatisfactory result as at first. And now, being a trifle choleric in his temperament, the lieutenant-governor uplifted the heavy hilt of his sword, wherewith he so beat and banged upon the door, that, as some of the bystanders whispered, the racket might have disturbed the dead. Be that as it might, it seemed to produce no awakening effect on Colonel Pyncheon. When the sound subsided, the silence through the house was deep, dreary and oppressive, notwithstanding that the tongues of many of the guests had already been loosened by a surreptitious cup or two of wine or spirits.

"Strange, forsooth!—very strange!" cried the lieutenant-governor, whose smile was changed to a frown. "But seeing that our host sets us the good example of forgetting ceremony, I shall likewise throw it aside, and make free to intrude on his privacy!"

He tried the door, which yielded to his hand, and was flung wide open by a sudden gust of wind that passed, as with a loud sigh, from the outermost portal, through all the passages and apartments of the new house. It rustled the silken garments of the ladies, and waved the long curls of the gentlemen's wigs, and shook the window-hangings and the curtains of the bed-chambers; causing everywhere a singular stir, which yet was more like a hush. A shadow of awe and half-fearful anticipation—nobody knew wherefore, nor of what—had all at once fallen over the company.

They thronged, however, to the now open door, pressing the lieutenant-governor, in the eagerness of their curiosity, into the room in advance of them. At the first glimpse, they beheld nothing extraordinary: a handsomely-furnished room, of moderate size, somewhat darkened by curtains; books arranged on shelves; a large map on the wall, and likewise a portrait of Colonel Pyncheon, beneath which sat the original colonel himself, in an oaken elbow-chair, with a pen in his hand. Letters, parchments, and blank sheets of paper, were on the table before him. He appeared to gaze at the curious crowd, in front of which stood the lieutenant-governor; and there was a frown on his dark and massive countenance, as if sternly resentful of the boldness that had impelled them into his private retirement.

A little boy—the colonel's grandchild, and the only human being that ever dared to be familiar with him—now made his way among the guests, and ran towards the seated figure; then pausing half-way, he began to shriek with terror. The company, tremulous as the leaves of a tree, when all are shaking together, drew nearer, and perceived that there was an unnatural distortion in the fixedness of Colonel Pyncheon's stare; that there was blood on his ruff, and that his hoary beard was saturated with it. It was too late to give assistance. The iron-hearted Puritan, the relentless persecutor, the grasping and strong-willed man, was dead! Dead, in his new house! There is a tradition, only worth alluding to, as lending a tinge of superstitious awe to a scene perhaps gloomy enough without it, that a voice spoke loudly among the guests, the tones of which were like those of old Matthew Maule, the executed wizard,—"God hath given him blood to drink!"

Thus early had that one guest—the only guest who is certain, at one time or another, to find his way into every human dwelling—thus early had Death stepped across the threshold of the House of the Seven Gables!

Colonel Pyncheon's sudden and mysterious end made a vast deal of noise in its day. There were many rumors, some of which have vaguely drifted down to the present time, how that appearances indicated violence; that there were the marks of fingers on his throat, and the print of a bloody hand on his plaited ruff; and that his peaked beard was dishevelled, as if it had been fiercely clutched and pulled. It was averred, likewise, that the lattice-window, near the colonel's chair, was open; and that only a few minutes before the fatal oc currence, the figure of a man had been seen clambering over the garden-fence, in the rear of the house. But it were folly to lay any stress on stories of this kind, which are sure to spring up around such an event as that now related, and which, as in the present case, sometimes prolong themselves for ages afterwards, like the toadstools that indicate where the fallen and buried trunk of a tree has long since mouldered into the earth. For our own part, we allow them just as little credence as to that other fable of the skeleton hand which the lieutenant-governor was said to have seen at the colonel's throat, but which vanished away, as he advanced further into the room. Certain it is, however, that there was a great consultation and dispute of doctors over the dead body. One—John Swinnerton by name—who appears to have been a man of eminence, upheld it, if we have rightly understood his terms of art, to be a case of apoplexy. His professional brethren, each for himself, adopted various hypotheses, more or less plausible, but all dressed out in a perplexing mystery of phrase, which, if it do not show a bewilderment of mind in these erudite physicians, certainly causes it in the unlearned peruser of their opinions. The coroner's jury sat upon the corpse, and, like sensible men, returned an unassailable verdict of "Sudden Death!"

It is indeed difficult to imagine that there could have been a serious suspicion of murder, or the slightest grounds for implicating any particular individual as the perpetrator. The rank, wealth, and eminent character of the deceased, must have insured the strictest scrutiny into every ambiguous circumstance. As none such is on record, it is safe to assume that none existed. Tradition—which sometimes brings down truth that history has let slip, but is oftener the wild babble of the time, such as was formerly spoken at the fireside, and now congeals in newspapers—tradition is responsible for all contrary averments. In Colonel Pyncheon's funeral sermon, which was printed, and is still extant, the Rev. Mr. Higginson enumerates, among the many felicities of his distinguished parishioner's earthly career, the happy seasonableness of his death. His duties all performed,—the highest prosperity attained,—his race and future generations fixed on a stable basis, and with a stately roof to shelter them, for centuries to come,—what other upward step remained for this good man to take, save the final step from earth to the golden gate of heaven! The pious clergyman surely would not have uttered words like these, had he in the least suspected that the colonel had been thrust into the other world with the clutch of violence upon his throat.

The family of Colonel Pyncheon, at the epoch of his death, seemed destined to as fortunate a permanence as can anywise consist with the inherent instability of human affairs. It might fairly be anticipated that the progress of time would rather increase and ripen their prosperity, than wear away and destroy it. For, not only had his son and heir come into immediate enjoyment of a rich estate, but there was a claim, through an Indian deed, confirmed by a subsequent grant of the General Court, to a vast and as yet unexplored and unmeasured tract of eastern lands. These possessions—for as such they might almost certainly be reckoned—comprised the greater part of what is now known as Waldo County, in the State of Maine, and were more extensive than many a dukedom, or even a reigning prince's territory, on European soil. When the pathless forest, that still covered this wild principality, should give place—as it inevitably must, though perhaps not till ages hence—to the golden fertility of human culture, it would be the source of incalculable wealth to the Pyncheon blood. Had the colonel survived only a few weeks longer, it is probable that his great political influence, and powerful connections, at home and abroad, would have consummated all that was necessary to render the claim available. But, in spite of good Mr. Higginson's congratulatory eloquence, this appeared to be the one thing which Colonel Pyncheon, provident and sagacious as he was, had allowed to go at loose ends. So far as the prospective territory was concerned, he unquestionably died too soon. His son lacked not merely the father's eminent position, but the talent and force of character to achieve it: he could, therefore, effect nothing by dint of political interest; and the bare justice or legality of the claim was not so apparent, after the colonel's decease, as it had been pronounced in his lifetime. Some connecting link had slipped out of the evidence, and could not anywhere be found.

Efforts, it is true, were made by the Pyncheons, not only then, but at various periods for nearly a hundred years afterwards, to obtain what they stubbornly persisted in deeming their right. But, in course of time, the territory was partly re-granted to more favored individuals, and partly cleared and occupied by actual settlers. These last, if

they ever heard of the Pyncheon title, would have laughed at the idea of any man's asserting a right—on the strength of mouldy parchments, signed with the faded autographs of governors and legislators long dead and forgotten—to the lands which they or their fathers had wrested from the wild hand of nature, by their own sturdy toil. This impalpable claim, therefore, resulted in nothing more solid than to cherish, from generation to generation, an absurd delusion of family importance, which all along characterized the Pyncheons. It caused the poorest member of the race to feel as if he inherited a kind of nobility, and might yet come into the possession of princely wealth to support it. In the better specimens of the breed, this peculiarity threw an ideal grace over the hard material of human life, without stealing away any truly valuable quality. In the baser sort, its effect was to increase the liability to sluggishness and dependence, and induce the victim of a shadowy hope to remit all self-effort, while awaiting the realization of his dreams. Years and years after their claim had passed out of the public memory, the ·Pyncheons were accustomed to consult the colonel's ancient map, which had been projected while Waldo County was still an unbroken wilderness. Where the old land-surveyor had put down woods, lakes, and rivers, they marked out the cleared spaces, and dotted the villages and towns, and calculated the progressively increasing value of the territory, as if there were yet a prospect of its ultimately forming a princedom for themselves.

In almost every generation, nevertheless, there happened to be some one descendant of the family gifted with a portion of the hard, keen sense, and practical energy, that had so remarkably distinguished the original founder. His character, indeed, might be traced all the way down, as distinctly as if the colonel himself, a little diluted, had been gifted with a sort of intermittent immortality on earth. At two or three epochs, when the fortunes of the family were low, this representative of hereditary qualities had made his appearance, and caused the traditionary gossips of the town to whisper among themselves: —"Here is the old Pyncheon come again! Now the Seven Gables will be new-shingled!" From father to son, they clung to the ancestral house, with singular tenacity of home attachment. For various reasons, however, and from impressions often too vaguely founded to be put on paper, the writer cherishes the belief that many, if not most, of the successive proprietors of this estate, were troubled with doubts as to their moral right to hold it. Of their legal tenure there could be no question; but old Matthew Maule, it is to be feared, trode downward from his own age to a far later one, planting a heavy footstep, all the way, on the conscience of a Pyncheon. If so, we are left to dispose of the awful query, whether each inheritor of the property—conscious of wrong, and failing to rectify it—did not commit anew the great guilt of his ancestor, and incur all its original responsibilities. And supposing such to be the case, would it not be a far truer mode of expression to say, of the Pyncheon family, that they inherited a great misfortune, than the reverse?

We have already hinted, that it is not our purpose to trace down the history of the Pyncheon family, in its unbroken connection with the House of the Seven Gables; nor to show, as in a magic picture, how the rustiness and infirmity of age gathered over the venerable house itself. As regards its interior life, a large, dim looking-glass used to hang in one of the rooms, and was fabled to contain within its depths all the shapes that had ever been reflected there,—the old colonel himself, and his many descendants, some in the garb of antique babyhood, and others in the bloom of feminine beauty or manly prime, or saddened with the wrinkles of frosty age. Had we the secret of that mirror, we would gladly sit down before it, and transfer its revelations to our page. But there was a story, for which it is difficult to conceive any foundation, that the posterity of Matthew Maule had some connection with the mystery of the looking-glass, and that, by what appears to have been a sort of mesmeric process, they could make its inner region all alive with the departed Pyncheons; not as they had shown themselves to the world, nor in their better and happier hours, but as doing over again some deed of sin, or in the crisis of life's bitterest sorrow. The popular imagination, indeed, long kept itself busy with the affair of the old Puritan Pyncheon and the wizard Maule; the curse, which the latter flung from his scaffold, was remembered, with the very important addition, that it had become a part of the Pyncheon inheritance. If one of the family did but gurgle in his throat, a bystander would be likely enough to whisper, between jest and earnest,—"He has Maule's blood to drink!" The sudden death of a Pyncheon, about a hundred years ago, with circumstances very similar to what have been related of the colonel's exit, was held as giving additional probability to the received opinion on this topic. It was considered, moreover, an ugly and ominous circumstance, that Colonel Pyncheon's picture —in obedience, it was said, to a provision of his will—remained affixed to the wall of the room in which he died. Those stern, immitigable features seemed to symbolize an evil influence, and so darkly to mingle the shadow of their presence with the sunshine of the passing hour, that no good thoughts or purposes could ever spring up and blossom there. To the thoughtful mind, there will be no tinge of superstition in what we figuratively express, by affirming that the ghost of a dead progenitor —perhaps as a portion of his own punishment—is often doomed to become the Evil Genius of his family.

The Pyncheons, in brief, lived along, for the better part of two centuries, with perhaps less of outward vicissitude than has attended most other New England families, during the same period of time. Possessing very distinctive traits of their own, they nevertheless took the general characteristics of the little community in which they dwelt; a town noted for its frugal, discreet, well-ordered, and home-loving inhabitants, as well as for the somewhat confined scope of its sympathies; but in which, be it said, there are odder individuals, and, now and then, stranger occurrences, than one meets with almost anywhere else. During the Revolution, the Pyncheon of that epoch, adopting the royal side, became a refugee; but repented, and made his reappearance, just at the point of time to preserve the House of the Seven Gables from confiscation. For the last seventy years, the most noted

event in the Pyncheon annals had been likewise the heaviest calamity that ever befell the race; no less than the violent death—for so it was adjudged—of one member of the family, by the criminal act of another. Certain circumstances, attending this fatal occurrence, had brought the deed irresistibly home to a nephew of the deceased Pyncheon. The young man was tried and convicted of the crime; but either the circumstantial nature of the evidence, and possibly some lurking doubt in the breast of the executive, or, lastly,—an argument of greater weight in a republic than it could have been under a monarchy,— the high respectability and political influence of the criminal's connections, had availed to mitigate his doom from death to perpetual imprisonment. This sad affair had chanced about thirty years before the action of our story commences. Latterly, there were rumors (which few believed, and only one or two felt greatly interested in) that this long-buried man was likely, for some reason or other, to be summoned forth from his living tomb.

It is essential to say a few words respecting the victim of this now almost forgotten murder. He was an old bachelor, and possessed a great wealth, in addition to the house and real estate which constituted what remained of the ancient Pyncheon property. Being of an eccentric and melancholy turn of mind, and greatly given to rummaging old records and hearkening to old traditions, he had brought himself, it is averred, to the conclusion, that Matthew Maule, the wizard, had been foully wronged out of his homestead, if not out of his life. Such being the case, and he, the old bachelor, in possession of the ill-gotten spoil—with the black stain of blood sunken deep into it, and still to be scented by conscientious nostrils—the question occurred, whether it were not imperative upon him, even at this late hour, to make restitution to Maule's posterity. To a man living so much in the past, and so little in the present, as the secluded and antiquarian old bachelor, a century and a half seemed not so vast a period as to obviate the propriety of substituting right for wrong. It was the belief of those who knew him best, that he would positively have taken the very singular step of giving up the House of the Seven Gables to the representative of Matthew Maule, but for the unspeakable tumult which a suspicion of the old gentleman's project awakened among his Pyncheon relatives. Their exertions had the effect of suspending his purpose; but it was feared that he would perform, after death, by the operation of his last will, what he had so hardly been prevented from doing, in his proper lifetime. But there is no one thing which men so rarely do, whatever the provocation or inducement, as to bequeath patrimonial property away from their own blood. They may love other individuals far better than their relatives,—they may ever cherish dislike, or positive hatred, to the latter; but yet, in view of death, the strong prejudice of propinquity revives, and impels the testator to send down his estate in the line marked out by custom so immemorial that it looks like nature. In all the Pyncheons, this feeling had the energy of disease. It was too powerful for the conscientious scruples of the old bachelor; at whose death, accordingly, the mansion-house, together with most of his other riches,

passed into the possession of his next legal representative.

This was a nephew, the cousin of the miserable young man who had been convicted of the uncle's murder. The new heir, up to the period of his accession, was reckoned rather a dissipated youth, but had at once reformed, and made himself an exceedingly respectable member of society. In fact, he showed more of the Pyncheon quality, and had won higher eminence in the world, than any of his race, since the time of the original Puritan. Applying himself in earlier manhood to the study of the law, and having a natural tendency towards office, he had attained, many years ago, to a judicial situation in some inferior court, which gave him for life the very desirable and imposing title of judge. Later, he had engaged in politics, and served a part of two terms in Congress, besides making a considerable figure in both branches of the state legislature. Judge Pyncheon was unquestionably an honor to his race. He had built himself a country-seat within a few miles of his native town, and there he spent such portions of his time as could be spared from public service in the display of every grace and virtue—as a newspaper phrased it, on the eve of an election—befitting the Christian, the good citizen, the horticulturalist, and the gentleman.

There were few of the Pyncheons left to sun themselves in the glow of the judge's prosperity. In respect to natural increase, the breed had not thriven; it appeared rather to be dying out. The only members of the family known to be extant were, first, the judge himself, and a single surviving son, who was now travelling in Europe; next, the thirty years prisoner, already alluded to, and a sister of the latter, who occupied, in an extremely retired manner, the House of the Seven Gables, in which she had a life-estate by the will of the old bachelor. She was understood to be wretchedly poor, and seemed to make it her choice to remain so; inasmuch as her affluent cousin, the judge, had repeatedly offered her all the comforts of life, either in the old mansion or his own modern residence. The last and youngest Pyncheon was a little country-girl of seventeen, the daughter of another of the judge's cousins, who had married a young woman of no family or property, and died early, and in poor circumstances. His widow had recently taken another husband.

As for Matthew Maule's posterity, it was supposed now to be extinct. For a very long period after the witchcraft delusion, however, the Maules had continued to inhabit the town where their progenitor had suffered so unjust a death. To all appearance, they were a quiet, honest, well meaning race of people, cherishing no malice against individuals or the public, for the wrong which had been done them; or if, at their own fireside, they transmitted, from father to child, any hostile recollection of the wizard's fate, and their lost patrimony, it was never acted upon, nor openly expressed. Nor would it have been singular had they ceased to remember that the House of the Seven Gables was resting its heavy frame-work on a foundation that was rightfully their own. There is something so massive, stable, and almost irresistibly imposing, in the exterior presentment of established rank and great possessions, that their very existence seems to give them

a right to exist; at least, so excellent a counterfeit of right, that few poor and humble men have moral force enough to question it, even in their secret minds. Such is the case now, after so many ancient prejudices have been overthrown; and it was far more so in ante-revolutionary days, when the aristocracy could venture to be proud, and the low were content to be abased. Thus the Maules, at all events, kept their resentments within their own breasts. They were generally poverty-stricken; always plebeian and obscure; working with unsuccessful diligence at handicrafts; laboring on the wharves, or following the sea, as sailors before the mast; living here and there about the town, in hired tenements, and coming finally to the almshouse, as the natural home of their age. At last, after creeping, as it were, for such a length of time, along the utmost verge of the opaque puddle of obscurity, they had taken that downright plunge, which, sooner or later, is the destiny of all families, whether princely or plebeian. For thirty years past, neither town-record, nor gravestone, nor the directory, nor the knowledge or memory of man, bore any trace of Matthew Maule's descendants. His blood might possibly exist elsewhere; here, where its lowly current could be traced so far back, it had ceased to keep an onward course.

So long as any of the race were to be found, they had been marked out from other men—not strikingly, nor as with a sharp line, but with an effect that was felt, rather than spoken of— by an hereditary character of reserve. Their companions, or those who endeavored to become such, grew conscious of a circle round about the

Maules, within the sanctity or the spell of which, in spite of an exterior of sufficient frankness and good-fellowship, it was impossible for any man to step. It was this indefinable peculiarity, perhaps, that, by insulating them from human aid, kept them always so unfortunate in life. It certainly operated to prolong, in their case, and to confirm to them, as their only inheritance, those feelings of repugnance and superstitious terror with which the people of the town, even after awakening from their frenzy, continued to regard the memory of the reputed witches. The mantle, or rather the ragged cloak, of old Matthew Maule, had fallen upon his children. They were half believed to inherit mysterious attributes; the family eye was said to possess strange power. Among other good-for-nothing properties and privileges, one was especially assigned them: of exercising an influence over people's dreams. The Pyncheons, if all stories were true, haughtily as they bore themselves in the noon-day streets of their native town, were no better than bond-servants to these plebeian Maules, on entering the topsy-turvy commonwealth of sleep. Modern psychology, it may be, will endeavor to reduce these alleged necromancies within a system, instead of rejecting them as altogether fabulous.

A descriptive paragraph or two, treating of the seven-gabled mansion in its more recent aspect, will bring this preliminary chapter to a close. The street in which it upreared its venerable peaks has long ceased to be a fashionable quarter of the town; so that, though the old edifice was surrounded by habitations of modern date, they were mostly small. built entirely of wood, and

typical of the most plodding uniformity of common life. Doubtless, however, the whole story of human existence may be latent in each of them, but with no picturesqueness, externally, that can attract the imagination or sympathy to seek it there. But as for the old structure of our story, its white-oak frame, and its boards, shingles and crumbling plaster, and even the huge, clustered chimney in the midst, seemed to constitute only the least and meanest part of its reality. So much of mankind's varied experience had passed there,— so much had been suffered, and something, too, enjoyed,—that the very timbers were oozy, as with the moisture of a heart. It was itself like a great human heart, with a life of its own, and full of rich and sombre reminiscences.

The deep projection of the second story gave the house such a meditative look, that you could not pass it without the idea that it had secrets to keep, and an eventful history to moralize upon. In front, just on the edge of the unpaved sidewalk, grew the Pyncheon-elm, which, in reference to such trees as one usually meets with, might well be termed gigantic. It had been planted by a great-grandson of the first Pyncheon, and, though now fourscore years of age, or perhaps nearer a hundred, was still in its strong and broad maturity, throwing its shadow from side to side of the street, overtopping the seven gables, and sweeping the whole black roof with its pendent foliage. It gave beauty to the old edifice, and seemed to make it a part of nature. The street having been widened about forty years ago, the front gable was now precisely on a line with it. On either side extended a ruinous wooden fence, of open lattice-work, through which could be seen a grassy yard, and, especially in the angles of the building, an enormous fertility of burdocks, with leaves, it is hardly an exaggeration to say, two or three feet long. Behind the house there appeared to be a garden, which undoubtedly had once been extensive, but was now infringed upon by other enclosures, or shut in by habitations and out-buildings that stood on another street. It would be an omission, trifling, indeed, but unpardonable, were we to forget the green moss that had long since gathered over the projections of the windows, and on the slopes of the roof; nor must we fail to direct the reader's eye to a crop, not of weeds, but flower-shrubs, which were growing aloft in the air, not a great way from the chimney, in the nook between two of the gables. They were called Alice's Posies. The tradition was, that a certain Alice Pyncheon had flung up the seeds, in sport, and that the dust of the street and the decay of the roof gradually formed a kind of soil for them, out of which they grew, when Alice had long been in her grave. However the flowers might have come there, it was both sad and sweet to observe how nature adopted to herself this desolate, decaying, gusty, rusty old house of the Pyncheon family; and how the ever-returning summer did her best to gladden it with tender beauty, and grew melancholy in the effort.

There is one other feature, very essential to be noticed, but which, we greatly fear, may damage any picturesque and romantic impression which we have been willing to throw over our sketch of this respectable edifice. In the front gable, under the impending brow of the second story, and contiguous to the street, was a shop-door, divided horizontally in the midst, and with a window for its upper segment, such as is often seen in dwellings of a somewhat ancient date. This same shop-door had been a subject of no slight mortification to the present occupant of the august Pyncheon-house, as well as to some of her predecessors. The matter is disagreeably delicate to handle; but, since the reader must needs be let into the secret, he will please to understand, that, about a century ago, the head of the Pyncheons found himself involved in serious financial difficulties. The fellow (gentleman, as he styled himself) can hardly have been other than a spurious interloper; for, instead of seeking office from the king or the royal governor, or urging his hereditary claim to eastern lands, he bethought himself of no better avenue to wealth than by cutting a shop-door through the side of his ancestral residence. It was the custom of the time, indeed, for merchants to store their goods and transact business in their own dwellings. But there was something pitifully small in this old Pyncheon's mode of setting about his commercial operations; it was whispered, that, with his own hands, all be-ruffled as they were, he used to give change for a shilling, and would turn a half-penny twice over, to make sure that it was a good one. Beyond all question, he had the blood of a petty huckster in his veins, through whatever channel it may have found its way there.

Immediately on his death, the shop-door had been locked, bolted, and barred, and, down to the period of our story, had probably never once been opened. The old counter, shelves, and other fixtures of the little shop, remained just as he had left them. It used to be affirmed, that the dead shopkeeper, in a white wig, a faded velvet coat, an apron at his waist, and his ruffles carefully turned back from his wrist, might be seen through the chinks of the shutters, any night of the year, ransacking his till, or poring over the dingy pages of his day-brook. From the look of unutterable woe upon his face, it appeared to be his doom to spend eternity in a vain effort to make his accounts balance.

And now—in a very humble way, as will be seen—we proceed to open our narrative.

CHAPTER II

THE LITTLE SHOP-WINDOW

It still lacked half an hour of sunrise, when Miss Hepzibah Pyncheon—we will not say awoke; it being doubtful whether the poor lady had so much as closed her eyes, during the brief night of midsummer—but, at all events, arose from her solitary pillow, and began what it would be mockery to term the adornment of her person. Far from us be the indecorum of assisting, even in imagination, at a maiden lady's toilet! Our story must therefore await Miss Hepzibah at the threshold of her chamber; only presuming, meanwhile, to note some of the heavy sighs that labored from her bosom, with little restraint as to their lugubrious depth and volume of sound, inasmuch as they could be audible to nobody, save a disembodied listener like ourself. The Old Maid was alone in the old house. Alone, except for a certain respectable and orderly young man, an artist in the daguerreotype line, who, for about three months back, had been a lodger in a remote gable,—quite a house by itself, indeed, —with locks, bolts, and oaken bars, on all the intervening doors. Inaudible, consequently, were poor Miss Hepzibah's gusty sighs. Inaudible, the creaking joints of her stiffened knees, as she knelt down by the bedside. And inaudible, too, by mortal ear, but heard with all-comprehending love and pity in the furthest heaven, that almost agony of prayer—now whispered, now a groan, now a struggling silence—wherewith she besought the Divine assistance through the day! Evidently, this is to be a day of more than ordinary trial to Miss Hepzibah, who, for above a quarter of a century gone by, has dwelt in strict seclusion, taking no part in the business of life, and just as little in its intercourse and pleasures. Not with such fervor prays the torpid recluse, looking forward to the cold, sunless, stagnant calm of a day that is to be like innumerable yesterdays!

The maiden lady's devotions are concluded. Will she now issue forth over the threshold of our story? Not yet, by many moments. First, every drawer in the tall, old-fashioned bureau is to be opened; with difficulty, and with a succession of spasmodic jerks; then, all must close again, with the same fidgety reluctance. There is a rustling of stiff silks; a tread of backward and forward footsteps, to and fro, across the chamber. We suspect Miss Hepzibah, moreover, of taking a step upward into a chair, in order to give heedful regard to her appearance, on all sides, and at full length, in the oval, dingy-framed toilet-glass, that hangs above her table. Truly! well, indeed! who would have thought it! Is all this precious time to be lavished on the matutinal repair and beautifying of an elderly person, who never goes abroad, whom nobody ever visits, and from whom, when she shall have done her utmost, it were the best charity to turn one's eyes another way?

Now she is almost ready. Let us pardon her one other pause; for it is given to the sole sentiment, or, we might better say—heightened and rendered intense, as it has been, by sorrow and seclusion—to the strong passion, of her life. We heard the turning of a key in a small lock; she has opened a secret drawer of an escritoire, and is probably looking at a certain miniature, done in Malbone's most perfect style, and representing a face worthy of no less delicate a pencil. It was once our good fortune to see this picture. It is a likeness of a young man, in a silken dressing-gown of an old fashion, the soft richness of which is well adapted to the countenance of reverie, with its full, tender lips, and beautiful eyes, that seem to indicate not so much capacity of thought, as gentle and voluptuous emotion. Of the possessor of such features we shall have a right to ask nothing,

except that he would take the rude world easily, and make himself happy in it. Can it have been an early lover of Miss Hepzibah? No; she never had a lover—poor thing, how could she?—nor ever knew, by her own experience, what love technically means. And yet, her undying faith and trust, her fresh remembrance, and continual devotedness towards the original of that miniature, have been the only substance for her heart to feed upon.

She seems to have put aside the miniature, and is standing again before the toilet-glass. There are tears to be wiped off. A few more footsteps to and fro; and here, at last—with another pitiful sigh, like a gust of chill, damp wind out of a long-closed vault, the door of which has accidentally been set ajar—here comes Miss Hepzibah Pyncheon! Forth she steps into the dusky, time-darkened passage; a tall figure, clad in black silk, with a long and shrunken waist, feeling her way towards the stairs like a near-sighted person, as in truth she is.

The sun, meanwhile, if not already above the horizon, was ascending nearer and nearer to its verge. A few clouds, floating high upward, caught some of the earliest light, and threw down its golden gleam on the windows of all the houses in the street, not forgetting the House of the Seven Gables, which —many such sunrises as it had witnessed—looked cheerfully at the present one. The reflected radiance served to show, pretty distinctly, the aspect and arrangement of the room which Hepzibah entered, after descending the stairs. It was a low-studded room, with a beam across the ceiling, panelled with dark wood, and having a large chimney-piece, set round with pictured tiles, but now closed by an iron fire-board, through which ran the funnel of a modern stove. There was a carpet on the floor, originally of rich texture, but so worn and faded, in these latter years, that its once brilliant figure had quite vanished into one indistinguishable hue. In the way of furniture, there were two tables: one, constructed with perplexing intricacy, and exhibiting as many feet as a centipede; the other, most delicately wrought, with four long and slender legs, so apparently frail that it was almost incredible what a length of time the ancient tea-table had stood upon them. Half a dozen chairs stood about the room, straight and stiff, and so ingeniously contrived for the discomfort of the human person that they were irksome even to sight, and conveyed the ugliest possible idea of the state of society to which they could have been adapted. One exception there was, however, in a very antique elbow-chair, with a high back, carved elaborately in oak, and a roomy depth within its arms, that made up, by its spacious comprehensiveness, for the lack of any of those artistic curves which abound in a modern chair.

As for ornamental articles of furniture, we recollect but two, if such they may be called. One was a map of the Pyncheon territory at the eastward, not engraved, but the handiwork of some skilful old draftsman, and grotesquely illuminated with pictures of Indians and wild beasts, among which was seen a lion; the natural history of the region being as little known as its geography, which was put down most fantastically awry. The other adornment was the portrait of old Colonel Pyncheon, at two-thirds length, representing the stern features of a puritanic-looking personage, in a skull cap, with a laced band and a grizzly beard; holding a Bible with one hand, and in the other uplifting an iron sword-hilt. The latter object, being more successfully depicted by the artist, stood out in far greater prominence than the sacred volume. Face to face with this picture, on entering the apartment, Miss Hepzibah Pyncheon came to a pause; regarding it with a singular scowl, a strange contortion of the brow, which, by people who did not know her, would probably have been interpreted as an expression of bitter anger and ill-will. But it was no such thing. She, in fact, felt a reverence for the pictured visage of which only a far-descended and time-stricken virgin could be susceptible; and this forbidding scowl was the innocent result of her near-sightedness, and an effort so to concentrate her powers of vision as to substitute a firm outline of the object instead of a vague one.

We must linger a moment on this unfortunate expression of poor Hepzibah's brow. Her scowl—as the world, or such part of it as sometimes caught a transitory glimpse of her at the window, wickedly persisted in calling it—her scowl had done Miss Hepzibah a very ill office, in establishing her character as an ill-tempered old maid; nor does it appear improbable, that, by often gazing at herself in a dim looking-glass, and perpetually encountering her own frown within its ghostly sphere, she had been led to interpret the expression almost as unjustly as the world did. "How miserably cross I look!" she must often have whispered to herself;—and ultimately have fancied herself so, by a sense of inevitable doom. But her heart never frowned. It was naturally tender, sensitive, and full of little tremors and palpitations; all of which weaknesses it retained, while her visage was growing so perversely stern, and even fierce. Nor had Hepzibah ever any hardihood, except what came from the very warmest nook in her affections.

All this time, however, we are loitering faint-heartedly on the threshold of our story. In very truth, we have an invincible reluctance to disclose what Miss Hepzibah Pyncheon was about to do.

It has already been observed, that, in the basement story of the gable fronting on the street, an unworthy ancestor, nearly a century ago, had fitted up a shop. Ever since the old gentleman retired from trade, and fell asleep under his coffin-lid, not only the shop-door, but the inner arrangements, had been suffered to remain unchanged; while the dust of ages gathered inch-deep over the shelves and counter, and partly filled an old pair of scales, as if it were of value enough to be weighed. It treasured itself up, too. in the half-opened till, where there still lingered a base sixpence, worth neither more nor less than the hereditary pride which had here been put to shame. Such had been the state and condition of the little shop in old Hepzibah's childhood, when she and her brother used to play at hide-and-seek in its forsaken precincts. So it had remained, until within a few days past.

But now, though the shop-window was still closely curtained from the public gaze, a remarkable change had taken place in its interior. The rich and heavy festoons of cobweb, which it had cost a long ancestral succession

of spiders their life's labor to spin and weave, had been carefully brushed away from the ceiling. The counter, shelves, and floor, had all been scoured, and the latter was overstrewn with fresh blue sand. The brown scales, too, had evidently undergone rigid discipline, in an unavailing effort to rub off the rust, which, alas! had eaten through and through their substance. Neither was the little old shop any longer empty of merchantable goods. A curious eye, privileged to take an account of stock, and investigate behind the counter, would have discovered a barrel,—yea, two or three barrels and half ditto,— one containing flour, another apples, and a third, perhaps, Indian meal. There was likewise a square box of pine-wood, full of soap in bars; also, another of the same size, in which were tallow candles, ten to the pound. A small stock of brown sugar, some white beans and split peas, and a few other commodities of low price, and such as are constantly in demand, made up the bulkier portion of the merchandise. It might have been taken for a ghostly or phantasmagoric reflection of the old shopkeeper Pyncheon's shabbily-provided shelves, save that some of the articles were of a description and outward form which could hardly have. been known in his day. For instance, there was a glass pickle-jar, filled with fragments of Gibraltar rock; not, indeed, splinters of the veritable stone foundation of the famous fortress, but bits of delectable candy, neatly done up in white paper. Jim Crow, moreover, was seen executing his world-renowned dance, in gingerbread. A party of leaden dragoons were galloping along one of the shelves, in equipments and uniform of modern cut; and there were some sugar figures, with no strong resemblance to the humanity of any epoch, but less unsatisfactorily representing our own fashions than those of a hundred years ago. Another phenomenon, still more strikingly modern, was a package of lucifer matches, which, in old times, would have been thought actually to borrow their instantaneous flame from the nether fires of Tophet.

In short, to bring the matter at once to a point, it was incontrovertibly evident that somebody had taken the shop and fixtures of the long-retired and forgotten Mr. Pyncheon, and was about to renew the enterprise of that departed worthy, with a different set of customers. Who could this bold adventurer be? And, of all places in the world, why had he chosen the House of the Seven Gables as the scene of his commercial speculations?

We return to the elderly maiden. She at length withdrew her eyes from the dark countenance of the colonel's portrait, heaved a sigh,—indeed, her breast was a very cave of Æolus, that morning,—and stept across the room on tip-toe, as is the customary gait of elderly women. Passing through an intervening passage, she opened a door that communicated with the shop, just now so elaborately described. Owing to the projection of the upper story—and still more to the thick shadow of the Pyncheon-elm, which stood almost directly in front of the gable—the twilight, here, was still as much akin to night as morning. Another heavy sigh from Miss Hepzibah! After a moment's pause on the threshold, peering towards the window with her near-sighted scowl, as if frowning down some bitter enemy,

she suddenly projected herself into the shop. The haste, and, as it were, the galvanic impulse of the movement, were really quite startling.

Nervously—in a sort of frenzy, we might almost say—she began to busy herself in arranging some children's play-things, and other little wares, on the shelves and at the shop-window. In the aspect of this dark-arrayed, pale-faced, lady-like old figure, there was a deeply tragic character, that contrasted irreconcilably with the ludicrous pettiness of her employment. It seemed a queer anomaly, that so gaunt and dismal a personage should take a toy in hand; a miracle, that the toy did not vanish in her grasp; a miserably absurd idea, that she should go on perplexing her stiff and sombre intellect with the question how to tempt little boys into her premises! Yet such is undoubtedly her object. Now she places a gingerbread elephant against the window, but with so tremulous a touch that it tumbles upon the floor, with the dismemberment of three legs and its trunk; it has ceased to be an elephant, and has become a few bits of musty gingerbread. There, again, she has upset a tumbler of marbles, all of which roll different ways, and each individual marble, devil-directed, into the most difficult obscurity that it can find Heaven help our poor old Hepzibah, and forgive us for taking a ludicrous view of her position! As her rigid and rusty frame goes down upon its hands and knees, in quest of the absconding marbles, we positively feel so much the more inclined to shed tears of sympathy, from the very fact that we must needs turn aside and laugh at her. For here —and if we fail to impress it suitably upon the reader, it is our own fault, not that of the theme—here is one of the truest points of melancholy interest that occur in ordinary life. It was the final throe of what called itself old gentility. A lady—who had fed herself from childhood with the shadowy food of aristocratic reminiscences, and whose religion it was that a lady's hand soils itself irremediably by doing aught for bread—this born lady, after sixty years of narrowing means, is fain to step down from her pedestal of imaginary rank. Poverty, treading closely at her heels for a life-time, has come up with her at last. She must earn her own food, or starve! And we have stolen upon Miss Hepzibah Pyncheon, too irreverently, at the instant of time when the patrician lady is to be transformed into the plebeian woman.

In this republican country, amid the fluctuating waves of our social life, somebody is always at the drowning-point. The tragedy is enacted with as continual a repetition as that of a popular drama on a holiday; and, nevertheless, is felt as deeply, perhaps, as when an hereditary noble sinks below his order. More deeply; since, with us, rank is the grosser substance of wealth and a splendid establishment, and has no spiritual existence after the death of these, but dies hopelessly along with them. And, therefore, since we have been unfortunate enough to introduce our heroine at so inauspicious a juncture, we would entreat for a mood of due solemnity in the spectators of her fate. Let us behold, in poor Hepzibah, the immemorial lady,—two hundred years old, on this side of the water, and thrice as many on the other,—with her antique portraits, pedigrees, coats

of arms, records and traditions, and her claim, as joint heiress, to that princely territory at the eastward, no longer a wilderness, but a populous fertility,—born, too, in Pyncheon-street, under the Pyncheon-elm, and in the Pyncheon-house, where she has spent all her days, —reduced now, in that very house, to be the hucksteress of a cent-shop!

This business of setting up a petty shop is almost the only resource of women, in circumstances at all similar to those of our unfortunate recluse. With her near-sightedness, and those tremulous fingers of hers, at once inflexible and delicate, she could not be a seamstress; although her sampler, of fifty years gone-by, exhibited some of the most recondite specimens of ornamental needle-work. A school for little children had been often in her thoughts; and, at one time, she had begun a review of her early studies in the New England primer, with a view to prepare herself for the office of instructress. But the love of children had never been quickened in Hepzibah's heart, and was now torpid, if not extinct; she watched the little people of the neighborhood from her chamber-window, and doubted whether she could tolerate a more intimate acquaintance with them. Besides, in our day, the very A B C has become a science, greatly too abstruse to be any longer taught by pointing a pin from letter to letter. A modern child could teach old Hepzibah more than old Hepzibah could teach the child. So—with many a cold, deep heart-quake at the idea of at last coming into sordid contact with the world, from which she had so long kept aloof, while every added day of seclusion had rolled another stone against the cavern-door of her hermitage—the poor thing bethought herself of the ancient shop-window, the rusty scales, and dusty till. She might have held back a little longer; but another circumstance, not yet hinted at, had somewhat hastened her decision. Her humble preparations, therefore, were duly made, and the enterprise was now to be commenced. Nor was she entitled to complain of any remarkable singularity in her fate; for, in the town of her nativity, we might point to several little shops of a similar description; some of them in houses as ancient as that of the seven gables; and one or two, it may be, where a decayed gentlewoman stands behind the counter, as grim an image of family pride as Miss Hepzibah Pyncheon herself.

It was overpoweringly ridiculous—we must honestly confess it—the deportment of the maiden lady while setting her shop in order for the public eye. She stole on tiptoe to the window, as cautiously as if she conceived some bloody-minded villain to be watching behind the elm-tree, with intent to take her life. Stretching out her long, lank arm, she put a paper of pearl-buttons, a Jew's-harp, or whatever the small article might be, in its destined place, and straightway vanished back into the dusk, as if the world need never hope for another glimpse of her. It might have been fancied, indeed, that she expected to minister to the wants of the community unseen, like a disembodied divinity, or enchantress, holding forth her bargains to the reverential and awe-stricken purchaser, in an invisible land. But Hepzibah had no such flattering dream. She was well aware that she must ultimately come forward, and stand revealed in her proper individuality; but, like other sensitive persons, she could not bear to be observed in the gradual process, and chose rather to flash forth on the world's astonished gaze at once.

The inevitable moment was not much longer to be delayed. The sunshine might now be seen stealing down the front of the opposite house, from the windows of which came a reflected gleam, struggling through the boughs of the elm-tree, and enlightening the interior of the shop more distinctly than heretofore. The town appeared to be waking up. A baker's cart had already rattled through the street, chasing away the latest vestige of night's sanctity with the jingle-jangle of its dissonant bells. A milkman was distributing the contents of his cans from door to door; and the harsh peal of a fisherman's conch-shell was heard far off, around the corner. None of these tokens escaped Hepzibah's notice. The moment had arrived. To delay longer would be only to lengthen out her misery. Nothing remained, except to take down the bar from the shop-door, leaving the entrance free—more than free—welcome, as if all were household friends—to every passer-by, whose eyes might be attracted by the commodities at the window. This last act Hepzibah now performed, letting the bar fall with what smote upon her excited nerves as a most astounding clatter. Then—as if the only barrier betwixt herself and the world had been thrown down, and a flood of evil consequences would come tumbling through the gap—she fled into the inner parlor, threw herself into the ancestral elbow-chair, and wept.

Our miserable old Hepzibah! It is a heavy annoyance to a writer, who endeavors to represent nature, its various attitudes and circumstances, in a reasonably correct outline and true coloring, that so much of the mean and ludicrous should be hopelessly mixed up with the purest pathos which life anywhere supplies to him. What tragic dignity, for example, can be wrought into a scene like this! How can we elevate our history of retribution for the sin of long ago, when, as one of our most prominent figures, we are compelled to introduce—not a young and lovely woman, nor even the stately remains of beauty, storm-shattered by affliction—but a gaunt, sallow, rusty-jointed maiden, in a long-waisted silk gown, and with the strange horror of a turban on her head! Her visage is not even ugly. It is redeemed from insignificance only by the contraction of her eyebrows into a near-sighted scowl. And, finally, her great life-trial seems to be, that, after sixty years of idleness, she finds it convenient to earn comfortable bread by setting up a shop in a small way. Nevertheless, if we look through all the heroic fortunes of mankind, we shall find this same entanglement of something mean and trivial with whatever is noblest in joy or sorrow. Life is made up of marble and mud. And, without all the deeper trust in a comprehensive sympathy above us, we might hence be led to suspect the insult of a sneer, as well as an immitigable frown, on the iron countenance of fate. What is called poetic insight is the gift of discerning, in this sphere of strangely-mingled elements, the beauty and the majesty which are compelled to assume a garb so sordid.

CHAPTER III

THE FIRST CUSTOMER

MISS HEPZIBAH PYNCHEON sat in the oaken elbow-chair, with her hands over her face, giving way to that heavy down-sinking of the heart which most persons have experienced, when the image of hope itself seems ponderously moulded of lead, on the eve of an enterprise at once doubtful and momentous. She was suddenly startled by the tinkling alarum—high, sharp, and irregular —of a little bell. The maiden lady arose upon her feet, as pale as a ghost at cock-crow; for she was an enslaved spirit, and this the talisman to which she owed obedience. This little bell— to speak in plainer terms—being fastened over the shop-door, was so contrived as to vibrate by means of a steel spring, and thus convey notice to the inner regions of the house, when any customer should cross the threshold. Its ugly and spiteful little din (heard now for the first time, perhaps, since Hepzibah's periwigged predecessor had retired from trade) at once set every nerve of her body in responsive and tumultuous vibration. The crisis was upon her! Her first customer was at the door!

Without giving herself time for a

second thought, she rushed into the shop, pale, wild, desperate in gesture and expression, scowling portentously, and looking far better qualified to do fierce battle with a house-breaker than to stand smiling behind the counter, bartering small wares for a copper recompense. Any ordinary customer, indeed, would have turned his back and fled. And yet there was nothing fierce in Hepzibah's poor old heart; nor had she, at the moment, a single bitter thought against the world at large, or one individual man or woman. She wished them all well, but wished, too, that she herself were done with them, and in her quiet grave.

The applicant, by this time, stood within the doorway. Coming freshly, as he did, out of the morning light, he appeared to have brought some of its cheery influences into the shop along with him. It was a slender young man, not more than one or two and twenty years old, with rather a grave and thoughtful expression, for his years, but likewise a springy alacrity and vigor. These qualities were not only perceptible, physically, in his make and motions, but made themselves felt almost immediately in his character. A brown beard, not too silken in its texture, fringed his chin, but as yet without completely hiding it; he wore a short moustache, too, and his dark, high-featured countenance looked all the better for these natural ornaments. As for his dress, it was of the simplest kind; a summer sack of cheap and ordinary material, thin, checkered pantaloons, and a straw hat, by no means of the finest braid. Oak Hall might have supplied his entire equipment. He was chiefly marked as a gentleman—if such,

indeed, he made any claim to be—by the rather remarkable whiteness and nicety of his clean linen.

He met the scowl of old Hepzibah without apparent alarm, as having heretofore encountered it, and found it harmless.

"So, my dear Miss Pyncheon," said the daguerreotypist,—for it was that sole other occupant of the seven-gabled mansion,—"I am glad to see that you have not shrunk from your good purpose. I merely look in to offer my best wishes, and to ask if I can assist you any further in your preparations."

People in difficulty and distress, or in any manner at odds with the world, can endure a vast amount of harsh treatment, and perhaps be only the stronger for it; whereas, they give way at once before the simplest expression of what they perceive to be genuine sympathy. So it proved with poor Hepzibah; for, when she saw the young man's smile,—looking so much the brighter on a thoughtful face,—and heard his kindly tone, she broke first into a hysteric giggle, and then began to sob.

"Ah, Mr. Holgrave," cried she, as soon as she could speak, "I never can go through with it! Never, never, never! I wish I were dead, and in the old family-tomb, with all my forefathers! With my father, and my mother, and my sister! Yes, and with my brother, who had far better find me there than here! The world is too chill and hard, —and I am too old, and too feeble, and too hopeless!"

"O, believe me, Miss Hepzibah," said the young man, quietly, "these feelings will not trouble you any longer, after you are once fairly in the midst of your enterprise. They are unavoidable at this moment, standing, as you do, on the outer verge of your long seclusion, and peopling the world with ugly shapes, which you will soon find to be as unreal as the giants and ogres of a child's story-book. I find nothing so singular in life, as that everything appears to lose its substance, the instant one actually grapples with it. So it will be with what you think so terrible."

"But I am a woman!" said Hepzibah, piteously. "I was going to say, a lady, —but I consider that as past."

"Well; no matter if it be past!" answered the artist, a strange gleam of half-hidden sarcasm flashing through the kindliness of his manner. "Let it go! You are the better without it. I speak frankly, my dear Miss Pyncheon; for are we not friends? I look upon this as one of the fortunate days of your life. It ends an epoch, and begins one. Hitherto, the life-blood has been gradually chilling in your veins, as you sat aloof, within your circle of gentility, while the rest of the world was fighting out its battle with one kind of necessity or another. Henceforth, you will at least have the sense of healthy and natural effort for a purpose, and of lending your strength—be it great or small—to the united struggle of mankind. This is success—all the success that anybody meets with!"

"It is natural enough, Mr. Holgrave, that you should have ideas like these," rejoined Hepzibah, drawing up her gaunt figure, with slightly offended dignity. "You are a man, a young man, and brought up, I suppose, as almost everybody is now-a-days, with a view to seeking your fortune. But I was born a lady and have always lived one; no

matter in what narrowness of means, always a lady!"

"But I was not born a gentleman; neither have I lived like one," said Holgrave, slightly smiling; "so, my dear madam, you will hardly expect me to sympathize with sensibilities of this kind; though, unless I deceive myself, I have some imperfect comprehension of them. These names of gentlemen and lady had a meaning, in the past history of the world, and conferred privileges, desirable or otherwise, on those entitled to bear them. In the present—and still more in the future condition of society —they imply, not privilege, but restriction!"

"These are new notions," said the old gentlewoman, shaking her head. "I shall never understand them; neither do I wish it."

"We will cease to speak of them, then," replied the artist, with a friendlier smile than his last one, "and I will leave you to feel whether it is not better to be a true woman than a lady. Do you really think, Miss Hepzibah, that any lady of your family has ever done a more heroic thing, since this house was built, than you are performing in it to-day? Never; and if the Pyncheons had always acted so nobly, I doubt whether an old wizard Maule's anathema, of which you told me once, would have had much weight with Providence against them."

"Ah—no, no!" said Hepzibah, not displeased at this allusion to the sombre dignity of an inherited curse. "If old Maule's ghost, or a descendant of his, could see me behind the counter to-day, he would call it the fulfilment of his worst wishes. But I thank you for your kindness, Mr. Holgrave, and will do my utmost to be a good shop-keeper."

"Pray do," said Holgrave, "and let me have the pleasure of being your first customer. I am about taking a walk to the sea-shore, before going to my rooms, where I misuse Heaven's blessed sunshine, by tracing out human features, through its agency. A few of those biscuits, dipt in sea-water, will be just what I need for breakfast. What is the price of half a dozen?"

"Let me be a lady a moment longer," replied Hepzibah, with a manner of antique stateliness, to which a melancholy smile lent a kind of grace. She put the biscuits into his hand, but rejected the compensation. "A Pyncheon must not, at all events, under her forefathers' roof, receive money for a morsel of bread, from her only friend!"

Holgrave took his departure, leaving her, for the moment, with spirits not quite so much depressed. Soon, however, they had subsided nearly to their former dead level. With a beating heart, she listened to the footsteps of early passengers, which now began to be frequent along the street. Once or twice, they seemed to linger; these strangers, or neighbors, as the case might be, were looking at the display of toys and petty commodities in Hepzibah's shop-window. She was doubly tortured; in part, with a sense of overwhelming shame, that strange and unloving eyes should have the privilege of gazing, and partly because the idea occurred to her, with ridiculous importunity, that the window was not arranged so skilfully, nor nearly to so much advantage, as it might have been. It seemed as if the whole fortune or failure of her shop

might depend on the display of a differ-ent set of articles, or substituting a fairer apple for one which appeared to be specked. So she made the change, and straightway fancied that everything was spoiled by it; not recognizing that it was the nervousness of the juncture, and her own native squeamishness, as an old maid, that wrought all the seeming mischief.

Anon, there was an encounter, just at the door-step, betwixt two laboring men, as their rough voices denoted them to be. After some slight talk about their own affairs, one of them chanced to notice the shop-window, and directed the other's attention to it.

"See here!" cried he; "what do you think of this? Trade seems to be looking up, in Pyncheon-street!"

"Well, well, this is a sight, to be sure!" exclaimed the other. "In the old Pyncheon-house, and underneath the Pyncheon-elm! Who would have thought it? Old Maid Pyncheon is setting up a cent-shop!"

"Will she make it go, think you, Dixey?" said his friend. "I don't call it a very good stand. There's another shop, just around the corner."

"Make it go!" cried Dixey, with a most contemptuous expression, as if the very idea were impossible to be conceived. "Not a bit of it! Why, her face—I've seen it, for I dug her garden for her, one year—her face is enough to frighten the Old Nick himself, if he had ever so great a mind to trade with her. People can't stand it, I tell you! She scowls dreadfully, reason or none, out of pure ugliness of temper!"

"Well, that's not so much matter," remarked the other man. "These sour-tempered folks are mostly handy at business, and know pretty well what they are about. But, as you say, I don't think she'll do much. This business of keeping cent-shops is overdone, like all other kinds of trade, handicraft, and bodily labor. I know it, to my cost! My wife kept a cent-shop three months, and lost five dollars on her outlay!"

"Poor business!" responded Dixey, in a tone as if he were shaking his head, —"poor business!"

For some reason or other, not very easy to analyze, there had hardly been so bitter a pang, in all her previous misery about the matter, as what thrilled Hepzibah's heart, on overhearing the above conversation. The testimony in regard to her scowl was frightfully important; it seemed to hold up her image, wholly relieved from the false light of her self-partialities, and so hideous that she dared not look at it.

She was absurdly hurt, moreover, by the slight and idle effect that her setting up shop—an event of such breathless interest to herself—appeared to have upon the public, of which these two men were the nearest representatives. A glance; a passing word or two; a coarse laugh; and she was doubtless forgotten, before they turned the corner! They cared nothing for her dignity, and just as little for her degradation. Then, also, the augury of ill-success, uttered from the sure wisdom of experience, fell upon her half-dead hope like a clod into a grave. The man's wife had already tried the same experiment, and failed! How could the born lady—the recluse of half a lifetime, utterly unpractised in the world, at sixty years of age—how could she ever dream of succeeding, when the hard, vulgar, keen, busy, hackneyed New England

woman, had lost five dollars on her little outlay! Success presented itself as an impossibility, and the hope of it as a wild hallucination.

Some malevolent spirit, doing his utmost to drive Hepzibah mad, unrolled before her imagination a kind of panorama, representing the great thoroughfare of a city, all astir with customers. So many and so magnificent shops as there were! Groceries, toy-shops, dry-goods stores, with their immense panes of plate-glass, their gorgeous fixtures, their vast and complete assortments of merchandise, in which fortunes had been invested; and those noble mirrors at the further end of each establishment, doubling all this wealth by a brightly-burnished vista of unrealities! On one side of the street, this splendid bazaar, with a multitude of perfumed and glossy salesmen, smirking, smiling, bowing, and measuring out the goods. On the other the dusky old House of the Seven Gables, with the antiquated shop-window under its projecting story, and Hepzibah herself, in a gown of rusty black silk, behind the counter, scowling at the world as it went by! This mighty contrast thrust itself forward, as a fair expression of the odds against which she was to begin her struggle for a subsistence. Success? Preposterous! She would never think of it again! The house might just as well be buried in an eternal fog, while all other houses had the sunshine on them; for not a foot would ever cross the threshold, nor a hand so much as try the door!

But, at this instant, the shop-bell, right over her head, tinkled as if it were bewitched. The old gentlewoman's heart seemed to be attached to the same steel spring, for it went through a series of sharp jerks, in unison with the sound. The door was thrust open, although no human form was perceptible on the other side of the half-window. Hepzibah, nevertheless, stood at a gaze, with her hands clasped, looking very much as if she had summoned up an evil spirit, and were afraid, yet resolved, to hazard the encounter.

"Heaven help me!" she groaned, mentally. "Now is my hour of need!"

The door, which moved with difficulty on its creaking and rusty hinges, being forced quite open, a square and sturdy little urchin became apparent, with cheeks as red as an apple. He was clad rather shabbily (but, as it seemed, more owing to his mother's carelessness than his father's poverty), in a blue apron, very wide and short trousers, shoes somewhat out at the toes, and a chip-hat, with the frizzles of his curly hair sticking through its crevices. A book and a small slate, under his arm, indicated that he was on his way to school. He stared at Hepzibah a moment, as an elder customer than himself would have been likely enough to do, not knowing what to make of the tragic attitude and queer scowl wherewith she regarded him.

"Well, child," said she, taking heart at sight of a personage to little formidable,—"well, my child, what did you wish for?"

"That Jim Crow, there, in the window," answered the urchin, holding out a cent, and pointing to the gingerbread figure that had attracted his notice, as he loitered along to school; "the one that has not a broken foot."

So Hepzibah put forth her lank arm, and taking the effigy from the shop-window, delivered it to her first customer.

"No matter for the money," said she, giving him a little push towards the door; for her old gentility was contumaciously squeamish at sight of the copper coin, and, besides, it seemed such pitiful meanness to take the child's pocket-money in exchange for a bit of stale gingerbread. "No matter for the cent. You are welcome to Jim Crow."

The child, staring, with round eyes, at this instance of liberality, wholly unprecedented in his large experience of cent-shops, took the man of gingerbread, and quitted the premises. No sooner had he reached the sidewalk (little cannibal that he was!) than Jim Crow's head was in his mouth. As he had not been careful to shut the door, Hepzibah was at the pains of closing it after him, with a pettish ejaculation or two about the troublesomeness of young people, and particularly of small boys. She had just placed another representative of the renowned Jim Crow at the window, when again the shop-bell tinkled clamorously, and again the door being thrust open, with its characteristic jerk and jar, disclosed the same sturdy little urchin who, precisely two minutes ago, had made his exit. The crumbs and discoloration of the cannibal feast, as yet hardly consummated, were exceedingly visible about his mouth.

"What is it now, child?" asked the maiden lady, rather impatiently; "did you come back to shut the door?"

"No," answered the urchin, pointing to the figure that had just been put up; "I want that other Jim Crow."

"Well, here it is for you," said Hepzibah, reaching it down; but, recog-

zing that this pertinaceous customer
ould not quit her on any other terms,
 long as she had a gingerbread figure
 her shop, she partly drew back her
 tended hand,—"Where is the cent?"
The little boy had the cent ready, but,
ke a true-born Yankee, would have
referred the better bargain to the
orse. Looking somewhat chagrined, he
ut the coin into Hepzibah's hand, and
eparted, sending the second Jim Crow
 quest of the former one. The new
hop-keeper dropped the first sordid
esult of her commercial enterprise into
e till. It was done! The sordid stain of
hat copper coin could never be washed
way from her palm. The little school-
oy, aided by the impish figure of the
egro dancer, had wrought an irrepar-
ble ruin. The structure of ancient aris-
cracy had been demolished by him,
ven as if his childish gripe had torn
own the seven-gabled mansion! Now
t Hepzibah turn the old Pyncheon
ortraits with their faces to the wall,
nd take the map of her eastern terri-
ry to kindle the kitchen fire, and blow
p the flame with the empty breath of
er ancestral traditions! What had she
o do with ancestry? Nothing; no more
an with posterity! No lady, now, but
mply Hepzibah Pyncheon, a forlorn
ld maid, and keeper of a cent-shop!

Nevertheless, even while she paraded
hese ideas somewhat ostentatiously
hrough her mind, it is altogether sur-
rising what a calmness had come over
er. The anxiety and misgivings which
ad tormented her, whether asleep or
n melancholy day-dreams, ever since
er project began to take an aspect
f solidity, had now vanished quite
way. She felt the novelty of her posi-
on, indeed, but no longer with dis-

turbance or affright. Now and then,
there came a thrill of almost youthful
enjoyment. It was the invigorating
breath of a fresh outward atmosphere,
after the long torpor and monotonous
seclusion of her life. So wholesome is
effort! So miraculous the strength that
we do not know of! The healthiest glow
that Hepzibah had known for years had
come now, in the dreaded crisis, when,
for the first time, she had put forth
her hand to help herself. The little
circlet of the schoolboy's copper coin—
dim and lustreless though it was, with
the small services which it had been
doing, here and there about the world
—had proved a talisman, fragrant with
good, and deserving to be set in gold
and worn next her heart. It was as
potent, and perhaps endowed with the
same kind of efficacy, as a galvanic ring!
Hepzibah, at all events, was indebted
to its subtile operation, both in body
and spirit; so much the more, as it
inspired her with energy to get some
breakfast, at which, still the better to
keep up her courage, she allowed herself an extra spoonful in her infusion
of black tea.

Her introductory day of shop-keeping
did not run on, however, without many
and serious interruptions of this mood
of cheerful vigor. As a general rule,
Providence seldom vouchsafes to mortals any more than just that degree
of encouragement which suffices to keep
them at a reasonably full exertion of
their powers. In the case of our old
gentlewoman, after the excitement of
her new effort had subsided, the despondency of her whole life threatened,
ever and anon, to return. It was like
the heavy mass of clouds which we
may often see obscuring the sky, and

making a gray twilight everywhere, until, towards nightfall, it yields temporarily to a glimpse of sunshine. But, always, the envious cloud strives to gather again across the streak of celestial azure.

Customers came in, as the forenoon advanced, but rather slowly; in some cases, too, it must be owned, with little satisfaction either to themselves or Miss Hepzibah; nor, on the whole, with an aggregate of very rich emolument to the till. A little girl, sent by her mother to match a skein of cotton thread, of a peculiar hue, took one that the near-sighted old lady pronounced extremely like, but soon came running back, with a blunt and cross message, that it would not do, and, besides, was very rotten! Then, there was a pale, care-wrinkled woman, not old but haggard, and already with streaks of gray among her hair, like silver ribbons; one of those women, naturally delicate, whom you at once recognize as worn to death by a brute—probably a drunken brute—of a husband, and at least nine children. She wanted a few pounds of flour, and offered the money, which the decayed gentlewoman silently rejected, and gave the poor soul better measure than if she had taken it. Shortly afterwards, a man in a blue cotton frock, much soiled, came in and bought a pipe, filling the whole shop, meanwhile, with the hot odor of strong drink, not only exhaled in the torrid atmosphere of his breath, but oozing out of his entire system, like an inflammable gas. It was impressed on Hepzibah's mind that this was the husband of the care-wrinkled woman. He asked for a paper of tobacco; and as she had neglected to provide herself with the article, her brutal customer dashed down his newly-bought pipe, and left the shop, muttering some unintelligible words, which had the tone and bitterness of a curse. Hereupon Hepzibah threw up her eyes, unintentionally scowling in the face of Providence!

No less than five persons, during the forenoon, inquired for ginger-beer, or root-beer, or any drink of a similar brewage, and, obtaining nothing of the kind, went off in an exceedingly bad humor. Three of them left the door open, and the other two pulled it so spitefully in going out that the little bell played the very deuce with Hepzibah's nerves. A round, bustling, fire-ruddy housewife of the neighborhood burst breathlessly into the shop, fiercely demanding yeast; and when the poor gentlewoman, with her cold shyness of manner, gave her hot customer to understand that she did not keep the article this very capable housewife took upon herself to administer a regular rebuke.

"A cent-shop, and no yeast!" quoth she; "that will never do! Who ever heard of such a thing? Your loaf will never rise, no more than mine will to-day. You had better shut up shop at once."

"Well," said Hepzibah, heaving a deep sigh, "perhaps I had!"

Several times, moreover, besides the above instance, her ladylike sensibilities were seriously infringed upon by the familiar, if not rude tone, with which people addressed her. They evidently considered themselves not merely her equals, but her patrons and superiors. Now, Hepzibah had unconsciously flattered herself with the idea that there would be a gleam or halo, of some kind or other, about her person, which would

sure an obeisance to her sterling gen-
ity, or, at least, a tacit recognition
it. On the other hand, nothing tor-
red her more intolerably than when
is recognition was too prominently
pressed. To one or two rather officious
ers of sympathy, her responses were
tle short of acrimonious; and, we
gret to say, Hepzibah was thrown into
positively unchristian state of mind,
y the suspicion that one of her cus-
mers was drawn to the shop not by
iy real need of the article which she
etended to seek, but by a wicked wish
stare at her. The vulgar creature
as determined to see for herself what
rt of a figure a mildewed piece of
istocracy, after wasting all the bloom,
id much of the decline of her life,
part from the world, would cut behind
counter. In this particular case, how-
ver mechanical and innocuous it might
e at other times, Hepzibah's contortion
f brow served her in good stead.

"I never was so frightened in my
fe!" said the curious customer, in de-
cribing the incident to one of her
cquaintances. "She's a real old vixen,
ike my word of it! She says little,
o be sure; but if you could only see
he mischief in her eye!"

On the whole, therefore, her new
xperience led our decayed gentlewoman
o very disagreeable conclusions as to
he temper and manners of what she
ermed the lower classes, whom hereto-
ore she had looked down upon with
gentle and pitying complaisance, as
erself occupying a sphere of unques-
ionable superiority. But, unfortunately,

she had likewise to struggle against a
bitter emotion of a directly opposite
kind: a sentiment of virulence, we mean,
towards the idle aristocracy to which
it had so recently been her pride to
belong. When a lady, in a delicate
and costly summer garb, with a floating veil and gracefully-swaying gown,
and, altogether, an ethereal lightness
that made you look at her beautifully-
slippered feet, to see whether she trod
on the dust or floated in the air,—
when such a vision happened to pass
through this retired street, leaving it
tenderly and delusively fragrant with
her passage, as if a bouquet of tea-
roses had been borne along,—then,
again, it is to be feared, old Hepzibah's scowl could no longer vindicate
itself entirely on the plea of near-
sightedness.

"For what end," thought she, giving
vent to that feeling of hostility which
is the only real abasement of the poor,
in presence of the rich,—"for what
good end, in the wisdom of Providence,
does that woman live? Must the whole
world toil, that the palms of her hands
may be kept white and delicate?"

Then, ashamed and penitent, she hid
her face.

"May God forgive me!" said she.

Doubtless, God did forgive her. But,
taking the inward and outward history
of the first half-day into consideration,
Hepzibah began to fear that the shop
would prove ner ruin in a moral and
religious point of view, without contributing very essentially towards even her
temporal welfare.

CHAPTER IV

A DAY BEHIND THE COUNTER

TOWARDS noon, Hepzibah saw an elderly gentleman, large and portly, and of remarkably dignified demeanor, passing slowly along, on the opposite side of the white and dusty street. On coming within the shadow of the Pyncheon-elm, he stopt, and (taking off his hat, meanwhile, to wipe the perspiration from his brow) seemed to scrutinize, with especial interest, the dilapidated and rusty-visaged House of the Seven Gables. He himself, in a very different style, was as well worth looking at as the house. No better model need be sought, nor could have been found, of a very high order of respectability, which, by some indescribable magic, not merely expressed itself in his looks and gestures, but even governed the fashion of his garments, and rendered them all proper and essential to the man. Without appearing to differ, in any tangible way, from other people's clothes, there was yet a wide and rich gravity about them, that must have been a characteristic of the wearer, since it could not be defined as pertaining either to the cut or material. His gold-headed cane, too,—a serviceable staff, of dark, polished wood,—had similar traits, and had it chosen to take a walk by itself, would have been recognized anywhere as a tolerably adequate representative of its master. This character—which showed itself so strikingly in everything about him, and the effect of which we seek to convey to the reader—went no deeper than his station, habits of life, and external circumstances. One perceived him to be personage of mark, influence, and authority; and, especially, you could feel just as certain that he was opulent as if he had exhibited his bank account or as if you had seen him touching the twigs of the Pyncheon-elm, and Midaslike, transmuting them to gold.

In his youth, he had probably been considered a handsome man; at his present age, his brow was too heavy, his temples too bare, his remaining hair too gray, his eye too cold, his lips too closely compressed, to bear any relation to mere personal beauty. He would have made a good and massive portrait; better now, perhaps, than at any previous period of his life, although his look might grow positively harsh, in the process of being fixed upon the canvas. The artist would have found it desirable to study his face, and prove its capacity for varied expression; to darken it with a frown,—to kindle it up with a smile.

While the elderly gentleman stood looking at the Pyncheon-house, both the frown and the smile passed successively over his countenance. His eyes rested on the shop-window, and, putting up a pair of gold-bowed spectacles, which he held in his hand, he minutely surveyed Hepzibah's little arrangement of toys and commodities. At first it seemed not to please him,—nay, to cause him exceeding displeasure,—and yet, the very next moment, he smiled. While this latter expression was yet on his lips, he caught a glimpse of Hepzibah, who

d involuntarily bent forward to the
indow; and then the smile changed
om acrid and disagreeable to the sun-
est complacency and benevolence. He
owed, with a happy mixture of dignity
nd courteous kindliness, and pursued
s way.

"There he is!" said Hepzibah to her-
lf, gulping down a very bitter emo-
on, and, since she could not rid her-
lf of it, trying to drive it back into
er heart. "What does he think of it,
wonder? Does it please him? Ah!—
e is looking back!"

The gentleman had paused in the
reet, and turned himself half about,
ill with his eyes fixed on the shop-
indow. In fact, he wheeled wholly
ound, and commenced a step or two,
s if designing to enter the shop; but,
s it chanced, his purpose was antici-
ated by Hepzibah's first customer, the
ttle cannibal of Jim Crow, who, star-
g up at the window, was irresistibly
ttracted by an elephant of gingerbread.
Vhat a grand appetite had this small
rchin!—two Jim Crows, immediately
fter breakfast!—and now an elephant,
s a preliminary whet before dinner!
y the time this latter purchase was
ompleted, the elderly gentleman had
esumed his way, and turned the street
orner.

"Take it as you like, Cousin Jaf-
rey!" muttered the maiden lady, as
ne drew back, after cautiously thrust-
g out her head, and looking up and
own the street. "Take it as you like!
ou have seen my little shop-window!
Vell!—What have you to say?—is not
ne Pyncheon-house my own, while I'm
live?"

After this incident, Hepzibah re-
reated to the back parlor, where she

at first caught up a half-finished stocking, and began knitting at it with nervous and irregular jerks; but quickly
finding herself at odds with the stitches,
she threw it aside, and walked hurriedly
about the room. At length, she paused
before the portrait of the stern old
Puritan, her ancestor, and the founder
of the house. In one sense, this picture
had almost faded into the canvas, and
hidden itself behind the duskiness of
age; in another, she could not but fancy
that it had been growing more prominent, and strikingly expressive, ever
since her earliest familiarity with it,
as a child. For, while the physical outline and substance were darkening away
from the beholder's eye, the bold, hard,
and, at the same time, indirect character
of the man, seemed to be brought out
in a kind of spiritual relief. Such an
effect may occasionally be observed in
pictures of antique date. They acquire
a look which an artist (if he have anything like the complacency of artists
now-a-days) would never dream of presenting to a patron as his own characteristic expression, but which, nevertheless, we at once recognize as reflecting
the unlovely truth of a human soul.
In such cases, the painter's deep conception of his subject's inward traits has
wrought itself into the essence of the
picture, and is seen after the superficial
coloring has been rubbed off by time.

While gazing at the portrait, Hepzibah trembled under its eye. Her hereditary reverence made her afraid to judge
the character of the original so harshly
as a perception of the truth compelled
her to do. But still she gazed, because
the face of the picture enabled her—
at least, she fancied so—to read more
accurately, and to a greater depth, the

face which she had just seen in the street.

"This is the very man!" murmured she to herself. "Let Jaffrey Pyncheon smile as he will, there is that look beneath! Put on him a skull-cap, and a band, and a black cloak, and a Bible in one hand and a sword in the other, —then let Jaffrey smile as he might, —nobody would doubt that it was the old Pyncheon come again! He has proved himself the very man to build up a new house! Perhaps, too, to draw down a new curse!"

Thus did Hepzibah bewilder herself with these fantasies of the old time. She had dwelt too much alone, too long in the Pyncheon-house,—until her very brain was impregnated with the dry rot of its timbers. She needed a walk along the noon-day street, to keep her sane.

By the spell of contrast, another portrait rose up before her, painted with more daring flattery than any artist would have ventured upon, but yet so delicately touched that the likeness remained perfect. Malbone's miniature, though from the same original, was far inferior to Hepzibah's air-drawn picture, at which affection and sorrowful remembrance wrought together. Soft, mildly, and cheerfully contemplative, with full, red lips, just on the verge of a smile, which the eyes seemed to herald by a gentle kindling-up of their orbs! Feminine traits, moulded inseparably with those of the other sex! The miniature, likewise, had this last peculiarity; so that you inevitably thought of the original as resembling his mother, and she, a lovely and lovable woman, with perhaps some beautiful infirmity of character, that made it all the pleas-

anter to know, and easier to love her. "Yes," thought Hepzibah, with grief of which it was only the more tolerable portion that welled up from her heart to her eyelids, "they persecuted his mother in him! He never was a Pyncheon!"

But here the shop-bell rang; it was like a sound from a remote distance —so far had Hepzibah descended into the sepulchral depths of her reminiscences. On entering the shop, she found an old man there, a humble resident of Pyncheon-street, and whom, for a great many years past, she had suffered to be a kind of familiar of the house. He was an immemorial personage, who seemed always to have had a white head and wrinkles, and never to have possessed but a single tooth, and that a half-decayed one, in the front of the upper jaw. Well advanced as Hepzibah was, she could not remember when Uncle Venner, as the neighborhood called him, had not gone up and down the street, stooping a little and drawing his feet heavily over the gravel or pavement. But still there was something tough and vigorous about him, that not only kept him in daily breath, but enabled him to fill a place which would else have been vacant in the apparently crowded world. To go of errands, with his slow and shuffling gait, which made you doubt how he ever was to arrive anywhere; to saw a small household's foot or two of fire-wood, or knock to pieces an old barrel, or split up a pine board, for kindling-stuff; in summer, to dig the few yards of garden ground appertaining to a low-rented tenement, and share the produce of his labor at the halves; in winter, to shovel away the snow from the side-walk, or open paths

the wood-shed or along the clothes-
ne; such were some of the essential
ices which Uncle Venner performed
nong at least a score of families.
ithin that circle, he claimed the same
rt of privilege, and probably felt as
uch warmth of interest, as a clergyman
es in the range of his parishioners.
ot that he laid claim to the tithe pig;
at, as an analogous mode of reverence,
e went his rounds, every morning, to
ther up the crumbs of the table and
verflowings of the dinner-pot, as food
r a pig of his own.

In his younger days—for, after all,
ere was a dim tradition that he had
en, not young, but younger—Uncle
enner was commonly regarded as
ther deficient, than otherwise, in his
ts. In truth, he had virtually pleaded
uilty to the charge, by scarcely aiming
such success as other men seek, and
taking only that humble and modest
art, in the intercourse of life, which
longs to the alleged deficiency. But,
w, in his extreme old age,—whether
were that his long and hard experi-
ce had actually brightened him, or
at his decaying judgment rendered him
ss capable of fairly measuring himself,
-the venerable man made pretensions
no little wisdom, and really enjoyed
e credit of it. There was likewise, at
mes, a vein of something like poetry
him; it was the moss or wall-flower
his mind in its small dilapidation,
id gave a charm to what might have
en vulgar and common-place in his
rlier and middle life. Hepzibah had a
gard for him, because his name was
acient in the town, and had formerly
en respectable. It was a still better
ason for awarding him a species of
amiliar reverence, that Uncle Venner

was himself the most ancient existence,
whether of man or thing, in Pyncheon-
street, except the House of the Seven
Gables, and perhaps the elm that overshadowed it.

This patriarch now presented himself
before Hepzibah, clad in an old blue
coat, which had a fashionable air, and
must have accrued to him from the cast-
off wardrobe of some dashing clerk. As
for his trousers, they were of tow-cloth,
very short in the legs, and bagging down
strangely in the rear, but yet having a
suitableness to his figure which his other
garment entirely lacked. His hat had
relation to no other part of his dress,
and but very little to the head that wore
it. Thus Uncle Venner was a miscellaneous old gentleman, partly himself,
but, in good measure, somebody else;
patched together, too, of different
epochs; an epitome of times and
fashions.

"So you have really begun trade,"
said he,—"really begun trade! Well, I'm
glad to see it. Young people should
never live idle in the world, nor old
ones neither, unless when the rheuma-
tize gets hold of them. It has given me
warning already; and in two or three
years longer, I shall think of putting
aside business, and retiring to my farm.
That's yonder—the great brick house,
you know—the workhouse, most folks
call it; but I mean to do my work first,
and go there to be idle and enjoy myself. And I'm glad to see you beginning
to do your work, Miss Hepzibah!"

"Thank you, Uncle Venner," said
Hepzibah, smiling; for she always felt
kindly towards the simple and talkative
old man. Had he been an old woman,
she might probably have repelled the
freedom which she now took in good

part. "It is time for me to begin work, indeed! Or, to speak the truth, I have just begun, when I ought to be giving it up."

"O, never say that, Miss Hepzibah," answered the old man. "You are a young woman yet. Why, I hardly thought myself younger than I am now, it seems so little while ago since I used to see you playing about the door of the old house, quite a small child! Oftener, though, you used to be sitting at the threshold, and looking gravely into the street; for you had always a grave kind of way with you,—a grown-up air, when you were only the height of my knee. It seems as if I saw you now; and your grandfather with his red cloak, and his white wig, and his cocked hat, and his cane, coming out of the house, and stepping so grandly up the street! Those old gentlemen that grew up before the Revolution used to put on grand airs. In my young days, the great man of the town was commonly called King; and his wife, not Queen to be sure, but Lady. Now-a-days, a man would not dare to be called King; and if he feels himself a little above common folks, he only stoops so much the lower to them. I met your cousin, the judge, ten minutes ago; and, in my old tow-cloth trousers, as you see, the judge raised his hat to me, I do believe! At any rate, the judge bowed and smiled!"

"Yes," said Hepzibah, with something bitter stealing unawares into her tone; "my cousin Jaffrey is thought to have a very pleasant smile!"

"And so he has!" replied Uncle Venner. "And that's rather remarkable in a Pyncheon; for, begging your pardon, Miss Hepzibah, they never had the name of being an easy and agreeable set of folks. There was no getting close t them. But now, Miss Hepzibah, if a old man may be bold to ask, why don Judge Pyncheon, with his great mean step forward, and tell his cousin to shu up her little shop at once? It's for you credit to be doing something; but it' not for the judge's credit to let you!"

"We won't talk of this, if you please Uncle Venner," said Hepzibah, coldly "I ought to say, however, that if choose to earn bread for myself, it not Judge Pyncheon's fault. Neither wi he deserve the blame," added she, mor kindly, remembering Uncle Venner privileges of age and humble familiarity "if I should, by-and-by, find it con venient to retire with you to you farm."

"And it's no bad place, neither, tha farm of mine!" cried the old ma cheerily, as if there were somethin positively delightful in the prospect "No bad place is the great brick farm house, especially for them that will fin a good many old cronies there, as wi be my case. I quite long to be amon them, sometimes, of the winter evenings for it is but dull business for a lonesom elderly man, like me, to be nodding, b the hour together, with no company bu his air-tight stove. Summer or winte there's a great deal to be said in favo of my farm. And, take it in the au tumn, what can be pleasanter than t spend a whole day on the sunny sid of a barn or a wood-pile, chatting wit somebody as old as one's self; or, per haps, idling away the time with a natura born simpleton, who knows how to b idle, because even our busy Yankee never have found out how to put hir to any use? Upon my word, Miss Hepzi bah, I doubt whether I've ever been s comfortable as I mean to be at my farm, which most folks call the workhouse. But you,—you're a young woman yet,—you never need go there! Something still better will turn up for you. I'm sure of it!"

Hepzibah fancied that there was something peculiar in her venerable friend's look and tone; insomuch, that she gazed into his face with considerable earnestness, endeavoring to discover what secret meaning, if any, might be lurking there. Individuals whose affairs have reached an utterly desperate crisis almost invariably keep themselves alive with hopes, so much the more airily magnificent, as they have the less of solid matter within their grasp, whereof to mould any judicious and moderate expectation of good. Thus, all the while Hepzibah was perfecting the scheme of her little shop, she had cherished an unacknowledged idea that some harlequin trick of fortune would intervene in her favor. For example, an uncle—who had sailed for India, fifty years before, and never been heard of since—might yet return, and adopt her to be the comfort of his very extreme and decrepit age, and adorn her with pearls, diamonds, and oriental shawls and turbans, and make her the ultimate heiress of his unreckonable riches. Or the member of parliament, now at the head of the English branch of the family,—with which the elder stock, on this side of the Atlantic, had held little or no intercourse for the last two centuries,—this eminent gentleman might invite Hepzibah to quit the ruinous House of the Seven Gables, and come over to dwell with her kindred at Pyncheon Hall. But, for reasons the most imperative, she could not yield to this request. It was

more probable, therefore, that the descendants of a Pyncheon who had emigrated to Virginia, in some past generation, and become a great planter there,—hearing of Hepzibah's destitution, and impelled by the splendid generosity of character with which their Virginian mixture must have enriched the New England blood,—would send her a remittance of a thousand dollars, with a hint of repeating the favor, annually. Or—and, surely, anything so undeniably just could not be beyond the limits of reasonable anticipation—the great claim to the heritage of Waldo County might finally be decided in favor of the Pyncheons; so that, instead of keeping a cent-shop, Hepzibah would build a palace, and look down from its highest tower on hill, dale, forest, field, and town, as her own share of the ancestral territory.

These were some of the fantasies which she had long dreamed about; and, aided by these, Uncle Venner's casual attempt at encouragement kindled a strange festal glory in the poor, bare, melancholy chambers of her brain, as if that inner world were suddenly lighted up with gas. But either he knew nothing of her castles in the air—as how should he?—or else her earnest scowl disturbed his recollection, as it might a more courageous man's. Instead of pursuing any weightier topic, Uncle Venner was pleased to favor Hepzibah with some sage counsel in her shop-keeping capacity.

"Give no credit!"—these were some of his golden maxims,—"Never take paper money! Look well to your change! Ring the silver on the four-pound weight! Shove back all English half-pence and base copper tokens, such as are very plenty about town! At your leisure hours knit children's woollen socks and mittens! Brew your own yeast, and make your own ginger-beer!"

And while Hepzibah was doing her utmost to digest the hard little pellets of his already uttered wisdom, he gave vent to his final, and what he declared to be his all-important advice, as follows:—

"Put on a bright face for your customers, and smile pleasantly as you hand them what they ask for! A stale article, if you dip it in a good, warm, sunny smile, will go off better than a fresh one that you've scowled upon."

To this last apothegm poor Hepzibah responded with a sigh so deep and heavy that it almost rustled Uncle Venner quite away, like a withered leaf,—as he was,—before an autumnal gale. Recovering himself, however, he bent forward, and, with a good deal of feeling in his ancient visage, beckoned her nearer to him.

"When do you expect him home?" whispered he.

"Whom do you mean?" asked Hepzibah, turning pale.

"Ah! you don't love to talk about it," said Uncle Venner. "Well, well! we'll say no more, though there's word of it, all over town. I remember him, Miss Hepzibah, before he could run alone!"

During the remainder of the day, poor Hepzibah acquitted herself even less creditably, as a shopkeeper, than in her earlier efforts. She appeared to be walking in a dream; or, more truly, the vivid life and reality assumed by her emotions made all outward occurrences unsubstantial, like the teasing phantasms of a half-conscious slumber. She still responded, mechanically, to the frequent summons of the shop-bell, and, at the demand of her customers, went prying with vague eyes about the shop, proffering them one article after another, and, thrusting aside—perversely, as most of them supposed—the identical thing they asked for. There is sad confusion, indeed, when the spirit thus flits away into the past, or into the more awful future, or, in any manner, steps across the spaceless boundary betwixt its own region and the actual world; where the body remains to guide itself, as best it may, with little more than the mechanism of animal life. It is like death, without death's quiet privilege,—its freedom from mortal care. Worst of all, when the actual duties are comprised in such petty details as now vexed the brooding soul of the old gentlewoman. As the animosity of fate would have it, there was a great influx of custom in the course of the afternoon. Hepzibah blundered to and fro about her small place of business, committing the most unheard of errors: now stringing up twelve, and now seven tallow-candles, instead of ten to the pound; selling ginger for Scotch snuff, pins for needles, and needles for pins; misreckoning her change, sometimes to the public detriment, and much oftener to her own; and thus she went on, doing her utmost to bring chaos back again, until, at the close of the day's labor, to her inexplicable astonishment, she found the money-drawer almost destitute of coin. After all her painful traffic, the whole proceeds were perhaps half a dozen coppers, and a questionable ninepence, which ultimately proved to be copper likewise.

At this price, or at whatever price, she rejoiced that the day had reached

ts end. Never before had she had such
a sense of the intolerable length of time
that creeps between dawn and sunset,
and of the miserable irksomeness of
having aught to do, and of the better
wisdom that it would be, to lie down
at once, in sullen resignation, and let
life, and its toils and vexations, trample
over one's prostrate body, as they may!
Hepzibah's final operation was with the
little devourer of Jim Crow and the
elephant, who now proposed to eat a
camel. In her bewilderment, she offered
him first a wooden dragoon, and next a
handful of marbles; neither of which
being adapted to his else omniverous
appetite, she hastily held out her whole
remaining stock of natural history in
gingerbread, and huddled the small customer out of the shop. She then muffled
the bell in an unfinished stocking, and
put up the oaken bar across the door.

During the latter process, an omnibus
came to a standstill under the branches
of the elm-tree. Hepzibah's heart was
in her mouth. Remote and dusky, and
with no sunshine on all the intervening
space, was that region of the Past
whence her only guest might be expected
to arrive! Was she to meet him now?

Somebody, at all events, was passing
from the furthest interior of the omnibus towards its entrance. A gentleman
alighted; but it was only to offer his
hand to a young girl, whose slender
figure, nowise needing such assistance,
now lightly descended the steps, and
made an airy little jump from the final
one to the sidewalk. She rewarded her
cavalier with a smile, the cheery glow
of which was seen reflected on his own
face, as he reëntered the vehicle. The
girl then turned towards the House of
the Seven Gables; to the door of which,

meanwhile,—not the shop-door, but the
antique portal,—the omnibus-man had
carried a light trunk and a band-box.
First giving a sharp rap of the old iron
knocker, he left his passenger and her
luggage at the door-step, and departed.

"Who can it be?" thought Hepzibah,
who had been screwing her visual organs
into the acutest focus of which they
were capable. "The girl must have mistaken the house!"

She stole softly into the hall, and,
herself invisible, gazed through the dusty
side-lights of the portal at the young,
blooming, and very cheerful face, which
presented itself for admittance into the
gloomy old mansion. It was a face to
which almost any door would have
opened of its own accord.

The young girl, so fresh, so uncon-
ventional, and yet so orderly and
obedient to common rules, as you at
once recognized her to be, was widely in
contrast, at that moment, with everything about her. The sordid and ugly
luxuriance of gigantic weeds that grew
in the angle of the house, and the heavy
projection that overshadowed her, and
the time-worn frame-work of the door,
—none of these things belonged to her
sphere. But, even as a ray of sunshine,
fall into what dismal place it may, instantaneously creates for itself a propriety in being there, so did it seem
altogether fit that the girl should be
standing at the threshold. It was no less
evidently proper that the door should
swing open to admit her. The maiden
lady herself, sternly inhospitable in her
first purposes, soon began to feel that
the door ought to be shoved back, and
the rusty key be turned in the reluctant
lock.

"Can it be Phœbe?" questioned she

within herself. "It must be little Phœbe; for it can be nobody else,—and there is a look of her father about her, too! But what does she want here? And how like a country cousin, to come down upon a poor body in this way, without so much as a day's notice, or asking whether she would be welcome! Well; she must have a night's lodging, I suppose; and to-morrow the child shall go back to her mother!"

Phœbe, it must be understood, was that one little off-shoot of the Pyncheon race to whom we have already referred, as a native of a rural part of New England, where the old fashions and feelings of relationship are still partially kept up. In her own circle, it was re-garded as by no means improper fo[r] kinsfolk to visit one another, withou[t] invitation, or preliminary and ceremoni[-]ous warning. Yet, in consideration o[f] Miss Hepzibah's recluse way of life, [a] letter had actually been written an[d] despatched, conveying information o[f] Phœbe's projected visit. This epistle, fo[r] three or four days past, had been in th[e] pocket of the penny-postman, who, hap[-]pening to have no other business i[n] Pyncheon-street, had not yet made i[t] convenient to call at the House of th[e] Seven Gables.

"No!—she can stay only one night," said Hepzibah, unbolting the door. "I[f] Clifford were to find her here, it migh[t] disturb him!"

CHAPTER V

MAY AND NOVEMBER

PHŒBE PYNCHEON slept, on the night of her arrival, in a chamber that looked down on the garden of the old house. It fronted towards the east, so that at a very seasonable hour a glow of crimson light came flooding through the window, and bathed the dingy ceiling and paper-hangings in its own hue. There were curtains to Phœbe's bed; a dark, antique canopy and ponderous festoons, of a stuff which had been rich, and even magnificent, in its time; but which now brooded over the girl like a cloud, making a night in that one corner, while elsewhere it was beginning to be day. The morning light, however, soon stole into the aperture at the foot of the bed, betwixt those faded curtains. Finding the new guest there,—with a bloom on her cheeks like the morning's own, and a gentle stir of departing slumber in her limbs, as when an early breeze moves the foliage,—the dawn kissed her brow[.] It was the caress which a dewy maiden —such as the dawn is, immortally— gives to her sleeping sister, partly from the impulse of irresistible fondness, and partly as a pretty hint that it is time now to unclose her eyes.

At the touch of those lips of light, Phœbe quietly awoke, and, for a mo[-]ment, did not recognize where she was[,] nor how those heavy curtains chance[d] to be festooned around her. Nothing indeed, was absolutely plain to her, ex[-]cept that it was now early morning, an[d] hat, whatever might happen next, it was proper, first of all, to get up and say her prayers. She was the more inlined to devotion, from the grim aspect of the chamber and its furniture, especially the tall, stiff chairs; one of which stood close by her bedside, and looked as if some old-fashioned personage had been sitting there all night, and had vanished only just in season to escape discovery.

When Phœbe was quite dressed, she peeped out of the window, and saw a rose-bush in the garden. Being a very tall one, and of luxurious growth, it had been propped up against the side of the house, and was literally covered with a rare and very beautiful species of white rose. A large portion of them, as the girl afterwards discovered, had blight or mildew at their hearts; but, viewed at a fair distance, the whole rose-bush looked as if it had been brought from Eden that very summer, together with the mould in which it grew. The truth was, nevertheless, that it had been planted by Alice Pyncheon, —she was Phœbe's great-great-grandaunt,—in soil which, reckoning only its cultivation as a garden-plat, was now unctuous with nearly two hundred years of vegetable decay. Growing as they did, however, out of the old earth, the flowers still sent a fresh and sweet incense up to their Creator; nor could it have been the less pure and acceptable, because Phœbe's young breath mingled with it, as the fragrance floated past the window. Hastening down the creaking and carpetless staircase, she found her way into the garden, gathered some of the most perfect of the roses, and brought them to her chamber.

Little Phœbe was one of those persons who possess, as their exclusive patrimony, the gift of practical arrangement. It is a kind of natural magic that enables these favored ones to bring out the hidden capabilities of things around them; and particularly to give a look of comfort and habitableness to any place which, for however brief a period, may happen to be their home. A wild hut of underbrush, tossed together by wayfarers through the primitive forest, would acquire the home aspect by one night's lodging of such a woman, and would retain it long after her quiet figure had disappeared into the surrounding shade. No less a portion of such homely witchcraft was requisite, to reclaim, as it were, Phœbe's waste, cheerless, and dusky chamber, which had been untenanted so long—except by spiders, and mice, and rats, and ghosts— that it was all overgrown with the desolation which watches to obliterate every trace of man's happier hours. What was precisely Phœbe's process, we find it impossible to say. She appeared to have no preliminary design, but gave a touch here, and another there; brought some articles of furniture to light, and dragged others into the shadow; looped up or let down a window-curtain; and, in the course of half an hour, had fully succeeded in throwing a kindly and hospitable smile over the apartment. No longer ago than the night before, it had resembled nothing so much as the old maid's heart; for there was neither sunshine nor household-fire in one nor the other, and, save for ghosts and ghostly reminiscences, not a guest, for many years gone-by, had entered the heart or the chamber.

There was still another peculiarity of this inscrutable charm. The bed-cham ber, no doubt, was a chamber of very great and varied experience, as a scene of human life: the joy of bridal nights had throbbed itself away here; new immortals had first drawn earthly breath here; and here old people had died. But —whether it were the white roses, or whatever the subtle influence might be —a person of delicate instinct would have known, at once, that it was now a maiden's bed-chamber, and had been purified of all former evil and sorrow by her sweet breath and happy thoughts. Her dreams of the past night, being such cheerful ones, had exorcised the gloom, and now haunted the chamber in its stead.

After arranging matters to her satisfaction, Phœbe emerged from her chamber, with a purpose to descend again into the garden. Besides the rose-bush, she had observed several other species of flowers, growing there in a wilderness of neglect, and obstructing one another's development (as is often the parallel case in human society) by their uneducated entanglement and confusion. At the head of the stairs, however, she met Hepzibah, who, it being still early, invited her into a room which she would probably have called her boudoir, had her education embraced any such French phrase. It was strewn about with a few old books, and a work-basket, and a dusty writing-desk; and had, on one side, a large, black article of furniture, of very strange appearance, which the old gentlewoman told Phœbe was a harpsichord. It looked more like a coffin than anything else; and, indeed,— not having been played upon, or opened, for years,—there must have been a vast deal of dead music in it, stifled for want of air. Human finger was hardly

known to have touched its chords since the days of Alice Pyncheon, who had learned the sweet accomplishment of melody in Europe.

Hepzibah bade her young guest sit down, and, herself taking a chair near by, looked as earnestly at Phœbe's trim little figure as if she expected to see right into its springs and motive secrets. "Cousin Phœbe," said she, at last, "I really can't see my way clear to keep you with me."

These words, however, had not the inhospitable bluntness with which they may strike the reader; for the two relatives, in a talk before bedtime, had arrived at a certain degree of mutual understanding. Hepzibah knew enough to enable her to appreciate the circumstances (resulting from the second marriage of the girl's mother) which made it desirable for Phœbe to establish herself in another home. Nor did she misinterpret Phœbe's character, and the genial activity pervading it,—one of the most valuable traits of the true New England woman,—which had impelled her forth, as might be said, to seek her fortune, but with a self-respecting purpose to confer as much benefit as she could anywise receive. As one of her nearest kindred, she had naturally betaken herself to Hepzibah, with no idea of forcing herself on her cousin's protection, but only for a visit of a week or two, which might be indefinitely extended, should it prove for the happiness of both.

To Hepzibah's blunt observation, therefore, Phœbe replied, as frankly, and more cheerfully.

"Dear cousin, I cannot tell how it will be," said she. "But I really think we may suit one another much better than you suppose."

"You are a nice girl,—I see it plainly," continued Hepzibah; "and it is not any question as to that point which makes me hesitate. But, Phœbe, this house of mine is but a melancholy place for a young person to be in. It lets in the wind and rain, and the snow, too, in the garret and upper chambers, in winter-time; but it never lets in the sunshine! And as for myself, you see what I am,—a dismal and lonesome old woman (for I begin to call myself old, Phœbe), whose temper, I am afraid, is none of the best, and whose spirits are as bad as can be. I cannot make your life pleasant, Cousin Phœbe, neither can I so much as give you bread to eat."

"You will find me a cheerful little body," answered Phœbe, smiling, and yet with a kind and gentle dignity; "and I mean to earn my bread. You know I have not been brought up a Pyncheon. A girl learns many things in a New England village."

"Ah! Phœbe," said Hepzibah, sighing, "your knowledge would do but little for you here! And then it is a wretched thought, that you should fling away your young days in a place like this. Those cheeks would not be so rosy, after a month or two. Look at my face!"— and, indeed, the contrast was very striking,—"you see how pale I am! It is my idea that the dust and continual decay of these old houses are unwholesome for the lungs."

"There is the garden,—the flowers to be taken care of," observed Phœbe. "I should keep myself healthy with exercise in the open air."

"And, after all, child," exclaimed Hepzibah, suddenly arising, as if to dismiss the subject, "it is not for me to say who shall be a guest or inhabitant of the old Pyncheon-house. Its master is coming."

"Do you mean Judge Pyncheon?" asked Phœbe, in surprise.

"Judge Pyncheon!" answered her cousin, angrily. "He will hardly cross the threshold while I live! No, no! But, Phœbe, you shall see the face of him I speak of."

She went in quest of the miniature already described, and returned with it in her hand. Giving it to Phœbe, she watched her features narrowly, and with a certain jealousy as to the mode in which the girl would show herself affected by the picture.

"How do you like the face?" asked Hepzibah.

"It is handsome!—it is very beautiful!" said Phœbe, admiringly. "It is as sweet a face as a man's can be, or ought to be. It has something of a child's expression,—and yet not childish,—only, one feels so very kindly towards him! He ought never to suffer anything. One would bear much for the sake of sparing him toil or sorrow. Who is it, Cousin Hepzibah?"

"Did you never hear," whispered her cousin, bending towards her, "of Clifford Pyncheon?"

"Never! I thought there were no Pyncheons left, except yourself and our cousin Jaffrey," answered Phœbe. "And yet I seem to have heard the name of Clifford Pyncheon. Yes!—from my father, or my mother; but has he not been a long while dead?"

"Well, well, child, perhaps he has!" said Hepzibah, with a sad, hollow laugh; "but, in old houses like this, you know, dead people are very apt to come back again! We shall see. And, Cousin Phœbe, since, after all that I have said, your courage does not fail you, we will not part so soon. You are welcome, my child, for the present, to such a home as your kinswoman can offer you."

With this measured, but not exactly cold assurance of a hospitable purpose, Hepzibah kissed her cheek.

They now went below stairs, where Phœbe—not so much assuming the office as attracting it to herself, by the magnetism of innate fitness—took the most active part in preparing breakfast. The mistress of the house, meanwhile, as is usual with persons of her stiff and unmalleable cast, stood mostly aside; willing to lend her aid, yet conscious that her natural inaptitude would be likely to impede the business in hand. Phœbe, and the fire that boiled the teakettle, were equally bright, cheerful, and efficient, in their respective offices. Hepzibah gazed forth from her habitual sluggishness, the necessary result of long solitude, as from another sphere. She could not help being interested, however, and even amused, at the readiness with which her new inmate adapted herself to the circumstances, and brought the house, moreover, and all its rusty old appliances, into a suitableness for her purposes. Whatever she did, too, was done without conscious effort, and with frequent outbreaks of song, which were exceedingly pleasant to the ear. This natural tunefulness made Phœbe seem like a bird in a shadowy tree; or conveyed the idea that the stream of life warbled through her heart as a brook sometimes warbles through a pleasant little dell. It betokened the cheeriness of an active temperament, finding joy in its activity, and, therefore, rendering it beautiful; it

was a New England trait,—the stern old stuff of Puritanism, with a gold thread in the web.

Hepzibah brought out some old silver spoons, with the family crest upon them, and a China tea-set, painted over with grotesque figures of man, bird, and beast, in as grotesque a landscape. These pictured people were odd humorists, in a world of their own,—a world of vivid brilliancy, so far as color went, and still unfaded, although the tea-pot and small cups were as ancient as the custom itself of tea-drinking.

"Your great-great-great-great-grandmother had these cups, when she was married," said Hepzibah to Phœbe. "She was a Davenport, of a good family. They were almost the first tea-cups ever seen in the colony; and if one of them were to be broken, my heart would break with it. But it is nonsense to speak so about a brittle tea-cup, when I remember what my heart has gone through without breaking."

The cups—not having been used, perhaps, since Hepzibah's youth—had contracted no small burthen of dust, which Phœbe washed away with so much care and delicacy as to satisfy even the proprietor of this invaluable china.

"What a nice little housewife you are!" exclaimed the latter, smiling, and, at the same time, frowning so prodigiously that the smile was sunshine under a thunder-cloud. "Do you do other things as well? Are you as good at your book as you are at washing tea-cups?"

"Not quite, I am afraid," said Phœbe, laughing at the form of Hepzibah's question. "But I was school-mistress for the little children in our district, last summer, and might have been so still."

"Ah! 'tis all very well!" observed the maiden lady, drawing herself up.—"But these things must have come to you with your mother's blood. I never knew a Pyncheon that had any turn for them."

It is very queer, but not the less true, that people are generally quite as vain, or even more so, of their deficiencies, than of their available gifts; as was Hepzibah of this native inapplicability, so to speak, of the Pyncheons, to any useful purpose. She regarded it as an hereditary trait; and so, perhaps, it was, but, unfortunately, a morbid one, such as is often generated in families that remain long above the surface of society.

Before they left the breakfast-table, the shop-bell rang sharply, and Hepzibah set down the remnant of her final cup of tea, with a look of sallow despair that was truly piteous to behold. In cases of distasteful occupation, the second day is generally worse than the first; we return to the rack with all the soreness of the preceding torture in our limbs. At all events, Hepzibah had fully satisfied herself of the impossibility of ever becoming wonted to this peevishly obstreperous little bell. Ring as often as it might, the sound always smote upon her nervous system rudely and suddenly. And especially now, while, with her crested tea-spoons and antique china, she was flattering herself with ideas of gentility, she felt an unspeakable disinclination to confront a customer.

"Do not trouble yourself, dear cousin!" cried Phœbe, starting lightly up. "I am shopkeeper to-day."

"You, child!" exclaimed Hepzibah. "What can a little country-girl know of such matters?"

"O, I have done all the shopping for the family, at our village store," said Phœbe. "And I have had a table at a fancy fair, and made better sales than anybody. These things are not to be learnt; they depend upon a knack, that comes, I suppose," added she, smiling, "with one's mother's blood. You shall see that I am as nice a little saleswoman as I am a housewife!"

The old gentlewoman stole behind Phœbe, and peeped from the passageway into the shop, to note how she would manage her undertaking. It was a case of some intricacy. A very ancient woman, in a white short gown, and a green petticoat, with a string of gold beads about her neck, and what looked like a night-cap on her head, had brought a quantity of yarn to barter for the commodities of the shop. She was probably the very last person in town who still kept the time-honored spinning-wheel in constant revolution. It was worth while to hear the croaking and hollow tones of the old lady, and the pleasant voice of Phœbe, mingling in one twisted thread of talk; and still better, to contrast their figures,—so light and bloomy—so decrepit and dusky,—with only the counter betwixt them, in one sense, but more than three-score years, in another. As for the bargain, it was wrinkled slyness and craft pitted against native truth and sagacity.

"Was not that well done?" asked Phœbe, laughing, when the customer was gone.

"Nicely done, indeed, child!" answered Hepzibah. "I could not have gone through with it nearly so well. As you say, it must be a knack that belongs to you on the mother's side."

It is a very genuine admiration, that

with which persons too shy or too awkward to take a due part in the bustling world regard the real actors in life's stirring scenes; so genuine, in fact, that the former are usually fain to make it palatable to their self-love, by assuming that these active and forcible qualities are incompatible with others, which they chose to deem higher and more important. Thus, Hepzibah was well content to acknowledge Phœbe's vastly superior gifts as a shopkeeper; she listened, with compliant ear, to her suggestion of various methods whereby the influx of trade might be increased, and rendered profitable, without a hazardous outlay of capital. She consented that the village maiden should manufacture yeast, both liquid and in cakes; and should brew a certain kind of beer, nectareous to the palate, and of rare stomachic virtues; and, moreover, should bake and exhibit for sale some little spice-cakes, which whosoever tasted would longingly desire to taste again. All such proofs of a ready mind, and skilful handiwork, were highly acceptable to the aristocratic hucksteress, so long as she could murmur to herself, with a grim smile, and a half-natural sigh, and a sentiment of mixed wonder, pity, and growing affection,—

"What a nice little body she is! If she could only be a lady, too!—but that's impossible! Phœbe is no Pyncheon. She takes everything from her mother."

As to Phœbe's not being a lady, or whether she were a lady or no, it was a point, perhaps, difficult to decide, but which could hardly have come up for judgment at all, in any fair and healthy mind. Out of New England, it would be impossible to meet with a person combining so many ladylike attributes with so many others that form no necessary (if compatible) part of the character. She shocked no canon of taste; she was admirably in keeping with herself, and never jarred against surrounding circumstances. Her figure, to be sure,—so small as to be almost childlike, and so elastic that motion seemed as easy or easier to it than rest,—would hardly have suited one's idea of a countess. Neither did her face—with the brown ringlets on either side, and the slightly piquant nose, and the wholesome bloom, and the clear shade of tan, and the half a dozen freckles, friendly remembrancers of the April sun and breeze—precisely give us a right to call her beautiful. But there was both lustre and depth in her eyes. She was very pretty; as graceful as a bird, and graceful much in the same way; as pleasant about the house as a gleam of sunshine, falling on the floor through a shadow of twinkling leaves, or as a ray of firelight that dances on the wall, while evening is drawing nigh. Instead of discussing her claim to rank among ladies, it would be preferable to regard Phœbe as the example of feminine grace and availability combined, in a state of society, if there were any such, where ladies did not exist. There it should be woman's office to move in the midst of practical affairs, and to gild them all, the very homeliest, —were it even the scouring of pots and kettles,—with an atmosphere of loveliness and joy.

Such was the sphere of Phœbe. To find the born and educated lady, on the other hand, we need look no further than Hepzibah, our forlorn old maid, in her rustling and rusty silks, with her deeply-cherished and ridiculous consciousness of long descent, her shadowy claims to princely territory, and, in the way of accomplishment, her recollections, it may be, of having formerly thrummed on a harpsichord, and walked a minuet, and worked an antique tapestry-stitch on her sampler. It was a fair parallel between new Plebeianism and old Gentility.

It really seemed as if the battered visage of the House of the Seven Gables, black and heavy-browed as it still certainly looked, must have shown a kind of cheerfulness glimmering through its dusky windows, as Phœbe passed to and fro in the interior. Otherwise, it is impossible to explain how the people of the neighborhood so soon became aware of the girl's presence. There was a great run of custom, setting steadily in, from about ten o'clock until towards noon, —relaxing, somewhat, at dinner-time, but re-commencing in the afternoon, and, finally, dying away a half an hour or so before the long day's sunset. One of the staunchest patrons was little Ned Wiggins, the devourer of Jim Crow and the elephant, who to-day had signalized his omnivorous prowess by swallowing two dromedaries and a locomotive. Phœbe laughed, as she summed up her aggregate of sales, upon the slate, while Hepzibah, first drawing on a pair of silk gloves, reckoned over the sordid accumulation of copper coin, not without silver intermixed, that had jingled into the till.

"We must renew our stock, Cousin Hepzibah!" cried the little saleswoman. "The gingerbread figures are all gone, and so are those Dutch wooden milk-maids, and most of our other playthings. There has been constant inquiry for cheap raisins, and a great cry for whis-tles, and trumpets, and Jew's-harps; and at least a dozen little boys have asked for molasses-candy. And we must contrive to get a peck of russet apples, late in the season as it is. But, dear cousin, what an enormous heap of copper! Positively a copper mountain!"

"Well done! well done! well done!" quoth Uncle Venner, who had taken occasion to shuffle in and out of the shop several times, in the course of the day. "Here's a girl that will never end her days at my farm! Bless my eyes, what a brisk little soul!"

"Yes, Phœbe is a nice girl!" said Hepzibah, with a scowl of austere approbation. "But, Uncle Venner, you have known the family a great many years. Can you tell me whether there ever was a Pyncheon whom she takes after?"

"I don't believe there ever was," answered the venerable man. "At any rate, it never was my luck to see her like among them, nor, for that matter, anywhere else. I've seen a great deal of the world, not only in people's kitchens and back-yards, but at the street-corners, and on the wharves, and in other places where my business calls me; and I'm free to say, Miss Hepzibah, that I never knew a human creature do her work so much like one of God's angels as this child Phœbe does!"

Uncle Venner's eulogium, if it appear rather too high-strained for the person and occasion, had, nevertheless, a sense in which it was both subtle and true. There was a spiritual quality in Phœbe's activity. The life of the long and busy day—spent in occupations that might so easily have taken a squalid and ugly aspect—had been made pleasant, and even lovely, by the spontaneous grace with which these homely duties seemed to bloom out of her character; so that labor, while she dealt with it, had the easy and flexible charm of play. Angels do not toil, but let their good works grow out of them; and so did Phœbe.

The two relatives—the young maid and the old one—found time, before nightfall, in the intervals of trade, to make rapid advances towards affection and confidence. A recluse, like Hepzibah, usually displays remarkable frankness, and at least temporary affability, on being absolutely cornered, and brought to the point of personal intercourse; like the angel whom Jacob wrestled with, she is ready to bless you, when once overcome.

The old gentlewoman took a dreary and proud satisfaction in leading Phœbe from room to room of the house, and recounting the traditions with which, as we may say, the walls were lugubriously frescoed. She showed the indentations made by the lieutenant-governor's sword-hilt in the door-panels of the apartment where old Colonel Pyncheon, a dead host, had received his affrighted visitors with an awful frown. The dusky terror of that frown, Hepzibah observed, was thought to be lingering ever since in the passage-way. She bade Phœbe step into one of the tall chairs and inspect the ancient map of the Pyncheon territory at the eastward. In a tract of land on which she laid her finger, there existed a silver mine, the locality of which was precisely pointed out in some memoranda of Colonel Pyncheon himself, but only to be made known when the family claim should be recognized by government. Thus it was for the interest of all New England that the Pyncheons should have justice done them.

She told, too, how that there was undoubtedly an immense treasure of English guineas hidden somewhere about the house, or in the cellar, or possibly in the garden.

"If you should happen to find it, Phœbe," said Hepzibah, glancing aside at her, with a grim yet kindly smile, "we will tie up the shop-bell for good and all!"

"Yes, dear cousin," answered Phœbe; "but, in the meantime, I hear somebody ringing it!"

When the customer was gone, Hepzibah talked rather vaguely, and at great length, about a certain Alice Pyncheon, who had been exceedingly beautiful and accomplished in her lifetime, a hundred years ago. The fragrance of her rich and delightful character still lingered about the place where she had lived, as a dried rose-bud scents the drawer where it has withered and perished. This lovely Alice had met with some great and mysterious calamity, and had grown thin and white, and gradually faded out of the world. But, even now, she was supposed to haunt the House of the Seven Gables, and, a great many times,—especially when one of the Pyncheons was to die,—she had been heard playing sadly and beautifully on the harpsichord. One of these tunes, just as it had sounded from her spiritual touch, had been written down by an amateur of music; it was so exquisitely mournful that nobody, to this day, could bear to hear it played, unless when a great sorrow had made them know the still profounder sweetness of it.

"Was it the same harpsichord that you showed me?" inquired Phœbe.

"The very same," said Hepzibah. "It was Alice Pyncheon's harpsichord. When

I was learning music, my father would never let me open it. So, as I could only play on my teacher's instrument, I have forgotten all my music, long ago."

Leaving these antique themes, the old lady began to talk about the daguerreotypist, whom, as he seemed to be a well-meaning and orderly young man, and in narrow circumstances, she had permitted to take up his residence in one of the seven gables. But, on seeing more of Mr. Holgrave, she hardly knew what to make of him. He had the strangest companions imaginable: men with long beards, and dressed in linen blouses, and other such new-fangled and ill-fitting garments; reformers, temperance lecturers, and all manner of cross-looking philanthropists; community-men and come-outers, as Hepzibah believed, who acknowledged no law, and ate no solid food, but lived on the scent of other people's cookery, and turned up their noses at the fare. As for the daguerreotypist, she had read a paragraph in a penny-paper, the other day, accusing him of making a speech full of wild and disorganizing matter, at a meeting of his banditti-like associates. For her own part, she had reason to believe that he practised animal magnetism, and, if such things were in fashion now-a-days, should be apt to suspect him of studying the Black Art, up there in his lonesome chamber.

"But, dear cousin," said Phœbe, "if the young man is so dangerous, why do you let him stay? If he does nothing worse, he may set the house on fire!"

"Why, sometimes," answered Hepzibah, "I have seriously made it a question, whether I ought not to send him away. But, with all his oddities, he is a quiet kind of a person, and has such a way of taking hold of one's mind, that, without exactly liking him (for I don't know enough of the young man), I should be sorry to lose sight of him entirely. A woman clings to slight acquaintances, when she lives so much alone as I do."

"But if Mr. Holgrave is a lawless person!" remonstrated Phœbe, a part of whose essence it was to keep within the limits of law.

"O!" said Hepzibah, carelessly,—for, formal as she was, still, in her life's experience, she had gnashed her teeth against human law,—"I suppose he has a law of his own!"

CHAPTER

MAULE'S WELL

AFTER an early tea, the little country-girl strayed into the garden. The enclosure had formerly been very extensive, but was now contracted within small compass, and hemmed about, partly by high wooden fences, and partly by the out-buildings of houses that stood on another street. In its centre was a grass-plat, surrounding a ruinous little structure, which showed just enough of its original design to indicate that it had once been a summer-house. A hop-vine, springing from last year's root, was beginning to clamber over it, but would be long in covering the roof with its green mantle. Three of the seven gables either fronted or looked side-ways, with a dark solemnity of aspect, down into the garden.

The black, rich soil had fed itself with the decay of a long period of time; such as fallen leaves, the petals of flowers, and the stalks and seed-vessels of vagrant and lawless plants, more useful after their death than ever while flaunting in the sun. The evil of these departed years would naturally have sprung up again, in such rank weeds (symbolic of the transmitted vices of society) as are always prone to root themselves about human dwellings. Phœbe saw, however, that their growth must have been checked by a degree of careful labor, bestowed daily and systematically on the garden. The white double rose-bush had evidently been propped up anew against the house, since the commencement of the season; and a pear-tree and three damson-trees, which, except a row of currant-bushes, constituted the only varieties of fruit, bore marks of the recent amputation of several superfluous or defective limbs. There were also a few species of antique and hereditary flowers, in no very flourishing condition, but scrupulously weeded; as if some person, either out of love or curiosity, had been anxious to bring them to such perfection as they were capable of attaining. The remainder of the garden presented a well-selected assortment of esculent vegetables, in a praiseworthy state of advancement. Summer squashes, almost in their golden blossom; cucumbers, now evincing a tendency to spread away from the main stock, and ramble far and wide; two or three rows of string-beans, and as many more that were about to festoon themselves on poles; tomatoes, occupying a site so sheltered and sunny that the plants were already gigantic, and promised an early and abundant harvest.

Phœbe wondered whose care and toil it could have been that had planted these vegetables, and kept the soil so clean and orderly. Not, surely, her cousin Hepzibah's, who had no taste nor spirits for the lady-like employment of cultivating flowers, and—with her recluse habits, and tendency to shelter herself within the dismal shadow of the house—would hardly have come forth, under the speck of open sky, to weed and hoe among the fraternity of beans and squashes.

It being her first day of complete estrangement from rural objects, Phœbe found an unexpected charm in this little nook of grass, and foliage, and aristocratic flowers, and plebeian vegetables. The eye of Heaven seemed to look down into it pleasantly, and with a peculiar smile, as if glad to perceive that nature, elsewhere overwhelmed, and driven out of the dusty town, had here been able to retain a breathing-place. The spot acquired a somewhat wilder grace, and yet a very gentle one, from the fact that a pair of robins had built their nest in the pear-tree, and were making themselves exceedingly busy and happy in the dark intricacy of its boughs. Bees, too,—strange to say,—had thought it worth their while to come hither, possibly from the range of hives beside some farm-house, miles away. How many aerial voyages might they have made, in quest of honey, or honey-laden, betwixt dawn and sunset! Yet, late as it now was, there still arose a pleasant hum out of one or two of the squash-blossoms, in the depths of which these bees were plying their golden labor. There was one other object in the garden which nature might fairly claim as her inalienable property, in spite of whatever man could do to render it his own. This was a fountain, set round with a rim of old, mossy stones, and paved, in its bed, with what appeared to be a sort of Mosaic-work of variously colored pebbles. The play and slight agitation of the water, in its upward gush, wrought magically with these variegated pebbles, and made a continually shifting apparition of quaint figures, vanishing too suddenly to be definable. Thence, swelling over the rim of moss-grown stones, the water stole away under the fence, through what we regret to call a gutter, rather than a channel.

Nor must we forget to mention a hen-coop of very reverend antiquity that stood in the further corner of the garden, not a great way from the fountain. It now contained only Chanticleer, his two wives, and a solitary chicken. All of them were pure specimens of a breed which had been transmitted down as an heir-loom in the Pyncheon family, and were said, while in their prime, to have attained almost the size of turkeys, and, on the score of delicate flesh, to be fit for a prince's table. In proof of the authenticity of this legendary renown, Hepzibah could have exhibited the shell of a great egg, which an ostrich need hardly have been ashamed of. Be that as it might, the hens were now scarcely larger than pigeons, and had a queer, rusty, withered aspect, and a gouty kind of movement, and a sleepy and

melancholy tone throughout all the variations of their clucking and cackling. It was evident that the race had degenerated, like many a noble race besides, in consequence of too strict a watchfulness to keep it pure. These feathered people had existed too long in their distinct variety; a fact of which the present representatives, judging by their lugubrious deportment, seemed to be aware. They kept themselves alive, unquestionably, and laid now and then an egg, and hatched a chicken; not for any pleasure of their own, but that the world might not absolutely lose what had once been so admirable a breed of fowls. The distinguishing mark of the hens was a crest of lamentably scanty growth, in these latter days, but so oddly and wickedly analogous to Hepzibah's turban, that Phœbe—to the poignant distress of her conscience, but inevitably—was led to fancy a general resemblance betwixt these forlorn bipeds and her respectable relative.

The girl ran into the house to get some crumbs of bread, cold potatoes, and other such scraps as were suitable to the accommodating appetite of fowls. Returning, she gave a peculiar call, which they seemed to recognize. The chicken crept through the pales of the coop, and ran, with some show of liveliness to her feet; while Chanticleer and the ladies of his household regarded her with queer, sidelong glances, and then croaked one to another, as if communicating their sage opinions of her character. So wise, as well as antique, was their aspect, as to give color to the idea, not merely that they were the descendants of a time-honored race, but that they had existed, in their individual capacity, ever since the House of the

Seven Gables was founded, and were somehow mixed up with its destiny. They were a species of tutelary sprite, or Banshee; although winged and feathered differently from most other guardian angels.

"Here, you odd little chicken!" said Phœbe; "here are some nice crumbs for you!"

The chicken, hereupon, though almost as venerable in appearance as its mother, —possessing, indeed, the whole antiquity of its progenitors, in miniature, —mustered vivacity enough to flutter upward and alight on Phœbe's shoulder.

"That little fowl pays you a high compliment!" said a voice behind Phœbe.

Turning quickly, she was surprised at sight of a young man, who had found access into the garden by a door opening out of another gable than that whence she had emerged. He had a hoe in his hand, and, while Phœbe was gone in quest of the crumbs, had begun to busy himself with drawing up fresh earth about the roots of the tomatoes.

"The chicken really treats you like an old acquaintance," continued he, in a quiet way, while a smile made his face pleasanter than Phœbe at first fancied it. "Those venerable personages in the coop, too, seem very affably disposed. You are lucky to be in their good graces so soon! They have known me much longer, but never honor me with any familiarity, though hardly a day passes without my bringing them food. Miss Hepzibah, I suppose, will interweave the fact with her other traditions, and set it down that the fowls know you to be a Pyncheon!"

"The secret is," said Phœbe, smiling, "that I have learned how to talk with hens and chickens."

"Ah! but these hens," answered the young man,—"these hens of aristocratic lineage would scorn to understand the vulgar language of a barn-yard fowl. I prefer to think,—and so would Miss Hepzibah,—that they recognize the family tone. For you are a Pyncheon?"

"My name is Phœbe Pyncheon," said the girl, with a manner of some reserve; for she was aware that her new acquaintance could be no other than the daguerreotypist, of whose lawless propensities the old maid had given her a disagreeable idea. "I did not know that my cousin Hepzibah's garden was under another person's care."

"Yes," said Holgrave, "I dig, and hoe, and weed, in this black old earth, for the sake of refreshing myself with what little nature and simplicity may be left in it. after men have so long sown and reaped here. I turn up the earth by way of pastime. My sober occupation, so far as I have any, is with a lighter material. In short, I make pictures out of sunshine; and, not to be too much dazzled with my own trade, I have prevailed with Miss Hepzibah to let me lodge in one of these dusky gables. It is like a bandage over one's eyes, to come into it. But would you like to see a specimen of my productions?"

"A daguerreotype likeness, do you mean?" asked Phœbe, with less reserve; for, in spite of prejudice, her own youthfulness sprang forward to meet his. "I don't much like pictures of that sort— they are so hard and stern; besides dodging away from the eye, and trying to escape altogether. They are conscious of looking very unamiable, I suppose, and therefore hate to be seen."

"If you would permit me," said the artist. looking at Phœbe, "I should like to try whether the daguerreotype can bring out disagreeable traits on a perfectly amiable face. But there certainly is truth in what you have said. Most of my likenesses do look unamiable; but the very sufficient reason, I fancy, is, because the originals are so. There is a wonderful insight in Heaven's broad and simple sunshine. While we give it credit only for depicting the merest surface, it actually brings out the secret character with a truth that no painter would ever venture upon, even could he detect it. There is, at least, no flattery in my humble line of art. Now, here is a likeness which I have taken over and over again, and still with no better result. Yet the original wears, to common eyes, a very different expression. It would gratify me to have your judgment on this character."

He exhibited a daguerreotype miniature, in a morocco case. Phœbe merely glanced at it and gave it back.

"I know the face," she replied; "for its stern eye has been following me about, all day. It is my Puritan ancestor, who hangs yonder in the parlor. To be sure, you have found some way of copying the portrait without its black velvet cap and gray beard, and have given him a modern coat and satin cravat, instead of his cloak and band. I don't think him improved by your alterations."

"You would have seen other differences, had you looked a little longer," said Holgrave, laughing, yet apparently much struck. "I can assure you that this is a modern face, and one which you will very probably meet. Now, the remarkable point is, that the original wears, to the world's eye,—and, for aught I know, to his most intimate

friends,—an exceedingly pleasant countenance, indicative of benevolence, openness of heart, sunny good-humor, and other praiseworthy qualities of that cast. The sun, as you see, tells quite another story, and will not be coaxed out of it, after half a dozen patient attempts on my part. Here we have the man, sly, subtle, hard, imperious, and, withal, cold as ice. Look at that eye! Would you like to be at its mercy? At that mouth! Could it ever smile? And yet, if you could only see the benign smile of the original! It is so much the more unfortunate, as he is a public character of some eminence, and the likeness was intended to be engraved."

"Well, I don't wish to see it any more," observed Phœbe, turning away her eyes. "It is certainly very like the old portrait. But my cousin Hepzibah has another picture,—a miniature. If the original is still in the world, I think he might defy the sun to make him look stern and hard."

"You have seen that picture, then!" exclaimed the artist, with an expression of much interest. "I never did, but have a great curiosity to do so. And you judge favorably of the face?"

"There never was a sweeter one," said Phœbe. "It is almost too soft and gentle for a man's."

"Is there nothing wild in the eye?" continued Holgrave, so earnestly that it embarrassed Phœbe, as did also the quiet freedom with which he presumed on their so recent acquaintance. "Is there nothing dark or sinister, anywhere? Could you not conceive the original to have been guilty of a great crime?"

"It is nonsense," said Phœbe, a little impatiently. "for us to talk about a picture which you have never seen. You mistake it for some other. A crime, indeed! Since you are a friend of my cousin Hepzibah's, you should ask her to show you the picture."

"It will suit my purpose still better to see the original," replied the daguerreotypist, coolly. "As to his character, we need not discuss its points; they have already been settled by a competent tribunal, or one which called itself competent. But, stay? Do not go yet, if you please! I have a proposition to make you."

Phœbe was on the point of retreating, but turned back, with some hesitation; for she did not exactly comprehend his manner, although, on better observation, its feature seemed rather to be lack of ceremony than any approach to offensive rudeness. There was an odd kind of authority, too, in what he now proceeded to say, rather as if the garden were his own than a place to which he was admitted merely by Hepzibah's courtesy.

"If agreeable to you," he observed, "it would give me pleasure to turn over these flowers, and those ancient and respectable fowls, to your care. Coming fresh from country air and occupations, you will soon feel the need of some such out-of-door employment. My own sphere does not so much lie among flowers. You can trim and tend them, therefore, as you please; and I will ask only the least trifle of a blossom, now and then, in exchange for all the good, honest kitchen-vegetables with which I propose to enrich Miss Hepzibah's table. So we will be fellow-laborers, somewhat on the community system."

Silently, and rather surprised at her own compliance, Phœbe accordingly betook herself to weeding a flower-bed, but busied herself still more with cogitations respecting this young man, with whom she so unexpectedly found herself on terms approaching to familiarity. She did not altogether like him. His character perplexed the little country-girl, as it might a more practised observer; for, while the tone of his conversation had generally been playful, the impression left on her mind was that of gravity, and, except as his youth modified it, almost sternness. She rebelled, as it were, against a certain magnetic element in the artist's nature, which he exercised towards her, possibly without being conscious of it.

After a little while, the twilight, deepened by the shadows of the fruit-trees, and the surrounding buildings, threw an obscurity over the garden.

"There," said Holgrave, "it is time to give over work! That last strike of the hoe has cut off a beanstalk. Goodnight, Miss Phœbe Pyncheon! Any bright day, if you will put one of those rose-buds in your hair, and come to my rooms in Central-street, I will seize the purest ray of sunshine, and make a picture of the flower and its wearer."

He retired towards his own solitary gable, but turned his head, on reaching the door, and called to Phœbe, with a tone which certainly had laughter in it, yet which seemed to be more than half in earnest.

"Be careful not to drink at Maule's well!" said he. "Neither drink nor bathe your face in it!"

"Maule's well!" answered Phœbe. "Is that it with the rim of mossy stones? I have no thought of drinking there— but why not?"

"O," rejoined the daguerreotypist,

"because, like an old lady's cup of tea, it is water bewitched!"

He vanished; and Phœbe, lingering a moment, saw a glimmering light, and then the steady beam of a lamp, in a chamber of the gable. On returning into Hepzibah's department of the house, she found the low-studded parlor so dim and dusky that her eyes could not penetrate the interior. She was indistinctly aware, however, that the gaunt figure of the old gentlewoman was sitting in one of the straight-back chairs, a little withdrawn from the window, the faint gleam of which showed the blanched paleness of her cheek, turned sideway towards a corner.

"Shall I light a lamp, Cousin Hepzibah?" she asked.

"Do, if you please, my dear child," answered Hepzibah. "But put it on the table in the corner of the passage. My eyes are weak; and I can seldom bear the lamp-light on them."

What an instrument is the human voice! How wonderfully responsive to every emotion of the human soul! In Hepzibah's tone, at that moment, there was a certain rich depth and moisture, as if the words, common-place as they were, had been steeped in the warmth of her heart. Again, while lighting the lamp in the kitchen, Phœbe fancied that her cousin spoke to her.

"In a moment, cousin!" answered the girl. "These matches just glimmer, and go out."

But, instead of a response from Hepzibah, she seemed to hear the murmur of an unknown voice. It was strangely indistinct, however, and less like articulate words than an unshaped sound, such as would be the utterance of feeling and sympathy, rather than of the intellect. So vague was it, that its impression or echo in Phœbe's mind was that of unreality. She concluded that she must have mistaken some other sound for that of the human voice; or else that it was altogether in her fancy.

She set the lighted lamp in the passage, and again entered the parlor. Hepzibah's form, though its sable outline mingled with the dusk, was now less imperfectly visible. In the remoter parts of the room, however, its walls being so ill adapted to reflect light, there was nearly the same obscurity as before.

"Cousin," said Phœbe, "did you speak to me just now?"

"No, child!" replied Hepzibah.

Fewer words than before, but with the same mysterious music in them! Mellow, melancholy, yet not mournful, the tone seemed to gush up out of the deep well of Hepzibah's heart, all steeped in its profoundest emotion. There was a tremor in it, too, that— as all strong feeling is electric—partly communicated itself to Phœbe. The girl sat silently for a moment. But soon, her senses being very acute, she became conscious of an irregular respiration in an obscure corner of the room. Her physical organization, moreover, being at once delicate and healthy, gave her a perception, operating with almost the effect of a spiritual medium, that somebody was near at hand.

"My dear cousin," asked she, overcoming an indefinable reluctance, "is there not some one in the room with us?"

"Phœbe, my dear little girl," said Hepzibah, after a moment's pause, "you were up betimes, and have been busy all day. Pray go to bed; for I am sure you must need rest. I will sit in the parlor a while, and collect my thoughts. It has been my custom for more years, child, than you have lived!"

While thus dismissing her, the maiden lady stept forward, kissed Phœbe, and pressed her to her heart, which beat against the girl's bosom with a strong, high, and tumultuous swell. How came there to be so much love in this desolate old heart, that it could afford to well over this abundantly?

"Good-night, cousin," said Phœbe, strangely affected by Hepzibah's manner. "If you begin to love me, I am glad!"

She retired to her chamber, but did not soon fall asleep, nor then very profoundly. At some uncertain period in the depths of night, and, as it were, through the thin veil of a dream, she was conscious of a footstep mounting the stairs, heavily, but not with force and decision. The voice of Hepzibah, with a hush through it, was going up along with the footsteps; and, again, responsive to her cousin's voice, Phœbe heard that strange, vague murmur, which might be likened to an indistinct shadow of human utterance.

———

CHAPTER VII

THE GUEST

WHEN Phœbe awoke,—which she did with the early twittering of the conjugal couple of robins in the pear-tree, —she heard movements below stairs, and, hastening down, found Hepzibah already in the kitchen. She stood by a window, holding a book in close contiguity to her nose, as if with the hope of gaining an olfactory acquaintance with its contents, since her imperfect vision made it not very easy to read them. If any volume could have manifested its essential wisdom in the mode suggested, it would certainly have been the one now in Hepzibah's hand; and the kitchen, in such an event, would forthwith have steamed with the fragrance of venison, turkeys, capons, larded partridges, puddings, cakes, and Christmas-pies, in all manner of elaborate mixture and concoction. It was a cookery book, full of innumerable old fashions of English dishes, and illustrated with engravings, which represented the arrangements of the table at such banquets as it might have befitted a nobleman to give, in the great hall of his castle. And, amid these rich and potent devices of the culinary art (not one of which, probably, had been tested, within the memory of any man's grandfather), poor Hepzibah was seeking for some nimble little titbit, which, with what skill she had, and such materials as were at hand, she might toss up for breakfast.

Soon, with a deep sigh, she put aside the savory volume, and inquired of Phœbe whether old Speckle, as she called one of the hens, had laid an egg the preceding day. Phœbe ran to see, but returned without the expected treasure in her hand. At that instant, however, the blast of a fish-dealer's conch was heard, announcing his approach along the street. With energetic raps at the shop-window, Hepzibah summoned the man in, and made purchase of what he warranted as the finest mackerel in his cart, and as fat a one as ever he felt with his finger so early in the season. Requesting Phœbe to roast some coffee,—which she casually observed was the real Mocha, and so long kept that each of the small berries ought to be worth its weight in gold,—the maiden lady heaped fuel into the vast receptacle of the ancient fireplace in such quantity as soon to drive the lingering dusk out of the kitchen. The country-girl, willing to give her utmost assistance, proposed to make an Indian cake, after her mother's peculiar method, of easy manufacture, and which she could vouch for as possessing a richness, and, if rightly prepared, a delicacy, unequalled by any other mode of breakfast-cake. Hepzibah, gladly assenting, the kitchen was soon the scene of savory preparation. Perchance, amid their proper element of smoke, which eddied forth from the ill-constructed chimney, the ghosts of departed cook-maids looked wonderingly on, or peeped down the great breadth of the flue, despising the simplicity of the projected meal, yet ineffectually pining to thrust their shadowy hands into each inchoate dish. The half-starved rats, at any rate, stole visibly out of their hiding-places, and sat on their hind-legs, snuffing the funny atmosphere, and wistfully awaiting an opportunity to nibble.

Hepzibah had no natural turn for cookery, and, to say the truth, had fairly incurred her present meagreness,

by often choosing to go without her dinner, rather than be attendant on the rotation of the spit, or ebullition of the pot. Her zeal over the fire, therefore, was quite an heroic test of sentiment. It was touching, and positively worthy of tears (if Phœbe, the only spectator, except the rats and ghosts aforesaid, had not been better employed than in shedding them), to see her rake out a bed of fresh and glowing coals, and proceed to broil the mackerel. Her usually pale cheeks were all a-blaze with heat and hurry. She watched the fish with as much tender care and minuteness of attention as if,—we know not how to express it otherwise,—as if her own heart were on the gridiron, and her immortal happiness were involved in its being done precisely to a turn!

Life, within doors, has few pleasanter prospects than a neatly-arranged and well-provisioned breakfast-table. We come to it freshly, in the dewy youth of the day, and when our spiritual and sensual elements are in better accord than at a later period; so that the material delights of the morning meal are capable of being fully enjoyed, without any very grievous reproaches, whether gastric or conscientious, for yielding even a trifle over-much to the animal department of our nature. The thoughts, too, that run around the ring of familiar guests, have a piquancy and mirthfulness, and oftentimes a vivid truth, which more rarely find their way into the elaborate intercourse of dinner. Hepzibah's small and ancient table, supported on its slender and graceful legs, and covered with a cloth of the richest damask, looked worthy to be the scene and centre of one of the cheerfullest of parties. The vapor of the broiled fish arose like incense from the shrine of a barbarian idol, while the fragrance of the Mocha might have gratified the nostrils of a tutelary Lar, or whatever power has scope over a modern breakfast-table. Phœbe's Indian cakes were the sweetest offering of all,—in their hue befitting the rustic altars of the innocent and golden age,—or, so brightly yellow were they, resembling some of the bread which was changed to glistening gold, when Midas tried to eat it. The butter must not be forgotten,—butter which Phœbe herself had churned, in her own rural home, and brought it to her cousin as a propitiatory gift,— smelling of clover-blossoms, and diffusing the charm of pastoral scenery through the dark-panelled parlor. All this, with the quaint gorgeousness of the old China cups and saucers, and the crested spoons, and a silver cream-jug (Hepzibah's only other article of plate, and shaped like the rudest porringer), set out a board at which the stateliest of old Colonel Pyncheon's guests need not have scorned to take his place. But the Puritan's face scowled down out of the picture, as if nothing on the table pleased his appetite.

By way of contributing what grace she could, Phœbe gathered some roses and a few other flowers, possessing either scent or beauty, and arranged them in a glass pitcher, which, having long ago lost its handle, was so much the fitter for a flower-vase. The early sunshine—as fresh as that which peeped into Eve's bower, while she and Adam sat at breakfast there—came twinkling through the branches of the pear-tree, and fell quite across the table. All was now ready. There were chairs and plates for three. A chair and plate for Hepzibah,—the same for Phœbe,—but what other guest did her cousin look for?

Throughout this preparation, there had been a constant tremor in Hepzibah's frame; an agitation so powerful that Phœbe could see the quivering of her gaunt shadow, as thrown by the fire-light on the kitchen wall, or by the sunshine on the parlor floor. Its manifestations were so various, and agreed so little with one another, that the girl knew not what to make of it. Sometimes it seemed an ecstasy of delight and happiness. At such moments, Hepzibah would fling out her arms and enfold Phœbe in them, and kiss her cheek as tenderly as ever her mother had; she appeared to do so by an inevitable impulse, and as if her bosom were oppressed with tenderness, of which she must needs pour out a little, in order to gain breathing-room. The next moment, without any visible cause for the change, her unwonted joy shrank back, appalled as it were, and clothed itself in mourning; or it ran and hid itself, so to speak, in the dungeon of her heart, where it had long lain chained, while a cold, spectral sorrow took the place of the imprisoned joy, that was afraid to be enfranchised—a sorrow as black as that was bright. She often broke into a little, nervous, hysteric laugh, more touching than any tears could be; and forthwith, as if to try which was the most touching, a gust of tears would follow, or perhaps the laughter and tears came both at once, and surrounded our poor Hepzibah, in a moral sense, with a kind of pale, dim rainbow. Towards Phœbe, as we have said, she was affectionate, —far tenderer than ever before, in their brief acquaintance, except for that one kiss on the preceding night,—yet with a continually recurring pettishness and irritability. She would speak sharply to her; then, throwing aside all the starched reserve of her ordinary manner, ask pardon, and the next instant renew the just-forgiven injury.

At last, when their mutual labor was all finished, she took Phœbe's hand in her own trembling one.

"Bear with me, my dear child," she cried; "for truly my heart is full to the brim! Bear with me; for I love you, Phœbe, though I speak so roughly! Think nothing of it, dearest child! By-and-by, I shall be kind, and only kind!"

"My dearest cousin, cannot you tell me what has happened?" asked Phœbe, with a sunny and tearful sympathy. "What is it that moves you so?"

"Hush! hush! He is coming!" whispered Hepzibah, hastily wiping her eyes. "Let him see you first, Phœbe; for you are young and rosy, and cannot help letting a smile break out, whether or no. He always liked bright faces! And mine is old, now, and the tears are hardly dry on it. He never could abide tears. There; draw the curtain a little, so that the shadow may fall across his side of the table! But let there be a good deal of sunshine, too; for he never was fond of gloom, as some people are. He has had but little sunshine in his life,—poor Clifford,—and, oh, what a black shadow! Poor, poor Clifford!"

Thus murmuring, in an under tone, as if speaking rather to her own heart than to Phœbe, the old gentlewoman stepped on tiptoe about the room, making such arrangements as suggested themselves at the crisis.

Meanwhile, there was a step in the passage-way, above stairs. Phœbe recog-nized it as the same which had passed upward, as through her dream, in the night-time. The approaching guest, who-ever it might be, appeared to pause at the head of the staircase; he paused twice or thrice in the descent; he paused again at the foot. Each time, the delay seemed to be without purpose, but rather from a forgetfulness of the pur-pose which had set him in motion, or as if the person's feet came involun-tarily to a stand-still, because the mo-tive power was too feeble to sustain his progress. Finally, he made a long pause at the threshold of the parlor. He took hold of the knob of the door; then loosened his grasp, without open-ing it. Hepzibah, her hands convulsively clasped, stood gazing at the entrance.

"Dear Cousin Hepzibah, pray don't look so!" said Phœbe, trembling; for her cousin's emotion, and this mysteri-ously reluctant stop, made her feel as if a ghost were coming into the room. "You really frighten me! Is something awful going to happen?"

"Hush!" whispered Hepzibah. "Be cheerful! whatever may happen, be nothing but cheerful!"

The final pause at the threshold proved so long, that Hepzibah, unable to endure the suspense, rushed forward, threw open the door, and led in the stranger by the hand. At the first glance, Phœbe saw an elderly personage, in an old-fashioned dressing-gown of faded damask, and wearing his gray, or almost white hair, of an unusual length. It quite overshadowed his forehead, except when he thrust it back, and stared vaguely about the room. After a very brief in-spection of his face, it was easy to conceive that his footstep must neces-sarily be such an one as that which, slowly, and with as indefinite an aim as a child's first journey across a floor, had just brought him hitherward. Yet there were no tokens that his physical strength might not have sufficed for a free and determined gait. It was the spirit of the man that could not walk. The expression of his countenance—while, not withstanding, it had the light of reason in it—seemed to waver, and glimmer, and nearly to die away, and feebly to recover itself again. It was like a flame which we see twinkling among half-extinguished embers; we gaze at it more intently than if it were a positive blaze, gushing vividly upward,—more intently, but with a certain impatience, as if it ought either to kindle itself into satisfactory splendor, or be at once extinguished.

For an instant after entering the room, the guest stood still, retaining Hepzibah's hand, instinctively, as a child does that of the grown person who guides it. He saw Phœbe, however, and caught an illumination from her youthful and pleasant aspect, which, indeed, threw a cheerfulness about the parlor, like the circle of reflected brilliancy around the glass vase of flowers that was standing in the sunshine. He made a salutation, or, to speak nearer the truth, an ill-defined, abortive attempt at courtesy. Imperfect as it was, however, it conveyed an idea, or, at least, gave a hint, of indescribable grace, such as no practiced art of external manners could have attained. It was too slight to seize upon, at the instant; yet, as recollected afterwards, seemed to transfigure the whole man.

"Dear Clifford," said Hepzibah, in the 'one with which one soothes a wayward infant, "this is our cousin Phœbe,—little Phœbe Pyncheon,—Arthur's only child, you know. She has come from the country to stay with us a while; for our old house has grown to be very lonely now."

"Phœbe? — Phœbe Pyncheon? — Phœbe?" repeated the guest, with a strange, sluggish, ill-defined utterance. "Arthur's child! Ah, I forget! No matter! She is very welcome!"

"Come, dear Clifford, take this chair, said Hepzibah, leading him to his place. "Pray, Phœbe, lower the curtain a very little more. Now let us begin breakfast."

The guest seated himself in the place assigned him, and looked strangely around. He was evidently trying to grapple with the present scene, and bring it home to his mind with a more satisfactory distinctness. He desired to be certain, at least, that he was here, in the low-studded, cross-beamed, oaken-panelled parlor, and not in some other spot, which had stereotyped itself into his senses. But the effort was too great to be sustained with more than a fragmentary success. Continually, as we may express it, he faded away out of his place; or, in other words, his mind and consciousness took their departure, leaving his wasted, gray, and melancholy figure,—a substantial emptiness, a material ghost,—to occupy his seat at table. Again, after a blank moment, there would be a flickering, taper-gleam in his eye-balls. It betokened that his spiritual part had returned, and was doing its best to kindle the heart's household fire, and light up intellectual lamps in the dark and ruinous mansion, where it was doomed to be a forlorn inhabitant.

At one of these moments, of less torpid, yet still imperfect animation,

Phœbe became convinced of what she had at first rejected as too extravagant and startling an idea. She saw that the person before her must have been the original of the beautiful miniature in her cousin Hepzibah's possession. Indeed, with a feminine eye for costume, she had at once identified the damask dressing-gown, which enveloped him, as the same in figure, material, and fashion, with that so elaborately represented in the picture. This old, faded garment, with all its pristine brilliancy extinct, seemed, in some indescribable way, to translate the wearer's untold misfortune, and make it perceptible to the beholder's eye. It was the better to be discerned, by the exterior type, how worn and old were the soul's more immediate garments; that form and countenance, the beauty and grace of which had almost transcended the skill of the most exquisite of artists. It could the more adequately be known that the soul of the man must have suffered some miserable wrong, from its earthly experience. There he seemed to sit, with a dim veil of decay and ruin betwixt him and the world, but through which, at flitting intervals, might be caught the same expression, so refined, so softly imaginative, which Malbone—venturing a happy touch, with suspended breath—had imparted to the miniature! There had been something so innately characteristic in this look, that all the dusky years, and the burthen of unfit calamity which had fallen upon him, did not suffice utterly to destroy it.

Hepzibah had now poured out a cup of deliciously fragrant coffee, and presented it to her guest. As his eyes met hers, he seemed bewildered and disquieted.

"Is this you, Hepzibah?" he murmured, sadly; then, more apart, and perhaps unconscious that he was overheard, "How changed! how changed! And is she angry with me? Why does she bend her brow so?"

Poor Hepzibah! It was that wretched scowl, which time, and her near-sightedness, and the fret of inward discomfort, had rendered so habitual that any vehemence of mood invariably evoked it. But, at the indistinct manner of his words, her whole face grew tender, and even lovely, with sorrowful affection;— the harshness of her features disappeared, as it were, behind the warm and misty glow.

"Angry!" she repeated; "angry with you, Clifford!"

Her tone, as she uttered the exclamation, had a plaintive and really exquisite melody thrilling through it, yet without subduing a certain something which an obtuse auditor might still have mistaken for asperity. It was as if some transcendent musician should draw a soul-thrilling sweetness out of a cracked instrument, which makes its physical imperfection heard in the midst of ethereal harmony—so deep was the sensibility that found an organ in Hepzibah's voice!

"There is nothing but love, here, Clifford," she added,—"nothing but love! You are at home!"

The guest responded to her tone by a smile, which did not half light up his face. Feeble as it was, however, and gone in a moment, it had a charm of wonderful beauty. It was followed by a coarser expression; or one that had the effect of coarseness on the fine mould and outline of his countenance, because there was nothing intellectual to temper it. It was a look of appetite. He ate food with what might almost be termed voracity; and seemed to forget himself, Hepzibah, the young girl, and everything else around him, in the sensual enjoyment which the bountifully spread table afforded. In his natural system, though high-wrought and delicately refined, a sensibility to the delights of the palate was probably inherent. It would have been kept in check, however, and even converted into an accomplishment, and one of the thousand modes of intellectual culture, had his more ethereal characteristics retained their vigor. But, as it existed now, the effect was painful, and made Phœbe droop her eyes.

In a little while the guest became sensible of the fragrance of the yet untasted coffee. He quaffed it eagerly. The subtle essence acted on him like a charmed draught, and caused the opaque substance of his animal being to grow transparent, or, at least, translucent; so that a spiritual gleam was transmitted through it, with a clearer lustre than hitherto.

"More, more!" he cried, with nervous haste in his utterance, as if anxious to retain his grasp of what sought to escape him. "This is what I need! Give me more!"

Under this delicate and powerful influence, he sat more erect, and looked out from his eyes with a glance that took note of what it rested on. It was not so much that his expression grew more intellectual; this, though it had its share, was not the most peculiar effect. Neither was what we call the moral nature so forcibly awakened as to present itself in remarkable prominence. But a certain fine temper of

being was now,—not brought out in full relief, but changeably and imperfectly betrayed,—of which it was the function to deal with all beautiful and enjoyable things. In a character where it should exist as the chief attribute, it would bestow on its possessor an exquisite taste, and an enviable susceptibility of happiness. Beauty would be his life; his aspirations would all tend toward it; and, allowing his frame and physical organs to be in consonance, his own developments would likewise be beautiful. Such a man should have nothing to do with sorrow; nothing with strife; nothing with the martyrdom which, in an infinite variety of shapes, awaits those who have the heart, and will, and conscience, to fight a battle with the world. To these heroic tempers, such martyrdom is the richest meed in the world's gift. To the individual before us, it could only be a grief, intense in due proportion with the severity of the infliction. He had no right to be a martyr; and, beholding him so fit to be happy, and so feeble for all other purposes, a generous, strong, and noble spirit would, methinks, have been ready to sacrifice what little enjoyment it might have planned for itself,—it would have flung down the hopes, so paltry in its regard, —if thereby the wintry blasts of our rude sphere might come tempered to such a man.

Not to speak it harshly or scornfully, it seemed Clifford's nature to be a Sybarite. It was perceptible, even there, in the dark old parlor, in the inevitable polarity with which his eyes were attracted towards the quivering play of sunbeams through the shadowy foliage. It was seen in his appreciating notice of the vase of flowers, the scent of which he inhaled with a zest almost peculiar to a physical organization so refined that spiritual ingredients are moulded in with it. It was betrayed in the unconscious smile with which he regarded Phœbe, whose fresh and maidenly figure was both sunshine and flowers,—their essence, in a prettier and more agreeable mode of manifestation. Not less evident was this love and necessity for the Beautiful, in the instinctive caution with which, even so soon, his eyes turned away from his hostess, and wandered to any quarter rather than come back. It was Hepzibah's misfortune,—not Clifford's fault. How could he,—so yellow as she was, so wrinkled, so sad of mien, with that odd uncouthness of a turban on her head, and that most perverse of scowls contorting her brow,—how could he love to gaze at her? But, did he owe her no affection for so much as she had silently given? He owed her nothing. A nature like Clifford's can contract no debts of that kind. It is,—we say it without censure, nor in diminution of the claim which it indefeasibly possesses on beings of another mould,—it is always selfish in its essence; and we must give it leave to be so, and heap up our heroic and disinterested love upon it so much the more, without a recompense. Poor Hepzibah knew his truth, or, at least, acted on the instinct of it. So long estranged from what was lovely, as Clifford had been, she rejoiced,—rejoiced, though with a present sigh, and a secret purpose to shed tears in her own chamber,—that he had brighter objects now before his eyes than her aged and uncomely features. They never possessed a charm; and if

they had, the canker of her grief for him would long since have destroyed it.

The guest leaned back in his chair. Mingled in his countenance with a dreamy delight, there was a troubled look of effort and unrest. He was seeking to make himself more fully sensible of the scene around him; or, perhaps, dreading it to be a dream, or a play of imagination, was vexing the fair moment with a struggle for some added brilliancy and more durable illusion.

"How pleasant!—How delightful!" he murmured, but not as if addressing any one. "Will it last? How balmy the atmosphere, through that open window! An open window! How beautiful that play of sunshine! Those flowers, how very fragrant! That young girl's face, how cheerful, how blooming!—a flower with the dew on it, and sunbeams in the dewdrops! Ah! this must be all a dream! A dream! A dream! But it has quite hidden the four stone walls!"

Then his face darkened, as if the shadow of a cavern or a dungeon had come over it; there was no more light in its expression than might have come through the iron grates of a prison window,—still lessening, too, as if he were sinking further into the depths. Phœbe (being of that quickness and activity of temperament that she seldom long refrained from taking a part, and generally a good one, in what was going forward) now felt herself moved to address the stranger.

"Here is a new kind of rose, which I found this morning, in the garden," said she, choosing a small crimson one from among the flowers in the vase. "There will be but five or six on the bush, this season. This is the most perfect of them all; not a speck of blight or mildew in it. And how sweet it is! —sweet like no other rose! One can never forget that scent!"

"Ah!—let me see!—let me hold it!" cried the guest, eagerly seizing the flower. which, by the spell peculiar to remembered odors, brought innumerable associations along with the fragrance that it exhaled. "Thank you! This has gone me good. I remember how I used to prize this flower—long ago, I suppose, very long ago!—or was it only yesterday? It makes me feel young again! Am I young? Either this remembrance is singularly distinct, or this consciousness strangely dim! But how kind of the fair young girl! Thank you! Thank you!"

The favorable excitement derived from this little crimson rose afforded Clifford the brightest moment which he enjoyed at the breakfast-table. It might have lasted longer, but that his eyes happened, soon afterwards, to rest on the face of the old Puritan, who, out of his dingy frame and lustreless canvas, was looking down on the scene like a ghost, and a most ill-tempered and ungenial one. The guest made an impatient gesture of the hand, and addressed Hepzibah with what might easily be recognized as the licensed irritability of a petted member of the family.

"Hepzibah!—Hepzibah!" cried he, with no little force and distinctness, —"why do you keep that odious picture on the wall? Yes, yes!—that is precisely your taste! I have told you, a thousand times, that it was the evil genius of the house!—my evil genius particularly! Take it down, at once!"

"Dear Clifford," said Hepzibah, sadly, "you know it cannot be!"

"Then, at all events," continued he, still speaking with some energy, "pray cover it with a crimson curtain, broad enough to hang in folds, and with a golden border and tassels. I cannot bear it! It must not stare me in the face!"

"Yes, dear Clifford, the picture shall be covered," said Hepzibah, soothingly "There is a crimson curtain in a trunk above stairs,—a little faded and moth eaten, I'm afraid,—but Phœbe and I will do wonders with it."

"This very day, remember!" said he and then added, in a low, self-communing voice,—"Why should we live in this dismal house at all? Why not go to the south of France?—to Italy?—Paris Naples, Venice, Rome? Hepzibah will say, we have not the means. A droll idea, that!"

He smiled to himself, and threw a glance of fine sarcastic meaning toward Hepzibah.

But the several moods of feeling faintly as they were marked, through which he had passed, occurring in so brief an interval of time, had evidently wearied the stranger. He was probably accustomed to a sad monotony of life not so much flowing in a stream, however sluggish, as stagnating in a poo around his feet. A slumberous veil diffused itself over his countenance, and had an effect, morally speaking, on it naturally delicate and elegant outline like that which a brooding mist, with no sunshine in it, throws over the features of a landscape. He appeared to become grosser,—almost cloddish. If aught of interest or beauty—even ruined beauty—had heretofore been visible in this man, the beholder might now begin to doubt it, and to accuse his own imagination of deluding him with whateve grace had flickered over that visage, and whatever exquisite lustre had gleamed in those filmy eyes.

Before he had quite sunken away, however, the sharp and peevish tinkle of the shop-bell made itself audible. Striking most disagreeably on Clifford's auditory organs and the characteristic sensibility of his nerves, it caused him to start upright out of his chair.

"Good Heavens, Hepzibah! what horrible disturbance have we now in the house?" cried he, wreaking his resentful impatience—as a matter of course, and a custom of old—on the one person in the world that loved him. "I have never heard such a hateful clamor! Why do you permit it? In the name of all dissonance, what can it be?"

It was, very remarkable into what prominent relief—even as if a dim picture should leap suddenly from its canvas—Clifford's character was thrown, by this apparently trifling annoyance. The secret was, that an individual of his temper can always be pricked more acutely through his sense of the beautiful and harmonious than through his heart. It is even possible—for similar cases have often happened—that if Clifford, in his foregoing life, had enjoyed the means of cultivating his taste to its utmost perfectability, that subtle attribute might, before this period, have completely eaten out or filed away his affections. Shall we venture to pronounce, therefore, that his long and black calamity may not have had a redeeming drop of mercy at the bottom?

"Dear Clifford, I wish I could keep the sound from your ears," said Hepzibah, patiently, but reddening with a painful suffusion of shame. "It is very disagreeable even to me. But, do you know, Clifford, I have something to tell you? This ugly noise,—pray run, Phœbe, and see who is there!—this naughty little tinkle is nothing but our shop-bell!"

"Shop-bell!" repeated Clifford, with a bewildered stare.

"Yes, our shop-bell," said Hepzibah, a certain natural dignity, mingled with deep emotion, now asserting itself in her manner. "For you must know, dearest Clifford, that we are very poor. And there was no other resource, but either to accept assistance from a hand that I would push aside (and so would you!) were it to offer bread when we were dying for it,—no help, save from him, or else to earn our subsistence with my own hands! Alone, I might have been content to starve. But you were to be given back to me! Do you think, then, dear Clifford," added she, with a wretched smile, "that I have brought an irretrievable disgrace on the old house, by opening a little shop in the front gable? Our great-great-grandfather did the same, when there was far less need! Are you ashamed of me?"

"Shame! Disgrace! Do you speak these words to me, Hepzibah?" said Clifford,—not angrily, however; for when a man's spirit has been thoroughly crushed, he may be peevish at small offences, but never resentful of great ones. So he spoke with only a grieved emotion. "It was not kind to say so, Hepzibah! What shame can befall me now?"

And then the unnerved man—he that had been born for enjoyment, but had met a doom so very wretched—burst into a woman's passion of tears. It was but of brief continuance, however; soon leaving him in a quiescent, and, to judge by his countenance, not an uncomfortable state. From this mood, too, he partially rallied, for an instant, and looked at Hepzibah with a smile, the keen, half-derisory purport of which was a puzzle to her.

"Are we so very poor, Hepzibah?" said he.

Finally, his chair being deep and softly cushioned, Clifford fell asleep. Hearing the more regular rise and fall of his breath—(which, however, even then, instead of being strong and full, had a feeble kind of tremor, corresponding with the lack of vigor in his character)—hearing these tokens of settled slumber, Hepzibah seized the opportunity to peruse his face more attentively than she had yet dared to do. Her heart melted away in tears; her profoundest spirit sent forth a moaning voice, low, gentle, but inexpressibly sad. In this depth of grief and pity, she felt that there was no irreverence in gazing at his altered, aged, faded, ruined face. But no sooner was she a little relieved than her conscience smote her for gazing curiously at him, now that he was so changed; and, turning hastily away, Hepzibah let down the curtain over the sunny window, and left Clifford to slumber there.

CHAPTER VIII

THE PYNCHEON OF TO-DAY

PHŒBE, on entering the shop, beheld there the already familiar face of the little devourer—if we can reckon his mighty deeds aright—of Jim Crow, the elephant, the camel, the dromedaries, and the locomotive. Having expended his private fortune, on the two preceding days, in the purchase of the above unheard-of luxuries, the young gentleman's present errand was on the part of his mother, in quest of three eggs and half a pound of raisins. These articles Phœbe accordingly supplied, and, as a mark of gratitude for his previous patronage, and a slight super-added morsel after breakfast, put likewise into his hands a whale! The great fish, reversing his experience with the prophet of Nineveh, immediately began his progress down the same red pathway of fate, whither so varied a caravan had preceded him. This remarkable urchin, in truth, was the very emblem of old Father Time, both in respect of his all devouring appetite for men and things, and because he, as well as Time, after engulfing thus much of creation, looked almost as youthful as if he had been just that moment made.

After partly closing the door, the child turned back, and mumbled something to Phœbe, which, as the whale was but half disposed of, she could not perfectly understand.

"What did you say, my little fellow?" asked she.

"Mother wants to know," repeated Ned Higgins, more distinctly, "how Old Maid Pyncheon's brother does? Folks say he has got home."

"My cousin Hepzibah's brother!" exclaimed Phœbe, surprised at this sudden explanation of the relationship between Hepzibah and her guest. "Her brother! And where can he have been?"

The little boy only put his thumb to his broad snub-nose, with that look of shrewdness which a child, spending much of his time in the street, so soon learns to throw over his features, however unintelligent in themselves. Then, as Phœbe continued to gaze at him, without answering his mother's message, he took his departure.

As the child went down the steps, a gentleman ascended them, and made his entrance into the shop. It was the portly, and, had it possessed the advantage of a little more height, would have been the stately figure of a man considerably in the decline of life, dressed in a black suit of some thin stuff, resembling broadcloth as closely as possible. A gold-headed cane, of rare oriental wood, added materially to the high respectability of his aspect, as did also a white neckcloth of the utmost snowy purity, and the conscientious polish of his boots. His dark, square countenance, with its almost shaggy depth of eyebrows, was naturally impressive, and would, perhaps, have been rather stern, had not the gentleman considerately taken upon himself to mitigate the harsh effect by a look of exceeding good-humor and benevolence. Owing, however, to a somewhat massive accumulation of animal substance about the lower region of his face, the look was, perhaps, unctuous, rather than spiritual, and had, so to speak, a kind of fleshly effulgence, not altogether so satisfactory as he doubtless intended it to be. A susceptible observer, at any rate, might

have regarded it as affording very little evidence of the genuine benignity of soul whereof it purported to be the outward reflection. And if the observer chanced to be ill-natured, as well as acute and susceptible, he would probably suspect that the smile on the gentleman's face was a good deal akin to the shine on his boots, and that each must have cost him and his boot-black, respectively, a good deal of hard labor to bring out and preserve them.

As the stranger entered the little shop, where the projection of the second story and the thick foliage of the elm-tree, as well as the commodities at the window, created a sort of gray medium, his smile grew as intense as if he had set his heart on counteracting the whole gloom of the atmosphere (besides any moral gloom pertaining to Hepzibah and her inmates) by the unassisted light of his countenance. On perceiving a young rose-bud of a girl, instead of the gaunt presence of the old maid, a look of surprise was manifest. He at first knit his brows; then smiled with more unctuous benignity than ever.

"Ah, I see how it is!" said he, in a deep voice,—a voice which, had it come from the throat of an uncultivated man, would have been gruff, but, by dint of careful training, was now sufficiently agreeable,—"I was not aware that Miss Hepzibah Pyncheon had commenced business under such favorable auspices. You are her assistant, I suppose?"

"I certainly am," answered Phœbe, and added, with a little air of ladylike assumption (for, civil as the gentleman was, he evidently took her to be a young person serving for wages), "I am a cousin of Miss Hepzibah, on a visit to her."

"Her cousin?—and from the country? Pray pardon me, then," said the gentleman, bowing and smiling, as Phœbe never had been bowed to nor smiled on before; "in that case, we must be better acquainted; for, unless I am sadly mistaken, you are my own little kinswoman likewise! Let me see,—Mary?—Dolly?—Phœbe? yes, Phœbe is the name! Is it possible that you are Phœbe Pyncheon, only child of my dear cousin and classmate, Arthur? Ah, I see your father now, about your mouth! Yes, yes! we must be better acquainted! I am your kinsman, my dear. Surely you must have heard of Judge Pyncheon?"

As Phœbe courtesied in reply, the judge bent forward, with the pardonable and even praiseworthy purpose—considering the nearness of blood, and the difference of age—of bestowing on his young relative a kiss of acknowledged kindred and natural affection. Unfortunately (without design, or only with such instinctive design as gives no account of itself to the intellect), Phœbe, just at the critical moment, drew back; so that her highly respectable kinsman, with his body bent over the counter, and his lips protruded, was betrayed into the rather absurd predicament of kissing the empty air. It was a modern parallel to the case of Ixion embracing a cloud, and was so much the more ridiculous, as the judge prided himself on eschewing all airy matter, and never mistaking a shadow for a substance. The truth was,—and it is Phœbe's only excuse,—that, although Judge Pyncheon's glowing benignity might not be absolutely unpleasant to the feminine beholder, with the width of a street,

or even an ordinary-sized room, interposed between, yet it became quite too intense, when this dark, full-fed physiognomy (so roughly bearded, too, that no razor could ever make it smooth) sought to bring itself into actual contact with the object of its regards. The man, the sex, somehow or other, was entirely too prominent in the judge's demonstrations of that sort. Phœbe's eyes sank, and, without knowing why, she felt herself blushing deeply under his look. Yet she had been kissed before, and without any particular squeamishness, by perhaps half a dozen different cousins, younger, as well as older, than this dark-browed, grisly-bearded, white-neckclothed, and unctuously-benevolent judge! Then, why not by him?

On raising her eyes, Phœbe was startled by the change in Judge Pyncheon's face. It was quite as striking, allowing for the difference of scale, as that betwixt a landscape under a broad sunshine and just before a thunderstorm; not that it had the passionate intensity of the latter aspect, but was cold, hard, immitigable, like a day-long brooding cloud.

"Dear me! what is to be done now?" thought the country-girl to herself. "He looks as if there were nothing softer in him than a rock, nor milder than the east wind! I meant no harm! Since he is really my cousin, I would have let him kiss me, if I could!"

Then, all at once, it struck Phœbe that this very Judge Pyncheon was the original of the miniature which the daguerreotypist had shown her in the garden, and that the hard, stern, relentless look, now on his face, was the same that the sun had so inflexibly persisted in bringing out. Was it, therefore, no momentary mood, but, however skilfully concealed, the settled temper of his life? And not merely so, but was it hereditary in him, and transmitted down, as a precious heirloom, from that bearded ancestor, in whose picture both the expression, and, to a singular degree, the features, of the modern judge were shown as by a kind of prophecy. A deeper philosopher than Phœbe might have found something very terrible in this idea. It implied that the weaknesses and defects, the bad passions, the mean tendencies, and the moral diseases, which lead to crime, are handed down from one generation to another, by a far surer process of transmission than human law has been able to establish, in respect to the riches and honors which it seeks to entail upon posterity.

But, as it happened, scarcely had Phœbe's eyes rested again on the judge's countenance, than all its ugly sternness vanished; and she found herself quite overpowered by the sultry, dog-day heat, as it were, of benevolence, which this excellent man diffused out of his great heart into the surrounding atmosphere;—very much like a serpent, which, as a preliminary to fascination, is said to fill the air with his peculiar odor.

"I like that, Cousin Phœbe!" cried he, with an emphatic nod of approbation. "I like it much, my little cousin! You are a good child, and know how to take care of yourself. A young girl —especially if she be a very pretty one —can never be too chary of her lips."

"Indeed, sir," said Phœbe, trying to laugh the matter off, "I did not mean to be unkind."

Nevertheless, whether or no it were entirely owing to the inauspicious commencement of their acquaintance, she still acted under a certain reserve, which was by no means customary to her frank and genial nature. The fantasy would not quit her, that the original Puritan, of whom she had heard so many sombre traditions,—the progenitor of the whole race of New England Pyncheons, the founder of the House of the Seven Gables, and who had died so strangely in it,—had now stept into the shop. In these days of off-hand equipment, the matter was easily enough arranged. On his arrival from the other world, he had merely found it necessary to spend a quarter of an hour at a barber's, who had trimmed down the Puritan's full beard into a pair of grizzled whiskers; then, patronizing a ready-made clothing establishment, he had exchanged his velvet doublet and sable cloak, with the richly-worked band under his chin, for a white collar and cravat, coat, vest, and pantaloons; and lastly, putting aside his steel-hilted broadsword to take up a gold-headed cane, the Colonel Pyncheon, of two centuries ago, steps forward as the judge, of the passing moment!

Of course, Phœbe was far too sensible a girl to entertain this idea in any other way than as a matter for a smile. Possibly, also, could the two personages have stood together before her eye, many points of difference would have been perceptible, and perhaps only a general resemblance. The long lapse of intervening years, in a climate so unlike that which had fostered the ancestral Englishman, must inevitably have wrought important changes in the physical system of his descendant. The judge's volume of muscle could hardly be the same as the colonel's; there was undoubtedly less beef in him. Though looked upon as a weighty man among his contemporaries, in respect of animal substance, and as favored with a remarkable degree of fundamental development, well adapting him for the judicial bench, we conceive that the modern Judge Pyncheon, if weighed in the same balance with his ancestor, would have required at least an old-fashioned fifty-six to keep the scale in equilibrio. Then the judge's face had lost the ruddy English hue, that showed its warmth through all the duskiness of the colonel's weather-beaten cheek, and had taken a sallow shade, the established complexion of his countrymen. If we mistake not, moreover, a certain quality of nervousness had become more or less manifest, even in so solid a specimen of Puritan descent as the gentleman now under discussion. As one of its effects, it bestowed on his countenance a quicker mobility than the old Englishman's had possessed, and keener vivacity, but at the expense of a sturdier something, on which these acute endowments seemed to act like dissolving acids. This process, for aught we know, may belong to the great system of human progress, which, with every ascending footstep, as it diminishes the necessity for animal force, may be destined gradually to spiritualize us, by refining away our grosser attributes of body. If so, Judge Pyncheon could endure a century or two more of such refinement, as well as most other men.

The similarity, intellectual and moral, between the judge and his ancestor, appears to have been at least as strong as the resemblance of mien and feature would afford reason to anticipate. In old Colonel Pyncheon's funeral discourse, the clergyman absolutely canonized his deceased parishioner, and opening, as it were, a vista through the roof of the church, and thence through the firmament above, showed him seated, harp in hand, among the crowned choristers of the spiritual world. On his tombstone, too, the record is highly eulogistic; nor does history, so far as he holds a place upon its page, assail the consistency and uprightness of his character. So also, as regards the Judge Pyncheon of to-day, neither clergyman, nor legal critic, nor inscriber of tomb-stones, nor historian of general or local politics, would venture a word against this eminent person's sincerity as a Christian, or respectability as a man, or integrity as a judge, or courage and faithfulness as the often-tried representative of his political party. But, besides these cold, formal, and empty words of the chisel that inscribes, the voice that speaks, and the pen that writes, for the public eye and for distant time,—and which inevitably lose much of their truth and freedom by the fatal consciousness of so doing,—there were traditions about the ancestor, and private diurnal gossip about the judge, remarkably accordant in their testimony. It is often instructive to take the woman's, the private and domestic view of a public man; nor can anything be more curious than the vast discrepancy between portraits intended for engraving, and the pencil-sketches that pass from hand to hand, behind the original's back.

For example, tradition affirmed that the Puritan had been greedy of wealth; the judge, too, with all the show of liberal expenditure, was said to be as close-fisted as if his gripe were of iron.

The ancestor had clothed himself in a grim assumption of kindliness, a rough heartiness of word and manner, which most people took to be the genuine warmth of nature, making its way through the thick and inflexible hide of a manly character. His descendant, in compliance with the requirements of a nicer age, had etherealized this rude benevolence into that broad benignity of smile, wherewith he shone like a noonday sun along the streets, or glowed like a household fire in the drawingrooms of his private acquaintance. The Puritan—if not belied by some singular stories, murmured, even at this day, under the narrator's breath—had fallen into certain transgressions to which men of his great animal development, whatever their faith or principles, must continue liable, until they put off impurity, along with the gross earthly substance that involves it. We must not stain our page with any contemporary scandal to a similar purport, that may have been whispered against the judge. The Puritan, again, an autocrat in his own household, had worn out three wives, and, merely by the remorseless weight and hardness of his character in the conjugal relation, had sent them, one after another, broken-hearted, to their graves. Here, the parallel, in some sort, fails. The judge had wedded but a single wife, and lost her in the third or fourth year of their marriage. There was a fable, however,—for such we choose to consider it, though, not impossibly, typical of Judge Pyncheon's marital deportment,—that the lady got her death-blow in the honey-moon, and never smiled again, because her husband compelled her to serve him with coffee, every morning, at his bedside, in token

of fealty to her liege-lord and master.

But it is too fruitful a subject, this of hereditary resemblances,—the frequent recurrence of which, in a direct line, is truly unaccountable, when we consider how large an accumulation of ancestry lies behind every man, at the distance of one or two centuries. We shall only add, therefore, that the Puritan—so, at least, says chimney-corner tradition, which often preserves traits of character with marvellous fidelity— was bold, imperious, relentless, crafty; laying his purposes deep, and following them out with an inveteracy of pursuit that knew neither rest nor conscience; trampling on the weak, and, when essential to his ends, doing his utmost to beat down the strong. Whether the judge in any degree resembled him, the further progress of our narrative may show.

Scarcely any of the items in the above-drawn parallel occurred to Phœbe, whose country birth and residence, in truth, had left her pitifully ignorant of most of the family traditions, which lingered, like cobwebs and incrustations of smoke, about the rooms and chimneycorners of the House of the Seven Gables. Yet there was a circumstance, very trifling in itself, which impressed her with an odd degree of horror. She had heard of the anathema flung by Maule, the executed wizard, against Colonel Pyncheon and his posterity,— that God would give them blood to drink,—and likewise of the popular notion, that this miraculous blood might now and then be heard gurgling in their throats. The latter scandal—as became a person of sense, and, more especially, a member of the Pyncheon family— Phœbe had set down for the absurdity which it unquestionably was. But ancient superstitions, after being steeped in human hearts, and embodied in human breath, and passing from lip to ear, in manifold repetition, through a series of generations, become imbued with an effect of homely truth. The smoke of the domestic hearth has scented them, through and through. By long transmission among household facts, they grow to look like them, and have such a familiar way of making themselves at home, that their influence is usually greater than we suspect. Thus it happened, that when Phœbe heard a certain noise in Judge Pyncheon's throat,—rather habitual with him, not altogether voluntary, yet indicative of nothing, unless it were a slight bronchial complaint, or, as some people hinted, an apoplectic symptom,—when the girl heard this queer and awkward ingurgitation (which the writer never did hear, and therefore cannot describe), she, very foolishly, started, and clasped her hands.

Of course, it was exceedingly ridiculous in Phœbe to be discomposed by such a trifle, and still more unpardonable to show her discomposure to the individual most concerned in it. But the incident chimed in so oddly with her previous fancies about the colonel and the judge, that, for the moment, it seemed quite to mingle their identity.

"What is the matter with you, young woman?" said Judge Pyncheon, giving her one of his harsh looks. "Are you afraid of anything?"

"O, nothing, sir,—nothing in the world!" answered Phœbe, with a little laugh of vexation at herself. "But perhaps you wish to speak with my cousin Hepzibah. Shall I call her?"

"Stay a moment, if you please," said the judge, again beaming sunshine out of his face. "You seem to be a little nervous, this morning. The town air, Cousin Phœbe, does not agree with your good, wholesome country habits. Or, has anything happened to disturb you?—anything remarkable in Cousin Hepzibah's family?—An arrival, eh? I thought so! No wonder you are out of sorts, my little cousin. To be an inmate with such a guest may well startle an innocent young girl!"

"You quite puzzle me, sir," replied Phœbe, gazing inquiringly at the judge. "There is no frightful guest in the house, but only a poor, gentle, child-like man, whom I believe to be Cousin Hepzibah's brother. I am afraid (but you, sir, will know better than I) that he is not quite in his sound senses; but so mild and quiet he seems to be, that a mother might trust her baby with him; and I think he would play with the baby, as if he were only a few years older than itself. He startle me!—O, no indeed!"

"I rejoice to hear so favorable and so ingenuous an account of my cousin Clifford," said the benevolent judge. "Many years ago, when we were boys and young men together, I had a great affection for him, and still feel a tender interest in all his concerns. You say, Cousin Phœbe, he appears to be weak-minded. Heaven grant him at least enough of intellect to repent of his past sins!"

"Nobody, I fancy," observed Phœbe, "can have fewer to repent of."

"And is it possible, my dear," rejoined the judge, with a commiserating look, "that you have never heard of Clifford Pyncheon?—that you know nothing of his history? Well, it is all right; and your mother has shown a very proper regard for the good name of the family with which she connected herself. Believe the best you can of this unfortunate person, and hope the best! It is a rule which Christians should always follow, in their judgments of one another; and especially is it right and wise among near relatives, whose characters have necessarily a degree of mutual dependence. But is Clifford in the parlor? I will just step in and see."

"Perhaps, sir, I had better call my cousin Hepzibah," said Phœbe; hardly knowing, however, whether she ought to obstruct the entrance of so affectionate a kinsman into the private regions of the house. "Her brother seemed to be just falling asleep, after breakfast; and I am sure she would not like him to be disturbed. Pray, sir, let me give her notice!"

But the judge showed a singular determination to enter unannounced; and as Phœbe, with the vivacity of a person whose movements unconsciously answer to her thoughts, had stepped towards the door, he used little or no ceremony in putting her aside.

"No, no, Miss Phœbe!" said Judge Pyncheon, in a voice as deep as a thunder-growl, and with a frown as black as the cloud whence it issues. "Stay you here! I know the house, and know my cousin Hepzibah, and know her brother Clifford likewise!—nor need my little country cousin put herself to the trouble of announcing me!"—in these latter words, by-the-by, there were symptoms of a change from his sudden harshness into his previous benignity of manner.—"I am at home here, Phœbe, you must recollect, and you are the stranger. I will just step in, therefore,

and see for myself how Clifford is, and assure him and Hepzibah of my kindly feelings and best wishes. It is right, at this juncture, that they should both hear from my own lips how much I desire to serve them. Ha! here is Hepzibah herself!"

Such was the case. The vibrations of the judge's voice had reached the old gentlewoman in the parlor, where she sat, with face averted, waiting on her brother's slumber. She now issued forth, as would appear, to defend the entrance, looking, we must needs say, amazingly like the dragon which, in fairy tales, is wont to be the guardian over an enchanted beauty. The habitual scowl of her brow was, undeniably, too fierce, at this moment, to pass itself off on the innocent score of near-sightedness; and it was bent on Judge Pyncheon in a way that seemed to confound, if not alarm him, so inadequately had he estimated the moral force of a deeply-grounded antipathy. She made a repelling gesture with her hand, and stood, a perfect picture of prohibition, at full length, in the dark frame of the doorway. But we must betray Hepzibah's secret, and confess that the native timorousness of her character even now developed itself, in a quick tremor, which, to her own perception, set each of her joints at variance with its fellows.

Possibly, the judge was aware how little true hardihood lay behind Hepzibah's formidable front. At any rate, being a gentleman of steady nerves, he soon recovered himself, and failed not to approach his cousin with outstretched hand; adopting the sensible precaution, however, to cover his advance with a smile, so broad and sultry, that, had it been only half as warm as it looked, a trellis of grapes might at once have turned purple under its summer-like exposure. It may have been his purpose, indeed, to melt poor Hepzibah on the spot, as if she were a figure of yellow wax.

"Hepzibah, my beloved cousin, I am rejoiced!" exclaimed the judge, most emphatically. "Now, at length, you have something to live for. Yes, and all of us, let me say, your friends and kindred, have more to live for than we had yesterday. I have lost no time in hastening to offer any assistance in my power towards making Clifford comfortable. He belongs to us all. I know how much he requires,—how much he used to require,—with his delicate taste, and his love of the beautiful. Anything in my house,—pictures, books, wine, luxuries at the table,—he may command them all! It would afford me most heart-felt gratification to see him! Shall I step in, this moment?"

"No," replied Hepzibah, her voice quivering too painfully to allow of many words. "He cannot see visitors!"

"A visitor, my dear cousin!—do you call me so?" cried the judge, whose sensibility, it seems, was hurt by the coldness of the phrase. "Nay, then, let me be Clifford's host, and your own likewise. Come at once to my house. The country air, and all the conveniences— I may say luxuries—that I have gathered about me, will do wonders for him. And you and I, dear Hepzibah, will consult together, and watch together, and labor together, to make our dear Clifford happy. Come! why should we make more words about what is both a duty and a pleasure, on my part? Come to me at once!"

On hearing these so hospitable offers, and such generous recognition of the claims of kindred, Phœbe felt very much in the mood of running up to Judge Pyncheon, and giving him, of her own accord, the kiss from which she had so recently shrunk away. It was quite otherwise with Hepzibah; the judge's smile seemed to operate on her acerbity of heart like sunshine upon vinegar, making it ten times sourer than ever.

"Clifford," said she,—still too agitated to utter more than an abrupt sentence, —"Clifford has a home here!"

"May Heaven forgive you, Hepzibah," said Judge Pyncheon,—reverently lifting his eyes towards that high court of equity to which he appealed,—"if you suffer any ancient prejudice or animosity to weigh with you in this matter! I stand here, with an open heart, willing and anxious to receive yourself and Clifford into it. Do not refuse my good offices,—my earnest propositions for your welfare! They are such, in all respects, as it behooves your nearest kinsman to make. It will be a heavy responsibility, cousin, if you confine your brother to this dismal house and stifled air, when the delightful freedom of my country-seat is at his command."

"It would never suit Clifford," said Hepzibah, as briefly as before.

"Woman!" broke forth the judge, giving way to his resentment, "what is the meaning of all this? Have you other resources? Nay, I suspected as much! Take care, Hepzibah, take care! Clifford is on the brink of as black a ruin as ever befell him yet! But why do I talk with you, woman as you are? Make way!—I must see Clifford!"

Hepzibah spread out her gaunt figure across the door, and seemed really to increase in bulk; looking the more terrible, also, because there was so much terror and agitation in her heart. But Judge Pyncheon's evident purpose of forcing a passage was interrupted by a voice from the inner room; a weak, tremulous, wailing voice, indicating helpless alarm, with no more energy for self-defence than belongs to a frightened infant.

"Hepzibah, Hepzibah!" cried the voice; "go down on your knees to him! Kiss his feet! Entreat him not to come in! O, let him have mercy on me! Mercy!—mercy!"

For the instant, it appeared doubtful whether it were not the judge's resolute purpose to set Hepzibah aside, and step across the threshold into the parlor, whence issued that broken and miserable murmur of entreaty. It was not pity that restrained him, for, at the first sound of the enfeebled voice, a red fire kindled in his eyes, and he made a quick pace forward, with something inexpressibly fierce and grim darkening forth, as it were, out of the whole man. To know Judge Pyncheon, was to see him at that moment. After such a revelation, let him smile with what sultriness he would, he could much sooner turn grapes purple, or pumpkins yellow, than melt the iron-branded impression out of the beholder's memory. And it rendered his aspect not the less, but more frightful, that it seemed not to express wrath or hatred, but a certain hot fellness of purpose, which annihilated everything but itself.

Yet, after all, are we not slandering an excellent and amiable man? Look at the judge now! He is apparently conscious of having erred, in too energetically pressing his deeds of loving-kindness on persons unable to appreciate them. He will await their better mood, and hold himself as ready to assist them, then, as at this moment. As he draws back from the door, an all-comprehensive benignity blazes from his visage, indicating that he gathers Hepzibah, little Phœbe, and the invisible Clifford, all three, together with the whole world besides, into his immense heart, and gives them a warm bath in its flood of affection.

"You do me great wrong, dear Cousin Hepzibah!" said he, first kindly offering her his hand, and then drawing on his glove preparatory to departure. "Very great wrong! But I forgive it, and will study to make you think better of me. Of course, our poor Clifford being in so unhappy a state of mind, I cannot think of urging an interview at present. But I shall watch over his welfare, as if he were my own beloved brother; nor do I at all despair, my dear cousin, of constraining both him and you to acknowledge your injustice. When that shall happen, I desire no other revenge than your acceptance of the best offices in my power to do you."

With a bow to Hepzibah, and a degree of paternal benevolence in his parting nod to Phœbe, the judge left the shop, and went smiling along the street. As is customary with the rich, when they aim at the honors of a republic, he apologized, as it were, to the people, for his wealth, prosperity, and elevated station, by a free and hearty manner towards those who knew him; putting off the more of his dignity, in due proportion with the humbleness of the man whom he saluted. and thereby proving a haughty consciousness of his advantages as irrefragably as if he had marched forth preceded by a troop of lackeys to clear the way. On this particular forenoon, so excessive was the warmth of Judge Pyncheon's kindly aspect, that (such, at least, was the rumor about town) an extra passage of the water-carts was found essential, in order to lay the dust occasioned by so much extra sunshine!

No sooner had he disappeared than Hepzibah grew deadly white, and, staggering towards Phœbe, let her head fall on the young girl's shoulder.

"O, Phœbe!" murmured she, "that man has been the horror of my life! Shall I never, never have the courage, —will my voice never cease from trembling long enough to let me tell him what he is?"

"Is he so very wicked?" asked Phœbe. "Yet his offers were surely kind!"

"Do not speak of them,—he has a heart of iron!" rejoined Hepzibah. "Go, now, and talk to Clifford! Amuse and keep him quiet! It would disturb him wretchedly to see me so agitated as I am. There, go, dear child, and I will try to look after the shop."

Phœbe went, accordingly, but perplexed herself, meanwhile, with queries as to the purport of the scene which she had just witnessed, and also, whether judges, clergymen, and other characters of that eminent stamp and respectability, could really, in any single instance, be otherwise than just and upright men. A doubt of this nature has a most disturbing influence, and, if shown to be a fact, comes with fearful and startling effect, on minds of the trim, orderly, and limit-loving class, in which we find our little country-girl. Dispositions more boldly speculative may derive a stern enjoyment from the discovery, since there must be evil in the world, that a high man is as likely to grasp his share of it as a low one. A wider scope of view, and a deeper insight, may see rank, dignity, and station, all proved illusory, so far as regards their claims to human reverence, and yet not feel as if the universe were thereby tumbled headlong into chaos. But Phœbe, in order to keep the universe in its old place, was fain to smother, in some degree, her own intuitions as to Judge Pyncheon's character. And as for her cousin's testimony in disparagement of it, she concluded that Hepzibah's judgment was embittered by one of those family feuds, which render hatred the more deadly, by the dead and corrupted love that they intermingle with its native poison.

CHAPTER IX

CLIFFORD AND PHŒBE

TRULY was there something high, generous, and noble, in the native composition of our poor old Hepzibah! Or else,—and it was quite as probably the case,—she had been enriched by poverty, developed by sorrow, elevated y the strong and solitary affection of er life, and thus endowed with heroism, which never could have characerized her in what are called happier ircumstances. Through dreary years, Hepzibah had looked forward—for the most part despairingly, never with any confidence of hope, but always with the feeling that it was her brightest possibility—to the very position in which he now found herself. In her own behalf, she had asked nothing of Providence, but the opportunity of devoting herself to this brother, whom she had so loved,—so admired for what he was, or might have been,—and to whom she had kept her faith, alone of all the world, wholly, unfalteringly, at every instant, and throughout life. And here, in his late decline, the lost one had come back out of his long and strange misfortune, and was thrown on her sympathy, as it seemed, not merely for the bread of his physical existence, but for everything that should keep him morally alive. She had responded to the call. She had come forward,—our poor, gaunt Hepzibah, in her rusty silks, with her rigid joints, and the sad perversity of her scowl,—ready to do her utmost; and with affection enough, if that were all, to do a hundred times as much! There could be few more tearful sights, —and Heaven forgive us, if a smile insist on mingling with our conception of it!—few sights with truer pathos in them, than Hepzibah presented, on that first afternoon.

How patiently did she endeavor to wrap Clifford up in her great, warm love, and make it all the world to him, so that he should retain no torturing sense of the coldness and dreariness without! Her little efforts to amuse him!

How pitiful, yet magnanimous, they were!

Remembering his early love of poetry and fiction, she unlocked a bookcase, and took down several books that had been excellent reading in their day. There was a volume of Pope, with the Rape of the Lock in it, and another of the Tatler, and an odd one of Dryden's Miscellanies, all with tarnished gilding on their covers, and thoughts of tarnished brilliancy inside. They had no success with Clifford. These, and all such writers of society, whose new works glow like the rich texture of a just-woven carpet, must be content to relinquish their charm, for every reader, after an age or two, and could hardly be supposed to retain any portion of it for a mind that had utterly lost its estimate of modes and manners. Hepzibah then took up Rasselas, and began to read of the Happy Valley, with a vague idea that some secret of a contented life had there been elaborated, which might at least serve Clifford and herself for this one day. But the Happy Valley had a cloud over it. Hepzibah troubled her auditor, moreover, by innumerable sins of emphasis, which he seemed to detect, without any reference to the meaning; nor, in fact, did he appear to take much note of the sense of what she read, but evidently felt the tedium of the lecture, without harvesting its profit. His sister's voice, too, naturally harsh, had, in the course of her sorrowful lifetime, contracted a kind of croak, which, when it once gets into the human throat, is as ineradicable as sin. In both sexes, occasionally, this lifelong croak, accompanying each word of joy or sorrow, is one of the symptoms of a settled melancholy; and wherever it occurs, the whole history of misfortune is conveyed in its slightest accent. The effect is as if the voice had been dyed black; or,—if we must use a more moderate simile,—this miserable croak, running through all the variations of the voice, is like a black silken thread, on which the crystal beads of speech are strung, and whence they take their hue. Such voices have put on mourning for dead hopes; and they ought to die and be buried along with them!

Discerning that Clifford was not gladdened by her efforts, Hepzibah searched about the house for the means of more exhilarating pastime. At one time, her eyes chanced to rest on Alice Pyncheon's harpsichord. It was a moment of great peril; for,—despite the traditionary awe that had gathered over this instrument of music, and the dirges which spiritual fingers were said to play on it,—the devoted sister had solemn thoughts of thrumming on its chords for Clifford's benefit, and accompanying the performance with her voice. Poor Clifford! Poor Hepzibah! Poor harpsichord! All three would have been miserable together. By some good agency, —possibly, by the unrecognized interposition of the long-buried Alice herself,—the threatening calamity was averted.

But the worst of all,—the hardest stroke of fate for Hepzibah to endure, and perhaps for Clifford too,—was his invincible distaste for her appearance. Her features, never the most agreeable, and now harsh with age and grief, and resentment against the world for his sake; her dress, and especially her turban; the queer and quaint manners, which had unconsciously grown upon her in solitude;—such being the poor gentlewoman's outward characteristics, it is no great marvel, although the mournfullest of pities, that the instinctive lover of the Beautiful was fain to turn away his eyes. There was no help for it. It would be the latest impulse to die within him. In his last extremity, the expiring breath stealing faintly through Clifford's lips, he would doubtless press Hepzibah's hand, in fervent recognition of all her lavished love, and close his eyes,—but not so much to die, as to be constrained to look no longer on her face! Poor Hepzibah! She took counsel with herself what might be done, and thought of putting ribbons on her turban; but, by the instant rush of several guardian angels, was withheld from an experiment that could hardly have proved less than fatal to the beloved object of her anxiety.

To be brief, besides Hepzibah's disadvantages of person, there was an uncouthness pervading all her deeds; a clumsy something, that could but ill adapt itself for use, and not at all for ornament. She was a grief to Clifford, and she knew it. In this extremity, the antiquated virgin turned to Phœbe. No grovelling jealousy was in her heart. Had it pleased Heaven to crown the heroic fidelity of her life by making her personally the medium of Clifford's happiness, it would have rewarded her for all the past, by a joy with no bright tints, indeed, but deep and true, and worth a thousand gayer ecstasies. This could not be. She therefore turned to Phœbe, and resigned the task into the young girl's hands. The latter took it up, cheerfully, as she did everything, but with no sense of a mission to perform, and succeeding all the better for that same simplicity.

By the involuntary effect of a genial temperament, Phœbe soon grew to be absolutely essential to the daily comfort, if not the daily life, of her two forlorn companions. The grime and sordidness of the House of the Seven Gables seemed to have vanished, since her appearance there; the gnawing tooth of the dry-rot was stayed, among the old timbers of its skeleton frame; the dust had ceased to settle down so densely, from the antique ceilings, upon the floors and furniture of the rooms below;—or, at any rate, there was a little wife, as light-footed as the breeze that sweeps a garden walk, gliding hither and thither, to brush it all away. The shadows of gloomy events, that haunted the else lonely and desolate apartments; the heavy, breathless scent which death had left in more than one of the bedchambers, ever since his visits of long ago;—these were less powerful than the purifying influence scattered throughout the atmosphere of the household by the presence of one youthful, fresh, and thoroughly wholesome heart. There was no morbidness in Phœbe; if there had been, the old Pyncheon-house was the very locality to ripen it into incurable disease. But now her spirit resembled, in its potency, a minute quantity of ottar of rose in one of Hepzibah's huge, iron-bound trunks, diffusing its fragrance through the various articles of linen and wrought-lace, kerchiefs, caps, stockings, folded dresses, gloves, and whatever else was treasured there. As every article in the great trunk was the sweeter for the rose-scent, so did all the thoughts and emotions of Hepzibah and Clifford, sombre as they might seem, acquire a subtle attribute of happiness from

Phœbe's intermixture with them. Her activity of body, intellect, and heart, impelled her continually to perform the ordinary little toils that offered themselves around her, and to think the thought proper for the moment, and to sympathize,—now with the twittering gayety of the robins in the pear-tree, and now to such a depth as she could with Hepzibah's dark anxiety, or the vague moan of her brother. This facile adaptation was at once the symptom of perfect health, and its best preservative.

A nature like Phœbe's has invariably its due influence, but is seldom regarded with due honor. Its spiritual force, however, may be partially estimated by the fact of her having found a place for herself, amid circumstances so stern as those which surrounded the mistress of the house; and also by the effect which she produced on a character of so much more mass than her own. For the gaunt, bony frame and limbs of Hepzibah, as compared with the tiny lightsomeness of Phœbe's figure, were perhaps in some fit proportion with the moral weight and substance, respectively, of the woman and the girl.

To the guest,—to Hepzibah's brother,—or Cousin Clifford, as Phœbe now began to call him,—she was especially necessary. Not that he could ever be said to converse with her, or often manifest, in any other very definite mode, his sense of a charm in her society. But, if she were a long while absent, he became pettish and nervously restless, pacing the room to and fro, with the uncertainty that characterized all his movements; or else would sit broodingly in his great chair, resting his head on his hands, and evincing life only by an electric sparkle of ill-humor, whenever Hepzibah endeavored to arouse him. Phœbe's presence, and the contiguity of her fresh life to his blighted one, was usually all that he required. Indeed, such was the native gush and play of her spirit, that she was seldom perfectly quiet and undemonstrative, any more than a fountain ever ceases to dimple and warble with its flow. She possessed the gift of song, and that, too, so naturally, that you would as little think of inquiring whence she had caught it, or what master had taught her, as of asking the same questions about a bird, in whose small strain of music we recognize the voice of the Creator as distinctly as in the loudest accents of his thunder. So long as Phœbe sang, she might stray at her own will about the house. Clifford was content, whether the sweet, airy homeliness of her tones came down from the upper chambers, or along the passage-way from the shop, or was sprinkled through the foliage of the pear-tree, inward from the garden, with the twinkling sunbeams. He would sit quietly, with a gentle pleasure gleaming over his face, brighter now, and now a little dimmer, as the song happened to float near him, or was more remotely heard. It pleased him best, however, when she sat on a low foot-stool at his knee.

It is perhaps remarkable, considering her temperament, that Phœbe oftener chose a strain of pathos than of gayety. But the young and happy are not ill pleased to temper their life with a transparent shadow. The deepest pathos of Phœbe's voice and song, moreover, came sifted through the golden texture of a cheery spirit, and was somehow so interfused with the quality thence acquired, that one's heart felt all the lighter for having wept at it. Broad mirth, in the sacred presence of dark misfortune, would have jarred harshly and irreverently with the solemn symphony that rolled its undertone through Hepzibah's and her brother's life. Therefore, it was well that Phœbe so often chose sad themes, and not amiss that they ceased to be so sad while she was singing them.

Becoming habituated to her companionship, Clifford readily showed how capable of imbibing pleasant tints and gleams of cheerful light from all quarters his nature must originally have been. He grew youthful, while she sat by him. A beauty,—not precisely real, even in its utmost manifestation, and which a painter would have watched long to seize and fix upon his canvas, and, after all, in vain,—beauty, nevertheless, that was not a mere dream, would sometimes play upon and illuminate his face. It did more than to illuminate; it transfigured him with an expression that could only be interpreted as the glow of an exquisite and happy spirit. That gray hair, and those furrows,—with their record of infinite sorrow, so deeply written across his brow, and so compressed, as with a futile effort to crowd in all the tale, that the whole inscription was made illegible,—these, for the moment, vanished. An eye, at once tender and acute, might have beheld in the man some shadow of what he was meant to be. Anon, as age came stealing, like a sad twilight, back over his figure, you would have felt tempted to hold an argument with Destiny, and affirm, that either this being should not have been made mortal, or mortal existence should have been tempered to his qualities. There seemed no necessity for his having drawn breath, at all;—the world never wanted him;—but, as he had breathed, it ought always to have been the balmiest of summer air. The same perplexity will invariably haunt us with regard to natures that tend to feed exclusively upon the Beautiful, let their earthly fate be as lenient as it may.

Phœbe, it is probable, had but a very imperfect comprehension of the character over which she had thrown so beneficent a spell. Nor was it necessary. The fire upon the hearth can gladden a whole semi-circle of faces round about it, but need not know the individuality of one among them all. Indeed, there was something too fine and delicate in Clifford's traits to be perfectly appreciated by one whose sphere lay so much in the Actual as Phœbe's did. For Clifford, however, the reality, and simplicity, and thorough homeliness, of the girl's nature, were as powerful a charm as any that she possessed. Beauty, it is true, and beauty almost perfect in its own style, was indispensable. Had Phœbe been coarse in feature, shaped clumsily, of a harsh voice, and uncouthly mannered, she might have been rich with all good gifts, beneath this unfortunate exterior, and still, so long as she wore the guise of woman, she would have shocked Clifford, and depressed him by her lack of beauty. But nothing more beautiful—nothing prettier, at least—was ever made than Phœbe. And, therefore, to this man,—whose whole poor and impalpable enjoyment of existence, heretofore, and until both his heart and fancy died within him, had been a dream,—whose images of women

had more and more lost their warmth and substance, and been frozen, like the pictures of secluded artists, into the chillest ideality,—to him, this little figure of the cheeriest household life was just what he required to bring him back into the breathing world. Persons who have wandered, or been expelled, out of the common track of things, even were it for a better system, desire nothing so much as to be led back. They shiver in their loneliness, be it on a mountain-top or in a dungeon. Now, Phœbe's presence made a home about her,—that very sphere which the outcast, the prisoner, the potentate,—the wretch beneath mankind, the wretch aside from it, or the wretch above it,—instinctively pines after,—a home! She was real! Holding her hand, you felt something; a tender something; a substance, and a warm one: and so long as you should feel its grasp, soft as it was, you might be certain that your place was good in the whole sympathetic chain of human nature. The world was no longer a delusion.

By looking a little further in this direction, we might suggest an explanation of an often-suggested mystery. Why are poets so apt to choose their mates, not for any similarity of poetic endowment, but for qualities which might make the happiness of the rudest handicraftsman as well as that of the ideal craftsman of the spirit? Because, probably, at his highest elevation, the poet needs no human intercourse; but he finds it dreary to descend, and be a stranger.

There was something very beautiful in the relation that grew up between this pair, so closely and constantly linked together, yet with such a waste of gloomy and mysterious years from his birth-day to hers. On Clifford's part, it was the feeling of a man naturally endowed with the liveliest sensibility to feminine influence, but who had never quaffed the cup of passionate love, and knew that it was now too late. He knew it, with the instinctive delicacy that had survived his intellectual decay. Thus, his sentiment for Phœbe, without being paternal, was not less chaste than if she had been his daughter. He was a man, it is true, and recognized her as a woman. She was his only representative of womankind. He took unfailing note of every charm that appertained to her sex, and saw the ripeness of her lips, and the virginal development of her bosom. All her little womanly ways, budding out of her like blossoms on a young fruit-tree, had their effect on him, and sometimes caused his very heart to tingle with the keenest thrills of pleasure. At such moments,—for the effect was seldom more than momentary,—the half-torpid man would be full of harmonious life, as a long-silent harp is full of sound, when the musician's fingers sweep across it. But, after all, it seemed rather a perception, or a sympathy, than a sentiment belonging to himself as an individual. He read Phœbe, as he would a sweet and simple story; he listened to her, as if she were a verse of household poetry, which God, in requital of his bleak and dismal lot, had permitted some angel, that most pitied him, to warble through the house. She was not an actual fact for him, but the interpretation of all that he had lacked on earth, brought warmly home to his conception; so that this mere symbol, or lifelike picture, had almost the comfort of reality.

But we strive in vain to put the idea into words. No adequate expression of the beauty and profound pathos with which it impressed us is attainable. This being, made only for happiness, and heretofore so miserably failing to be happy,—his tendencies so hideously thwarted, that, some unknown time ago, the delicate springs of his character, never morally or intellectually strong, had given way, and he was now imbecile,—this poor, forlorn voyager from the Islands of the Blest, in a frail bark, on a tempestuous sea, had been flung, by the last mountain-wave of his shipwreck, into a quiet harbor. There, as he lay more than half lifeless on the strand, the fragrance of an earthly rosebud had come to his nostrils, and, as odors will, had summoned up reminiscences or visions of all the living and breathing beauty amid which he should have had his home. With his native susceptibility of happy influences, he inhales the slight, ethereal rapture into his soul, and expires!

And how did Phœbe regard Clifford? The girl's was not one of those natures which are most attracted by what is strange and exceptional in human character. The path which would best have suited her was the well-worn track of ordinary life; the companions in whom she would most have delighted were such as one encounters at every turn. The mystery which enveloped Clifford, so far as it affected her at all, was an annoyance, rather than the piquant harm which many women might have found in it. Still, her native kindliness was brought strongly into play, not by what was darkly picturesque in his situation, nor so much even, by the finer grace of his character, as by the simple appeal of a heart so forlorn as his to one so full of genuine sympathy as hers. She gave him an affectionate regard, because he needed so much love, and seemed to have received so little. With a ready tact, the result of ever-active and wholesome sensibility, she discerned what was good for him, and did it. Whatever was morbid in his mind and experience, she ignored; and thereby kept their intercourse healthy, by the incautious, but, as it were, heaven-directed freedom of her whole conduct. The sick in mind, and, perhaps, in body, are rendered more darkly and hopelessly so, by the manifold reflection of their disease, mirrored back from all quarters, in the deportment of those about them; they are compelled to inhale the poison of their own breath, in infinite repetition. But Phœbe afforded her poor patient a supply of purer air. She impregnated it, too, not with a wild-flower scent,—for wildness was no trait of hers,—but with the perfume of garden-roses, pinks, and other blossoms of much sweetness, which nature and man have consented together in making grow, from summer to summer, and from century to century. Such a flower was Phœbe, in her relation with Clifford, and such the delight that he inhaled from her.

Yet, it must be said, her petals sometimes drooped a little, in consequence of the heavy atmosphere about her. She grew more thoughtful than heretofore. Looking aside at Clifford's face, and seeing the dim, unsatisfactory elegance, and the intellect almost quenched, she would try to inquire what had been his life. Was he always thus? Had this veil been over him from his birth?—this veil, under which far more of his spirit was hidden than revealed, and through which he so imperfectly discerned the actual world,—or was its gray texture woven of some dark calamity? Phœbe loved no riddles, and would have been glad to escape the perplexity of this one. Nevertheless, there was so far a good result of her meditations on Clifford's character, that, when her involuntary conjectures, together with the tendency of every strange circumstance to tell its own story, had gradually taught her the fact, it had no terrible effect upon her. Let the world have done him what vast wrong it might, she knew Cousin Clifford too well—or fancied so—ever to shudder at the touch of his thin, delicate fingers.

Within a few days after the appearance of this remarkable inmate, the routine of life had established itself with a good deal of uniformity in the old house of our narrative. In the morning, very shortly after breakfast, it was Clifford's custom to fall asleep in his chair; nor, unless accidentally disturbed, would he emerge from a dense cloud of slumber, or the thinner mists that flitted to and fro, until well towards noonday. These hours of drowsy head were the season of the old woman's attendance on her brother, while Phœbe took charge of the shop; an arrangement which the public speedily understood, and evinced their decided preference of the younger shopwoman by the multiplicity of their calls during her administration of affairs. Dinner over, Hepzibah took her knitting-work,—a long stocking of gray yarn, for her brother's winter-wear,—and with a sigh, and a scowl of affectionate farewell to Clifford, and a gesture enjoining watchfulness on Phœbe, went to take her seat behind the counter. It was now the young girl's turn to be the nurse,—the guardian, the playmate,—or whatever is the fitte phrase,—of the gray-haired man.

CHAPTER X

THE PYNCHEON-GARDEN

CLIFFORD, except for Phœbe's more active instigation, would ordinarily have yielded to the torpor which had crept through all his modes of being, and which sluggishly counselled him to sit in his morning chair till even-tide. But the girl seldom failed to propose a removal to the garden, where Uncle Venner and the daguerrotypist had made such repairs on the roof of the ruinous arbor, or summer-house, that it was now a sufficient shelter from sunshine and casual showers. The hop-vine, too, had begun to grow luxuriantly over the sides of the little edifice, and made an interior of verdant seclusion, with innumerable peeps and glimpses into the wider solitude of the garden.

Here, sometimes, in this green playplace of flickering light, Phœbe read to Clifford. Her acquaintance, the artist, who appeared to have a literary turn, had supplied her with works of fiction, in pamphlet-form, and a few volumes of poetry, in altogether a different style and taste from those which Hepzibah selected for his amusement. Small thanks were due to the books, however, if the girl's readings were in any degree more successful than her elderly cousin's. Phœbe's voice had always a pretty music in it, and could either enliven Clifford by its sparkle and gayety of tone, or soothe him by a continued flow of pebbly and brook-like cadences. But the fictions—in which the country-girl, unused to works of that nature often became deeply absorbed—inter ested her strange auditor very little, o not at all. Pictures of life, scenes of passion or sentiment, wit, humor, and pathos, were all thrown away, or worse than thrown away, on Clifford; either because he lacked an experience by which to test their truth, or because his own griefs were a touch-stone of reality that few feigned emotions could withstand. When Phœbe broke into a peal of merry laughter at what she read, he would now and then laugh for sympathy, but oftener respond with a troubled, questioning look. If a tear—a maiden's sunshiny tear, over imaginary woe—dropped upon some melancholy page, Clifford either took it as a token of actual calamity, or else grew peevish, and angrily motioned her to close the volume. And wisely, too! Is not the world sad enough, in genuine earnest, without making a pastime of mock-sorrows?

With poetry, it was rather better. He delighted in the swell and subsidence of the rhythm, and the happily-recurring rhyme. Nor was Clifford incapable of feeling the sentiment of poetry,—not, perhaps, where it was highest or deepest, but where it was most flitting and

thereal. It was impossible to foretell
in what exquisite verse the awakening
spell might lurk; but, on raising her
eyes from the page to Clifford's face,
Phœbe would be made aware, by the
light breaking through it, that a more
delicate intelligence than her own had
caught a lambent flame from what she
read. One glow of this kind, however,
was often the precursor of gloom for
many hours afterward; because, when
the glow left him, he seemed conscious
of a missing sense and power, and
groped about for them, as if a blind man
should go seeking his lost eyesight.

It pleased him more, and was better
for his inward welfare, that Phœbe
should talk, and make passing occur-
ences vivid to his mind by her accompanying description and remarks. The
life of the garden offered topics enough
for such discourse as suited Clifford
best. He never failed to inquire what
flowers had bloomed since yesterday.
His feeling for flowers was very exquisite, and seemed not so much a taste
as an emotion; he was fond of sitting
with one in his hand, intently observing
it, and looking from its petals into
Phœbe's face, as if the garden-flower
were the sister of the household-maiden.
Not merely was there a delight in the
flower's perfume, or pleasure in its beautiful form, and the delicacy of brightness of its hue; but Clifford's enjoyment
was accompanied with a perception of
life, character, and individuality, that
made him love these blossoms of the
garden, as if they were endowed with
sentiment and intelligence. This affection and sympathy for flowers is almost
exclusively a woman's trait. Men, if endowed with it by nature, soon lose,
forget, and learn to despise it, in their

contact with coarser things than flowers.
Clifford, too, had long forgotten it; but
found it again, now, as he slowly revived from the chill torpor of his life.

It is wonderful how many pleasant
incidents continually came to pass in
that secluded garden-spot, when once
Phœbe had set herself to look for them.
She had seen or heard a bee there, on
the first day of her acquaintance with
the place. And often,—almost continually, indeed,—since then, the bees kept
coming thither. Heaven knows why, or
by what pertinacious desire for far-
fetched sweets, when, no doubt, there
were broad clover-fields, and all kinds
of garden-growth, much nearer home
than this. Thither the bees came, however, and plunged into the squash-blossoms, as if there were no other squash-
vines within a long day's flight, or as
if the soil of Hepzibah's garden gave
its productions just the very quality
which these laborious little wizards
wanted, in order to impart the Hymet-
tus odor to their whole hive of New
England honey. When Clifford heard
their sunny, buzzing murmur, in the
heart of the great yellow blossoms, he
looked about him with a joyful sense
of warmth, and blue sky, and green
grass, and of God's free air in the whole
height from earth to heaven. After all,
there need be no question why the bees
came to that one green nook, in the
dusty town. God sent them thither, to
gladden our poor Clifford. They brought
the rich summer with them, in requital
of a little honey.

When the bean-vines began to flower
on the poles, there was one particular
variety which bore a vivid scarlet blossom. The daguerreotypist had found
these beans in a garret, over one of the

seven gables, treasured up in an old chest of drawers, by some horticultural Pyncheon of days gone by, who, doubtless, meant to sow them the next summer, but was himself first sown in Death's garden-ground. By way of testing whether there was still a living germ in such ancient seeds, Holgrave had planted some of them; and the result of his experiment was a splendid row of bean-vines, clambering, early, to the full height of the poles, and arraying them, from top to bottom, in a spiral profusion of red blossoms. And, ever since the unfolding of the first bud, a multitude of humming-birds had been attracted thither. At times, it seemed as if for every one of the hundred blossoms there was one of these tiniest fowls of the air; a thumb's bigness of burnished plumage, hovering and vibrating about the bean-poles. It was with indescribable interest, and even more than childish delight, that Clifford watched the humming-birds. He used to thrust his head softly out of the arbor, to see them the better; all the while, too, motioning Phœbe to be quiet, and snatching glimpses of the smile upon her face, so as to heap his enjoyment up the higher with her sympathy. He had not merely grown young;—he was a child again.

Hepzibah, whenever she happened to witness one of these fits of miniature enthusiasm, would shake her head, with a strange mingling of the mother and sister, and of pleasure and sadness, in her aspect. She said that it had always been thus with Clifford, when the humming-birds came,—always, from his babyhood,—and that his delight in them had been one of the earliest tokens by which he showed his love for beautiful

things. And it was a wonderful coincidence, the good lady thought, that the artist should have planted these scarlet-flowering beans—which the humming-birds sought far and wide, and which had not grown in the Pyncheon-garden before for forty years—on the very summer of Clifford's return.

Then would the tears stand in poor Hepzibah's eyes, or overflow them with a too abundant gush, so that she was fain to betake herself into some corner, lest Clifford should espy her agitation. Indeed, all the enjoyments of this period were provocative of tears. Coming so late as it did, it was a kind of Indian summer, with a mist in its balmiest sunshine, and decay and death in its gaudiest delight. The more Clifford seemed to taste the happiness of a child, the sadder was the difference to be recognized. With a mysterious and terrible Past, which had annihilated his memory, and a blank Future before him, he had only this visionary and impalpable Now, which, if you once look closely at it, is nothing. He himself, as was perceptible by many symptoms, lay darkly behind his pleasure, and knew it to be a baby-play, which he was to toy and trifle with, instead of thoroughly believing. Clifford saw, it may be, in the mirror of his deeper consciousness, that he was an example and representative of that great class of people whom an inexplicable Providence is continually putting at cross-purposes with the world; breaking what seems its own promise in their nature; withholding their proper food and setting poison before them for a banquet; and thus,—when it might so easily, as one would think, have been adjusted otherwise,—making their existence a strangeness, a solitude, and torment. All his life long, he had been learning how to be wretched, as one learns a foreign tongue; and now, with the lesson thoroughly at heart he could with difficulty comprehend his little airy happiness. Frequently, there was a dim shadow of doubt in his eyes. "Take my hand, Phœbe," he would say, "and pinch it hard with your little fingers! Give me a rose, that I may press its thorns, and prove myself awake, by the sharp touch of pain!" Evidently, he desired this prick of a trifling anguish, in order to assure himself, by that quality which he best knew to be real, that the garden, and the seven weather-beaten gables, and Hepzibah's scowl and Phœbe's smile, were real, likewise. Without this signet in his flesh, he could have attributed no more substance to them than to the empty confusion of imaginary scenes with which he had fed his spirit, until even that poor sustenance was exhausted.

The author needs great faith in his reader's sympathy; else he must hesitate to give details so minute, and incidents apparently so trifling, as are essential to make up the idea of this garden-life. It was the Eden of a thunder smitten Adam, who had fled for refuge thither out of the same dreary and perilous wilderness into which the original Adam was expelled.

One of the available means of amusement, of which Phœbe made the most, in Clifford's behalf, was that feathered society, the hens, a breed of whom, as we have already said, was an immemorial heirloom in the Pyncheon family. In compliance with a whim of Clifford, as it troubled him to see them in confinement, they had been set at liberty, and now roamed at will about the garden;

doing some little mischief, but hindered from escape by buildings, on three sides, and the difficult peaks of a wooden fence, on the other. They spent much of their abundant leisure on the margin of Maule's well, which was haunted by a kind of snail, evidently a titbit to their palates; and the brackish water itself, however nauseous to the rest of the world, was so greatly esteemed by these fowls, that they might be seen tasting, turning up their heads, and smacking their bills, with precisely the air of wine-bibbers round a probationary cask. Their generally quiet, yet often brisk, and constantly diversified talk, one to another, or sometimes in soliloquy,— as they scratched worms out of the rich, black soil, or pecked at such plants as suited their taste,—had such a domestic tone, that it was almost a wonder why you could not establish a regular interchange of ideas about household matters, human and gallinaceous. All hens are well worth studying, for the piquancy and rich variety of their manners; but by no possibility can there have been other fowls of such odd appearance and deportment as these ancestral ones. They probably embodied the traditionary peculiarities of their whole line of progenitors, derived through an unbroken succession of eggs; or else this individual Chanticleer and his two wives had grown to be humorists, and a little crack-brained withal, on account of their solitary way of life, and out of sympathy for Hepzibah, their lady-patroness.

Queerly, indeed, they looked! Chanticleer himself, though stalking on two stilt-like legs, with the dignity of interminable descent in all his gestures was hardly bigger than an ordinary partridge; his two wives were about the size of quails; and as for the one chicken, it looked small enough to be still in the egg, and, at the same time, sufficiently old, withered, wizened, and experienced, to have been the founder of the antiquated race. Instead of being the youngest of the family, it rather seemed to have aggregated into itself the ages, not only of these living specimens of the breed, but of all its forefathers and foremothers, whose united excellences and oddities were squeezed into its little body. Its mother evidently regarded it as the one chicken of the world, and as necessary, in fact, to the world's continuance, or, at any rate, to the equilibrium of the present system of affairs, whether in church or state. No lesser sense of the infant fowl's importance could have justified, even in a mother's eyes, the perseverance with which she watched over its safety, ruffling her small person to twice its proper size, and flying in everybody's face that so much as looked towards her hopeful progeny. No lower estimate could have vindicated the indefatigable zeal with which she scratched, and her unscrupulousness in digging up the choicest flower or vegetable, for the sake of the fat earth-worm at its root. Her nervous cluck, when the chicken happened to be hidden in the long grass or under the squash-leaves; her gentle croak of satisfaction, while sure of it beneath her wing; her note of ill-concealed fear and obstreperous defiance, when she saw her arch-enemy, a neighbor's cat, on the top of the high fence; —one or other of these sounds was to be heard at almost every moment of the day. By degrees, the observer came to feel nearly as much interest in this chicken of illustrious race as the mother hen did.

Phœbe, after getting well acquainted with the old hen, was sometimes permitted to take the chicken in her hand which was quite capable of grasping it cubic inch or two of body. While she curiously examined its hereditary marks —the peculiar speckle of its plumage the funny tuft on its head, and a knob on each of its legs,—the little biped, as she insisted, kept giving her a sagacious wink. The daguerreotypist once whispered her that these marks betoken the oddities of the Pyncheon family, and that the chicken itself was a symbol of the life of the old house, embodying its interpretation, likewise, although an unintelligible one, as such clues generally are. It was a feathered riddle; a mystery hatched out of an egg, and just as mysterious as if the egg had been addle!

The second of Chanticleer's two wives, ever since Phœbe's arrival, had been in a state of heavy despondency, caused, as it afterwards appeared, by her inability to lay an egg. One day however, by her self-important gait, the side-way turn of her head, and the cock of her eye, as she pried into one and another nook of the garden,—croaking to herself, all the while, with inexpressible complacency,—it was made evident that this identical hen, much as mankind under-valued her, carried something about her person, the worth of which was not to be estimated either in gold or precious stones. Shortly after, there was a prodigious cackling and gratulation of Chanticleer and all his family, including the wizened chicken who appeared to understand the matter quite as well as did his sire, his mother, or his aunt. That afternoon Phœbe found a diminutive egg,—not in the regular nest—it was far too precious to be trusted there,—but cunningly hidden under the currant-bushes, on some dry stalks of last year's grass. Hepzibah, on learning the fact, took possession of the egg and appropriated it to Clifford's breakfast, on account of a certain delicacy of flavor, for which, as she affirmed, these eggs had always been famous. Thus unscrupulously did the old gentlewoman sacrifice the continuance, perhaps, of an ancient feathered race, with no better end then to supply her brother with a dainty that hardly filled the bowl of a tea-spoon! It must have been in reference to this outrage that Chanticleer, the next day, accompanied by the bereaved mother of the egg, took his post in front of Phœbe and Clifford, and delivered himself of a harangue that might have proved as long as his own pedigree, but for a fit of merriment on Phœbe's part. Hereupon, the offended fowl stalked away on his long stilts, and utterly withdrew his notice from Phœbe and the rest of human nature, until she made her peace with an offering of spice-cake, which, next to snails, was the delicacy most in favor with his aristocratic taste.

We linger too long, no doubt, beside this paltry rivulet of life that flowed through the garden of the Pyncheon-house. But we deem it pardonable to record these mean incidents, and poor delights, because they proved so greatly to Clifford's benefit. They had the earth-smell in them, and contributed to give him health and substance. Some of his occupations wrought less desirably upon him. He had a singular propensity, for example, to hang over Maule's well, and look at the constantly shifting phantas-

magoria of figures produced by the agitation of the water over the mosaic-work of colored pebbles at the bottom. He said that faces looked upward to him there,—beautiful faces, arrayed in betwitching smiles,—each momentary face so fair and rosy, and every smile so sunny, that he felt wronged at its departure, until the same flitting witchcraft made a new one. But sometimes he would suddenly cry out, "The dark face gazes at me!" and be miserable the whole day afterwards. Phœbe, when she hung over the fountain by Clifford's side, could see nothing of all this,—neither the beauty nor the ugliness,—but only the colored pebbles, looking as if the gush of the water shook and disarranged them. And the dark face, that so troubled Clifford, was no more than the shadow thrown from a branch of one of the damson-trees, and breaking the inner light of Maule's well. The truth was, however, that his fancy—reviving faster than his will and judgment, and always stronger than they—created shapes of loveliness that were symbolic of his native character, and now and then a stern and dreadful shape, that typified his fate.

On Sundays, after Phœbe had been at church,—for the girl had a church-going conscience, and would hardly have been at ease had she missed either prayer, singing, sermon, or benediction, —after church-time, therefore, there was, ordinarily, a sober little festival in the garden. In addition to Clifford, Hepzibah and Phœbe, two guests made up the company. One was the artist, Holgrave, who, in spite of his consociation with reformers, and his other queer and questionable traits, continued to hold an elevated place in Hepzibah's regard. The other, we are almost ashamed to say, was the venerable Uncle Venner, in a clean shirt, and a broadcloth coat, more respectable than his ordinary wear, inasmuch as it was neatly patched on each elbow, and might be called an entire garment, except for a slight inequality in the length of its skirts. Clifford, on several occasions, had seemed to enjoy the old man's intercourse, for the sake of his mellow, cheerful vein, which was like the sweet flavor of a frost-bitten apple, such as one picks up under the tree in December. A man at the very lowest point of the social scale was easier and more agreeable for the fallen gentleman to encounter than a person at any of the intermediate degrees; and, moreover, as Clifford's young manhood had been lost, he was fond of feeling himself comparatively youthful, now, in apposition with the patriarchal age of Uncle Venner. In fact, it was sometimes observable that Clifford half wilfully hid from himself the consciousness of being stricken in years, and cherished visions of an earthly future still before him; visions, however, too indistinctly drawn to be followed by disappointment—though, doubtless, by depression—when any casual incident or recollection made him sensible of the withered leaf.

So this oddly-composed little social party used to assemble under the ruinous arbor. Hepzibah—stately as ever, at heart, and yielding not an inch of her old gentility, but resting upon it so much the more, as justifying a princess-like condescension—exhibited a not ungraceful hospitality. She talked kindly to the vagrant artist, and took sage counsel—lady as she was—with the woodsawyer, the messenger of everybody's petty

errands, the patched philosopher. And Uncle Venner, who had studied the world at street-corners, and at other posts equally well adapted for just observation, was as ready to give out his wisdom as a town-pump to give water.

"Miss Hepzibah, ma'am," said he once, after they had all been cheerful together, "I really enjoy these quiet little meetings, of a Sabbath afternoon. They are very much like what I expect to have, after I retire to my farm!"

"Uncle Venner," observed Clifford, in a drowsy, inward tone, "is always talking about his farm. But I have a better scheme for him, by-and-by. We shall see!"

"Ah, Mr. Clifford Pyncheon!" said the man of patches, "you may scheme for me as much as you please; but I'm not going to give up this one scheme of my own, even if I never bring it really to pass. It does seem to me that men make a wonderful mistake in trying to heap up property upon property. If I had done so, I should feel as if Providence was not bound to take care of me; and, at all events, the city wouldn't be! I'm one of those people who think that infinity is big enough for us all,—and eternity long enough!"

"Why, so they are, Uncle Venner," remarked Phœbe, after a pause; for she had been trying to fathom the profundity and appositeness of this concluding apothegm. "But, for this short life of ours, one would like a house and a moderate garden-spot of one's own."

"It appears to me," said the daguerreotypist, smiling, "that Uncle Venner has the principles of Fourier at the bottom of his wisdom; only they have not quite so much distinctness, in his mind, as in that of the systematizing renchman."

"Come, Phœbe," said Hepzibah, "it is
ime to bring the currants."

And then, while the yellow richness
of the declining sunshine still fell into
he open space of the garden, Phœbe
brought out a loaf of bread, and a
China-bowl of currants, freshly gath-
red from the bushes, and crushed with
ugar. These, with water,—but not from
he fountain of ill omen, close at hand,
—constituted all the entertainment.
Meanwhile, Holgrave took some pains
o establish an intercourse with Clifford,
actuated, it might seem, entirely by an
impulse of kindliness, in order that the
present hour might be cheerfuller than
most which the poor recluse had spent,
or was destined yet to spend. Neverthe-
ess, in the artist's deep, thoughtful, all-
observant eyes, there was, now and
hen, an expression, not sinister, but
questionable; as if he had some other
interest in the scene than a stranger, a
youthful and unconnected adventurer,
might be supposed to have. With great
nobility of outward mood, however, he
pplied himself to the task of enliven-
ng the party; and with so much suc-
ess, that even dark-hued Hepzibah
hrew off one tint of melancholy, and
made what shift she could with the remaining portion. Phœbe said to herself,
—"How pleasant he can be!" As for
Uncle Venner, as a mark of friendship
nd approbation, he readily consented
o afford the young man his counte-
ance in the way of his profession,—
ot metaphorically, be it understood,
ut literally, by allowing a daguerreo-
ype of his face, so familiar to the town,
o be exhibited at the entrance of Hol-
rave's studio.

Clifford, as the company partook of

their little banquet, grew to be the
gayest of them all. Either it was one of
those up-quivering flashes of the spirit,
to which minds in an abnormal state are
liable, or else the artist had subtly
touched some chord that made musical
vibration. Indeed, what with the pleasant summer evening, and the sympathy
of this little circle of not unkindly
souls, it was perhaps natural that a
character so susceptible as Clifford's
should become animated, and show itself readily responsive to what was said
around him. But he gave out his own
thoughts, likewise, with an airy and
fanciful glow; so that they glistened, as
it were, through the arbor, and made
their escape among the interstices of the
foliage. He had been as cheerful, no
doubt, while alone with Phœbe, but
never with such tokens of acute, although partial intelligence.

But, as the sunlight left the peaks of
the seven gables, so did the excitement
fade out of Clifford's eyes. He gazed
vaguely and mournfully about him, as
if he missed something precious, and
missed it the more drearily for not
knowing precisely what it was.

"I want my happiness!" at last he
murmured, hoarsely and indistinctly,
hardly shaping out the words. "Many,
many years, have I waited for it! It
is late! It is late! I want my happiness!"

Alas, poor Clifford! You are old, and
worn with troubles that ought never to
have befallen you. You are partly crazy,
and partly imbecile; a ruin, a failure, as
almost everybody is,—though some in
less degree, or less perceptibly, than
their fellows. Fate has no happiness in
store for you; unless your quiet home
in the old family residence with the

faithful Hepzibah, and your long summer afternoons with Phœbe, and these Sabbath festivals with Uncle Venner and the daguerreotypist, deserve to be called happiness! Why not? If not the thing itself, it is marvellously like it, and the more so for that ethereal and intangible quality which causes it all to vanish, at too close an introspection. Take it, therefore, while you may! Murmur not,—question not,—but make the most of it!

·   ———

CHAPTER XI

THE ARCHED WINDOW

FROM the inertness, or what we may term the vegetative character, of his ordinary mood, Clifford would perhaps have been content to spend one day after another, interminably,—or, at least, throughout the summer-time,—in just the kind of life described in the preceding pages. Fancying, however, that it might be for his benefit occasionally to diversify the scene, Phœbe sometimes suggested that he should look out upon the life of the street. For this purpose, they used to mount the staircase together, to the second story of the house, where, at the termination of a wide entry, there was an arched window of uncommonly large dimensions, shaded by a pair of curtains. It opened above the porch, where there had formerly been a balcony, the balustrade of which had long since gone to decay, and been removed. At this arched window, throwing it open, but keeping himself in comparative obscurity by means of the curtain, Clifford had an opportunity of witnessing such a portion of the great world's movement as might be supposed to roll through one of the retired streets of a not very populous city. But he and Phœbe made a sight as well worth seeing as any that the city could exhibit. The pale, gray, childish, aged, melancholy, yet often simply cheerful, and sometimes delicately intelligent aspect of Clifford, peering from behind the faded crimson of the curtain,—watching the monotony of every-day occurrences with a kind of inconsequential interest and earnestness, and, at every petty throb of his sensibility, turning for sympathy to the eyes of the bright young girl!

If once he were fairly seated at the window, even Pyncheon-street would hardly be so dull and lonely but that somewhere or other along its extent Clifford might discover matter to occupy his eyes, and titillate, if not engross, his observation. Things familiar to the youngest child that had begun its outlook at existence seemed strange to him. A cab; an omnibus, with its populous interior, dropping here and there a passenger, and picking up another, and thus typifying that vast rolling vehicle, the world, the end of whose journey is everywhere and nowhere;—these objects he followed eagerly with his eye, but forgot them, before the dust raised by the horses and wheels had settled along their track. As regarded novelties among which cabs and omnibuses were to be reckoned), his mind appeared to have lost its proper gripe and retentiveness. Twice or thrice, for example, during the sunny hours of the day, a water-cart went along by the Pyncheon-house, leaving a broad wake of moistened earth, instead of the white dust that had risen at a lady's lightest footfall; it was like a summer shower, which the city authorities had caught and tamed, and compelled it into the commonest routine of their convenience. With the water-cart Clifford could never grow familiar; it always affected him with just the same surprise as at first. His mind took apparently sharp impression from it, but lost the recollection of this peramulatory shower, before its next reappearance, as completely as did the street itself, along which the heat so quickly strewed the white dust again. It was the same with the railroad. Clifford could hear the obstreperous howl of the steam-devil, and, by leaning a little way from the arched window, could catch a glimpse of the trains of cars, flashing a brief transit across the extremity of the street. The idea of terrible energy, thus forced upon him, was new at every recurrence, and seemed to affect him as disagreeably, and with almost as much surprise, the hundredth time as the first. Nothing gives a sadder sense of decay than this loss or suspension of the power to deal with unaccustomed things, and to keep up with the swiftness of the passing moment. It can merely be a suspended animation; for, were the power actually to perish, there would be little use of immortality. We are less than ghosts, for the time being, whenever this calamity befalls us.

Clifford was indeed the most inveterate of conservatives. All the antique fashions of the street were dear to him; even such as were characterized by a rudeness that would naturally have annoyed his fastidious senses. He loved the old rumbling and jolting carts, the former track of which he still found in his long-buried remembrance, as the observer of to-day finds the wheel-tracks of ancient vehicles, in Herculaneum. The butcher's cart, with its snowy canopy, was an acceptable object; so was the fish-cart, heralded by its horn; so, likewise, was the countryman's cart of vegetables, plodding from door to door, with long pauses of the patient horse, while his owner drove a trade in turnips, carrots, summer-squashes, string-beans, green peas, and new potatoes, with half the housewives of the neighborhood. The baker's cart, with the harsh music of its bells, had a pleasant effect on Clifford, because, as few things else did, it jingled the very dissonance of yore. One afternoon, a scissor-grinder chanced to set his wheel a-going under the Pyncheon-elm, and just in front of the arched window. Children came running with their mothers' scissors, or the carving-knife, or the paternal razor, or anything else that lacked an edge (except, indeed, poor Clifford's wits), that the grinder might apply the article to his magic wheel, and give it back as good as new. Round went the busily-revolving machinery, kept in motion by the scissor-grinder's foot, and wore away the hard steel against the hard stone, whence issued an intense and spiteful prolongation of a hiss, as fierce as those emitted by Satan and his compeers in Pandemonium, though squeezed into smaller compass. It was an ugly, little, venomous serpent of a noise, as ever did petty violence to human ears. But Clifford listened with rapturous delight. The sound, however disagreeable, had very brisk life in it, and, together with the circle of curious children watching the revolutions of the wheel, appeared to give him a more vivid sense of active, bustling, and sunshiny existence, than he had attained in almost any other way. Nevertheless, its charm lay chiefly in the past; for the scisssor-grinder's wheel had hissed in his childish ears.

He sometimes made doleful complaint that there were no stage-coaches, now-a-days. And he asked, in an injured tone, what had become of all those old square-top chaises, with wings sticking out on either side, that used to be drawn by a plough-horse, and driven by a farmer's wife and daughter, pedling whortleberries and blackberries, about the town. Their disappearance made him doubt, he said, whether the berries had not left off growing in the broad pastures, and along the shady country lanes.

But anything that appealed to the sense of beauty, in however humble a way, did not require to be recommended by these old associations. This was observable when one of those Italian boys (who are rather a modern feature of our streets) came along with his barrel-organ, and stopped under the wide and cool shadows of the elm. With his quick professional eye, he took note of the two faces watching him from the arched window, and, opening his instrument, began to scatter its melodies abroad. He had a monkey on his shoulder, dressed in a Highland plaid; and, to complete the sum of splendid attractions wherewith he presented himself to the public, there was a company of little

figures, whose sphere and habitation wa in the mahogany case of his organ, an whose principle of life was the music which the Italian made it his business to grind out. In all their variety of occu pation,—the cobbler, the blacksmith the soldier, the lady with her fan, th toper with his bottle, the milk-maid sit ting by her cow,—this fortunate littl society might truly be said to enjoy harmonious existence, and to make lif literally a dance. The Italian turned crank; and, behold! every one of thes small individuals started into the mos curious vivacity. The cobbler wrough upon a shoe; the blacksmith hammere his iron; the soldier waved his glitterin blade; the lady raised a tiny breeze wit her fan; the jolly toper swigged lustil at his bottle; a scholar opened his bool with eager thirst for knowledge, an turned his head to and fro along th page; the milk-maid energeticall drained her cow; and a miser counte gold into his strong box;—all at th same turning of a crank. Yes; and moved by the self-same impulse, a love saluted his mistress on her lips! Po sibly, some cynic, at once merry an bitter, had desired to signify, in th pantomimic scene, that we mortal whatever our business or amusement,— however serious, however trifling,—a dance to one identical tune, and, in spi of our ridiculous activity, bring nothir finally to pass. For the most remarkab aspect of the affair was, that, at th cessation of the music, everybody wa petrified, at once, from the most e travagant life into a dead torpo Neither was the cobbler's shoe finishe nor the blacksmith's iron shaped ou nor was there a drop less of brandy i the toper's bottle, nor a drop more milk in the milk-maid's pail, nor one additional coin in the miser's strong-box, nor was the scholar a page deeper in his book. All were precisely in the same condition as before they made themselves so ridiculous by their haste to toil, to enjoy, to accumulate gold, and to become wise. Saddest of all, moreover, the lover was none the happier for the maiden's granted kiss! But, rather than swallow this last too acrid ingredient, we reject the whole moral of the show.

The monkey, meanwhile, with a thick tail curling out into preposterous prolixity from beneath his tartans, took his station at the Italian's feet. He turned a wrinkled and abominable little visage to every passer-by, and to the circle of children that soon gathered round, and to Hepzibah's shop-door, and upward to the arched window, whence Phœbe and Clifford were looking down. Every moment, also, he took off his Highland-bonnet, and performed a bow and scrape. Sometimes, moreover, he made personal application to individuals, holding out his small black palm, and otherwise plainly signifying his excessive desire for whatever filthy lucre might happen to be in anybody's pocket. The mean and low, yet strangely man-like expression of his wilted countenance; the prying and crafty glance, that showed him ready to gripe at every miserable advantage; his enormous tail (too enormous to be decently concealed under his gabardine), and the deviltry of nature which it betokened;—take this monkey just as he was, in short, and you could desire no better image of the Mammon of copper-coin, symbolizing the grossest form of the love of money. Neither was there any possibil-

ity of satisfying the covetous little devil. Phœbe threw down a whole handful of cents, which he picked up with joyless eagerness, handed them over to the Italian for safe-keeping, and immediately recommenced a series of pantomimic petitions for more.

Doubtless, more than one New Englander—or, let him be of what country he might, it is as likely to be the case—passed by, and threw a look at the monkey, and went on, without imagining how nearly his own moral condition was here exemplified. Clifford, however, was a being of another order. He had taken childish delight in the music, and smiled, too, at the figures which it set in motion. But, after looking a while at the long-tailed imp, he was so shocked by his horrible ugliness, spiritual as well as physical, that he actually began to shed tears; a weakness which men of merely delicate endowments, and destitute of the fiercer, deeper, and more tragic power of laughter, can hardly avoid, when the worst and meanest aspect of life happens to be presented to them.

Pyncheon-street was sometimes enlivened by spectacles of more imposing pretensions than the above, and which brought the multitude along with them. With a shivering repugnance at the idea of personal contact with the world, a powerful impulse still seized on Clifford, whenever the rush and roar of the human tide grew strongly audible to him. This was made evident, one day, when a political procession, with hundreds of flaunting banners, and drums, fifes, clarions, and cymbals, reverberating between the rows of buildings, marched all through town, and trailed its length of trampling footsteps, and most infrequent uproar, past the ordinarily quiet House of the Seven Gables. As a mere object of sight, nothing is more deficient in picturesque features than a procession, seen in its passage through narrow streets. The spectator feels it to be fool's play, when he can distinguish the tedious common-place of each man's visage, with the perspiration and weary self-importance on it, and the very cut of his pantaloons, and the stiffness or laxity of his shirt-collar, and the dust on the back of his black coat. In order to become majestic, it should be viewed from some vantage-point, as it rolls its slow and long array through the centre of a wide plain, or the stateliest public square of a city; for then, by its remoteness, it melts all the petty personalities, of which it is made up, into one broad mass of existence,—one great life,—one collected body of mankind, with a vast, homogeneous spirit animating it. But, on the other hand, if an impressible person, standing alone over the brink of one of these processions, should behold it, not in its atoms, but in its aggregate,—as a mighty river of life, massive in its tide, and black with mystery, and, out of its depths, calling to the kindred depth within him,—then the contiguity would add to the effect. It might so fascinate him that he would hardly be restrained from plunging into the surging stream of human sympathies.

So it proved with Clifford. He shuddered; he grew pale; he threw an appealing look at Hepzibah and Phœbe, who were with him at the window. They comprehended nothing of his emotions, and supposed him merely disturbed by the unaccustomed tumult. At last, with tremulous limbs, he started up, set his foot on the window-sill, and, in an instant more, would have been in the unguarded balcony. As it was, the whole procession might have seen him, a wild haggard figure, his gray locks floating in the wind that waved their banners; a lonely being, estranged from his race, but now feeling himself man again, by virtue of the irrepressible instinct that possessed him. Had Clifford attained the balcony, he would probably have leaped into the street; but whether impelled by the species of terror that sometimes urges its victim over the very precipice which he shrinks from, or by a natural magnetism, tending towards the great centre of humanity, it were not easy to decide. Both impulses might have wrought on him at once.

But his companions, affrighted by his gesture,—which was that of a man hurried away, in spite of himself,—seized Clifford's garment and held him back. Hepzibah shrieked. Phœbe, to whom all extravagance was a horror, burst into sobs and tears.

"Clifford, Clifford! are you crazy?" cried his sister.

"I hardly know, Hepzibah," said Clifford, drawing a long breath. "Fear nothing,—it is over now,—but had I taken that plunge, and survived it, methinks it would have made me another man!"

Possibly, in some sense, Clifford may have been right. He needed a shock; or perhaps he required to take a deep, deep plunge into the ocean of human life, and to sink down and be covered by its profoundness, and then to emerge, sobered, invigorated, restored to the world and to himself. Perhaps, again, he required nothing less than the great final remedy—death!

A similar yearning to renew the

roken links of brotherhood with his ind sometimes showed itself in a milder orm; and once it was made beautiful y the religion that lay even deeper han itself. In the incident now to be ketched, there was a touching recognition, on Clifford's part, of God's care nd love towards him,—towards this oor, forsaken man, who, if any mortal ould, might have been pardoned for egarding himself as thrown aside, forotten, and left to be the sport of some end, whose playfulness was an ecstasy f mischief.

It was the Sabbath morning; one of hose bright, calm Sabbaths, with its wn hallowed atmosphere, when Heaven eems to diffuse itself over the earth's ace in a solemn smile, no less sweet han solemn. On such a Sabbath morn, vere we pure enough to be its medium, ve should be conscious of the earth's atural worship ascending through our rames, on whatever spot of ground we tood. The church-bells, with various ones, but all in harmony, were calling ut, and responding to one another—"It the Sabbath!—The Sabbath!—Yea; he Sabbath!"—and over the whole city he bells scattered the blessed sounds, ow slowly, now with livelier joy, now ne bell alone, now all the bells together, crying earnestly—"It is the Sabath!" and flinging their accents afar ff, to melt into the air, and pervade it vith the holy word. The air, with God's weetest and tenderest sunshine in it, vas meet for mankind to breathe into heir hearts, and send it forth again as he utterance of prayer.

Clifford sat at the window, with Hepibah, watching the neighbors as they tepped into the street. All of them, owever unspiritual on other days, were transfigured by the Sabbath influence; so that their very garments—whether it were an old man's decent coat, well brushed for the thousandth time, or a little boy's first sack and trousers, finished yesterday by his mother's needle —had somewhat of the quality of ascension-robes. Forth, likewise, from the portal of the old house, stepped Phœbe, putting up her small green sunshade, and throwing upward a glance and smile of parting kindness to the faces at the arched window. In her aspect there was a familiar gladness, and a holiness that you could play with, and yet reverence it as much as ever. She was like a prayer, offered up in the homeliest beauty of one's mother-tongue. Fresh was Phœbe, moreover, and airy and sweet in her apparel; as if nothing that she wore—neither her gown, nor her small straw bonnet, nor her little kerchief, any more than her snowy stockings—had ever been put on before; or, if worn, were all the fresher for it, and with a fragrance as if they had lain among the rose-buds.

The girl waved her hand to Hepzibah and Clifford, and went up the street; a religion in herself, warm, simple, true, with a substance that could walk on earth, and a spirit that was capable of heaven.

"Hepzibah," asked Clifford, after watching Phœbe to the corner, "do you never go to church?"

"No, Clifford!" she replied,—"not these many, many years!"

"Were I to be there," he rejoined, "it seems to me that I could pray once more, when so many human souls were praying all around me!"

She looked into Clifford's face, and beheld there a soft, natural effusion; for his heart gushed out, as it were, and ran over at his eyes, in delightful reverence for God, and kindly affection for his human brethren. The emotion communicated itself to Hepzibah. She yearned to take him by the hand, and go and kneel down, they two together,—both so long separate from the world, and, as she now recognized, scarcely friends with Him above,—to kneel down among the people, and be reconciled to God and man at once.

"Dear brother," said she, earnestly, "let us go! We belong nowhere. We have not a foot of space in any church to kneel upon; but let us go to some place of worship, even if we stand in the broad aisle. Poor and forsaken as we are, some pew-door will be opened to us!"

So Hepzibah and her brother made themselves ready,—as ready as they could, in the best of their old-fashioned garments, which had hung on pegs, or been laid away in trunks, so long that the dampness and mouldy smell of the past was on them,—made themselves ready, in their faded bettermost, to go to church. They descended the staircase together,—gaunt, sallow Hepzibah, and pale, emaciated, age-stricken Clifford! They pulled open the front door, and stepped across the threshold, and felt, both of them, as if they were standing in the presence of the whole world, and with mankind's great and terrible eye on them alone. The eye of their Father seemed to be withdrawn, and gave them no encouragement. The warm sunny air of the street made them shiver. Their hearts quaked within them, at the idea of taking one step further.

"It cannot be, Hepzibah!—it is too late," said Clifford, with deep sadness.—"We are ghosts! We have no right among human beings,—no right anywhere, but in this old house, which has a curse on it, and which therefore we are doomed to haunt! And, besides," he continued, with a fastidious sensibility, inalienably characteristic of the man "it would not be fit nor beautiful to go! It is an ugly thought, that I should be frightful to my fellow-beings, and that children would cling to their mothers' gowns, at sight of me!"

They shrank back into the dusky passage-way, and closed the door. But, going up the staircase again, they found the whole interior of the house ten-fold more dismal, and the air closer and heavier, for the glimpse and breath of freedom which they had just snatched. They could not flee; their jailer had but left the door ajar, in mockery, and stood behind it, to watch them stealing out. At the threshold, they felt his pitiless gripe upon them. For, what other dungeon is so dark as one's own heart! What jailer so inexorable as one's self!

But it would be no fair picture of Clifford's state of mind, were we to represent him as continually or prevailingly wretched. On the contrary, there was no other man in the city, we are bold to affirm, of so much as half his years, who enjoyed so many lightsome and griefless moments as himself. He had no burthen of care upon him; there were none of those questions and contingencies with the future to be settled, which wear away all other lives, and render them not worth having by the process of providing for their support. In this respect, he was a child,—a child for the whole term of his existence, be it long or short. Indeed, his life seemed to be standing still at a period little in advance of childhood, and to cluster all

is reminiscences about that epoch; just
s, after the torpor of a heavy blow,
ne sufferer's reviving consciousness goes
ack to a moment considerably behind
he accident that stupefied him. He
ometimes told Phœbe and Hepzibah his
reams, in which he invariably played
he part of a child, or a very young
an. So vivid were they, in his relation
f them, that he once held a dispute
rith his sister as to the particular figure
f print of a chintz morning-dress, which
e had seen their mother wear, in the
ream of the preceding night. Hepzibah,
iquing herself on a woman's accuracy
n such matters, held it to be slightly
ifferent from what Clifford described;
ut, producing the very gown from an
ld trunk, it proved to be identical with
is remembrance of it. Had Clifford,
very time that he emerged out of
reams so life-like, undergone the tor-
ure of transformation from a boy into
n old and broken man, the daily recur-
ence of the shock would have been too
nuch to bear. It would have caused an
cute agony to thrill, from the morning
wilight, all the day through, until bed-
me; and even then would have mingled
 dull, inscrutable pain, and pallid hue
f misfortune, with the visionary bloom
nd adolescence of his slumber. But the
ightly moonshine interwove itself with
he morning mist, and enveloped him
s in a robe, which he hugged about his
erson, and seldom let realities pierce
hrough; he was not often quite awake,
ut slept open-eyed, and perhaps fancied
imself most dreaming then.

Thus, lingering always so near his
hildhood, he had sympathies with chil-
ren, and kept his heart the fresher
hereby, like a reservoir into which rivu-
ets were pouring, not far from the

fountain-head. Though prevented, by a
subtle sense of propriety, from desiring
to associate with them, he loved few
things better than to look out of the
arched window, and see a little girl driving her hoop along the sidewalk, or
schoolboys at a game of ball. Their
voices, also, were very pleasant to him,
heard at a distance, all swarming and
intermingling together, as flies do in a
sunny room.

Clifford would, doubtless, have been
glad to share their sports. One afternoon, he was seized with an irresistible
desire to blow soap-bubbles; an amusement, as Hepzibah told Phœbe apart,
that had been a favorite one with her
brother, when they were both children.
Behold him, therefore, at the arched
window, with an earthern pipe in his
mouth! Behold him, with his gray hair,
and a wan, unreal smile over his countenance, where still hovered a beautiful
grace, which his worst enemy must have
acknowledged to be spiritual and immortal, since it had survived so long!
Behold him, scattering airy spheres
abroad, from the window into the street!
Little impalpable worlds were those
soap-bubbles, with the big world depicted, in hues bright as imagination,
or the nothing of their surface. It was
curious to see how the passers-by regarded these brilliant fantasies, as they
came floating down, and made the dull
atmosphere imaginative about them.
Some stopped to gaze, and, perhaps,
carried a pleasant recollection of the
bubbles onward as far as the street-
corner; some looked angrily upward, as
if poor Clifford wronged them, by setting
an image of beauty afloat so near their
dusty pathway. A great many put out
their fingers or their walking-sticks. to

touch, withal; and were perversely gratified, no doubt, when the bubble, with all its pictured earth and sky scene, vanished as if it had never been.

At length, just as an elderly gentleman of very dignified presence happened to be passing, a large bubble sailed majestically down, and burst right against his nose! He looked up,—at first with a stern, keen glance, which penetrated at once into the obscurity behind the arched window,—then with a smile, which might be conceived as diffusing a dog-day sultriness for the space of several yards about him.

"Aha, Cousin Clifford!" cried Judge Pyncheon. "What! still blowing soap bubbles!"

The tone seemed as if meant to be kind and soothing, but yet had a bitterness of sarcasm in it. As for Clifford, an absolute palsy of fear came over him. Apart from any definite cause of dread which his past experience might have given him, he felt that native and original horror of the excellent judge which is proper to a weak, delicate and apprehensive character, in the presence of massive strength. Strength is incomprehensible by weakness, and, therefore the more terrible. There is no greater bugbear than a strong-willed relative, in the circle of his own connections.

CHAPTER XII

THE DAGUERREOTYPIST

It must not be supposed that the life of a personage naturally so active as Phœbe could be wholly confined within the precincts of the old Pyncheon-house. Clifford's demands upon her time were usually satisfied, in those long days, considerably earlier than sunset. Quiet as his daily existence seemed, it nevertheless drained all the resources by which he lived. It was not physical exercise that over-wearied him; for—except that he sometimes wrought a little with a hoe, or paced the garden-walk, or, in rainy weather, traversed a large, unoccupied room—it was his tendency to remain only too quiescent, as regarded any toil of the limbs and muscles. But, either there was a smouldering fire within him that consumed his vital energy, or the monotony that would have dragged itself with benumbing effect over a mind differently situated was no monotony to Clifford. Possibly, he was in a state of second growth and recovery, and was constantly assimilating nutriment for his spirit and intellect from sights, sounds, and events, which passed as a perfect void to persons more practised with the world. As all is activity and vicissitude to the new mind of a child, so might it be, likewise, to a mind that had undergone a kind of new creation, after its long-suspended life.

Be the cause what it might, Clifford commonly retired to rest, thoroughly exhausted, while the sunbeams were still melting through his window-curtains, or were thrown with late lustre on the chamber wall. And while he thus slept early, as other children do, and dreamed of childhood, Phœbe was free to follow her own tastes for the remainder of the day and evening.

This was a freedom essential to the health even of a character so little susceptible of morbid influences as that of Phœbe. The old house, as we have already said, had both the dry-rot and the damp-rot in its walls; it was not good to breathe no other atmosphere than that. Hepzibah, though she had her valuable and redeeming traits, had grown to be a kind of lunatic, by imprisoning herself so long in one place, with no other company than a single series of ideas, and but one affection, and one bitter sense of wrong. Clifford, the reader may perhaps imagine, was too inert to operate morally on his fellow-creatures, however intimate and exclusive their relations with him. But the sympathy or magnetism among human beings is more subtle and universal than we think; it exists, indeed, among different classes of organized life, and vibrates from one to another. A flower, for instance, as Phœbe herself observed, always began to droop sooner in Clifford's hand, or Hepzibah's, than in her own; and by the same law, converting her whole daily life into a flower-fragrance for these two sickly spirits, the blooming girl must inevitably droop and fade much sooner than if worn on a younger and happier breast. Unless she had now and then indulged her brisk impulses, and breathed rural air in a suburban walk, or ocean-breezes along the shore,—had occasionally obeyed the impulse of nature, in New England girls, by attending a meta-physical or philosophical lecture, or viewing a seven-mile panorama, or listening to a concert,—had gone shopping about the city, ransacking entire depôts of splendid merchandise, and bringing home a ribbon,—had employed, likewise, a little time to read the Bible in her chamber, and had stolen a little more to think of her mother and her native place,—unless for such moral medicines as the above, we should soon have beheld our poor Phœbe grow thin, and put on a bleached, unwholesome aspect, and assume strange, shy ways, prophetic of old-maidenhood and a cheerless future.

Even as it was, a change grew visible; a change partly to be regretted, although whatever charm it infringed upon was repaired by another, perhaps more precious. She was not so constantly gay, but had her moods of thought, which Clifford, on the whole, liked better than her former phase of unmingled cheerfulness; because now she understood him better and more delicately, and sometimes even interpreted him to himself. Her eyes looked larger, and darker, and deeper; so deep, at some silent moments, that they seemed like Artesian wells, down, down, into the infinite. She was less girlish than when we first beheld her, alighting from the omnibus; less girlish, but more a woman.

The only youthful mind with which Phœbe had an opportunity of frequent intercourse was that of the daguerreotypist. Inevitably, by the pressure of the seclusion about them, they had been brought into habits of some familiarity. Had they met under different circumstances, neither of these young persons would have been likely to bestow much thought upon the other; unless, indeed, their extreme dissimilarity should have proved a principle of mutual attraction. Both, it is true, were characters proper to New England life, and possessing a common ground, therefore, in their more external developments; but as unlike, in their respective interiors, as if their native climes had been at world-wide distance. During the early part of their acquaintance, Phœbe had held back rather more than was customary with her frank and simple manners from Holgrave's not very marked advances. Nor was she yet satisfied that she knew him well, although they almost daily met and talked together, in a kind, friendly, and what seemed to be a familiar way.

The artist, in a desultory manner, had imparted to Phœbe something of his history. Young as he was, and had his career terminated at the point already attained, there had been enough of incident to fill, very creditably, an autobiographic volume. A romance on the plan of Gil Blas, adapted to American society and manners, would cease to be a romance. The experience of many individuals among us, who think it hardly worth the telling, would equal the vicissitudes of the Spaniard's earlier life; while their ultimate success, or the point whither they tend, may be incomparably higher than any that a novelist would imagine for his hero. Holgrave, as he told Phœbe, somewhat proudly, could not boast of his origin, unless as being exceedingly humble, nor of his education, except that it had been the scantiest possible, and obtained by a few winter-months' attendance at a district school. Left early to his own guidance, he had begun to be self-dependent while yet a boy; and it was a condition aptly suited to his natural force of will. Though now but twenty-two years old (lacking some months, which are years in such a life), he had already been, first, a country schoolmaster; next, a salesman in a country store; and, either at the same time or afterwards, the political editor of a country newspaper. He had subsequently travelled New England and the Middle States, as a pedler, in the employment of a Connecticut manufactory of a cologne-water and other essences. In an episodical way, he had studied and practised dentistry, and with very flattering success, especially in many of the factory-towns along our inland streams. As a supernumerary official, of some kind or other, aboard a packet-ship, he had visited Europe, and found means, before his return, to see Italy, and part of France and Germany. At a later period, he had spent some months in a community of Fourierists. Still more recently, he had been a public lecturer on Mesmerism, for which science (as he assured Phœbe, and, indeed, satisfactorily proved, by putting Chanticleer, who happened to be scratching near by, to sleep) he had very remarkable endowments.

His present phase, as a daguerreotypist, was of no more importance in his own view, nor likely to be more permanent, than any of the preceding ones. It had been taken up with the careless alacrity of an adventurer, who had his bread to earn. It would be thrown aside as carelessly, whenever he should choose to earn his bread by some other equally digressive means. But what was most remarkable, and, perhaps, showed a more than common poise in the young man, was the fact, that, amid all these personal vicissitudes, he had never lost his identity. Homeless as he had been,—continually changing his whereabout, and, therefore, responsible neither to public opinion nor to individuals,—putting off one exterior, and snatching up another, to be soon shifted for a third,—he had never violated the innermost man, but had carried his conscience along with him. It was impossible to know Holgrave, without recognizing this to be the fact. Hepzibah had seen it. Phœbe soon saw it, likewise, and gave him the sort of confidence which such a certainty inspires. She was startled, however, and sometimes repelled,—not by any doubt of his integrity to whatever law he acknowledged,—but by a sense that his law differed from her own. He made her uneasy, and seemed to unsettle everything around her, by his lack of reverence for what was fixed, unless, at a moment's warning, it could establish its right to hold its ground.

Then, moreover, she scarcely thought him affectionate in his nature. He was too calm and cool an observer. Phœbe felt his eye, often; his heart, seldom, or never. He took a certain kind of interest in Hepzibah and her brother, and Phœbe herself. He studied them attentively, and allowed no slightest circumstance of their individualities to escape him. He was ready to do them whatever good he might; but, after all, he never exactly made common cause with them, nor gave any reliable evidence that he loved them better, in proportion as he knew them more. In his relations with them, he seemed to be in quest of mental food, not heart-sustenance. Phœbe could not conceive what interested him so much in her

friends and herself, intellectually, since he cared nothing for them, or, comparatively, so little, as objects of human affection.

Always, in his interviews with Phœbe, the artist made especial inquiry as to the welfare of Clifford, whom, except at the Sunday festival, he seldom saw.

"Does he still seem happy?" he asked, one day.

"As happy as a child," answered Phœbe; "but—like a child, too—very easily disturbed."

"How disturbed?" inquired Holgrave. "By things without, or by thoughts within?"

"I cannot see his thoughts! How should I?" replied Phœbe, with simple piquancy. "Very often, his humor changes without any reason that can be guessed at, just as a cloud comes over the sun. Latterly, since I have begun to know him better, I feel it to be not quite right to look closely into his moods. He has had such a great sorrow, that his heart is made all solemn and sacred by it. When he is cheerful,—when the sun shines into his mind,—then I venture to peep in, just as far as the light reaches, but no further. It is holy ground where the shadow falls!"

"How prettily you express this sentiment!" said the artist. "I can understand the feeling, without possessing it. Had I your opportunities, no scruples would prevent me from fathoming Clifford to the full depth of my plummet-line!"

"How strange that you should wish it!" remarked Phœbe, involuntarily. "What is Cousin Clifford to you?"

"O, nothing,—of course, nothing!" answered Holgrave, with a smile. "Only this is such an odd and incomprehensible world! The more I look at it, the more it puzzles me; and I begin to suspect that a man's bewilderment is the measure of his wisdom. Men and women, and children, too, are such strange creatures, that one never can be certain that he really knows them; nor ever guess what they have been, from what he sees them to be, now. Judge Pyncheon! Clifford! What a complex riddle—a complexity of complexities—do they present! It requires intuitive sympathy, like a young girl's, to solve it. A mere observer, like myself (who never have any intuitions, and am, at best, only subtile and acute), is pretty certain to go astray."

The artist now turned the conversation to themes less dark than that which they had touched upon. Phœbe and he were young together; nor had Holgrave, in his premature experience of life, wasted entirely that beautiful spirit of youth, which, gushing forth from one small heart and fancy, may diffuse itself over the universe, making it all as bright as on the first day of creation. Man's own youth is the world's youth; at least, he feels as if it were, and imagines that the earth's granite substance is something not yet hardened, and which he can mould into whatever shape he likes. So it was with Holgrave. He could talk sagely about the world's old age, but never actually believed what he said; he was a young man still, and therefore looked upon the world—that gray-bearded and wrinkled profligate, decrepit, without being venerable—as a tender stripling, capable of being improved into all that it ought to be, but scarcely yet had shown the remotest promise of becoming. He had that sense, or inward prophecy,—which a young

man had better never have been born than not to have, and a mature man had better die at once than utterly to relinquish,—that we are not doomed to creep on forever in the old, bad way, but that, this very now, there are the harbingers abroad of a golden era, to be accomplished in his own lifetime. It seemed to Holgrave—as doubtless it has seemed to the hopeful of every century, since the epoch of Adam's grandchildren —that in this age, more than ever before, the moss-grown and rotten Past is to be torn down, and lifeless institutions to be thrust out of the way, and their dead corpses buried, and everything to begin anew.

As to the main point,—may we never live to doubt it!—as to the better centuries that are coming, the artist was surely right. His error lay in supposing that this age, more than any past or future one, is destined to see the tattered garments of Antiquity exchanged for a new suit, instead of gradually renewing themselves by patchwork; in applying his own little life-span as the measure of an interminable achievement; and, more than all, in fancying that it mattered anything to the great end in view, whether he himself should contend for it or against it. Yet it was well for him to think so. This enthusiasm, infusing itself through the calmness of his character, and thus taking an aspect of settled thought and wisdom, would serve to keep his youth pure, and make his aspirations high. And when, with the years settling down more weightily upon him, his early faith should be modified by inevitable experience, it would be with no harsh and sudden revolution of his sentiments. He would still have faith in man's brightening destiny, and perhaps love him all the better, as he should recognize his helplessness in his own behalf; and the haughty faith, with which he began life, would be well bartered for a far humbler one, at its close, in discerning that man's best-directed effort accomplishes a kind of dream, while God is the sole worker of realities.

Holgrave had read very little, and that little in passing through the thoroughfare of life, where the mystic language of his books was necessarily mixed up with the babble of the multitude, so that both one and the other were apt to lose any sense that might have been properly their own. He considered himself a thinker, and was certainly of a thoughtful turn, but, with his own path to discover, had perhaps hardly yet reached the point where an educated man begins to think. The true value of his character lay in that deep consciousness of inward strength, which made all his past vicissitudes seem merely like a change of garments; in that enthusiasm, so quiet that he scarcely knew of its existence, but which gave a warmth to everything that he laid his hand on; in that personal ambition, hidden—from his own as well as other eyes—among his more generous impulses, but in which lurked a certain efficacy, that might solidify him from a theorist into the champion of some practicable cause. Altogether, in his culture and want of culture,—in his crude, wild, and misty philosophy, and the practical experience that counteracted some of its tendencies; in his magnanimous zeal for man's welfare, and his recklessness of whatever the ages had established in man's behalf; in his faith, and in his infidelity; in what he had, and in what he lacked,—the artist might fitly enough stand forth as the representative of many compeers in his native land.

His career it would be difficult to prefigure. There appeared to be qualities in Holgrave, such as, in a country where everything is free to the hand that can grasp it, could hardly fail to put some of the world's prizes within his reach. But these matters are delightfully uncertain. At almost every step in life, we meet with young men of just about Holgrave's age, for whom we anticipate wonderful things, but of whom, even after much and careful inquiry, we never happen to hear another word. The effervescence of youth and passion, and the fresh gloss of the intellect and imagination, endow them with a false brilliancy, which makes fools of themselves and other people. Like certain chintzes, calicoes, and ginghams, they show finely in their first newness, but cannot stand the sun and rain, and assume a very sober aspect after washing-day.

But our business is with Holgrave as we find him on this particular afternoon, and in the arbor of the Pyncheon-garden. In that point of view, it was a pleasant sight to behold this young man, with so much faith in himself, and so fair an appearance of admirable powers, —so little harmed, too, by the many tests that had tried his metal,—it was pleasant to see him in his kindly intercourse with Phœbe. Her thought had scarcely done him justice, when it pronounced him cold; or, if so, he had grown warmer now. Without such purpose on her part, and unconsciously on his, she made the House of the Seven Gables like a home to him, and the garden a familiar precinct. With the insight on which he prided himself, he fancied that he could look through Phœbe, and all around her, and could read her off like a page of a child's story-book. But these transparent natures are often deceptive in their depth; those pebbles at the bottom of the fountain are further from us than we think. Thus the artist, whatever he might judge of Phœbe's capacity, was beguiled, by some silent charm of hers, to talk freely of what he dreamed of doing in the world. He poured himself out as to another self. Very possibly, he forgot Phœbe while he talked to her, and was moved only by the inevitable tendency of thought, when rendered sympathetic by enthusiasm and emotion, to flow into the first safe reservoir which it finds. But, had you peeped at them through the chinks of the garden-fence, the young man's earnestness and heightened color might have led you to suppose that he was making love to the young girl!

At length, something was said by Holgrave that made it apposite for Phœbe to inquire what had first brought him acquainted with her cousin Hepzibah, and why he now chose to lodge in the desolate old Pyncheon-house. Without directly answering her, he turned from the Future, which had heretofore been the theme of his discourse, and began to speak of the influences of the Past. One subject, indeed, is but the reverberation of the other.

"Shall we never, never get rid of this Past?" cried he, keeping up the earnest tone of his preceding conversation.—"It lies upon the Present like a giant's dead body! In fact, the case is just as if a young giant were compelled to waste all

his strength in carrying about the corpse of the old giant, his grandfather, who died a long while ago, and only needs to be decently buried. Just think a moment, and it will startle you to see what slaves we are to by-gone times,—to Death, if we give the matter the right word!"

"But I do not see it," observed Phœbe.

"For example, then," continued Holgrave; "a dead man, if he happen to have made a will, disposes of wealth no longer his own; or, if he die intestate, it is distributed in accordance with the notions of men much longer dead than he. A dead man sits on all our judgment-seats; and living judges do but search out and repeat his decisions. We read in dead men's books! We laugh at dead men's jokes, and cry at dead men's pathos! We are sick of dead men's diseases, physical and moral, and die of the same remedies with which dead doctors killed their patients! We worship the living Deity according to dead men's forms and creeds! Whatever we seek to do, of our own free motion, a dead man's icy hand obstructs us! Turn our eyes to what point we may, a dead man's white, immitigable face encounters them, and freezes our very heart! And we must be dead ourselves, before we can begin to have our proper influence on our own world, which will then be no longer our world, but the world of another generation, with which we shall have no shadow of a right to interfere. I ought to have said, too, that we live in dead men's houses; as, for instance, in this of the seven gables!"

"And why not," said Phœbe, "so long as we can be comfortable in them?"

"But we shall live to see the day, I

trust," went on the artist, "when no man shall build his house for posterity. Why should he? He might just as reasonably order a durable suit of clothes, —leather, or gutta percha, or whatever else lasts longest,—so that his great-grandchildren should have the benefit of them, and cut precisely the same figure in the world that he himself does. If each generation were allowed and expected to build its own houses, that single change, comparatively unimportant in itself, would imply almost every reform which society is now suffering for. I doubt whether even our public edifices —our capitols, state-houses, courthouses, city-halls, and churches—ought to be built of such permanent materials as stone or brick. It were better that they should crumble to ruin, once in twenty years, or thereabouts, as a hint to the people to examine into and reform the institutions which they symbolize."

"How you hate everything old!" said Phœbe, in dismay. "It makes me dizzy to think of such a shifting world!"

"I certainly love nothing mouldy," answered Holgrave. "Now, this old Pyncheon-house! Is it a wholesome place to live in, with its black shingles, and the green moss that shows how damp they are?—its dark, low-studded rooms?—its grime and sordidness, which are the crystallization on its walls of the human breath, that has been drawn and exhaled here, in discontent and anguish? The house ought to be purified with fire,—purified till only its ashes remain!"

"Then why do you live in it?" asked Phœbe, a little piqued.

"O, I am pursuing my studies here; not in books, however," replied Hol-

grave. "The house, in my view, is expressive of that odious and abominable Past, with all its bad influences, against which I have just been declaiming. I dwell in it for a while, that I may know the better how to hate it. By-the-by, did you ever hear the story of Maule, the wizard, and what happened between him and your immeasurably great-grandfather?"

"Yes indeed!" said Phœbe; "I heard it long ago, from my father, and two or three times from my cousin Hepzibah, in the month that I have been here. She seems to think that all the calamities of the Pyncheons began from that quarrel with the wizard, as you call him. And you, Mr. Holgrave, look as if you thought so too! How singular, that you should believe what is so very absurd, when you reject many things that are a great deal worthier of credit!"

"I do believe it," said the artist, seriously; "not as a superstition, however, but as proved by unquestionable facts, and as exemplifying a theory. Now, see; —under those seven gables, at which we now look up,—and which old Colonel Pyncheon meant to be the house of his descendants, in prosperity and happiness, down to an epoch far beyond the present,—under that roof, through a portion of three centuries, there has been perpetual remorse of conscience, a constantly defeated hope, strife amongst kindred, various misery, a strange form of death, dark suspicion, unspeakable disgrace,—all, or most of which calamity, I have the means of tracing to the old Puritan's inordinate desire to plant and endow a family. To plant a family! This idea is at the bottom of most of the wrong and mischief which men do. The truth is, that, once in every half century, at longest, a family should be merged into the great, obscure mass of humanity, and forget all about its ancestors. Human blood, in order to keep its freshness, should run in hidden streams, as the water of an aqueduct is conveyed in subterranean pipes. In the family existence of these Pyncheons, for instance,—forgive me, Phœbe; but I cannot think of you as one of them,— in their brief New England pedigree, there has been time enough to infect them all with one kind of lunacy or another!"

"You speak very unceremoniously of my kindred," said Phœbe, debating with herself whether she ought to take offence.

"I speak true thoughts to a true mind!" answered Holgrave, with a vehemence which Phœbe had not before witnessed in him. "The truth is as I say! Furthermore, the original perpetrator and father of this mischief appears to have perpetuated himself, and still walks the street,—at least, his very image, in mind and body,—with the fairest prospect of transmitting to posterity as rich and as wretched an inheritance as he has received! Do you remember the daguerreotype, and its resemblance to the old portrait?"

"How strangely in earnest you are!" exclaimed Phœbe, looking at him with surprise and perplexity: half alarmed, and partly inclined to laugh. "You talk of the lunacy of the Pyncheons;—is it contagious?"

"I understand you!" said the artist, coloring and laughing. "I believe I am a little mad. This subject has taken hold of my mind with the strangest tenacity of clutch, since I have lodged in yonder old gable. As one method of throwing it off, I have put an incident of the Pyncheon family history, with which I happen to be acquainted, into the form of a legend, and mean to publish it in a magazine."

"Do you write for the magazines?" inquired Phœbe.

"Is it possible you did not know it?" cried Holgrave.—"Well, such is literary fame! Yes. Miss Phœbe Pyncheon, among the multitude of my marvellous gifts, I have that of writing stories; and my name has figured, I can assure you, on the covers of Graham and Godey, making as respectable an appearance, for aught I could see, as any of the canonized bead-roll with which it was associated. In the humorous line, I am thought to have a very pretty way with me; and as for pathos, I am as provocative of tears as an onion. But shall I read you my story?"

"Yes, if it is not very long," said Phœbe,—and added, laughingly,—"nor very dull."

As this latter point was one which the daguerreotypist could not decide for himself, he forthwith produced his roll of manuscript, and, while the late sunbeams gilded the seven gables, began to read.

CHAPTER XIII

ALICE PYNCHEON

THERE was a message brought, one day, from the worshipful Gervayse Pyncheon to young Matthew Maule, the carpenter, desiring his immediate presence at the House of the Seven Gables.

"And what does your master want with me?" said the carpenter to Mr. Pyncheon's black servant. "Does the house need any repair? Well it may, by this time; and no blame to my father who built it, neither! I was reading the old colonel's tombstone, no longer ago than last Sabbath; and reckoning from that date, the house has stood seven-and-thirty years. No wonder if there should be a job to do on the roof."

"Don't know what massa wants," answered Scipio. "The house is a berry good house, and old Colonel Pyncheon think so too, I reckon;—else why the old man haunt it so, and frighten a poor nigga, as he does?"

"Well, well, friend Scipio; let your master know that I'm coming," said the carpenter, with a laugh. "For a fair, workman-like job, he'll find me his man. And so the house is haunted, is it? It will take a tighter workman than I am to keep the spirits out of the seven gables. Even if the colonel would be quit," he added, muttering to himself, "my old grandfather, the wizard, will be pretty sure to stick to the Pyncheons, as long as their walls hold together."

"What's that you mutter to yourself, Matthew Maule?" asked Scipio. "And what for do you look so black at me?"

"No matter, darkey!" said the carpenter. "Do you think nobody is to look black but yourself? Go tell your master I'm coming; and if you happen to see Mistress Alice, his daughter, give Matthew Maule's humble respects to her. She has brought a fair face from Italy,—fair, and gentle, and proud,—has that same Alice Pyncheon!"

"He talk of Mistress Alice!" cried Scipio, as he returned from his errand. "The low carpenter-man! He no business so much as to look at her a great way off!"

This young Matthew Maule, the carpenter, it must be observed, was a person little understood, and not very generally liked, in the town where he resided; not that anything could be alleged against his integrity, or his skill and diligence in the handicraft which he exercised. The aversion (as it might justly be called) with which many persons regarded him, was partly the result of his own character and deportment, and partly an inheritance.

He was the grandson of a former Matthew Maule, one of the early settlers of the town, and who had been a famous and terrible wizard, in his day. This old reprobate was one of the sufferers when Cotton Mather and his brother ministers, and the learned judges, and other wise men, and Sir William Phipps, the sagacious governor, made such laudable efforts to weaken the great enemy of souls, by sending a multitude of his adherents up the rocky pathway of Gallows Hill. Since those days, no doubt, it had grown to be suspected, that, in consequence of an unfortunate overdoing of a work praiseworthy in itself, the proceedings against the witches had proved far less acceptable to the Beneficent Father than to that very Arch Enemy whom they were intended to distress and utterly overwhelm. It is not the less certain, however, that awe and terror brooded over the memories of those who died for this horrible crime of witchcraft. Their graves, in the crevices of the rocks, were supposed to be incapable of retaining the occupants who had been so hastily thrust into them. Old Matthew Maule, especially, was known to have as little hesitation or difficulty in rising out of his grave as an ordinary man in getting out of bed, and was as often seen at midnight as living people at noonday. This pestilent wizard (in whom his just punishment seemed to have wrought no manner of amends) had an inveterate habit of haunting a certain mansion, styled the House of the Seven Gables, against the owner of which he pretended to hold an unsettled claim for ground-rent. The ghosts, it appears,—with the pertinacity which was one of his distinguishing characteristics while alive,—insisted that he was the rightful proprietor of the site upon which the house stood. His terms were, that either the aforesaid ground-rent, from the day when the cellar began to be dug, should be paid down, or the mansion itself given up; else he, the ghostly creditor, would have his finger in all the affairs of the Pyncheons, and make everything go wrong with them, though it should be a thousand years after his death. It was a wild story, perhaps, but seemed not altogether so incredible, to those who could remember what an inflexibly obstinate old fellow this wizard Maule had been.

Now, the wizard's grandson, the young Matthew Maule of our story, was popularly supposed to have inherited some of his ancestor's questionable traits. It is wonderful how many absurdities were promulgated in reference to the young man. He was fabled, for example, to have a strange power of getting into people's dreams, and regulating matters there according to his own fancy, pretty much like the stage-manager of a theatre. There was a great deal of talk among the neighbors, particularly the petticoated ones, about what they called the witchcraft of Maule's eye. Some said that he could look into people's minds; others, that, by the marvellous power of this eye, he could draw people into his own mind, or send them, if he pleased, to do errands to his grandfather, in the spiritual world; others, again, that it was what is termed an Evil Eye, and possessed the valuable faculty of blighting corn, and drying children into mummies with the heart-burn. But, after all, what worked most to the young carpenter's disadvantage was, first, the reserve and sternness of his natural disposition, and next, the fact of his not being a church-communicant, and the suspicion of his holding heretical tenents in matters of religion and polity.

After receiving Mr. Pyncheon's message, the carpenter merely tarried to finish a small job, which he happened to have in hand, and then took his way towards the House of the Seven Gables. This noted edifice, though its style might be getting a little out of fashion, was still as respectable a family residence as that of any gentleman in town. The present owner, Gervayse Pyncheon, was said to have contracted a dislike to the house, in consequence of a shock to his sensibility, in early childhood, from the sudden death of his grandfather. In the very act of running to climb Colonel Pyncheon's knee, the boy had discovered the old Puritan to be a corpse! On arriving at manhood, Mr. Pyncheon had visited England, where he married a lady of fortune, and had subsequently spent many years, partly in the mother country, and partly in various cities on the continent of Europe. During this period, the family mansion had been consigned to the charge of a kinsman, who was allowed to make it his home, for the time being, in consideration of keeping the premises in thorough repair. So faithfully had this contract been fulfilled, that now, as the carpenter approached the house, his practised eye could detect nothing to criticize in its condition. The peaks of the seven gables rose up sharply; the shingled roof looked thoroughly watertight; and the glittering plaster-work entirely covered the exterior walls, and sparkled in the October sun, as if it had been new only a week ago.

The house had that pleasant aspect of life which is like the cheery expression of comfortable activity in the human countenance. You could see, at once, that there was the stir of a large family within it. A huge load of oak-wood was passing through the gateway, towards the out-buildings in the rear; the fat cook—or probably it might be the housekeeper—stood at the side-door, bargaining for some turkeys and poultry, which a countryman had brought for sale. Now and then, a maid-servant, neatly dressed, and now the shining sable face of a slave, might be seen bustling across the windows, in the lower part of the house. At an open window of a room in the second story, hanging over some pots of beautiful and delicate flowers,—exotics, but which had never known a more genial sunshine than that of the New England autumn,—was the figure of a young lady, an exotic, like the flowers, and beautiful and delicate as they. Her presence imparted an indescribable grace and faint witchery to the whole edifice. In other respects, it was a substantial, jolly-looking mansion, and seemed fit to be the residence of a patriarch, who might establish his own head-quarters in the front gable, and assign one of the remainder to each of his six children; while the great chimney in the centre should symbolize the old fellow's hospitable heart, which kept them all warm, and made a great whole of the seven smaller ones.

There was a vertical sun-dial on the front gable; and as the carpenter passed beneath it, he looked up and noted the hour.

"Three o'clock!" said he to himself. "My father told me that dial was put up only an hour before the old colonel's death. How truly it has kept time these seven-and-thirty years past! The shadow creeps and creeps, and is always looking over the shoulder of the sunshine!"

It might have befitted a craftsman, like Matthew Maule, on being sent for to a gentleman's house, to go to the back-door, where servants and work-people were usually admitted; or at least to the side-entrance, where the better class of tradesmen made application. But the carpenter had a great deal of pride and stiffness in his nature; and, at this moment, moreover, his heart was bitter with the sense of hereditary wrong, because he considered the great

Pyncheon-house to be standing on soil which should have been his own. On this very site, beside a spring of delicious water, his grandfather had felled the pine-trees and built a cottage, in which children had beeh born to him; and it was only from a dead man's stiffened fingers that Colonel Pyncheon had wrestled away the title-deeds. So young Maule went straight to the principal entrance, beneath a portal of carved oak, and gave such a peal of the iron knocker that you would have imagined the stern old wizard himself to be standing at the threshold.

Black Scipio answered the summons, in a prodigious hurry; but showed the whites of his eyes, in amazement, on beholding only the carpenter.

"Lord-a-mercy! what a great man he be, this carpenter fellow!" mumbled Scipio, down in his throat. "Anybody think he beat on the door with his biggest hammer!"

"Here I am!" said Maule, sternly. "Show me the way to your master's parlor!"

As he stept into the house, a note of sweet and melancholy music thrilled and vibrated along the passage-way, proceeding from one of the rooms above stairs. It was the harpsichord which Alice Pyncheon had brought with her from beyond the sea. The fair Alice bestowed most of her maiden leisure between flowers and music, although the former were apt to droop, and the melodies were often sad. She was of foreign education, and could not take kindly to the New England modes of life, in which nothing beautiful had ever been developed.

As Mr. Pyncheon had been impatiently awaiting Maule's arrival, black

Scipio, of course, lost no time in ushering the carpenter into his master's presence. The room in which this gentleman sat was a parlor of moderate size, looking out upon the garden of the house, and having its windows partly shadowed by the foliage of fruit-trees. It was Mr. Pyncheon's peculiar apartment, and was provided with furniture, in an elegant and costly style, principally from Paris; the floor (which was unusual, at that day) being covered with a carpet, so skilfully and richly wrought, that it seemed to glow as with living flowers. In one corner stood a marble woman, to whom her own beauty was the sole and sufficient garment. Some pictures—that looked old, and had a mellow tinge diffused through all their artful splendor—hung on the walls. Near the fireplace was a large and very beautiful cabinet of ebony, inlaid with ivory; a piece of antique furniture, which Mr. Pyncheon had bought in Venice, and which he used as the treasure-place for medals, ancient coins, and whatever small and valuable curiosities he had picked up, on his travels. Through all this variety of decoration, however, the room showed its original characteristics; its low stud, its cross-beam, its chimney-piece, with the old-fashioned Dutch tiles; so that it was the emblem of a mind industriously stored with foreign ideas, and elaborated into artificial refinement, but neither larger, nor, in its proper self, more elegant, than before.

There were two objects that appeared rather out of place in this very handsomely furnished room. One was a large map, or surveyor's plan, of a tract of land, which looked as if it had been drawn a good many years ago, and was now dingy with smoke, and soiled, here and there, with the touch of fingers. The other was a portrait of a stern old man, in a Puritan garb, painted roughly, but with a bold effect, and a remarkably strong expression of character.

At a small table, before a fire of English sea-coal, sat Mr. Pyncheon, sipping coffee, which had grown to be a very favorite beverage with him in France. He was a middle-aged and really handsome man, with a wig flowing down upon his shoulders; his coat was of blue velvet, with lace on the borders and at the buttonholes; and the fire-light glistened on the spacious breadth of his waistcoat, which was flowered all over with gold. On the entrance of Scipio, ushering in the carpenter, Mr. Pyncheon turned partly round, but resumed his former position, and proceeded deliberately to finish his cup of coffee, without immediate notice of the guest whom he had summoned to his presence. It was not that he intended any rudeness, or improper neglect,—which, indeed, he would have blushed to be guilty of,— but it never occurred to him that a person in Maule's station had a claim on his courtesy, or would trouble himself about it, one way or the other.

The carpenter, however, stepped at once to the hearth, and turned himself about, so as to look Mr. Pyncheon in the face.

"You sent for me," said he. "Be pleased to explain your business, that I may go back to my own affairs."

"Ah! excuse me," said Mr. Pyncheon, quietly. "I did not mean to tax your time without a recompense. Your name, I think, is Maule,—Thomas or Matthew Maule,—a son or grandson of the builder of this house?"

"Matthew Maule," replied the car-penter,—"son of him who built the house,—grandson of the rightful proprietor of the soil."

"I know the dispute to which you allude," observed Mr. Pyncheon, with undisturbed equanimity. "I am well aware that my grandfather was compelled to resort to a suit at law, in order to establish his claim to the foundation-site of this edifice. We will not, if you please, renew the discussion. The matter was settled at the time, and by the competent authorities,—equitably, it is to be presumed,—and, at all events, irrevocably. Yet, singularly enough, there is an incidental reference to this very subject in what I am now about to say to you. And this same inveterate grudge, —excuse me, I mean no offence,—this irritability, which you have just shown, is not entirely aside from the matter."

"If you can find anything for your purpose, Mr. Pyncheon," said the car-penter, "in a man's natural resentment for the wrongs done to his blood, you are welcome to it!"

"I take you at your word, Goodman Maule," said the owner of the seven gables, with a smile, "and will proceed to suggest a mode in which your hereditary resentments—justifiable, or otherwise—may have had a bearing on my affairs. You have heard, I suppose, that the Pyncheon family, ever since my grandfather's days, have been prosecuting a still unsettled claim to a very large extent of territory at the eastward?"

"Often," replied Maule,—and it is said that a smile came over his face,— "very often,—from my father!"

"This claim," continued Mr. Pyncheon, after pausing a moment, as if to consider what the carpenter's smile might mean, "appeared to be on the very verge of a settlement and full allowance, at the period of my grandfather's decease. It was well known, to those in his confidence, that he anticipated neither difficulty nor delay. Now, Colonel Pyncheon, I need hardly say, was a practical man, well acquainted with public and private business, and not at all the person to cherish ill-founded hopes, or to attempt the following out of an impracticable scheme. It is obvious to conclude, therefore, that he had grounds, not apparent to his heirs, for his confident anticipation of success in the matter of this eastern claim. In a word, I believe,—and my legal advisers coincide in the belief, which, moreover, is authorized, to a certain extent, by the family traditions,— that my grandfather was in possession of some deed, or other document, essential to this claim, but which has since disappeared."

"Very likely," said Matthew Maule, —and again, it is said, there was a dark smile on his face,—"but what can a poor carpenter have to do with the grand affairs of the Pyncheon family?"

"Perhaps nothing," returned Mr. Pyncheon,—"possibly, much!"

Here ensued a great many words between Matthew Maule and the proprietor of the seven gables, on the subject which the latter had thus broached. It seems (although Mr. Pyncheon had some hesitation in referring to stories so exceedingly absurd in their aspect) that the popular belief pointed to some mysterious connection and dependence, existing between the family of the Maules and these vast, unrealized possessions of the Pyncheons. It was an ordinary saying, that the old wizard,

hanged though he was, had obtained the best end of the bargain, in his contest with Colonel Pyncheon; inasmuch as he had got possession of the great eastern claim, in exchange for an acre or two of garden-ground. A very aged woman, recently dead, had often used the metaphorical expression, in her fireside talk, that miles and miles of the Pyncheon lands had been shovelled into Maule's grave; which, by-the-by, was but a very shallow nook, between two rocks, near the summit of Gallows Hill. Again, when the lawyers were making inquiry for the missing document, it was a by-word, that it would never be found, unless in the wizard's skeleton-hand. So much weight had the shrewd lawyers assigned to these fables, that—(but Mr. Pyncheon did not see fit to inform the carpenter of the fact)—they had secretly caused the wizard's grave to be searched. Nothing was discovered, however, except that, unaccountably, the right hand of the skeleton was gone.

Now what was unquestionably important, a portion of these popular rumors could be traced, though rather doubtfully and indistinctly, to chance words and obscure hints of the executed wizard's son, and the father of this present Matthew Maule. And here Mr. Pyncheon could bring an item of his own personal evidence into play. Though but a child at the time, he either remembered or fancied that Matthew's father had had some job to perform, on the day before, or possibly the very morning of the colonel's decease, in the private room where he and the carpenter were at this moment talking. Certain papers belonging to Colonel Pyncheon, as his grandson distinctly recollected, had been spread out on the table.

Matthew Maule understood the insinuated suspicion.

"My father," he said,—but still there was that dark smile, making a riddle of his countenance,—"my father was an honester man than the bloody old colonel! Not to get his rights back again would he have carried off one of those papers!"

"I shall not bandy words with you," observed the foreign-bred Mr. Pyncheon, with haughty composure. "Nor will it become me to resent any rudeness towards either my grandfather or myself. A gentleman, before seeking intercourse with a person of your station and habits, will first consider whether the urgency of the end may compensate for the disagreeableness of the means. It does so, in the present instance."

He then renewed the conversation, and made great pecuniary offers to the carpenter, in case the latter should give information leading to the discovery of the lost document, and the consequent success of the eastern claim. For a long time Matthew Maule is said to have turned a cold ear to these propositions. At last, however, with a strange kind of laugh, he inquired whether Mr. Pyncheon would make over to him the old wizard's homestead-ground, together with the House of the Seven Gables, now standing on it, in requital of the documentary evidence so urgently required.

The wild, chimney-corner legend (which, without copying all its extravagances, my narrative essentially follows) here gives an account of some very strange behavior on the part of Colonel Pyncheon's portrait. This picture, it must be understood, was supposed to be so intimately connected with the fate of the house, and so magically built into the walls, that, if once it should be removed, that very instant the whole edifice would come thundering down in a heap of dusty ruin. All through the foregoing conversation between Mr. Pyncheon and the carpenter, the portrait had been frowning, clenching its fist, and giving many such proofs of excessive discomposure, but without attracting the notice of either of the two colloquists. And finally at Matthew Maule's audacious suggestion of a transfer of the seven-gabled structure, the ghostly portrait is averred to have lost all patience, and to have shown itself on the point of descending bodily from its frame. But such incredible incidents are merely to be mentioned aside.

"Give up this house!" exclaimed Mr. Pyncheon, in amazement at the proposal. "Were I to do so, my grandfather would not rest quiet in his grave!"

"He never has, if all stories are true," remarked the carpenter composedly. "But that matter concerns his grandson more than it does Matthew Maule. I have no other terms to propose."

Impossible as he at first thought it to comply with Maule's conditions, still, on a second glance, Mr. Pyncheon was of opinion that they might at least be made matter of discussion. He himself had no personal attachment for the house, nor any pleasant associations connected with his childish residence in it. On the contrary, after seven-and-thirty years, the presence of his dead grandfather seemed still to pervade it, as on that morning when the affrighted boy had beheld him, with so ghastly an aspect, stiffening in his chair. His long abode in foreign parts, moreover, and familiarity with many of the castles and ancestral halls of England, and the marble palaces of Italy, had caused him to look contemptuously at the House of the Seven Gables, whether in point of splendor or convenience. It was a mansion exceedingly inadequate to the style of living which it would be incumbent on Mr. Pyncheon to support, after realizing his territorial rights. His steward might deign to occupy it, but never, certainly, the great landed proprietor himself. In the event of success, indeed, it was his purpose to return to England; nor, to say the truth, would he recently have quitted that more congenial home, had not his own fortune, as well as his deceased wife's begun to give symptoms of exhaustion. The eastern claim once fairly settled, and put upon the firm basis of actual possession, Mr. Pyncheon's property— to be measured by miles, not acres— would be worth an earldom, and would reasonably entitle him to solicit, or enable him to purchase, that elevated dignity from the British monarch. Lord Pyncheon!—or the Earl of Waldo!— how could such a magnate be expected to contract his grandeur within the pitiful compass of seven shingled gables?

In short, on an enlarged view of the business, the carpenter's terms appeared so ridiculously easy, that Mr. Pyncheon could scarcely forbear laughing in his face. He was quite ashamed, after the foregoing reflections, to propose any diminution of so moderate a recompense for the immense service to be rendered.

"I consent to your proposition, Maule," cried he. "Put me in possession of the document essential to establish my rights, and the House of the Seven Gables is your own!"

According to some versions of the story, a regular contract to the above effect was drawn up by a lawyer, and signed and sealed in the presence of witnesses. Others say that Matthew Maule was contented with a private written agreement, in which Mr. Pyncheon pledged his honor and integrity, to the fulfilment of the terms concluded upon. The gentleman then ordered wine, which he and the carpenter drank together, in confirmation of their bargain. During the whole preceding discussion and subsequent formalities, the old Puritan's portrait seems to have persisted in its shadowy gestures of disapproval; but without effect, except that, as Mr. Pyncheon set down the emptied glass, he thought he beheld his grandfather frown.

"This sherry is too potent a wine for me; it has affected my brain already," he observed, after a somewhat startled look at the picture. "On returning to Europe, I shall confine myself to the more delicate vintages of Italy and France, the best of which will not bear transportation."

"My Lord Pyncheon may drink what wine he will, and wherever he pleases," replied the carpenter, as if he had been privy to Mr. Pyncheon's ambitious projects. "But first, sir, if you desire tidings of this lost document, I must crave the favor of a little talk with your fair daughter Alice."

"You are mad, Maule!" exclaimed Mr. Pyncheon, haughtily; and now, at last, there was anger mixed up with his pride. "What can my daughter have to do with a business like this?"

Indeed, at this new demand on the carpenter's part, the proprietor of the seven gables was even more thunderstruck than at the cool proposition to surrender his house. There was, at least, an assignable motive for the first stipulation; there appeared to be none whatever, for the last. Nevertheless, Matthew Maule sturdily insisted on the young lady being summoned, and even gave her father to understand, in a mysterious kind of explanation,—which made the matter considerably darker than it looked before,—that the only chance of acquiring the requisite knowledge was through the clear, crystal medium of a pure and virgin intelligence, like that of the fair Alice. Not to encumber our story with Mr. Pyncheon's scruples, whether of conscience, pride, or fatherly affection, he at length ordered his daughter to be called. He well knew that she was in her chamber, and engaged in no occupation that could not readily be laid aside; for, as it happened, ever since Alice's name had been spoken, both her father and the carpenter had heard the sad and sweet music of her harpsichord, and the airier melancholy of her accompanying voice.

So Alice Pyncheon was summoned, and appeared. A portrait of this young lady, painted by a Venetian artist, and left by her father in England, is said to have fallen into the hands of the present Duke of Devonshire, and to be now preserved at Chatsworth; not on account of any associations with the original, but for its value as a picture, and the high character of beauty in the countenance. If ever there was a lady born, and set apart from the world's vulgar mass by a certain gentle and cold stateliness, it was this very Alice Pyncheon. Yet there was the womanly mixture in her; the tenderness, or, at least, the tender capabilities. For the sake of that redeeming quality, a man of generous nature would have forgiven all her pride, and have been content, almost, to lie down in her path, and let Alice set her slender foot upon his heart. All that he would have required, was simply the acknowledgment that he was indeed a man, and a fellow-being, moulded of the same elements as she.

As Alice came into the room, her eyes fell upon the carpenter, who was standing near its centre, clad in a green woollen jacket, a pair of loose breeches, open at the knees, and with a long pocket for his rule, the end of which protruded; it was as proper a mark of the artisan's calling, as Mr. Pyncheon's full-dress sword of that gentleman's aristocratic pretensions. A glow of artistic approval brightened over Alice Pyncheon's face; she was struck with admiration—which she made no attempt to conceal—of the remarkable comeliness, strength and energy, of Maule's figure. But that admiring glance (which most other men, perhaps, would have cherished as a sweet recollection, all through life) the carpenter never forgave. It must have been the devil himself that made Maule so subtile in his perception.

"Does the girl look at me as if I were a brute beast?" thought he, setting his teeth. "She shall know whether I have a human spirit; and the worse for her, if it prove stronger than her own!"

"My father, you sent for me," said Alice, in her sweet and harp-like voice. "But, if you have business with this young man, pray let me go again. You know I do not love this room, in spite of that Claude, with which you try to bring back sunny recollections."

"Stay a moment, young lady, if you please!" said Matthew Maule. "My business with your father is over. With yourself, it is now to begin!"

Alice looked towards her father, in surprise and inquiry.

"Yes, Alice," said Mr. Pyncheon, with some disturbance and confusion. "This young man—his name is Matthew Maule—professes, so far as I can understand him, to be able to discover, through your means, a certain paper or parchment, which was missing long before your birth. The importance of the document in question renders it advisable to neglect no possible, even if improbable, method of regaining it. You will therefore oblige me, my dear Alice, by answering this person's inquiries, and complying with his lawful and reasonable requests, so far as they may appear to have the aforesaid object in view. As I shall remain in the room, you need apprehend no rude nor unbecoming deportment, on the young man's part; and, at your slightest wish, of course, the investigation, or whatever we may call it, shall immediately be broken off."

"Mistress Alice Pyncheon," remarked Matthew Maule, with the utmost deference, but yet a half-hidden sarcasm in his look and tone, "will no doubt feel herself quite safe in her father's presence, and under his all-sufficient protection."

"I certainly shall entertain no manner of apprehension, with my father at hand," said Alice, with maidenly dignity. "Neither do I conceive that a lady, while true to herself, can have aught to fear, from whomsoever, or in any circumstances!"

Poor Alice! By what unhappy impulse did she thus put herself at once on terms of defiance against a strength which she could not estimate?

"Then, Mistress Alice," said Matthew Maule, handing a chair,—gracefully enough, for a craftsman,—"will it please you only to sit down. and do me the favor (though altogether beyond a poor carpenter's deserts) to fix your eyes on mine!"

Alice complied. She was very proud. Setting aside all advantages of rank, this fair girl deemed herself conscious of a power,—combined of beauty, high, unsullied purity, and the preservative force of womanhood,—that could make her sphere impenetrable, unless betrayed by treachery within. She instinctively knew, it may be, that some sinister or evil potency was now striving to pass her barriers; nor would she decline the contest. So Alice put woman's might against man's might; a match not often equal, on the part of woman.

Her father, meanwhile, had turned away, and seemed absorbed in the contemplation of a landscape by Claude, where a shadowy and sun-streaked vista penetrated so remotely into an ancient wood, that it would have been no wonder if his fancy had lost itself in the picture's bewildering depths. But, in truth, the picture was no more to him, at that moment, than the blank wall against which it hung. His mind was haunted with the many and strange tales which he had heard, attributing mysterious if not supernatural endowments to these Maules, as well the grandson, here present, as his two immediate ancestors. Mr. Pyncheon's long residence abroad, and intercourse with men of wit and fashion,—courtiers, worldlings, and free-thinkers,—had done much towards obliterating the grim Puritan superstitions, which no man of New England birth, at that early period, could entirely escape. But, on the other hand, had not a whole community believed Maule's grandfather to be a wizard? Had not the crime been proved? Had not the wizard died for it? Had he not bequeathed a legacy of hatred against the Pyncheons to this only grandson, who, as it appeared, was now about to exercise a subtle influence over the daughter of his enemy's house? Might not this influence be the same that was called witchcraft?

Turning half around, he caught a glimpse of Maule's figure in the looking-glass. At some paces from Alice, with his arms uplifted in the air, the carpenter made a gesture, as if directing downward a slow, ponderous, and invisible weight upon the maiden.

"Stay, Maule!" exclaimed Mr. Pyncheon, stepping forward. "I forbid your proceeding further!"

"Pray, my dear father, do not interrupt the young man," said Alice, without changing her position. "His efforts, I assure you, will prove very harmless."

Again Mr. Pyncheon turned his eyes towards the Claude. It was then his daughter's will, in opposition to his own, that the experiment should be fully tried. Henceforth, therefore, he did but consent, not urge it. And was it not for her sake, far more than for his own, that he desired its success? That lost parchment once restored, the beautiful Alice Pyncheon, with the rich dowry which he could then bestow, might wed an English duke, or a German reigning-prince instead of some New England clergyman or lawyer! At the thought, the ambitious father almost consented, in his heart, that, if the devil's power

were needed to the accomplishment of this great object, Maule might evoke him. Alice's own purity would be her safeguard.

With his mind full of imaginary magnificence, Mr. Pyncheon heard a half-uttered exclamation from his daughter. It was very faint and low; so indistinct that there seemed but half a will to shape out the words, and too undefined a purport to be intelligible. Yet it was a call for help!—his conscience never doubted it;—and, little more than a whisper to his ear, it was a dismal shriek, and long reëchoed so, in the region round his heart! But, this time, the father did not turn.

After a further interval, Maule spoke. "Behold your daughter!" said he.

Mr. Pyncheon came hastily forward. The carpenter was standing erect in front of Alice's chair, and pointing his finger towards the maiden with an expression of triumphant power, the limits of which could not be defined, as, indeed, its scope stretched vaguely towards the unseen and the infinite. Alice sat in an attitude of profound repose, with the long brown lashes drooping over her eyes.

"There she is!" said the carpenter. "Speak to her!"

"Alice! My daughter!" exclaimed Mr. Pyncheon. "My own Alice!"

She did not stir.

"Louder!" said Maule, smiling.

"Alice! Awake!" cried her father. "It troubles me to see you thus! Awake!"

He spoke loudly, with terror in his voice, and close to that delicate ear, which had always been so sensitive to every discord. But the sound evidently reached her not. It is indescribable wha a sense of remote, dim, unattainable distance, betwixt himself and Alice, was impressed on the father by this impossibility of reaching her with his voice.

"Best touch her!" said Matthew Maule. "Shake the girl, and roughly too! My hands are hardened with too much use of axe, saw, and plane,—else I might help you!"

Mr. Pyncheon took her hand, and pressed it with the earnestness of startled emotion. He kissed her, with so great a heart-throb in the kiss, that he thought she must needs feel it. Then, in a gust of anger at her insensibility, he shook her maiden form, with a violence which, the next moment, it affrighted him to remember. He withdrew his encircling arms, and Alice—whose figure, though flexible, had been wholly impassive—relapsed into the same attitude as before these attempts to arouse her. Maule having shifted his position, her face was turned towards him, slightly, but with what seemed to be a reference of her very slumber to his guidance.

Then it was a strange sight to behold how the man of conventionalities shook the powder out of his periwig; how the reserved and stately gentleman forgot his dignity; how the gold-embroidered waistcoat flickered and glistened in the fire-light, with the convulsion of rage, terror, and sorrow, in the human heart that was beating under it.

"Villain!" cried Mr. Pyncheon, shaking his clenched fist at Maule. "You and the fiend together have robbed me of my daughter! Give her back, spawn of the old wizard, or you shall climb Gallows Hill in your grandfather's footsteps!"

"Softly, Mr. Pyncheon!" said the carpenter, with scornful composure. "Softly, an' it please your worship, else you will spoil those rich lace ruffles, at your wrists! Is it my crime if you have sold your daughter for the mere hope of getting a sheet of yellow parchment into your clutch? There sits Mistress Alice, quietly asleep! Now let Matthew Maule try whether she be as proud as the carpenter found her a while since."

He spoke, and Alice responded, with a soft, subdued, inward acquiesence, and a bending of her form towards him, like the flame of a torch when it indicates a gentle draft of air. He beckoned with his hand, and, rising from her chair,—blindly, but undoubtingly, as tending to her sure and inevitable centre,—the proud Alice approached him. He waved her back, and, retreating, Alice sank again into her seat.

"She is mine!" said Matthew Maule. "Mine, by the right of the strongest spirit!"

In the further progress of the legend, there is a long, grotesque, and occasionally awe-striking account of the carpenter's incantations (if so they are to be called), with a view of discovering the lost document. It appears to have been his object to convert the mind of Alice into a kind of telescopic medium, through which Mr. Pyncheon and himself might obtain a glimpse into the spiritual world. He succeeded, accordingly, in holding an imperfect sort of intercourse, at one remove, with the departed personages, in whose custody the so much valued secret had been carried beyond the precincts of earth. During her trance, Alice described three figures as being present to her spiritualized perception. One was an aged, dignified, stern-looking gentleman, clad, as for a solemn festival, in grave and costly attire, but with a great blood-stain on his richly-wrought band; the second, an aged man, meanly dressed, with a dark and malign countenance, and a broken halter about his neck; the third, a person not so advanced in life as the former two, but beyond the middle age, wearing a coarse woollen tunic and leather breeches, and with a carpenter's rule sticking out of his side-pocket. These three visionary characters possessed a mutual knowledge of the missing document. One of them, in truth,—it was he with the blood-stain on his band,—seemed, unless his gestures were misunderstood, to hold the parchment in his immediate keeping, but was prevented, by his two partners in the mystery, from disburthening himself of the trust. Finally, when he showed a purpose of shouting forth his secret, loudly enough to be heard from his own sphere into that of mortals, his companions struggled with him, and pressed their hands over his mouth; and forthwith—whether that he were choked by it, or that the secret itself was of a crimson hue—there was a fresh flow of blood upon his band. Upon this, the two meanly-dressed figures mocked and jeered at the much-abashed old dignitary, and pointed their fingers at the stain.

At this juncture, Maule turned to Mr. Pyncheon.

"It will never be allowed," said he. "The custody of this secret, that would so enrich his heirs, makes part of your grandfather's retribution. He must choke with it until it is no longer of any value. And keep you the House of the Seven Gables! It is too dear-bought an inheritance, and too heavy with the curse upon it, to be shifted yet a while from the colonel's posterity!"

Mr. Pyncheon tried to speak, but—what with fear and passion—could make only a gurgling murmur in his throat. The carpenter smiled.

"Aha, worshipful sir!—so, you have old Maule's blood to drink!" said he jeeringly.

"Fiend in man's shape! why dost thou keep dominion over my child?" cried Mr. Pyncheon, when his choked utterance could make way. "Give me back my daughter! Then go thy ways; and may we never meet again!"

"Your daughter!" said Matthew Maule. "Why, she is fairly mine! Nevertheless, not to be too hard with fair Mistress Alice, I will leave her in your keeping; but I do not warrant you that she shall never have occasion to remember Maule, the carpenter."

He waved his hands with an upward motion; and, after a few repetitions of similar gestures, the beautiful Alice Pyncheon awoke from her strange trance. She awoke, without the slightest recollection of her visionary experience; but as one losing herself in a momentary reverie, and returning to the consciousness of actual life, in almost as brief an interval as the down-sinking flame of the hearth should quiver again up the chimney. On recognizing Matthew Maule, she assumed an air of somewhat cold but gentle dignity; the rather, as there was a certain peculiar smile on the carpenter's visage, that stirred the native pride of the fair Alice. So ended, for that time, the quest for the lost title-deed of the Pyncheon territory at the eastward; nor, though often subsequently renewed, has it ever yet befallen a Pyncheon to set his eye upon that parchment.

But, alas for the beautiful, the gentle, yet too haughty Alice! A power, that she little dreamed of, had laid its grasp upon her maiden soul. A will, most unlike her own, constrained her to do its grotesque and fantastic bidding. Her father, as it proved, had martyred his poor child to an inordinate desire for measuring his land by miles, instead of acres. And, therefore, while Alice Pyncheon lived, she was Maule's slave, in a bondage more humiliating, a thousand fold, than that which binds its chain around the body. Seated by his humble fireside, Maule had but to wave his hand; and, wherever the proud lady chanced to be,—whether in her chamber, or entertaining her father's stately guests, or worshipping at church,—whatever her place or occupation, her spirit passed from beneath her own control, and bowed itself to Maule. "Alice, laugh!"—the carpenter, beside his hearth, would say; or perhaps intensely will it, without a spoken word. And, even were it prayer-time, or at a funeral, Alice must break into wild laughter. "Alice, be sad!"—and, at the instant, down would come her tears, quenching all the mirth of those around her, like sudden rain upon a bonfire. "Alice, dance!"—and dance she would, not in such court-like measures as she had learned abroad, but some high-paced jig, or hop-skip rigadoon, befitting the brisk lasses at a rustic merry-making. It seemed to be Maule's impulse not to ruin Alice, nor to visit her with any black or gigantic mischief, which would have crowned her sorrows with the grace of tragedy, but to wreak a low, ungenerous scorn upon her. Thus all the dignity of life was lost. She felt herself too much abased, and longed to change natures with some worm!

One evening, at a bridal-party—(but not her own; for, so lost from self-control, she would have deemed it sin to marry)—poor Alice was beckoned forth by her unseen despot, and constrained, in her gossamer white dress and satin slippers, to hasten along the street to the mean dwelling of a laboring-man. There was laughter and good cheer within; for Matthew Maule, that night, was to wed the laborer's daughter, and had summoned proud Alice Pyncheon to wait upon his bride. And so she did; and when the twain were one, Alice awoke out of her enchanted sleep. Yet, no longer proud,—humbly, and with a smile all steeped in sadness, —she kissed Maule's wife, and went her way. It was an inclement night; the south-east wind drove the mingled snow and rain into her thinly-sheltered bosom; her satin slippers were wet through and through, as she trod the muddy sidewalks. The next day, a cold; soon, a settled cough; anon, a hectic cheek, a wasted form, that sat beside the harpsichord, and filled the house with music! Music, in which a strain of the heavenly choristers was echoed! O, joy! For Alice had borne her last humiliation! O, greater joy! For Alice was penitent of her one earthly sin, and proud no more!

The Pyncheons made a great funeral for Alice. The kith and kin were there, and the whole respectability of the town besides. But, last in the procession, came Matthew Maule, gnashing his teeth, as if he would have bitten his own heart in twain—the darkest and wofullest man that ever walked behind a corpse! He meant to humble Alice —not to kill her;—but he had taken a woman's delicate soul into his rude gripe, to play with,—and she was dead!

CHAPTER XIV

PHŒBE'S GOOD-BY

HOLGRAVE, plunging into his tale with the energy and absorption natural to a young author, had given a good deal of action to the parts capable of being developed and exemplified in that manner. He now observed that a certain remarkable drowsiness (wholly unlike that with which the reader possibly feels himself affected) had been flung over the senses of his auditress. It was the effect, unquestionably, of the mystic gesticulations by which he had sought to bring bodily before Phœbe's perception the figure of the memerizing carpenter. With the lids drooping over her eyes,—now lifted, for an instant, and drawn down again, as with leaden weights,—she leaned slightly towards him, and seemed almost to regulate her breath by his. Holgrave gazed at her, as he rolled up his manuscript, and recognized an incipient stage of that curious psychological condition, which, as he had himself told Phœbe, he possessed more than an ordinary faculty of producing. A veil was beginning to be muffled about her, in which she could behold only him, and live only in his thoughts and emotions. His glance, as he fastened it on the young girl, grew involuntarily more concentrated; in his attitude there was the consciousness of power, investing his hardly mature figure with a dignity that did not belong

to its physical manifestation. It was evident, that, with but one wave of his hand, and a corresponding effort of his will, he could complete his mastery over Phœbe's yet free and virgin spirit: he could establish an influence over this good, pure, and simple child, as dangerous, and perhaps as disastrous, as that which the carpenter of his legend had acquired and exercised over the ill-fated Alice.

To a disposition like Holgrave's at once speculative and active, there is no temptation so great as the opportunity of acquiring empire over the human spirit; nor any idea more seductive to a young man than to become the arbiter of a young girl's destiny. Let us, therefore,—whatever his defects of nature and education, and in spite of his scorn for creeds and institutions, —concede to the daguerreotypist the rare and high quality of reverence for another's individuality. Let us allow him integrity, also, forever after to be confided in; since he forbade himself to twine that one link more which might have rendered his spell over Phœbe indissoluble.

He made a slight gesture upward with his hand.

"You really mortify me, my dear Miss Phœbe!" he exclaimed, smiling half-sarcastically at her. "My poor story, it is but too evident, will never do for Godey or Graham! Only think of your falling asleep at what I hoped the newspaper critics would pronounce a most brilliant, powerful, imaginative, pathetic, and original winding up! Well, the manuscript must serve to light lamps with;—if, indeed, being so imbued with my gentle dulness, it is any longer capable of flame!"

"Me asleep! How can you say so?" answered Phœbe, as unconscious of the crisis through which she had passed as an infant of the precipice to the verge of which it has rolled. "No, no! I consider myself as having been very attentive; and, though I don't remember the incidents quite distinctly, yet I have an impression of a vast deal of trouble and calamity,—so, no doubt, the story will prove exceedingly attractive."

By this time, the sun had gone down, and was tinting the clouds towards the zenith with those bright hues which are not seen there until some time after sunset, and when the horizon has quite lost its richer brilliancy. The moon, too, which had long been climbing overhead, and unobtrusively melting its disk into the azure,—like an ambitious demagogue, who hides his aspiring purpose by assuming the prevalent hue of popular sentiment,—now began to shine out, broad and oval, in its middle pathway. These silvery beams were already powerful enough to change the character of the lingering daylight. They softened and embellished the aspect of the old house; although the shadows fell deeper into the angles of its many gables, and lay brooding under the projecting story, and within the half-open door. With the lapse of every moment,

the garden grew more picturesque; the fruit-trees, shrubbery and flower-bushes, had a dark obscurity among them. The common-place characteristics,—which, at noontide, it seemed to have taken a century of sordid life to accumulate,—were now transfigured by a charm of romance. A hundred mysterious years were whispering among the leaves, whenever the slight sea-breeze found its way thither and stirred them. Through the foliage that roofed the little summer-house the moonlight flickered to and fro, and fell silvery white on the dark floor, the table and the circular bench, with a continual shift and play, according as the chinks and wayward crevices among the twigs admitted or shut out the glimmer.

So sweetly cool was the atmosphere, after all the feverish day, that the summer eve might be fancied as sprinkling dews and liquid moonlight, with a dash of icy temper in them, out of a silver vase. Here and there, a few drops of this freshness were scattered on a human heart, and gave it youth again, and sympathy with the eternal youth of nature. The artist chanced to be one on whom the reviving influence fell. It made him feel—what he sometimes almost forgot, thrust so early as he had been into the rude struggle of man with man—how youthful he still was.

"It seems to me," he observed, "that I never watched the coming of so beautiful an eve, and never felt anything so very much like happiness as at this moment. After all, what a good world we live in! How good, and beautiful! How young it is, too, with nothing really rotten or age-worn in it! This old house, for example, which sometimes has positively oppressed my breath with its smell of decaying timber! And this garden, where the black mould always clings to my spade, as if I were a sexton, delving in a graveyard! Could I keep the feeling that now possesses me, the garden would every day be virgin soil, with the earth's first freshness in the flavor of its beans and squashes; and the house!—it would be like a bower in Eden, blossoming with the earliest roses that God ever made. Moonlight, and the sentiment in man's heart responsive to it, are the greatest of renovators and reformers. And all other reform and renovation, I suppose, will prove to be no better than moonshine!"

"I have been happier than I am now; at least, much gayer," said Phœbe, thoughtfully. "Yet I am sensible of a great charm in this brightening moonlight; and I love to watch how the day, tired as it is, lags away reluctantly, and hates to be called yesterday so soon. I never cared much about moonlight before. What is there, I wonder, so beautiful in it, to-night?"

"And you have never felt it before?" inquired the artist, looking earnestly at the girl, through the twilight.

"Never," answered Phœbe; "and life does not look the same, now that I have felt it so. It seems as if I had looked at everything, hitherto, in broad daylight, or else in the ruddy light of a cheerful fire, glimmering and dancing through a room. Ah, poor me!" she added, with a half-melancholy laugh. "I shall never be so merry as before I knew Cousin Hepzibah and poor Cousin Clifford. I have grown a great deal older, in this little time. Older, and, I hope, wiser, and,—not exactly sadder,—but certainly, with not half so

much lightness in my spirits! I have given them my sunshine, and have been glad to give it; but, of course, I cannot both give and keep it. They are welcome, notwithstanding!"

"You have lost nothing, Phœbe, worth keeping, nor which it was possible to keep," said Holgrave, after a pause. "Our first youth is of no value; for we are never conscious of it, until after it is gone. But sometimes—always, I suspect, unless one is exceedingly unfortunate—there comes a sense of second youth, gushing out of the heart's joy at being in love; or, possibly, it may come to crown some other grand festival in life, if any other such there be. This bemoaning of one's self (as you do now) over the first careless, shallow gayety of youth departed, and this profound happiness at youth regained, —so much deeper and richer than that we lost,—are essential to the soul's development. In some cases, the two states come almost simultaneously, and mingle the sadness and the rapture in one mysterious emotion."

"I hardly think I understand you," said Phœbe.

"No wonder," replied Holgrave, smiling; "for I have told you a secret which I hardly began to know, before I found myself giving it utterance. Remember it, however; and when the truth becomes clear to you, then think of this moonlight scene!"

"It is entirely moonlight now, except only a little flush of faint crimson, upward from the west, between those buildings," remarked Phœbe. "I must go in. Cousin Hepzibah is not quick at figures, and will give herself a headache over the day's accounts, unless I help her."

But Holgrave detained her a little longer.

"Miss Hepzibah tells me," observed he, "that you return to the country, in a few days."

"Yes, but only for a little while," answered Phœbe; "for I look upon this as my present home. I go to make a few arrangements, and to take a more deliberate leave of my mother and friends. It is pleasant to live where one is much desired, and very useful; and I think I may have the satisfaction of feeling myself so, here."

"You surely may, and more than you imagine," said the artist. "Whatever health, comfort and natural life, exists in the house, is embodied in your person. These blessings came along with you, and will vanish when you leave the threshold. Miss Hepzibah, by secluding herself from society, has lost all true relation with it, and is, in fact, dead; although she galvanizes herself into a semblance of life, and stands behind her counter, afflicting the world with a greatly-to-be-deprecated scowl. Your poor cousin Clifford is another dead and long-buried person, on whom the governor and council have wrought a necromantic miracle. I should not wonder if he were to crumble away, some morning, after you are gone, and nothing be seen of him more, except a heap of dust. Miss Hepzibah, at any rate, will lose what little flexibility she has. They both exist by you."

"I should be very sorry to think so," answered Phœbe, gravely. "But it is true that my small abilities were precisely what they needed; and I have a real interest in their welfare,—an odd kind of motherly sentiment,—which I wish you would not laugh at! And

let me tell you frankly, Mr. Holgrave, I am sometimes puzzled to know whether you wish them well or ill."

"Undoubtedly," said the daguerreotypist, "I do feel an interest in this antiquated, poverty-stricken old maiden-lady, and this degraded and shattered gentleman,—this abortive lover of the beautiful. A kindly interest, too, helpless old children that they are! But you have no conception what a different kind of heart mine, is from your own. It is not my impulse, as regards these two individuals, either to help or hinder; but to look on, to analyze, to explain matters to myself, and to comprehend the drama which, for almost two hundred years, has been dragging its slow length over the ground where you and I now tread. If permitted to witness the close, I doubt not to derive a moral satisfaction from it, go matters how they may. There is a conviction within me that the end draws nigh. But, though Providence sent you hither to help, and sends me only as a privileged and meet spectator, I pledge myself to lend these unfortunate beings whatever aid I can!"

"I wish you would speak more plainly," cried Phœbe, perplexed and displeased; "and, above all, that you would feel more like a Christian and a human being! How is it possible to see people in distress, without desiring, more than anything else, to help and comfort them? You talk as if this old house were a theatre; and you seem to look at Hepzibah's and Clifford's misfortunes, and those of generations before them, as a tragedy, such as I have seen acted in the hall of a country hotel. only the present one appears to be played exclusively for your amusement.

I do not like this. To play costs the performers too much, and the audience is too cold-hearted."

"You are severe," said Holgrave, compelled to recognize a degree of truth in this piquant sketch of his own mood.

"And then," continued Phœbe, "what can you mean by your conviction, which you tell me of, that the end is drawing near? Do you know of any new trouble hanging over my poor relatives? If so, tell me at once, and I will not leave them!"

"Forgive me, Phoebe!" said the daguerreotypist, holding out his hand, to which the girl was constrained to yield her own. "I am somewhat of a mystic, it must be confessed. The tendency is in my blood, together with the faculty of mesmerism, which might have brought me to Gallows Hill, in the good old times of witchcraft. Believe me, if I were really aware of any secret, the disclosure of which would benefit your friends,—who are my own friends, likewise,—you should learn it before we part. But I have no such knowledge."

"You hold something back!" said Phœbe.

"Nothing,—no secrets but my own," answered Holgrave. "I can perceive, indeed, that Judge Pyncheon still keeps his eye on Clifford, in whose ruin he had so large a share. His motives and intentions, however, are a mystery to me. He is a determined and relentless man, with the genuine character of an inquisitor; and had he any object to gain by putting Clifford to the rack, I verily believe that he would wrench his joints from their sockets, in order to accomplish it. But, so wealthy and eminent as he is,—so powerful in his own strength, and in the support of

society, on all sides,—what can Judge Pyncheon have to hope or fear from the imbecile, branded, half-torpid Clifford?"

"Yet," urged Phœbe, "you did speak as if misfortune were impending!"

"O, that was because I am morbid!" replied the artist. "My mind has a twist aside, like almost everybody's mind, except your own. Moreover, it is so strange to find myself an inmate of this old Pyncheon-house, and sitting in this old garden—(hark, how Maule's well is murmuring!)—that, were it only for this one circumstance, I cannot help fancying that Destiny is arranging its fifth act for a catastrophe."

"There!" cried Phœbe with renewed vexation; for she was by nature as hostile to mystery as the sunshine to a dark corner. "You puzzle me more than ever!"

"Then let us part friends!" said Holgrave, pressing her hand. "Or, if not friends, let us part before you entirely hate me. You, who love everybody else in the world!"

"Good-by, then," said Phœbe, frankly. "I do not mean to be angry a great while, and should be sorry to have you think so. There has Cousin Hepzibah been standing in the shadow of the door-way, this quarter of an hour past! She thinks I stay too long in the damp garden. So, good-night, and good-by!"

On the second morning thereafter, Phœbe might have been seen, in her straw bonnet, with a shawl on one arm and a little carpet-bag on the other, bidding adieu to Hepzibah and Cousin Clifford. She was to take a seat in the next train of cars, which would transport her to within half a dozen miles of her country village.

The tears were in Phœbe's eyes; a smile, dewy with affectionate regret, was glimmering around her pleasant mouth. She wondered how it came to pass, that her life of a few weeks, here in this heavy-hearted old mansion, had taken such hold of her, and so melted into her associations, as now to seem a more important centre-point of remembrance than all which had gone before. How had Hepzibah—grim, silent, and irresponsive to her overflow of cordial sentiment—contrived to win so much love? And Clifford,—in his abortive decay, with the mystery of fearful crime upon him, and the close prison-atmosphere yet lurking in his breath.—how had he transformed himself into the simplest child, whom Phœbe felt bound to watch over, and be, as it were, the providence of his unconsidered hours! Everything, at that instant of farewell, stood out prominently to her view. Look where she would, lay her hand on what she might, the object responded to her consciousness, as if a moist human heart were in it.

She peeped from the window into the garden, and felt herself more regretful at leaving this spot of black earth, vitiated with such an age-long growth of weeds, than joyful at the idea of again scenting her pine-forests and fresh clover-fields. She called Chanticleer, his two wives, and the venerable chicken, and threw them some crumbs of bread from the breakfast-table. These being hastily gobbled up, the chicken spread its wings, and alighted close by Phœbe on the window-sill, where it looked gravely into her face and vented its emotions in a croak. Phœbe bade it be a good old chicken during her absence, and promised to bring it a little bag of buckwheat.

"Ah, Phœbe!" remarked Hepzibah, "you do not smile so naturally as when you came to us! Then the smile chose to shine out; now, you choose it should. It is well that you are going back, for a little while, into your native air. There has been too much weight on your spirits. The house is too gloomy and lonesome; the shop is full of vexations; and as for me, I have no faculty of making things look brighter than they are. Dear Clifford has been your only comfort!"

"Come hither, Phœbe," suddenly cried her cousin Clifford, who had said very little, all the morning. "Close!—closer! —and look me in the face!"

Phœbe put one of her small hands on each elbow of his chair, and leaned her face towards him, so that he might peruse it as carefully as he would. It is probable that the latent emotions of this parting hour had revived, in some degree, his bedimmed and enfeebled faculties. At any rate, Phœbe soon felt that, if not the profound insight of a seer, yet a more than feminine delicacy of appreciation, was making her heart the subject of its regard. A moment before, she had known nothing which she would have sought to hide. Now, as if some secret were hinted to her own consciousness through the medium of another's perception, she was fain to let her eyelids droop beneath Clifford's gaze. A blush, too,—the redder, because she strove hard to keep it down,— ascended higher and higher, in a tide of fitful progress, until even her brow was all suffused with it.

"It is enough, Phœbe," said Clifford, with a melancholy smile. "When I first saw you, you were the prettiest little maiden in the world; and now you have deepened into beauty! Girlhood has passed into womanhood; the bud is a bloom! Go, now!—I feel lonelier than I did."

Phœbe took leave of the desolate couple, and passed through the shop, twinkling her eyelids to shake off a dew-drop; for—considering how brief her absence was to be, and therefore the folly of being cast down about it —she would not so far acknowledge her tears as to dry them with her handkerchief. On the doorstep, she met the little urchin whose marvellous feats of gastronomy have been recorded in the earlier pages of our narrative. She took from the window some specimen or other of natural history,—her eyes being too dim with moisture to inform her accurately whether it was a rabbit or a hippopotamus,—put it into the child's hand, as a parting gift, and went her way. Old Uncle Venner was just coming out of his door, with a wood-horse and saw on his shoulder; and, trudging along the street, he scrupled not to keep company with Phœbe, so far as their paths lay together; nor, in spite of his patched coat and rusty beaver, and the curious fashion of his tow-cloth trousers, could she find it in her heart to outwalk him.

"We shall miss you, next Sabbath afternoon," observed the street philosopher. "It is unaccountable how little while it takes some folks to grow just as natural to a man as his own breath; and, begging your pardon, Miss Phœbe (though there can be no offence in an old man's saying it), that's just what you've grown to me! My years have

been a great many, and your life is but just beginning; and yet, you are somehow as familiar to me as if I had found you at my mother's door, and you had blossomed, like a running vine, all along my pathway since. Come back soon, or I shall be gone to my farm; for I begin to find these wood-sawing jobs a little too tough for my back-ache."

"Very soon, Uncle Venner," replied Phœbe.

"And let it be all the sooner, Phœbe, for the sake of those poor souls yonder," continued her companion. "They can never do without you, now,—never, Phœbe, never!—no more than if one of God's angels had been living with them, and making their dismal house pleasant and comfortable! Don't it seem to you they'd be in a sad case, if, some pleasant summer morning like this, the angel should spread his wings, and fly to the place he came from? Well, just so they feel, now that you're going home by the railroad! They can't bear it, Miss Phœbe; so be sure to come back!"

"I am no angel, Uncle Venner," said Phœbe, smiling, as she offered him her hand at the street-corner. "But, I suppose, people never feel so much like angels as when they are doing what little good they may. So I shall certainly come back!"

Thus parted the old man and the rosy girl; and Phœbe took the wings of the morning, and was soon flitting almost as rapidly away as if endowed with the aerial locomotion of the angels to whom Uncle Venner had so graciously compared her.

CHAPTER XV

THE SCOWL AND SMILE

SEVERAL days passed over the seven gables, heavily and drearily enough. In fact (not to attribute the whole gloom of sky and earth to the one inauspicious circumstance of Phœbe's departure), an easterly storm had set in, and indefatigably applied itself to the task of making the black roof and walls of the old house look more cheerless than ever before. Yet was the outside not half so cheerless as the interior. Poor Clifford was cut off, at once, from all his scanty resources of enjoyment. Phœbe was not there; nor did the sunshine fall upon the floor. The garden, with its muddy walks, and the chill, dripping foliage of its summer-house, was an image to be shuddered at. Nothing flourished in the cold, moist, pitiless atmosphere, drifting with the brackish scud of sea-breezes, except the moss along the joints of the shingle-roof, and the great bunch of weeds, that had lately been suffering from drought, in the angle between the two front gables.

As for Hepzibah, she seemed not merely possessed with the east wind, but to be, in her very person, only another phase of this gray and sullen spell of weather; the east wind itself, grim and disconsolate, in a rusty black silk gown, and with a turban of cloud-wreaths on its head. The custom of the shop fell off because a story got abroad that she soured her small beer and other damageable commodities, by scowling on them. It is, perhaps, true that the public had something reasonably to complain of in her deportment; but towards Clifford she was neither ill-tempered nor unkind, nor felt less warmth of heart than always, had it been possible to make it reach him. The inutility of her best efforts, however, palsied the poor old gentlewoman. She could do little else than sit silently in a corner of the room, when the wet pear-tree branches, sweeping across the small windows, created a noon-day dusk, which Hepzibah unconsciously darkened with her woe-begone aspect. It was no fault of Hepzibah's. Everything—even the old chairs and tables, that had known what weather was for three or four such lifetimes as her own—looked as damp and chill as if the present were their worst experience. The picture of the Puritan colonel shivered on the wall. The house itself shivered, from every attic of its seven gables, down to the great kitchen fireplace, which served all the better as an emblem of the mansion's heart, because, though built for warmth, it was now so comfortless and empty.

Hepzibah attempted to enliven matters by a fire in the parlor. But the storm-demon kept watch above, and, whenever a flame was kindled, drove the smoke back again, choking the chimney's sooty throat with its own breath. Nevertheless, during four days of this miserable storm, Clifford wrapt himself in an old cloak, and occupied his customary chair. On the morning of the fifth, when summoned to breakfast, he responded only by a broken-hearted murmur, expressive of a determination not to leave his bed. His sister made no attempt to change his purpose. In fact, entirely as she loved him. Hepzibah could hardly have borne any longer the wretched duty—so impracticable by her few and rigid faculties—of seeking pastime for a still sensitive, but ruined mind, critical and fastidious, without force or volition. It was, at least, something short of positive despair, that, to-day, she might sit shivering alone, and not suffer continually a new grief, and unreasonable pang of remorse, at every fitful sigh of her fellow-sufferer.

But Clifford, it seemed, though he did not make his appearance below stairs, had, after all, bestirred himself in quest of amusement. In the course of the forenoon, Hepzibah heard a note of music, which (there being no other tuneful contrivance in the House of the Seven Gables) she knew must proceed from Alice Pyncheon's harpsichord. She was aware that Clifford, in his youth, had possessed a cultivated taste for music, and a considerable degree of skill in its practice. It was difficult, however, to conceive of his retaining an accomplishment to which daily exercise is so essential, in the measure indicated by the sweet, airy, and delicate, though most melancholy strain, that now stole upon her ear. Nor was it less marvellous that the long-silent instrument should be capable of so much melody. Hepzibah involuntarily thought of the ghostly harmonies, prelusive of death in the family, which were attributed to the legendary Alice. But it was, perhaps, proof of the agency of other than spiritual fingers, that, after a few touches, the chords seemed to snap asunder with their own vibrations, and the music ceased.

But a harsher sound succeeded to the mysterious notes; nor was the easterly day fated to pass without an event sufficient in itself to poison, for Hepzibah and Clifford, the balmiest air that ever brought the humming-birds along with it. The final echoes of Alice Pyncheon's performance (or Clifford's, if his we must consider it) were driven away by no less vulgar a dissonance than the ringing of the shop-bell. A foot was heard scraping itself on the threshold, and thence somewhat ponderously stepping on the floor. Hepzibah delayed a moment, while muffling herself in a faded shawl, which had been her defensive armor in a forty years' warfare against the east wind. A characteristic sound, however,—neither a cough nor a hem, but a kind of rumbling and reverberating spasm in somebody's capacious depth of chest,—impelled her to hurry forward, with that aspect of fierce faint-heartedness so common to women in cases of perilous emergency. Few of her sex, on such occasions, have ever looked so terrible as our poor scowling Hepzibah. But the visitor quietly closed the shop-door behind him, stood up his umbrella against the counter, and turned a visage of composed benignity, to meet the alarm and anger which his appearance had excited.

Hepzibah's presentiment had not deceived her. It was no other than Judge Pyncheon, who, after in vain trying the front door, had now effected his entrance into the shop.

"How do you do, Cousin Hepzibah? —and how does this most inclement weather affect our poor Clifford?" began the judge; and wonderful it seemed, indeed, that the easterly storm was not put to shame, or, at any rate, a little mollified, by the genial benevolence of his smile. "I could not rest without calling to ask, once more, whether I can in any manner promote his comfort, or your own."

"You can do nothing," said Hepzibah, controlling her agitation as well as she could. "I devote myself to Clifford. He has every comfort which his situation admits of."

"But, allow me to suggest, dear cousin," rejoined the judge, "you err, —in all affection and kindness, no doubt, and with the very best intentions,—but you do err, nevertheless, in keeping your brother so secluded. Why insulate him thus from all sympathy and kindness? Clifford, alas! has had too much of solitude. Now let him try society,—the society, that is to say, of kindred and old friends. Let me, for instance, but see Clifford; and I will answer for the good effect of the interview."

"You cannot see him," answered Hepzibah. "Clifford has kept his bed since yesterday."

"What! How! Is he ill?" exclaimed Judge Pyncheon, starting with what seemed to be angry alarm; for the very frown of the old Puritan darkened through the room as he spoke. "Nay, then, I must and will see him! What if he should die?"

"He is in no danger of death," said Hepzibah,—and added, with bitterness that she could repress no longer, "none; —unless he shall be persecuted to death, now, by the same man who long ago attempted it!"

"Cousin Hepzibah," said the judge, with an impressive earnestness of manner, which grew even to tearful pathos, as he proceeded, "is it possible that you do not perceive how unjust, how unkind, how unchristian, is this constant, this long-continued bitterness against me, for a part which I was constrained by duty and conscience, by the force of law, and at my own peril, to act? What did I do, in detriment to Clifford, which it was possible to leave undone? How could you, his sister,—if, for your never-ending sorrow, as it has been for mine, you had known what I did,—have shown greater tenderness? And do you think, cousin, that it has cost me no pang?—that it has left no anguish in my bosom, from that day to this, amidst all the prosperity with which Heaven has blessed me?— or that I do not now rejoice, when it is deemed consistent with the dues of public justice and the welfare of society that this dear kinsman, this early friend, this nature so delicately and beautifully constituted,—so unfortunate, let us pronounce him, and forbear to say, so guilty,—that our own Clifford, in fine, should be given back to life, and its possibilities of enjoyment? Ay, you little know me, Cousin Hepzibah! You little know this heart! It now throbs at the thought of meeting him! There lives not the human being (except yourself, —and you not more than I) who has shed so many tears for Clifford's calamity! You behold some of them now. There is none who would so delight to promote his happiness! Try me, Hepzibah!—try me, cousin!—try the man whom you have treated as your enemy and Clifford's!—try Jaffrey Pyncheon, and you shall find him true, to the heart's core!"

"In the name of Heaven," cried Hepzibah, provoked only to intenser indignation by this out-gush of the inestimable tenderness of a stern nature,—

"in God's name, whom you insult, and whose power I could almost question, since he hears you utter so many false words, without palsying your tongue, —give over, I beseech you, this loathsome pretense of affection for your victim! You hate him! Say so, like a man! You cherish, at this moment, some black purpose against him, in your heart! Speak it out, at once!—or, if you hope so to promote it better, hide it till you can triumph in its success! But never speak again of your love for my poor brother! I cannot bear it! It will drive me beyond a woman's decency! It will drive me mad! Forbear! Not another word! It will make me spurn you!"

For once, Hepzibah's wrath had given her courage. She had spoken. But, after all, was this unconquerable distrust of Judge Pyncheon's integrity, and this utter denial, apparently, of his claim to stand in the ring of human sympathies,—were they founded in any just perception of his character, or merely the offspring of a woman's unreasonable prejudice, deduced from nothing?

The judge, beyond all question, was a man of eminent respectability. The church acknowledged it; the state acknowledged it. It was denied by nobody. In all the very extensive sphere of those who knew him, whether in his public or private capacities, there was not an individual—except Hepzibah, and some lawless mystic, like the daguerreotypist, and, possibly, a few political opponents—who would have dreamed of seriously disputing his claim to a high and honorable place in the world's regard. Nor (we must do him the further justice to say) did Judge Pyncheon himself, probably, entertain many or very frequent doubts, that his enviable reputation accorded with his deserts. His conscience, therefore, usually considered the surest witness to a man's integrity, —his conscience, unless it might be for the little space of five minutes in the twenty-four hours, or, now and then, some black day in the whole year's circle,—his conscience bore an accordant testimony with the world's laudatory voice. And yet, strong as this evidence may seem to be, we should hesitate to peril our own conscience on the assertion, that the judge and the consenting world were right, and that poor Hepzibah, with her solitary prejudice, was wrong. Hidden from mankind,— forgotten by himself, or buried so deeply under a sculptured and ornamented pile of ostentatious deeds that his daily life could take no note of it,—there may have lurked some evil and unsightly thing. Nay, we could almost venture to say, further, that a daily guilt might have been acted by him, continually renewed, and reddening forth afresh, like the miraculous blood-stain of a murder, without his necessarily and at every moment being aware of it.

Men of strong minds, great force of character, and a hard texture of the sensibilities, are very capable of falling into mistakes of this kind. They are ordinarily men to whom forms are of paramount importance. Their field of action lies among the external phenomena of life. They possess vast ability in grasping, and arranging, and appropriating to themselves, the big, heavy, solid unrealities, such as gold, landed estate, offices of trust and emolument, and public honors. With these materials, and with deeds of goodly aspect, done in the public eye, an individual of this class builds up, as it were, a tall and stately edifice, which, in the view of other people, and ultimately in his own view, is no other than the man's character, or the man himself. Behold, therefore, a palace! Its splendid halls, and suites of spacious apartments, are floored with a mosaic-work of costly marbles; its windows, the whole height of each room, admit the sunshine through the most transparent of plate-glass; its high cornices are gilded, and its ceilings gorgeously painted; and a lofty dome—through which, from the central pavement, you may gaze up to the sky, as with no obstructing medium between—surmounts the whole. With what fairer and nobler emblem could any man desire to shadow forth his character? Ah! but in some low and obscure nook,—some narrow closet on the ground-floor, shut, locked, and bolted, and the key flung away,—or beneath the marble pavement, in a stagnant water-puddle, with the richest pattern of mosaic-work above,—may lie a corpse, half decayed, and still decaying, and diffusing its death-scent all through the palace! The inhabitant will not be conscious of it, for it has long been his daily breath! Neither will the visitors, for they smell only the rich odors which the master sedulously scatters through the palace, and the incense which they bring, and delight to burn before him! Now and then, perchance, comes in a seer, before whose sadly-gifted eye the whole structure melts into thin air, leaving only the hidden nook, the bolted closet, with the cobwebs festooned over its forgotten door, or the deadly hole under the pavement, and the decaying corpse within. Here, then, we are to seek the true emblem of the man's character, and of the deed that gives whatever reality it possesses to his life. And, beneath the show of a marble palace, that pool of stagnant water, foul with many impurities, and, perhaps, tinged with blood,—that secret abomination, above which, possibly, he may say his prayers, without remembering it,—is this man's miserable soul!

To apply this train of remark somewhat more closely to Judge Pyncheon. —We might say (without in the least imputing crime to a personage of his eminent respectability) that there was enough of splendid rubbish in his life to cover up and paralyze a more active and subtile conscience than the judge was ever troubled with. The purity of his judicial character, while on the bench; the faithfulness of his public service in subsequent capacities; his devotedness to his party, and the rigid consistency with which he had adhered to its principles; or, at all events, kept pace with its organized movements; his remarkable zeal as president of a Bible society; his unimpeachable integrity as treasurer of a widow's and orphan's fund; his benefits to horticulture, by producing two much-esteemed varieties of the pear, and to agriculture, through the agency of the famous Pyncheon-bull; the cleanliness of his moral deportment, for a great many years past; the severity with which he had frowned upon, and finally cast off, an expensive and dissipated son, delaying forgiveness until within the final quarter of an hour of the young man's life; his prayers at morning and eventide, and graces at meal-time; his efforts in furtherance of the temperance cause; his confining himself, since the last attack of the gout, to five diurnal glasses of old sherry wine; the snowy whiteness of his linen the polish of his boots, the handsomeness of his gold-headed cane, the square and roomy fashion of his coat, and the fineness of its material, and, in general, the studied propriety of his dress and equipment; the scrupulousness with which he paid public notice, in the street, by a bow, a lifting of the hat, a nod, or a motion of the hand, to all and sundry his acquaintances, rich or poor; the smile of broad benevolence wherewith he made it a point to gladden the whole world;—what room could possibly be found for darker traits, in a portrait made up of lineaments like these? This proper face was what he beheld in the looking-glass. This admirably arranged life was what he was conscious of, in the progress of every day. Then, might not he claim to be its result and sum, and say to himself and the community,—"Behold Judge Pyncheon there"?

And, allowing that, many, many years ago, in his early and reckless youth, he had committed some one wrong act,—or that, even now, the inevitable force of circumstances should occasionally make him do one questionable deed, among a thousand praiseworthy, or, at least, blameless ones,—would you characterize the judge by that one necessary deed, and that half-forgotten act, and let it overshadow the fair aspect of a lifetime? What is there so ponderous in evil, that a thumb's bigness of it should outweigh the mass of things not evil which were heaped into the other scale! This scale and balance system is a favorite one with people of Judge Pyncheon's brotherhood. A hard, cold man, thus unfortunately situated, seldom or never looking inward, and resolutely taking his idea of himself from what purports to be his image as reflected in the mirror of public opinion, can scarcely arrive at true self-knowledge, except through loss of property and reputation. Sickness will not always help him to it; not always the death-hour!

But our affair now is with Judge Pyncheon as he stood confronting the fierce outbreak of Hepzibah's wrath. Without premeditation, to her own surprise, and indeed terror, she had given vent, for once, to the inveteracy of her resentment, cherished against this kinsman for thirty years.

Thus far, the judge's countenance had expressed mild forbearance,—grave and almost gentle deprecation of his cousin's unbecoming violence,—free and Christian-like forgiveness of the wrong inflicted by her words. But, when those words were irrevocably spoken, his look assumed sternness, the sense of power, and immitigable resolve; and this with so natural and imperceptible a change, that it seemed as if the iron man had stood there from the first, and the meek man not at all. The effect was as when the light vapory clouds, with their soft coloring, suddenly vanish from the stony brow of a precipitous mountain, and leave there the frown which you at once feel to be eternal. Hepzibah almost adopted the insane belief that it was her old Puritan ancestor, and not the modern judge, on whom she had just been wreaking the bitterness of her heart. Never did a man show stronger proof of the lineage attributed to him than Judge Pyncheon, at this crisis, by his unmistakable resemblance to the picture in the inner room.

"Cousin Hepzibah," said he, very calmly, "it is time to have done with this."

"With all my heart!" answered she. "Then, why do you persecute us any longer? Leave poor Clifford and me in peace. Neither of us desires anything better!"

"It is my purpose to see Clifford before I leave this house," continued the judge. "Do not act like a mad-woman, Hepzibah! I am his only friend, and an all-powerful one. Has it never occurred to you,—are you so blind as not to have seen,—that, without not merely my consent, but my efforts, my representations, the exertion of my whole influence, political, official, personal, Clifford would never have been what you call free? Did you think his release a triumph over me? Not so, my good cousin; not so, by any means! The furthest possible from that! No; but it was the accomplishment of a purpose long entertained on my part. I set him free!"

"You!" answered Hepzibah. "I never will believe it! He owed his dungeon to you;—his freedom to God's providence!"

"I set him free!" reaffirmed Judge Pyncheon, with the calmest composure. "And I come hither now to decide whether he shall retain his freedom. It will depend upon himself. For this purpose, I must see him."

"Never!—it would drive him mad!" exclaimed Hepzibah, but with an irresoluteness sufficiently perceptible to the keen eye of the judge; for, without the slightest faith in his good intentions, she knew not whether there was most to dread in yielding or resistance. "And why should you wish to see this wretched, broken man, who retains hardly a fraction of his intellect, and will hide even that from an eye which has no love in it?"

"He shall see love enough in mine, if that be all!" said the judge, with well-grounded confidence in the benignity of his aspect. "But, Cousin Hepzibah, you confess a great deal, and very much to the purpose. Now, listen, and I will frankly explain my reasons for insisting on this interview. At the death, thirty years since, of our uncle Jaffrey, it was found,—I know not whether the circumstance ever attracted much of your attention, among the sadder interests that clustered round that event.—but it was found that his visible estate. of every kind, fell far short of any estimate ever made of it. He was supposed to be immensely rich. Nobody doubted that he stood among the weightiest men of his day. It was one of his eccentricities, however,—and not altogether a folly, neither,—to conceal the amount of his property by making distant and foreign investments, perhaps under other names than his own, and by various means, familiar enough to capitalists, but unnecessary here to be specified. By Uncle Jaffrey's last will and testament, as you are aware, his entire property was bequeathed to me, with the single exception of a life interest to yourself in this old family mansion, and the strip of patrimonial estate remaining attached to it."

"And do you seek to deprive us of that?" asked Hepzibah, unable to restrain her bitter contempt. "Is this your price for ceasing to persecute poor Clifford?"

"Certainly not, my dear cousin!" answered the judge, smiling benevolently. "On the contrary, as you must do me the justice to own, I have constantly expressed my readiness to double or treble your resources, whenever you should make up your mind to accept any kindness of that nature at the hands of your kinsman. No, no! But here lies the gist of the matter. Of my uncle's unquestionably great estate, as I have said, not the half—no, not one third, as I am fully convinced—was apparent after his death. Now, I have the best possible reasons for believing that your brother Clifford can give me a clue to the recovery of the remainder."

"Clifford!—Clifford know of any hidden wealth?—Clifford have it in his power to make you rich?" cried the old gentlewoman, affected with a sense of something like ridicule, at the idea. "Impossible! You deceive yourself! It is really a thing to laugh at!"

"It is as certain as that I stand here!" said Judge Pyncheon, striking his gold-headed cane on the floor, and at the same time stamping his foot, as if to express his conviction the more forcibly by the whole emphasis of his substantial person. "Clifford told me so himself!"

"No, no!" exclaimed Hepzibah, incredulously. "You are dreaming, Cousin Jaffrey!"

"I do not belong to the dreaming class of men," said the judge, quietly. "Some months before my uncle's death, Clifford boasted to me of the possession of the secret of incalculable wealth. His purpose was to taunt me, and excite my curiosity. I know it well. But, from a pretty distinct recollection of the particulars of our conversation, I am thoroughly convinced that there was truth in what he said. Clifford, at this moment, if he chooses,—and choose he must!—can inform me where to find the schedule, the documents, the evi-

dences, in whatever shape they exist, of the vast amount of Uncle Jaffrey's missing property. He has the secret. His boast was no idle word. It had a directness, an emphasis, a particularity, that showed a back-bone of solid meaning within the mystery of his expression."

"But what could have been Clifford's object," asked Hepzibah, "in concealing it so long?"

"It was one of the bad impulses of our fallen nature," replied the judge, turning up his eyes. "He looked upon me as his enemy. He considered me as the cause of his overwhelming disgrace, his imminent peril of death, his irretrievable ruin. There was no great probability, therefore, of his volunteering information, out of his dungeon, that should elevate me still higher on the ladder of prosperity. But the moment has now come when he must give up his secret."

"And what if he should refuse?" inquired Hepzibah. "Or,—as I steadfastly believe,—what if he has not knowledge of this wealth?"

"My dear cousin," said Judge Pyncheon, with a quietude which he had the power of making more formidable than any violence, "since your brother's return, I have taken the precaution (a highly proper one in the near kinsman and natural guardian of an individual so situated) to have his deportment and habits constantly and carefully overlooked. Your neighbors have been eye-witnesses to whatever has passed in the garden. The butcher, the baker, the fishmonger, some of the customers of your shop, and many a prying old woman have told me several of the secrets of your interior. A still larger circle—I myself, among the rest—can testify to his extravagances at the arched window. Thousands beheld him, a week or two ago, on the point of flinging himself thence into the street. From all this testimony, I am led to apprehend—reluctantly, and with deep grief—that Clifford's misfortunes have so affected his intellect, never very strong, that he cannot safely remain at large. The alternative, you must be aware,—and its adoption will depend entirely on the decision which I am now about to make, —the alternative is his confinement, probably for the remainder of his life, in a public asylum, for persons in his unfortunate state of mind."

"You cannot mean it!" shrieked Hepzibah.

"Should my cousin Clifford," continued Judge Pyncheon, wholly undisturbed, "from mere malice, and hatred of one whose interests ought naturally to be dear to him,—a mode of passion that, as often as any other, indicates mental disease,—should he refuse me the information so important to myself, and which he assuredly possesses, I shall consider it the one needed jot of evidence to satisfy my mind of his insanity. And, once sure of the course pointed out by conscience, you know me too well, Cousin Hepzibah, to entertain a doubt that I shall pursue it."

"O, Jaffrey—Cousin Jaffrey!" cried Hepzibah, mournfully, not passionately, "it is you that are diseased in mind, not Clifford! You have forgotten that a woman was your mother!—that you have had sisters, brothers, children of your own!—or that there ever was affection between man and man, or pity from one man to another, in this miserable world! Else, how could you have dreamed of this? You are not young,

Cousin Jaffrey!—no, nor middle-aged,—but already an old man! The hair is white upon your head! How many years have you to live? Are you not rich enough for that little time? Shall you be hungry,—shall you lack clothes, or a roof to shelter you,—between this point and the grave? No! but, with the half of what you now possess, you could revel in costly food and wines, and build a house twice as splendid as you now inhabit, and make a far greater show to the world,—and yet leave riches to your only son, to make him bless the hour of your death! Then, why should you do this cruel, cruel thing?—so mad a thing, that I know not whether to call it wicked! Alas, Cousin Jaffray, this hard and grasping spirit has run in our blood these two hundred years! You are but doing over again, in another shape, what your ancestor before you did, and sending down to your posterity the curse inherited from him!"

"Talk sense, Hepzibah, for Heaven's sake!" exclaimed the judge, with the impatience natural to a reasonable man, on hearing anything so utterly absurd as the above, in a discussion about matters of business. "I have told you my determination. I am not apt to change. Clifford must give up his secret, or take the consequences. And let him decide quickly; for I have several affairs to attend to, this morning, and an important dinner engagement with some political friends."

"Clifford has no secret!" answered Hepzibah. "And God will not let you do the thing you meditate!"

"We shall see," said the unmoved judge. "Meanwhile, choose whether you will summon Clifford, and allow this business to be amicably settled by an interview between two kinsmen, or drive me to harsher measures, which I should be most happy to feel myself justified in avoiding. The responsibility is altogether on your part."

"You are stronger than I," said Hepzibah, after a brief consideration; "and you have no pity in your strength! Clifford is not now insane; but the interview which you insist upon may go far to make him so. Nevertheless, knowing you as I do, I believe it to be my best course to allow you to judge for yourself as to the improbability of his possessing any valuable secret. I will call Clifford. Be merciful in your dealings with him!—be far more merciful than your heart bids you be!—for God is looking at you, Jaffrey Pyncheon!"

The judge followed his cousin from the shop, where the foregoing conversation had passed, into the parlor, and flung himself heavily into the great ancestral chair. Many a former Pyncheon had found repose in its capacious arms: —rosy children, after their sports; young men, dreamy with love; grown men, weary with cares; old men, burthened with winters;—they had mused, and slumbered, and departed to a yet profounder sleep. It had been a long tradition, though a doubtful one, that this was the very chair, seated in which, the earliest of the judge's New England forefathers—he whose picture still hung upon the wall—had given a dead man's silent and stern reception to the throng of distinguished guests. From that hour of evil omen, until the present, it may be,—though we know not the secret of his heart,—but it may be that no wearier and sadder man had ever sunk into the chair than this same Judge Pyncheon, whom we have just beheld so immitigably hard and resolute. Surely, it must have been at no slight cost that he had thus fortified his soul with iron. Such calmness is a mightier effort than the violence of weaker men. And there was yet a heavy task for him to do. Was it a little matter,—a trifle to be prepared for in a single moment, and to be rested from in another moment,— that he must now, after thirty years, encounter a kinsman risen from a living tomb, and wrench a secret from him, or else consign him to a living tomb again?

"Did you speak?" asked Hepzibah, looking in from the threshold of the parlor; for she imagined that the judge had uttered some sound which she was anxious to interpret as a relenting impulse. "I thought you called me back."

"No, no!" gruffly answered Judge Pyncheon, with a harsh frown, while his brow grew almost a black purple, in the shadow of the room. "Why should I call you back? Time flies! Bid Clifford come to me!"

The judge had taken his watch from his vest-pocket, and now held it in his hand, measuring the interval which was to ensue before the appearance of Clifford.

CHAPTER XVI

CLIFFORD'S CHAMBER

NEVER had the old house appeared so dismal to poor Hepzibah as when she departed on that wretched errand. There was a strange aspect in it. As she trode along the foot-worn passages, and opened one crazy door after another, and ascended the creaking staircase, she gazed wistfully and fearfully around. It would have been no marvel, to her excited mind, if, behind or beside her, there had been the rustle of dead people's garments, or pale visages awaiting her on the landing-place above. Her nerves were set all ajar by the scene of passion and terror through which she had just struggled. Her colloquy with Judge Pyncheon, who so perfectly represented the person and attributes of the founder of the family, had called back the dreary past. It weighed upon her heart. Whatever she had heard, from legendary aunts and grandmothers, concerning the good or evil fortunes of the Pyncheons,—stories which had heretofore been kept warm in her remembrance by the chimney-corner glow that was associated with them,—now recurred to her, sombre, ghastly, cold, like most passages of family history, when brooded over in melancholy mood. The whole seemed little else but a series of calamity, reproducing itself in successive generations, with one general hue, and varying in little, save the outline. But Hepzibah now felt as if the judge, and Clifford, and herself,—they three together,—were on the point of adding another incident to the annals of the house, with a bolder relief of wrong and sorrow, which would cause it to stand out from all the rest. Thus it is that the grief of the passing moment takes upon itself an individuality, and a character of climax, which it is destined to lose, after a while, and to fade into the dark gray tissue common to the grave or glad events of many years ago. It is but for a moment, comparatively, that anything looks strange or startling;—a truth that has the bitter and the sweet in it.

But Hepzibah could not rid herself of the sense of something unprecedented at that instant passing, and soon to be accomplished. Her nerves were in a shake. Instinctively she paused before the arched window, and looked out upon the street, in order to seize its permanent objects with her mental grasp, and thus to steady herself from the reel and vibration which affected her more immediate sphere. It brought her up, as we may say, with a kind of shock, when she beheld everything under the same appearance as the day before, and numberless preceding days, except for the difference between sunshine and sullen storm. Her eyes travelled along the street, from door-step to door-step, noting the wet sidewalks, with here and there a puddle in hollows that had been imperceptible until filled with water. She screwed her dim optics to their acutest point, in the hope of making out, with greater distinctness, a certain window, where she half saw, half guessed, that a tailor's seamstress was sitting at her work. Hepzibah flung herself upon that unknown woman's companionship, even thus far off. Then she was attracted by a chaise rapidly passing, and watched its moist and glistening top, and its splashing wheels, until it had turned the corner, and refused to carry any further her idly trifling, because appalled and overburthened, mind. When the vehicle had disappeared, she allowed herself still another loitering moment; for the patched figure of good Uncle Venner was now visible, coming slowly from the head of the street downward, with a rheumatic limp, because the east wind had got into his joints. Hepzibah wished that he would pass yet more slowly, and befriend her shivering solitude a little longer. Anything that would take her out of the grievous present, and interpose human beings betwixt herself and what was nearest to her,—whatever would defer, for an instant, the inevitable errand on which she was bound,—all such impediments were welcome. Next to the lightest heart, the heaviest is apt to be most playful.

Hepzibah had little hardihood for her own proper pain, and far less for what she must inflict on Clifford. Of so slight a nature, and so shattered by his previous calamities, it could not well be short of utter ruin to bring him face to face with the hard, relentless man, who had been his evil destiny through life. Even had there been no bitter recollections, nor any hostile interest now at stake between them, the mere natural repugnance of the more sensitive system to the massive, weighty, and unimpressible one, must, in itself, have been disastrous to the former. It would be like flinging a porcelain vase, with already a crack in it, against a granite column. Never before had Hepzibah so adequately estimated the powerful charac-

ter of her cousin Jaffrey,—powerful by intellect, energy of will, the long habit of acting among men, and, as she believed, by his unscrupulous pursuit of selfish ends through evil means. It did but increase the difficulty, that Judge Pyncheon was under a delusion as to the secret which he supposed Clifford to possess. Men of his strength of purpose, and customary sagacity, if they chance to adopt a mistaken opinion in practical matters, so wedge it and fasten it among things known to be true, that to wrench it out of their minds is hardly less difficult than pulling up an oak. Thus, as the judge required an impossibility of Clifford, the latter, as he could not perform it, must needs perish. For what, in the grasp of a man like this, was to become of Clifford's soft, poetic nature, that never should have had a task more stubborn than to set a life of beautiful enjoyment to the flow and rhythm of musical cadences! Indeed, what had become of it already? Broken! Blighted! All but annihilated! Soon to be wholly so!

For a moment, the thought crossed Hepzibah's mind, whether Clifford might not really have such knowledge of their deceased uncle's vanished estate as the judge imputed to him. She remembered some vague intimations, on her brother's part, which—if the supposition were not essentially preposterous—might have been so interpreted. There had been schemes of travel and residence abroad, day-dreams of brilliant life at home, and splendid castles in the air, which it would have required boundless wealth to build and realize. Had this wealth been in her power, how gladly would Hepzibah have bestowed it all upon her iron-hearted kinsman, to buy for Clifford the freedom and seclusion of the desolate old house! But she believed that her brother's schemes were as destitute of actual substance and purpose as a child's pictures of its future life, while sitting in a little chair by its mother's knee. Clifford had none but shadowy gold at his command; and it was not the stuff to satisfy Judge Pyncheon!

Was there no help, in their extremity? It seemed strange that there should be none, with a city round about her. It would be so easy to throw up the window, and send forth a shriek, at the strange agony of which everybody would come hastening to the rescue, well understanding it to be the cry of a human soul, at some dreadful crisis! But how wild, how almost laughable, the fatality, —and yet how continually it comes to pass, thought Hepzibah, in this dull delirium of a world,—that whosoever, and with however kindly a purpose, should come to help, they would be sure to help the strongest side! Might and wrong combined, like iron magnetized, are endowed with irresistible attraction. There would be Judge Pyncheon,—a person eminent in the public view, of high station and great wealth, a philanthropist, a member of congress and of the church, and intimately associated with whatever else bestows good name, —so imposing, in these advantageous lights, that Hepzibah herself could hardly help shrinking from her own conclusions as to his hollow integrity. The judge, on one side! And who, on the other? The guilty Clifford! Once a byword! Now, an indistinctly-remembered ignominy!

Nevertheless, in spite of this perception that the judge would draw all human aid to his own behalf, Hepzibah was so unaccustomed to act for herself, that the least word of counsel would have swayed her to any mode of action. Little Phœbe Pyncheon would at once have lighted up the whole scene, if not by any available suggestion, yet simply by the warm vivacity of her character. The idea of the artist occurred to Hepzibah. Young and unknown, mere vagrant adventurer as he was, she had been conscious of a force in Holgrave which might well adapt him to be the champion of a crisis. With this thought in her mind, she unbolted a door, cobwebbed and long disused, but which had served as a former medium of communication between her own part of the house and the gable where the wandering daguerreotypist had now established his temporary home. He was not there. A book, face downward, on the table, a roll of manuscript, a half-written sheet, a newspaper, some tools of his present occupation, and several rejected daguerreotypes, conveyed an impression as if he were close at hand. But, at this period of the day, as Hepzibah might have anticipated, the artist was at his public rooms. With an impulse of idle curiosity, that flickered among her heavy thoughts, she looked at one of the daguerreotypes, and beheld Judge Pyncheon frowning at her! Fate stared her in the face. She turned back from her fruitless quest, with a heart-sinking sense of disappointment. In all her years of seclusion, she had never felt, as now, what it was to be alone. It seemed as if the house stood in a desert, or, by some spell, was made invisible to those who dwelt around, or passed beside it; so that any mode of misfortune, miserable accident, or crime, might happen in it, without the possibility of aid. In her grief and wounded pride, Hepzibah had spent her life in divesting herself of friends;—she had wilfully cast off the support which God has ordained his creatures to need from one another;—and it was now her punishment, that Clifford and herself would fall the easier victims to their kindred enemy.

Returning to the arched window, she lifted her eyes,—scowling, poor, dim-sighted Hepzibah, in the face of Heaven!—and strove hard to send up a prayer through the dense gray pavement of clouds. Those mists had gathered, as if to symbolize a great, brooding mass of human trouble, doubt, confusion, and chill indifference, between earth and the better regions. Her faith was too weak; the prayer too heavy to be thus uplifted. It fell back, a lump of lead, upon her heart. It smote her with the wretched conviction that Providence intermeddled not in these petty wrongs of one individual to his fellow, nor had any balm for these little agonies of a solitary soul; but shed its justice, and its mercy, in a broad, sunlike sweep, over half the universe at once. Its vastness made it nothing. But Hepzibah did not see that, just as there comes a warm sunbeam into every cottage window, so comes a love-beam of God's care and pity, for every separate need.

At last, finding no other pretext for deferring the torture that she was to inflict on Clifford,—her reluctance to which was the true cause of her loitering at the window, her search for the artist, and even her abortive prayer,—dreading, also, to hear the stern voice of Judge Pyncheon from below stairs, chiding her delay,—she crept slowly, a pale, grief-stricken figure, a dismal shape of woman, with almost torpid limbs, slowly to her brother's door, and knocked!

There was no reply!

And how should there have been? Her hand, tremulous with the shrinking purpose which directed it, had smitten so feebly against the door that the sound could hardly have gone inward. She knocked again. Still, no response! Nor was it to be wondered at. She had struck with the entire force of her heart's vibration, communicating, by some subtle magnetism, her own terror to the summons. Clifford would turn his face to the pillow, and cover his head beneath the bed-clothes, like a startled child at midnight. She knocked a third time, three regular strokes, gentle, but perfectly distinct, and with meaning in them; for, modulate it with what cautious art we will, the hand cannot help playing some tune of what we feel, upon the senseless wood.

Clifford returned no answer.

"Clifford! dear brother!" said Hepzibah. "Shall I come in?"

A silence.

Two or three times, and more, Hepzibah repeated his name, without result; still, thinking her brother's sleep unwontedly profound, she undid the door, and entering, found the chamber vacant. How could he have come forth, and when, without her knowledge? Was it possible that, in spite of the stormy day, and worn out with the irksomeness within doors, he had betaken himself to his customary haunt in the garden, and was now shivering under the cheerless shelter of the summer-house? She hastily threw up a window, thrust forth her turbaned head and the half of her gaunt figure, and searched the whole garden through, as completely as her dim vision would allow. She could see the interior of the summer-house, and its circular seat, kept moist by the droppings of the roof. It had no occupant. Clifford was not thereabouts; unless, indeed, he had crept for concealment— (as, for a moment, Hepzibah fancied might be the case)—into a great wet mass of tangled and broad-leaved shadow, where the squash-vines were clambering tumultuously upon an old wooden frame-work, set casually aslant against the fence. This could not be, however; he was not there; for, while Hepzibah was looking, a strange grimalkin stole forth from the very spot, and picked his way across the garden. Twice he paused to snuff the air, and then anew directed his course towards the parlor-window. Whether it was only on account of the stealthy, prying manner common to the race, or that this cat seemed to have more than ordinary mischief in his thoughts, the old gentlewoman, in spite of her much perplexity, felt an impulse to drive the animal away, and accordingly flung down a window-stick. The cat stared up at her, like a detected thief or murderer, and, the next instant, took to flight. No other living creature was visible in the garden. Chanticleer and his family had either not left their roost, disheartened by the interminable rain, or had done the next wisest thing, by seasonably returning to it. Hepzibah closed the window.

But where was Clifford? Could it be, that, aware of the presence of his Evil Destiny, he had crept silently down the staircase, while the judge and Hepzibah stood talking in the shop, and had softly undone the fastenings of the outer door, and made his escape into the street? With that thought, she seemed to behold his gray, wrinkled, yet childlike aspect, in the old-fashioned garments which she wore about the house; a figure such as one sometimes imagines himself to be, with the world's eye upon him, in a troubled dream. This figure of her wretched brother would go wandering through the city, attracting all eyes, and everybody's wonder and repugnance, like a ghost, the more to be shuddered at because visible at noontide. To incur the ridicule of the younger crowd, that knew him not,—the harsher scorn and indignation of a few old men, who might recall his once familiar features! To be the sport of boys, who, when old enough to run about the streets, have no more reverence for what is beautiful and holy, nor pity for what is sad,—no more sense of sacred misery, sanctifying the human shape in which it embodies itself,—than if Satan were the father of them all! Goaded by their taunts, their loud, shrill cries, and cruel laughter,—insulted by the filth of the public ways, which they would fling upon him,—or, as it might well be, distracted by the mere strangeness of his situation, though nobody should afflict him with so much as a thoughtless word,—what wonder if Clifford were to break into some wild extravagance, which was certain to be interpreted as lunacy? Thus Judge Pyncheon's fiendish scheme would be ready accomplished to his hands!

Then Hepzibah reflected that the town was almost completely watergirdled. The wharves stretched out towards the centre of the harbor, and, in this inclement weather, were deserted by the ordinary throng of merchants, laborers, and sea-faring men; each wharf a solitude, with the vessels moored stem and stern, along its misty length. Should her brother's aimless footsteps stray thitherward, and he but bend, one moment, over the deep, black tide, would be not bethink himself that here was the sure refuge within his reach, and that, with a single step, or the slightest over-balance of his body, he might be forever beyond his kinsman's gripe? O, the temptation! To make of his ponderous sorrow a security! To sink, with its leaden weight upon him, and never rise again!

The horror of this last conception was too much for Hepzibah. Even Jaffrey Pyncheon must help her now! She hastened down the staircase, shrieking as she went.

"Clifford is gone!" she cried. "I cannot find my brother! Help, Jaffrey Pyncheon! Some harm will happen to him!"

She throw open the parlor-door. But, what with the shade of branches across the windows, and the smoke-blackened ceiling, and the dark oak-panelling of the walls, there was hardly so much daylight in the room that Hepzibah's imperfect sight could accurately distinguish the judge's figure. She was certain, however, that she saw him sitting in the ancestral armchair, near the centre of the floor, with his face somewhat averted, and looking towards a window. So firm and quiet is the nervous system of such men as Judge Pyncheon, that he had perhaps stirred not more than once since her departure, but, in the hard composure of his temperament, retained the position into which accident had thrown him.

"I tell you, Jaffray," cried Hepzibah, impatiently, as she turned from the parlor-door to search other rooms, "my brother is not in his chamber! You must help me seek him!"

But Judge Pyncheon was not the man to let himself be startled from an easy-chair with haste ill-befitting either the dignity of his character or his broad personal basis, by the alarm of an hysteric woman. Yet, considering his own interest in the matter, he might have bestirred himself with a little more alacrity.

"Do you hear me, Jaffrey Pyncheon?" screamed Hepzibah, as she again approached the parlor-door, after an ineffectual search elsewhere. "Clifford is gone!"

At this instant, on the threshold of the parlor, emerging from within, appeared Clifford himself. His face was preternaturally pale; so deadly white, indeed, that, through all the glimmering indistinctness of the passage-way, Hepzibah could discern his features, as if a light fell on them alone. Their vivid and wild expression seemed likewise sufficient to illuminate them; it was an expression of scorn and mockery, coinciding with the emotions indicated by his gesture. As Clifford stood on the threshold, partly turning back, he pointed his finger within the parlor, and shook it slowly, as though he would have summoned, not Hepzibah alone, but the whole world, to gaze at some object inconceivably ridiculous. This action, so ill-timed and extravagant,—accompanied, too, with a look that showed more like joy than any other kind of excitement,—compelled Hepzibah to dread that her stern kinsman's ominous visit had driven her poor brother to absolute insanity. Nor could she otherwise account for the judge's quiescent mood than by supposing him craftily on the watch, while Clifford developed these symptoms of a distracted mind.

"Be quiet, Clifford!" whispered his

sister, raising her hand, to impress caution. "O, for Heaven's sake, be quiet!"

"Let him be quiet! What can he do better?" answered Clifford, with a still wilder gesture, pointing into the room which he had just quitted. "As for us, Hepzibah, we can dance now!—we can sing, laugh, play, do what we will! The weight is gone, Hepzibah! it is gone off this weary old world; and we may be as light-hearted as little Phœbe herself!"

And, in accordance with his words, he began to laugh, still pointing his finger at the object, invisible to Hepzibah, within the parlor. She was seized with a sudden intuition of some horrible thing. She thrust herself past Clifford, and disappeared into the room; but almost immediately returned, with a cry choking in her throat. Gazing at her brother, with an affrighted glance of inquiry, she beheld him all in a tremor and a quake, from head to foot, while, amid these commoted elements of passion or alarm, still flickered his gusty mirth.

"My God! what is to become of us?" gasped Hepzibah.

"Come!" said Clifford, in a tone of brief decision, most unlike what was usual with him. "We stay here too long! Let us leave the old house to our cousin Jaffrey! He will take good care of it!"

Hepzibah now noticed that Clifford had on a cloak,—a garment of long ago,—in which he had constantly muffled himself during these days of easterly storm. He beckoned with his hand, and intimated, so far as she could comprehend him, his purpose that they should go together from the house. There are chaotic, blind, or drunken moments, in the lives of persons who lack real force of character,—moments of test, in which courage would most assert itself,—but where these individuals, if left to themselves, stagger aimlessly along, or follow implicitly whatever guidance may befall them, even if it be a child's. No matter how preposterous or insane, a purpose is a God-send to them. Hepzibah had reached this point. Unaccustomed to action or responsibility,—full of horror at what she had seen, and afraid to inquire, or almost to imagine, how it had come to pass,—affrighted at the fatality which seemed to pursue her brother,—stupefied by the dim, thick, stifling atmosphere of dread, which filled the house as with a death-smell, and obliterated all definiteness of thought,—she yielded without a question, and on the instant, to the will which Clifford expressed. For herself, she was like a person in a dream, when the will always sleeps. Clifford, ordinarily so destitute of this faculty, had found it in the tension of the crisis.

"Why do you delay so?" cried he, sharply. "Put on your cloak and hood, or whatever it pleases you to wear! No matter what;—you cannot look beautiful nor brilliant, my poor Hepzibah! Take your purse, with money in it, and come along!"

Hepzibah obeyed these instructions, as if nothing else were to be done or thought of. She began to wonder, it is true, why she did not wake up, and at what still more intolerable pitch of dizzy trouble her spirit would struggle out of the maze, and make her conscious that nothing of all this had actually happened. Of course, it was not real; no such black, easterly day as this had yet begun to be; Judge Pyncheon had not talked with her; Clifford had not laughed, pointed, beckoned her away with him; but she had merely been afflicted—as lonely sleepers often are—with a great deal of unreasonable misery, in a morning dream!

"Now—now—I shall certainly awake!" thought Hepzibah, as she went to and fro, making her little preparations. "I can bear it no longer! I must wake up now!"

But it came not, that awakening moment! It came not, even when, just before they left the house, Clifford stole to the parlor-door, and made a parting obeisance to the sole occupant of the room.

"What an absurd figure the old fellow cuts now!" whispered he to Hepzibah. "Just when he fancied he had me completely under his thumb! Come, come; make haste! or he will start up, like Giant Despair in pursuit of Christian and Hopeful, and catch us yet!"

As they passed into the street, Clifford directed Hepzibah's attention to something on one of the posts of the front door. It was merely the initials of his own name, which, with somewhat of his characteristic grace about the forms of the letters, he had cut there, when a boy. The brother and sister departed, and left Judge Pyncheon sitting in the old home of his forefathers, all by himself; so heavy and lumpish that we can liken him to nothing better than a defunct nightmare, which had perished in the midst of its wickedness, and left its flabby corpse on the breast of the tormented one, to be gotten rid of as it might!

CHAPTER XVII

THE FLIGHT OF TWO OWLS

SUMMER as it was, the east wind set poor Hepzibah's few remaining teeth chattering in her head, as she and Clifford faced it, on their way up Pyncheon-street, and towards the centre of the town. Not merely was it the shiver which this pitiless blast brought to her frame (although her feet and hands, especially, had never seemed so death-a-cold as now), but there was a moral sensation, mingling itself with the physical chill, and causing her to shake more in spirit than in body. The world's broad, bleak atmosphere was all so comfortless! Such, indeed, is the impression which it makes on every new adventurer, even if he plunge into it while the warmest tide of life is bubbling through his veins. What, then, must it have been to Hepzibah and Clifford,—so time-stricken as they were, yet so like children in their inexperience,—as they left the door-step, and passed from beneath the wide shelter of the Pyncheon-elm! They were wandering all abroad, on precisely such a pilgrimage as a child often meditates, to the world's end, with perhaps a sixpence and a biscuit in his pocket. In Hepzibah's mind, there was the wretched consciousness of being adrift. She had lost the faculty of self-guidance; but, in view of the difficulties around her, felt it hardly worth an effort to regain it, and was, moreover, incapable of making one.

As they proceeded on their strange expedition, she now and then cast a look sidelong at Clifford, and could not but observe that he was possessed and swayed by a powerful excitement. It was this, indeed, that gave him the control which he had at once, and so irresistibly, established over his movements. It not a little resembled the exhilaration of wine. Or, it might more fancifully be compared to a joyous piece of music, played with wild vivacity, but upon a disordered instrument. As the cracked jarring note might always be heard, and as it jarred loudest amid the loftiest exultation of the melody, so was there a continual quake through Clifford, causing him most to quiver while he wore a triumphant smile, and seemed almost under a necessity to skip in his gait.

They met few people abroad, even on passing from the retired neighborhood of the House of the Seven Gables into what was ordinarily the more thronged and busier portion of the town. Glistening sidewalks, with little pools of rain, here and there, along their unequal surface; umbrellas displayed ostentatiously in the shop-windows, as if the life of trade had concentred itself in that one article; wet leaves of the horse-chestnut or elm trees, torn off untimely by the blast, and scattered along the public way; an unsightly accumulation of mud in the middle of the street, which perversely grew the more unclean for its long and laborious washing;—these were the more definable points of a very sombre picture. In the way of movement, and human life, there was the hasty rattle of a cab or coach, its driver protected by a water-proof cap over his head and shoulders; the forlorn figure of an old man, who seemed to have crept out of some subterranean sewer, and was stooping along the kennel, and poking the wet rubbish with a stick, in quest of rusty nails; a merchant or two, at the door of the post-office, together with an editor, and a miscellaneous politician, awaiting a dilatory mail; a few visages of retired sea-captains at the window of an insurance office, looking out vacantly at the vacant street, blaspheming at the weather, and fretting at the dearth as well of public news as local gossip. What a treasure-trove to these venerable quidnuncs, could they have guessed the secret which Hepzibah and Clifford were carrying along with them! But their two figures attracted hardly so much notice as that of a young girl, who passed at the same instant, and happened to raise her skirt a trifle too high above her ankles. Had it been a sunny and cheerful day, they could hardly have gone through the streets without making themselves obnoxious to remark. Now, probably, they were felt to be in keeping with the dismal and bitter weather, and therefore did not stand out in strong relief, as if the sun were shining on them, but melted into the gray gloom, and were forgotten as soon as gone.

Poor Hepzibah! Could she have understood this fact, it would have brought her some little comfort; for, to all her other troubles—strange to say!—there was added the womanish and old-maiden-like misery arising from a sense of unseemliness in her attire. Thus, she was fain to shrink deeper into herself, as it were, as if in the hope of making people suppose that here was only a cloak and hood, threadbare and wofully faded, taking an airing in the midst of the storm, without any wearer!

As they went on, the feeling of indistinctness and unreality kept dimly hovering round about her, and so diffusing itself into her system that one of her hands was hardly palpable to the touch of the other. Any certainty would have been preferable to this. She whispered to herself, again and again,—"Am I awake? —Am I awake?"—and sometimes exposed her face to the chill spatter of the wind, for the sake of its rude assurance that she was. Whether it was Clifford's purpose, or only chance, had led them thither, they now found themselves passing beneath the arched entrance of a large structure of gray stone. Within, there was a spacious breadth, and an airy height from floor to roof, now partially filled with smoke and steam, which eddied voluminously upward, and formed a mimic cloud-region over their heads. A train of cars was just ready for a start; the locomotive was fretting and fuming, like a steed impatient for a headlong rush; and the bell rang out its hasty peal, so well expressing the brief summons which life vouchsafes to us, in its hurried career. Without question or delay,—with the irresistible decision, if not rather to be called recklessness, which had so strangely taken possession of him, and through him of Hepzibah,—Clifford impelled her towards the cars, and assisted her to enter. The signal was given; the engine puffed forth its short, quick breaths; the train began its movement; and, along with a hundred other passengers, these two unwonted travellers sped onward like the wind.

At last, therefore, and after so long estrangement from everything that the world acted or enjoyed, they had been drawn into the great current of human life, and were swept away by it, as by the suction of fate itself.

Still haunted with the idea that not one of the past incidents, inclusive of Judge Pyncheon's visit, could be real, the recluse of the seven gables murmured in her brother's ear,—

"Clifford! Clifford! Is not this a dream?"

"A dream, Hepzibah!" repeated he, almost laughing in her face. "On the contrary, I have never been awake before!"

Meanwhile, looking from the window, they could see the world racing past them. At one moment, they were rattling through a solitude; the next, a village had grown up around them; a few breaths more, and it had vanished, as if swallowed by an earthquake. The spires of meeting-houses seemed set adrift from their foundations; the broad-based hills glided away. Everything was unfixed from its age-long rest, and moving at whirlwind speed in a direction opposite to their own.

Within the car, there was the usual interior life of the railroad, offering little to the observation of other passengers, but full of novelty for this pair of strangely enfranchised prisoners. It was novelty enough, indeed, that there were fifty human beings in close relation with them, under one long and narrow roof, and drawn onward by the same mighty influence that had taken their two selves into its grasp. It seemed marvellous how all these people could remain so quietly in their seats, while so much noisy strength was at work in their behalf. Some, with tickets in their hats (long travellers these, before whom lay a hundred miles of railroad), had plunged into the English scenery and adventures of pamphlet novels, and were keeping company with dukes and earls. Others, whose briefer span forbade their devoting themselves to studies so abstruse, beguiled the little tedium of the way with penny-papers. A party of girls, and one young man, on opposite sides of the car, found huge amusement in a game of ball. They tossed it to and fro, with peals of laughter that might be measured by mile-lengths; for, faster than the nimble ball could fly, the merry players fled unconsciously along, leaving the trail of their mirth afar behind, and ending their game under another sky than had witnessed its commencement. Boys, with apples, cakes, candy, and rolls of variously tinctured lozenges,—merchandise that reminded Hepzibah of her deserted shop,—appeared at each momentary stopping-place, doing up their business in a hurry, or breaking it short off, lest the market should ravish them away with it. New people continually entered. Old acquaintances—for such they soon grew to be, in this rapid current of affairs—continually departed. Here and there, amid the rumble and the tumult, sat one asleep. Sleep; sport; business; graver or lighter study; and the common and inevitable movement onward! It was life itself!

Clifford's naturally poignant sympathies were all aroused. He caught the color of what was passing about him, and threw it back more vividly than he received it, but mixed, nevertheless, with a lurid and portentous hue. Hepzibah, on the other hand, felt herself more apart from human kind than even in the seclusion which she had just quitted.

"You are not happy, Hepzibah!" said Clifford, apart, in a tone of reproach. "You are thinking of that dismal old house, and of Cousin Jaffrey,"—here came the quake through him,—"and of Cousin Jaffrey sitting there, all by himself! Take my advice,—follow my example,—and let such things slip aside. Here we are, in the world, Hepzibah!— in the midst of life!—in the throng of our fellow-beings! Let you and I be happy! As happy as that youth, and those pretty girls, at their game of ball!"

"Happy!" thought Hepzibah, bitterly conscious, at the word, of her dull and heavy heart, with the frozen pain in it. "Happy! He is mad already; and, if I could once feel myself broad awake, I should go mad too!"

If a fixed idea be madness, she was perhaps not remote from it. Fast and far as they had rattled and clattered along the iron track, they might just as well, as regarded Hepzibah's mental images, have been passing up and down Pyncheon-street. With miles and miles of varied scenery between, there was no scene for her, save the seven old gable-peaks, with their moss, and the tuft of weeds in one of the angles, and the shop-window, and a customer shaking the door, and compelling the little bell to jingle fiercely, but without disturbing Judge Pyncheon! This one old house was everywhere! It transported its great, lumbering bulk, with more than railroad speed, and set itself phlegmatically down on whatever spot she glanced at. The quality of Hepzibah's mind was too unmalleable to take new impressions so readily as Clifford's. He had a winged nature; she was rather of the vegetable kind, and could hardly be kept long alive, if drawn up by the roots. Thus it happened that the relation heretofore existing between her brother and herself was changed. At home, she was his guardian; here, Clifford had become hers, and seemed to comprehend whatever belonged to their new position with a singular rapidity of intelligence. He had been startled into manhood and intellectual vigor; or, at least, into a condition that resembled them, though it might be both diseased and transitory.

The conductor now applied for their tickets; and Clifford, who had made himself the purse-bearer, put a banknote into his hand, as he had observed others do.

"For the lady and yourself?" asked the conductor. "And how far?"

"As far as that will carry us," said Clifford. "It is no great matter. We are riding for pleasure, merely!"

"You choose a strange day for it, sir!" remarked a gimlet-eyed old gentleman, on the other side of the car, looking at Clifford and his companion, as if curious to make them out. "The best chance of pleasure, in an easterly rain, I take it, is in a man's own house, with a nice little fire in the chimney."

"I cannot precisely agree with you," said Clifford, courteously bowing to the old gentleman, and at once taking up the clue of conversation which the latter had proffered. "It had just occurred to me, on the contrary, that this admirable invention of the railroad—with the vast and inevitable improvements to be looked for, both as to speed and convenience—is destined to do away with those stale ideas of home and fireside, and substitute something better."

"In the name of common sense," asked the old gentleman, rather testily, "what can be better for a man than his own parlor and chimney-corner?"

"These things have not the merit which many good people attribute to them," replied Clifford. "They may be said, in few and pithy words, to have ill-served a poor purpose. My impression is, that our wonderfully increased and still increasing facilities of locomotion are destined to bring us round again to the nomadic state. You are aware, my dear sir,—you must have observed it, in your own experience,—that all human progress is in a circle; or, to use a more accurate and beautiful figure, in an ascending spiral curve. While we fancy ourselves going straight forward, and attaining, at every step, an entirely new position of affairs, we do actually return to something long ago tried and abandoned, but which we now find etherealized, refined, and perfected to its ideal. The past is but a coarse and sensual prophecy of the present and the future. To apply this truth to the topic now under discussion.—In the early epochs of our race, men dwelt in temporary huts, or bowers of branches, as easily constructed as a bird's nest and which they built,—if it should be called building, when such sweet homes of a summer solstice rather grew than were made with hands,—which Nature, we will say, assisted them to rear, where fruit abounded, where fish and game were plentiful, or, most especially, where the sense of beauty was to be gratified by a lovelier shade than elsewhere, and a more exquisite arrangement of lake, wood, and hill. This life possessed a charm, which, ever since man quitted it, has vanished from existence. And it typified something better than itself. It had its drawbacks; such as hunger and thirst, inclement weather, hot sunshine, and weary and foot-blistering marches over barren and ugly tracts, that lay between the sites desirable for their fertility and beauty. But, in our ascending spiral, we escape all this. These railroads—could but the whistle be made musical, and the rumble and the jar got rid of—are positively the greatest blessing that the ages have wrought out for us. They give us wings; they annihilate the toil and dust of pilgrimage; they spiritualize travel! Transition being so facile, what can be any man's inducement to tarry in one spot? Why, therefore, should he build a more cumbrous habitation than can readily be carried off with him? Why should he make himself a prisoner for life in brick, and stone, and old worm-eaten timber, when he may just as easily dwell, in one sense, nowhere,—in a better sense, wherever the fit and beautiful shall offer him a home?"

Clifford's countenance glowed, as he divulged this theory; a youthful character shone out from within, converting the wrinkles and pallid duskiness of age into an almost transparent mask. The merry girls let their ball drop upon the floor, and gazed at him. They said to themselves, perhaps, that, before his hair was gray and the crow's feet tracked his temples, this now decaying man must have stamped the impress of his features on many a woman's heart. But, alas! no woman's eye had seen his face while it was beautiful!

"I should scarcely call it an improved state of things," observed Clifford's new acquaintance, "to live everywhere and nowhere!"

"Would you not?" exclaimed Clifford, with singular energy. "It is as clear to me as sunshine,—were there any in the sky,—that the greatest possible stumbling-blocks in the path of human happiness and improvement are these heaps of bricks and stones, consolidated with mortar, or hewn timber, fastened together with spike-nails, which men painfully contrive for their own torment and call them house and home! The soul needs air; a wide sweep and frequent change of it. Morbid influences in a thousand-fold variety, gather about hearths, and pollute the life of households. There is no such unwholesome atmosphere as that of an old home, rendered poisonous by one's defunct forefathers and relatives. I speak of what I know. There is a certain house within my familiar recollection,—one of those peaked-gable (there are seven of them) projecting-storied edifices, such as you occasionally see, in our elder towns,—a rusty, crazy, creaky, dry-rotted, damp-rotted, dingy, dark, and miserable old dungeon, with an arched window over the porch, and a little shop-door on one side, and a great, melancholy elm before it! Now, sir, whenever my thoughts recur to this seven-gabled mansion—(the fact is so very curious that I must needs mention it)—immediately I have a vision or image of an elderly man, of remarkably stern countenance, sitting in an oaken elbow-chair, dead, stone-dead, with an ugly flow of blood upon his shirt-bosom! Dead, but with open eyes! He taints the whole house, as I remember it. I could never flourish there, nor be happy, nor do nor enjoy what God meant me to do and enjoy!"

His face darkened, and seemed to contract, and shrivel itself up, and wither into age.

"Never, sir!" he repeated. "I could never draw cheerful breath there!"

"I should think not," said the old gentleman, eyeing Clifford earnestly, and rather apprehensively. "I should conceive not, sir, with that notion in your head!"

"Surely not," continued Clifford; "and it were a relief to me if that house could be torn down, or burnt up, and so the earth be rid of it, and grass be sown abundantly over its foundation. Not that I should ever visit its site again! for, sir, the further I get away from it, the more does the joy, the lightsome freshness, the heart-leap, the intellectual dance, the youth, in short,—yes, my youth, my youth!—the more does it come back to me. No longer ago than this morning, I was old. I remember looking in the glass, and wondering at my own gray hair, and the wrinkles, many and deep, right across my brow, and the furrows down my cheeks, and the prodigious trampling of crow's feet about my temples! It was too soon! I could not bear it! Age had no right to come! I had not lived! But now do I look old? If so, my aspect belies me strangely; for—a great weight being off my mind —I feel in the very hey-dey of my youth, with the world and my best days before me!"

"I trust you may find it so," said the old gentleman, who seemed rather embarrassed, and desirous of avoiding the observation which Clifford's wild talk drew on them both. "You have my best wishes for it."

"For Heaven's sake, dear Clifford, be quiet!" whispered his sister. "They think you mad."

"Be quiet yourself, Hepzibah!" returned her brother. "No matter what they think! I am not mad. For the first time in thirty years, my thoughts gush up and find words ready for them. I must talk, and I will!"

He turned again towards the old gentleman, and renewed the conversation.

"Yes, my dear sir," said he, "it is my firm belief and hope, that these terms of roof and hearth-stone, which have so long been held to embody something sacred, are soon to pass out of men's daily use, and be forgotten. Just imagine, for a moment, how much of human evil will crumble away, with this one change! What we call real estate—the solid ground to build a house on—is the broad foundation on which nearly all the guilt of this world rests. A man will commit almost any wrong,—he will heap up an immense pile of wickedness, as hard as granite, and which will weigh as heavily upon his soul, to eternal ages,—only to build a great, gloomy, dark-chambered mansion, for himself to die in, and for his posterity to be miserable in. He lays his own dead corpse beneath the underpinning, as one may say, and hangs his frowning picture on the wall, and, after thus converting himself into an evil destiny, expects his remotest great-grandchildren to be happy there! I do not speak wildly. I have just such a house in my mind's eye!"

"Then, sir," said the old gentleman, getting anxious to drop the subject, "you are not to blame for leaving it."

"Within the lifetime of the child already born," Clifford went on, "all this will be done away. The world is growing too ethereal and spiritual to bear these enormities a great while longer. To me, —though, for a considerable period of time, I have lived chiefly in retirement, and know less of such things than most men,—even to me, the harbingers of a better era are unmistakable. Mesmerism, now! Will that effect nothing, think you, towards purging away the grossness out of human life?"

"All a humbug!" growled the old gentleman.

"These rapping spirits, that little Phœbe told us of, the other day," said Clifford,—"what are these but the messengers of the spiritual world, knocking at the door of substance? And it shall be flung wide open!"

"A humbug, again!" cried the old gentleman, growing more and more testy, at these glimpses of Clifford's metaphysics. "I should like to rap with a good stick on the empty pates of the dolts who circulate such nonsense!"

"Then there is electricity;—the demon, the angel, the mighty physical power, the all-pervading intelligence!" exclaimed Clifford. "Is that a humbug, too? Is it a fact—or have I dreamt it—that, by means of electricity, the world of matter has become a great nerve, vibrating thousands of miles in a breathless point of time? Rather, the round globe is a vast head, a brain, instinct with intelligence! Or, shall we say, it is itself a thought, nothing but thought, and no longer the substance which we deemed it!"

"If you mean the telegraph," said the old gentleman, glancing his eye toward its wire, alongside the rail-track, "it is an excellent thing;—that is, of course, if the speculators in cotton and politics don't get possession of it. A great thing, indeed, sir; particularly as regards the detection of bank-robbers and murderers."

"I don't quite like it, in that point of view," replied Clifford. "A bank-robber, and what you call a murderer, likewise, has his rights, which men of enlightened humanity and conscience should regard in so much the more liberal spirit, because the bulk of society is prone to controvert their existence. An almost spiritual medium, like the electric telegraph, should be consecrated to high, deep, joyful, and holy missions. Lovers, day by day,—hour by hour, if so often moved to do it,—might send their heart-throbs from Maine to Florida, with some such words as these,—'I love you forever!'—'My heart runs over with love!'—'I love you more than I can!'—and, again, at the next message,—'I have lived an hour longer, and love you twice as much!' Or, when a good man has departed, his distant friend should be conscious of an electric thrill, as from the world of happy spirits, telling him,—'Your dear friend is in bliss!' Or, to an absent husband, should come tidings thus,—'An immortal being, of whom you are the father, has this moment come from God!'—and immediately its little voice would seem to have reached so far, and to be echoing in heart. But for these poor rogues, the bank-robbers —who, after all, are about as honest as nine people in ten, except that they disregard certain formalities, and prefer to transact business at midnight, rather than 'Change-hours,—and for these murderers, as you phrase it, who are often excusable in the motives of their deed, and deserve to be ranked among public benefactors, if we consider only its result,—for unfortunate individuals like these, I really cannot applaud the enlistment of an immaterial and miraculous power in the universal world-hunt at their heels!"

"You can't, hey?" cried the old gentleman, with a hard look.

"Positively, no!" answered Clifford. "It puts them too miserably at disadvantage. For example, sir, in a dark, low, cross-beamed, panelled room of an old house, let us suppose a dead man, sitting in an arm-chair, with a blood-stain on his shirt-bosom,—and let us add to our hypothesis another man, issuing from the house, which he feels to be over-filled with the dead man's presence, —and let us lastly imagine him fleeing, Heaven knows whither, at the speed of a hurricane, by railroad! Now, sir, if the fugitive alight in some distant town, and find all the people babbling about that self-same dead man, whom he has fled so far to avoid the sight and thought of, will you not allow that his natural rights have been infringed? He has been deprived of his city of refuge, and, in my humble opinion, has suffered infinite wrong!"

"You are a strange man, sir!" said the old gentleman, bringing his gimlet-eye to a point on Clifford, as if determined to bore right into him. "I can't see through you!"

"No, I'll be bound you can't!" cried Clifford, laughing. "And yet, my dear sir, I am as transparent as the water of Maule's well! But come, Hepzibah! We have flown far enough for once. Let us alight, as the birds do, and perch ourselves on the nearest twig, and consult whither we shall fly next!"

Just then, as it happened, the train reached a solitary way-station. Taking advantage of the brief pause, Clifford left the car, and drew Hepzibah along with him. A moment afterwards, the train—with all the life of its interior, amid which Clifford had made himself so conspicuous an object—was gliding

away in the distance, and rapidly lessening to a point, which, in another moment, vanished. The world had fled away from these two wanderers. They gazed drearily about them. At a little distance stood a wooden church, black with age, and in a dismal state of ruin and decay, with broken windows, a great rift through the main body of the edifice, and a rafter dangling from the top of the square tower. Further off was a farm-house, in the old style, as venerably black as the church, with a roof sloping downward from the three-story peak, to within a man's height of the ground. It seemed uninhabited. There were the relics of a wood-pile, indeed, near the door, but with grass sprouting up among the chips and scattered logs. The small rain-drops came down aslant; the wind was not turbulent, but sullen, and full of chilly moisture.

Clifford shivered from head to foot. The wild effervescence of his mood—which had so readily supplied thoughts, fantasies, and a strange aptitude of words, and impelled him to talk from the mere necessity of giving vent to this bubbling-up gush of ideas—had entirely subsided. A powerful excitement had given him energy and vivacity. Its operation over, he forthwith began to sink.

"You must take the lead now, Hepzibah!" murmured he, with a torpid and reluctant utterance. "Do with me as you will!"

She knelt down upon the platform where they were standing, and lifted her clasped hands to the sky. The dull, gray weight of clouds made it invisible; but it was no hour for disbelief;—no juncture this, to question that there was a sky above, and an Almighty Father looking down from it!

"O, God!"—ejaculated poor, gaunt Hepzibah,—then paused a moment to consider what her prayer should be,— "O, God,—our Father,—are we not thy children? Have mercy on us!"

CHAPTER XVIII

GOVERNOR PYNCHEON

JUDGE PYNCHEON, while his two relatives have fled away with such ill-considered haste, still sits in the old parlor, keeping house, as the familiar phrase is, in the absence of its ordinary occupants. To him, and to the venerable House of the Seven Gables, does our story now betake itself, like an owl, bewildered in the daylight, and hastening back to his hollow tree.

The judge has not shifted his position for a long while now. He has not stirred hand or foot, nor withdrawn his eyes so much as a hair's breadth from their fixed gaze towards the corner of the room, since the footsteps of Hepzibah and Clifford creaked along the passage, and the outer door was closed cautiously behind their exit. He holds his watch in his left hand, but clutched in such a manner that you cannot see the dial-plate. How profound a fit of meditation! Or, supposing him asleep, how infantile a quietude of conscience, and what wholesome order in the gastric region, are betokened by slumber so entirely undisturbed with starts, cramp, twitches, muttered dream-talk, trumpet-blasts through the nasal organ, or any the slightest irregularity of breath! You must hold your own breath, to satisfy yourself whether he

breathes at all. It is quite inaudible. You hear the ticking of his watch; his breath you do not hear. A most refreshing slumber, doubtless! And yet, the judge cannot be asleep. His eyes are open! A veteran politician, such as he, would never fall asleep with wide-open eyes, lest some enemy or mischief-maker, taking him thus at unawares, should peep through these windows into his consciousness, and make strange discoveries among the reminiscences, projects, hopes, apprehensions, weaknesses, and strong points, which he has heretofore shared with nobody. A cautious man is proverbially said to sleep with one eye open. That may be wisdom. But not with both; for this were heedlessness! No, no! Judge Pyncheon cannot be asleep.

It is odd, however, that a gentleman so burthened with engagements—and noted, too, for punctuality—should linger thus in an old lonely mansion, which he has never seemed very fond of visiting. The oaken chair, to be sure, may tempt him with its roominess. It is, indeed, a spacious, and, allowing for the rude age that fashioned it, a moderately easy seat, with capacity enough, at all events, and offering no restraint to the judge's breadth of beam.

A bigger man might find ample accommodation in it. His ancestor, now pictured upon the wall, with all his English beef about him, used hardly to present a front extending from elbow to elbow of this chair, or a base that would cover its whole cushion. But there are better chairs than this—mahogany, black-walnut, rosewood, spring-seated and damask-cushioned, with varied slopes, and innumerable artifices to make them easy, and obviate the irksomeness of too tame an ease;—a score of such might be at Judge Pyncheon's service. Yes! in a score of drawing-rooms he would be more than welcome. Mamma would advance to meet him, with outstretched hand; the virgin daughter, elderly as he has now got to be,—an old widower, as he smilingly describes himself,—would shake up the cushion for the judge, and do her pretty little utmost to make him comfortable. For the judge is a prosperous man. He cherishes his schemes, moreover, like other people, and reasonably brighter than most others; or did so, at least, as he lay abed, this morning, in an agreeable half-drowse, planning the business of the day, and speculating on the probabilities of the next fifteen years. With his firm health, and the little inroad that age has made upon him, fifteen years or twenty—yes, or perhaps five-and-twenty!—are no more than he may fairly call his own. Five-and-twenty years for the enjoyment of his real estate in town and country, his railroad, bank, and insurance shares, his United States stock,—his wealth, in short, however invested, now in possession, or soon to be acquired; together with the public honors that have fallen upon him, and the weightier ones that are yet to fall!

It is good! It is excellent! It is enough!

Still lingering in the old chair! If the judge has a little time to throw away, why does not he visit the insurance office, as is his frequent custom, and sit a while in one of their leathern-cushioned arm-chairs, listening to the gossip of the day, and dropping some deeply-designed chance-word, which will be certain to become the gossip of tomorrow! And have not the bank directors a meeting, at which it was the judge's purpose to be present, and his office to preside? Indeed they have; and the hour is noted on a card, which is, or ought to be, in Judge Pyncheon's right vest-pocket. Let him go thither, and loll at ease upon his money-bags! He has lounged long enough in the old chair!

This was to have been such a busy day! In the first place, the interview with Clifford. Half an hour, by the judge's reckoning, was to suffice for that; it would probably be less, but—taking into consideration that Hepzibah was first to be dealt with, and that these women are apt to make many words where a few would do much better—it might be safest to allow half an hour. Half an hour? Why, judge, it is already two hours, by your own undeviatingly accurate chronometer! Glance your eye down at it, and see? Ah! he will not give himself the trouble either to bend his head, or elevate his hand, so as to bring the faithful time-keeper within his range of vision! Time, all at once, appears to have become a matter of no moment with the judge!

And has he forgotten all the other items of his memoranda? Clifford's affair arranged, he was to meet a State-street broker, who has undertaken to procure a heavy percentage, and the best of paper, for a few loose thousands which the judge happens to have by him, uninvested. The wrinkled note-shaver will have taken his railroad trip in vain. Half an hour later, in the street next to this, there was to be an auction of real estate, including a portion of the old Pyncheon property, originally belonging to Maule's garden-ground. It has been alienated from the Pyncheons these fourscore years; but the judge had kept it in his eye, and had set his heart on re-annexing it to the small demesne still left around the seven gables;—and now, during this odd fit of oblivion, the fatal hammer must have fallen, and transferred our ancient patrimony to some alien possessor! Possibly, indeed, the sale may have been postponed till fairer weather. If so, will the judge make it convenient to be present, and favor the auctioneer with his bid, on the proximate occasion?

The next affair was to buy a horse for his own driving. The one heretofore his favorite stumbled, this very morning, on the road to town, and must be at once discarded. Judge Pyncheon's neck is too precious to be risked on such a contingency as a stumbling steed. Should all the above business be seasonably got through with, he might attend the meeting of a charitable society; the very name of which, however, in the multiplicity of his benevolence, is quite forgotten; so that this engagement may pass unfulfilled, and no great harm done. And if he have time, amid the press of more urgent matters, he must take measures for the renewal of Mrs. Pyncheon's tombstone, which, the sexton tells him, has fallen on its marble face, and is cracked quite in twain. She was a praiseworthy woman enough, thinks the judge, in spite of her nervousness, and the tears that she was so oozy with, and her foolish behavior about the coffee; and as she took her departure so seasonably, he will not grudge the second tombstone. It is better, at least, than if she had never needed any! The next item on his list was to give orders for some fruit-trees, of a rare variety, to be delivered at his country-seat, in the ensuing autumn. Yes, buy them, by all means; and may the peaches be luscious in your mouth; Judge Pyncheon! After this comes something more important. A committee of his political party has besought him for a hundred or two of dollars, in addition to his previous disbursements, towards carrying on the fall campaign. The judge is a patriot; the fate of the country is staked on the November election; and besides, as will be shadowed forth in another paragraph, he has no trifling stake of his own, in the same great game. He will do what the committee asks; nay, he will be liberal beyond their expectations; they shall have a check for five hundred dollars, and more anon, if it be needed. What next? A decayed widow, whose husband was Judge Pyncheon's early friend, has laid her case of destitution before him, in a very moving letter. She and her fair daughter have scarcely bread to eat. He partly intends to call on her, to-day,—perhaps so—perhaps not,—accordingly as he may happen to have leisure, and a small bank-note.

Another business, which, however, he puts no great weight on—(it is well, you know, to be heedful, but not over anxious, as respects one's personal health)—another business, then, was to consult his family physician. About what, for Heaven's sake? Why, it is rather difficult to describe the symptoms. A mere dimness of sight and dizziness of brain, was it?—or a disagreeable choking, or stifling, or gurgling, or bubbling, in the region of the thorax, as the anatomists say?—or was it a pretty severe throbbing and kicking of the heart, rather creditable to him than otherwise, as showing that the organ had not been left out of the judge's physical contrivance? No matter what it was. The doctor, probably, would smile at the statement of such trifles in his professional ear; the judge would smile, in his turn; and meeting one another's eyes, they would enjoy a hearty laugh together! But a fig for medical advice! The judge will never need it.

Pray, pray, Judge Pyncheon, look at your watch, now! What—not a glance! It is within ten minutes of the dinner-hour! It surely cannot have slipped your memory that the dinner of to-day is to be the most important, in its consequences, of all the dinners you ever ate. Yes, precisely the most important; although, in the course of your somewhat eminent career, you have been placed high towards the head of the table, at splendid banquets, and have poured out your festive eloquence to ears yet echoing with Webster's mighty organ-tones. No public dinner this, however. It is merely a gathering of some dozen or so of friends from several districts of the state; men of distinguished character and influence, assembling, almost casually, at the house of a common friend, likewise distinguished, who will make them welcome to a little better than his ordinary fare. Nothing in the way of French cookery, but an excellent dinner, nevertheless! Real turtle,

we understand, and salmon, tautog, canvas-backs, pig, English mutton, good roastbeef or dainties of that serious kind, fit for substantial country gentlemen, as these honorable persons mostly are. The delicacies of the season, in short, and flavored by a brand of old Madeira which has been the pride of many seasons. It is the Juno brand; a glorious wine, fragrant, and full of gentle might; a bottled-up happiness, put by for use; a golden liquid, worth more than liquid gold; so rare and admirable, that veteran wine-bibbers count it among their epochs to have tasted it! It drives away the heart-ache, and substitutes no head-ache! Could the judge but quaff a glass, it might enable him to shake off the unaccountable lethargy which—(for the ten intervening minutes, and five to boot, are already past)—has made him such a laggard at this momentous dinner. It would all but revive a dead man! Would you like to sip it now, Judge Pyncheon?

Alas, this dinner! Have you really forgotten its true object? Then let us whisper it, that you may start at once out of the oaken chair, which really seems to be enchanted, like the one in Comus, or that in which Moll Pitcher imprisoned your own grandfather. But ambition is a talisman more powerful than witchcraft. Start up, then, and hurrying through the streets, burst in upon the company, that they may begin before the fish is spoiled! They wait for you; and it is little for your interest that they should wait. These gentlemen —need you be told of it?—have assembled, not without purpose, from every quarter of the state. They are practised politicians, every man of them, and skilled to adjust those preliminary measures which steal from the people, without its knowledge, the power of choosing its own rulers. The popular voice, at the next gubernatorial election, though loud as thunder, will be really but an echo of what these gentlemen shall speak, under their breath, at your friend's festive board. They meet to decide upon their candidate. This little knot of subtle schemers will control the convention, and, through it, dictate to the party. And what worthier candidate, —more wise and learned, more noted for philanthropic liberality, truer to safe principles, tried oftener by public trusts, more spotless in private character, with a larger stake in the common welfare, and deeper grounded, by hereditary descent, in the faith and practice of the Puritans,—what man can be presented for the suffrage of the people, so eminently combining all these claims to the chief-rulership as Judge Pyncheon here before us?

Make haste, then! Do your part! The meed for which you have toiled, and fought, and climbed, and crept, is ready for your grasp! Be present at this dinner!—drink a glass or two of that noble wine!—make your pledges in as low a whisper as you will!—and you rise up from table virtually governor of the glorious old state! Governor Pyncheon, of Massachusetts!

And is there no potent and exhilarating cordial in a certainty like this? It has been the grand purpose of half your lifetime to obtain it. Now, when there needs little more than to signify your acceptance, why do you sit so lumpishly in your great-great-grandfather's oaken chair, as if preferring it to the gubernatorial one? We have all heard of King Log; but, in these jostling times, one

of that royal kindred will hardly win the race for an elective chief-magistracy.

Well! it is absolutely too late for dinner? Turtle, salmon, tautog, woodcock, boiled turkey, South-Down mutton, pig, roast beef, have vanished, or exist only in fragments, with lukewarm potatoes, and gravies crusted over with cold fat. The judge, had he done nothing else, would have achieved wonders with his knife and fork. It was he, you know, of whom it used to be said, in reference to his ogre-like appetite, that his Creator made him a great animal, but that the dinner-hour made him a great beast. Persons of his large sensual endowments must claim indulgence, at their feeding-time. But, for once, the judge is entirely too late for dinner! Too late, we fear, even to join the party at their wine! The guests are warm and merry; they have given up the judge; and, concluding that the free-soilers have him, they will fix upon another candidate. Were our friend now to stalk in among them, with that wide-open stare, at once wild and stolid, his ungenial presence would be apt to change their cheer. Neither would it be seemly in Judge Pyncheon, generally so scrupulous in his attire, to show himself at a dinner-table with that crimson stain upon his shirt-bosom. By-the-by, how came it there? It is an ugly sight, at any rate; and the wisest way for the judge is to button his coat closely over his breast, and, taking his horse and chaise from the livery-stable, to make all speed to his own house. There, after a glass of brandy and water, and a mutton-chop, a beef-steak, a broiled fowl, or some such hasty little dinner and supper all in one, he had better spend the evening by the fireside. He must toast his slippers a long while, in order to get rid of the chilliness which the air of this vile old house has sent curdling through his veins.

Up, therefore, Judge Pyncheon, up! You have lost a day. But to-morrow will be here anon. Will you rise, betimes, and make the most of it? To-morrow! To-morrow! To-morrow! We, that are alive, may rise betimes to-morrow. As for him that died to-day, his morrow will be the resurrection morn.

Meanwhile the twilight is glooming upward out of the corners of the room. The shadows of the tall furniture grow deeper, and at first become more definite; then, spreading wider, they lose their distinctness of outline in the dark gray tide of oblivion, as it were, that creeps slowly over the various objects, and the one human figure sitting in the midst of them. The gloom has not entered from without; it has brooded here all day, and now, taking its own inevitable time, will possess itself of everything. The judge's face, indeed, rigid, and singularly white, refuses to melt into this universal solvent. Fainter and fainter grows the light. It is as if another double-handful of darkness had been scattered through the air. Now it is no longer gray, but sable. There is still a faint appearance at the windows; neither a glow, nor a gleam, nor a glimmer,—any phrase of light would express something far brighter than this doubtful perception, or sense, rather, that there is a window there. Has it yet vanished? No!—yes!—not quite! And there is still the swarthy whiteness,— we shall venture to marry these ill-agreeing words,—the swarthy whiteness of Judge Pyncheon's face. The features are all gone; there is only the paleness of them left. And how looks it now?

There is no window! There is no face! An infinite, inscrutable blackness has annihilated sight! Where is our universe? All crumbled away from us; and we, adrift in chaos, may hearken to the gusts of homeless wind, that go sighing and murmuring about, in quest of what was once a world!

Is there no other sound? One other, and a fearful one. It is the ticking of the judge's watch, which, ever since Hepzibah left the room in search of Clifford, he has been holding in his hand. Be the cause what it may, this little, quiet, never-ceasing throb of Time's pulse, repeating its small strokes with such busy regularity, in Judge Pyncheon's motionless hand, has an effect of terror, which we do not find in any other accompaniment of the scene.

But, listen! That puff of the breeze was louder; it had a tone unlike the dreary and sullen one which has bemoaned itself, and afflicted all mankind with miserable sympathy, for five days past. The wind has veered about! It now comes boisterously from the northwest, and, taking hold of the aged frame-work of the seven gables, gives it a shake, like a wrestler that would try strength with his antagonist. Another and another sturdy tussle with the blast! The old house creaks again, and makes a vociferous but somewhat unintelligible bellowing in its sooty throat— (the big flue, we mean, of its wide chimney)—partly in complaint at the rude wind, but rather, as befits their century and a half of hostile intimacy, in tough defiance. A rumbling kind of a bluster roars behind the fireboard. A door has slammed above-stairs. A window, perhaps, has been left open, or else is driven in by an unruly gust. It is not to be conceived, beforehand, what wonderful wind-instruments are these old timber mansions, and how haunted with the strangest noises, which immediately begin to sing, and sigh, and sob, and shriek,—and to smite with sledge-hammers, airy, but ponderous, in some distant chamber,—and to tread along the entries as with stately foot-steps, and rustle up and down the stair-case, as with silks miraculously stiff,—whenever the gale catches the house with a window open, and gets fairly into it! Would that we were not an attendant spirit here! It is too awful! This clamor of the wind through the lonely house; the judge's quietude, as he sits invisible; and that pertinacious ticking of his watch!

As regards Judge Pyncheon's invisibility, however, that matter will soon be remedied. The north-west wind has swept the sky clear. The window is distinctly seen. Through its panes, moreover, we dimly catch the sweep of the dark, clustering foliage, outside, fluttering with a constant irregularity of movement, and letting in a peep of starlight, now here, now there. Oftener than any other object, these glimpses illuminate the judge's face. But here comes more effectual light. Observe that silvery dance upon the upper branches of the pear-tree, and now a little lower, and now on the whole mass of boughs, while, through their shifting intricacies, the moonbeams fall aslant into the room. They play over the judge's figure, and show that he has not stirred throughout the hours of darkness. They follow the shadows, in changeful sport, across his unchanging features. They gleam upon his watch. His grasp conceals the dial-plate; but we know that the faithful hands have met; for one of the city clocks tells midnight.

A man of sturdy understanding, like Jaffrey Pyncheon, cares no more for twelve o'clock at night than for the corresponding hour of noon. However just the parallel drawn, in some of the preceding pages, between his Puritan ancestors and himself, it fails in this point. The Pyncheon of two centuries ago, in common with most of his contemporaries, professed his full belief in spiritual ministrations, although reckoning them chiefly of a malignant character. The Pyncheon of to-night, who sits in yonder arm-chair, believes in no such nonsense. Such, at least, was his creed, some few hours since. His hair will not bristle, therefore, at the stories which—in times when chimney-corners had benches in them, where old people sat poking into the ashes of the past, and raking out traditions like live coals —used to be told about this very room of his ancestral house. In fact, these tales are too absurd to bristle even childhood's hair. What sense, meaning, or moral, for example, such as even ghost-stories should be susceptible of, can be traced in the ridiculous legend, that, at midnight, all the dead Pyncheons are bound to assemble in this parlor? And, pray, for what? Why, to see whether the portrait of their ancestor still keeps its place upon the wall, in compliance with his testamentary directions! Is it worth while to come out of their graves for that?

We are tempted to make a little sport with the idea. Ghost-stories are hardly to be treated seriously, any longer. The family-party of the defunct Pyncheons, we presume, goes off in this wise.

First comes the ancestor himself, in

his black cloak, steeple-hat, and trunk-breeches, girt about the waist with a leathern belt, in which hangs his steel-hilted sword; he has a long staff in his hand, such as gentlemen in advanced life used to carry, as much for the dignity of the thing as for the support to be derived from it. He looks up at the portrait;— a thing of no substance, gazing at its own painted image! All is safe. The picture is still there. The purpose of his brain has been kept sacred thus long after the man himself has sprouted up in grave-yard grass. See! he lifts his ineffectual hand, and tries the frame. All safe! But is that a smile? —is it not, rather, a frown of deadly import, that darkens over the shadow of his features? The stout colonel is dissatisfied! So decided is his look of discontent as to impart additional distinctness to his features; through which, nevertheless, the moonlight passes, and flickers on the wall beyond. Something has strangely vexed the ancestor! With a grim shake of the head, he turns away. Here come other Pyncheons, the whole tribe, in their half a dozen generations, jostling and elbowing one another, to reach the picture. We behold aged men and grandames, clergyman with the Puritanic stiffness still in his garb and mien, and a red-coated officer of the old French war; and there comes the shop-keeping Pyncheon of a century ago, with the ruffles turned back from his wrists; and there the periwigged and brocaded gentleman of the artist's legend, with the beautiful and pensive Alice, who brings no pride out of her virgin grave. All try the picture-frame. What do these ghostly people seek? A mother lifts her child, that his little hands may touch it! There is evidently

a mystery about the picture, that perplexes these poor Pyncheons, when they ought to be at rest. In a corner, meanwhile, stands the figure of an elderly man, in a leather jerkin and breeches, with a carpenter's rule sticking out of his side-pocket; he points his finger at the bearded colonel and his descendants, nodding, jeering, mocking, and finally bursting into obstreperous, though inaudible laughter.

Indulging our fancy in this freak, we have partly lost the power of restraint and guidance. We distinguish an unlooked-for figure in our visionary scene. Among those ancestral people there is a young man, dressed in the very fashion of to-day; he wears a dark frock-coat, almost destitute of skirts, gray pantaloons, gaiter boots of patent leather, and has a finely-wrought gold chain across his breast, and a little silver-headed whalebone stick in his hand. Were we to meet this figure at noon-day, we should greet him as young Jaffrey Pyncheon, the judge's only surviving child, who has been spending the last two years in foreign travel. If still in life, how comes his shadow hither? If dead, what a misfortune! The old Pyncheon property, together with the great estate acquired by the young man's father, would devolve on whom? On poor, foolish Clifford, gaunt Hepzibah, and rustic little Phœbe! But another and a greater marvel greets us! Can we believe our eyes? A stout, elderly gentleman has made his appearance; he has an aspect of eminent respectability, wears a black coat and pantaloons, of roomy width, and might be pronounced scrupulously neat in his attire, but for a broad crimson stain across his snowy neckcloth and down his shirt-bosom. Is it the judge, or no? How can it be Judge Pyncheon? We discern his figure, as plainly as the flickering moonbeams can show us anything, still seated in the oaken chair! Be the apparition whose it may, it advances to the picture, seems to seize the frame, tries to peep behind it, and turns away, with a frown as black as the ancestral one.

The fantastic scene just hinted at must by no means be considered as forming an actual portion of our story. We were betrayed into this brief extravagance by the quiver of the moonbeams; they dance hand-in-hand with shadows, and are reflected in the looking-glass, which, you are aware, is always a kind of window or door-way into the spiritual world. We needed relief, moreover, from our too long and exclusive contemplation of that figure in the chair. This wild wind, too, has tossed our thoughts into strange confusion, but without tearing them away from their one determined centre. Yonder leaden judge sits immovably upon our soul. Will he never stir again? We shall go mad, unless he stirs! You may the better estimate his quietude by the fearlessness of a little mouse, which sits on its hind legs, in a streak of moonlight, close by Judge Pyncheon's foot, and seems to meditate a journey of exploration over this great black bulk. Ha! what has startled the nimble little mouse? It is the visage of Grimalkin, outside of the window, where he appears to have posted himself for a deliberate watch. This Grimalkin has a very ugly look. Is it a cat watching for a mouse, or the devil for a human soul? Would we could scare him from the window!

Thank Heaven, the night is well-nigh past! The moonbeams have no longer so silvery a gleam, nor contrast so strongly with the blackness of the shadows among which they fall. They are paler, now; the shadows look gray, not black. The boisterous wind is hushed. What is the hour? Ah! the watch has at last ceased to tick; for the judge's forgetful fingers neglected to wind it up, as usual, at ten o'clock, being half an hour, or so, before his ordinary bed-time;—and it has run down, for the first time in five years. But the great world-clock of Time still keeps its beat. The dreary night,—for, oh, how dreary seems its haunted waste, behind us!—gives place to a fresh, transparent, cloudless morn. Blessed, blessed radiance! The day-beam,—even what little of it finds its way into this always dusky parlor—seems part of the universal benediction, annulling evil, and rendering all goodness possible, and happiness attainable. Will Judge Pyncheon now rise up from his chair? Will he go forth, and receive the early sunbeams on his brow? Will he begin this new day,—which God has smiled upon, and blessed, and given to mankind,—will he begin it with better purposes than the many that have been spent amiss? Or are all the deep-laid schemes of yesterday as stubborn in his heart, and as busy in his brain, as ever?

In this latter case, there is much to do. Will the judge still insist with Hepzibah on the interview with Clifford? Will he buy a safe, elderly gentleman's horse? Will he persuade the purchaser of the old Pyncheon property to relinquish the bargain, in his favor? Will he see his family physician, and obtain a medicine that shall preserve him, to be an honor and blessing to his race. until the utmost term of patriarchal longevity? Will Judge Pyncheon, above all, make due apologies to that company of honorable friends, and satisfy them that his absence from the festive board was unavoidable, and so fully retrieve himself in their good opinion that he shall yet be Governor of Massachusetts? And, all these great purposes accomplished, will he walk the streets again, with that dog-day smile of elaborate benevolence, sultry enough to tempt flies to come and buzz in it? Or will he, after the tomb-like seclusion of the past day and night, go forth a humbled and repentant man, sorrowful, gentle, seeking no profit, shrinking from worldly honor, hardly daring to love God, but bold to love his fellow-man, and to do him what good he may? Will he bear about with him,—no odious grin of feigned benignity, insolent in its pretence, and loathsome in its falsehood,—but the tender sadness of a contrite heart, broken, at last, beneath its own weight of sin? For it is our belief, whatever show of honor he may have piled upon it, that there was heavy sin at the base of this man's being.

Rise up, Judge Pyncheon! The morning sunshine glimmers through the foliage, and. beautiful and holy as it is, shuns not to kindle up your face. Rise up, thou subtile, worldly, selfish, iron-hearted hypocrite, and make thy choice whether still to be subtile, worldly, selfish, iron-hearted, and hypocritical, or to tear these sins out of thy nature, though they bring the life-blood with them! The Avenger is upon thee! Rise up, before it be too late!

What! Thou art not stirred by this last appeal? No, not a jot! And there we see a fly,—one of your common house-flies, such as are always buzzing on the window-pane,—which has smelt out Governor Pyncheon, and alights, now on his forehead, now on his chin, and now, Heaven help us! is creeping over the bridge of his nose, towards the would-be chief-magistrate's wide-open eyes! Canst thou not brush the fly away? Art thou too sluggish? Thou man, that hadst so many busy projects, yesterday! Art thou too weak, that wast so powerful? Not brush away a fly! Nay, then, we give thee up!

And, hark! the shop-bell rings. After hours like these latter ones, through which we have borne our heavy tale, it is good to be made sensible that there is a living world, and that even this old, lonely mansion retains some manner of connection with it. We breathe more freely, emerging from Judge Pyncheon's presence into the street before the seven gables

---

CHAPTER XIX

ALICE'S POSIES

UNCLE VENNER, trundling a wheelbarrow, was the earliest person stirring in the neighborhood, the day after the storm.

Pyncheon-street, in front of the House of the Seven Gables, was a far pleasanter scene than a by-lane, confined by shabby fences, and bordered with wooden dwellings of the meaner class, could reasonably be expected to present. Nature made sweet amends, that morning, for the five unkindly days which had preceded it. It would have been enough to live for, merely to look up at the wide benediction of the sky, or as much of it as was visible between the houses, genial once more with sunshine. Every object was agreeable, whether to be gazed at in the breadth, or examined more minutely. Such, for example, were the well-washed pebbles and gravel of the sidewalk; even the sky-reflecting pools in the centre of the street; and the grass, now freshly verdant, that crept along the base of the fences, on the other side of which, if one peeped over, was seen the multifarious growth of gardens. Vegetable productions, of whatever kind, seemed more than negatively happy, in the juicy warmth and abundance of their life. The Pyncheon-elm, throughout its great circumference, was all alive, and full of the morning sun and a sweetly-tempered little breeze, which lingered within this verdant sphere, and set a thousand leafy tongues a-whispering all at once. This aged tree appeared to have suffered nothing from the gale. It had kept its boughs unshattered, and its full complement of leaves; and the whole in perfect verdure, except a single branch, that, by the earlier change with which the elm-tree sometimes prophesies the autumn, had been transmuted to bright gold. It was like the golden branch, that gained Æneas and the Sybil admittance into Hades.

This one mystic branch hung down before the main entrance of the seven gables, so nigh the ground that any passer-by might have stood on tiptoe and plucked it off. Presented at the door, it would have been a symbol of his right to enter, and be made acquainted with all the secrets of the house. So little faith is due to external appearance, that there was really an inviting aspect over the venerable edifice, conveying an idea that its history must be a decorous and happy one, and such as would be delightful for a fire-side tale. Its windows gleamed cheerfully in the slanting sunlight. The lines and tufts of green moss, here and there, seemed pledges of familiarity and sisterhood with Nature; as if this human dwelling-place, being of such old date, had established its prescriptive title among primeval oaks, and whatever other objects, by virtue of their long continuance, have acquired a gracious right to be. A person of imaginative temperament, while passing by the house, would turn, once and again, and peruse it well:—its many peaks, consenting together in the clustered chimney; the deep projection over its basement-story; the arched window, imparting a look, if not of grandeur, yet of antique gentility, to the broken portal over which it opened; the luxuriance of gigantic burdocks, near the threshold:—he would note all these characteristics, and be conscious of something deeper than he saw. He would conceive the mansion to have been the residence of the stubborn old Puritan, Integrity, who, dying in some forgotten generation, had left a blessing in all its rooms and chambers, the efficacy of which was to be seen in the religion, honesty, moderate competence, or upright poverty and solid happiness, of his descendants, to this day.

One object, above all others, would take root in the imaginative observer's memory. It was the great tuft of flowers,—weeds, you would have called them, only a week ago,—the tuft of crimson-spotted flowers, in the angle between the two front gables. The old people used to give them the name of Alice's Posies, in remembrance of fair Alice Pyncheon, who was believed to have brought their seeds from Italy. They were flaunting in rich beauty and full of bloom, to-day, and seemed, as it were, a mystic expression that something within the house was consummated.

It was but little after sunrise, when Uncle Venner made his appearance, as aforesaid, impelling a wheelbarrow along the street. He was going his matutinal rounds to collect cabbage-leaves, turnip-tops, potato-skins, and the miscellaneous refuse of the dinner-pot, which the thrifty housewives of the neighborhood were accustomed to put aside, as fit only to feed a pig. Uncle Venner's pig was fed entirely, and kept in prime order, on these eleemosynary contributions; insomuch that the patched philosopher used to promise that, before retiring to his farm, he would make a feast of the portly grunter, and invite all his neighbors to partake of the joints and spare-ribs which they had helped to fatten. Miss Hepzibah Pyncheon's housekeeping had so greatly improved, since Clifford became a member of the family, that her share of the banquet would have been no lean one; and Uncle Venner, accordingly, was a good deal disappointed not to find the large earthen-pan, full of fragmentary eatables, that ordinarily awaited his coming, at the back door-step of the seven gables.

"I never knew Miss Hepzibah so forgetful before," said the patriarch to himself. "She must have had a dinner yesterday,—no question of that! She always has one, now-a-days. So where's the pot-liquor and potato-skins, I ask? Shall I knock, and see if she's stirring yet? No, no,—'twon't do! If little Phœbe was about the house, I should not mind knocking; but Miss Hepzibah, likely as not, would scowl down at me, out of the window, and look cross, even if she felt pleasantly. So I'll come back at noon."

With these reflections, the old man was shutting the gate of the little backyard. Creaking on its hinges, however, like every other gate and door about the premises, the sound reached the ears of the occupant of the northern gable, one of the windows of which had a side-view towards the gate.

"Good-morning, Uncle Venner!" said the daguerreotypist, leaning out of the window. "Do you hear nobody stirring?"

"Not a soul," said the man of patches. "But that's no wonder. 'Tis barely half an hour past sunrise, yet. But I'm really glad to see you, Mr. Holgrave! There's a strange, lonesome look about this side of the house; so that my heart misgave me, somehow or other, and I felt as if there was nobody alive in it. The front of the house looks a good deal cheerier; and Alice's Posies are blooming there beautifully; and if I were a young man, Mr. Holgrave, my sweetheart should have one of these flowers in her bosom, though I risked my neck climbing for it! —Well! and did the wind keep you awake last night?"

"It did, indeed!" answered the artist,

smiling. "If I were a believer in ghosts,—and I don't quite know whether I am or not,—I should have concluded that all the old Pyncheons were running riot in the lower rooms, especially in Miss Hepzibah's part of the house. But it is very quiet now."

"Yes, Miss Hepzibah will be apt to over-sleep herself, after being disturbed, all night, with the racket," said Uncle Venner. "But it would be odd, now, wouldn't it, if the judge had taken both his cousins into the country along with him? I saw him go into the shop yesterday."

"At what hour?" inquired Holgrave.

"O, along the forenoon," said the old man. "Well, well! I must go my rounds, and so must my wheelbarrow. But I'll be back here at dinner-time; for my pig likes a dinner as well as a breakfast. No meal-time, and no sort of victuals, ever seems to come amiss to my pig. Good-morning to you! And, Mr. Holgrave, if I were a young man, like you, I'd get one of Alice's Posies, and keep it in water till Phœbe comes back."

"I have heard," said the daguerreotypist, as he drew in his head, "that the water of Maule's well suits those flowers best."

Here the conversation ceased, and Uncle Venner went on his way. For half an hour longer, nothing disturbed the repose of the seven gables; nor was there any visitor, except a carrier-boy, who, as he passed the front door-step, threw down one of his newspapers; for Hepzibah, of late, had regularly taken it in. After a while, there came a fat woman, making prodigious speed, and stumbling as she ran up the steps of the shop-door. Her face glowed with fire-heat, and it being a pretty warm morning, she bubbled and hissed, as it were, as if all a-fry with chimney-warmth, and summer-warmth, and the warmth of her own corpulent velocity. She tried the shop-door;—it was fast. She tried it again, with so angry a jar that the bell tinkled angrily back at her.

"The deuce take Old Maid Pyncheon!" muttered the irascible housewife. "Think of her pretending to set up a cent-shop, and then lying abed till noon! These are what she calls gentlefolk's airs, I suppose. But I'll either start her ladyship, or break the door down!"

She shook it accordingly, and the bell, having a spiteful little temper of its own, rang obstreperously, making its remonstrances heard,—not, indeed, by the ears for which they were intended,—but by a good lady on the opposite side of the street. She opened her window, and addressed the impatient applicant.

"You'll find nobody there, Mrs. Gubbins."

"But I must and will find somebody here!" cried Mrs. Gubbins, inflicting another outrage on the bell. "I want a half-pound of pork, to fry some first-rate flounders, for Mr. Gubbins's breakfast; and, lady or not, Old Maid Pyncheon shall get up and serve me with it!"

"But do hear reason, Mrs. Gubbins!" responded the lady opposite. "She, and her brother, too, have both gone to their cousin, Judge Pyncheon's, at his country-seat. There's not a soul in the house, but that young daguerreotype-man, that sleeps in the north gable. I saw old Hepzibah and Clifford go away yesterday; and a queer couple of ducks they were, paddling through the mud-puddles! They're gone, I'll assure you."

"And how do you know they're gone to the judge's?" asked Mrs. Gubbins. "He's a rich man; and there's been a quarrel between him and Hepzibah, this many a day, because he won't give her a living. That's the main reason of her setting up a cent-shop."

"I know that well enough," said the neighbor. "But they're gone,—that's one thing certain. And who but a blood-relation, that couldn't help himself, I ask you, would take in that awful-tempered old maid, and that dreadful Clifford? That's it, you may be sure."

Mrs. Gubbins took her departure, still brimming over with hot wrath against the absent Hepzibah. For another half hour, or, perhaps, considerably more, there was almost as much quiet on the outside of the house as within. The elm, however, made a pleasant, cheerful, sunny sigh, responsive to the breeze that was elsewhere imperceptible; a swarm of insects buzzed merrily under its drooping shadow, and became specks of light, whenever they darted into the sunshine; a locust sang, once or twice, in some inscrutable seclusion of the tree; and a solitary little bird, with plumage of pale gold, came and hovered about Alice's Posies.

At last, our small acquaintance, Ned Higgins, trudged up the street, on his way to school; and happening, for the first time in a fortnight, to be the possessor of a cent, he could by no means get past the shop-door of the seven gables. But it would not open. Again and again, however, and half a dozen other agains, with the inexorable pertinacity of a child intent upon some object important to itself, did he renew his efforts for admittance. He had,

doubtless, set his heart upon an elephant; or, possibly, with Hamlet, he meant to eat a crocodile. In response to his more violent attacks, the bell gave, now and then, a moderate tinkle, but could not be stirred into clamor by any exertion of the little fellow's childish and tiptoe strength. Holding by the door-handle, he peeped through a crevice of the curtain, and saw that the inner door, communicating with the passage towards the parlor, was closed.

"Miss Pyncheon!" screamed the child, rapping on the window-pane, "I want an elephant!"

There being no answer to several repetitions of the summons, Ned began to grow impatient; and his little pot of passion quickly boiling over, he picked up a stone, with a naughty purpose to fling it through the window; at the same time blubbering and sputtering with wrath. A man—one of two who happened to be passing by—caught the urchin's arm.

"What's the trouble, old gentleman?" he asked.

"I want old Hepzibah, or Phœbe, or any of them!" answered Ned, sobbing. "They won't open the door; and I can't get my elephant!"

"Go to school, you little scamp!" said the man. "There's another cent-shop round the corner. 'Tis very strange, Dixey," added he to his companion, "what's become of all these Pyncheons! Smith, the livery-stable keeper, tells me Judge Pyncheon put his horse up yesterday, to stand till after dinner, and has not taken him away yet. And one of the judge's hired men has been in, this morning, to make inquiry about him. He's a kind of person, they say, that seldom breaks his habits, or stays out o' nights."

"O, he'll turn up safe enough!" said Dixey. "And as for Old Maid Pyncheon, take my word for it, she has run in debt, and gone off from her creditors. I foretold, you remember, the first morning she set up shop, that her devilish scowl would frighten away customers. They couldn't stand it!"

"I never thought she'd make it go," remarked his friend. "This business of cent-shops is overdone among the women-folks. My wife tried it, and lost five dollars on her outlay!"

"Poor business!" said Dixey, shaking his head. "Poor business!"

In the course of the morning, there were various other attempts to open a communication with the supposed inhabitants of this silent and impenetrable mansion. The man of root-beer came, in his neatly-painted wagon, with a couple of dozen full bottles, to be exchanged for empty ones; the baker, with a lot of crackers which Hepzibah had ordered for her retail custom; the butcher, with a nice titbit which he fancied she would be eager to secure for Clifford. Had any observer of these proceedings been aware of the fearful secret hidden within the house, it would have affected him with a singular shape and modification of horror, to see the current of human life making this small eddy hereabouts;—whirling sticks, straws, and all such trifles, round and round, right over the black depth where a dead corpse lay unseen!

The butcher was so much in earnest with his sweetbread of lamb, or whatever the dainty might be, that he tried every accessible door of the seven gables, and at length came round again to the shop, where he ordinarily found admittance.

"It's a nice article, and I know the old lady would jump at it," said he to himself. "She can't be gone away! In fifteen years that I have driven my cart through Pyncheon-street, I've never known her to be away from home; though often enough, to be sure, a man might knock all day without bringing her to the door. But that was when she'd only herself to provide for."

Peeping through the same crevice of the curtain where, only a little while before, the urchin of elephantine appetite had peeped, the butcher beheld the inner door, not closed, as the child had seen it, but ajar, and almost wide open. However it might have happened, it was the fact. Through the passageway there was a dark vista into the lighter but still obscure interior of the parlor. It appeared to the butcher that he could pretty clearly discern what seemed to be the stalwart legs, clad in black pantaloons, of a man sitting in a large oaken chair, the back of which concealed all the remainder of his figure. This contemptuous tranquillity on the part of an occupant of the house, in response to the butcher's indefatigable efforts to attract notice, so piqued the man of flesh that he determined to withdraw.

"So," thought he, "there sits Old Maid Pyncheon's bloody brother, while I've been giving myself all this trouble! Why, if a hog hadn't more manners, I'd stick him! I call it demeaning a man's business to trade with such people; and from this time forth, if they want a sausage or an ounce of liver, they shall run after the cart for it!"

He tossed the titbit angrily into his cart, and drove off in a pet.

Not a great while afterwards, there was a sound of music turning the corner, and approaching down the street, with several intervals of silence, and then a renewed and nearer outbreak of brisk melody. A mob of children was seen moving onward, or stopping, in unison with the sound, which appeared to proceed from the centre of the throng; so that they were loosely bound together by slender strains of harmony, and drawn along captive; with ever and anon an accession of some little fellow in an apron and straw-hat, capering forth from door or gateway. Arriving under the shadow of the Pyncheon-elm, it proved to be the Italian boy, who, with his monkey and show of puppets, had once before played his hurdy-gurdy beneath the arched window. The pleasant face of Phœbe—and doubtless, too, the liberal recompense which she had flung him—still dwelt in his remembrance. His expressive features kindled up, as he recognized the spot where this trifling incident of his erratic life had chanced. He entered the neglected yard (now wilder than ever, with its growth of hogweed and burdock), stationed himself on the door-step of the main entrance, and opening his show-box, began to play. Each individual of the automatic community forthwith set to work, according to his or her proper vocation: the monkey, taking off his Highland bonnet, bowed and scraped to the bystanders most obsequiously, with ever an observant eye to pick up a stray cent; and the young foreigner himself, as he turned the crank of his machine, glanced upward to the arched window, expectant of a presence that would make his music the livelier and sweeter. The throng of

children stood near; some on the sidewalk; some within the yard; two or three establishing themselves on the very door-step; and one squatting on the threshold. Meanwhile, the locust kept singing in the great old Pyncheon-elm.

"I don't hear anybody in the house," said one of the children to another. "The monkey won't pick up anything here."

"There is somebody at home," affirmed the urchin on the threshold. "I heard a step!"

Still the young Italian's eye turned sidelong upward; and it really seemed as if the touch of genuine, though slight and almost playful emotion, communicated a juicier sweetness to the dry, mechanical process of his minstrelsy. These wanderers are readily responsive to any natural kindness—be it no more than a smile, or a word, itself not understood, but only a warmth in it—which befalls them on the roadside of life. They remember these things, because they are the little enchantments which, for the instant,—for the space that reflects a landscape in a soap-bubble,—build up a home about them. Therefore, the Italian boy would not be discouraged by the heavy silence with which the old house seemed resolute to clog the vivacity of his instrument. He persisted in his melodious appeals; he still looked upward, trusting that his dark, alien countenance would soon be brightened by Phœbe's sunny aspect. Neither could he be willing to depart without again beholding Clifford, whose sensibility, like Phœbe's smile, had talked a kind of heart's language to the foreigner. He repeated all his music, over and over again, until his auditors were getting weary. So were the little wooden people in his show-box, and the monkey most of all. There was no response, save the singing of the locust.

"No children live in this house," said a schoolboy, at last. "Nobody lives here but an old maid and an old man. You'll get nothing here! Why don't you go along?"

"You fool, you, why do you tell him?" whispered a shrewd little Yankee, caring nothing for the music, but a good deal for the cheap rate at which it was had. "Let him play as long as he likes! If there's nobody to pay him, that's his own look-out!"

Once more, however, the Italian ran over his round of melodies. To the common observer—who could understand nothing of the case, except the music and the sunshine on the hither side of the door—it might have been amusing to watch the pertinacity of the street-performer. Will he succeed at last? Will that stubborn door be suddenly flung open? Will a group of joyous children, the young ones of the house, come dancing, shouting, laughing, into the open air, and cluster round the show-box, looking with eager merriment at the puppets, and tossing each a copper for long-tailed Mammon, the monkey, to pick up?

But, to us, who know the inner heart of the seven gables, as well as its exterior face, there is a ghastly effect in this repetition of light popular tunes at its door-step. It would be an ugly business, indeed, if Judge Pyncheon (who would not have cared a fig for Paganini's fiddle, in his most harmonious mood) should make his appearance at the door, with a bloody shirt-bosom, and a grim frown on his swarthily-white visage, and motion the foreign vagabond away! Was ever before such a grinding out of jigs and waltzes, where nobody was in the cue to dance? Yes, very often. This contrast, or intermingling of tragedy with mirth, happens daily, hourly, momently. The gloomy and desolate old house, deserted of life, and with awful Death sitting sternly in its solitude, was the emblem of many a human heart, which, nevertheless, is compelled to hear the trill and echo of the world's gayety around it.

Before the conclusion of the Italian's performance, a couple of men happened to be passing, on their way to dinner.

"I say, you young French fellow!" called out one of them,—"come away from that door-step, and go somewhere else with your nonsense! The Pyncheon family live there; and they are in great trouble, just about this time. They don't feel musical to-day. It is reported, all over town, that Judge Pyncheon, who owns the house, has been murdered; and the city marshal is going to look into the matter. So be off with you, at once!"

As the Italian shouldered his hurdy-gurdy, he saw on the door-step a card, which had been covered, all the morning, by the newspaper that the carrier had flung upon it, but was now shuffled into sight. He picked it up, and perceiving something written in pencil, gave it to the man to read. In fact, it was an engraved card of Judge Pyncheon's, with certain pencilled memoranda on the back, referring to various businesses, which it had been his purpose to transact during the preceding day. It formed a prospective epitome of the day's history; only that affairs had not turned out altogether in accordance with the

rogramme. The card must have been
ost from the judge's vest-pocket, in his
preliminary attempt to gain access by
he main entrance of the house. Though
well-soaked with rain, it was still par-
ially legible.

"Look here, Dixey!" cried the man.
This has something to do with Judge
Pyncheon. See!—here's his name printed
on it; and here, I suppose, is some of
his hand-writing."

"Let's go to the city marshal with it!"
said Dixey. "It may give him just the
clue he wants. After all," whispered he
in his companion's ear, "it would be no
wonder if the judge has gone into that
door, and never come out again! A
certain cousin of his may have been at
his old tricks. And Old Maid Pyncheon,
having got herself in debt by the cent-
shop,—and the judge's pocket-book being well filled,—and bad blood amongst
them already! Put all these things together, and see what they make!"

"Hush, hush!" whispered the other.
"It seems like a sin to be the first to
speak of such a thing. But I think, with
you, that we had better go to the city
marshal."

"Yes, yes!" said Dixey. "Well!—I
always said there was something devilish
in that woman's scowl!"

The men wheeled about, accordingly,
and retraced their steps up the street.
The Italian, also, made the best of his
way off, with a parting glance up at the
arched window. As for the children,
they took to their heels, with one accord, and scampered as if some giant or
ogre were in pursuit, until, at a good
distance from the house, they stopped
as suddenly and simultaneously as they
had set out. Their susceptible nerves
took an indefinite alarm from what they

had overheard. Looking back at the
grotesque peaks and shadowy angles of
the old mansion, they fancied a gloom
diffused about it, which no brightness of
the sunshine could dispel. An imaginary
Hepzibah scowled and shook her finger
at them, from several windows at the
same moment. An imaginary Clifford
—for (and it would have deeply wounded him to know it) he had always been
a horror to these small people—stood
behind the unreal Hepzibah, making
awful gestures, in a faded dressing-
gown. Children are even more apt, if
possible, than grown people, to catch
the contagion of a panic terror. For
the rest of the day, the more timid
went whole streets about, for the sake
of avoiding the seven gables; while the
bolder signalized their hardihood by
challenging their comrades to race past
the mansion at full speed.

It could not have been more than
half an hour after the disappearance of
the Italian boy, with his unseasonable
melodies, when a cab drove down the
street. It stopped beneath the Pyncheon-
elm; the cabman took a trunk, a
canvas-bag, and a band-box, from the
top of his vehicle, and deposited them
on the door-step of the old house; a
straw bonnet, and then the pretty figure
of a young girl, came into view from
the interior of the cab. It was Phœbe!
Though not altogether so blooming as
when she first tripped into our story,—
for, in the few intervening weeks, her
experiences had made her graver, more
womanly, and deeper-eyed, in token of
a heart that had begun to suspect its
depths,—still there was the quiet glow
of natural sunshine over her. Neither
had she forfeited her proper gift of
making things look real, rather than

fantastic, within her sphere. Yet we feel it to be a questionable venture, even for Phœbe, at this juncture, to cross the threshold of the seven gables. Is her healthful presence potent enough to chase away the crowd of pale, hideous, and sinful phantoms, that have gained admittance there since her departure? Or will she, likewise, fade, sicken, sadden, and grow into deformity, and be only another pallid phantom, to glide noiselessly up and down the stairs, and affright children, as she pauses at the window?

At least, we would gladly forewarn the unsuspecting girl that there is nothing in human shape or substance to receive her, unless it be the figure of Judge Pyncheon, who—wretched spectacle that he is, and frightful in our remembrance, since our night-long vigil with him!—still keeps his place in the oaken chair.

Phœbe first tried the shop-door. It did not yield to her hand; and the white curtain, drawn across the window which formed the upper section of the door, struck her quick perceptive faculty as something unusual. Without making another effort to enter here, she betook herself to the great portal, under the arched window. Finding it fastened, she knocked. A reverberation came from the emptiness within. She knocked again, and a third time; and, listening intently, fancied that the floor creaked, as if Hepzibah were coming, with her ordinary tiptoe movement, to admit her. But so dead a silence ensued upon this imaginary sound, that she began to question whether she might not have mistaken the house, familiar as she thought herself with its exterior.

Her notice was now attracted by a child's voice, at some distance. It appeared to call her name. Looking in the direction whence it proceeded, Phœbe saw little Ned Higgins, a good way down the street, stamping, shaking his head violently, making deprecatory gestures with both hands, and shouting to her a mouth-wide screech.

"No, no, Phœbe!" he screamed "Don't you go in! There's somethin wicked there! Don't—don't—don't g in!"

But, as the little personage could no be induced to approach near enough t explain himself, Phœbe concluded tha he had been frightened, on some of hi visits to the shop, by her cousin Hepzi bah; for the good lady's manifestations in truth, ran about an equal chance o scaring children out of their wits, o compelling them to unseemly laughter Still, she felt the more, for this incident how unaccountably silent and impene trable the house had become. As her next resort, Phœbe made her way into the garden, where, on so warm and bright a day as the present, she had little doubt of finding Clifford, and per haps Hepzibah also, idling away the noontide in the shadow of the arbor Immediately on her entering the garden gate, the family of hens half ran, half flew, to meet her; while a strange Grimalkin, which was prowling under the parlor-window, took to his heels clambered hastily over the fence, and vanished. The arbor was vacant, and its floor, table, and circular bench, were still damp, and bestrewn with twigs, and the disarray of the past storm. The growth of the garden seemed to have got quite out of bounds; the weeds had taken advantage of Phœbe's absence and the long-continued rain, to run rampant over the flowers and kitchen-vegetables. Maule's well had overflowed its stone border, and made a pool of formidable breadth, in that corner of the garden.

The impression of the whole scene was that of a spot where no human foot had left its print for many preceding days,—probably not since Phœbe's departure,—for she saw a side-comb of her own under the table of the arbor, where it must have fallen on the last afternoon when she and Clifford sat there.

The girl knew that her two relatives were capable of far greater oddities than that of shutting themselves up in their old house, as they appeared now to have done. Nevertheless, with indistinct misgivings of something amiss, and apprehensions to which she could not give

shape, she approached the door that formed the customary communication between the house and garden. It was secured within, like the two which she had already tried. She knocked, however; and immediately, as if the application had been expected, the door was drawn open, by a considerable exertion of some unseen person's strength, not widely, but far enough to afford her a side-long entrance. As Hepzibah, in order not to expose herself to inspection from without, invariably opened a door in this manner, Phœbe necessarily concluded that it was her cousin who now admitted her.

Without hesitation, therefore, she stepped across the threshold, and had no sooner entered than the door closed behind her.

CHAPTER XX

THE FLOWER OF EDEN

PHŒBE, coming so suddenly from the sunny daylight, was altogether bedimmed in such density of shadow as lurked in most of the passages of the old house. She was not at first aware by whom she had been admitted. Before her eyes had adapted themselves to the obscurity, a hand grasped her own, with a firm but gentle and warm pressure, thus imparting a welcome which caused her heart to leap and thrill with an indefinable shiver of enjoyment. She felt herself drawn along, not towards the parlor, but into a large and unoccupied apartment, which had formerly been the

grand reception-room of the seven gables. The sunshine came freely into all the uncurtained windows of this room, and fell upon the dusty floor; so that Phœbe now clearly saw—what, indeed, had been no secret, after the encounter of a warm hand with hers—that it was not Hepzibah nor Clifford, but Holgrave, to whom she owed her reception. The subtle, intuitive communication, or, rather, the vague and formless impression of something to be told, had made her yield unresistingly to his impulse. Without taking away her hand, she looked eagerly in his face, not quick to forebode evil, but unavoidably conscious that the state of the family had changed since her departure, and therefore anxious for an explanation.

The artist looked paler than ordinary; there was a thoughtful and severe contraction of his forehead, tracing a deep vertical line between the eyebrows. His smile, however, was full of genuine warmth, and had in it a joy, by far the most vivid expression that Phœbe had ever witnessed, shining out of the New England reserve with which Holgrave habitually masked whatever lay near his heart. It was the look wherewith a man, brooding alone over some fearful object, in a dreary forest or illimitable desert, would recognize the familiar aspect of his dearest friend, bringing up all the peaceful ideas that belong to home, and the gentle current of everyday affairs. And yet, as he felt the necessity of responding to her look of inquiry, the smile disappeared.

"I ought not to rejoice that you have come, Phœbe," said he. "We meet at a strange moment!"

"What has happened?" she exclaimed. "Why is the house so deserted? Where are Hepzibah and Clifford?"

"Gone! I cannot imagine where they are!" answered Holgrave. "We are alone in the house!"

"Hepzibah and Clifford gone?" cried Phœbe. "It is not possible! And why have you brought me into this room, instead of the parlor? Ah, something terrible has happened! I must run and see!"

"No, no, Phœbe!" said Holgrave, holding her back. "It is as I have told you. They are gone, and I know not whither. A terrible event has, indeed, happened, but not to them, nor, as I undoubtingly believe, through any agency of theirs. If I read your character rightly, Phœbe," he continued, fixing his eyes on hers, with stern anxiety, intermixed with tenderness, "gentle as you are, and seeming to have your sphere among common things, you yet possess remarkable strength. You have wonderful poise, and a faculty which, when tested, will prove itself capable of dealing with matters that fall far out of the ordinary rule."

"O, no, I am very weak!" replied Phœbe, trembling. "But tell me what has happened!"

"You are strong!" persisted Holgrave. "You must be both strong and wise; for I am all astray, and need your counsel. It may be you can suggest the one right thing to do!"

"Tell me!—tell me!" said Phœbe, all in a tremble. "It oppresses,—it terrifies me,—this mystery! Anything else I can bear!"

The artist hesitated. Notwithstanding what he had just said, and most sincerely, in regard to the self-balancing power with which Phœbe impressed him, it still seemed almost wicked to bring the awful secret of yesterday to her knowledge. It was like dragging a hideous shape of death into the cleanly and cheerful space before a household fire where it would present all the uglier aspect, amid the decorousness of everything about it. Yet it could not be concealed from her; she must needs know it.

"Phœbe," said he, "do you remember this?"

He put into her hand a daguerreotype; the same that he had shown her at their first interview, in the garden, nd which so strikingly brought out the ard and relentless traits of the original.

"What has this to do with Hepzibah and Clifford?" asked Phœbe, with impatient surprise that Holgrave should so rifle with her, at such a moment. "It s Judge Pyncheon! You have shown it :o me before!"

"But here is the same face, taken vithin this half-hour," said the artist, presenting her with another miniature. 'I had just finished it, when I heard you it the door."

"This is death!" shuddered Phœbe, urning very pale. "Judge Pyncheon lead!"

"Such as there represented," said Holgrave, "he sits in the next room. The udge is dead, and Clifford and Hepzibah have vanished! I know no more. All beyond is conjecture. On returning to ny solitary chamber, last evening, I noticed no light, either in the parlor, or Hepzibah's room, or Clifford's; no stir nor footstep about the house. This morning there was the same death-like quiet. From my window, I overheard the testimony of a neighbor, that your relatives were seen leaving the house, in the midst of yesterday's storm. A rumor reached me, too, of Judge Pyncheon being missed. A feeling which I cannot describe—an indefinite sense of some catastrophe, or consummation—impelled me to make my way into this part of the house, where I discovered what you see. As a point of evidence that may be useful to Clifford, and also as a memorial valuable to myself,—for, Phœbe, here are hereditary reasons that connect me strangely with that man's fate, —I used the means at my disposal to preserve this pictorial record of Judge Pyncheon's death."

Even in her agitation, Phœbe could not help remarking the calmness of Holgrave's demeanor. He appeared, it is true, to feel the whole awfulness of the judge's death, yet had received the fact into his mind without any mixture of surprise, but as an event pre-ordained, happening inevitably, and so fitting itself into past occurrences that it could almost have been prophesied.

"Why have you not thrown open the doors, and called in witnesses?" inquired she, with a painful shudder. "It is terrible to be here alone!"

"But Clifford!" suggested the artist. "Clifford and Hepzibah! We must consider what is best to be done in their behalf. It is a wretched fatality, that they should have disappeared! Their flight will throw the worst coloring over this event of which it is susceptible. Yet how easy is the explanation, to those who know them! Bewildered and terror-stricken by the similarity of this death to a former one, which was attended with such disastrous consequences to Clifford, they have had no idea but of removing themselves from the scene. How miserably unfortunate! Had Hepzibah but shrieked aloud,— had Clifford flung wide the door, and proclaimed Judge Pyncheon's death,— it would have been, however awful in itself, an event fruitful of good consequences to them. As I view it, it would have gone far towards obliterating the black stain on Clifford's character."

"And how," asked Phœbe, "could any good come from what is so very dreadful?"

"Because," said the artist, "if the matter can be fairly considered, and candidly interpreted, it must be evident that Judge Pyncheon could not have come unfairly to his end. This mode of death has been an idiosyncrasy with his family, for generations past; not often occurring, indeed, but, when it does occur, usually attacking individuals about the judge's time of life, and generally in the tension of some mental crisis, or, perhaps, in an excess of wrath. Old Maule's prophecy was probably founded on a knowledge of this physical predisposition in the Pyncheon race. Now, there is a minute and almost exact similarity in the appearances connected with the death that occurred yesterday and those recorded of the death of Clifford's uncle, thirty years ago. It is true, there was a certain arrangement of circumstances, unnecessary to be recounted, which made it possible,—nay, as men look at these things, probable, or even certain,—that old Jaffrey Pyncheon came to a violent death, and by Clifford's hands."

"Whence came those circumstances?" exclaimed Phœbe; "he being innocent, as we know him to be!"

"They were arranged," said Holgrave,—"at least, such has long been my conviction,—they were arranged, after the uncle's death, and before it was made public, by the man who sits in yonder parlor. His own death, so like that former one, yet attended with none of those suspicious circumstances, seems the stroke of God upon him, at once a punishment for his wickedness, and making plain the innocence of Clifford. But this flight,—it distorts everything! He may be in concealment, near at hand. Could we but bring him back before the discovery of the judge's death, the evil might be rectified."

"We must not hide this thing a moment longer!" said Phœbe. "It is dreadful to keep it so closely in our hearts Clifford is innocent. God will make i manifest! Let us throw open the doors and call all the neighborhood to see th truth!"

"You are right, Phœbe," rejoined Holgrave. "Doubtless you are right."

Yet the artist did not feel the horror which was proper to Phœbe's sweet and order-loving character, at thus finding herself at issue with society, and brought in contact with an event that transcended ordinary rules. Neither was he in haste, like her, to betake himself within the precincts of common life. On the contrary, he gathered a wild enjoyment,—as it were, a flower of strange beauty, growing in a desolate spot, and blossoming in the wind,—such a flower of momentary happiness he gathered from his present position. It separated Phœbe and himself from the world, and bound them to each other, by their exclusive knowledge of Judge Pyncheon's mysterious death, and the counsel which they were forced to hold respecting it. The secret, so long as it should continue such, kept them within the circle of a spell, a solitude in the midst of men, a remoteness as entire as that of an island in mid-ocean;—once divulged, the ocean would flow betwixt them, standing on its widely-sundered shores. Meanwhile, all the circumstances of their situation seemed to draw them together; they were like two children who go hand in hand, pressing closely to one another's side, through a shadow-haunted passage. The image of awful Death, which filled the house, held them united by his stiffened grasp.

These influences hastened the development of emotions that might not otherwise have flowered so soon. Possibly, ndeed, it had been Holgrave's purpose o let them die in their undeveloped ;erms.

"Why do we delay so?" asked Phœbe. 'This secret takes away my breath! Let us throw open the doors!"

"In all our lives, there can never :ome another moment like this!" said Holgrave. "Phœbe, is it all terror?— nothing but terror? Are you conscious of no joy, as I am, that has made this he only point of life worth living for?"

"It seems a sin," replied Phœbe, trembling, "to think of joy at such a ime!"

"Could you but know, Phœbe, how it was with me, the hour before you :ame!" exclaimed the artist. "A dark, :old, miserable hour! The presence of yonder dead man threw a great black shadow over everything; he made the universe, so far as my perception could reach, a scene of guilt, and of retribution more dreadful than the guilt. The sense of it took away my youth. I never hoped to feel young again! The world looked strange, wild, evil, hostile;—my past life, so lonesome and dreary; my future, a shapeless gloom, which I must mould into gloomy shapes! But, Phœbe, you crossed the threshold; and hope, warmth and joy, came in with you! The black moment became at once a blissful one. It must not pass without the spoken word. I love you!"

"How can you love a simple girl like me?" asked Phœbe, compelled by his earnestness to speak. "You have many, many thoughts, with which I should try in vain to sympathize. And I,—I, too,— I have tendencies with which you would sympathize as little. That is less matter. But I have not scope enough to make you happy."

"You are my only possibility of happiness!" answered Holgrave. "I have no faith in it, except as you bestow it on me!"

"And then—I am afraid!" continued Phœbe, shrinking towards Holgrave, even while she told him so frankly the doubts with which he affected her. "You will lead me out of my own quiet path. You will make me strive to follow you, where it is pathless. I cannot do so. It is not my nature. I shall sink down and perish!"

"Ah, Phœbe!" exclaimed Holgrave, with almost a sigh, and a smile that was burthened with thought. "It will be far otherwise than as you forebode. The world owes all its onward impulses to men ill at ease. The happy man inevitably confines himself within ancient limits. I have a presentiment that, hereafter, it will be my lot to set out trees, to make fences,—perhaps, even, in due time, to build a house for another generation,—in a word, to conform myself to laws, and the peaceful practice of society. Your poise will be more powerful than any oscillating tendency of mine."

"I would not have it so!" said Phœbe, earnestly.

"Do you love me?" asked Holgrave. "If we love one another, the moment has room for nothing more. Let us pause upon it, and be satisfied. Do you love me, Phœbe?"

"You look into my heart," said she, letting her eyes drop. "You know I love you!"

And it was in this hour, so full of doubt and awe, that the one miracle was wrought, without which every human existence is a blank. The bliss, which makes all things true, beautiful, and holy, shone around this youth and maiden. They were conscious of nothing sad nor old. They transfigured the earth, and made it Eden again, and themselves the two first dwellers in it. The dead man, so close beside them, was forgotten. At such a crisis, there is no death; for immortality is revealed anew, and embraces everything in its hallowed atmosphere.

But how soon the heavy earth-dream settled down again!

"Hark!" whispered Phœbe. "Somebody is at the street door!"

"Now let us meet the world!" said Holgrave. "No doubt, the rumor of Judge Pyncheon's visit to this house, and the flight of Hepzibah and Clifford, is about to lead to the investigation of the premises. We have no way but to meet it. Let us open the door at once."

But, to their surprise, before they could reach the street door,—even before they quitted the room in which the foregoing interview had passed,—they heard footsteps in the further passage. The door, therefore, which they supposed to be securely locked,—which Holgrave, indeed, had seen to be so, and at which Phœbe had vainly tried to enter,—must have been opened from without. The sound of footsteps was not harsh, bold, decided, and intrusive, as the gait of strangers would naturally be, making authoritative entrance into a dwelling where they knew themselves unwelcome. It was feeble, as of persons either weak or weary; there was the mingled murmur of two voices, familiar to both the listeners.

"Can it be?" whispered Holgrave.

"It is they!" answered Phœbe. "Than' God!—thank God!"

And then, as if in sympathy wit] Phœbe's whispered ejaculation, the heard Hepzibah's voice, more distinctly

"Thank God, my brother, we are a home!"

"Well!—Yes!—thank God!" respond ed Clifford. "A dreary home, Hepzibah But you have done well to bring m hither! Stay! That parlor-door is open I cannot pass by it! Let me go and res me in the arbor, where I used,—oh, very long ago, it seems to me, after what ha befallen us,—where I used to be s happy with little Phœbe!"

But the house was not altogether s dreary as Clifford imagined it. They ha not made many steps,—in truth, the were lingering in the entry, with the list lessness of an accomplished purpose uncertain what to do next,—whe Phœbe ran to meet them. On beholdin her, Hepzibah burst into tears. With a her might, she had staggered onwar beneath the burden of grief and re sponsibility, until now that it was saf to fling it down. Indeed, she had no energy to fling it down, but had cease to uphold it, and suffered it to press he to the earth. Clifford appeared th stronger of the two.

"It is our own little Phœbe!—Ah! and Holgrave with her," exclaimed he, witl a glance of keen and delicate insight and a smile, beautiful, kind, but melancholy. "I thought of you both, as we came down the street, and beheld Alice's Posies in full bloom. And so the flower of Eden has bloomed, likewise in thi old, darksome house, to-day!"

CHAPTER XXI

THE DEPARTURE

THE sudden death of so prominent a member of the social world as the Honorable Judge Jaffrey Pyncheon created a sensation (at least, in the circles more immediately connected with the deceased) which had hardly quite subsided in a fortnight.

It may be remarked, however, that, of all the events which constitute a person's biography, there is scarcely one— one, certainly, of anything like a similar importance—to which the world so easily reconciles itself as to his death. In most other cases and contingencies, the individual is present among us, mixed up with the daily revolution of affairs, and affording a definite point for observation. At his decease, there is only a vacancy, and a momentary eddy,— very small, as compared with the apparent magnitude of the ingurgitated object,—and a bubble or two, ascending out of the black depth, and bursting at the surface. As regarded Judge Pyncheon, it seemed probable, at first blush, that the mode of his final departure might give him a larger and longer posthumous vogue than ordinarily attends the memory of a distinguished man. But when it came to be understood, on the highest professional authority, that the event was a natural, and—except for some unimportant particulars, denoting a slight idiosyncrasy— by no means an unusual form of death, the public, with its customary alacrity, proceeded to forget that he had ever lived. In short, the honorable judge was beginning to be a stale subject, before half the county newspapers had found time to put their columns in mourning, and publish his exceedingly eulogistic obituary.

Nevertheless, creeping darkly through the places which this excellent person had haunted in his lifetime, there was a hidden stream of private talk, such as it would have shocked all decency to speak loudly at the street-corners. It is very singular, how the fact of a man's death often seems to give people a truer idea of his character, whether for good or evil, than they have ever possessed while he was living and acting among them. Death is so genuine a fact that it excludes falsehood, or betrays its emptiness; it is a touchstone that proves the gold, and dishonors the baser metal. Could the departed, whoever he may be, return in a week after his decease, he would almost invariably find himself at a higher or lower point than he had formerly occupied, on the scale of public appreciation. But the talk, or scandal, to which we now allude, had reference to matters of no less old a date than the supposed murder, thirty or forty years ago, of the late Judge Pyncheon's uncle. The medical opinion, with regard to his own recent and regretted decease, had almost entirely obviated the idea that a murder was committed, in the former case. Yet, as the record showed, there were circumstances irrefragably indicating that some person had gained access to old Jaffrey Pyncheon's private apartments, at or near the moment of his death. His desk and private drawers, in a room contiguous to his bedchamber, had been ransacked; money and valuable articles were missing; there was a bloody hand-print on the old man's linen; and, by a powerfully welded chain of deductive evidence, the guilt of the robbery and apparent murder had been fixed on Clifford, then residing with his uncle in the House of the Seven Gables.

Whencesoever originating, there now arose a theory that undertook so to account for these circumstances as to exclude the idea of Clifford's agency. Many persons affirmed that the history and elucidation of the facts, long so mysterious, had been obtained by the daguerreotypist from one of those mesmerical seers, who, now-a-days, so strangely perplex the aspect of human affairs, and put everybody's natural vision to the blush, by the marvels which they see with their eyes shut.

According to this version of the story, Judge Pyncheon, exemplary as we have portrayed him in our narrative, was, in his youth, an apparently irreclaimable scapegrace. The brutish, the animal instincts, as is often the case, had been developed earlier than the intellectual qualities, and the force of character, for which he was afterwards remarkable. He had shown himself wild, dissipated, addicted to low pleasures, little short of ruffianly in his propensities, and recklessly expensive, with no other resources than the bounty of his uncle. This course of conduct had alienated the old bachelor's affection, once strongly fixed upon him. Now, it is averred,—but whether on authority available in a court of justice, we do not pretend to have investigated.—that the young man was tempted by the

devil, one night, to search his uncle' private drawers, to which he had unsus pected means of access. While thu criminally occupied, he was startled by the opening of the chamber-door. Ther stood old Jaffrey Pyncheon, in his night clothes! The surprise of such a dis covery, his agitation, alarm, and horror brought on the crisis of a disorder t which the old bachelor had an heredi tary liability;—he seemed to choke with blood, and fell upon the floor, striking his temple a heavy blow against the corner of a table. What was to be done? The old man was surely dead! Assist ance would come too late! What a mis fortune, indeed, should it come too soon since his reviving consciousness would bring the recollection of the ignominiou offence which he had beheld his nephew in the very act of committing!

But he never did revive. With the cool hardihood that always pertained to him, the young man continued his search of the drawers, and found a will of recent date, in favor of Clifford,— which he destroyed,—and an older one in his own favor, which he suffered to remain. But, before retiring, Jaffrey bethought himself of the evidence, in these ransacked drawers, that some one had visited the chamber with sinister purposes. Suspicion, unless averted, might fix upon the real offender. In the very presence of the dead man, therefore, he laid a scheme that should free himself at the expense of Clifford, his rival, for whose character he had at once a contempt and a repugnance. It is not probable, be it said, that he acted with any set purpose of involving Clifford in a charge of murder. Knowing that his uncle did not die by violence, it may not have occurred to him, in the

urry of the crisis, that such an in-
erence might be drawn. But, when the
ffair took this darker aspect, Jaffrey's
previous steps had already pledged him
o those which remained. So craftily
ad he arranged the circumstances, that,
t Clifford's trial, his cousin hardly
ound it necessary to swear to anything
alse, but only to withhold the one de-
isive explanation, by refraining to state
vhat he had himself done and witnessed.

Thus Jaffrey Pyncheon's inward
riminality, as regarded Clifford, was,
ndeed, black and damnable; while its
nere outward show and positive com-
nission was the smallest that could
ossibly consist with so great a sin.
'his is just the sort of guilt that a
nan of eminent respectability finds it
asiest to dispose of. It was suffered to
ade out of sight, or be reckoned a
enial matter, in the Honorable Judge
'yncheon's long subsequent survey of
is own life. He shuffled it aside, among
he forgotten and forgiven frailties of
is youth, and seldom thought of it
gain.

We leave the judge to his repose. He
ould not be styled fortunate, at the
our of death. Unknowingly, he was a
hildless man, while striving to add
nore wealth to his only child's in-
eritance. Hardly a week after his de-
ease, one of the Cunard steamers
rought intelligence of the death, by
holera, of Judge Pyncheon's son, just
t the point of embarkation for his
ative land. By this misfortune, Clifford
ecame rich; so did Hepzibah; so did
ur little village-maiden, and, through
er, that sworn foe of wealth and all
nanner of conservatism,—the wild re-
ormer,—Holgrave!

It was now far too late in Clifford's
life for the good opinion of society to
be worth the trouble and anguish of a
formal vindication. What he needed was
the love of a very few; not the admiration, or even the respect, of the
unknown many. The latter might probably have been won for him, had those
on whom the guardianship of his welfare had fallen deemed it advisable to
expose Clifford to a miserable resusci-
tation of past ideas, when the condition
of whatever comfort he might expect
lay in the calm of forgetfulness. After
such wrong as he had suffered, there is
no reparation. The pitiable mockery of
it, which the world might have been
ready enough to offer, coming so long
after the agony had done its utmost
work, would have been fit only to pro-
voke bitterer laughter than poor Clifford was ever capable of. It is a truth
(and it would be a very sad one, but for
the higher hopes which it suggests) that
no great mistake, whether acted or endured, in our mortal sphere, is ever
really set right. Time, the continual
vicissitude of circumstances, and the
invariable inopportunity of death, render it impossible. If, after long lapse
of years, the right seems to be in our
power, we find no niche to set it in.
The better remedy is for the sufferer
to pass on, and leave what he once
thought his irreparable ruin far behind
him.

The shock of Judge Pyncheon's death
had a permanently invigorating and
ultimately beneficial effect on Clifford.
That strong and ponderous man had
been Clifford's night-mare. There was
no free breath to be drawn, within the
sphere of so malevolent an influence.
The first effect of freedom, as we have
witnessed in Clifford's aimless flight, was

a tremulous exhilaration. Subsiding from it, he did not sink into his former intellectual apathy. He never, it is true, attained to nearly the full measure of what might have been his faculties. But he recovered enough of them partially to light up his character, to display some outline of the marvellous grace that was abortive in it, and to make him the object of no less deep, although less melancholy interest than heretofore. He was evidently happy. Could we pause to give another picture of his daily life, with all the appliances now at command to gratify his instinct for the Beautiful, the garden scenes, that seemed so sweet to him, would look mean and trivial in comparison.

Very soon after their change of fortune, Clifford, Hepzibah, and little Phœbe, with the approval of the artist, concluded to remove from the dismal old House of the Seven Gables, and take up their abode, for the present, at the elegant country-seat of the late Judge Pyncheon. Chanticleer and his family had already been transported thither, where the two hens had forthwith begun an indefatigable process of egg-laying, with an evident design, as a matter of duty and conscience, to continue their illustrious breed under better auspices than for a century past. On the day set for their departure, the principal personages of our story, including good Uncle Venner, were assembled in the parlor.

"The country-house is certainly a very fine one, so far as the plan goes," observed Holgrave, as the party were discussing their future arrangements. "But I wonder that the late judge—being so opulent, and with a reasonable prospect of transmitting his wealth to

descendants of his own—should n[ot] have felt the propriety of embodying s[o] excellent a piece of domestic archite[c]ture in stone, rather than in wood. The[n] every generation of the family mig[ht] have altered the interior, to suit its ow[n] taste and convenience; while the e[x]terior, through the lapse of years, mig[ht] have been adding venerableness to i[ts] original beauty, and thus giving tha[t] impression of permanence which I con[si]der essential to the happiness of an[y] one moment."

"Why," cried Phœbe, gazing int[o] the artist's face with infinite amaze[]ment, "how wonderfully your ideas ar[e] changed! A house of stone, indeed! I[t] is but two or three weeks ago, that yo[u] seemed to wish people to live in some[]thing as fragile and temporary as [a] bird's nest!"

"Ah, Phœbe, I told you how it woul[d] be!" said the artist, with a hal[f] melancholy laugh. "You find me a con[]servative already! Little did I thin[k] ever to become one. It is especially un[]pardonable in this dwelling of so muc[h] hereditary misfortune, and under th[e] eye of yonder portrait of a model con[]servative, who, in that very characte[r] rendered himself so long the evil destin[y] of his race."

"That picture!" said Clifford, seemin[g] to shrink from its stern glance. "When[]ever I look at it, there is an old, dream[] recollection haunting me, but keepin[g] just beyond the grasp of my mind[.] Wealth, it seems to say!—boundles[s] wealth!—unimaginable wealth! I coul[d] fancy that, when I was a child, or [a] youth, that portrait had spoken, an[d] told me a rich secret, or had held fort[h] its hand, with the written record o[f] hidden opulence. But those old matter[s]

re so dim with me, now-a-days! What
ould this dream have been?"

"Perhaps I can recall it," answered
Holgrave. "See! There are a hundred
chances to one, that no person, unacquainted with the secret, would ever
touch this spring."

"A secret spring!" cried Clifford. "Ah,
I remember now! I did discover it, one
summer afternoon, when I was idling
and dreaming about the house, long,
long ago. But the mystery escapes me."

The artist put his finger on the contrivance to which he had referred. In
former days, the effect would probably
have been to cause the picture to start
forward. But, in so long a period of
concealment, the machinery had been
eaten through with rust; so that, at
Holgrave's pressure, the portrait, frame
and all, tumbled suddenly from its
position, and lay face downward on the
floor. A recess in the wall was thus
brought to light, in which lay an object
so covered with a century's dust that it
could not immediately be recognized as
a folded sheet of parchment. Holgrave
opened it, and displayed an ancient
deed, signed with the hieroglyphics of
several Indian sagamores, and conveying to Colonel Pyncheon and his heirs,
forever, a vast extent of territory at the
eastward.

"This is the very parchment the attempt to recover which cost the beautiful Alice Pyncheon her happiness and
life," said the artist, alluding to his
legend. "It is what the Pyncheons
sought in vain, while it was valuable;
and now that they find the treasure, it
has long been worthless."

"Poor Cousin Jaffrey! This is what
deceived him," exclaimed Hepzibah.
"When they were young together, Clif-

ford probably made a kind of fairy-tale
of this discovery. He was always dreaming hither and thither about the house,
and lighting up its dark corners with
beautiful stories. And poor Jaffrey, who
took hold of everything as if it were
real, thought my brother had found out
his uncle's wealth. He died with this
delusion in his mind!"

"But," said Phœbe, apart to Holgrave, "how came you to know the
secret?"

"My dearest Phœbe," said Holgrave,
"how will it please you to assume the
name of Maule? As for the secret, it is
the only inheritance that has come down
to me from my ancestors. You should
have known sooner (only that I was
afraid of frightening you away) that,
in this long drama of wrong and retribution, I represent the old wizard, and am
probably as much of a wizard as ever
he was. The son of the executed
Matthew Maule, while building this
house, took the opportunity to construct
that recess, and hide away the Indian
deed, on which depended the immense
land-claim of the Pyncheons. Thus they
bartered their eastern territory for
Maule's garden-ground."

"And now," said Uncle Venner, "I
suppose their whole claim is not worth
one man's share in my farm yonder!"

"Uncle Venner," cried Phœbe, taking
the patched philosopher's hand, "you
must never talk any more about your
farm! You shall never go there, as long
as you live! There is a cottage in
our new garden,—the prettiest little
yellowish-brown cottage you ever saw;
and the sweetest-looking place, for it
looks just as if it were made of gingerbread,—and we are going to fit it up
and furnish it, on purpose for you. And

you shall do nothing but what you choose, and shall be as happy as the day is long, and shall keep Cousin Clifford in spirits with the wisdom and pleasantness which is always dropping from your lips!"

"Ah! my dear child," quoth good Uncle Venner, quite overcome, "if you were to speak to a young man as you do to an old one, his chance of keeping his heart another minute would not be worth one of the buttons on my waistcoat! And—soul alive!—that great sigh, which you made me heave, has burst off the very last of them! But never mind! It was the happiest sigh I ever did heave; and it seems as if I must have drawn in a gulp of heavenly breath, to make it with. Well, well, Miss Phœbe! They'll miss me in the gardens, hereabouts, and round by the back-doors; and Pyncheon-street, I'm afraid, will hardly look the same without old Uncle Venner, who remembers it with a mowing field on one side, and the garden of the seven gables on the other. But either I must go to your country-seat, or you must come to my farm—that's one of two things certain; and I leave you to choose which!"

"O, come with us, by all means, Uncle Venner!" said Clifford, who had a remarkable enjoyment of the old man's mellow, quiet, and simple spirit. "I want you always to be within five minutes' saunter of my chair. You are the only philosopher I ever knew of, whose wisdom has not a drop of bitter essence at the bottom!"

"Dear me!" cried Uncle Venner, beginning partly to realize what manner of man he was. "And yet folks used to set me down among the simple ones, in my younger days! But I suppose I am

like a Roxbury russet,—a great deal th better, the longer I can be kept. Yes and my words of wisdom, that you an Phœbe tell me of, are like the golde dandelions, which never grow in th hot months, but may be seen glistenin among the withered grass, and unde the dry leaves, sometimes as late a December. And you are welcom friends, to my mess of dandelions, i there were twice as many!"

A plain, but handsome, dark-gree barouche had now drawn up in fror of the ruinous portal of the old mansio house. The party came forth, and (wit the exception of good Uncle Venne who was to follow in a few days) pr ceeded to take their places. They wer chatting and laughing very pleasantl together; and—as proves to be often th case, at moments when we ought t palpitate with sensibility—Clifford an Hepzibah bade a final farewell to th abode of their forefathers, with hardl more emotion than if they had mad it their arrangement to return thither a tea-time. Several children were draw to the spot by so unusual a spectac as the barouche and pair of gray horses Recognizing little Ned Higgins amon them, Hepzibah put her hand into he pocket, and presented the urchin, he earliest and staunchest customer, wit silver enough to people the Domdanie cavern of his interior with as variou a procession of quadrupeds as passe into the ark.

Two men were passing, just as th barouche drove off.

"Well, Dixey," said one of them "what do you think of this? My wif kept a cent-shop three months, and los five dollars on her outlay. Old Mai Pyncheon has been in trade just abou

s long, and rides off in her carriage
ith a couple of hundred thousand,—
eckoning her share, and Clifford's, and
hœbe's,—and some say twice as much!
f you choose to call it luck, it is all
ery well; but if we are to take it as the
ill of Providence, why, I can't exactly
thom it!"

"Pretty good business!" quoth the
agacious Dixey. "Pretty good business!"

Maule's well, all this time, though left
a solitude, was throwing up a succes-
ion of kaleidoscopic pictures, in which
gifted eye might have seen fore-
adowed the coming fortunes of Hepzi-
ah and Clifford, and the descendant of
the legendary wizard, and the village-
maiden, over whom he had thrown
love's web of sorcery. The Pyncheon-
elm, moreover, with what foliage the
September gale had spared to it, whispered unintelligible prophecies. And wise
Uncle Venner, passing slowly from the
ruinous porch, seemed to hear a strain
of music, and fancied that sweet Alice
Pyncheon—after witnessing these deeds,
this by-gone woe, and this present
happiness, of her kindred mortals—had
given one farewell touch of a spirit's joy
upon her harpsichord, as she floated
heavenward from the HOUSE OF THE
SEVEN GABLES!